River Rising

A Cherokee Odyssey

A Novel By

Frank Stewart

River Rising
A Cherokee Odyssey

Copyright © 1997
Wohali Press
First Printing 1998

Published by: **Wohali Press**
P. O. Box 27740
Las Vegas, NV 89126

E-Mail: wohalipress@mindspring.com

Cover: Frank Stewart

ISBN: 0-9663853-0-6

Library of Congress
Catalog Card Number: 98-60320

Printed in the USA by
BookCrafters
613 E. Industrial Drive ▪ Chelsea, MI 48118-0370 ▪ 734-475-9145

Dedication

For my wife, Gill, and Mōnka Lēka,
both of whom have inspired, encouraged
and comforted me.

And for my grandson, River, who
is a light and an inspiration
to us all.

Acknowledgments

This story, though a work of fiction, is presented as a candle of truth in honor of those Cherokees who suffered and died in the American prison camps and on The Trail Of Tears and as a tribute to those who survived to carry on The Eternal Flame.

My earnest prayer is that *River Rising* might inspire the reader to question the history we have been taught in our schools, to look beyond the untruths, half-truths and misinformation fed to school children across the decades. Always ask yourself, "Is this the truth, the whole truth and nothing but the truth?" Learn to search beyond the much-heralded achievements—often apocryphal at best—of those whom our leaders and educators have placed upon pedestals to be worshipped and portrayed in pageants, parades and festive ceremonies. Ferret out the less-than-flattering and often shameful truth that lurks in the darkened corners behind the busts and portraits of our so-called national heroes.

Wa-do to *Blue*, a blue-eyed, full-blood Cherokee medicine man deep in the hills of Eastern Oklahoma, who told me I had to write this story; and to Ralph Powell, who became my friend and first introduced me to the story of the Cherokees.

A heartfelt thanks to some very special California folks at *Hawk's Hill Ranch* in San Luis Obispo County, at *Rancho Aliso* in the Santa Clarita Valley, and to my loved ones at Ben Bheula, Arrochar, Scotland. For me, these three places have become meccas of spiritual rejuvenation and fountainheads of creativity.

To all my dear friends and family who have believed in me and encouraged me through the years, a simple *thank you* cannot begin to convey the depth of my gratitude.

My thanks to Mary Sieffert and Selena Sieffert for their help in proofreading and preparing the manuscript for publication. If you find punctuation or grammatical errors, blame them!

And, finally, mortal words could never express the depth of my love and gratitude for my friends and teachers from The Dream Time. They are to me Water and Light.

The author can be reached on the Internet at:

| e-mail: | riverrising@mindspring.com |
| web site: | www.cherokee7.com |

v

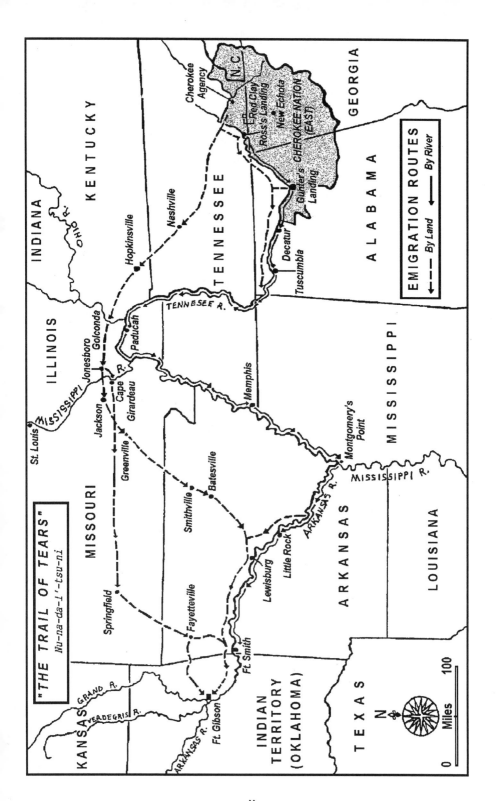

"THE TRAIL OF TEARS"
Nu-na-da-ǔ'-tsu-ni

EMIGRATION ROUTES
--- By Land
→ By River

INDIANA
KENTUCKY
ILLINOIS
MISSOURI
TENNESSEE
GEORGIA
N.C.
ALABAMA
MISSISSIPPI
ARKANSAS
LOUISIANA
INDIAN TERRITORY (OKLAHOMA)
TEXAS
KANSAS

Cherokee Agency
Red Clay
Ross's Landing
New Echota
CHEROKEE NATION (EAST)
Gunter's Landing
Decatur
Tuscumbia
Nashville
Hopkinsville
St. Louis
Golconda
Jonesboro
Paducah
Cape Girardeau
Jackson
Greenville
Smithville
Batesville
Memphis
Montgomery's Point
Little Rock
Lewisburg
Springfield
Fayetteville
Ft. Smith
Ft. Gibson

OHIO R.
MISSISSIPPI R.
TENNESEE R.
R.
ARKANSAS R.
MISSISSIPPI R.
GRAND R.
VERDEGRIS R.
ARKANSAS R.

N

Miles
0   100

vii

CHEROKEE SYLLABLES

Ꭰ a	Ꭱ e	Ꭲ i	Ꭳ o	Ꭴ u	Ꭵ v
Ꭶ ga Ꭷ ka	Ꭸ ge	Ꭹ gi	Ꭺ go	Ꭻ gu	Ꭼ gv
Ꭽ ha	Ꭾ he	Ꭿ hi	Ꮀ ho	Ꮁ hu	Ꮂ hv
Ꮃ la	Ꮄ le	Ꮅ li	Ꮆ lo	Ꮇ lu	Ꮈ lv
Ꮉ ma	Ꮊ me	Ꮋ mi	Ꮌ mo	Ꮍ mu	
Ꮎ na Ꮏ hna Ꮐ nah	Ꮑ ne	Ꮒ ni	Ꮓ no	Ꮔ nu	Ꮕ nv
Ꮖ qua	Ꮗ que	Ꮘ qui	Ꮙ quo	Ꮚ quu	Ꮛ quv
Ꮜ sa Ꮝ s	Ꮞ se	Ꮟ si	Ꮠ so	Ꮡ su	Ꮢ sv
Ꮣ da Ꮤ ta	Ꮥ de Ꮦ te	Ꮧ di Ꮨ ti	Ꮩ do	Ꮪ du	Ꮫ dv
Ꮬ dla Ꮭ tla	Ꮮ tle	Ꮯ tli	Ꮰ tlo	Ꮱ tlu	Ꮲ tlv
Ꮳ tsa	Ꮴ tse	Ꮵ tsi	Ꮶ tso	Ꮷ tsu	Ꮸ tsv
Ꮹ wa	Ꮺ we	Ꮻ wi	Ꮼ wo	Ꮽ wu	Ꮾ wv
Ꮿ ya	Ᏸ ye	Ᏹ yi	Ᏺ yo	Ᏻ yu	Ᏼ yv

Sounds Represented by Vowels

a, as a in father, or short as a in rival

e, as a in hate, or short as e in met

i, as i in pique, or short as i in pit

o, as o in note, approaching aw in law

u, as oo in fool, or short as u in pull

v, as u in but, nasalized

Consonant Sounds

g nearly as in English, but approaching to k. d nearly as in English but approaching to t. h k l m n q s t w y as in English. Syllables beginning with g except Ꭶ (ga) have sometimes the power of k. Ꭺ (go), Ꮪ (du), Ꮫ (dv) are sometimes sounded to, tu, tv and syllables written with tl except Ꮭ (tla) sometimes vary to dl.

The English letters beside the Cherokee symbols are *not* part of the symbol. They show how that symbol is to be written in English and how it is to be pronounced (in accordance with the explanation below the chart).

Note the syllables in the sixth column—*v, gv, hv, lv, nv, quv, sv, dv, tlv, tsv, wv, yv*. The "v" is pronounced as a nasalized "u", similar to "-ung" in *sung* or *hung*, dropping the final "g". For readers unfamiliar with Cherokee, it is sometimes difficult to get used to seeing this "v" and remembering to convert it to a nasalized "u". Therefore, in *River Rising*, I have taken the liberty of substituting "ŭ" for "v", so the characters in the sixth column become ŭ, gŭ, hŭ, lŭ, nŭ, quŭ, sŭ, dŭ, tlŭ, tsŭ, wŭ and yŭ.

PREFACE

If you are unfamiliar with the history, customs and culture of the Cherokee Nation, you are asked to clear from your mind all preconceived ideas and myths about Native Americans, particularly as historically presented in pulp novels of the 19th Century and by Hollywood in the 20th Century. Fortunately—albeit decades too late—many novels, films and television programs in recent years have made a conscientious effort to portray Native Americans more realistically and with more historical accuracy. Such a departure from the "Indian" stereotype is especially critical in assessing the events and settings of *River Rising*, for, as you will discover, the *Tsa-la-gi* (Cherokee) are a nation vastly different from the *Plains Indians* and *Southwest Indians* more often portrayed in fiction, film and TV.

History and Geography

Before the white man came to North America, the Cherokees controlled an area of approximately 120,000 square miles in the southeastern part of the continent in the present states of Kentucky, West Virginia, Virginia, Tennessee, North Carolina, South Carolina, Georgia and Alabama. The Cherokees' first contact with Europeans is said to have come in 1540 when DeSoto and his Spanish explorers came up into Cherokee territory from Florida to the south. But this was only a passing encounter. It was not until years later when English, Scottish, Irish and German trappers and traders began working the forests and rivers of Cherokee territory that integration with the white man truly began.

Many Cherokee leaders recognized early on that the tide of white encroachment would not, could not be stemmed. Their only hope for survival as a people, many felt, was to learn from and adapt to the ways of the Europeans. Tribal leaders taken abroad as "exhibits" greatly impressed the courts of Europe with their handsome appearance, regal bearing, intelligence and statesmanship.

In the French-Indian War of the 18th Century (1754-1763), a young military commander named George Washington relied heavily on his Cherokee allies and once said he preferred a half-dozen Cherokee warriors to a company of white soldiers because of the Cherokees' superior cunning, intelligence and bravery.

When the American colonists declared their independence from English rule, the Cherokees made what was, for them, the only intelligent choice: fight on the side of the British Crown, because the

Crown's purpose was to curtail growth and slow colonial expansion in the new world. It proved an unfortunate decision for the Cherokees. Soon after the Revolutionary War there began the inevitable and seemingly endless string of treaties between the Cherokees and the new government of the United States. And with each treaty, the Cherokee lands grew smaller. By the time of *River Rising* (1830-1839), Cherokee territory had been reduced to approximately 12,000 square miles—barely one-tenth its original size—occupying northwest Georgia, northeast Alabama, southeast Tennessee and southwest North Carolina.

Nevertheless, many of the Cherokees continued their efforts to successfully interweave the white man's culture with their own. Young Cherokee men were educated in the finest colleges and universities of the northeast. The daughters of wealthier Cherokees attended finishing schools in Richmond, Charleston and Atlanta. Missionary schools proliferated throughout Cherokee towns and villages, bringing both education and Christianity. Cherokees and whites freely intermarried. Many great Cherokee leaders possessed only a fraction of Cherokee blood, yet so deep was their love of their Cherokee heritage, coupled with their matriarchal identification through the Cherokee clan system, that they considered themselves *Tsa-la-gi* when they could easily have "passed" for white. (A prime example is John Ross, known in his youth as *Tsan-u-s-di*—Little John—and later by his Cherokee name, *Gu-wi-s-gu-wi*. Ross was sandy-haired, blue-eyed and only one-eighth Cherokee, yet he served as principal chief for a period spanning 5 decades, during some of the most difficult times in Cherokee history.)

There were, by contrast, many full-blood *traditionalists* who disdained the white man's culture and preferred to cling to their ancient ways. Over time, this division among the Cherokees would become a sensitive target of land-greedy whites who wished to drive a wedge of dissension between the two factions, thereby undermining the strength of the Cherokee nation as a whole.

The Language

The linguistic history of the Cherokees is unique. They were the first (and only) indigenous tribe to create their own written language, using a system of characters devised in the early Nineteenth Century by *Sequoyah*. Each character represents a *syllable* rather than a single letter, as in the English alphabet. Hence, the collection of Cherokee characters is, in the truest sense, a *syllabary*, although many refer to it—inaccurately—as an alphabet. Sequoyah's contribution represents one of the most phenomenal achievements in the history of mankind. In the span of a single generation, the Cherokees advanced from a strictly oral language* to a reading/writing literacy level well over 90 percent. The Cherokees went on to have their own written constitution and laws and were the only Native American tribe in their time to publish a newspaper in their own language.

Cherokee is written in two different ways. In order to read and write Cherokee in its true form, one must learn the special characters and the sounds of the syllables they represent. (See the Cherokee Syllabary on p. *ix*.) Another way—the method used in *River Rising*—is to present the syllables written in the English alphabet, representing the *sounds* of the Cherokee syllables. For example, the Cherokee characters for the word *Cherokee* look much like this: **C W Y**, similar in appearance to the 3rd, 23d and 25th letters of the English alphabet. The syllables represented by these characters, **C W Y**, would be presented as *tsa-la-gi*, pronounced *cha la GEE*, or *cha la KEE*. (The "G" in Cherokee is always the "hard" English G, as in "great", or the English K, as in "kitten". There is no "soft g" in Cherokee like in the English "George").

Cherokee is a smooth-flowing, almost musical sounding language. There are dialectic variations, especially between the Western Cherokee (of Oklahoma) and the Eastern Cherokee (North Carolina). In an attempt to maintain a degree of authenticity, I have used many Cherokee words and phrases in *River Rising*. The linguistic purists might well take me to task for using the Western dialect almost exclusively, even in those portions of the story set in the east. As my intent is more to add a Cherokee flavor to the story than to provide a completely accurate linguistic rendering, I yield the point.

In reading the story it might be more enjoyable to have a little knowledge of the pronunciation of the Cherokee syllables. It is especially worth noting one particular sound in Cherokee that can not be accurately represented by a single letter or syllable in English. In most presentations of Cherokee-as-English-letters, it is shown as the letter "**V**", though it is not sounded at all like the 22nd letter of the English alphabet. It represents a very nasalized "u", similar to

---

*   There are theories extant that in ancient times there was a written Cherokee language. However, nothing exists today to substantiate such claims.

the "-ung" in the English words "sung" or "hung", but without actually pronouncing the "g" at the end. Since most readers will not necessarily be students of the language, I have chosen to present this sound using "ŭ" rather than "v", merely as a convenience to the reader.

A *Glossary* is presented at the end of the book which contains most of the Cherokee words and phrases (along with an approximate pronunciation guide) used in *River Rising*.

Adolph Hitler once said that he based his **solution** *to the* **problem** *of the European Jews in part on what England and the United States had done to the Native Americans.*

Never forget...

* * * * * * *

Ka-ma-ma

In the Cherokee language there is but one word for both **elephant** *and* **butterfly**.

Learn to see...

PROLOGUE

Tulsa, Oklahoma
Present Day

She'd been following me around the house all morning. My mother. I flung my clothes into the suitcase she'd given me for high school graduation four years earlier.

"I don't see why you have to leave so soon, Elizabeth," she over-enunciated—halting after each word—from outside the closed bedroom door. I could just see her, hands on hips, staring straight at the doorknob as though the force of her words alone would actually turn it. It wasn't locked, but I knew my mother. She had this thing about closed doors. If the door was shut, she always knocked, and even then she'd wait for you to invite her in. "When do you register for classes? Next Thursday? Why can't you stay at least through the weekend? I need to talk to you, Elizabeth. You left some of your things in the bathroom. Your birth control pills. When did you start taking birth control pills? Do we need to talk?"

I hated it when she called me Elizabeth. Since I turned twelve I had been Liz to everyone. Even to Mother, when she could remember, which wasn't often. She could recall everything my older brother, Michael, and I had ever said or done to cause her pain or grief, but she couldn't remember to call me Liz.

"I'm twenty-two years old, Mom, not fifteen!"

"You've been taking birth control pills since you were fifteen?!" Characteristically, she made the unintended connection. Refusing to honor her ridiculous inference with a response, I punched the play button on my boom box and cranked up the volume of a *Rokker* CD. It was the *Leave Your Mother* track. My favorite. I loved its driving, primal beat, not to mention the profound message of the lyrics.

"I know you're doing that just to annoy me!" her muffled accusation penetrated from the hallway. I spun the volume up two more notches before opening the door. There she stood. My mother, Janet Pierce. Immaculately groomed and perfectly coiffed in a late-Fifties-June-Cleaver look that was so her. I sometimes caught myself thinking she should have been in black-and-white like the old TV reruns Michael and I had grown up watching. And what puzzled us even more—she was only forty-eight years old, not even having reached adulthood during the Fifties. She would have seen the original runs of *Leave It To Beaver, Father Knows Best, Donna Reed* and all those *we've-got-our-cute-little-problems-but-thank-God-we're-*

1

not-dysfunctional TV sitcoms of the era at the age of ten or twelve. We could only figure that at some point she had made a conscious choice to act this way as an adult. If she dressed, groomed and behaved like June Cleaver, she must have reasoned in her twisted way, her problems in life would never be more serious than those June had faced. So why was she now aging, alone and afraid, after two failed marriages?

"Elizabeth, I know you're doing that just to annoy me," she repeated, glaring at the boom box as though it were an animate, willing co-conspirator.

"I heard you the first time."

"Loud music and rush-rush-rush. You're going to end up with an ulcer."

"Mom, you know it's an all day drive to Austin." I was starting to get more than a little irritated. "I want to get back and chill out for a day or two before the semester starts." I buried myself in packing my make-up kit, ignoring the shoe box she placed on top of the suitcase. I knew what was in the box and I knew what she wanted me to do with it. "Forget it, Mom. I'm going straight to Austin."

"It isn't that far out of your way, Elizabeth. You can't do your mother this one little favor? I ask so little..."

"Mom, you know I hate it when you call me Elizabeth! Talk about annoying! How many times..." I trailed off. What was the use?

She stepped to the window and split the Venetian blinds with her Lee Press-Ons. Even above the deafening boom box there was no mistaking the throaty rumble of Michael's jacked-up mini-jeep as it spun into the driveway. I zipped the make-up bag closed, swung it over to the bed and shoved the shoe box off my suitcase. "Christmas is four months away, for Christ's sake!"

"Don't swear in this house," she admonished with a routine flatness as she turned from the window. "Just take this to your grandmother." Mom adjusted the thick rubber band holding the lid in place and repositioned the shoe box on the suitcase. Just as determined, I removed it again.

"Hi, Mom!" Michael grinned from the doorway. At twenty-four he still displayed a youthful effervescence I often found more a defensive insulation for his dissolute life style than a quaint example of Oklahoma good-ol'-boy charm. But then, he was my obnoxious older brother. I was, by birth, entitled to such judgments. His grin widened when he looked toward me. "Thought you were going back today. What are you still doing here?"

I dropped *Rokker* down a couple of notches before stuffing a few last-minute items into the already bulging Samsonite. I didn't want Michael to miss a word of my brilliant rejoinder. "Me? *I'm* in my final year of college. A year from now *I'll* be starting law school. With a place of my own. A *career* of my own. A *life* of my own. The question is, big brother, what are *you* still doing here?"

Beaming proudly, he whipped out a yellow hard-hat from behind his back. "I got the job with Phillips! In Bartlesville. I start Monday!"

"All the more reason you should move out and get your own apartment." I refused to buy into another of his sugar-coated diversions. To tell the truth, I had always enjoyed bursting his bubble. Bringing him down whenever the opportunity presented itself, and not just a notch or two—I'm talking crash-and-burn. It was by now a conditioned reaction, resulting from years of getting knocked around as a child in what I had dramatically described to Mom at the time as *savage, brutal attacks*. An indictment which, on those rare occasions when she even bothered to get involved, would invariably get pleaded down to a lesser charge of *playing too rough*. And just as inevitably, my bitter protests denied, the appellate opinion came in the form of a shrug of dismissal and a *boys will be boys*.

"You two don't start," came Mom's habitual nasal reaction to our sibling bickering. "I like having Michael here. Since your father and I divorced, this house feels so big and empty." Michael, still holding the hard-hat, draped his arm over Mom's shoulder, shooting me a little smirk of victory. And, as usual, Mom enlisted him on her side. "All I ask of her is one small favor—"

"Small favor! Right!" I slammed the suitcase shut.

"Just take the present to Grandmother Pierce. Is that so difficult?"

I concentrated on tucking a suitcase strap, the tip of a sock and the edge of some underwear back inside the overstuffed bag. "You always *mail* her Christmas present. Why do I have to *go* there?"

"She claims they never got there the past two years," Mom came over to help, but I shifted my position to block her. She knew she would win on the Christmas present issue, but I'd be damned if I let her touch my suitcase. "Besides," she continued, "you haven't seen your grandmother in—what's it been—eight years? The summer you were fourteen."

I powered off the boom box and hoisted the strap of the cosmetics bag over my shoulder. Sliding the heavy suitcase off the bed with a loud thump, I looked at Michael, who was still grinning from the doorway. What was I thinking—that he might help? As if! I pushed my way through, making sure to bang the suitcase into my vexatious brother. "No, that's all right, Michael," I fired sarcastically. "I can manage. But thanks so much for offering."

Outside, I refused to let either of them help get the suitcase into the old milk-chocolate Toyota Corolla hatchback sitting in the driveway facing the street. Directly opposite us, old Mr. Murcheson had waddled out in his boxer shorts and T-shirt to retrieve his paper from where it had been skillfully tossed into his wife's bed of geraniums. He peered over the half-cut bifocals perched on the end of his bulbous nose. Great, I thought, just what I need—an audience for the street theater about to unfold. The perky *click-click* of Mother's high heels followed me down the hall—*Jesus! Who wears high heels around the house?!*—and I spoke without looking back. "I've seen her, what, three times my whole life?" It was a last-ditch plea. More like just trying to whine my way out of it. "I mean, my God, she lives so far back in the boonies! I'll get lost! Anyway, it's just a stupid ol' fruitcake."

"And some hand lotion," Mom corrected.

"Hand lotion?" Sometimes I just couldn't believe my mother. "Hand lotion! For a ninety year old Cherokee squaw?!"

"I don't know why I even bother!" Mom gripped her forehead and tilted her head back. "She's your father's mother, not mine! And she's *only* eighty-five."

I didn't want to talk about it any more. I knew I would make the detour to deliver the package. She knew it. End of discussion. I checked my watch and looked up and down the street, then glared directly at old Mr. Murcheson until he bojangled on back inside. We had lived on South 82nd East Avenue in Tulsa for as long as I could remember. When I was growing up, Mom had often spoken of a much nicer house in the hills. A place she had loved. A place we'd been forced to give up when Dad lost his job at the plant in Bartlesville. I often wondered if there had actually been such a house or if this were merely a fairy-tale fragment Mom had used to humiliate Dad and remind him what a disappointing failure he had turned out to be as a man, as a father, as a husband.

I had spoken with Dad the day before by phone. He'd promised to drop by before I left for Austin. I had deliberately dragged around all morning, delaying my departure by more than an hour, just to make sure I didn't miss him. But I knew he wouldn't show. Not because he didn't love me or didn't want to see me. Dad was just Dad. He was probably still sleeping off last night's bottle. Wrestling with the demons. His drinking had steadily increased since Mom kicked him out almost five years ago, my junior year in high school. I got into a lot of trouble that year and almost got expelled from school for ditching class too many times. One day he had busted me hanging out with some friends at the Seven-Eleven. He had pulled up in his ratty old pickup before we could book. But he was cool. Dad always made a point of not embarrassing us in front of our friends. He bought us all Big Gulps then piled us into the back of his pickup and drove us back to school. When we first realized we were busted, we had all expected a substantial dose of swearing, followed by a lecture and threats of exposure to the parents of all concerned. I have never forgotten his compassion and understanding. He was firm. He let us know what we had done was wrong, but he treated us as misguided adults, not as newspaper-chewing dogs to be yelled at and whipped. And now I wanted to tell him how well I was doing at U.T. I knew he'd be proud. And I especially wanted Mom and Michael to see me share it with him. I looked again at my watch and leaned against the Corolla. It was almost two hours past the time he'd said he would be there. I hated that Mom and Michael knew I was waiting for him.

"Dad promised he'd stop by before I left," I offered weakly.

"As usual, your father's on Indian time," she patted my arm in her condescending way that said *You poor thing...you're just the victim of another one of your father's countless shortcomings.*

"Better get goin', Sis!" Michael leaned against his Suzuki Samurai, flipping his yellow hard-hat in the air repeatedly. "You're the *Fruitcake Express*—when it positively has to be there before Christmas."

"Why can't Michael take it," I made one last entreaty. "When's the last time *he* saw Grandma Mary?"

"Six years," his answer came too quickly. He had anticipated my move and was ready. "Jimmy Clayton and me went by there right after high school graduation. That makes it your turn!" He tossed the hard-hat into the passenger seat of the Samurai and jumped in behind the wheel. "Besides, I gotta go buy some steel-toed boots for my new job. Later, Sis! Mom." Michael leaned out the window and gave me one of his harder-than-just-playful punches on the shoulder, then shoved the Suzuki into reverse before I could swing back at him.

I could hear him loudly singing, *"Here comes Santa Claus, here comes Santa Claus..."* even above the thundering muffler as he sped off down the street. I glanced toward the stop sign at the end of the block on the off chance Dad's old pickup might magically appear, but the intersection was empty. I made one last palms-up, pleading whine, "Mom...."

"Honey, just give her the presents, sit and talk to her for a few minutes. Have some tea or coffee or something, and you're back on the road. Be nice. Do this for me. Do it for your father." She knew exactly which buttons to push and when to push them.

"All right. All right." I got in behind the wheel and ground the starter four or five times before the old clunker kicked itself to life. "But you owe me! Big time!" She just smiled her plastic, pleasant smile, knowing she had won. Again.

* * * * * * *

As I drove southwest on I-44, I fought the overwhelming urge to keep going and connect up with the Okmulgee Expressway, down to McAlester where US-69 would take me back to Texas. I glanced down at the shoe box containing the fruitcake and hand lotion resting on the seat beside me. Another couple of hours and that fruitcake would begin to smell. Bad. Really bad. That and the consuming dread of one of Mom's endless telephone harangues was all it took to force the Toyota onto the Broken Arrow Expressway.

Over the river and through the woods... I hoped I could find my way to Grandmother's house. Grandma Mary. Dad's mother. It was State Highway 51 East to Wagoner, I remembered. The same little Mom-and-Pop convenience store with the same old nonfunctioning, 1940's glass reservoir gas pump was still there. Dad had stopped and got us snacks the few times I had been here before, all by the age of fourteen. I pulled in and got a Dr. Pepper and a Peanut Patty. The same old Indian couple ran the place. And I had that same feeling I used to get when I was a kid that they were watching every move I made like I might boost a Snickers or something.

I crossed the Grand River and drove through a wide spot in the road called Hulbert. The turn-off was somewhere between there and Tahlequah. I tried looking at a road map as I drove but abandoned that useless effort after forcing a farmer and his tractor off into the ditch. Then I saw it. The giant dead oak in the corner of a field. I had forgotten all about it, but the instant it came into view, I knew that was where I had to turn.

The narrow, winding dirt road led me deeper into the hill country of Eastern Oklahoma. Indian Territory. Cherokee land. But once I got beyond the great dead oak, nothing looked familiar. I vaguely recalled there was one more turn to make—onto an even narrower, rougher dirt trail. I passed an ancient Indian man in a rickety wagon pulled by a scrawny old mule. The driver saluted me with a gnarled, arthritic hand lifted beside a toothless smile. I drove another hundred yards and stopped at what appeared to be a two-rut path leading into some trees. Was this the one? What the hell, I shrugged, I couldn't get any more lost than I already was. I made a right onto the little road from which the old wagon had just emerged.

Nothing I saw registered as familiar. Yet somehow I knew this was the way. A strange feeling swept over me. At first just a tingling in the stomach, then the overpowering sense you sometimes get that you're being watched. But there was no one in sight. Not even the odd grazing cow or the tediously circling buzzard. Still, someone—or something—was watching me. I felt it.

The little two rut lane—I could hear and feel the weeds and tall grass scratching and thumping the underside of the Corolla—hugged the shadows of a thick stand of blackjack oak and sweetgum alongside a field of anemic and broken cornstalks. Then I veered sharply left and disappeared into the trees beckoning me to enter another world. A few hundred yards later I emerged from the tunnel of overhanging branches into the clearing where my grandmother's frame house stood. It was, indeed, another world—a relic from a strange and distant past. A past that was somehow connected to my father and his mother, but which had nothing to do with me, with the present, and certainly bore no relation to my future.

From the few times in my life I had seen my grandmother, I remembered her as a soft-spoken woman with a twinkle in her eye that belied her years and a strange sense of humor that would set her chuckling at things that left Michael and me staring at each other in puzzlement. I eased the Toyota to a stop and stared in amazement through the dust-covered windshield. It was a picture frozen in time, exactly as I remembered it from eight years before. And all the years before that. The corner of the front porch sagged as it always had. The chickens pecked idly in the sand out front. The floppy-eared hound dog that had seemed ancient to me even as a child occupied the same spot in the cool, dusty shade beside the steps. And there, tottering back and forth in her creaking old rocking chair sat Grandma Mary Pierce. Even her plain dress that had once been a deep blue floral print—now bleached almost colorless—looked familiar. I was sure it was the only dress I had ever seen her wear over the years. Her hair was pulled back in a single long, thick braid that hung down in front of her shoulder. The dark gray that I recalled from childhood had turned to snowy white. Her bony forefinger, crooked around the long, slender stem of her pipe, twitched as she lifted it in greeting as though it were the most natural thing to see me driving up. Like she'd been expecting me all along. But I hadn't seen her in eight years. How could she have known? Did she even recognize me? Probably not. I stepped out of the car and shaded my eyes against the sun.

"Grandma Mary! Hi! It's Liz. Remember me?" I retrieved the shoe box from the car seat and started toward the porch steps.

"Liz. Did you bring my fruitcake?"

I stopped, looked down at the box in my hands, then back at Grandma Mary. "How did you know? It's only August. Fruitcakes are for Christmas." I continued toward the steps. The old dog—I tried but couldn't recall his name—lifted his head, rolled his blood-shot eyes and greeted me with a protracted grunt. He was a stain-toothed, bony-hipped old mongrel whose sad, drooping eyes seemed to confess—and at the same time apologize for—some long-ago, vaguely remembered canine sin.

"Down, Boomer!" Grandma said softly and pointed to the lethargic hound who had hardly stirred, then smiled at me. "The Little People told me you were coming."

"What little people?" I asked, thinking it must be some quaint Cherokee version of the more familiar *A little birdie told me*. She ignored my question and, with the pipe clenched between her teeth, stiffly pushed herself up out of the rocker. The sagging screen door creaked with a long-forgotten but comforting familiarity.

"*Gi-yŭ-ha!* Come on in! Get in this house, girl."

She looked even tinier than I remembered. And more stooped. Each movement was deliberate and calculated, as though by sheer concentration and force of will she could overcome the withering stiffness of arthritis and the tremors of age. The house—like Grandma Mary—appeared smaller than I recalled. Nothing had moved in my eight-year absence. The old pendulum clock which ticked methodically but never had the correct time hung on the wall near the front door. A dusty, antique upright piano Grandma claimed to have played back in the Twenties as

8

accompaniment to silent movies in Tahlequah was now home to a collection of bric-a-brac, books, a hymnal and a few dusty, framed photographs. Here and there on the walls were other old cracked and faded photos of people I didn't know. Mostly Cherokees—stark, intense, unsmiling. The entire house exuded the odor of fried food, Pine Sol and baked bread that I remembered and found strangely comforting. I realized it was an assemblage of smells I identified with Grandma Mary herself.

She went into the cramped but immaculate kitchen where she brewed coffee in what Michael and I had always called the *cowboy pot*, made of gray-flecked blue metal with a triangular spout. Not a word was spoken when she returned to the main room and sat down at the oak dining table where she carved the fruitcake into perfectly equal slices. She stared at me while she consumed one piece and then began another.

"You're the only person I know who actually *eats* my mother's fruitcake," I said, sipping the rich, strong coffee. Grandma Mary washed down a mouthful of the gooey confection, then pushed a slice toward me. "No thanks. I grabbed something on the road," I declined. "It's for you. For Christmas."

Her eyes never left me the whole time she was eating, as though she had been challenged and was determined to prove she could devour the whole thing. When she had consumed all but the final slice, she carefully licked each finger before pushing back from the table and disappearing into the adjacent bedroom. I heard her rustling around. A closet door creaked. A bureau drawer scraped open, then closed. I pinched a corner off the last slice of fruitcake, tasted it and immediately spit it out into my hand. I looked around for a place to put it, then tossed it through the hole in the screen door and felt only sympathy for the poor, stupid chickens that rushed over and began pecking at it.

"Now. *I* have a present for *you*," Grandma Mary spoke from the other room. I had just reclaimed my seat when she brought in a very old wooden box cradled in her withered hands. The edges of the leather hinges were frayed with age, but the beautifully hand-carved designs with inlaid silver, turquoise and mother-of-pearl reflected a craftsmanship that had withstood the ravages of time. She pushed the fruitcake aside and carefully placed the box in the center of the table. I didn't know what it held, but clearly it was very important to her. As children Michael and I had seen the box and often wondered what was inside, but whenever we asked, Grandma had always just smiled and said, "Someday, we'll get into

9

all that." I couldn't understand why she'd want to give something like this to a granddaughter she barely knew.

With trembling fingers she unhooked the tiny latch and lifted the lid like some priestess of antiquity opening the sacred ark. And with that same spiritual reverence, she removed from the box what appeared to be a leather letter pouch, tattered, cracked and heavily worn.

"That's some really old leather," I whispered, then stood up and leaned over for a closer look.

"Like me. Really old leather," she chuckled softly in that way I remembered.

"What's in it?"

"Nothing," she answered, staring at it as though her words carried some hidden meaning.

"Why do you keep it, if it's not important?" I was curious.

"Didn't say it wasn't important. Said there was nothing in it." She continued gazing at the pouch and offered no further explanation.

"Oh, so at one point, it did contain something important. What was it?"

"Nothing," she repeated with a hint of a smile.

"I don't understand."

"Sit down," she motioned me back into my chair.

"No, I can't. Really." I looked at my watch. "I have to get on the road."

"*U-wo-la.* Sit," her crooked finger gestured at the chair, but her eyes never left the cracked leather pouch. "Sit." Carefully she laid the letter pouch aside and brought out the next item—the threadbare remains of what appeared to have been a hand-made doll. The once-delicate features of the porcelain head were almost faded away, chipped and cracked. The material of the dress, though tattered, worn and stained, was unmistakably an exquisite lace that might once have been part of the finest wedding dress of its day. Her old fingers quivered as she tenderly caressed the fabric. Was it an emotional reaction or merely the palsy of age?

"There's a story about this old doll..." her voice yielded sadly to another time. I stood and rested a hand on her shoulder.

"I'm sure there is, Grandma, but I really do have to get going. It's a long way to Austin." Did I really feel pressed to get to Austin, or merely to avoid the long, rambling story that was eminent? Some meandering tale that held no meaning for me.

"I'll make some fry bread," she broke from her reverie and

started toward the kitchen. "You used to like my fry bread when you were a little girl. Sit down. *U-wo-la.*"

"How long does fry bread take?" I asked, checking my watch again. Another hour wouldn't make that much difference.

She turned back to face me, her piercing hazel eyes burning deep into mine. "Do you learn anything at that school?"

"At school?" I asked, caught off guard. "The University of Texas? Grandma, it's one of the finest schools in the country."

"Not what I asked you." She never blinked.

"Yes. All right. I learn a lot."

"Sit!" she repeated, her gnarled old hand on my shoulder pressed me down into the chair with surprising strength. "You will learn something here. Now. Today. I will tell it to you as it was told to me."

"Grandma...will this take long?"

"It takes as long as it takes," she tapped the old box emphasizing each word, then toddled off to the kitchen. I knew I dare not move. I watched through the kitchen door until sometime later she was depositing a plate of steaming hot Indian fry bread on the table beside the ornate treasure box. I glanced again at my watch. If I got on the road within the next half hour, I could still make Austin by dark.

"That's a nice watch," Grandma Mary had caught me checking the time. "Can I see it?" I extended my wrist and the Longine toward her. She squinted and beckoned to bring it closer. I loosened the tiny clasp and slipped the watch off, handing it to her. She held it admiringly toward the light, then dropped it into the side pocket of her dress.

"Grandma...?" I knew it was useless to ask for the watch back. With that devilish smile I remembered, she piled her plate high and settled back in her chair. As she meticulously doctored a piece of fry bread with butter and honey, Grandma Mary began to unfold a story.

"Over four hundred years ago," she started, intently studying the bread, "before the *yo-neg**—the white man—came to our land, the *Tsa-la-gi* lived in what is now the Carolinas, Georgia, Alabama and Tennessee."

"That's a lot of territory." I immediately wished I could

---

*   *Yo-neg* is a dialectic rendering of *u-ne-ga* (or *u-ne-ka*), which is, simply, the Cherokee word for *white*.

retract my patronizing response.

"I talk. You listen," Grandma said without taking her eyes off the bread. There was no way I was going to make Austin before nightfall.

"And Kentucky, Virginia and West Virginia," she continued. "Now, *that's* a lot of territory. Over 120,000 square miles. Mountains, forests, beautiful rivers...all given to our fathers by *A-da-nv-do*, the Great Spirit." She paused to savor a big bite of the dripping pastry. I looked out through the screen door at my car and thought about bolting. As if reading my mind, Grandma Mary picked the largest, perfectly-browned, crisp-around-the-edges piece of fry bread off the platter, put it on a saucer and pushed it over in front of me. It had been years since I had tasted this native delicacy, soaked with butter and smothered in honey. It was worth the wait.

"The first treaty that really began chipping away at this territory," she resumed, "was in 1721 at Charlestown. And once they started taking our land, it was the beginning of the end. Always, the *yo-neg* wanted more...and more...and more...until, finally, our land was very small. And still they wanted more...."

1

Northwest Georgia
1830

The village of Pine Hill sat nestled on a promontory flanked on three sides by a meandering bend of the Conasauga River in the foothills of the southern Blue Ridge Mountains. A couple of warehouses and loading docks lined the bank adjacent to the ferry crossing. The general store, a multi-denominational church, the blacksmith shop and livery stable took up the north side of Pine Hill's main street. Across the village square from the general store was the Indian agent's office, squeezed in between a local government building and the town jail. A pleasant muddle of little businesses clustered around the square completed the center of this bustling town of almost 2,000, founded by early Scottish and Irish traders who had been dealing with the Cherokee and Creek towns up and down these rivers for more than a century.

Pine Hill's multi-cultural population included whites, Cherokees, full-bloods and mixed-blood descendants of the early white settlers. By 1830 it was difficult to distinguish one group from another. A number of *yo-negs* had lived among the Cherokees for decades, had married Cherokee women—sometimes two or three!—and had fathered a multitude of mixed-blood children. Many of these white men had adopted the Cherokee way of regarding things both natural and spiritual. Their attire usually included the traditional Cherokee turban, hunting jacket and knee-high, fringed leather boots. They bore little resemblance in appearance, thought or deed to their white counterparts who remained distant and aloof. And, conversely, many mixed-bloods had gravitated toward the *yo-neg* ways over the generations. Knowing that their very survival hinged on coexisting with the perpetual white wave that would inevitably seep into their country, many influential *Tsa-la-gi* had sent their sons to New England's finest universities and their daughters to finishing schools in Charleston, Atlanta and Savannah.

Within the tribe itself, great advancements had been made. It had taken *Sequoyah*, whose *yo-neg* name was George Guess or Gist, more than twelve years to create a set of written symbols that represented all the syllables used in the Cherokee language. He had travelled to the *Tsa-la-gi* river towns and to the mountain villages teaching his people the mysteries of the *talking leaves*. Most

Cherokees—from children to the very elderly—learned to read and write their language in about six weeks. This amazing little man—small in stature but a giant intellectually—led his people to a level of literacy that far exceeded that of most *yo-negs* in the area. This was especially remarkable because many of the *Tsa-la-gi* became literate in both Cherokee and English while many of their white counterparts were functionally illiterate in English and knew nothing of the Cherokee language. The tribe's laws had been codified, there was a written constitution and a sophisticated judicial system that dispensed justice under the legal guidance of the national tribal council. A newspaper, *The Cherokee Phoenix*, was published simultaneously in English and Cherokee. The Moravians, the Methodists and other religious sects had been allowed to establish schools and missions throughout the territory. Yet all the trappings of social and cultural assimilation the Cherokees had been told would be their only hope of survival weren't enough. The *Tsa-la-gi—heathen* and *cultured* alike—stood between greedy whites and the beautiful native Cherokee lands. The whites lusted after the orchards, the fertile fields, the lush forests and the rich streams and rivers the Cherokees had farmed, hunted and fished since the days of their ancestors. And the discovery of gold a year earlier in the *Tsa-la-gi* region of northern Georgia had only magnified the white man's catabolic appetite and intensified the urgent necessity of removing the Cherokees. More to the point, the Indians must go. Or die.

Regardless of their outward reactions to the white man or their ostensible assimilation of *yo-neg* ways, most Cherokees knew exactly how the white man felt and could predict their behavior with uncanny accuracy. Because of this, many had agreed to move to the Arkansas territory west of the great Father of Waters, the Mississippi. Those who stayed believed—because they had to—that they would never be compelled to leave their beloved hills, their mountains, their valleys or the Cherokee towns that stretched up and down the rivers—Broom Town, Little Hogs Town, Pole Cat Town, Acpactoniche, Turkey Town, Cosat, Chiaha, Chattooga and others. Wishful thinking made some of them believe their adaptability would protect them. Surely the *Tsa-la-gi's* acceptance of the white Christian religion, white educational system and the white call for civilization would bolster their legal claim to their ancestral lands. After all, hadn't it been promised in every treaty to date between the Cherokee and the United States?

Unfortunately, after nearly thirty years, it was clear that

14

those first skeptical Cherokee emigrants were justified in their gloomy predictions. The officially anti-expansionist treaties designed to protect Indian lands from further encroachment weren't worth the paper they were written on. The United States government had turned a deaf ear, a blind eye and a cold heart to the impassioned pleas and logical arguments of anyone who disagreed with their actual expansionist manifesto. Once again, Cherokee leaders were split in their approach to the future. More and more of them realized they had to face facts—their earlier optimism had been in vain. If they were to recoup any sort of compensation for their losses and be granted safe passage to the Arkansas Territory, they'd better get going. The rest decided to ride out the flood. Realistically, the river of white invasion continued to rise, and soon any choices would be washed away, the Eternal Flame drenched forever. The wait-and-see group, led by the principal chief, *Gu-wi-s-gu-wi*, simply wouldn't see the peril they were all in. Although he constantly met with the president and congress, he, too, failed to appreciate the imminent danger. In the end, everyone waited too long.

*   *   *   *   *   *   *

The cool rain had brought refreshing relief from the torturously hot, sleepless summer nights. By morning, the road sloping up from the river was a slippery quagmire. In fact, it seemed like any other wet, summer morning in Pine Hill. Nothing could have been farther from the truth. An ill wind was blowing in across the Conasauga that would forever destroy its still waters and peaceful reflections.

Two wagons were parked in front of the general store. One was loaded with baskets of fresh peaches and ripe melons. The second held a crude cage fashioned from inch-thick saplings tightly bound with strips of rawhide. Inside the cage a large sow grunted, more out of curiosity than from anxiety or discontent. Two spirited ponies tied to the rear of the pig wagon each wore a beautifully crafted saddle adorned with intricately designed silver inlay. Several teenage boys milled around on the rough plank boardwalk running the length of the general store. Fourteen-year-old Michael Drummond, with his deep tan, dark hair and eyes, looked more like a Cherokee than his full-blood best friend, James Walker. In fact, James, who was also fourteen, had hazel eyes and lighter skin than Michael's. But no one would ever mistake for Cherokee the tall, blond, blue-eyed, seventeen-year-old Peter Tanner. Peter was at his happiest when dominating a group of his peers. He viewed himself as a feudal overlord who wanted the younger white boys to admire him when he bullied the Indians. He'd learned to hate and hurt the *Tsa-la-gi* from his father, a former Army Colonel whose official position was that of advisor to local Indian agents. In practice, however, Karl Tanner was a master of bigotry, deception and self-justification who spent most of his time enjoying every devious method possible to cheat the Indians out of their cattle, their crops or—the most valued prize—their land.

Peter, surrounded by Charles, a soft, chunky sixteen-year-old white boy, and two Cherokee boys, twelve and fourteen, studied some strange markings James had just scrawled with charcoal on a broken piece of board. Michael and James stood together, a pace or two apart from the others.

"That's just chicken scratch!" Peter sneered. "It ain't writing! It's just some kind of stupid Injun trick."

"It's no trick," James countered. "It's Cherokee writing."

"*Sequoyah* invented it," Michael jumped in, making it clear whose side he was on. "So his people could read and write their own language."

"Horse shit!" Peter shook his head and gestured toward James with the board. "He's just a stupid Injun. What the hell does he know about reading and writing?"

"I can so read!" James fired back. "We even have our own newspaper. *The Phoenix*. Tell him, Michael!"

Michael had never liked Peter Tanner nor his crude and cruel behavior. Quick tempered and fiercely loyal to his friends, Michael had no intention of letting things go unchallenged. He stepped in front of Peter, glaring up at the older boy who was also considerably taller. "How dare you—of all people!—call him stupid!" Michael exclaimed.

"Everybody knows ain't no Injun smart as a white man!" Peter considered Michael to be as puzzling as Michael found Peter to be repugnant. "He's nothin' but a Injun and you're nothin' but a Injun lover!"

"My Pa says all Injuns is stupid," the pasty Charles validated Peter.

"Your Pa is the stupid one!" James blasted him.

"You better take that back, Injun!" Peter would brook no disrespect from a lowly Cherokee.

Michael's firm grip on James's arm held his friend in check. It wasn't the right time for a fight. Not yet. "Hold on!" Michael

16

stepped between them. "We can settle this," he said and pointed at the gloating Tanner. "Peter, how many languages do you know?"

"What the hell difference does that make? I know the only one *worth* knowing!"

"And you, James?" Michael held up a hand to silence Peter. "How many?"

"Oh, English. Some Greek and Latin from the missionary school. Creek. Choctaw. And, of course, *Tsa-la-gi*. But—"

Michael cut him off with the same gesture and turned back to Peter. "He knows *six*, and you don't do too well with the *one* you know! So, who's callin' who stupid?"

"Oh, no! Three of his are Injun," Peter argued. "They don't count. They aren't *cultured* languages."

The other boys bristled with anticipation, hoping Michael and James would make Peter eat his words. James poked a stick through the bars of the cage and idly scratched the pig's head.

"That *cultured yo-neg* isn't fit to kiss this pig's ass," James mused in his native tongue. When Michael and the other Cherokee boys burst out laughing, Peter demanded to know what was so funny.

"Oh, nothing. He was just wonderin' how many languages the pig speaks," Michael stifled his laughter.

"He damn well better not be sayin' nothin' else!" Peter's eyes narrowed with suspicion.

"The pig smells better, too," James again mumbled in Cherokee. The boys' spewing outburst enraged Peter. "What did he say?!" Michael, choking with laughter, waved him off. The much larger Peter jerked Michael up by the collar and shrieked, "Tell me, damn you!"

Michael patted Peter on the chest and held up a hand to say *Give me a chance to catch my breath.* Peter relaxed his grip. Michael stepped back, holding onto the wagon wheel, and interpreted. "All he said was he could probably have a more *cultured* conversation with the pig than with you!"

Even Charles—gutless toadie that he usually was—snorted at Peter. "Well, then," Peter said, "if he likes pigs so damn much, he might as well waller in the mud like one," and knocked James off the boardwalk.

With lightning speed, Michael threw a perfect punch to the taller boy's stomach. Peter landed on his back with a loud splat in the red mud, and before he could react, the smaller Michael was on top of him, pounding away, flailing wildly, driving both his fists against ribs, stomach, nose and jaw. So suddenly had it happened, so forceful was Michael's attack, that Peter couldn't even muster enough breath to scream, curse or cry out in pain.

But it ended as quickly as it had begun. A broad, angular hand grabbed Michael's jacket from behind, lifting him into the air and depositing him on the boardwalk in front of the general store. At six-foot-four, William Drummond, Michael's father, towered over both boys. This handsome man of forty, humble and soft-spoken, always moved with a confident purpose that quietly announced a presence of irrefutable physical power. He rarely had to use it, but everyone knew it was there. William was the only lawyer anywhere around and was widely regarded as a good and honest man. Although honest lawyers were in short supply, William was the exception and was often called on to render his services in places as far away as Savannah or Charleston. Since he insisted on fair treatment of the Indians, he'd caused a lot of trouble for himself in the white quarter by representing many Cherokee and Creek clients in their legal efforts to make *yo-negs* live up to their contracts. Naturally, many whites felt perfectly justified in flagrantly—and frequently—breaching their contracts with the Indians. William had proven himself very adept at reminding them that the laws weren't just for the protection of the whites. However, even those who hated him were forced to respect him.

"Michael! What have I told you about fighting?!" William thundered.

"I know, Father, but—"

"Peter started it, Mr. Drummond." Now that an adult was present, Charles was perfectly willing to sell Peter out to save his own skin. He scrambled to the other side of the wagon.

Michael grasped at the suggested defense. "He insulted James and his sister! He insulted the whole Cherokee nation!"

Since no one had trouble believing that, all eyes were on Peter as he dragged himself out of the muck. Sheepish and completely covered with mud, he couldn't look any of them in the eye. His embarrassment at having been pounded by a much smaller assailant was evident to all. "We was only joking around, Mr. Drummond," he said, discovering the blood streaming from his nose. "Mostly I just slipped."

Charles completed his defection by joining the others and whining, "Mostly he just whupped yer ass!"

The angrier Peter Tanner became, the more the other boys laughed. "Break it up now," William cheerfully instructed. As much

18

fun as they were having, the boys decided they'd better *git while the gittin' was good.* Just as the group was breaking up, James climbed out of the mud in time to greet his father.

Thomas Walker was a traditional full-blood, much shorter than his friend William, but just as powerfully built. A blue and red turban hid all of his hair but a long, thin braid that hung down just behind his left ear and to which was attached a Creek arrowhead. It was a trophy he had pulled from his own thigh in 1814 at the Battle of the Horseshoe where he, like so many of his fellow Cherokees, had served under Andrew Jackson against the British and their Creek Red Stick allies in what the *yo-negs* referred to as the War of 1812.

A solemn and dignified man, Thomas was also a warm and loyal one. He was a good worker who modestly minded his own business, so the *yo-negs* favorably viewed him as the quintessential *good Indian.* Like William, he carried himself with a quiet blend of confidence and humility. Though considered poor by white standards, Thomas, like so many of the Cherokees—especially the full-bloods—counted himself wealthy beyond all *yo-neg* understanding. Money meant nothing to him compared to the treasure of the mountains, rivers, lakes and trees he had been free to roam and claim as his own from the days of his earliest memories.

Under one arm Thomas clutched two bolts of new cloth, one red and one blue, matching the colors of his turban. He looked at the mud-covered Michael and glanced across the street at the other boys disappearing around the side of the blacksmith shop. A twinkle as his eyes met William's showed that Thomas had surmised the gist of the incident without hearing the details.

"*Si-yo,* Thomas," William acknowledged his friend with the traditional Cherokee greeting. "*To-hi-tsu?*"

"*O-s-da,*" Thomas answered, gesturing with the bolts of cloth at their muddy sons. It was a subtle granting of permission for William to include James in his fatherly rebuke.

"I brought you boys into town to work, not to fight," William lectured. "Now, unload this wagon. Put these melons and peaches in the back of Mr. Clancey's store, then load up our supplies."

Thomas seconded William's tone in addressing James. "Take this pig over to MacDougal's warehouse. I traded it for a rifle, three pots and two bolts of cloth."

Neither boy had to be told twice. Michael began unloading the peaches and melons while James led the pig-wagon toward the warehouse down by the river, passing three riders headed straight toward William and Thomas.

Titus Ogilvie's ragged bay mount was a reflection of its shabby owner. The heavyset, bearded Scot, the soggy tails of his long black coat draped over his stumpy thighs, rode in front of his two burly sons, thick-necked replicas of their father. Cephus, the brighter one, was nineteen and had a stringy, skimpy beard. His younger brother Alton, eighteen, not only had trouble remembering what day of the week it was, he often forgot the names of the days themselves and wasn't entirely convinced they always came in the same order, week after week.

William and Thomas watched the riders approach and stop before them. Titus removed his wide-brimmed black hat and smeared the sweat across his forehead with the back of his sleeve. He and his family had barely escaped from their native Scotland when his plans to swindle all the local farmers out of their land had gone awry. He might have achieved his goal of cheating the farmers—along with half the local villagers—had he not compounded his commercial efforts with more unforgivable behavior. When his liaisons with both the wife and the daughter of the local tavern keeper came to light, he realized he'd better get as far away as he could—as soon as possible. He followed his wife's advice to leave for the New World where new rubes and new maidens awaited. And, since he hadn't been completely unsuccessful, funds were readily available for the hastily arranged trip. The closer he got to America, the better his luck ran. The ocean crossing was rough, and the dysentery was ready to claim anyone unfortunate enough to catch it. Nineteen days out to sea, Mrs. Ogilvie had contracted the dreaded disease. Her survivors could barely conceal their disinterest as the ship's crew consigned her to a watery grave somewhere in the Atlantic. Upon reaching the new world, Titus Ogilvie wasted no time in securing a new bride, Amanda, the less-than-come-hither sister of influential Atlanta businessman, Shadrach Bogen. Out of undying gratitude, Bogen had financed several of his new brother-in-law's entrepreneurial ventures.

Titus dismounted and eyed Thomas Walker condescendingly, categorizing him swiftly as one of those full-blood Indians not worthy of his attention. His hand went out only to William and he spoke with a thick, Scottish brogue. "Good marnin' to ye, sir. Ogilvie's the name. Titus Ogilvie, merchant and tradesman."

"William Drummond, attorney at law," William accepted the handshake. "How do you do?"

"I'm the new representative for Charleston Mercantile,"

20

Ogilvie offered, then gestured back at his mud-spattered offspring. "My boys, Cephus and Alton. We're lookin' for—"

"This is my good friend, Thomas Walker," William interrupted. Thomas reached out and Ogilvie reluctantly responded with a hasty, insincere handshake. The slight wasn't lost on the soft-spoken Cherokee who turned his back completely on Ogilvie, a gesture of supreme insult among the *Tsa-la-gi.*

"So, William," Thomas said, "you and your family will come tonight?"

"It will be an honor, my friend. Elizabeth is looking forward to it."

"Beggin' yer pardon, but we was lookin' fer—" Ogilvie tried to get back into the conversation, but William and Thomas ignored him for the time being.

"And after," Thomas concluded, "we all go to the council meeting."

"Yes...well...like I was sayin', I'm with Charleston Mercantile," Ogilvie inched around to face them once more. "And I'm lookin' for the chief of the Cherokee Injuns. The boy at the ferry said I might find him here in town." William and Thomas eyed each other while Ogilvie dug a piece of paper from his pocket. "Cooweescoowee," Ogilvie squinted, struggling with the pronunciation. "I tell you, these people have some strange names." Continuing to ignore Thomas—one of *these people*—Titus grinned up at William, then followed William's gaze in the direction of the warehouse.

Carefully navigating his way along a string of high spots in the muddy street, a handsome man of medium build, about William's age, with sandy hair and blue-gray eyes, made his way toward them. Though only five feet five inches tall, he was an authoritative figure, dressed in a new black suit, a radiant white shirt with a high collar rising above a blue tie. William stepped off the boardwalk.

"John! John, come here for a minute," he beckoned. "There's someone here I want you to meet." William gently pivoted Ogilvie to face the newcomer. "Mr. Ogilvie, this is John Ross." Ogilvie was quick to spot a man whose sartorial presence exceeded his own. He wiped his hand on his vest before extending it toward Ross.

"Pleased to meet you, Mr. Ogilvie. *Si-yo, Wi-li.* Thomas." Ross first shook hands with his friends before accepting Ogilvie's.

"Ross. Now, that's a fine Scottish name!" Ogilvie bubbled.

"Scottish it is, indeed."

"Mr. Ogilvie's the new Charleston Mercantile agent," William explained. "He's come to trade with the Cherokees."

"I understand the Cherokee in these parts have some damn fine cattle," Ogilvie wanted to ingratiate himself to this obviously successful businessman.

"It's true," Ross confirmed. "Along with some wonderful fruit orchards. And this year's corn crop looks to be an excellent one."

Ogilvie rubbed his hands together in anticipation. "Good. Good. They do love their beef up in Charleston. And peaches. God knows, they love those peaches!" He picked a plump, ripe peach from William's wagon and took a huge bite, the juice and dangling pulp streaming down his beard. Following his father's lead, Cephus leaned down from his horse and grabbed a couple of peaches, tossing one to Alton.

"And what will you trade for cattle, corn and peaches, Mr. Ogilvie?" Ross inquired.

"Ha!" Ogilvie shook the juice from his hand and wiped it again on his vest. "Thar's the best part! A few blankets, mirrors, trinkets. Some pots and pans. They're like children, you know. You have to indulge them. Play up to their chiefs. That sort of thing."

"Oh, is that how it works?" Ross acted grateful for the enlightenment. He exchanged a glance with William and Thomas. They didn't miss his suppressed smile.

"Yes," William added. "Ignorant savages, for the most part. Easily duped."

"Well, gentlemen," Ross said, adjusting a cuff, "I must run along. I have some cattle and peaches to sell. If I can find the right buyer."

Ogilvie shifted to get in front of Ross. "Then you are a local merchant, Mr. Ross?"

"Of sorts, yes," Ross answered. "And, please—call me John. Or, as my family and my Cherokee friends call me—*Gu-wi-s-gu-wi*." The Cherokee chief side-stepped Ogilvie for a parting remark to his friends. "*Wi-li*. Thomas. See you tonight at the council house." He made a polite half-bow to Ogilvie but refused the dripping hand offered him. He nodded to Cephus and Alton and strode away.

Ogilvie was silent, the peach juice dripping from his beard down onto his huge stomach. "Cooweescoowee. He was joking, of course..."

"That, Mr. Ogilvie," William savored the moment, "is John Ross—or *Gu-wi-s-gu-wi*—principal chief of the Cherokee Nation."

The stunned agent of Charleston Mercantile could only mutter, "Well, I'll be a son of a bitch..." and watch the handsome chief heading back toward the warehouse.

"No doubt." William tossed Thomas a peach. "No doubt."

CHAPTER

2

Some might have referred to the spacious, two-story early southern home as an estate. Under a different owner, it might even have born some pretentious title. William Drummond called it simply *the house*. Elm, sweetgum, chinaberry and ancient oaks canopied the sandy-rutted lane that wound its way up from the main road and curled beneath the carriage cover before sloping gently across the clearing down to the large barn backed up against the peach orchard to the south. Beyond the open field behind the barn was a stand of tall pines, a few slender cedars, and more sprawling oaks and sweetgum. The forest was alive with the clatter of crickets and thackle of cicadas, the chatter of jays and mockingbirds, the rapid fire *tick-tick-tick* of woodpeckers, and a creekside chorus of night frogs.

Ezekiel Campbell drove the Drummonds' family carriage up from the barn. Thin and well over six feet tall, the soft-spoken freedman moved with a dignified fluidity of motion. Slow to speak, his words were usually as wise as they were brief. He could make others laugh and forget their anger. Almost twenty years earlier, Ezekiel had been William's first client when he was a young attorney just setting up his practice. Ezekiel was taking two steers to an auction outside of Milledgeville, the capital of Georgia, when suddenly he found himself surrounded by more than a dozen white men. They accused him of being both a runaway slave and a cattle thief. Despite Ezekiel's protest that he was a property owner as well as a freedman, they had severely beaten him—the standard treatment for runaways—and would have hanged or shot him as a cattle thief had William Drummond not happened along. After rescuing him, William took the wounded Ezekiel into his home to recover from the beating. In the following two weeks, William had earned not only Ezekiel's gratitude but his trust as well and had finally convinced the reluctant freedman to bring charges against his attackers.

As the story unfolded in court, it turned out that on his way to Milledgeville Ezekiel had stopped at the Buchanan Plantation to see Reba, a slave girl. They had fallen in love a few months before and wanted to see each other. This wasn't the first time he'd gone there only to meet with a hostile reception. Even though he'd visited on Sunday evenings when slaves were allowed to socialize, Ezekiel had always been chased away under a hail of curses and threats by

Mr. Buchanan, his three sons and their pack of vicious dogs. White slave owners didn't tolerate their niggers associating with freedmen who, they feared, might inspire their captive brothers and sisters to thoughts of freedom and independence. William had volunteered to assist the young state's attorney who had shown little enthusiasm for prosecuting all three sons of the powerful Buchanan family. But nobody—not even the eloquent young William Drummond—could have convinced twelve white jurors that doing justice was worth incurring the Buchanans' wrath. After all, it wasn't as though they had injured a white man. Although William and Ezekiel had lost the case, in one of those conundrum verdicts that flies in the face of logic, the same all-white jury had ordered the defendants to reimburse Ezekiel for the two steers they had shot and left to rot in the road. The senseless slaughter of good cattle shouldn't go unpunished. Even old man Buchanan had personally thanked each juror for teaching his boys a worthwhile lesson about the value of property.

But the court's decree had never been enforced and Ezekiel had never received the payment due him. Nevertheless, word had spread of the unprecedented decision in which a white jury had ordered white landowners to pay restitution to a black man. It was hailed as a moral victory for the downtrodden, and, as a result, William Drummond had become something of a legend among both blacks and Cherokees. At the same time, he had garnered the displeasure of the Buchanans and other whites who, by and large, had subsequently excluded William and his wife, Elizabeth, from the local social registry. The act was not entirely unappreciated by the Drummonds who were not given to a great deal of boring, time-wasting teas and cotillions fraught with frozen smiles, deferential nods and trivial gossip. The one such indulgence which they enjoyed—especially Elizabeth—was the annual governor's ball held in Atlanta. Their social ostracism, however, was occasionally eclipsed by the need for adept legal representation when one of these same whites unexpectedly found himself—or an errant son—facing a serious legal entanglement from which there appeared little likelihood of successful extrication.

Every evening for the first few days following Ezekiel's attack, Reba had slipped away from the Buchanan's plantation and had hurried through the darkness to William's house to care for Ezekiel until his recovery was assured. Her affection for this strong, quiet man was genuine and evident. Elizabeth, William's young bride, had immediately bonded with Reba. Then one night Reba failed to

25

appear. She had been caught by the Buchanans' slave master and had received a beating nearly as severe as the one that had been visited upon her beloved Ezekiel.

For some time, Ezekiel had been saving his money to buy Reba's freedom, but that would have to wait, because Ezekiel felt honor bound to pay the legal fees due this lone white man who had stood up for him. But William not only refused to accept payment for the case he had lost, he also advanced Ezekiel the balance of the money needed to purchase Reba's freedom. William had even transacted the deal, bargaining Buchanan down on the price because Reba was obviously a problem slave. An habitual runaway. Hadn't she just been beaten for sneaking off?

Ezekiel had agreed to work off William's fee, after which he and Reba had planned to go north in search of Ezekiel's relatives somewhere in Illinois. Elizabeth, who by that time had become very fond of Reba, suggested that the couple could discharge the debt much sooner if Reba worked for Mrs. Drummond in the house. Elizabeth's battle with recurring respiratory ailments had left her with a fragile constitution at an early age. She could use the help. Frequently Elizabeth endured protracted spells of sickness interspersed with periods of general malaise and weakness. She often became exhausted after a single trip up the stairs. But William and Elizabeth, it seemed, had never remembered to withhold any of Ezekiel's or Reba's wages to repay the debt which William had refused to acknowledge in the first place. They had given Ezekiel and Reba full pay from the beginning. When both Ezekiel and Reba protested, William argued that they had proven themselves to be worth far more than they had originally agreed to work for, and were, therefore, to consider accounts in balance.

With each passing season, the trip to Illinois had faded with the leaves of autumn and dripped away with the thaws of early spring. Reba had mid-wifed the births of Elizabeth's daughter, Susanna, and son, Michael—both deliveries having nearly claimed the life of this fragile flower. Ezekiel, in his plodding, unassuming way, had proven himself the true master of William's estate. There was nothing he couldn't repair when broken, nothing he couldn't build when needed. His superior husbandry and agrarian intuition had not only enhanced the farm's productivity but had also made possible William's successful law practice by allowing him the luxury of extended absences not always afforded other landed professionals.

"All ready, Mister Drummond," Ezekiel hailed from his carriage seat to William who had just stepped out onto the front porch.

"Thank you, Ezekiel."

William watched Michael riding up from the barn on Midnight, his black stallion, scattering chickens and a few guinea hens before him. "Come on, ladies!" William called back into the house. "We need to travel while it's still light!"

Elizabeth Drummond emerged from the door, patting down her dress, checking every pleat and button. Soft-spoken and beautiful, she never complained about the physical ailments that had plagued her most of her thirty-eight years. And despite her frail constitution, she had always been a source of strength to her family. She had to be to raise the head-strong Michael and the even more intractable Susanna, who hurried out behind Elizabeth. Long, auburn ringlets framed the face of this fifteen-year-old heiress to her mother's beauty. Large, brown eyes and a flawless complexion with the exotic hint of an olive hue might easily have deceived the uninitiated. Few would have suspected that behind those soft, doe eyes lurked an outspoken, strong-willed, often rude young lady. She was being herded toward the carriage by Reba Campbell who had been waging an endless battle against Susanna's caustic tongue since the day the child had first spoken.

Ezekiel assisted Elizabeth and Susanna into the carriage while Reba darted back inside to retrieve a blanket which she placed in Elizabeth's lap. "It's like to be chilly on yo' way home, Miz 'Liz'beth. You'll be needin' this."

"Thank you, Reba," Elizabeth patted Reba's calloused hand with affection.

"Any idea what time you'll be back, Mistah Drummond?" Ezekiel stood holding the reins.

"It'll be late," William said. He climbed up into the seat and took the reins. "Don't wait up. I'll have Michael take care of the horse and the carriage."

"Good 'nuff, then," Ezekiel patted the horse's neck and stepped back. William slapped the reins, jolting the carriage into motion.

* * * * * * *

The leaves of the oak, walnut and sweetgum branches overhanging the road danced like red embers suspended on invisible filaments, fueled by the last rays of a brilliant sunset. William drove with Elizabeth and Susanna behind him in the two-seated carriage.

Michael trotted alongside, quite the independent young man atop his animated ebony stallion. He couldn't resist a grin in reply to the bitter glare from his sister, who considered herself an unwilling prisoner for the evening.

"Whatever in the world possessed you, Father," she leaned forward, still scowling at Michael, "to agree to dine with these people—in the middle of the forest and in the middle of the night?"

Elizabeth gently pulled her daughter back against the seat. "Susanna. They're our friends."

"Well, they aren't *my* friends!" Susanna crossed her arms. "And why must we go to this dreadful all-night gathering of theirs?"

William spoke back over his shoulder. "It's an honor to be invited to a meeting of the Cherokee National Council."

"Why?" Susanna whined. "It has absolutely nothing to do with us! Can't we just have dinner and then go home?" In front of her, William shook his head, hiding his amused expression. "And I'm not eating any strange animals!" Susanna firmly proclaimed. "If I don't recognize it, I don't eat it."

Elizabeth patted her daughter's arm. "Susanna. Please. Promise me..."

It was the familiar conciliatory words, tone and gesture Susanna had come to identify as an inseparable part of her mother. "Promise what?"

This time William twisted in his seat to make sure she didn't miss the full force of his admonition. "You know full well what she's talking about, Susanna. Mind your tongue. Now and for the rest of the evening."

Susanna pulled her arm from beneath her mother's touch and squirmed back against the leather seat, silent, sulking. And no one deluded themselves into believing for an instant that she would allow the day to expire without more sarcasm, insult and confrontation.

* * * * * * *

The Walkers' two-room log cabin, in its bleak simplicity a stark contrast to the elegance of the Drummond house, was no less a home. A large wooden table occupied the center of the main room. The hand-hewn table's surface had been worn smooth over the decades, sealed with the grease and drippings of countless stews and fried Cherokee delicacies. The few other simple pieces of hand-made furniture attracted little attention and clung as mere blemishes to the log walls. A robust blaze crackled in the stone fireplace, its light like soft, golden fingers of a sightless spirit curiously exploring the faces of its visitors.

William and Elizabeth were seated on one side of the table with Susanna safely book-ended between them. The parents were genuinely enjoying the rabbit stew while their daughter picked idly at the large pieces of carrots and potatoes and the chunks of tender meat on the plate before her. Across from them Michael, elbows on the table, one forearm almost surrounding his plate, hungrily devoured his favorite dish. James Walker and his twin sister, Annie, watched silently from their seats atop two wooden barrels placed against the wall. The tattered old dress Annie wore couldn't disguise the beauty of her flawless olive complexion and her piercing hazel eyes. Her hair, a shade lighter than her brother's, was a river of silky brown molasses, pulled behind her head and loosely twisted into a single braid that hung down in front of her left shoulder. Around her waist Annie wore a bright red sash, fashioned from the bolt of cloth her father had bartered for at MacDougal's store earlier in the day.

A few feet away from James and Annie sat their mother's grandfather, an ancient, toothless little man whose face was deeply etched with the history of winters no longer reckoned. His eyes burned with the wisdom whispered from the Other Side, which now had a stronger pull on his spirit than did the things of this world. He studied his guests with a quiet intensity and a hint of a smile.

"Susanna, please!" Elizabeth pleaded under her breath. "I asked you—"

"But it's true, Mother! It's the height of ill manners!" Susanna had demonstratively protested the noted absence from the room of Thomas Walker and his wife. "They invite us to this—this hovel—then they—"

Michael leaned across the table, close to Susanna's face. "That's enough, sister! How dare you insult my friends—right here in their own home!"

"Well, it *is* rude!" she defended herself, gesturing at the food. "They invite us to dinner, serve us this—this—whatever it is, then leave the room! They don't even sit here with us! If we have to eat it, so should they!"

For the first time, James spoke from his seat against the wall. "The food is for our guests. Not for us. When you have finished eating, we will all join you. It is our custom. To honor you."

The Old One was drawn to this beautiful young *yo-neg* girl who seemed so troubled. Beneath her anger and rude arrogance the

Old One sensed a depth the others didn't see. There was a current. A deep, strong current. A current that would someday rise to become the full flow of a mighty river. Suddenly Susanna smiled at him. A warm, genuine smile. Then, just as quickly, she looked away. *Why on earth did I do that,* she wondered. Perhaps she merely found his clown-like, toothless expression and his twitching facial antics amusing.

When Susanna turned from The Old One, she looked directly into the eyes of Thomas Walker and *Tse-ni-si,* or Janice, his wife, visible in the glow of the lantern from the adjoining room. Janice, the obvious source of her daughter's rare beauty, was *A-ni-wa-ya,* of the Wolf Clan. She was a quiet, hard working woman whose subdued personality was perfectly synchronized with her low-keyed husband's quiet demeanor. They were not, however, a couple devoid of passion and humor. Their devotion to each other was deep and binding; their love-making could be quiet, playful or ravenous. They honored, loved, respected and, most importantly, enjoyed their children.

All other eyes in the room were on Susanna following her *faux pas.* If her socially cruel remarks had caused within her even an embryonic fluttering of remorse, she kept it hidden from the others with years of practiced ease. For a fraction of a second she had felt something in the pit of her stomach when she saw the hurt in their eyes, but she knew it wasn't embarrassment. How could it be? In front of a bunch of Indians? And it certainly wouldn't have been compassion or empathy. How could it be? These were Indians.

"Well. It's a nice enough custom, I suppose. Still...quite odd." She analyzed the stew-like concoction before her. With a grand flourish she took a bite, unable to mask her astonishment at its good taste.

"*Tsisdu,*" Annie spoke softly, then translated. "It's rabbit."

"Of course it is. Any idiot would know that," Susanna said and took another bite.

* * * * * * *

Exactly as James had said, once the meal was finished and the table cleared, Thomas and *Tse-ni-si* joined the Drummonds in the main room. A well-worn family ceremonial pipe was lit and started around, beginning with The Old One, who then passed it to William. Elizabeth coughed and declined, but Thomas and Janice both smoked. With that subtle sense of humor characteristic of the

Cherokees, Thomas offered the pipe to Susanna and feigned disappointment when she shook her head, scrunched her nose and held up a hand to keep him at a distance. Then, in a gesture intended to respectfully acknowledge the approaching manhood of James and Michael, Thomas passed the pipe on to the boys. He then concluded his account to The Old One of the meeting earlier in the day between the new merchant, Titus Ogilvie, and Chief John Ross.

"...and William told the fat man: that was John Ross—*Gu-wi-s-gu-wi*—principal chief of the *Tsa-la-gi*."

The boys and Annie laughed, perhaps as much at the gleeful cackle and toothless grin of The Old One, for whom James had been translating, as at the humor of the story itself. William smiled broadly, fully aware of the honor accorded him as the central figure in a story that had just been officially initiated into and would henceforth remain a part of the Walker family's oral tradition.

Elizabeth kept her eye on Michael and wanted to protest when James passed him the pipe. But William, anticipating her, made a little silencing gesture with his hand. Michael took a long draft. The muscles in his chest and shoulders tightened visibly. He was determined not to cough, which could have been misinterpreted as a sign that he hadn't yet fully achieved manhood. What neither William nor Elizabeth missed was what occurred when Annie took the pipe from Michael. Her hand lingered on his longer than was really necessary to receive the instrument, which she then passed back to her great grandfather. The Old One took the pipe, his hand touching her's exactly as hers had Michael's. His wrinkle-framed eyes were slits from the smile he wore. There was—had always been—a special bond between these two. He knew Annie was gifted with a third eye, the ability to see, to hear, to sense things that hadn't yet happened, or simultaneously to feel them as they were happening at a great distance. He had seen in her eyes this hidden light—which he well knew could be at once a blessing and a curse—from the time she was a child.

On one occasion at the age of five, Annie had been playing in the shade of the cabin under his watchful eye while Thomas and Janice were away. Inexplicably she had begun to cry. She sprang to her feet and raced to the corner to look out behind the cabin. The chickens were still scratching and pecking at the grain thrown out for them earlier. A mother hen and her six baby chicks were Annie's favorites. Her little fingers tugged anxiously at a strip of bark on one of the cabin logs. Within seconds a *ta-wo-di*, or chicken hawk, had swooped down out of nowhere and snatched two of the chicks.

The rest of the birds scattered in a storm of squawks and feathers, the remaining chicks bouncing like tiny balls of fuzzy sunlight after their hysterical mother.

Yet another time—at an even earlier age—Annie had come to The Old One and, without speaking, had begun tapping hard on his left forearm and calling out her brother's name—*Tsi-mi! Tsi-mi! Tsi-mi!* Half an hour later her father had returned to the cabin carrying her twin. James had climbed up into a tree to retrieve a squirrel Thomas had shot with a blow dart. The animal had lodged in the tree's branches in its fall. An expert climber even at so young an age, *Tsi-mi* had stepped out onto a dead limb which snapped beneath him. He had fallen and broken his left forearm in the exact spot Annie had indicated. Since her early childhood The Old One had guided Annie in the direction of the Great Spirit and the mysteries of the Eternal Flame. Indeed, she could be, he sometimes thought, a *Gi-ga-u*, or Beloved Woman. She was, after all, of the Wolf Clan.

After the pipe was passed around again, there followed a long silence which, among the Cherokee, was entirely appropriate and viewed as a sign of balance and serenity. Susanna, however, couldn't abide the disconcerting quiet, punctuated only by the slapping of the dog's tail against the dirt floor where he lay beside the fireplace.

"I'm going to finishing school," she announced. No one responded. "In Charleston," she added. "In the Fall." Another long silence followed while the pipe went around once more. The only one bothered or embarrassed was Susanna. "I suppose that was a foolish thing to say," she cocked her chin to one side and looked around her. "Under the circumstances..."

"It's all right," Annie said, her compassion for her guest's discomfort had outweighed Susanna's condescending air of superiority. "Many Cherokee girls have gone to your finishing schools."

"Really?" Susanna was genuinely surprised.

"It has taught them to be polite," Mrs. Walker added, her meaning grasped by all but Susanna.

"Perhaps she will become a lady," Michael teased his sister.

"Yes, and an Abolitionist," Susanna proclaimed.

"Susanna. That's enough," her mother cautioned.

"It's true!" Susanna refused to let it rest. "I am an Abolitionist! No man should be slave to another!"

"Susie..." William's voice was soft but firm.

Thomas gently exhaled the smoke and passed the pipe to

William before speaking. "Many of the wealthier *Tsa-la-gi* have *di-gi-tsi-na-tla-i*, the black slaves."

"Well, it's *wrong!*" Susanna crossed her arms with a truculent thrust of her chin. The pipe made the circle again, eventually coming back to Thomas. Finally he spoke.

"Yes. It is wrong."

"Father, you don't own slaves," Susanna felt obliged to expound. "You pay Ezekiel and Reba. They stay because they like working for you, but they could leave at any time."

"True," William agreed. "They are free to go."

"Then why do you get upset when I speak out against owning slaves?"

With an apologetic glance to Thomas and Janice, Elizabeth answered for her husband. "Dear, it's just that a young woman should fix her thoughts on spinning, sewing and cooking. Taking care of her home and her children."

"Oh, I think not, Mother!" Susanna hated it when her mother—or anyone else—assumed her destiny lay, without question, in the same path as the generations of mothers and grandmothers who had gone before her. It wasn't a new argument, nor was it the first time she had incurred a stern glare from her father for her bellicose tone. "With all due respect, dear Mother..." she added, then marked the end of the discussion by rising and crossing the room to examine the artifacts hanging on the wall. There were two doe-skin quivers filled with arrows, crossed and hanging beneath a shield painted with designs, figures and glyphic markings she couldn't decipher. Nearby hung a collection of traditional Cherokee blow guns of varying lengths along with a couple of pouches containing their feather-tipped darts. She traced her finger across a doe-skin stretched out on the wall, held in place by wooden pegs, and was surprised by it's delicate softness. Susanna knew all eyes were on her and made a point of keeping her back to the others. It was her familiar way of not dealing with a socially awkward situation when she, in fact, had been the very author of the unpleasantness.

As had been the case all their lives, Michael felt compelled to vie for his parents' attention. "Tomorrow I'm going with James to see his uncles. They're teaching us to be hunters and warriors."

"Of course you are, little brother," Susanna snorted over her shoulder. "You're going to become a big, brave warrior and slay your enemies!"

"Susanna..." came Elizabeth's familiar petition.

Susanna ignored her mother and continued torturing James.

"Why your uncles? Why doesn't your father teach you?" She was genuinely curious but couldn't resist concluding with her familiar sarcasm, "Don't tell me...it's your custom."

"Already James is amazing with the knife and the blow gun," Michael boasted.

"And you should see Michael shoot the rifle," James returned the compliment with equal enthusiasm. "With the eye of an eagle!"

"Go ahead, James! Show them—with the knife!" Michael urged. "Show them!"

Michael saw his mother's face cloud with concern. "That's all right, James," Elizabeth said. "We'll take Michael's word for it."

James reached down and pulled a wood-handled knife from his boot. In one smooth, fast motion he hurled the weapon across the room. It pierced Thomas's hat hanging on a peg beside the door, only inches from Susanna's head. Elizabeth and Susanna gasped while The Old One cackled with glee.

"See!" Michael beamed proudly. "Right in the middle!"

Encouraged by the reaction, James grabbed a four-foot-long blow gun from the wall and loaded a feathered dart. He held the tube to his mouth and his cheeks ballooned like a chipmunk's. There was a soft but definite *poof* and the four-inch dart shuddered where it had landed in the wooden handle of the knife. William and Elizabeth were breathless. Susanna's eyes anchored on the knife and the dart only inches away. Thomas, pleased with his son's performance, proudly took in the reactions of the others.

"So," William broke the silence. "You're pretty good with the rifle, then, are you, son?"

Michael swelled with pride.

"Please! Let's not have a demonstration just now!" his mother's quiet plea brought chuckles from the Walkers. Annie translated for The Old One who grinned and nodded in agreement.

Thomas added to the praise of his friend's son. "He is perhaps the best. John and Andrew, my wife's brothers, say it is so."

Susanna didn't like her brother and his friend commanding all the attention. It was time to reclaim center stage. "Then I'm sure it must be true," she said. She glided along the logs, past the knife and dart, to the stuffed head of a wolf mounted at the end of the room, centered on the wall by itself. "Tell me," she continued, "what's the significance of this smelly old thing? Another of your quaint little customs?"

"It's *wa-ya*, the wolf," James answered.

"Well, any idiot can see that," Susanna snorted with a supercilious flick of her curled locks.

"It's our clan. The Wolf Clan. *A-ni-wa-ya,*" Annie explained.

"The *Tsa-la-gi* have seven clans," James added. "The Bird clan, the Deer, the Wolf. The Blue clan and the Paint clan. The Long Hair and the Wild Potato, which we sometimes call the Bear Clan."

"We came from clans in Scotland, didn't we, Father?" Susanna said, venturing to touch the wolf's nose with a fingertip, then recoiling with disgust.

"Yes," William answered, "but it isn't exactly the same."

"Well," Susanna offered her perfected smile of feigned sincerity, "it's all so very, very fascinating."

William pulled the watch from his vest pocket and popped it open. The Old One's eyes sparkled with delight at the shiny time piece. "Perhaps we should be getting on to the council grounds," William suggested.

"My, yes," Susanna snipped under her breath, "we certainly don't want to miss *that!*"

"Susanna..." Elizabeth cautioned.

"All right, Mother. All right."

Everyone reached for hats, shawls and jackets. Thomas gave James a glare of mock severity as he retrieved his punctured hat from the wall and swatted playfully at his son. Thomas rehung the hat on its peg, opting instead for the turban which he gracefully and expertly twisted around his head. The jostling and preparation for departure found Michael and Annie pushed together in the corner near the door.

"That's a pretty sash, Annie," Michael fumbled to make conversation. He slipped into his fringed hunting shirt and joined James. Annie acknowledged the compliment with a smile but didn't speak. Her eyes remained locked on Michael. Though she had never spoken of it to anyone—not even to The Old One—Annie knew even at the tender age of fourteen that her own destiny was intertwined with that of Michael Drummond. Just how that destiny was to unfold she didn't know. She had received no presentiment to enlighten this particular mystery, and she wasn't sure she even wanted to know. Some things were better left to their own time.

The Old One reached up and hooked his finger under the chain lying against William's vest, lifting the gold watch from its tiny pocket. He stretched the tether to its full length, holding the timepiece to his ear—*tick-tick-tick*—and broke into his familiar toothless grin. While William stood there indulging The Old One's playful curiosity, James tapped his friend's father respectfully on the arm and said softly, "Thank you for letting Michael go with me tomorrow."

Before William could reply, The Old One pushed the watch back into William's hand, clung tightly to William's wrist and mumbled a few unintelligible words in Cherokee. William looked to Thomas, who translated.

"He says in your heart you must have *Tsa-la-gi* blood."

"And in his head he has corn meal mush!" Susanna spoke aside to her mother. "He's allowing Michael to turn himself into one of *them*!"

"I'm certain it's only a phase. It will pass," Elizabeth assured her with an entreating gesture to keep her voice down. "Now, please, just..."

"I know, Mother," Susanna cut her off. "Mind my tongue."

On her way to the door, Annie stopped to place a blanket around The Old One's shoulders. He expressed his appreciation with a trembling pat of her arm and looked up at her. Annie's eyes were still on Michael, watching him and James add a few more wedges of wood to the fire. Susanna inched her way past The Old One toward the cabin door. When he grasped her hand, she emitted a short, shrill yelp and attempted to pull away, but The Old One held fast. It was as though through this physical contact he could, with the wisdom of his years, see inside her soul. Just as he had done with William, The Old One mumbled in his native tongue. Everyone in the room was motionless, and for a fleeting instant Susanna's expression bore a seed of profound understanding. But before that seed could blossom into any meaningful thought, it was replaced by a nose-wrinkled grimace of revulsion. When she tried to free her hand a second time, The Old One relinquished his grip but kept his eyes locked on Susanna's. The recoil of her escape caused her to brush against her brother.

"What did he say?" she asked.

"Something about your spirit."

"He doesn't even know me," her voice dripped with disdain. Unconsciously she wiped her hand on Michael's sleeve. "What could he possibly have to say about my spirit?"

With a customary toss of her hair, Susanna washed the entire incident from the slate of her experience and moved on to the door, leaving The Old One staring after her, still muttering softly to himself.

* * * * * * *

Since the beginning of Cherokee time the number seven had been sacred among the people. Over the years *Tsa-la-gi* social, religious and political structures had evolved around sevens. There were, of course, the seven tribal clans. The sacred ceremonial fires were kindled from seven different kinds of wood—hickory, oak, maple, locust, birch, beech and ash. There were seven directions. In addition to the four customary ordinals of north, south, east and west, there were the directions of up, down and, not the least important, within, or where one was at the moment. The Cherokee held many celebrations throughout the year, but there were seven special festivals always held during a new moon: the First New Moon of Spring, usually coming in late March or early April; the New Green Corn Ceremony, *Se-lu Tsu-ni-gi-s-ti-s-ti*, normally in early August when the first sweet roasting ears were ready to eat; the Ripe Corn Ceremony, *Do-na-go-hu-ni*, in September in honor of the mature or ripened corn; the Great New Moon Ceremony, *Nu-wa-ti-e-qua*, in late September or early October at the first new moon of autumn—and marking the Cherokee New Year; the *A-to-hu-na*, or Reconciliation and New Friends Ceremony, which usually came ten days after the last festival; the Bouncing Bush Feast, *E-la-wa-ta-le-gi*, whose time would be set only at the first new moon of autumn; and the *U-ku*, or peace chief's dance, which came around only every seventh year and replaced the Great New Moon Ceremony. At this festival, the peace chief, clad entirely in yellow, solemnly rededicated himself to leading his people and prayed to the Great Spirit for wisdom and guidance.

The seven-sided Cherokee council house at New Echota sat in a clearing on the highest point of ground in the immediate area. A new permanent capital had been established by resolution of the Cherokee Nation's legislative Council less than five years earlier, in November of 1825, on the site of what had up until then been called New Town. It was renamed New Echota in honor of their beloved Echota on the Little Tennessee River, which had served as their principal city for many years. But blood hostilities between the whites and the Cherokees of the Upper, Middle and Overhill towns ranging throughout northern Georgia, Tennessee and western Northern Carolina had forced them to relocate. The new capital was situated on the south side of the confluence of the Coosawattee and Conasauga Rivers where they came together to form the Oostanula. This, it was believed, approximated the geographical center of what remained of the once vast Cherokee lands and would be accessible to the Cherokees from all directions.

A hundred one-acre lots had been marked off, with the town square taking two acres. The main street was sixty feet wide, with other streets set a bit narrower at fifty feet. In addition to the council house there was a building set aside for the *Tsa-la-gi* Supreme Court, and adjacent to it stood the print shop where Elias Boudinot oversaw the publication of the Cherokee-English newspaper, *The Cherokee Phoenix.*

The council house, supported on log poles—straight, smoothly polished and thicker than a man's leg—was an open-sided structure with a tightly thatched roof and a hole in the center to emit smoke from the council fire that burned in the specially made stone pit. On all seven sides, which symbolically represented the seven tribal clans, rows of log benches pie-wedged toward the center for those in attendance, a section of seats assigned to members of each clan. The closer one sat toward the center, the more esteemed was one's position in conducting tribal affairs. The principal chief occupied a place in the center near the fire. Close to him were his assistant chiefs, former chiefs and other highly respected tribal leaders. Many of them over the years had been women. Also near the chief was a special seat for any honored guest—a visiting Cherokee or an emissary from another Indian tribe—who would speak to the assembly.

Only whites of great importance—direct representatives of the President of the United States or the state governor—who were scheduled to address the council were allowed to sit with the chiefs and tribal leaders at the center of the council house. The run-of-the-mill Indian agents and other visitors—whites, Indians from other tribes, traders and merchants—were consigned to the perimeter, counting themselves esteemed enough if they managed to command a seat or even a standing position under the outer edge of the roof. Most Cherokees believed it was their role—without rancor or complaint—to confront and somehow overcome the harshness of winter's bitter cold or harvest time's hunger after a long summer's denying drought. Only then could they claim their seat at the council fire as true *Tsa-la-gi*, the People of the Eternal Flame.

No children were allowed inside during a council meeting, and even when no meeting was in progress, any child entering the council house did so with the utmost reverence and respect.

On this evening the grounds were packed. Dozens of fires winked from the surrounding woods. No formal starting time had been set and no announcement had been made. The Cherokees intuitively knew when it was time for the meeting to commence. The men, many in their turbans of red or blue, others wearing European-style hats, moved up the gentle slope. The traditional Cherokee jackets worn by many, bound at the waist by a brightly colored sash, marked the occasion as a meeting of great importance. Behind them came the women, teens and visitors, most of whom would remain outside the council house. The speeches that would ring out from beside the council fire would carry words to be weighed carefully, calling for decisions to be salted with the wisdom of the elders, the outcome of which would undoubtedly have grave consequences for the *Tsa-la-gi* people.

The mass of humanity flowed in a quiet and orderly manner, drawn through the darkness by some invisible magnet. The Drummonds stayed close to the Walkers. Susanna noticed that many of the Cherokees moving alongside them wore fringed, doe-skin hunting shirts like Michael's, and many—both men and women—had on the fringed moccasin-type boots that reached almost to the knee. There were also, she noted, a number of other whites who had come to observe, as well as many mixed-bloods and full-bloods who had abandoned their native dress in favor of the *yo-neg* style of clothing and were, for all intents and purposes, hardly discernible from the whites.

Thomas Walker stopped halfway up the grade to greet another Cherokee family. *"Si-yo, Tsa-li,"* Thomas uttered the familiar greeting to the wiry man with deep-set eyes that, to a stranger, were neither instantly warm and accepting nor cold and distant. They said with caution, *Be a friend and you have found a friend; show hostility or lack of respect and you have made a deadly enemy.* William had known *Tsa-li* Swimmer, or Charlie, even longer than he had known Thomas Walker. In William's opinion there was no better man—Indian, white or black—in the state of Georgia for shoeing a horse or doctoring a sick animal. The men shook hands and waited for their women to catch up. *E-wi* (Eva) Swimmer was at least two to three inches taller than her husband. This attractive twenty-nine-year-old full-blood stood erect with a stately, even regal bearing. She was noticeably pregnant with their third child.

"Dear, you remember Charlie Swimmer," William said. Elizabeth nodded.

"Nice to see you again, Eva." She squeezed the hand of the quiet, proud woman before her. "Our daughter, Susanna."

Susanna ignored the offered hand and refused to meet Eva's

eyes, staring instead in the direction of the council house, pretending to be searching for someone in particular. William scowled but let the incident pass.

"And Michael," Eva said with a smile. "Yes, we know *Mi-ki* well. He and James have taken *Tsu-tsu* fishing with them when many of the older boys wouldn't." She placed her hand on the shoulder of her seven-year-old son, the bright-eyed *Tsu-tsu* (Martin) Swimmer. He slipped from beneath her mothering touch to join Michael and James. He felt proud and important to be accepted into the company of these boys twice his age. They were his heroes.

Annie Walker smiled and spoke to *Tsu-tsu's* bashful, ten-year-old sister. "*Si-yo, Ma-di*." Martha Swimmer smiled and lowered her eyes.

"And our daughter, Martha," Eva completed the introduction.

Michael and James, with Martin strutting proudly behind them, joined some other boys headed up the hill. Their excitement was evident, but in a quiet, restrained way without the usual rowdiness of boys their age. The rest took the cue to resume their trek up the slope.

"It will be good talk tonight," Charlie Swimmer predicted.

"*Ŭ-ŭ*," Thomas grunted the nasal Cherokee affirmative.

Susanna her arms wrapped protectively around herself, kept close to her father. She glanced from side to side, her curiosity about these strange people exceeded only by her apprehension of the unfamiliar. They moved past numerous fires. At each one a medicine man, or *di-da-nŭ-wi-s-gi*, muttered incantations while *fixing* a clump of tobacco or exhorted a gathering about some indeterminate matter of great significance.

When William strode on ahead with Thomas and Charlie, Susanna positioned herself safely between her mother and Janice Walker on one side and Eva Swimmer on the other. And, as far as Susanna was concerned, Annie Walker and Martha Swimmer might as well not have existed.

* * * * * * *

The council house was packed. The log benches near the blazing fire were filled with tribal leaders and dignitaries, including the venerable old chiefs, Whitepath, Situwakee and *Tsunaluska*. The latter had, at the Battle of Horseshoe Bend in the War of 1812, actually saved Andrew Jackson from certain death at the hand of a Creek Red Stick warrior. The Creeks, ordinarily friends of the *Tsa-*

la-gi, had been enlisted to fight on the side of the British. The Red Stick warrior had the American commander bent backwards over a fallen log with his blood-red war ax raised for the death blow. *Tsunaluska* had leaped out of nowhere to seize the Creek warrior's arm while driving his own knife into the Red Stick's side. It was an act which, ironically, had elevated *Tsunaluska* to great status, both among the whites and his own people, by saving the life of the man who, since his election as President in 1828, had made it a personal crusade to see the Cherokees driven from their beloved homeland.

Susanna Drummond, in her detached observation of the quaint and the curious, eventually drifted from her mother's side and soon found herself surrounded by unfamiliar faces. She stifled an initial flash of panic and glanced around for Annie Walker, the only face she expected to recognize among these young Cherokees. It took a while to locate Annie several feet away where she was surrounded by a group of Cherokee girls her and Susanna's ages. Their eyes met briefly before Annie looked down, intimidated by Susanna's condescending arrogance. No help there, Susanna thought, dismissing Annie as useless in any social sense. She was nothing more than a visual point of reference.

Susanna spotted a handsome, fair-haired young man a few feet away from Annie and her friends. Obviously the son of one of the merchants or Indian agents attending the council, Susanna concluded. His deep blue eyes found hers and answered with a smile. With a toss of her curls and a glance toward Annie that said *There! Who needs you, after all?*, Susanna edged past the Cherokee girls toward her newfound compatriot.

"Hello, there," Susanna purred, taking his arm as if this gesture united the two of them amidst a sea of Cherokee inferiority. "This is my first time to one of these things," she confided.

The young man looked at her and listened politely with a faint smile, allowing her to finish before he softly replied in Cherokee, "*A-wi-u-s-di...a-s-ga-s-di...*"

Reacting like the frightened little deer the young mixed-blood had just described, Susanna jerked her hand away as though she had unwittingly embraced a leper. She took a step backwards, her eyes locked on the puzzled boy, searching his face for the signs she had obviously missed in the diminished light, signs that should have alerted her not to talk to him, he's one of *them*. Susanna took another step back and bumped into someone. She spun around to find herself face to face with her brother and James Walker. She grabbed Michael's arm, exhaling a mixture of relief and irritation.

41

"Stay right here! Don't you leave me!"

"Where's Mother?"

"There," Susanna pointed. "Behind Father."

Elizabeth stood between Janice Walker and Eva Swimmer at the outer edge of the council house. Directly in front of them, seated on the outermost log bench, were their husbands. James spotted them and spoke softly to Michael.

"My father and Charlie Swimmer think very highly of your father. They have taken him inside the council house."

Susanna reached up and tugged at the edge of Michael's turban. "Get that silly thing off your head. It looks ridiculous." James's expression went stone again. Susanna caught the hurt in his eyes in the instant before he looked away.

"I only meant because he isn't Cherokee," she lied to soften the insult.

"Hello, Susanna Drummond."

Susanna looked up at the tall and not unhandsome Peter Tanner. She smiled and immediately forgot her request for the security of her brother's presence. It was evident that she liked this young man and coyly made certain he was aware of it as well.

"Hello yourself, Peter Tanner. Goodness me! What on earth happened to your face?" she focused on the swelling and discoloration about Peter's left eye. Michael and James answered Peter's nasty glare with smirks of amused defiance. Susanna realized Peter's wound had something to do with the dreadful story recounted over dinner at the Walker's cabin—a boring anecdote to which she had paid little attention. "And what brings you to a place like this" she recaptured his vision, stepping between Peter and her brother.

"Father says I should study the Cherokees," Peter replied with importance. "Get to know them. See how they live. How they think." He didn't miss the expression of contempt that passed between Michael and James. Peter elaborated for Susanna. "Father says that after I go to West Point, my first assignment as an officer might well be right here to control these people."

"*These people*?" Michael was outraged. "What makes you think the *Tsa-la-gi* need to be *controlled*? Especially by the likes of you!"

"No one's talking to you," Peter tried to appear smugly superior. At the same time, he unconsciously inched back from Michael.

"That's right," Susanna agreed. "Be quiet, Michael."

James playfully pushed the end of his nose up with his thumb to simulate a pig's snout and grunted softly. Little *Tsu-tsu* Swimmer repeated the gesture from the safety of his position between Michael and James. Peter pointed a finger right in James's face. "You'll get yours, Injun boy. Sooner or later," he promised in a chilling tone, then took a swat at *Tsu-tsu*, who nimbly ducked out of reach.

James nudged Michael with quiet excitement and pointed to the center of the council house. He raised a hand to call for silence and said in a soft voice, "The Ridge is going to speak!" Until now the chiefs, sub-chiefs and elders at the center of the council house had been engaged in routine discussions of quotidian tribal affairs that held little interest for the average Cherokee—especially teenage boys—and meant absolutely nothing to those *yo-negs* who were merely there to observe.

A hush fell over the gathering. From a bench next to the council fire there arose a tall, distinguished full-blood Cherokee dressed in European-style clothing except for his native, knee-high boots. His olive skin stretched darkly across high, prominent cheek bones, his expansive forehead was furrowed, his eyebrows exploded in great, gray tufts. The Ridge had been born in the mountainous region of eastern Tennessee along the Hiwassee River and for years had been considered by many to be the most electrifying orator among the *Tsa-la-gi*. He and his brother, *Oo-watie*, The Ancient One, were members of the Deer Clan and, it was told, were descendants of the great chief, *Attacullaculla*, The Little Carpenter, whose reputation as a statesman and negotiator were legend, both among Cherokees and whites. In his early years, The Ridge had ridden with Doublehead and his brother, Pumpkin Boy, two of the most savage warriors among the Chickamaugan band. He had taken his first scalp at seventeen in raids following the Hopewell Treaty of 1785. But Ridge had been considered too soft by some of the Chickamaugans because of the compassion he often displayed and his distaste for the random, wanton murder of any and all whites. Later Ridge had moved to the southern part of the Cherokee lands—the Overhill Towns—and had married Susanna Wickett, or *Se-ho-ya*, a mixed-blood of great intelligence and beauty.

The Ridge had joined hundreds of his fellow Cherokees on the side of the Americans in the 1812 war with the British and the Creek Red Sticks. In the bitter winter of 1813-14, when Andrew Jackson was down to fewer than two hundred men and desperate for his first battle victory, Old Hickory had field promoted The Ridge to the rank of *major* for his efforts in raising additional forces from among the

Cherokees. Some whites viewed the rank as little more than the typical patronizing and condescending use of the word *chief* when addressing a *lowly Injun* or of *boss* when speaking to a black—freedman or slave. But The Ridge—now *Major* Ridge—knew his own value as a warrior and a leader and had chosen to take the title at its face value and wear it with pride.

From the time he first met and fell in love with *Sehoya*, she had been a stabilizing influence, and The Ridge's bloody ways had finally yielded to a more civilized lifestyle. He had, in fact, become one of the most influential landowners in the area, master of untold acres that supported hundreds of cattle and horses, extensive fruit orchards and rich fields of bountiful annual crops.

All eyes were riveted on his commanding presence. The nearly-sixty-year-old tribal leader curried his fingers through his long, gray, wavy hair. He stepped up to the council fire and held his hand above the flame for an inordinately long time, eyeing the diminutive mixed-blood dragoman who would translate his words into English. Though Ridge had become quite fluent in the white man's language, everyone knew he would address the council only in his native tongue. His baritone voice was melodic, resonant, almost hypnotic. In the respectful quiet the crackling of the fire sounded unusually loud. The Ridge's first words exploded the silence.

"People! Hear what I say. Listen with your heart!" he boomed in Cherokee. In a near monotone contrasting the speaker's delivery, the skinny translator with a shrivelled left hand echoed The Ridge's words in English. "For uncounted seasons our fathers and their fathers walked in these forests, given to us by the Great Spirit. Then the white man came. Those who came in peace, we welcomed as brothers. Those who came with their rifles and swords pointed at the *Tsa-la-gi*, we killed them or drove them from this land. But more whites came. With new weapons. More deadly than swords, rifles or cannons. Their new weapons were treaty talks and surveyor transits. Land stealers. They talked to our chiefs. And when the talks were done, our land was gone. *No more*, they said. *This is all the land we want. We will take no more.* Seasons passed. More talk. The whites made a new country called Georgia. Then the leaders of Georgia said they want all *Tsa-la-gi* land. But our Great Father in Washington said *No! Tsa-la-gi land belongs to Tsa-la-gi. No more for the white man.* And so it was written in a new treaty. Yet, still the whites continued to settle on *Tsa-la-gi* land. And when the snows came, I called on *Tsa-la-gi* warriors to ride with me..."

His brown eyes glazed over and settled, trance-like, on the

head of a bear staring down at him from one of the council house main cross beams above the section occupied by members of the Wild Potato Clan. All eyes and ears—of Cherokees, whites, and visiting members of other tribes—belonged to him as he described a land lying silent beneath the snow. Through the barren branches of the trees surrounding the clearing, he and twenty mounted warriors had watched the smoke curl up from the cabin of the white intruders who had built there illegally. Even after the treaty with the United States had strictly forbidden them to do so. He told of how he rode, in his leather leggings, bare from the waist up in the bitter cold, his entire upper body and face painted red, his war crown a horned buffalo head. He created a vivid word picture of his band of men. They were clad mostly in buckskins, but a few wore *yo-neg* hats and clothing, looking more like those they were riding to dispossess of their unlawful homestead than like Cherokee warriors.

He told how he and his men sat there in the cold, with their rifles resting across their saddles, watching the white settler lash his belongings to the rickety, overstuffed wagon he had been given one hour to load; how the settler's wife and daughter sat silently in the wagon, staring back at the *Tsa-la-gi* warriors; how the ten-year-old son had finally found his pet goat and had been placed with the rest of the family in the ox-drawn wagon which had then moved off into the thickening snowfall; how, above the crunching of the wagon wheels in the frozen mud, rose the crackling of the flames they had set to the squatters' cabin. Finally, The Ridge brought his eyes down to those nearest the council fire.

"Eighteen intruders we drove out that day. But only those who came *after* the law was made to keep them out. Our white brothers who came *before* that law was made have nothing to fear. But hear my words, *Tsa-la-gi*: we are at a crossroads. One road leads west. President *Tse-gi-si-ni* and those in Georgia, Tennessee, Alabama and Carolina—they want us to leave the land of our fathers and take that road west. But if we refuse to go, if we stay and fight for our land—I fear it is a road that will lead our nation into darkness. Our children into extinction. The white man's river of greed and hatred is rising out of its banks. Threatening to flood us out of existence. The time is coming when we must decide. Take these words into your hearts. The season is at hand. This is what I tell you. *A-ya a-gi-ha.*"

"I have spoken," came the translation of his final phrase, and The Ridge took his seat. The long silence that followed was marked only by an occasional scattered grunt—the traditional sign of

45

approval—from many of the tribal elders and minor chiefs.

William Drummond, himself schooled in the art of public oratory, leaned to whisper his assessment to Thomas Walker and Charlie Swimmer. Looking out across the crowd, William caught the eye of someone standing just outside the council house opposite them. A couple of onlookers shifted, giving William a clear view into the face of Titus Ogilvie. William nodded in acknowledgment with a hint of a smile. Ogilvie didn't miss his meaning. He frowned with embarrassment and looked away.

The sporadic grunts following The Ridge's speech gradually gave way to a soft buzz of whispers and low conversation regarding the suggestion that the *Tsa-la-gi* give serious thought to moving the tribe west of the Mississippi. This from a man who, years before, with fellow Cherokee avengers John Rogers and Alexander Saunders, had split the skull of Doublehead for violating tribal law by disposing of *Tsa-la-gi* land without full approval of the national council. With The Ridge's words had been planted the seeds of division that would eventually grow to threaten the very existence of this proud and noble people. A wedge of discord which would be driven between brother and sister, parent and child and which would sever the bond between the closest of friends.

Michael Drummond and James Walker moved through the crowd outside the council house to join their mothers and sisters. Peter Tanner stood a few feet away, glancing frequently at Susanna who reacted to his looks only enough to keep him interested. She made a point of ignoring him the rest of the time. To discourage sibling hostilities Elizabeth kept herself between Michael and Susanna. She appeared troubled by what she had heard through the interpreter.

"Those poor people. Burning their homes..."

"Mother, they were intruders!" Michael was incensed. "It was illegal for them to be there!"

"But in the dead of winter..." she persisted, unable to erase from her mind the indelible images of the freezing, displaced white family.

"It was a message, Mrs. Drummond," James explained respectfully. "No one was hurt. No blood was shed. It could've been much worse."

"It's barbaric," Susanna automatically took the position opposing Michael, who blasted back at her with an intensity that shocked no one.

"*Barbaric* is the Georgia Militia driving old Charlie Vann off his land, killing his son, and then giving his home and farm to some lazy white man from Milledgeville who never did an honest day's work in his life!"

Annie Walker had placed herself between James and Michael and seized the opportunity to make what, for her, was a bold move. Stirred by Michael's emotional defense of her people, she slipped her arm through his as though to sooth his passion. Her subtle move had not, however, gone unnoticed by Susanna, who looped behind her mother and pushed herself in between Michael and Annie. She took Michael's arm, openly mocking Annie's earlier move, her voice steeped in sarcasm.

"Most eloquently put, dear brother, *if* you were an Indian, which, I hasten to remind you, you are *not*," she said, cutting a superior look at James and Annie before continuing. "But not to worry. As you heard, they'll soon be gone west and you can turn your thoughts to the university and becoming a lawyer like Father. You know that's what he wants."

"Your compassion for an afflicted people is touching, dear sister," Michael's sarcasm equaled her own. He pulled his arm free and pushed her back to the other side of their mother, neither of them giving any weight to Elizabeth's impotent plea.

"Children, please don't argue..."

The usually shy Annie didn't look away this time. Her eyes burned into Susanna's, but Michael's sister dismissed the Cherokee girl with an insouciant flip of her long curls.

"Shh!" James got their attention. "Chief John Ross will speak now."

"He's the chief?" Susanna, astonished, shifted for a better look at the handsome, fair-skinned, sandy-haired principal chief of the Cherokee Nation who, by appearance, could as easily have been an old law school classmate of her father's. "He doesn't even look Indian! Is he as long winded as the last one?"

The crowd grew quiet when John Ross—*Gu-wi-s-gu-wi*—took his place at the center of the council house. The chief stood with rigid grace and looked around, making eye contact with the tribal elders closest to him, other tribal leaders scattered throughout the gathering and a few of those at the outer perimeter. He spied the new merchant, Titus Ogilvie, flanked on either side by his behemoth sons, Alton and Cephus. Embarrassed by the twinkle in Ross's eye and the hint of a smile tugging at the corner of the chief's mouth, Titus studied the mud at his feet. Alton and Cephus shifted uneasily.

The same gaunt mixed-blood translator who had converted The Ridge's Cherokee words into English now prepared to repeat in *Tsa-la-gi* the words *Gu-wi-s-gu-wi* would utter in English. *"Tsa-la-gi!"* the chief's voice split the night. "Listen carefully! I bring a heavy message. What Major Ridge said is true. We, as a nation, are indeed at a crossroads. One year ago, gold was found here in *Tsa-la-gi* territory. Gold. It poisons the minds and the souls of white men. Every day more miners arrive, their greedy squeals of delight echoing through our forests. They set up their illegal mud cities in Dahlondega. In Auraria. Anyplace there is gold. Now, the state of Georgia wants to take our land. And our gold. They have made new laws forbidding a Cherokee to dig gold from his own yard. A Cherokee can not testify in court against a white man. Indian contracts are no good without white witnesses. It is a dark day, my people. And, I fear, even darker days lie ahead. *A-ya a-gi-ha.*"

"A-ya a-gi-ha," the translator repeated in Cherokee, rather than translate the familiar phrase, *I have spoken*, that ended most council house speeches.

Though *Gu-wi-s-gu-wi's* speech was very brief and even somewhat ambiguous in its tone of ominous portent, the silence was every bit as palpable as that which had followed The Ridge's talk. Their chief, most felt, had failed to point them in any specific direction, nor had he delineated a particular course of action. He hadn't said prepare to move west; he hadn't said *don't* get ready to go west. A detailed battle plan would come later—perhaps years later—once all the trip stones and sinkholes of the battlefield had been identified and clearly marked. But there was definite trouble brewing where the whites were concerned, he had told them in his own way and in the presence of the *yo-negs* themselves. Be alert. Be watchful. Be ready. Because ultimately they would be pressed into making some monumental decisions regarding the fate of their nation—both its people and the lands they now occupied.

William Drummond exchanged a somber, reflective look with his friends, Thomas Walker and Charlie Swimmer. Their sons, a few feet behind them just outside the council house, mirrored their concern. The wives, Elizabeth Drummond, Janice Walker and Eva Swimmer, all shared a sense of foreboding, but for different reasons. Annie placed a comforting hand on her mother's arm. Even Susanna, normally insulated by her own self-involved detachment, was affected. She stepped closer to her mother and clung to Elizabeth. Across the council fire, the eyes of John Ross and Major Ridge found each other, each burdened by the portent their words held for the destiny of their people and the fate of their homeland. Even Titus Ogilvie recognized the opportunities suggested by the speeches. His might have been the only smiling face in the crowd as he whispered with quiet excitement to his sons.

* * * * * * *

The refreshing evening air was unseasonably cool for this time of summer. Full-bloods, mixed-bloods and whites made their way back down the slope from the council house toward their horses, wagons and carriages. Many Cherokees who had arrived on foot had already started along the forest trails that would take them back to cabins in the hills or to one of the many Cherokee towns networked up and down the rivers.

Good-byes were said to the Swimmers, and William helped Elizabeth and *Tse-ni-si* Walker into the Drummond's carriage. Thomas hitched his horse to the Walker's wagon where Annie waited silently, her eyes cutting at every opportunity to Michael and James. The boys sat their mounts with an adolescent air of importance and made quite a display of reining in their animated ponies while waiting for the homeward journey to begin.

"*Tsi-mi!* Drive Mr. Drummond's carriage," Thomas called to his son. James was openly disappointed.

"But *E-to-da*, Michael and I were going to race!"

"Drive the carriage," Thomas repeated flatly. "Mr. Drummond will ride with me. We need to talk. Annie will ride your horse."

Ordinarily Annie would have taken it as an insult—a suggestion that she wasn't responsible enough to drive the carriage that held her mother and the wife of an important white man. But Annie was unable to mask her delight. From the edge of the wagon she climbed onto the back of the roan pony behind her twin brother. Michael spun Midnight around and moved close to James's horse, *U-no-le*, aptly named *The Wind*.

"She's probably a better rider anyway!" Michael teased James.

"You'll pay for that!" James threw his leg over the horse's neck and dropped to the ground, then immediately sprang up into the driver's seat of the carriage. Annie, herself an excellent rider, pretended to have difficulty controlling *U-no-le*, allowing him to drift over and bump into Midnight. From her seat in the rear of the Drummonds' carriage, Susanna observed that Annie's gaze hadn't left Michael since the announcement that James would drive the carriage and Annie would ride his horse. She rolled her eyes in disgust at the absurdity of this interracial adolescent infatuation.

Michael and Annie trotted their ponies on ahead of the carriage. The Walker wagon brought up the rear. The full moon high overhead cast the riders' shadows across the pale sand of the road that curved among the towering pines. James glanced back at the wagon where his father rode with William Drummond.

"So. What did you think?" Thomas finally asked his *yo-neg* friend.

William studied the rear of the carriage in front of them as though he might discover the answer engraved there, and if he strained hard enough, he might be able to read it in the moonlight. "There was a lot of talk about the wrongs committed against the Cherokees," he began thoughtfully. "But it sounds like the worst is yet to come. What will your people do?"

"That is for us the great question," Thomas said. "Years ago, many *Tsa-la-gi* went west by their own choice. But this is our home. You heard *Gu-wi-s-gu-wi*. He didn't say it in words, but in his heart he believes we should stay and fight." He paused, weighing the ramifications of that position against the alternative presented by Major Ridge. "Others say the only way to survive as a people is to go where the white man can no longer take our land."

"There could be wisdom in those words as well," William offered.

"The Old One," Thomas said, speaking of his wife's grandfather, "says it makes no difference. Wherever we go, it's only a matter of time until the white man comes and takes what he wants." What could William say? History had already carved itself into that stone of truth.

"If you go west," William said earnestly, "we'll miss you." While he had always been a champion of Cherokee rights in the face of the white man's deceit and abuse, he couldn't escape a twinge of guilt-by-racial-affiliation as though somehow he had personally contributed to the present plight and impending hardship of his *Tsa-la-gi* friends. The two men studied their children up ahead. Thomas sensed his friend's discomfort and changed the subject—or at least shifted its direction.

"Michael's friendship has meant much to James," Thomas observed in his simple, straightforward manner, then added, "And to Annie." He and William exchanged a look, as men will do, making sure they concurred on the implied meaning. "Whatever we do,"

Thomas continued, "it won't be done soon. Indecision and fighting among ourselves—that's always been the *Tsa-la-gi's* worst enemy."

3

The flames of the fire danced in rhythm to the chant of the *di-da-nŭ-wi-s-gi* who sat cross-legged on the ground, rocking slowly back and forth in a pendulum of ancient mystery. With a wrinkled hand, the 80-year-old medicine man sprinkled tufts of twisted tobacco onto the fire. The dried shreds of pungent herb ignited immediately in a small explosion and sent a thick trail of smoke spiraling into the cool morning air. Michael Drummond and James Walker sat in like manner opposite the holy man. They were centered on the wizened old mystagogue charged with blessing their passage into manhood under the tutelage of James's maternal uncles in accordance with tribal clan laws. It was the *di-da-nŭ-wi-s-gi's* sacred obligation to assist the uncles in initiating the boys into the spiritual doctrines of *The Eternal Flame*. To guide them toward an understanding of what words could not express—what it meant to be *Tsa-la-gi* in the mind, in the heart, in the spirit.

On either side of James stood his uncles, John and Andrew Sixkiller, the only surviving brothers of Janice Walker. John, at fifty-four, was the oldest of the original five Sixkiller children. There had been four brothers, and they had all been delighted when their baby sister, *Tse-ni-si*, had come along. Throughout her childhood she had been the princess of Sixkiller Mountain in the verdant Blue Ridge range in western North Carolina. Against the protests of the three older brothers—John, Andrew and James—Matthew, the youngest boy, had insisted on accompanying them south to serve under General Andrew Jackson in 1814. Before they departed, however, James had suddenly taken ill and had swallowed his tongue during a seizure. He had choked to death while a frantic Janice held his head in her lap. Looking up at her, his eyes had fluttered spastically before rolling back in his head, and she knew she was the last thing he ever saw. Less than six months later word had come back to Sixkiller Mountain that Matthew had been killed at a place called The Horseshoe somewhere in Alabama. John and Andrew had never shared with her the grim details of the bloody battle in which the Cherokee had allied themselves with the Americans against the British and the Creek Indians. They never told Janice they had seen Matthew take a double-handed blow of a British soldier's saber that showered them in his blood and left Matthew's severed head hanging against his own chest by a finger's width of stretched skin. The same soldier had then thrust his saber at John's head. The point had entered John's mouth, and only an instinctive twist to the side had saved him. He tasted his baby brother's blood from the blade mixed with his own when the razor tip sliced open his cheek. In the same instant, Andrew drove his own knife into the soldier's stomach, ripping him open. The soldier dropped to his knees in the shallow, bloody water of the Tallapoosa River and stared down at his own shiny blue intestines hanging through his fingers as though a part of his uniform had inexplicably become detached and he couldn't quite think how to put it right. While John, himself bleeding profusely, gathered up the body—and the head—of his baby brother, Andrew scalped the British soldier who, through the blood running down into his own eyes, watched them walk out of the river as his own light began to dim.

None of this had they ever spoken to their sister, *Tse-ni-si*. All she was told was that her brother had been a great warrior, had killed many of his enemies and had died bravely in battle. And Janice's only words had been to wonder out loud about the sisters and the families of the British soldiers and the Creek warriors her own brothers might have slain. With time their wounds had healed. The slit that had opened John's face had, ironically, healed into a thickly scarred perpetual smile. Janice had named her firstborn son James in honor of her first brother to die. Her intention had been to call her next son Matthew, but the years had slipped by and she had born no more after the twins.

With hypnotic intensity all eyes were focused on the ribbon of smoke from the *di-da-nŭ-wi-s-gi's* fire. It bent first toward James and then wrapped around Michael before drifting up into the towering pines that stood as silent sentinels at the edge of the clearing in front of Andrew's cabin. Around them the padded forest floor was carpeted with the rusty brown of fallen pine needles and cedar shag; the prickly gray and black of rotting sweetgum balls.

The boys looked with eager anticipation to James's uncles for an interpretation of the smoke. John and Andrew exchanged a few muffled words with the ancient *di-da-nŭ-wi-s-gi*, then looked at Michael with an approving nod. Finally Andrew spoke softly to James in Cherokee, "The smoke says your white brother will make a big kill on today's hunt."

Though Michael knew much of the Cherokee language, he hadn't fully understood Andrew and was puzzled by James's look of disappointment. "What'd he say?" Michael asked. "I got something about the hunt."

"The strong smoke went to you first," James said

despondently. "You'll make a big kill."

"You, too, little brother, will find the mark," Uncle John knelt beside James. "The smoke did not forget you."

This seemed to assuage James. He and Michael uncrossed their legs and were about to rise when the *di-da-nŭ-wi-s-gi's* guttural bark froze them. A late piece of tobacco had popped loudly and burst into flame, sending another string of smoke snaking up into the pines. The ancient one, nearly blind in his advanced years, ran his tongue across his cracked lips, then spoke in his sing-song rhythm. "Death is red. Death is white. Death walks on two legs." Again, Michael looked to John and Andrew for explanation.

"Be careful today," Andrew said softly, his voice lacking its earlier enthusiasm. "Somebody could get killed."

Bare from the waist up and wearing their buckskin leggings, the boys gathered up their weapons. James had his bow and a doe-skin quiver. Annie had stitched a crude but discernible wolf's head design on it with colored beads. The quiver was filled with ten new arrows which his great grandfather, The Old One, had been secretly making in anticipation of this day. In addition, a sheath knotted to his belt held a new knife, its handle fashioned from deer antler. It was a gift from his father. Michael had his long-rifle and a bone-handled knife with a steel blade similar to the one James wore.

* * * * * * *

James walked naked into the cool, rippling waters of the Conasauga River up to his armpits. On the bank behind him Michael leaned against a low-slung limb, his knife and rifle lying at his feet with James's leggings, his bow, quiver of arrows, blowgun and knife. A few feet away Uncle Andrew Sixkiller stood at the water's edge, exhorting his nephew. *"I only hunt to eat,"* Andrew said in Cherokee.

"I thank my brothers the deer and the bear for their skins to keep me from the cold," James recited his practiced response in the lyrical liturgy of initiation.

"I do not kill my brother the wolf."

"My brother the wolf is messenger to the spirit world," James answered.

From his seat on a large rock jutting out into the stream, Uncle John Sixkiller studied Michael who was watching the proceedings intently, hanging on every word.

"Ha-ne-no-quŭ," John urged him. "Go."

Michael gestured toward the water to make sure he correctly understood.

"Yes, go to the water," John clarified in English. "It is good for the hunter."

Needing no further urging, Michael peeled his leggings and walked into the Conasauga, standing a few feet downstream from James. John and Andrew exchanged a look, pleased with their young charges.

"*The water makes me pure,*" Andrew resumed the ceremony.

"*The water is my protector,*" James said, concentrating to remember the right words that concluded the ritual of passage. Silently Michael mouthed the same words, eager to participate—but unobtrusively. James looked at his friend, somber and serious. Then with his palm he shot a stream of water directly at Michael's face, and the battle was on. Andrew joined his brother on the large rock where they shared a pipe while the boys played. They recognized it as the sheer joy of spirit within the boys and was in no way disrespectful to the ceremony of initiation for the hunter-warrior.

* * * * * * *

James and Michael moved silently through the thick woods, stopping to feel the sun's warmth on their shoulders in one of the few spots not blanketed in shade. Tied to James's belt was a rabbit, to Michael's a squirrel. The hunters' first take of the day. Michael was about to move on when James staid him with a forearm and pointed to the wild turkey scratching in the pine needles drifted up beneath a clump of brush.

"*Gŭ-ni,*" James whispered.

Michael slowly brought up his long rife, but James gently pushed the barrel down and slipped an arrow from his quiver, fitting it expertly to the bow string. Confidently he raised the bow, sighting on the bird. Aim and release smoothly. Don't snap the fingers off the string, he recalled his early training. *Whoosh.* The arrow sailed past the bird and thudded into the dirt fifteen feet beyond. The turkey squawked and jumped to one side, cocking its head curiously before strolling over to inspect the errant missile. Michael doubled over with silent laughter. He watched through tear-filled eyes as James, with tight-lipped frustration, fit another arrow to his bow string. Michael located a stone at his feet. From a kneeling position he fired it side-arm and hit the bird in the behind, sending the creature fluttering off into the shadows.

"It wasn't his day to die," James proclaimed with reverential acceptance.

"I'm sure his spirit thanks you," Michael tried not to laugh openly. James put his arrow away and gave Michael a playful shove before moving along the forest trail.

They spent the rest of the morning hunting until the sun was hot and high overhead. Despite having missed the turkey, James later had proven his superior ability with the blow gun by downing not one but two plump quail. They—along with the rabbit and squirrel—would make a tasty feast for the evening meal when the boys camped overnight in the woods before returning the next day to the Sixkiller cabin.

The two were more than ready for a swim when they finally reached the steep banks of Onion Creek that fed into the Conasauga a couple of miles to the south. They left their leggings, their weapons and the dead game in the shade of a large stump and slid naked down the clay slope into the waist-deep pool. Silently they agreed to forego boyish play, choosing rather to ceremoniously dip handfuls of the soothing water onto their chests, shoulders and back. They were hunters now. Men. Warriors. Fledgling, but warriors nonetheless. And this was how they'd seen their fathers and uncles enjoy the rivers and creeks on hot summer days.

Both boys heard it at the same time. Above the soft sounds of their own ablution, voices drifted to them from around the curve in the creek a few yards upstream. The words were unintelligible, but the male voices were clearly hostile. Michael and James hurriedly left the water and scrambled back up the steep bank. They looked toward the bend as they pulled on their leggings, grabbed their weapons and crept quietly through the brush toward the heated exchange.

It took them only a couple of minutes to angle across the heavily wooded promontory. From the safety of the thick brush they looked out onto a scene that would launch them full-fledged into the manhood they had been so eager to emulate. They were at the widest part of the creek for miles in either direction. On the opposite bank were two white miners, rough and scraggly Georgians who looked to be in their mid-to-late thirties. Their gear was spread all around where they had been panning for gold in a shallow pool formed just below some rapids. The miners' two donkeys were tied to a low limb in a grove of trees behind them. From the chaotic sprawl of the camp, the boys could tell that the men had been working this location for some time and, despite their proximity to the water, neither appeared to have bathed since establishing their operations here.

Zebulon was the thinner of the two miners. His beak-like nose was so disfigured from a lifetime of brawling that he gave the appearance of trying to sniff his own ear. He remained kneeling, swishing his large pan while occasionally eyeing his partner. Harlan, the other miner, growled through his tangled, encrusted beard at the two full-blood Cherokees facing him. James recognized one of them as Clarence Bearpaw, a friend of his father. The other man was known to him only as Willie No-Shoes.

"I say again—" Clarence repeated firmly without raising his voice, "this is *Tsa-la-gi* land. You go away. Now!"

Harlan chewed his tobacco and studied the Cherokees, trying to gauge just how far they would press their point. Zeb leaned back on his heels and squinted at his partner. "Keep your eye on 'em, Harlan! You know how sneaky they are."

"No sneak. Tell your face—get out!" Willie No-Shoes pointed toward the miners' donkeys.

"We ain't goin' nowhere, Chief!" Harlan answered, pointing to his musket leaning against a tree near the donkeys. "Now git yer sorry asses outa here and leave us alone or I'll get my gun!" Harlan broke into a victorious smile when Willie No-Shoes walked away, until he realized Willie was headed straight toward the other miner. "Watch him, Zeb!"

The warning was too late. Willie No-Shoes kicked the large, flat pan out of Zeb's hands. It flew out into the middle of the creek where it floated for a moment before tilting and slicing beneath the surface.

"Damn you!" Zeb watched the pan fade into the muddy water. "They was a nugget in there!"

"No! Damn *you*! Get off our land!" Willie No-Shoes pointed right at Zeb's face. The miner pushed himself up off his knees and lunged forward, driving his shoulder into Willie's stomach and knocking him to the ground. The Cherokee was instantly back on his feet. He drew a long-blade hunting knife from a fringed sheath at his waist. Zeb and Willie circled each other in a combative crouch, neither eager to make the next move.

Harlan and Clarence Bearpaw watched them, each realizing the confrontation had escalated to a potentially fatal level. "Georgia law says Injuns cain't dig gold no how! What's yer beef?" Harlan hoped to convince the Indians they were fighting a losing battle, and a couple of white miners wouldn't make much difference one way or the other. "If we don't get it, somebody else will!" he added.

"No one takes any more from *Tsa-la-gi*! Now you go," Clarence Bearpaw shook his head, refusing to adopt Harlan's logic. He began untying one of the donkeys. Harlan went to the other donkey and pulled two crusted flint-lock pistols from an old, stained saddle bag. Harlan held the guns down at each side and cocked them. He never uttered a word as he strode casually over to Clarence Bearpaw. With all the emotion of a man pushing closed a cabin door against an annoying winter wind, he raised one of the pistols to Clarence's stomach and fired.

From their hidden vantage point across the creek, Michael and James recoiled as though they themselves had been shot. Each sought—but did not find—an explanation in the eyes of the other before peering through the leaves back across the creek. Harlan held the pistol out to one side to distance himself from the acrid smoke still curling from the barrel and firing pan. Willie No-Shoes looked at his murdered friend. Clarence lay with his head two or three inches deep in the edge of the water, his feet higher up on the bank. Willie No-Shoes lunged for Zeb, slashing his forearm with the knife. Harlan glanced down to make sure Clarence wasn't moving, then stepped toward Willie and Zeb. He leveled the second pistol at Willie's face.

"Stop right there, you dog-eatin' piece of horse dung!" Willie froze, his eyes darting back and forth between Zeb and Harlan. "Only thing better'n a dead Injun is *two* dead Injuns!" Harlan said, inching his way around closer to Zeb. He motioned with the spent pistol toward Willie's dead companion. "So 'less you want some of what he just got, pick him up and get the hell outa here! And don't come back!" Willie's eyes remained on the pistol barrel pointed at his face. Harlan moved even closer.

In the thick brush perhaps fifty yards away, Michael raised his long rifle. James's eyes widened in disbelief, but he said nothing. This time he made no attempt to stop his friend. They watched the drama unfolding before them across the creek. Harlan, full of his own sense of omnipotence, confidently brandished the pistol, not realizing he had foolishly allowed himself to come within reach of Willie's knife. With the speed of a serpent's strike, the knife flashed up. A flick of the wrist had left a crimson slice across Harlan's left cheek, the dark liquid ribbons creeping down through his beard. Harlan staggered back a couple of steps. When Willie raised the knife and started toward him, Harlan fired the pistol. Willie was hit in the throat and died instantly. He slumped down the bank and came to rest near his friend's body at the water's edge.

Michael gently squeezed the trigger of his long-rifle as he had been taught when shooting at stumps or at squirrels. But now his target was neither rotting wood nor furry rodent. Harlan flew backwards off his feet from the impact of the rifle ball ripping through his heart. He hit the bank and slid down in a grotesque heap between the two dead Cherokees. The donkey Clarence had earlier untied bolted, disappearing into the brush. Zeb stood terrified, exposed in the open. Bug-eyed, he looked all around, not knowing where to go or what to do. Across the creek he spotted the smoking rifle barrel protruding from the brush, but he couldn't see its owner.

Zeb scrambled to take cover behind the other donkey straining at its tether, braying in answer to its companion in the forest.

"Don't shoot! Don't shoot!" Zeb pleaded. "I ain't got no gun!"

He grabbed the donkey's halter and tried to calm the skittish beast, peering over its back and across the creek. He searched the brush but saw nothing. No movement. No rifle. No smoke. Nothing. It took a few moments to convince himself the mystery shooter had gone. Then, still in a crouch, Zeb crept back around the donkey and down the bank toward Harlan's corpse. "Don't shoot! I'm leavin'!" he called loudly, in case the gunman was still across the creek, perhaps disappearing from sight just long enough to reload. "Jes' let me take the dead along! He deserves a Christian burial! Jes'...jes' don't shoot!"

With a strength fueled by fear, Zeb pulled Harlan's huge body onto his shoulders. He scampered back up the bank and flopped the corpse across the donkey's back, then nervously untied the animal. As they turned for the safety of the woods, Harlan's body slid off and rolled back down the embankment, almost to its original position sandwiched between the bodies of Willie No-Shoes and Clarence Bearpaw. Zeb whipped the donkey back around toward the creek. He tightly gripped the rope with one hand and scampered back down to the water's edge. But this time all he reached for was the tiny draw-string bag of nuggets tied to Harlan's belt before clawing his way back up the bank. He heard the *whoosh* and looked up. There was no time to dodge the arrow that buried itself in the right side of his chest just below the collar bone. Zeb dropped immediately to his knees, screaming from the searing heat that shot through his entire body and exploded in his head, ringing in his ears. His quivering hand clutched the shaft, but the slightest movement was so excruciating he knew he wouldn't be able to extract the arrow. With a guttural, beastly moan, he pushed himself back up onto his feet. Abandoning the donkey, Zeb staggered off into the brush, the tiny bag of gold pressed tightly against his stomach.

* * * * * * *

The late afternoon sun slashing in through the open doorway of the Walker cabin carried in its beams the fires of all the years Michael and James had aged in that single day. Seated across the table from them were their fathers, Thomas Walker and William Drummond, and James's uncles, Andrew and John Sixkiller. Annie peeked in from the other room, her attention locked on her twin brother and his friend. Her friend, too. She didn't fully understand the story they had just recited, but she knew they were telling the truth.

"*A-s-du-di!*" Thomas called to her in his familiar soft but firm voice. Janice Walker pulled her daughter back and obeyed her husband's command to close the door, but Annie pressed her face to the rough boards and watched through a crack. She saw Mr. Drummond rub his face and smooth his hair back, then stare up at the thatched roof and exhale an onerous sigh. It was a difficult situation for all of them, but especially for William, who had spent his entire adult life in reverential service of the law. Now he looked across the table at his fourteen-year-old son who had just killed another human being.

"One was Clarence Bearpaw," Andrew Sixkiller explained.

Michael and James had run all the way back to the Walker cabin. Even before they had finished the first telling of their story, Annie was on *U-no-le*, racing to the Drummond place to fetch William. Andrew and John had gone fishing on the Coosa with Thomas. The three of them had arrived back at the cabin only minutes before the boys came crashing through the brush into the clearing. While Annie was riding to get William, Thomas had stayed with the boys. Andrew and John had hurried back to the miner's camp.

"And Willie No-Shoes," John added. "Good men. We hid the bodies for now. We'll need to get them to their families."

"Does anyone else know about this?" William asked. Michael and James looked at each other for confirmation, then shook their heads, certain no one else had witnessed the incident.

"There is one other," Thomas reminded them all. "The miner who got away."

"James put an arrow in his chest, but it didn't kill him," Michael recalled.

"We didn't find a second *yo-neg*," John confirmed.

"He must have made it out," Andrew put in.

"What should we do?" Thomas posed the question each had been asking in his own mind.

William rose and walked to the front door, pushing it wider open to admit the curious breeze. He loomed large and black, silhouetted against the doorway. "As a lawyer—as an officer of the court—I never thought I'd say this," he paused for a long time before announcing his recommendation. "We do *nothing*." The others were silent, stunned by his words. "The Georgia authorities won't give a damn about two dead Cherokees," William reminded them of the harsh reality of the times in which they lived. "As for the dead miner—if they really *have* found gold, the other one doesn't want anyone else to know. He'll sneak back, bury his friend and keep his mouth shut. And that's exactly what we're going to do. Keep our mouths shut and bury this whole incident."

No one could present a stronger counter argument. No one wanted to. "It doesn't leave this room," Andrew expressed their collective thought.

"I'm afraid you might be right, *Wi-li*," Thomas Walker recalled his friend's words from the council meeting the night before. "The worst is yet to come."

Fall 1835
Five Years Later

The ancient Cherokee woman sat quietly on the stump at the edge of the narrow dirt road winding its way across the Georgia state line through the pine forest toward Red Clay, Tennessee. She couldn't say how long she'd been sitting there. She had walked many miles since daybreak and when her legs grew weary, she found a stump to sit on, oblivious to the light, steady rain that peppered her and the other travellers throughout the late morning and early afternoon. Finally the sun had broken through, but she was already soaked and in no great hurry to resume her trek.

In the criss-cross lines that channeled the old woman's face lay buried the secrets of the decades. Of love found in a forest glade. Of children born in that strange blend of joy and pain with medicine women, midwives and sisters gathered in a small cabin on a cold winter's night. Of the indescribable sadness that rips at the heart and devours the soul when burying a beloved grandchild stolen away by the white man's thief, cholera. Of saying good-bye to the man who had been at her side since before this beloved land, given to the *Tsa-la-gi* by the Great Spirit, had become what the *yo-negs* called their United States. With gnarled talons she pulled the blanket tighter around her shoulders and peered out through vacant eyes at the solemn procession of Cherokees streaming past.

In keeping with Cherokee custom, the men led the way, carrying rifles, lances, bows and arrows, or combinations of these. The children followed, with the women bringing up the rear, keeping the little ones safely in the middle. Most of the men wore the Cherokee turban, though a few had adopted *yo-neg* hats. Many had also donned the traditional tunic with a brightly colored sash at the waist; still others wore longer robes. But virtually every man marching was adorned with some form of drapery, giving the entire parade the peculiar semblance of biblical patriarchs. Nearly all went by foot, though a few old women and ancient men sat on horses led by grandsons or great nephews. The forest was strangely quiet, the only sound the crunching of feet in the dirt, a distant bird, the rustle of a light breeze tickling the leaves above them.

The thumping of confident hoofbeats preceded the appearance of a fancy carriage bearing Major Ridge and his wife, *Se-ho-ya,* or

Susanna. The Major's hair, still thick and full, was almost white, combed straight back on the top and sides. *Se-ho-ya* was a quiet woman of noble bearing, her auburn hair only lightly streaked with gray at the temples, pulled back in a single, thick braid that hung halfway down the middle of her back. With them rode their son, John Ridge, thin, cerebrotonic, of medium height. His beautiful wife, Sarah Bird Northrup Ridge, was the daughter of a wealthy Connecticut family. John had met and fallen passionately in love with her during his lengthy university stint in New England. To the consternation of her esteemed family, he had removed her—and not at all against her will—back to his native Cherokee territory. She supported him wholeheartedly in his commitment to work for the good of his people.

At a tug on his coattails, their black driver stopped the carriage even with the old Cherokee woman sitting on the stump. John jumped down and went to her, gently taking her hand.

"*E-he-na, a-ga-yŭ li-ge-i,*" he said softly, urging the old one to come with him. She shook her head firmly with a concrete expression. John gently persisted until finally she allowed him to help her into the carriage where Major Ridge and *Se-ho-ya* shifted to make room. No sooner had they resumed their journey than they were followed by the wagon of Thomas Walker. Riding with him were his wife, *Tse-ni-si*, and their friend, William Drummond. James Walker, striking in appearance at nineteen, with a compact, muscular build like his father's, followed behind the wagon on his roan pony, *U-no-le*. His conversation was lost on his two nineteen-year-old Cherokee companions who were clearly more interested in his beautiful twin sister, Annie, whose dangling bare feet enticed them from the tailgate of the wagon.

"*Tsi-mi!*" William called back to James, beckoning him to ride alongside the wagon. "I received some post yesterday from the university."

"A letter from Michael?" James was excited. "What does it say?"

William smiled down at Annie, who was hanging on his every word. He pulled the letter from his pocket. "Here," William extended it toward James. "Mrs. Drummond said to let you read it." James unfolded the letter and read, keeping pace with the wagon.

"What does it say?" Annie tried not to sound too eager.

"What do you care?" James teased. "He doesn't even mention you."

Annie looked down, shy and embarrassed. She watched

James out of the corner of her eye. William smiled, pulled a second letter from his coat and leaned over the wagon seat. "Annie...this one's especially for you." She took the letter and couldn't resist a look of victory at her twin brother.

* * * * * * *

Although New Echota, Georgia continued to serve as the seat of government for the Cherokee nation, their principal chief, John Ross, had relocated with his wife, Quatie, to an humble cabin just across the Tennessee state line near Red Clay. The Ross holdings had once included a thriving ferry business on the Tennessee River and a large, well-appointed home complete with peacocks, barns, corn-cribs, orchards, livestock, outbuildings and carriage house. Early in 1833, the chief had gone to Washington, D.C. to campaign against the incessant tide of illegal white immigrants into *Tsa-la-gi* territory and to bring federal pressure to bear on the state of Georgia for its repeated violation of Cherokee rights. When he had returned home in April, Ross found Quatie and their children confined to two small rooms of their spacious dwelling at *Head of Coosa*. His property had been assigned to the Georgia state land lottery and had been *won* by some whites who wasted little time taking over the estate. Ross immediately went to see Georgia Governor Wilson Lumpkin in protest, but Lumpkin had merely smiled and said that *Gu-wi-s-gu-wi* was, indeed, fortunate the new owners had graciously offered the Ross family the use of the two rooms, which was far more generosity than had been shown most dispossessed Cherokees. Rather than submit himself and his family to such indignity, *Gu-wi-s-gu-wi* sent the children to stay with relatives while he and Quatie moved over into neighboring Tennessee to the old cabin where his grandfather had once lived.

The sunny afternoon was sticky with humidity left by the morning rain. John Ross, in Cherokee tunic but without the familiar turban, leaned against the simple rail fence that separated the cabin from the road and chatted quietly with a few of the older men. Some who lived near the state line had come by foot, and the horses of the others were tied along the fence. A couple of the Cherokees acknowledged with a slight nod the thin-faced, middle-aged, bearded white man seated on a chair beside the cabin door. John Howard Payne, a well-known actor and playwright-turned-journalist with a consuming interest in the fate of the Cherokees, was there to write a series of articles for a London-based magazine. He had already met many of the Cherokee elders and chiefs and had been accepted as a friend of the tribe. Payne oserved quietly and occasionally jotted a few notes in his journal.

The conversations halted when The Ridge's carriage rolled up in front of the Ross cabin. True, the elder Ridge held an opposite view from the younger, yet no less morally meticulous chief on almost every weighted issue regarding the governing—indeed, the very fate—of the tribe. But he would never have considered riding past the Ross place on the way to the Red Clay council grounds without stopping to exchange a few words. Despite their well known political differences, the two men had, if not an affection, at least a deep-seated respect for one another. A number of the Cherokee men came over to pay their regards to *Se-ho-ya* Ridge and her daughter-in-law, Sarah. The women remained seated in the coach. John patted the arm of the old woman they had picked up by the side of the road and assured her they wouldn't be long. The Ridge ran both hands across his rain-matted hair as he walked up to Chief Ross at the gate. He eyed the *yo-neg* stranger sitting on Ross's porch but didn't speak to Payne.

"*O-si-yo, Gu-wi-s-gu-wi,*" Ridge addressed Ross with a formal air. Their exchange was polite, almost ceremonial, but the tension between the two men was evident.

"*Si-yo*, Ridge," Ross used the more familiar form of greeting, welcoming the venerable elder leader. "*U-li-he-li-s-di. To-hi-tsu?*"

"We are well," Ridge answered with stately decorum.

"I am glad you have come."

"It is an important council."

"Perhaps the most important in years," Ross agreed.

"May there be peace on our tongues, unity on our minds and love in our hearts," Ridge spoke with a natural eloquence which, despite his lack of formal education, had established his reputation as a great orator.

"May it be," Ross concurred and bid his respected tribal adversary good-bye. "*Do-na-da-go-hŭ-i.*"

"I will see you at the council house," Ridge concluded his brief conversation with the chief and began exchanging greetings with the other Cherokees who stood waiting to chat with the renowned elder statesman.

* * * * * * *

The small but picturesque *Gu-e-ha-le* River meandered

through the council grounds nestled in the Tennessee forest near Red Clay just north of the Georgia state line. The recent rains had left the air thick with the aroma of wet pine and honeysuckle. By evening a scattering of quickly constructed booths, huts and make- shift stores lined the dirt road running through the grounds up toward the council house which occupied the highest point in the area. Despite the bustling activity, the atmosphere was strangely quiet, ordered, almost reverent. Large, black pots suspended over star-stacked firewood awaited the *hog fry* that would follow the council meeting. Sides of beef and pork impaled on huge spits over charcoal trenches were rotated by adolescent girls and boys, intense with the magnitude of their assignment. Younger children, with equal solemnity, roasted chickens, rabbits and squirrels on green sticks over smaller fires.

As always when Cherokees gathered, there were whites present. Government representatives, Indian agents and traders, as well as those—both men and women—who were intermarried with or just good friends of the Cherokees. Inevitably, among the whites at these important tribal gatherings were the likes of Titus Ogilvie and his sons, Alton and Cephus, and others of their ilk, milling and lurking about, concocting some scheme whereby to cheat a Cherokee out of his mule or his land or lasciviously foisting their unwanted lecherous advances on Cherokee women and young girls.

Annie Walker helped her mother baste a side of beef, but when Janice resumed her conversation with the Cherokee women cooking in their immediate vicinity, Annie drifted off to visit with the other young women and the young men who swarmed around them like heel flies. At nineteen Annie was as beautiful as her twin brother, James, was handsome. She and the other girls either pretended to be annoyed by the boys or pretended to ignore them altogether. In truth, their proximity afforded the girls a certain feeling of safety against the prying eyes and vile thoughts of the Ogilvies and their kind.

Chief John Ross, accompanied by Thomas Walker, John and Andrew Sixkiller, Charlie Swimmer and a number of other Cherokees, walked comfortably among the crowd, greeting an old friend or acquaintance here, tasting a morsel of fresh pork or fry bread there. Trailing behind them was the journalist, John Howard Payne, listening intently to their soft-spoken yet animated exchanges. He made a few notes now and then but didn't engage anyone—white or Cherokee—in conversation. Tagging along with Payne was James Walker, apparently more interested in tribal affairs than in horsing around with the other young men his own age. Payne genuinely appreciated the company, though the two of them had scarcely spoken the entire evening.

When Chief Ross came upon William Drummond, he located Payne in the crowd and beckoned for the journalist to join him. "William, I'd like you to meet John Howard Payne. He's here from Europe to write a series of articles on the *Tsa-la-gi* for his London magazine. John, this is William Drummond. *Di-ti-yo-hi-hi.*" William was puzzled by that last phrase. Chief Ross grinned broadly and explained for both William and Payne. "An outstanding attorney. *Wi-li* frequently represents the Cherokees in claims against Georgia and Tennessee. And quite well, I might add."

"Not *the* John Howard Payne?" William shook hands with the journalist.

"I hope there aren't too many of us running around," Payne instantly liked the tall, quiet man before him.

"On the contrary, Mr. Payne," William reassured him. "I must say, both my wife and my daughter are most fond of your song, *Home, Sweet Home.*"

"Ah, the song," Payne chuckled politely, reliving an all-too-familiar exchange. "The damned song. I'm a journalist, Mr. Drummond. Not a minstrel. I must tell you, I'm quite sick of that song and sicker still of talking about it. It's just a little ditty. I was bored one rainy afternoon."

"And homesick, no doubt," William smiled. "But I won't mention it again. A pleasure to meet you."

"The pleasure's mine," Payne seemed relieved when William didn't press the issue of the popular song.

Chief Ross threaded his arm through William's to recapture the attorney's attention. "William, I'm assembling another delegation to go to Washington before the weather turns bad." He leaned close to the taller Drummond and said privately, "To meet with President Jackson. I'd very much like for you to go along as our representing counsel."

"I don't know, John," William shook his head. "My son's away at the university. There's only my man Ezekiel to run the farm. Besides, I'm not sure I could offer much help."

"Nonsense, William! You'd be a valuable asset to us in Washington. I'm counting on you."

Thomas Walker approved of the chief's selection. "Go ahead, William," he encouraged his friend. "James and I can help Ezekiel. Charlie Swimmer will help, too."

James stepped forward a little to confirm his father's words. Charlie Swimmer nodded in agreement. William looked each man directly in the eye. He understood that each one was asking, but he also knew none of them would beg. "All right," William turned to *Gu-wi-s-gu-wi.* "Let me know when."

"I knew we could count on you," Chief Ross squeezed William's arm in appreciation. The chief and his entourage moved on toward the Red Clay council house, passing numerous clusters of Cherokee men sitting around talking, smoking and discussing the ripening political climate that undoubtedly would soon impact their lives. Teenage boys and young men hung attentively at the fringes of each group, listening, learning, studying the ways of their fathers and their fathers' fathers in the mysteries of *Tsa-la-gi* politics.

* * * * * * *

A roaring fire—fueled by the seven traditional types of wood—had been built inside the council house, not only as the eternal symbol of the *Tsa-la-gi* but to cut the chill of the damp Tennessee autumn night. The ancient and venerable chief Womankiller, feet planted wide in the dust of the council house floor, commanded the full attention of the packed crowd. His voice was soft but firm and easily heard, even to the outer edges of the seven-sided structure. As he spoke, Womankiller tugged idly with a knotted hand at the wattles of skin that formed the front of his neck. His eyes occasionally rolled back in his head as though he were receiving wisdom from the Great Spirit above.

"My own sunset is upon me. Soon my old bones will be put under the ground. I want them to lie *here*, in the bosom of this earth we have received from our fathers who had it from the Great Being above. When I am asleep in forgetfulness, I hope you will not desert me." A master of such council speeches, the tremulous and gangling old warrior paused for maximum effect, staring coldly at the U. S. government representatives and Indian agents who occupied a seat across from the tribal leaders. This position of honor had once been granted to agents who had lived among the natives of the southeast and who had earned their trust and affection. In recent years, however, the Indian agents and other government men—federal, state and local—had adopted the practice of marching right into the council house and taking these seats. They acted like it was a right granted to them, if not by the Great Spirit, at least by the authority of their own governments over these hapless savages they would ultimately drive from their sacred homelands. It only remained, most of them believed, to give the official order and to work out the final details.

When each *yo-neg* had felt the heat of Womankiller's bitter glare, the old chief continued. "The United States wants to break the treaties. Trample the *Tsa-la-gi* under their feet. But we will not consent to this. And we will not betray our own people. These treaties were made in friendship, when our friendship was worth the price. Now, if they come and kill us for our land, we shall sleep with the spirits of our departed loved ones. But we will not give up our home. My old bones will not allow me to stand longer. I have spoken."

Womankiller hobbled back to his seat among the tribal leaders. The sound of his feet scraping in the dust could be heard from the farthest bench. Nods and grunts of approval followed from many in the crowd. The Sixkillers brothers, Thomas Walker and Charlie Swimmer all agreed with the ancient chief's sentiments. But there were also shaking heads and frowns of disapproval from others, indicative of the growing division among the *Tsa-la-gi* over the question of removal. William Drummond watched and listened, noting the polarity of responses. And he was painfully aware there were those whom he had come to admire and respect—even love—on both sides of the issue.

* * * * * * *

Major Ridge respectfully allowed time for reaction to Womankiller's talk to subside before rising to his full height and sweeping back his shock of nearly-white hair. There was a tangible strength in this man's deep set eyes, his rigid mouth and brooding deliberation; an aura that magnetically drew eyes and paralyzed lips. His presence modulated the very breathing of every man and woman there, including the whites, and commanded every aspect of their attention. He nodded to the translator that he was ready.

"Always I have listened to our wise chief, Womankiller. His wish is to sleep with our fathers when his spirit leaves this world. Here. Where our mothers and fathers have always slept." The Ridge's voice resonated through the assembly, and he nodded deferentially to the ancient leader. Then he looked around at the younger men and women inside and surrounding the council house. "But now we must think of our children. Do we want them to sleep before their sunset? Before they have seen many winters come and go? Just so we might say *Behold, they sleep with their fathers?* No one loves this land more than I. No one has paid a greater price to keep it sacred. Yet, even now the heavy hand of oppression is beating at our door. Only a fool would stand in his cabin, with the river rising up to his children's heads, about to swallow them, and say *We will stay here. Even if we die.* Hear me, *Tsa-la-gi!* You must get out while you can.... *A-ya a-gi-ha,"* he ended his talk with the familiar Cherokee council-fire proclamation, *I have spoken.*

While the crowd buzzed, The Ridge took his seat next to his son, John, who whispered his favorable review. John's eyes sought those of his wife Sarah, nicknamed Sally, who stood out near the edge of the council house. Her soft smile communicated her shared approval of her father-in-law's words. But John also saw that many good Cherokees whom he had known all his life—like Thomas Walker and Charlie Swimmer—were not pleased. Even young James Walker, standing with other young men just outside the open-sided council house, echoed his father's disapproval.

William Drummond, too, watched and listened. It was a question which had, indeed, taken on a life of its own and whose answer appeared far too complex for productive resolution. It would get a lot worse, William told himself, before it got better. William spotted John Howard Payne. By his expression, William concluded, Payne must have made an assessment of the situation not unlike his own. The journalist quietly scribbled in his notebook.

The murmured reaction to Major Ridge's address soon gave way to a hum of anticipation when Chief Ross rose to address the gathering. Though some twenty years The Ridge's junior and only one-eighth Cherokee by blood, *Gu-wi-s-gu-wi* had so completely and passionately embraced the *Tsa-la-gi* fraction of himself that he exacted a reverence and respect matching that accorded the full-blood Major Ridge. Ross's demeanor and speech were markedly different when addressing the council than when hatching political strategy with his friends, advisors and sub-chiefs. He made brief eye contact with the journalist, Payne, then, emulating the tactic used so effectively by Womankiller, he turned a dark scowl on the government representatives and Indian agents until they squirmed and the crowd had grown quiet.

"We do not understand your president," he began with genuine confusion in his voice. "Many years ago he sent us plows and hoes. *It is not good for my red children to hunt,* he said. *You must learn to cultivate the earth. You must become civilized, if you wish to live in peace with the white man.* We have done all that was asked. And more. We have a national government with a written constitution. We have a national court system. We have a written language. We have published our own newspaper. And we have created many schools. Our young people have studied at your best universities. Now the president has come full circle. He sends you to tell us: *Give up your homes. Your farms. Your orchards. Your livestock. Give up the lands of your fathers. If you will go west, we will give you rifles to hunt with!"*

Gu-wi-s-gu-wi paused, knowing full well that his people, with their keen sense of humor, wouldn't miss his subtle irony and sarcasm. All Cherokee eyes were on their *yo-neg* visitors, and those *yo-negs* not numbed by a drunken stupor felt the heat of Cherokee judgment. Ross then made a point of turning his back completely on the representatives of the white government in the familiar Cherokee gesture of greatest disrespect.

"Hear me, my people," he continued addressing the Cherokees. "This is *Tsa-la-gi* land. This is our home. As it should always be. But we have not held our lands throughout the ages without struggle. We must be strong. We must be prepared to stand our ground. I ask you not to even consider leaving. If we pick up and go west, we will only be taking our troubles with us. If we tuck tail and run, they will pursue us—like the cowardly dogs we would be—all the way west of the Mississippi, and there they would take whatever remained. The *Tsa-la-gi* have become a peace-loving people, but there are still many great warriors among us. It is time again to do battle. Not with the war lance and the tomahawk. We shall not give our enemies a reason to bring their armies against us. The battles that lie ahead must be fought on the white man's terms. In the halls of his own government and before the magistrates of his own courts. We must beat him on his own battlefield. It won't be easy, but if we remain together, strong, united in mind and purpose, I know we can win. We can keep our homeland."

Glances passed between those who had earlier supported the words of Womankiller and those who had indicated their backing of The Ridge. Ross knew too well that divisiveness among the Cherokees was exactly what the United States president and all his minions hoped to achieve. They were expert at creating and then exploiting such schisms. They had shown it too many times in the brief history of their *yo-neg* nation—first as colonies, then as the United States. Chief Ross knew it was the very thing he must prevent. Those who were practiced at dealing with the whites saw the gleam of greedy anticipation in the eyes of the *yo-neg* agents and merchants among them, even as they spoke. The chief raised his hand to still the crowd.

"If there is division among the *Tsa-la-gi*, the *yo-negs* will drive between us their wedge of fear and mistrust. They will turn brother against brother, father against son. Let it not be so." He paused to maximize the impact of his next words. Unlike many of his previously ambiguous speeches, this time Ross would recommend a specific plan of action. A show of resistance. "In the coming weeks, federal census takers will come among you. Do not help them. Do not talk to them. Send them on their way. They didn't come looking for us in 1830. We weren't important enough to count in 1820. Or ten years before that. They didn't come when they only wished to tally *citizens* of the United States. Though we were here first, we weren't good enough for that. Now they only want to count you and get your names to make sure they can find you when they're ready to drive you out. And they want to count your cattle and livestock and they want to know how many acres you are cultivating for one purpose only—so they can dream at night about everything they plan to steal from you! But we will give them nothing! I will go again to see the president. He cannot forever turn a deaf ear to our cries for truth and justice. We must not give up hope. *A-ya a-gi-ha*! I have spoken."

The buzz of agreement with *Gu-wi-s-gu-wi*'s words was more fervent and the rumble of dissension more pronounced, producing the exact opposite of the unifying effect the chief had so earnestly desired. A portentous thunder rumbled in from Alabama to the southwest. The looks that passed between Titus Ogilvie and his sons and the other whites outside the council house weren't looks of concern for the impending rainstorm that would drench them all before morning's light.

Thomas Walker, Charlie Swimmer, John and Andrew Sixkiller couldn't disguise their enthusiasm for the chief's talk. William Drummond, however, wasn't so strongly swayed. His eyes met those of John Howard Payne, who shared his concern.

"You see! We will win!" Thomas Walker said with controlled excitement.

"These lands belong to the *Tsa-la-gi*," Andrew Sixkiller concurred.

"To our fathers!" Charlie Swimmer added.

"And to their fathers before them!" John Sixkiller proclaimed.

The attorney in William felt compelled to temper their reactions with an unbiased assessment of what they had heard.

"Ridge says: *Save the children. Pack up and go west.* Chief Ross says: *Stay and fight. The Cherokees will win.* But who is right?" He looked to each man, not expecting any of them to actually offer a solution, but he hoped to persuade them to at least pause and reflect. "There is no easy answer," he continued. "You have to listen with your minds as well as with your hearts."

Had his words really given them something to ponder? William couldn't tell. They stared silently at him until their attention was drawn back to the council fire. Old Chief *Tsunaluska*, who had saved Andrew Jackson's life at The Horseshoe, had risen from his seat. He began to slowly circle the fire. After a few revolutions he was joined by another ancient chief, Whitepath. Then Situwakee. The faces of these once-fierce warriors who couldn't fathom leaving their homeland merely because it was coveted by a bunch of *yo-negs* remained rigid with a silent implacability. Soon a number of Cherokee chiefs and tribal leaders were circling the flames. *Tsunaluska* and Situwakee began to chant softly, accompanied by the steady, rhythmic beat of the ceremonial drum. Gradually they picked up the pace and drew into the dance a host of other Cherokees, including women with rattles made of land-turtle shells filled with pebbles strapped to their ankles and to their legs just below the knees. The chanting, the drums and the rattles filled the damp night air and, for a brief time, drove from the *Tsa-la-gi* all thoughts of being forced to choose between going west or staying and fighting for the lands given to them by the Great Creator. For a while they would sing and dance. Later there would be time enough to suffer and die. The chanting and dancing continued even after many of the council leaders had walked outside. A thick mist rolled in like a ghostly scout come to announce the impending storm with repeated flashes of lightning and peals of thunder.

William, Thomas, Charlie, Andrew and John huddled with several other Cherokee men. They smoked their pipes and discussed in low tones the implications of the evening's speeches, grunting their agreement or snorting their disapproval. James stood with them, quietly listening but never speaking. He watched with suspicion a pair of rough-looking, bearded Georgia *yo-negs*. Earlier he had heard them introduced to Titus Ogilvie and his sons simply as Brantley and Solmes. They whispered and glanced frequently in the direction of Chief Ross. Finally they mounted their horses and rode off into the night. James looked around to catch a reaction, but the only one who had noticed was the white journalist, the one they called Payne. His expression seemed more one of detached observation than suspicion or concern. James dismissed the incident as merely his innate dislike of Georgians. Payne continued to observe, listen and make his notes, but he had little to say. When the rain began, he tucked his notebook inside his coat. His interest surged when he saw Chief Ross dismiss himself from a huddle of government agents to join William and his group.

"A good talk, *'Tsu-ts'*," Andrew Sixkiller was eager to compliment the chief.

"*Wa-do*," Ross thanked him. "We can count on your help?"

"I will tell the census takers nothing," Andrew assured him.

"They won't even find my cabin," Charlie Swimmer proudly asserted. Ross gave him an approving clap on the back and then addressed James Walker.

"We have many strong, young men who will help us win this fight," he said, looking James in the eye. James tried not to let it show, but he was clearly bursting with pride. Even twelve-year-old *Tsu-tsu* Swimmer stood a little taller beside his father. Chief Ross tousled *Tsu-tsu's* hair before asking William, "And how is your boy doing at the university?"

"To be honest," William confided, "Michael has already been in trouble—more than a few times. He's quite vocal. Very passionate in his beliefs."

"Ah, the righteousness of youth," Ross answered with a knowing smile.

"His heterodox views on Indian affairs—particularly regarding the Cherokees—has not endeared him to the university's old guard."

"A great friend to the *Tsa-la-gi*. Following in his father's footsteps," Ross praised both father and son in his adept politician's manner.

"Sometimes I think Michael would rather follow in *your* footsteps," William returned the compliment.

Ross took on a more serious tone. "Flattering sentiments aside, William, the path these days is winding, confused and filled with anger."

"This whole removal issue does seem to invoke more passion than rational discourse," William agreed. "More separation than unity."

"If we aren't careful, we'll destroy ourselves from within."

"Which would please your enemies no end," William empathized with the Cherokee leader's concern. Major Ridge, just coming down from the council house, passed close by and stopped on hearing William's words. He acknowledged Ross, as usual, with respect, but always with unmistakable tension.

"Will you join our delegation to Washington?" the chief invited.

Major Ridge shook his head and said "Send my nephew, *De-ga-ta-ga.*"

"Stand Watie's a good man," Ross replied. "Perhaps he'll see more clearly than his uncle."

"If you keep our people here, they'll be destroyed." There was a sincere plea in The Ridge's voice.

"If you give away our land, you are violating tribal law," Ross countered with equal candor and added, "punishable by death."

"Don't tell me of tribal law and death!" Major Ridge snapped, trying to restrain his anger. "I, The Ridge, slew Chief Doublehead 30 years ago for giving away Cherokee land!"

"And now you would commit the same crime," Ross prodded.

"Doublehead acted for personal gain. I only do what I must to save my people," The Ridge said, regaining his composure.

"You wish to give up the land of our fathers and run away. What happened to the great warrior, The Ridge?"

Major Ridge side-stepped the question. "I'm calling for a national council at New Echota. In December."

"That would be a fatal mistake, my brother," Chief Ross warned. The two men dwelt for a long time in each other's eyes before Ross bid the elder tribesman good-bye. Despite their bitter rivalry, increased by their rapidly polarizing positions on the removal issue, the two men grasped each other's forearms like gladiators with mutual respect, oblivious to the constant drizzle.

"*Do-na-da-go-hŭ-i,*" The Ridge said with a finality that went much deeper than a mere *good-bye until I see you again.*

John Howard Payne leaned close to William. "What will become of these people?" he asked.

"I don't know, my friend," William spoke softly, his eyes still locked on the two *Tsa-la-gi* leaders. "But it won't be pleasant. For any of them."

"Just be thankful we're not part of it," Payne said. Chief Ross and The Ridge went their separate ways, each man's steps keeping pace with the drum beat, the chanting and the rhythmic rattling of the dancers' shells.

* * * * * * *

The rain fell hard all night long, as though *Tsa-la-gi* spirits were determined to wash away the white plague from Cherokee land, or, failing that, to at least purify the hearts and unify the minds of their own native children. The faint glow from the lanterns inside the Ross cabin seeped out through partially covered windows like troubled eyes seeking answers in the dripping darkness of the surrounding pines, blackjack oaks and chestnut trees.

Inside the chief's small but hospitable cabin the journalist, John Howard Payne, spectacles perched on the end of his nose, worked diligently at a scrivener's table copying Cherokee documents. He wrote very precisely, with the careful deliberation of an ancient holy scribe, dipping his scratchy quill pen often. He looked up from his papers to watch Quatie, the chief's wife. This tiny woman with a waist no larger than a lantern's base was constantly flitting about like a hummingbird. Despite her diminutive stature, she easily lifted the heavy kettle of boiling water from over the fire and refilled Payne's cup and her husband's. She was part white, Payne could tell, but her demeanor and bearing bespoke the same strength and quiet nobility he had seen in many of the women he'd met during his brief stay among the Cherokees.

"Thank you, Mrs. Ross," he said softly.

"Go to bed. Both of you. It's late," she urged, knowing her words were wasted.

"There's much work yet to do, dear Quatie," Ross said with a loving touch of her hand as she filled his cup.

"It'll all be here tomorrow. Go to bed."

She placed the kettle back on it's hook over the fire and retired at last to the adjacent bedroom. There was no door to close. Ordinarily she and John had no need for added privacy. Quatie would lie awake each night for hours, thinking of her children, praying for them before beginning her arduous pursuit of an elusive, fitful sleep. She lay down on top of the bed and spread a single, thin blanket over her legs.

Payne studied the chief, who watched his beloved wife with a smile for a little longer, then rummaged through a trunk full of papers until he found the document he was seeking. He took it to Payne who examined it in the lantern's light and shook his head in amazement. Ross looked on with quiet pride, relighting his pipe. Payne had just begun transcribing the new document when they were interrupted by the sharp barking of the Ross's dog which darted from his place at the foot of Quatie's bed and stood growling at the front door.

"*Gi-li! E-tla-we-i!*" Quatie ordered the dog to be quiet.

Finally, above the dog's low, throaty growl and the patter of the rain, the men heard and began to feel the approaching hoofbeats. Ross, cautious but not overly concerned, took an old rifle down from its pegs on the wall. Without speaking, he removed an old flint-lock pistol from a sideboard and laid it on the table in front of Payne. The journalist looked at the gun, then up at Ross, his expression asking *What am I supposed to do with this?*

The distant rumble grew steadily louder until it had become an ominous thunder, rolling closer and closer. From the bedroom doorway Quatie stared at her husband. Even *Gi-li* had stopped growling and looked back and forth from the front door to his master. The horses slowed and broke into individual clops of what sounded like twenty to twenty-five riders pulling up outside. Payne leaned toward the window and peered out into the darkness. The escaping lantern light reflected off the wet long-coats and slickers of the riders lined up in front of the cabin. Despite the dimness, there was no mistaking the men were heavily armed. Payne recognized two of the men nearest the window as Brantley and Solmes, the pair he and James Walker had observed slipping away from the council grounds earlier in the evening. The man who appeared to be their leader dismounted first, followed by half the others. The rest remained in their saddles. At a signal from the leader, those on the ground drew muskets from their saddle sheaths and affixed their bayonets.

Payne, more than a little concerned, looked to Ross, who was standing away from the window but positioned to see outside. The cabin's inhabitants had no choice but to wait. They weren't surprised by the anticipated loud, pounding knock.

"Who is it?" Chief Ross asked with all the authority he could muster. There was a short silence before the door exploded inward, hanging at an odd angle from the unsevered top hinge. Brantley and Solmes lunged into the room, their bayonets poised. There was something more than inelegant—downright brutish, almost simian—in the carriage of these two. *Gi-li* barked wildly, ready to attack. Solmes snarled back and jabbed with his bayonet, quite prepared—almost eager—to kill the dog. Quatie grabbed *Gi-li* by the scruff of the neck and pulled him to safety.

"Quiet, *Gi-li*," she pleaded.

Ross attempted to move closer to Quatie and the dog, but Brantley placed the point of his bayonet under the chief's chin. "I'll take that rifle," he growled.

"Who are you?" Ross demanded. "What do you want?"

77

The group's leader strolled into the room, followed by two more Georgia militiamen with bayonets and a third with a pistol held down at his side. Solmes alertly snatched the chief's pistol from the table in front of Payne.

"Colonel Absalom Bishop, Georgia State Militia," the commander boomed through his tangled, dirty beard, thrusting his huge stomach forward with the arrogance of power. His upper lip twitched, almost curling into a sneer as he looked the Cherokee leader up and down. He appeared curious—even amazed—that Ross looked more like a white man than the chief of one of the largest Indian tribes on the continent. "John Ross? I'm placing you under arrest."

Payne rose from his chair. Solmes, with tobacco juice trickling down the side of his chin, grinned menacingly and pointed the pistol at him.

"You can't do that!" Payne protested. "This is Tennessee. The Georgia Militia has no authority here!"

Solmes pushed him back down into his seat and placed the muzzle of the chief's old pistol right against Payne's cheek. "This is all the authority we need," he said, his words followed by a whistling, sucking sound as he tried to recapture an escaping string of tobacco spittle.

Chief Ross followed up on Payne's argument. "You can't just ride across the state line and—" His objection was cut short when Brantley pressed the bayonet's tip hard against his throat.

"I didn't see any state lines layin' across the road." Bishop's eyes remained on Ross as he addressed his militiamen. "Did you men see any lines?"

"No."

"I didn't see no lines."

"Me neither."

Payne rose again. He pushed the pistol barrel away from his face and stepped around the table, but Solmes kept the gun pointed right at the journalist's head.

"Why are you arresting Chief Ross?" he demanded. "What are the charges?"

Without warning, Solmes struck Payne on the side of the head with the butt of the pistol, knocking him to the floor.

"You'll find out soon enough," Solmes grinned and spat on the floor.

Colonel Bishop helped Payne to his feet. With a tone almost causal he explained, "I don't think you'll be wanting to upset

Sergeant Solmes. He's already had a nasty ride, and it's a long way back to Camp Benton."

The grinning Solmes spat again, drawing a stern look from Quatie. Brantley left Chief Ross and ambled over to the table where Payne had been transcribing. "I can read, you know," he announced, as though he had brilliantly foiled some sinister plot.

"Then you'll be able to see that these papers are harmless," Payne insisted. Quatie, ignoring the glares of the militiamen, dipped a washcloth in the porcelain bowl on the sideboard and dabbed at the bleeding wound above Payne's eye.

"What's this?" Brantley examined a paper written in the Cherokee characters.

"Important tribal documents. Please leave them alone," the chief implored.

With a sneer, Brantley crumpled the page and tossed it on the floor, then picked up another. "Looks to me like some kind of secret code, Colonel."

"They're written in the Cherokee language. Please..." Ross entreated once more.

Sergeant Solmes looked at the papers. "I think it's French," he smirked knowingly. "Yeah. It's French. I seen it in school once."

Payne reached for the paper, but Brantley pulled it away and pretended to read it. "Says here they're gonna overthrow the government. They're plotting a rebellion. Gonna join up with the nigger slaves and kill all the white folks."

"This is absurd!" Ross was outraged. "I must ask you to leave!"

Payne snatched the paper from Brantley. "You're an idiot!" he barked. "You probably can't even read English—much less French or Cherokee!" Without the slightest change in his expression, Solmes pushed Quatie out of the way and pistol whipped Payne on the other side of his face, knocking him to the floor again. Chief Ross wanted to go to the aid of his friend but was stopped by two bayonets. Quatie stood at her husband's side. Glaring defiantly at Solmes, she pushed aside one of the bayonets that, in her opinion, was too close to her husband's heart.

The noonday sun was warm and a gentle breeze from the south whispered through the tops of the loblolly pines and sweetgum trees lining the road. Midnight, the shiny black stallion with a blazed face and white stocking feet, trotted cockily along. His rider slid his three-cornered hat rakishly to one side and glanced behind him to check his belongings tied to the saddle. Michael Drummond pulled the stallion to a stop where a narrow trail led off into the woods. Smiling, he urged the horse to a gallop down the familiar shortcut.

* * * * * * *

Janice Walker emerged from the crackling dry corn stalks of the fading garden with a basket of late beans. Annie drove the hatchet forcefully into the top of a wedge of wood, splintering it into kindling. Her thin cotton dress clung to her shapely body in the light breeze. In the corral on the east side of the cabin James brushed *U-no-le*, his sleek roan pony, whose blazed face and white stockings were almost identical to the markings of Midnight, who shifted restlessly while Michael watched quietly from the shadows on the far side of the clearing where the narrow trail emerged from the trees.

When the breeze shifted, *U-no-le* caught the scent of Midnight and his rider. Annie paused from her wood chopping and wiped her brow with her forearm, brushing a few tendrils of wind-tossed hair from her eyes. She noticed that the dog lying in the shade had pricked up his ears and craned his head around toward the woods with a low growl. Annie followed his line of sight until she spotted Michael in the shadows. Her expression never changed as she calmly resumed her chopping with a subtle smile she made certain he couldn't see.

Michael walked his horse out into the sunlight. *U-no-le* snorted and whinnied softly, prompting James to look up. With the sun in his face, he reached for the rifle leaning against the fence, holding it casually in front of him. Just in case. He shielded his eyes and glanced around. His mother, about to enter the cabin, stopped when she heard *U-no-le*. But Annie kept working and didn't look up. Finally, James spotted their visitor.

"Michael..." he said softly, his heart soaring at the sight of his dearest friend. He leaned the rifle back against the post, sprang over the fence and trotted out to meet them. "Michael!" he shouted, then repeated the announcement to his mother and sister. "It's Michael!" Midnight trotted to close the distance and Michael dropped from the horse to embrace James.

"*Si-yo, tso-s-da-da-nŭ,*" Michael said with emotion.

"*Si-yo,* my brother," James echoed the greeting. "It's great to see you!"

Michael waved to James's mother in the cabin doorway. "*Si-yo,* Mrs. Walker. *To-hi-tsu?*"

Tse-ni-si Walker waved back with a smile. "*Si-yo,* Michael. Come. Eat with us. We have fresh beans. And *du-ma-tli.*" She knew how much Michael loved her juicy, vine-ripened tomatoes. Janice was very fond of Michael. He had been like a true brother to James since they were tiny children. The first time the two boys had met they couldn't have been more than three. Thomas had accompanied Charlie Swimmer to the Drummond place when William asked Charlie to recruit additional help for a major barn expansion project that would be something of a strain for William, Ezekiel and Charlie. A fourth worker would give them the balanced two-man teams they needed. Thomas had been reluctant at first. Charlie had assured him that William paid well and paid promptly. But for Thomas it wasn't the money. It was pride. He had never before worked for a *yo-neg* and had vowed many times that he never would. Eventually he had agreed to go, but only as a favor to Charlie, to make the day a little easier for his *Tsa-la-gi* friend. And to emphasize to the *yo-neg* that it was no more than a friendly outing, he had promptly yielded to James's cries to tag along.

James and Michael had bonded instantly as though their spirits had been companions in a pre-life and had finally been re-united following years of lonely separation. The barn project had taken on a life of its own and had swelled into a three-day job. Thomas had actually enjoyed the experience. On numerous occasions during the day William had sought his advice and actually implemented several of his suggestions, treating Thomas as an equal, without a hint of condescension. And Thomas had detected no patronizing air in the way William worked shoulder to shoulder with Ezekiel and Charlie.

At the end of the first day Thomas and William stood by the well, drinking the sweet water and washing sawdust and bark chips from their faces, necks, hands and arms. They watched their sons playing in the shade of the house. Elizabeth and Reba had insisted

Charlie and Thomas eat before leaving. Reba had spent all afternoon in the kitchen preparing fried chicken, roast pork, collard greens, sweet potatoes, rutabagas, purple-hull peas, cornbread and a peach cobbler. *Somebody's got to eat all this, 'cause I ain't throwin' it to the hogs*, she had pronounced indisputably when the shy Cherokees at first declined.

When Thomas and James left shortly after dark, William asked Thomas back the next day to help finish the barn, but only if he would accept pay—the same as Charlie and Ezekiel. With a smile William added the requirement that James come along to keep Michael company. Thomas accepted, but only because William didn't insult him by insisting on paying him for the first day after Thomas had made it clear he was working as a favor to his friend, Charlie Swimmer. From that time forward Thomas and William had been friends; Michael and James had been brothers. And in becoming a brother to James, Michael had gained a sister in Annie, James's twin.

As the children grew to adolescence, Janice and Thomas had noticed between Michael and their Annie the occasional lingering touch, the incidental brushing of bodies, the searching looks quickly diverted. Thomas had said little, but Janice knew his mind. She had, in the most secret recesses of her heart, nurtured a tiny dream for her only daughter's happiness that might involve this handsome young *yo-neg* from a kind and decent family, but she knew her husband viewed the situation through the prism of a harsher reality. Michael Drummond was the son of a prominent *yo-neg* lawyer. And though William had proven himself over the years to be a friend and a champion of *Tsa-la-gi* rights, Thomas also knew most white men who married Cherokee women fell into one of the categories of farmer, trader or merchant. Not doctors or lawyers. Yet, he admitted to her one night as they lay passion-spent in each other's arms, he supposed their precious Annie could do worse than this strong-spirited young Master Drummond. In the dark she smiled and, to the steady rhythm of his deep, peaceful breathing, fell asleep with her hand resting on his solid, sweat-moistened stomach.

"Thank you, Mrs. Walker," Michael's words were directed to Janice, but he was looking at Annie, now shading her eyes and squinting out toward Michael and James. "I'd better get on home. I just stopped by to say hello."

Tse-ni-si shrugged her acceptance and disappeared inside the cabin. Annie tried not to smile and went back to her work.

"What are you doing here?" James quizzed him. "We didn't

expect you until the end of December."

"It's a long story," Michael preferred to side-step the details of his dismissal from the university. He threw his arm around James's shoulder and led Midnight toward the cabin. "Let's just say I was invited to take an early holiday," Michael answered with his customary wry grin.

"What will your father say?"

"That's one reason I stopped by. I want you to ride home with me. Father might not get so angry if you're there." The whole time he spoke, Michael's eyes never left Annie, even when he and James reached the corral where they put Midnight in with *U-no-le*. Michael hadn't seen Annie for almost a year. He was intensely—even painfully—aware of how the breeze molded the thin dress to the outline of her breasts and hips. James placed the fence rail back into position enclosing the two horses. He noticed where Michael's attention was directed but said nothing. He had seen through the years the attraction between *Mi-ki* and his sister—though it had never been acknowledged or mentioned—and accepted it as part of the natural course of things.

"So...you think your father will be angry? I see," he teased. "And that's the only reason you stopped by."

"Of course not," Michael tore his eyes away from Annie and looked seriously at his friend. "I wanted to pay my respects to your mother." As they neared the cabin, Michael altered his path, drawn magnetically toward Annie. James slipped around to his other side—between Michael and Annie—and steered his friend toward a second corral on the opposite side of the cabin from where Annie was chopping wood.

"Come on," James feigned ignorance of Michael's interest in his sister. "You haven't seen my new horse! A little wild yet, so I keep her separated. But she's a beauty!"

They angled toward the temporary corral, but Michael's eyes drifted back over his shoulder. He had the fleeting impression Annie had been watching him and had looked quickly away. Perhaps it had only been the breeze blowing her hair, creating the illusion.

"Yes," he said softly, "she's a beauty."

* * * * * * *

Michael and James trotted their horses along the wooded trail that would eventually lead them across Onion Creek just downstream from where, five years earlier, they had witnessed the murder of Clarence Bearpaw and Willie No-Shoes. They exchanged a knowing glance but neither spoke of the incident. Michael struggled to formulate a defense for his scholastic expulsion which he hoped might dilute his father's anger. But the words wouldn't come. Perhaps because more than an irate outburst Michael feared William might wear a look of quiet disappointment, and that, he knew, would be even more painful. Anger voiced is soon dissipated. Disappointment swallowed can fester for seasons in the darker regions of the heart. Ultimately Michael accepted that he could neither predict nor control his father's reaction, so he forced it temporarily from his mind and challenged James to a race.

Two races had brought them to the creek where they stopped to let the horses drink. Michael had won the first race, James the second. And each one—as it had always been between them—had laughingly accused the other of cheating. *U-no-le* and Midnight had renewed their old acquaintance as though each animal was an extension of its owner's spirit and fully understood the bond that existed between their riders. When the horses had finished drinking, Michael took the lead, but when Midnight climbed out of the creek's steep banks, James noticed he was gradually veering away from the direction of the Drummond place.

"This isn't the way to your house," James said, urging *U-no-le* to catch up.

"I thought, since we're in the area, we should stop and see Uncle Andrew."

"You really dread going home, don't you, *'Tsu-ts'*?"

"No, of course not," Michael looked off into the trees, refusing to meet James's probing stare.

"Of course not," James repeated softly. Their new path took them on a wide detour, circling to the south. They rode in silence for quite some time before James spoke again. "Oh, yes. Uncle Andrew's place is *right on the way*."

"He's like my own uncle," Michael defended his ploy of procrastination.

"And he's going to kick your butt just like your father!" James laughed.

Michael was about to reply when both horses jolted to a stop, ears pricked forward, nostrils flared. The boys saw nothing. Then there was a rustling sound, like a small animal in the dry underbrush just ahead and slightly to their right. Michael and James exchanged a glance. A rabbit or a squirrel—even a skunk—wouldn't have startled the horses in this manner. They

84

heard twigs snapping and dried leaves crunching, then a Cherokee girl about four years old emerged from the foliage onto the trail in front of them. Terrified, she was glancing back over her shoulder. She froze in her tracks when she turned and saw the riders. Her eyes were wide with horror until she recognized her cousin, James. *"E-du-tsi Tsi-mi! E-du-tsi Tsi-mi!"* she called him uncle, as was the custom of many young Cherokee children when addressing an older cousin. She burst into tears and ran toward the horses. James dropped from *U-no-le* and scooped her up. Michael quickly dismounted and joined them, puzzled.

"It's Nancy!" James explained. "Uncle Andrew's youngest girl. Nancy! *Ga-to-u-s-di?* What's wrong?" he patted the sobbing child.

"U-ne-gŭ," she whimpered.

"White men?" Michael wasn't sure he had heard right.

"A-tsi-so-nŭ-nŭ e-ge-i," she blubbered through her tears that the white men were hurting her mother. Without another word, James hoisted the child into his saddle and sprang up behind her. Michael jumped back on Midnight and they were off.

* * * * * * *

James's Aunt Rebecca was on her knees in the clearing in front of the Sixkiller cabin. Her dress had been completely ripped off, and she was bent double, one arm folded protectively across her breasts, the other attempting to shield her head. Her back wore the criss-cross bloody stripes from a beating at the hands of the Georgia Militia. They had come to enforce the Cherokee's compliance with the demands of the two federal census agents. A few other guardsmen looked on with arms casually crossed as though observing nothing more than the punishment of an egg-sucking dog. Large contusions along Rebecca's side were already darkening to a splotchy, purplish-brown where she had been repeatedly kicked, punched and jabbed in the ribs with a rifle butt.

Rebecca had always been a favorite of both James and Michael. Not a woman of many words—either Cherokee or English—she always had a smile, an affectionate pat on the cheek or a subtle, teasing remark that exhibited her *Tsa-la-gi* sense of humor. She was from one of the upper towns and had met Andrew at the *U-ku*, or Peace Chief's Dance, held every seventh year. Their attraction had been immediate and Andrew found his hunting trips taking him farther north, closer to the town where Rebecca, or *We-gi*, lived.

Andrew, himself possessed of certain psychic abilities, had told her late one night as they lay on the soft pine needles near the creek behind her father's cabin that he had seen a vision of the two of them and their four children—two boys and two girls. Propped on her elbow and lying on her side, *We-gi* had lowered her shoulder and head to the ground, fluidly shifted onto her back and gently pulled him on top of her. Though certainly not lacking in the desire, Andrew was startled by her sudden actions. She reached up and cupped his strong, chiseled face in her hands. "Four *di-ni-yo-li?*" she said to him in a breathy voice. "Then we'd better get started." When he entered her for the first time, she arched her back to receive him and pulled his long hair down until his ear was at her lips. "Have you ever had a vision of *this?*" she whispered.

"More times than you could know," he answered softly.

Withdrawn to the side of the clearing opposite the Sixkiller cabin, a detail of five soldiers looked on dispassionately, as though the physical distance itself provided them an insulating moral detachment.

Andrew Sixkiller, also nude, appeared to be hugging a thick-trunked pine tree. A rope tied to each wrist was pulled tightly by two of the Georgia militiamen, holding Andrew firmly against the tree while a third *yo-neg* beat him with a black leather mule-skinner's whip. Andrew's and Rebecca's two sons, twelve-year-old Mark and ten-year-old Timothy, and their other daughter, Tiana, eight, were held at gunpoint to prevent them from helping their parents. Despite their youth, the boys glared at these white devils, their eyes burning with full blown adult hatred, murder and vengeance.

One of the Georgians buried the toe of his boot in Rebecca's ribs. She was so exhausted she could only exhale heavily from the force of the blow. "You tell these census folks these kids' names or I'll kick it outa you, one name at a time! Now talk, damn you!" Even the federal census takers, who, like most dedicated bureaucrats, considered their mission essential if not holy, were taken aback by the brutality of the state militiamen sent to assist them in gathering the information they so diligently sought.

The agent called Wallace, a thin, bowlegged man from New Jersey, leaned down over Rebecca as though convinced she simply didn't understand the rules by which they were legally compelled to operate. "The government of the United States," he clearly enunciated each word, "says you *must* give us this information."

Rebecca raised her eyes. She saw the black whip and heard

its whistle in the instant before it sank its fangs once more into her husband's back. Andrew grimaced, biting off a cry, determined to deny his tormentors the satisfaction. His eyes met *We-gi's* in a fleeting union from which each drew renewed tenacity. Arnot, the other census agent, held up his fat, stubby little hand to interrupt the flogging. He stepped closer to Andrew.

"How many horses do you own, Mr. Sixkiller? Just give us the number and we'll be on our way."

Andrew knew this wasn't about how many horses he owned. Or pigs or cows. They had merely to walk to his pens and count them. This was about *yo-negs* exercising complete dominance—and humiliation, if they could work that in—over a bunch of unfortunate, stupid Indians. But they were incapable of understanding the strength of will, the resolve of spirit they were encountering throughout *Tsa-la-gi* territory and dealt with it the only way they knew how—with brute force.

Andrew pressed his face hard against the pine tree until the bark cut into his cheek. Blood trickled from his bleeding lip and dripped off, blossoming like a crimson flower on his bare foot. A Georgia guardsman standing beside Andrew winked at one of the men holding the rope tied to Andrew's wrist. The grinning militiaman raised his rifle and pulled back the flint lock. Out of the corner of his eye Andrew saw him take aim and fire toward the sapling corral. Andrew forced his head as far back as he could and looked toward the pen just in time to see his prized horse drop on its front knees, then flop over onto its side. The two Georgian's holding his wrists jerked hard, slamming his face back into the tree.

"Give us the number, and we'll minus the dead one!" demanded the militiaman on his right wrist.

"Guess your Injun name'll have to be *Horsekiller!*" the one on the left cackled to the shooter. Until then, the soldiers had been content to sit idly by and allow the census agents and the militiamen to do whatever they deemed necessary in extracting information from these stubborn aboriginals. But killing good horse flesh was a giant step across the line of decency and good sense. The detail's commander, a raw young lieutenant, wheeled his horse and trotted over to the scene of the flogging.

"Hey! You're not to harm the livestock!" he yelled down at the shooter, but the weathered Georgians continued their laughter, ignoring the young officer. The shooter calmly tilted his powder horn to reload and flashed a snaggle-toothed smile up at the soldier.

"Sorry, Lieutenant. Sir. It sorta went off."

"Well...see it doesn't happen again," the young officer's voice broke with an adolescent crackle, further diluting his authority and eliciting a few snickers he couldn't pinpoint. Knowing this was the best he was going to get, he trotted his horse back toward his men, flinching but refusing to look back when he heard the whip biting once again into the flesh of Andrew's raw and bleeding back.

"One more time, Mr. Sixkiller," Arnot leaned in, "how many horses do you own? Not counting the dead one."

Michael and James had stopped their mounts in the shadows at the edge of the clearing. James kept Nancy pressed close to him to prevent her from witnessing the scene before them. Michael, outraged, wasted no time drawing his rifle from the saddle scabbard beneath his leg. James gently lowered Nancy from the horse, depositing her next to a large hickory.

"Stay here, Nancy. Right behind this tree," he whispered, then barked at Michael. "Let's go!" But before James could coax *U-no-le* into action, Michael grabbed the reins and held him back.

"You go charging in there, they'll put a bullet right through you!" he warned in a shouted whisper.

"Michael! We have to stop them!" James saw only his family being beaten and himiliated. Even from this distance they heard the whistling cry of the whip and another heavy grunt from Andrew. And they heard Tiana, unable to restrain herself any longer, cry out when Rebecca took another kick to the ribs. Mark, the oldest son, broke free from the man holding him and rushed the Georgian who had kicked his mother, only to be sent sprawling by a savage backhand. James's face contorted with anguish. *Something must be done...immediately!* his pained expression cried out.

Michael ripped the empty hunting sack from behind James's saddle and made slits in it with his knife. James, confused, shifted his attention back and forth between Michael and the Georgians. His eyes closed for an instant when they heard another shriek of the mule whip and another groan from Andrew.

"What are you doing?! Hurry!" James was beside himself. Another whiplash bit into Andrew's back.

"How many hogs, Mr. Sixkiller?" Arnot's squeaky voice carried across the clearing. Michael pulled the hunting sack down over his friend's head until James's wild, desperate eyes appeared at the slits. He swung his rifle up past James's head and rested the barrel in the crotch of a low branch.

"When I shoot, you ride like hell," he told James. "Fire over their heads. You don't want to hit anybody."

The hunting sack bobbed almost comically as James nodded. "Let's go!" came his muffled impatience.

Arnot scratched his groin and coughed up a fist-sized nugget of phlegm, depositing it next to Andrew's bloody foot before repeating his question. "I'm gon' ast you again, Mr. Sixkiller—how many hogs you got?"

As the whip-wielding Georgia guardsman drew back the leather snake for another blow, his hand exploded in a spray of red and the whip flew from his grasp. Horses skittered and whinnied. The wounded militiaman screamed in pain. The rest of the Georgians looked around for the source of the shot and the soldiers were instantly alert. James exploded from the trees across the clearing, driving *U-no-le* at full speed straight for the census agents and militiamen. Even the hunting sack couldn't stifle the blood-curdling yell that heralded his arrival. The Georgians scrambled to pull their pistols and raise their long rifles for a shot at the charging phantom.

U-no-le spun to one side and slid to a stop in the open, leaving James fully exposed to the barrage of rifle slugs and pistol balls singing all around him. He fired his own rifle in the general direction of the Georgians, remembering to shoot over their heads so as not to hit Andrew, Rebecca or the children. Taking advantage of the time the Georgians would need to reload, James jerked the reins and spun his horse around. Brandishing the rifle, he let out another piercing yell and rode hard toward the stunned young soldiers. *U-no-le* pulled up only a few feet from them and James sat facing the inept young lieutenant. James peered through the narrow slits in the fretsome sack that had shifted on his head. There was no mistaking—staring back at him was U. S. Army Second Lieutenant Peter Tanner. It was bad enough, James thought, that this unconscionable violation should have been visited upon his family by complete strangers. But here was someone he had known since childhood. They had never really been friends, but James found it inconceivable that Peter could sit calmly by and watch Aunt Rebecca and Uncle Andrew brutalized by these subhuman savages. Their eyes connected briefly before James wheeled *U-no-le* around and disappeared into the trees. The other soldiers sat motionless, mesmerized by the strange encounter they had just witnessed.

"After him!" Peter yelled. He led the soldiers in pursuit of James, who had accomplished his mission by engaging them long enough for Michael to reload his rifle. Census agent Arnot and another militiaman knelt beside the whip master who was cradling the bloody stump of what remained of his hand. The two Georgians holding Andrew used the large pine tree as cover, maintaining a firm grip on the ropes tied to Andrew's wrists. The others hurriedly reloaded their guns and fired ineffectually at the fleeing hooded rider.

"Stop shooting! Idiots! You'll hit the soldiers!" census agent Wallace shouted.

The guardsman who had killed Andrew's horse fired his rifle anyway, then drove the gun butt hard into Andrew's kidney. "Some of your Injun kinfolks?" he growled bitterly. The other Georgian kicked the cowering Rebecca in the middle of the back with the heel of his boot.

"Touch her again and I'll kill you!" the voice immediately behind him was soft but chilling. The Georgian and the census agents spun around to see Michael, a handkerchief covering his face like a highway robber, standing only a few feet away. The stock of his rifle was braced against his hip bone, leveled at the stomach of the guardsman who had kicked Rebecca. In his other hand Michael held a pearl-handled Collier repeating pistol. Most of the other guardsmen—caught in the midst of reloading following their futile volley at James—were slack-jawed with disbelief.

"Put 'em down! All of you!" Michael barked with authority.

"Who the hell are you?" the startled guardsman sneered.

"Another goddam Injun!" the half-handed Georgian snarled up at the man who had crippled him. "Look at his eyes."

Agent Arnot took a single, timorous step toward Michael. "You're not Indian," he said, then repeated it louder for the others. "He's no Indian!"

Michael ignored him and shifted his weapons from one to the other until they were all disarmed. Once their guns were down, Michael stepped closer to the guardsman who had kicked Rebecca and cracked him in the face with his pistol, breaking the Georgian's nose. Blood gushed everywhere. The dazed guardsman stumbled sideways and dropped to his knees. Michael swung the rifle barrel around only inches from his face. "Take off your coat," Michael said, the cold rage rumbling in his throat.

"What?"

"Give it to her!" Michael gestured toward Rebecca. "Now!"

Staring at the gaping rifle muzzle under his nose, the Georgian took off his long coat and draped it over Rebecca who lay on her side, curled in a fetal position. She looked up and, despite the mask, easily recognized Michael. Though she couldn't speak, her eyes expressed her love and gratitude. She pushed herself up onto her knees and pulled the coat closed around her. The children rushed to comfort their mother. Even little Nancy came running from the hickory tree across the clearing.

"Get over there..." Michael motioned for the Georgians to bunch closer together where he could watch them. A flurry of distant gunshots turned all heads but Michael's, who kept his eyes on his prisoners. He knew the soldiers were shooting at James, but he also knew they were no match for his Cherokee brother when it came to riding at break-neck speeds through the forest.

"Strip down," Michael raised the Collier pistol to the head of the man whose nose he had just broken. The confused guardsman gaped blankly at his youthful captor. "You heard me! Take off your clothes!" Michael snapped, raising the pistol as if to strike him again in the face.

"Now just a damn minute!" protested an older militia sergeant, the leader of the Georgia squad. He stepped out from the group and, without hesitation, Michael whipped the pistol around and shot him in the foot. The militia sergeant slumped to the ground, screaming, clutching at his boot where blood oozed from the bullet hole.

"I'm not playing games!" Michael yelled, his temper rising. "I'll kill every damn one of you!" The broken-nosed guardsman swiftly stripped down to his threadbare long underwear, stained from months of unwashed sweat and other bodily discharges. "All the way!" Michael gestured with the pistol. The grumbling guardsman removed his longjohns. "Now...hug that tree," Michael ordered and turned the rifle on two other guardsmen. "You...hold him."

Andrew, Rebecca and their children watched with the same curiosity as census agents Wallace and Arnot and the other Georgians. No one moved, including the two Georgians Michael had just ordered to hold their comrade to the tree. Exploding in a fury, Michael again struck the naked, broken-nosed guardsman on the side of the head. Then he drove the rifle butt into the gut of one of the men who had failed to obey him. They grabbed the naked man and held him tightly against the tree exactly as they had earlier done with Andrew.

Michael kicked the black mule-skinner's whip over in front of Andrew who had just pulled his trousers back on. Andrew, his back bloody and torn, hovered over Rebecca, talking softly to her in Cherokee. He picked up the whip and turned to the naked guardsman hugging the tree, but when he drew the whip back, he flinched with excruciating pain. The lacerated skin on his back and shoulders had begun to shrink and tighten. Any movement stretched open the wounds. He lowered the whip.

"You can't do this to him," census agent Wallace objected.

"Why not?" Michael argued. "You did it!" He handed the rifle to Andrew, then took the whip and rapidly delivered four searing blows above the howls of the man who had so savagely kicked Rebecca.

The militia sergeant, still clutching his wounded foot, snarled up at Michael. "I'll get you for this! I'll hunt you down like a God damned mad dog, whoever you are!"

Michael drew the whip back and snapped it forward, wrapping its sting around the sergeant's face. "I welcome the day, my friend!" he said. Then he walked over to the Georgians' horses, picked out a tall, good-looking roan and led the animal to Andrew. "Sorry about your horse. This looks like their best one. Guess we'll just have to call it even." Michael pointed his pistol at two more guardsmen and motioned toward their three wounded companions—the hand-shot whip master, the foot-shot sergeant, and the broken-nosed, mule-whipped woman kicker. "Put them on their horses and get the hell out of here," Michael ordered. He took back his rifle from Andrew and pushed it into the face of Arnot, the fat little census agent. "You, too. And if you're thinking of coming back, you'd better bring a whole army division, 'cause I'll be sitting up there in those trees—" he pointed to the towering pines, "—and I'll pick you off, one at a time. Now, get goin'!"

They all scrambled to obey the masked intruder. A couple of them were forced to ride double. Andrew led his replacement horse to his wife and children. Michael kept his weapons trained on the census agents and Georgia militiamen until they were out of sight. He waited to make sure they weren't doubling back, then mounted Midnight and said good-bye to the Sixkillers. Before he left, Michael cautioned them to keep all their hunting rifles loaded, their arrows ready and not to stray far from home for a couple of days. He suggested they post a guard in the woods in case some of the Georgians came back to set fire to the cabin.

* * * * * * *

Michael, still dusty from the afternoon's encounter at the Sixkiller cabin, looked out the window of his father's study. He kept his eyes on Midnight out in the corral so he wouldn't have to face his parents. William Drummond stood by the stone fireplace smoking his pipe and staring into the flame. Michael's mother sat with a blanket wrapped tightly about her shoulders. Her health, as always, was fragile at best. She dabbed at her tears and glanced at James, who was seated on a stool just inside the study door. James dipped his eyes, then felt foolish when he realized he was still clutching the slit hunting sack that had served as his mask. He and Michael had just risked their lives in defense of Uncle Andrew and his family, so why were they being made to feel as though they had done something wrong, he wondered.

"It's just so...so humiliating. Dismissed from the university!" Elizabeth lamented. "Have you no concern for your future, Michael? For the reputation of this family?"

Michael wheeled to face them. "I bow to no authority that is bent on the wanton destruction of a people," he barked the polemic of a strident university protest.

"Watch your tone, son. This is your mother," William's voice was soft but stern. Michael turned back to the window. In the corral Ezekiel was brushing Midnight. *U-no-le*, tied to the fence, had already been groomed by the black man who, along with Charlie Swimmer, had taught both boys their deep love and profound respect for horses. In front of the barn, Charlie pumped the hand bellows to bring the coals of his smithy fire to a glowing red as he prepared to re-shoe William's big gray, Clancey. His father's words subpoenaed Michael's fugitive thoughts back inside the study.

"Michael...you must learn to control your anger."

"I was only trying to help them. Someone had to."

"But don't you see?" William applied his lawyer logic, "In the long run you only make it worse. Two white men have been shot, another beaten. And ultimately the Cherokees will be blamed."

At least, Michael thought, the dreaded confrontation over his dismissal from the university had now been overshadowed by the Sixkiller incident. "What about all the Cherokees who've been shot and beaten by the whites?" he countered.

"Violence isn't the answer," Elizabeth echoed the words she'd heard her husband say countless times. "Civilized people settle their differences in a civilized manner."

Michael was about to lash out again, but a glance at his father softened his tone. "Civilized as in make a promise, then break it? Make a treaty, then violate it? Make laws to protect the whites, but not the Indians?"

"Well..." William drew the word out as he held a splinter of kindling in the fire, "perhaps I was wrong in expecting you to become an attorney."

"Yes," Michael's mother agreed. "You're much too emotional."

William relit his pipe. The crackle of the burning tobacco sounded unusually loud. "You could have been a great help to these people," William's words dripped with regret. Michael was hurt.

"I see you help them, Father. In court. But you don't have any real feeling for them!" Michael struck back. He hated the gnawing shame he felt had been unjustly heaped on him.

"I have very deep feelings for these people! I just wish you knew," William surprised his son with such an emotional response.

"Exactly my point, Father! How *could* I know? You're always so cold and aloof. Above it all. You've never shown me anything of how you feel!"

William, while capable of strong emotion, had never felt comfortable disclosing his feelings to others. Not even to his own son. William changed the subject. "Yes. Well. You're home now. Apparently to stay. I'm sure there's plenty of work to do."

"I'll pay you back, Father," Michael offered. "All the money for the university."

"Forget the money. It's not important."

"I suppose I must be a big disappointment to you as a son," Michael's eyes met William's, who had not missed the sadness in his son's voice. But Elizabeth wouldn't have sadness or disappointment under her roof, especially not between her husband and her son.

"You're still just a child. There are other universities. After Christmas, your father will write some letters." There. That should put an end to the unpleasantness. Enough had been said. Life would go on and they would all be happy. She would see to it.

James rose when Michael moved toward the door, taking him past his father. William's face was twisted with emotion. He kept his back to Elizabeth and grabbed the lapel of his son's coat.

"You may never become an attorney, but you will always be my son. You think I'm disappointed?" his voice almost cracked. He shook his head no. His voice was low, intense. Almost a whisper. "In so many ways, I admire you more than you'll ever know."

William straightened the jacket, brushed away a pine needle and placed a hand on the side of his son's face. Michael lowered his eyes, embarrassed by the unusual display from his normally stoic father. William's final pat on Michael's back sent him on his way, past James and out into the hallway. James backed toward the door

94

with a polite nod to William and Elizabeth.

"Mrs. Drummond...Mr. Drummond," he searched for the words. "If I may say it...perhaps your son is more of a man than you realize...."

After James had ducked out the door to follow Michael, Elizabeth fought off a cough and looked at William. "What do you suppose he meant by that?" she asked. William looked at her but didn't answer. The sound of hoofbeats coming up from the main road drew William to the window. Galloping toward the house were Major Ridge, his son, John, and four other Cherokee men. William had seen the other four at council meetings. What puzzled him was that two of the four he knew were aligned with The Ridge, while the other two had always sided with *Gu-wi-s-gu-wi*, the principal chief.

Michael had gone down to the barn to take over the grooming chore, freeing Ezekiel to help Charlie Swimmer re-shoe Clancey. Charlie and Ezekiel looked up at the approaching riders. William appeared on the front porch behind James. Michael handed the grooming brush to Charlie and leaped over the corral fence. He wiped his hands on his trouser legs and walked back up toward the house where the riders had stopped near William.

"*Si-yo*, Ridge," William greeted his guest.

"*Si-yo, Wi-li*," Ridge raised a hand in salute.

"Well, this is interesting. Ross men riding with The Ridge," William said. "Or have you switched sides?" There was no response from the chief's taciturn followers.

"It is true. There is trouble among our people," The Ridge acknowledged gravely. "Friction between Ross and me. But it disgraces all *Tsa-la-gi* when our principal chief is thrown into a cage like a wild dog."

Charlie and Ezekiel had ambled up from the barn in time to hear The Ridge's last remark. It was a puzzling—and troubling—report. All eyes were on William. He knew they hadn't ridden as a bipartisan group all the way out to his farm just to inform him of recent events. More was expected. Much more.

CHAPTER

6

Carriages, riders and pedestrians came and went with apparent purpose up and down the streets of Milledgeville, the bustling capital of Georgia nestled on the western bank of the Oconee River southeast of Atlanta. The capitol building, an imposing, three-story gothic structure with a gray textured finish and a tower in the center, occupied a plush green tree-lined square in the center of town. It served both as the seat of state government and as the Baldwin County courthouse. Immaculately tailored young black boys tended the horses and carriages of those who conducted mysterious and important business within. One serious-minded, light-skinned boy proudly minded the shiny black stallion and the big dappled gray of the two gentlemen who had ridden all the way down from Pine Hill.

The dark hallway smelled of burned lamp oil, polished wood, stale cigars and rancid spittoons. A wiry, beady-eyed clerk blinked with the rapidity of a nervous rodent from behind wire-rimmed spectacles as he wrestled with an oversized load of old court ledgers. His *peck-peck* footsteps echoed through the cavernous corridor. At last he reached the heavy oak door bearing an engraved sign: *Hon. Walter M. Barrington.* The clerk used the corner of a ledger to push his spectacles back up onto the bridge of his nose, then fumbled blindly for the handle. Finally he was forced to use his bony behind to open the door and backed into the judge's chambers.

William Drummond was seated across the vast mahogany desk from Judge Barrington, a man of sixty, nearly as tall as William, intelligent and sensitive. Michael stood gazing out the window, hands clasped behind him. The judge broke off his conversation mid-sentence when the clerk entered with the ledgers.

"Oh, yes...on the table there will be fine, Jernigan," he smiled with affection at the struggling little bureaucrat who deposited the oversized load on the table, brushed the dust from his pants and lifted the watch from his vest pocket.

"You're due in court in ten minutes, sir."

"Yes. Thank you, Jernigan," Barrington said. The devoted clerk dipped his head politely and backed out of the room. Barrington leaned forward over the papers on his desk. "As I was saying," he resumed with a glance at Michael, "no doubt this fine young man will follow in his father's footsteps in the practice of law?"

96

Michael pivoted from the window and looked at William, who smiled with slightly raised eyebrows. "We were discussing that very thing just yesterday, weren't we, Father?"

"With the rampant disrespect for the law these days," William answered the judge, "I'm not certain even I would choose this profession, if I had it to do over."

"Sad but true, William," Barrington concurred. "Sad but true." He dipped his feathered quill and scratched his signature on the papers. "This writ orders the release of Chief Ross. I wish you luck in getting it enforced." The judge saw William's expression cloud. "With President Jackson backing their position," Barrington continued, "these Georgia hooligans think they can pretty much do as they please. Court orders notwithstanding." He blew on the paper to dry the ink.

"Rumor has it you've been threatened because of your sympathetic views," William said. "I applaud your courage."

"Sympathy and courage have nothing to do with it. The law is the law. The Cherokees have their rights as much as any of us." This was the honest, straightforward, unbiased attitude with which Walter Barrington had dispensed justice for as long as anyone in his prefecture could recall.

"Someone should tell that to President Jackson," Michael injected.

"Indeed!" Barrington smiled at his young visitor. He gave William the paper and they shook hands. "Have a safe journey, William." Then to Michael he added, "Keep your powder dry, young man."

"And you yours, Judge Barrington. Thank you," Michael said and firmly shook the magistrate's hand. Barrington and William exchanged a smile, both impressed with the maturity of Michael's deportment.

* * * * * * *

The rotted Cherokee corpse spun slowly. The rope from the emaciated neck to the rough-hewn beam above whispered a soft creak of protest. The dank cell of the Camp Benton stockade at midnight left the eyes swimming in ink, but it was the denial of their other senses the three prisoners longed for as the stench of decaying human flesh raped its way into their nostrils and lungs and reached down into their stomachs to steal what wasn't there.

The prisoners—all seated in a line against the outer log

wall—heard the crunch of footsteps in the damp pea gravel just before the thick wooden cell door screeched open. They were blinded by the lantern light held close to their faces. One older full-blood, whose countenance was a mask of hard lines and bitterness, squinted up past the guard at William Drummond and Major Ridge. The spectral shadows cast by the low-slung lantern could have easily convinced the old *Tsa-la-gi* these were evil night messengers come to drag him off to yet another corner of hell. Once his eyes had adjusted, he recognized The Ridge, then glared with open hatred at the white man with him. "*Hi-tsa-la-gi-s-go?*" he asked if William was Cherokee. There was no reply. "*E-da-ni-gi-s-da,*" he growled. "Send him away."

The prisoner beside him leaned forward into the light. Through the scraggly growth of beard, the abrasions and the dirt, William and The Ridge barely recognized Chief John Ross. "*I-gi-s-de-nu-hi-ga,*" he reminded the other prisoner that William was there to help.

"We don't need this *yo-neg's* help," the old Cherokee prisoner snorted contemptuously before scooting back out of the lantern's glow.

"It's dark in here," William commented on the obvious in an effort to change the subject.

"He has helped the *Tsa-la-gi* many times," Ridge defended William.

Ross managed a faint smile and answered William. "When it's dark, you can't see the walls," he explained. "They could just as easily be fifty feet away. Quite roomy, you know?"

William appreciated the chief's innate ability to adapt and endure. When the guard shifted the lantern, William and Major Ridge saw the feet of the corpse. Their noses crinkled against the festering odor, each wondering—but neither asking—if it had been a suicide of despair or just another example of midnight justice—Georgia style.

"Can you get us out of here?" Ross asked his lawyer friend.

"I have a writ of release from Judge Barrington in Milledgeville. I'll talk to Colonel Bishop. I'm sure we can reason with him." William sounded less than convinced.

Another prisoner shifted forward into the light to join the conversation. It was the journalist, John Howard Payne. Large, crusted scabs had formed on the wounds from his pistol whipping. "Hauling the colonel out of bed in the middle of the night should put him in a receptive mood," he quipped.

"Thank you for coming, William," Ross was grateful for the effort.

Another guard stuck his head through the stockade door and announced, "Colonel's up." The lantern-toting guard motioned for William and The Ridge to leave the cell.

"See if you can get these men some decent food," Ross called out just before the cell door swung closed.

* * * * * * *

Grotesquely twisted greasy lips pulled and the thick, shiny tongue licked and leveraged until finally the stained teeth clamped down and ripped the last shreds of flesh from the massive turkey leg. Bits of fat and other food particles populated the scraggly moustache and beard surrounding the voracious orifice that was the mouth of Georgia's Militia Commander, Colonel Absalom Bishop. His eyelids sagged, heavy with sleep and gluttony.

"Makes me hungry. Gettin' up in the middle of the night. Always has. Real hungry." He gestured with the turkey bone toward the large platter, inviting his guests to partake.

William and Major Ridge glanced at each other before William politely shook his head no. Bishop shrugged indifferently and guzzled from a brown bottle, the dark fluid streaming down into his beard. He extended the bottle toward William who declined. Bishop poured from the bottle into a dirty mug and pushed it in front of William. It was clear Bishop would do or say nothing further until William had shared a drink, reinforcing the colonel's absolute control of the meeting. After staring at the cup for a long time, William took a sip and tried not to grimace too noticeably. The commandant appeared satisfied. William stretched his lips against the bitter ale before he spoke.

"It's a reasonable request, Colonel Bishop, to ask that you specify the charges for which Chief John Ross has been incarcerated."

"*Incarcerated*?" Bishop was genuinely puzzled by the ignorance of this supposedly educated man. "Hell, we didn't *burn* him, we just th'owed him in jail!"

"What are the charges?! Tell us!" Major Ridge demanded.

Bishop stopped chewing. His mouth hung open, food half in, half out. A guardsman by the door took a step toward the Cherokee leader. His hand rested meaningfully on the butt of the flint-lock pistol in his belt.

"Watch yer mouth, Injun," the sentry cautioned. Bishop resumed chewing and grinned up at his guests, fully enjoying the upper hand. William unfolded the writ from Judge Barrington and laid it on the table facing the militia commander.

"Either state the charges against Mr. Ross," William rephrased the request, "or release him. You can't just hold people—"

"You're forgetting one thing, counselor," Bishop interrupted, pushing the paper back toward William. "These is Cherokees. They ain't people."

"Mr. Payne isn't Cherokee," William corrected him.

"Payne? That writer fellow? I'm holdin' him for...Oh, I don't know...let's just say, aidin' and abettin'. How's that for a charge?"

"If you won't even say what Chief Ross is charged with," William argued logically, "how can Payne be guilty of aiding and abetting?"

Bishop took another drink, then danced the bottle back and forth, side to side on the table. With eyes half closed, he leaned his head back and drowsily mulled his visitors' demands. Finally, he nodded with pursed lips. "All right. I'll give you a charge for yer big-shot chief. How about subversion? Interferin' with federal census agents. Inciting to riot."

"That's absurd, and you know it!"

"Just the other day," Bishop shrugged, palms up, "a band of twenty-odd Cherokees and renegade whites attacked some census agents. Wounded three of my best men."

"Twenty? Did you say twenty?" William was incredulous at the colonel's exaggeration of the Sixkiller incident.

"Maybe more," the militia commander said in earnest.

William had heard enough. He picked up the writ and thrust it in Bishop's face. "This is a legal and binding court order. I demand you release these prisoners."

Bishop's grin vanished as he slammed the brown bottle down hard, shoved the paper aside and bolted out of his chair, oblivious to the liquid spilling onto the table and dripping through the cracks onto the floor. He pointed at William with the turkey leg bone. "You don't come in here demandin' a God damn thing! Understand?" he bellowed. "I decide when—or *if*—they can go! And if you don't want to join 'em, you'd best be gettin' out of my office. Out of Camp Benton!" William and Major Ridge stood silent in the face of this outburst. Bishop belched loudly, looked at the guard by the door and announced casually, "I'm goin' back to bed."

"You're a disgrace," William refused to be intimidated. "To the Militia. To the entire state of Georgia."

Bishop glanced at the guard who stepped forward, ready to take William into custody, but William held up a hand. "All right. All right," he swallowed his outrage with feigned respect. "We'd like another word with the prisoners. Sir. Please." Bishop, satisfied with William's newfound deference, motioned for the guard to step back. "And if it's all right...." William indicated the large platter of food Bishop had abandoned.

"Help yourself," the colonel gestured generously with the leg bone and grinned broadly when William picked up the entire tray.

* * * * * * *

Though famished, the Cherokee prisoners displayed better manners than had their white host. Quietly they picked the last morsels from the bones of the large bird. Chief Ross was genuinely grateful.

"It's all right, William. You did all you could. We appreciate the effort. Right now, you'll probably be more help to my people back at the Agency. Don't you agree?" he looked to Major Ridge who nodded.

From the shadows the bitter full-blood once more snorted, "As much help as he's been to us?"

"They can't hold you much longer," William said, ignoring the insult.

"They've made it painfully clear," Payne reminded him, "they can do whatever they damn well please."

"Let's go. That's long enough," the guard called from the cell door.

"I'll do all I can," William promised as he moved away.

"We know that, *Wi-li*," Ross said.

Major Ridge, the last to leave, paused near the door with an afterthought for Ross. "I've called for a council at New Echota to start on December 19th. I'm sure you'll be out by then."

"As chief, I can't sanction a council meeting whose purpose is to sign away our land," Ross said, clearly divining the reason for the proposed gathering.

"Our people must be saved, *Gu-wi-s-gu-wi*. I wish you could see that."

"Giving away our land isn't the answer. I wish you could see *that*."

"There's no other way."

"There will be severe consequences if such a treaty is signed."

"And worse consequences if it isn't," The Ridge stood his ground. The two leaders studied each other in the faint lantern light.

"*Do-da-da-go-hŭ-i*," Ridge bid them farewell.

"Good-bye," Ross answered in English. Darkness swallowed the prisoners once more when the guard swung the heavy door closed, taking with him the lantern's glow.

CHAPTER

7

The glass lantern chimney squeaked back into place, and the soft light feathered its way into the corners of Reba and Ezekiel Campbell's unadorned but impeccably clean two room house. Two straight-backed wooden chairs, a bed and a chest-of-drawers took up most of the bedroom. Clothing hung from four wooden pegs beside the door to the kitchen. Two wash pans sat on a work table beside a tiny pot-bellied stove. A gourd dipper was suspended from a nail in the wall over a bucket of drinking water. Butted up against a floor-to-ceiling pantry whose curtain was an old, threadbare blanket stood a simple oak table. Directly above a hand-carved Nativity scene on a cherry wood sideboard near the door hung a small wreath—the only signs of the imminent yuletide season.

Reba had awakened instantly at the sound of hoofbeats and carriage wheels. She jostled the groggy Ezekiel into a grudging, mumbling semi-consciousness.

"C'mon, Zeke," she prodded him in the back. "They here. Git yo' rickety ol' butt up there and build 'em a big fire. They bound to be froze half to death, out in a night like this! Let's go! You know how crabby Miss Susanna git when she ain't comf'table."

"Miss Susie! Oh, Lawd! Miss Susie!" The mention of the ever-demanding Susanna Drummond struck fear in the usually unflappable Ezekiel. He sprang up and grabbed his pants from the peg.

* * * * * * *

"Be careful! Must you be so clumsy?" Susanna complained when a single drop of hot milk splattered out of the cup Reba was filling. The black woman bit off a barbed response and added a mixture of freshly ground cocoa beans and brown sugar to the two cups. Ezekiel tossed more wood onto the fire. Susanna, still shivering from the night ride, pulled the blanket back up on her shoulder. Elizabeth, sickly as usual, occupied her favorite chair near the living room window. "Watch out for the sparks," Susanna criticized Ezekiel's every move. "You'll catch us all on fire! Get more wood. That won't be enough."

"Yes, Miss Susie."

"Thank you, Ezekiel. It's a wonderful fire," Elizabeth tried to ameliorate her daughter's harshness. "And thank you, Reba," she added as she received one cup of cocoa and watched Susanna take the second.

"I'm telling you, Mother, it was awful," Susanna continued her interrupted lamentation. "Someone said the ferry broke loose in the storm and drifted downstream. But the man at the landing suspected some Cherokees had cut it loose just for spite."

"Now why would they do such a thing?" Elizabeth preferred to believe that everyone in the world truly wanted to get along with one another as earnestly as she did.

"Who knows why these Indians do anything, Mother?" Susanna huffed her exasperation. "That's not the point! The point is, we had to wait three hours until another ferry came down from Haley's Landing!"

"Well, you're home safe now. It's Christmas. We should all be thankful."

William and Michael came in from the cold. Michael was loaded down with the remainder of Susanna's luggage. "Hope the horses don't get sick," William remarked to no one in particular. "Clancey's breathing doesn't sound so good."

"Would it be any wonder on a night like this?" Elizabeth commiserated.

"I thought you were just here for Christmas," Michael complained to his sister as he wrestled a stubborn bag through the doorway. "Looks like you're moving back home for good."

"No, dear brother," she sipped her cocoa and quipped with characteristic sarcasm, "*I* will be back in school. Unlike some others." Michael shot her a dirty look and resentfully slammed the bags down beside her. "Be careful, clumsy lout!" Susanna snapped.

"Children, don't start. Please. It's Christmas," came Elizabeth's habitual plea.

"*Fröliche Weinacht, lieber Brüder.* That's German. Merry Christmas, dear brother. *Joyeaux Noel, mon frere.* That's French. One learns such things if one stays long enough at the university," she was relentless in her teasing.

"I used to love to hear your Aunt Jane speak French," Elizabeth diverted the conversation. "She moved to Louisiana. Of course, that was before either of you were born." Susanna ignored her mother and glared defiantly at Michael, awaiting his barbed rejoinder. She felt disappointed when he silently turned his back and warmed his hands at the fire. Ezekiel brought in more wood and made a point of tossing two large pieces onto the fire, creating a shower of sparks.

"Sorry, Miss Susie," he feigned an apology before Susanna could chide him.

Ezekiel slouched toward the door with Reba right behind him. William watched the couple with loving appreciation. "Reba...please fix me a toddy. Make one for Ezekiel, too. And something for yourself."

"Why, thank you, Mistah D. I believe I could use a little somethin'," she said, cutting a glance at Susanna, "'cause they's definitely a chill in the air."

"Insolent old cow," Susanna muttered, making sure Reba heard her.

"Tomorrow we'll make candied apples," Elizabeth deplored friction among the people she loved. "You always liked those. Candied apples. And I'm sure Peter Tanner will come to pay you a visit. He asked about you in town the other day." At the mention of Peter Tanner, Michael glared down at his sister. She sipped her drink, refusing to look at him. She knew Michael had disliked Peter since they were children, and this made Peter imminently more attractive to her than he might otherwise have been.

* * * * * * *

The brightness of women's laughter broke through the morning air in stark contrast to the cold, overcast day. The Drummond's utility farm wagon, drawn by William's oldest, slowest nag, emerged from the woods across the meadow that spread eastward behind the barn. Reba drove the wagon, with Elizabeth seated beside her, wrapped as always in a heavy blanket. She occupied this position for warmth and to act as a barrier between Reba and Susanna. But Susanna had been uncommonly civil all day, a phenomenon primarily attributable to the presence of Peter Tanner. In his civilian clothes, the ax resting on his broad shoulders, he walked beside the wagon which carried the Christmas tree he had just chopped down.

"We really insist, Peter," Elizabeth repeated.

"Yes," Susanna echoed. "We insist."

"It's terribly kind, but I really couldn't impose..." Peter uttered the perfunctory, insincere refusal, knowing he would soon be outvoted and forced to capitulate.

"Nonsense!" Elizabeth countered predictably. "If your mother and father are going to be in Boston for the holiday, you must spend Christmas with us."

105

"Oh, Peter, please say yes!" Susie pleaded as though there were a chance he might actually decline. Peter enjoyed the attention. But his reluctance was less than convincing, and it was driving Reba to distraction.

"Oh, please, please, Mistah Peter," she mumbled. "I sho' do need another mouth to cook fo'."

"What are you mumbling about, Reba?" Susanna leaned forward to look across her mother.

"Nothin', Missy. Nothin' at all."

"We'll be expecting you then, Peter," Elizabeth made the final pronouncement. "We won't take no for an answer."

"Well, you've left me no choice!" Peter laughed. "All right. I'll be there."

"Well, I'm sho' glad that's settled," Reba muttered again. "The suspense was killin' me." She slapped the reins against the horse's rump to quicken the pace. "Giddyap!" Out of the corner of her eye, she saw Peter break into a trot to keep up. No one saw her smile.

William's large hands gripped the bow-saw, pushing, pulling, pushing, pulling. He finished cutting another eighteen-inch length off the log resting in the X-frame, kicked the newly cut piece out of the way and immediately began measuring off another. Michael placed the section his father had just cut on top of a large stump and halved it cleanly with one powerful blow of his ax, then proceeded to split each half into smaller wedges.

Ezekiel reined the mule team to a stop next to William's X-frame and unhitched another log dragged from the woods. Close behind came Charlie Swimmer, driving a team of horses. He deposited another log beside the one left by Ezekiel. Since sun up, all four men had been in the woods near the river at the back of the property where they had felled enough trees to keep them busy hauling, sawing, splitting and chopping for the rest of the day. They all paused from their labor at the sound of a rider coming up from the main road.

James Walker was bent low over *U-no-le*, riding at full speed. The horse locked in a stiff-legged halt right in front of William and Michael.

"It's Chief Ross!" James was bursting with excitement. "He's free! They let him go last night!"

"That's wonderful!" William wiped his face, dripping with perspiration despite the cool, crisp day. "Just in time for the council meeting in New Echota."

"He won't be going to the council," James's face grew serious. Michael, William and Charlie Swimmer exchanged puzzled looks. James dismounted and helped himself to a drink from the water bucket hanging on a fence post. "None of us will go," he continued, replacing the dipper. "*Gu-wi-s-gu-wi* wants us to spread the word. Stay away."

"I don't understand," William said. He handed the bow-saw to Ezekiel and began pulling off his gloves.

"Chief Ross says if we go, we'll all lose our land and be forced to go west. He wants to see you, Mr. Drummond. As soon as possible." William's brow furrowed as he started up toward the house.

"I'll go with you," Charlie said.

"I'm going, too!" Michael called out. William stopped. He was about to contradict Michael but changed his mind.

"Yes. All right. Saddle the horses."

Michael handed the ax to Ezekiel and headed for the barn with James. Charlie Swimmer unhitched his horse from the drag rig and handed the collar to Ezekiel. The black man considered the reins, tools and equipment in his hands.

"Well, don't s'pose Chief Ross'll be needin' Zeke's advice, so reckon I'll be cuttin' wood," he mumbled, then dropped the ax, reins and harness and began sawing on the log.

The Christmas tree wagon rounded the barn. Ezekiel looked up but kept on sawing. Reba had mercifully slowed the horse just enough for Peter to keep up at a brisk walk. He glanced down toward Ezekiel as they headed for the house. Susanna looked back at Peter, wondering why he had stopped. Reba clucked the horse and kept going.

Peter wasn't interested in Ezekiel and his wood cutting chores nor in Charlie Swimmer getting his saddle from the fence. He strode past the two men and went straight toward *U-no-le*, tied to the corral. Peter untied the reins from the sapling rail. Only then did he look at Ezekiel and Charlie.

"Who's horse is this?" Peter demanded.

"Mine. Don't touch him," the voice startled Peter. James had come up behind him from the barn door, with Michael right on his heels, leading Midnight and Clancey. Charlie Swimmer tugged quietly at his saddle girth and kept a watchful eye across his horse's back. Peter carefully examined *U-no-le's* saddle with its distinctive inlaid silver work and the hunting sack rolled up and tied behind the seat. He touched the sack and thought of unrolling it for a better look, certain he would find two eye-hole cut-outs.

"He told you not to touch his horse," Michael repeated. James wedged himself between Peter and *U-no-le*, deliberately bumping into Peter. Their eyes met before James sprang lightly into the saddle.

"A horse very much like this one," Peter's voice was slow, soft and controlled, "was used a couple of weeks ago in an attack on some federal census agents. I don't suppose you'd know anything about that?" James squinted down at Peter without answering. Peter searched Michael's eyes. "Or you?"

Michael maintained his inscrutable, granite expression, his voice dripping with casual innocence. "Was that out at Andrew Sixkiller's place?" He and Peter were locked in another of their icy duel of wills. And each knew it wouldn't be their last. Peter, though he hadn't seen Michael at the Sixkiller's cabin that day, was convinced Michael was hiding something. Michael expanded his question. "The attack you've been telling everybody about? Where *upwards of twenty wild Indians and outlaw whites ambushed a bunch of unarmed census agents and peaceful, innocent Georgia Militia by-standers?* That attack?" Peter knew Michael was toying with him and gave him a long, silent stare. Finally Michael answered the question. "No, we don't know anything about an attack fitting that description. Do we, James?"

"Don't recall anything like that," James agreed.

"Peter! Come on! Help us with the tree!" Susanna was standing in the wagon which had stopped as close to the back door as Reba could get it. William, wearing his coat and riding boots, strode back down from the house.

"The women are calling for you, Peter," Michael sneered. "You'd better go help them decorate the Christmas tree."

Peter shifted the ax off his shoulder and swung it with one hand, burying the blade in the ground not two inches from the side of Michael's foot, then headed up toward the house. William hadn't heard the conversation, but he had witnessed Peter's huffy departure. He looked at the ax, then at Michael and James.

"What was that all about?"

"Nothing," Michael said softly, his searing glare still on Peter's back. He handed Clancey's reins to William and they mounted up. Charlie Swimmer swung up onto his horse and joined them. He said nothing, but his eyes twinkled with quiet respect for *Wi-li* Drummond's young firebrand of a son.

* * * * * * *

The many horses tied to the fence along the front of John Ross's cabin twitched their ears and shifted nervously, sensing the tension in the sky that was pregnant with an impending storm. Whinnies of greeting announced the arrival of William, Michael, James and Charlie. They dismounted and tied their horses with the others.

The Cherokee chief opened the door. "William. Glad you could make it. *Tsa-li.* Michael. James." The four men wedged their way into the already crowded room. Michael and James said nothing, but both were flattered that *Gu-wi-s-gu-wi* had remembered their names.

"Sorry to hear about Mr. Payne," William voiced his concern for the journalist Colonel Bishop had refused to free along with the chief.

"We're hoping he'll be released soon," Ross said, then turned to the others in the room. "Gentlemen, this is William Drummond, the *di-ti-yo-hi-hi* I told you about. And you all know *Tsa-li* Swimmer." William, puzzled by the presence of so many men usually considered the chief's political foes, looked at Ross. "William, I believe you know John Ridge, Major Ridge's son," the chief made the formal introductions. "And this is his cousin, *Ga-le-gi-na*, Buck Watie. Sorry, Buck. He now goes by the name Elias Boudinot," Ross apologized. He knew it was important to keep things cordial.

"The editor of your newspaper, the *Cherokee Phoenix*," William was genuinely impressed by the bright young man who had been educated back east and had come home to serve his people. "I'm pleased to meet you, Mr. Boudinot. I hadn't pictured you such a young man. All the more to your credit." He shook hands with the thin young man with burning, brilliant eyes and finely sculpted features. In every aspect of speech, carriage and appearance, Boudinot could more likely have passed as young John Ridge's brother than his first cousin.

"And I believe you know Charles Hicks. George Lowrey. Joseph Vann," Ross added out of respect, aware that William was quite familiar with these tribal leaders. Lowrey, sixty-five, was Ross's right hand and assistant chief. Over the years he had earned the respect of all Cherokees—regardless of their political affiliation—and was renowned for his integrity, wisdom, sharp perception and mannerly conduct. William shook hands with each man. There was a somber air, void of banter and light conversation.

109

Sensing the gravity of the occasion, Michael and James pressed themselves against the wall where they remained still and silent.

"I must say, I'm pleasantly surprised to see these opposing factions gathered in council," William said.

Boudinot appeared to be the spokesman for his group. "We are here because Chief Ross has finally agreed to make a treaty."

William looked first to Charlie, who was as shocked as William himself. Michael and James held their breath, awaiting further detail. Ross cleared his throat, then spoke softly. "I'm proposing we go to Washington to negotiate a treaty. I'd like you to go with us, William."

"I—I don't know what to say," William was stunned. "This represents quite a shift...you're supporting a treaty, *Gu-wi-s-gu-wi?*"

John Ridge tapped the nail of his forefinger nervously on the corner of the table. "I must tell you, *Gu-wi-s-gu-wi*, my father is more than a little suspicious of your intentions."

"We'd like to know the basic elements of the treaty you intend to propose," Boudinot added.

"In due time, gentlemen. In due time. Right now, we should firm up plans for our trip."

"*Now, Gu-wi-s-gu-wi.* Tell us *now,*" John Ridge insisted.

"There will be no trip unless you tell us now," Boudinot echoed the demand.

Ross glanced at Hicks and Lowrey. They gave a slight nod, seen perhaps only by Ross himself. The chief took a seat at the end of the table, breathed tiredly and began. "Very well. I intend to propose that any *Tsa-la-gi* who desires to remain here in the east be granted legal title to the land he now claims and works. Those *Tsa-la-gi* driven from the state of Georgia are to be given, as compensation, equivalent property in Tennessee, Alabama or North Carolina. They will become normal, taxpaying citizens of those states, as well as full United States citizens."

Click. Click. Click. John Ridge's fingernail tapped. Someone in the room exhaled audibly. William thought it might have been Michael or James.

"Unacceptable," John Ridge finally spoke.

"President Jackson will never agree to such a treaty," Boudinot concurred.

Ross slapped the table with the palm of his hand, then interlocked his fingers tightly to prevent any further outbursts during the dialog to follow. "It is not Mr. Jackson's treaty!" the chief's voice trembled with anger. "It is the Senate that must ratify

110

a treaty. And we have many friends in the Senate."

"We'll end up with nothing!" John Ridge, normally very stoic and controlled like his father, could not conceal his emotion. "Our people will be living in squalor and degradation. This is no treaty, this is total surrender!"

Boudinot squared his chair around to face Ross. "What's to prevent Tennessee, Alabama and Carolina from ultimately driving us out and taking our land, just like Georgia is doing now?"

Ross tried to explain. "Once the Senate ratifies the treaty—"

"Has the history of our people taught you nothing?!" John Ridge interrupted the chief.

"They must have damaged your brain in that jail. You've taken leave of your senses!" Boudinot snapped and was instantly aware of the harsh glares from the senior tribesmen for his disrespect. John Ridge rose from his seat and pushed his way over to the window. The sky had grown darker and the horses were more restless than before. Finally he turned back to face Ross and the other leaders.

"Andrew Jackson and the United States government will honor a treaty *only* if it's in their best interest," he said in a controlled but passionate tone. "And it's in their best interest to take our land, our gold, our farms and—if we stand in their way—our lives!"

"*Tsi-ne-na,*" Boudinot pronounced sharply and started for the door. "Let's go! We were fools to come here!" John Ridge and Joseph Vann prepared to follow. Boudinot paused at the door and pointed back at Ross with an accusing finger. "It becomes clear to me now. This whole thing was just a trick to split us up. To drag us off to Washington when we are supposed to be here negotiating a removal treaty with Reverend Schermerhorn and Agent Benjamin Curry."

John Ridge piggy-backed on Boudinot's assessment. "If the principal chief and other tribal leaders are off in Washington, then you can later declare the treaty invalid, claiming it doesn't have the approval of the national council."

Gu-wi-s-gu-wi knew he couldn't prevent the hot-headed young men from leaving, and he no longer entertained any real hope of swaying them to his position. His voice held a grave sadness as he spoke. "That, gentlemen, will be true whether you go with us or not. I urge you to reconsider."

Without another word, John Ridge walked out, followed by the older Joseph Vann. Boudinot hung by the door and offered a parting observation. "You have always been a man of honor, *Gu-wi-s-gu-wi*. Don't let your *pride* destroy our people. I beg you." Not waiting for a reply, Boudinot left and closed the door behind him. Those who remained looked around the room at each other. They heard the retreating hoofbeats from down the road.

* * * * * * *

The oven door of the wood burning stove creaked open. Reba lifted the pan out and looked for a place to set it amid the growing pile of pots and cookware surrounding her Christmas feast preparations. The spacious kitchen of the Drummond house was a warm and friendly place where she spent a great deal of her time. Despite her habitual mumbling and grumbling, which the Drummonds appreciated as a part of her eccentric personality, it was her favorite place. Using a thin wooden spatula, she carefully transferred the freshly baked oatmeal-molasses cookies onto a platter by the window to cool. With a glance over her shoulder to check the door, she devoured one, pausing to savor its sweetness, licking the crumbs from the corner of her mouth. She took another cookie, flipping it from hand to hand until it had cooled enough to drop into her pocket. Later she would slip it to Ezekiel. Reba dolloped out another batch of cookie dough from the large wooden bowl and slid the pan into the oven, lifting the hot and heavy metal door closed with a handful of apron.

The recently cut Christmas tree filled an entire corner of the Drummond library. Elizabeth, wrapped in a blanket, sat near the window reading her Bible. Despite the cold, the morning light had broadened into a bright and cheery day; an observation which Elizabeth frequently made from the comfort of her chair to William, Reba or anyone else who ventured within earshot. Susanna was unpacking Christmas tree decorations from the wooden boxes scattered about the floor. Ezekiel brought in another box, adding it to the collection.

"Over here, Zeke!" Susanna snipped. "Closer to the tree. I do hope the candles are in that one. Mother, where are the candles!"

"You'll find them, dear," Elizabeth responded without looking up from the Scriptures. William poured over a stack of papers at his desk in the adjoining study which he used as his law office. He looked up at the two women in his life and smiled. Elizabeth had been delicate and frail for as long as he had known her, like some fragile but incredibly beautiful flower. Yet she was possessed of an inner strength which, William was convinced, few others even suspected.

Susanna had inherited her mother's physical beauty but not her frail constitution. She lacked, however, Elizabeth's gentleness and understanding. Since she was a tiny child, Susie had always been loud, pushy, demanding and critical. Sometimes even brutally insensitive. William and Elizabeth had often wondered what it would take to develop in her a sense of humanity, a compassionate empathy for the needs and feelings of others. So far, they agreed, everything was pretty much still dormant. Someday soon she'll fall in love with some nice young man and all that will change, Elizabeth had reassured him. It would be nice—for *his* sake, William had answered, if she could change *before*. Otherwise, she might never find that right man. William watched them for a long time before returning to the work on his desk.

Upstairs alone in his room, Michael sat on the bed cleaning his rifle and pistol. A large oil cloth was spread out with the partially disassembled weapons laid out in an organized manner. Michael looked up at the distant barking of Poke, the family dog. It sounded like he was down near the main road. Someone was coming. Soon Michael heard a single horse approaching at a leisurely pace. He stepped to the window.

Peter Tanner, in dress military uniform, had almost reached the house. From his window above, Michael noticed a large, bulging bag of Christmas gifts tied to the saddle behind him, eliciting from Michael a scowling assessment of the upcoming holiday. A fitting match, Michael thought with disgust. Peter Tanner and his sister, Susanna. No two people deserved each other more. Michael moved away from the window and continued cleaning his guns.

Susanna heard Poke barking and the Drummond horses whinny their greeting to the visitor's mount. "That must be Peter! He's early!"

Elizabeth glanced up from her Bible to the old clock. "Actually, he's right on time," she corrected her daughter. "So punctual. Military men are that way, you know. It's a nice quality to have."

Susanna dashed from the room. Elizabeth looked into the study and smiled at William. The front door opened and they heard a muffled exchange from the foyer. A delighted squeal preceded their daughter's appearance at the library door.

"Mother! Father, come in here! Look!" Susanna danced with excitement. Elizabeth closed the old Bible in her lap and peered over her wire-rim glasses.

"Why, yes. It's Peter. We were expecting him."

"No, silly! Look!" Susanna pointed to the new silver bar on the collar and to the epaulets of his uniform.

"Congratulations, Peter," William said from the study doorway. He went on to explain, in answer to his wife's puzzled look. "The silver bar, dear. Peter has been promoted to first lieutenant."

"Isn't it wonderful?" Susanna chirped. "He'll be a colonel before he's thirty!"

"Well, I wouldn't go so far as to say that..." Peter blushed but was obviously pleased with the flattering prediction about his future advancement.

"My, that is good news," Elizabeth applauded softly. "You should be very proud of yourself, First Lieutenant Tanner!"

"We're all proud of you, Peter!" Susanna grafted herself to him.

"Well, make yourself at home, Lieutenant," William said and went back to his work in the study.

"Thank you, sir."

Susanna steered Peter masterfully into the corner behind the partially decorated Tannenbaum. "You're just in time to help finish the tree. But I can't find the candles."

Reba came in from the kitchen carrying a serving tray loaded with freshly baked cookies and a pitcher of warm cider. Susanna eyed her petulantly and swung on Peter's arm with a little pout. "I suspect Reba hid them on purpose."

"Dat's right, Missy," Reba said, filling cups with the delicious, cinnamon-scented brew. "Reba got nothin' better to do than hide yo' candles!" She glanced frequently at the young couple while adjusting the cookies and clinking the cider cups on the tray. There was a lot of not-so-inadvertent bumping and touching going on back there. Reba set a cup and a plate on the table beside Elizabeth. "There. Reba brung y'all some cookies and cider," she said. Casually, she reached into the corner, took Peter's arm and pulled him out in front of the Christmas tree. "Here, Mistah Peter. You work out here where they's mo' room. Miss Susie gon' suffocate all pushed up in the corner that-a-way." She tugged him to the tray and pushed a mug into his hands. "Have some o' these cookies. Fresh outa the oven. An' some warm cider."

Susanna emerged from behind the tree. By the time Peter bit into his first cookie she had firmly reattached herself to his arm.

"Reba, we're doing just fine. We'll eat your ol' cookies when we're finished here." She took the half-eaten cookie from Peter and examined it, adding, "Besides, they look a little burned on the bottom to me."

Reba, hands on her hips, bit her tongue and glared at Susanna. "Whatever you say, Missy." There was no mistaking her sarcastic tone. She mumbled in her practiced make-sure-she-hears-it voice, "And I'd like to burn somebody's bottom..."

"Did you say something, Reba?" Susanna raised an eyebrow in her familiar smirk of victory.

"Naw, Missy. Reba ain't say nothin'."

* * * * * * *

The mid-afternoon sun slanted in through the windows, bathing the assembly in a false warmth of ochres and siennas reflecting off the floors and the rich wood panelling of the dining room. The Christmas feast had gone much as each member of the Drummond family had envisioned. But each held a distinct view of how the event should have unfolded. Susanna and Peter had been wrapped up in each other, their whispers punctuated with hushed giggles and soft laughter. Elizabeth was pleased to see her daughter so happy, while Michael tried to ignore them. William remained unaware of—or had simply chosen to disregard—the pronounced tension between Michael and Susanna. They had been at odds since the first time Michael decided he wouldn't do what his sister wanted—or ordered—him to do. That would have been somewhere around the age of two or three. William's wish for the holiday feast was simply that they all be together, that they all behave civilly toward one another and, most of all, that Elizabeth be happy at her favorite season of the year. When Michael finished eating, he wiped his mouth and looked directly at Peter for the first time.

"So, Lieutenant Tanner. Have you flogged any Cherokees lately?"

Not a sound. It was as though someone had thrown open the doors and windows to admit the icy wind that had been whipping around the house since before sunrise. William moved his hand a couple of inches toward Michael on the table top, but Michael kept his eyes locked on Peter.

"Well?"

"Michael..." William's voice, though soft, held warning of consequence.

"Ignore him, Peter. He's only trying to provoke you," Susanna tossed her hair and took a bite of bread, thrusting her chin defiantly at her brother. Peter sat up straight in his chair and mustered his academy-taught officer's diplomacy.

"I'm a guest in your house, Michael," he repeated the speech he'd rehearsed in his mind on the ride over in anticipation of this very moment. "I'm here to fellowship and to celebrate the birth of our Savior. We can have a political discussion some other time."

"Excellently put, Peter, dear," Susanna patted his hand. "Michael, must you always ruin everything?"

Michael refused to shift his scorching gaze from Peter. "I wonder what Andrew Sixkiller and his family are having for Christmas dinner. Horse meat? I understand his best mare was killed recently."

"Michael! That's quite enough!" William scolded louder than before.

"Perhaps I should be excused." Peter played the innocent victim and pushed his chair back from the table, but Susanna gripped his sleeve.

"It's all right. I'm leaving." Michael rose and stomped out of the room. His departure was followed by a tense silence before Elizabeth finally spoke.

"Peter, dear. Would you like some more sweet potato pie?"

Without waiting for his answer, Susanna spooned another serving onto his plate. Peter scooted his chair back up to the table and was about to take a bite when Michael reappeared at the dining room door. He had put on his riding boots, jacket and hat and had a bag slung across his shoulder.

"I'm going over to see James."

William nodded with approval. It was definitely a good idea for these two brash young men not to be under the same roof. "Wish them all a merry Christmas from us. Don't be too late."

"It looks like there might be a storm," Elizabeth added.

"Going to see James," Susanna mocked her brother. "You know very well he's going to be with that dreadful girl." William and Elizabeth both glanced up at Michael. Susanna defiantly met his glare. "Well, go! Go!" she said and continued to face the doorway even after they heard Michael exit the house. "Sometimes I just hate him. I really do," she said as she turned back to her dessert.

* * * * * * *

116

Michael rode Midnight at a brisk gallop all the way to the Walker cabin. He noticed the clouds gathering with darkened underbellies in the northern sky over Tennessee. The cold air had taken on an even icier sting from the increasing humidity. The wind spanked the tops of the hickories, birches and taller pines, flicking loose their cones and hurling them earthward in schools like frightened perch darting in synchronized panic in a stone-bottom pool of the Conasauga.

The humble interior of the Walker cabin was everything the Drummond household was not. Despite the stark contrast in furnishings and the absence of refined appointment, the warmth and spirit of the holiday was very much in evidence. Thomas and *Tse-ni-si* were seated on one side of the room opposite the door. James sat at one end of the rough-hewn wooden table. Annie was perched on a wooden box beside the door leading to the cabin's only other room. Mrs. Walker's superannuated grandfather sat beside the fireplace, a blanket draped across his lap and around his legs. He grinned with gap-toothed pleasure as Michael went from one to the other with his sack, passing out gifts like a young Kris Kringle. *Tse-ni-si* was the first to be honored. Michael presented her with a bolt of bright, new gingham cloth. Her eyes widened with surprise and she beamed up at Michael.

"*U-wo-du! Wa-do, U-we-tsi!*" In voicing her heartfelt gratitude, she affectionately called him her son.

"I made sure there's enough there for a dress, a bonnet, maybe even a new apron," Michael smiled down at her. This, to him, represented a truer celebration of the birth of Jesus of Nazareth, a simple man of humble origins. Never mind that Thomas and his family, though they all knew of Jesus, were not practicing Christians. Michael was convinced that each and every one of the Walkers embodied the values of Jesus Christ and His love more than any of the whites who proudly sat in sanctimonious judgement of the heathen savages inhabiting the continent they coveted.

Next Michael moved to The Old One. He pretended to search long and hard in the large sack, amused like the rest of the family by the old man's mounting excitement. His arthritic old fingers drummed eagerly on the blanket covering his legs. Finally Michael brought forth a leather pouch stuffed with fresh chewing tobacco. With sparkling eyes the ecstatic old man immediately began stuffing the moist shredded leaves into his cheek.

"*Wa-do! Wa-do!*" he mumbled with his mouth full.

Michael noticed Mrs. Walker frowning in anticipation of The

Old One's imminent need to spit. It couldn't be more than a minute away. Grinning, Michael pulled out the second part of the gift—a shiny, brass spittoon. Janice broke into a child-like laugh when her grandfather took the spittoon, stroked it lovingly and held it poised to receive his first oblation.

And then it was Thomas's turn. A smile appeared as he examined the gleaming new metal horn filled with gunpowder and the embroidered leather pouch full of shot. He nodded with sincere appreciation.

"Good hunting, *E-to-da,*" Michael said.

"*Ŭ-ŭ. Wa-do. Da-ni'-s-to-yo'-hi-hŭ!*" Thomas thanked Michael and wished him a merry Christmas. Next, Michael presented James with a small bundle wrapped in soft leather. James carefully opened it to reveal ten new black iron arrow heads. He looked up in astonishment at his dearest friend.

"They're from England," Michael informed him.

"We will hunt with them, *tso-da-da-nŭ,*" James proclaimed.

"Of course," Michael teased, "I'll have to teach you how to use them. So you don't hurt yourself." Thomas, Janice and The Old One laughed heartily.

They loved it when Michael and James ribbed each other. But their laughter subsided when Michael came to Annie. They all knew the friendship between Michael and Annie had been virtually as strong as the bond between Michael and James when they were all children growing up. But they were no longer children. Over the years there had been hints of an attraction between Michael and Annie that showed signs of going beyond a sibling-like friendship. Annie twisted a strand of her beautiful brown hair around a finger, her eyes locked on Michael's face while he probed the bottom of the sack. With a look of disappointment he flipped the bag inside out.

"I guess that's all there is," he said with an innocent shrug. The silence was broken by a distant rolling thunder and the pelting rain as it began its incessant tattoo on the cabin roof. Annie stood up and reached just inside the door to the other room.

"I have something for you, *Mi-ki,*" she said and produced a hand-made doe-skin hunting shirt. Michael was overwhelmed by the elegant beadwork, the artfully stitched embroidery and the finely cut fringe—it was the most beautiful garment he had ever seen. He knew it represented many hours of painstaking effort. When he reached out to touch it, Annie pulled it back with a playful smile.

"I know you have something for me," she challenged him.

Michael forced himself to keep a straight face. "No. Really.

I feel bad. Listen! *A-ga-s-ga!* It's raining!" he tried to change the subject. "I should probably start for home. I'm sorry I forgot your gift."

"*Ga-ye-go-gi!*" she flirted, calling him a liar.

"I'll just take my new hunting shirt and be on my way now," he kept up the charade, but she held the shirt just out of his reach while her free hand slipped inside his jacket, searching for her gift. The others watched them floating around the room in a mesmerizing *pas de deux*. Finally Annie's fingers discovered a package wrapped in blue paper.

"Uh-oh. What's that?" Michael acted surprised.

Annie handed him the doe-skin hunting shirt and eagerly tore open her gift, unfolding a large, triangular piece of beautiful red cloth that could be worn as a shawl, a head scarf, a turban or a waist sash. She was quietly impressed and her eyes found his as she held the smooth fabric against her face, stroking first one cheek, then the other.

"*Wa-do,*" her voice was barely audible.

"It isn't much," he shrugged.

"It's beautiful," she said a little louder, then shocked them all by kissing him on the lips—a fleeting but meaningful kiss. Michael was embarrassed in front of her family, but he couldn't take his eyes off Annie. With indescribable grace she coiled the sash around her waist. Tobacco juice streamed down The Old One's chin. He held out a trembling hand and grabbed the tail of Michael's jacket. The others laughed when he wouldn't let go. The Old One tugged and uttered something unintelligible in Cherokee.

"He says you belong here now," Thomas interpreted.

"He thinks you are part of the family," James added with a grin.

Michael felt a warmth and a love he hadn't experienced even in his own home. It was an inauspicious yet truly joyous holiday celebration. He looked from one to the other, unable to find the words in either English or Cherokee to express his love for each of them.

Annie unwound the sash from her waist and began twisting it as a turban around Michael's head. His eyes never left her, drinking in every move of her supple body, every ethereal gesture of her work-toughened yet delicate hands, every subtle volume written in her eyes, whispered in a single glance.

* * * * * * *

The national capital of the Cherokee nation was much like many of the other Cherokee towns scattered up and down the network of rivers in Tennessee, North Carolina, Georgia, Alabama, Kentucky—artificial state lines and arbitrary political boundaries drawn on maps by white men, dividing the land that had belonged to the *Tsa-la-gi* since the Great Creator had given it to them. Many of New Echota's cabins and board houses had recently been painted white with lime. Interspersed among them were sapling pole sheds with thatched roofs. These served as stores and barter booths whenever members of the tribe gathered from the other towns for an important council meeting, for a Green Corn Festival or any other celebration.

The special council meeting had been announced several days before Christmas, yet by December 29th scarcely more than forty Cherokees had assembled for what would prove to be one of the most significant council meetings in the tribe's long history. Individual campsites had been set up. Tent flaps and lean-to's sheltered their fires from the rain. Men and boys sat idly waiting, some soaked from their journey. Many of the older ones were strangely subdued and contemplative. Deeply etched lines in their sunbaked, impassive expressions formed disparate tributaries for the tiny rivers of rain coursing down their faces.

After many hours the heavy rains had stopped and the Cherokees began to dry out, only to be dampened now and again by the intermittent passing shower—just enough to keep them chilled and uncomfortable. During those infrequent reprieves, women fried bread and strips of pork in grease pots. Children clung to their mothers or squatted between their fathers and brothers in an attempt to keep dry and warm. The general atmosphere was quiet and somber. Soon they would all make their way up the slope to the council house. The word had come to them days before to gather here for an important tribal council meeting. Yet few of them had detected the usual flow of important tribal leaders who always attended such meetings. Where was *Gu-wi-s-gu-wi*, their chief? And George Lowrey? And Charles Hicks? Where was old *Tsunaluska*? Whitepath? Situwakee? None of these had been seen. Perhaps they were already up at the council house, many of the Cherokees must have thought.

But none of those men were in New Echota. Not one. The only acknowledged tribal leaders standing around in the shelter of the open sided council house, their backs to the warm council fire, were Major Ridge, his nephew Elias Boudinot, Joseph Vann and a half dozen lesser tribal dignitaries. With them were Indian Agent Ben Curry and the Reverend John Schermerhorn, authorized by the Jackson administration and the state of Georgia to negotiate a removal treaty with the Cherokees. Major Ridge confided to his nephew that he would have preferred to have his son, John Ridge, and Elias' brother, Stand Watie, present for this meeting, but they were off attending to business in Washington, D.C.

The Reverend Schermerhorn was a lecherous, rotund man, impressed with the power of his position and imminently more interested in potable spirits than in things spiritual. More adept at arranging a tryst than negotiating a treaty. His somber frown expressed his sense of personal insult at the low number of Cherokees. He pulled a fat flask from beneath his long, black coat and drained it.

Federal Indian Agent Benjamin Curry, a thin, dark-haired man with cavernous eyes and a long, droopy moustache, didn't dislike the Cherokees, neither did he see himself their champion. They were Indians. He was an Indian agent. It was his job to deal with these people—which included negotiating treaties—and he intended to do his job well.

"This is it?" Schermerhorn grumbled. "Three dozen rain-soaked Cherokees? I thought this was supposed to be a full-blown national council."

"I suspect John Ross has put out the word to avoid the meeting," Agent Curry said, bending his long, lanky frame toward the gray wetness, straining as though hoping to detect a wave of Cherokees washing up toward the council house.

"I'm sorry for the poor turnout, Reverend Schermerhorn," Elias Boudinot said, pacing back and forth behind the council fire. "Chief Ross led us to believe he would be willing to negotiate a treaty. All the while, he was telling his followers to stay away." He stopped in front of Major Ridge, who sat gazing into the fire, and pulled the sagging blanket back up onto his uncle's shoulders.

"*Gu-wi-s-gu-wi* is a sly fox," The Ridge said and repeated his habitual gesture of dragging his fingers back through his long, silver hair.

Schermerhorn pounded his fist against the thick support post. "He's a sneaky Injun bastard, that's what he is! No offense to you boys," he tossed them an insincere apology, then slapped the post with his open palm. "By God! We'll just negotiate our treaty without him!"

"It isn't that simple, Reverend," Elias Boudinot was

convinced the U. S. Senate would never ratify a treaty negotiated with a mere handful of old-and-fading and up-and-coming tribal leaders, absent the Cherokees' principal chief and virtually every other assistant chief, sub-chief and tribal leader of any significance. But the right Reverend Shermerhorn had a clearer, if less idealistic, view of his government than did young Boudinot.

"Sure it is!" Shermerhorn boomed enthusiastically. "That's exactly how simple it is!" His problem was solved. "Whoever shows up for the meeting, that's who gets to vote. Andy Jackson'll back me all the way on this." Boudinot exchanged a look of apprehension with his uncle, but Agent Curry was getting caught up in Schermerhorn's zeal.

"Got to hand it to Chief Ross. He'd have made one hell of a politician," Curry said and tugged with anticipation at his long moustache.

"He *is* one hell of a politician," Boudinot corrected him.

"Reckon he is, at that," Curry admitted.

"He's had many treaties overturned on the grounds they were for personal gain of a single individual or a select few who didn't represent the Cherokee nation," Elias reminded the *yo-negs*.

"Perhaps I should go and talk to him," Major Ridge rose stiffly.

"No, *E-du-tsi*," his nephew protested. "It is a waste of time talking to him. Perhaps enough people will show up and we can still negotiate this treaty."

Schermerhorn's mind was spinning. He was so certain of his success that a celebration was in order. "Say. Maybe you boys could get hold of a bottle of good whiskey. You reckon?"

"Whiskey is forbidden at Cherokee councils, John. You know that," Agent Curry reminded him.

"It ain't for *them*! It's for *me*!" Schermerhorn cackled with a conspiratorial wink. "I get toler'ble achy in the joints of a damp evening. The gout, don't you know? And the rheumatiz. I'd be mighty obliged," he looked pleadingly to Major Ridge, but the *Tsa-la-gi* leader's eyes never left the cleansing rain. Another hour passed. And another. The skies grew black and opened their floodgates once more with no hint of surcease. Shermerhorn managed to find a flask somewhere, nursed it sip by sip until it, too, was empty. He shifted nervously in search of another. No one had spoken a word for the better part of an hour. Strain as they might, none of them could see more than the forty-odd Cherokees who had been gathered outside the council house for some time. There were at most another forty

122

or fifty taking shelter in tents and lean-to's. No one else was coming.

"What do you figure?" Schermerhorn stepped up beside the taller Curry.

"Less than a hundred."

"This is never going to work," Elias Boudinot joined them.

Fortified with whiskey, the Reverend Schermerhorn refused to become discouraged. "Have faith, boys! Faith! We'll make it work. Jackson's going to love it. Take my word!"

* * * * * * *

By the time darkness found them, the rain had increased to angry torrents. The sweetgum leaves curled their tiny fingers into semi-fists and drifted down to earth where the rain softened them into slippery little rafts. For a while they would ride the rivulets down the hill but would ultimately tire and cling tenaciously to the roots and brush along the edges, afraid to launch themselves into the growing, maddening stream. The campfires had been drowned and most of the Cherokees had abandoned their camps and lean-to's below to seek refuge in the council house. Even a few more Cherokees had shown up near the end of the day. They had all come to hear the talk, and, despite the raging storm, many stood outside the council house as was their custom, reserving the comfort of the fire and a dry seat for the tribal leaders who, they well knew, would not appear.

Two new onlookers had joined those who elected to brave the elements. Unnoticed in the crowd, their hats pulled down over their eyes as much to avoid detection as to shield themselves from the downpour, were Michael Drummond and James Walker. They saw the puffs of smoke beneath the shelter from the pipes passed around the council fire. When they asked, someone told them who Schermerhorn and Curry were and why they were there. They knew The Ridge and Elias Boudinot and a few of the others who were huddled with the *yo-neg* agents.

"Looks like we got close to three hundred, boys," Schermerhorn made a characteristically hyperbolic assessment of the crowd's size. "I think this is going to work out just fine."

"Maybe two hundred at most, counting women and children," Major Ridge corrected him, not masking his distaste for the drunken clergyman-politician.

"There are over eighteen thousand Cherokees in this area,

Reverend Schermerhorn," Elias Boudinot didn't share the federal negotiator's blind fervor. "This is nothing. It's not enough."

"Don't tell me it's nothin', damn it!" Schermerhorn snapped, startling everyone. "I represent the United States government here! If I say it's enough, it's enough! Now, let's get started!" The few Cherokee leaders present, young and old alike, openly glared their dislike of Schermerhorn and disapproval of his outburst. He ignored their looks and drained the last drop from a flask discovered somewhere on his massive body. Major Ridge rose from his bench and went to the fire. The emaciated translator was about to join him but The Ridge waved him back to his seat. A master orator, The Ridge knew exactly how long to stand there, regal and silent, before beginning his talk with a thunderous start to instantly grab their attention and hold their ears captive for the duration.

"*Tsa-la-gi!*" his voice ripped the night. His next words were so soft everyone strained forward to be sure they heard. "I have hunted the deer and turkey in these lands for more than fifty years. I have fought your battles. I have defended your honor." He paused, took a deep breath and faced the whites present. "I have always been a friend to honest white men. But now the greedy hand of the Georgians is tight around our throat. They pass their laws. They harass our young men and make our children suffer and cry. I don't like it, but I understand. They believe the President is bound by the Treaty of 1802 to purchase this country for them. This is what they have been told. Right now they are willing to pay us for our land. But if we don't sell soon, they will simply take it."

The Ridge turned his dark, unnerving eyes on the whites as though giving them an opportunity to contradict his last statement, but no one there—Cherokee or white—questioned the accuracy of his words. "Yes, the *Tsa-la-gi* hold first title to this land. We obtained it from the living God above. The *yo-negs* got their title from a British king who has never even seen this country." He then spoke to his people—the few who were there. For the remainder of his talk he would not face the whites again. "Yet they are strong, and we are weak. They are many, we are few. We cannot remain here in safety and comfort. Yes, we love the graves of our fathers who have gone before us to be with the Great Spirit. We can never forget our homes here. But an unbending, iron necessity tells us we must leave. I would willingly die to save our home, but any forcible struggle will only cost us our lands, our lives and the lives of our children. There is only one path to a safe future for us as a nation. That path is open before you. Make a treaty of cession. Give up

124

these lands and go beyond the great Father of Waters. West of the Mississippi. *A-ya a-gi-ha*," he ended with the familiar declaration of Cherokee oratory. I have spoken.

Indeed, he had spoken. The honesty and simplicity of Major Ridge's words had moved many to tears. Some of the older men—though among them were no important tribal leaders—rose and surrounded The Ridge, taking him by the hand. On the fringe of the crowd outside, Michael and James had listened closely to every word. Though they considered themselves Ross supporters, they couldn't deny the truth of what they had heard.

"That was some strong talk," Michael said softly.

It was more of a struggle for James. He didn't want to betray his committed loyalty to *Gu-wi-s-gu-wi*. He gripped Michael's sleeve. "The old ones are too tired for battle. And the young ones—the children—what do they know? But there are plenty of young men who will fight!"

Michael could not so easily dismiss The Ridge's message. "There will be a lot of bloodshed, *Tsi-mi*."

"Whose side are you on?"

"Your side, *Tsi-mi*. Always. You know that. I'm only saying there's another side."

"*Di-ti-yo-hi-hi*." There was no respect in James's voice. "Spoken like a lawyer."

"No," Michael refused to be drawn into a name-calling argument, "spoken like someone who doesn't want to see his friends get slaughtered." Michael headed back down the slippery incline to where their horses were tied to a tree, well hidden in the darkness. They mounted their chilled, rain drenched ponies in silence. Midnight and *U-no-le* needed no prodding to head for home.

* * * * * * *

A single lantern in the front, first floor window cast its warm, orange glow out into the cold, wet night. The swirling wind lofted the raindrops against the infinite black space above. Below, a dozen horses and three mule-drawn wagons in front of Elias Boudinot's home were watched by three young Cherokee boys, wrapped in blankets and slickers, sitting patiently in the steady rain. The white, two story frame structure looked more like it might house the mayor of some Connecticut community than a rising young political figure in the Cherokee nation.

Inside, some twenty men had crowded into the parlor,

125

gathered there to sign the document which was destined to become the cornerstone of the *Tsa-la-gis'* greatest travail and which would launch one of this country's darkest chapters. Seated at the stained and polished oak table were Major Ridge, Reverend Schermerhorn, Agent Ben Curry, Elias Boudinot and a few other Cherokee men of note who had thrown their allegiance to the Ridge party. The rest of those present stood around the edge of the room, creating an image ironically not unlike paintings Elias Boudinot had seen on his trips back east of the Founding Fathers of the United States signing the *yo-negs'* Declaration of Independence.

The hand-written copies of the treaty lay on the rectangular table with a candle flanking the documents on either side. Everyone was quiet; there was nothing more to be said. Schermerhorn and Curry exchanged a nervous glance, waiting for one of the Cherokees to sign the treaty. They knew if Major Ridge would pick up the quill and make his mark, the rest of them would fall into line. But the old full-blood didn't stir. Schermerhorn drummed his fat fingers impatiently on the table. Finally, the Cherokee seated between Major Ridge and Elias Boudinot looked to the man on either side of him, then leaned forward and seized the pen.

"Well, by God, John Gunter isn't afraid to sign!"

The only sounds were Schermerhorn's labored breathing and the scratching of the quill on the paper. Gunter finished and handed the pen across the table to another Cherokee.

"Andrew Ross," there was challenge in Gunter's voice, "brother of John Ross. Are you willing to save your people?" All eyes awaited his response. Andrew Ross looked around at the men in the room. He took a deep breath, accepted the quill and began scribbling his name. Gradually the others stepped forward into the candles' glow awaiting their turn to sign. Around the room went the pen. The papers were shoved from one end of the table to the other to accommodate the signers.

Elias Boudinot affixed his signature, dipped the quill into the splattered ink bottle and handed it to the last man, his uncle, The Ridge. With a burdened sigh weightier than all the rest, The Ridge leaned forward and took the pen. He scratched the special symbol recognized by all present as his signature.

"Congratulations, gentlemen!" Reverend Schermerhorn could scarcely contain his excitement. "You have just signed a treaty that will save the Cherokee Nation."

The Ridge leaned back in his chair with a dismal expression reflected in the faces of many others in the room. "I think we have just signed our death warrant," he said with a contagious chill in his voice. The others stood silent, somber. No one contradicted him until Schermerhorn slapped his fat palm loudly on the table.

"Nonsense! The lives of your people should be better from here on! This is cause for celebration!" He fumbled in his coat for yet another flask he had somehow managed to procure, took a sip and offered to pass it around. No one accepted. Even Agent Curry declined. Reverend Schermerhorn shrugged indifferently and drained the flask. He was happy. He'd gotten what he came for.

C H A P T E R
8

Late Spring — 1836

The road to Pine Hill was lined with brightly colored wild flowers where countless bees and hummingbirds darted from stamen to stamen, and brilliant butterflies flitted gracefully in a staccato ballet of pollination. The spring had been a wet one, contributing not only to the vibrant natural garden bordering the highway but to the budding orchards that promised to be exploding with fruit and the verdant crops in the fields that would have baskets, wagons and cribs rupturing from an overabundant harvest.

Nearly six months had passed since that cold, wet December night in New Echota when names and symbols were scratched by candle light onto a treaty heralded as the tribe's salvation by those who had signed it and damned as the declaration of doom by those who had opposed it. But the truth was, while Chief John Ross had spent his time travelling back and forth to Washington, D.C. and throughout his own beloved Cherokee land speaking out against the treaty, not much had really come of it.

In May the United States Senate had ratified the Treaty of New Echota. By a single vote. Ironically, the senator who had committed to supporting the Cherokees and then had changed his vote at the last instant was named White. *Yo-neg.*

A grace period of two years had been granted for the Cherokees to dispose of their holdings in the southeast and begin moving west. The government promised equitable compensation for livestock, orchards, crops, fields and ferry landings held by Cherokees. Promises each side knew would, in all probability, never be honored. Compensation the Cherokees were fairly certain would never be forthcoming. And as the desperate sense of urgency subsided following the signing of the treaty, a strange, soporific inertia had settled over the nation. Very few of those who had supported the idea of *Take what we can get while we can get it and go west of the Mississippi and maybe, just maybe, the yo-negs will leave us alone* had, in fact, picked up and gone. Many of them had plowed their fields and put in crops for another season as though there was no hurry. Those opposed to the Treaty of New Echota, condemning it as the fiendish betrayal of a hand-picked few which in no way represented the wishes of the Cherokee nation, had done essentially the same thing. Crops were planted. Orchards tended.

128

Calves, kids and piglets were born and would increase the herds. And Chief Ross continued his message of hope and encouragement. *The treaty isn't valid. It will be struck down.* He would take it all the way to the United States Supreme Court. The Senate had granted them two years. Plenty of time to win this battle. To beat the greedy, land-lusting *yo-negs* in their own courts.

White settlers continued to pour into Cherokee territory, despite federal laws and long-standing treaties forbidding them to do so. But if the Cherokees were all going west, wouldn't the land eventually be open to them anyway? Why not get a head start? While the Cherokees resented the continued intrusion, it was certainly nothing new to them. Those who planned to go west figured the more whites there were in the area, the better deal they could strike for the land and livestock they would someday be expected to leave behind. If, indeed, that day ever came. Those who planned to stay and fight for their land naïvely conceded that if they just let the whites keep coming and didn't make a fuss, the government might see everyone getting along and the Cherokees wouldn't be driven from their land after all.

For many others—whites and Cherokees alike—the New Echota Treaty meant nothing. Many knew little or nothing of its existence. It was just another in a long line of treaties. Life had gone on. Life would continue to go on. Life as usual. Or so they believed.

* * * * * * *

The six-up stage coach glided along the rippled road beneath the shadows of silent Georgia pines, then burst into the sunlight and rolled past peach orchards and lush, grassy meadows. The gentle rain of the night before had settled the dust without turning it into mud, making for a pleasant afternoon ride. Tied to the rear of the coach was a well groomed, riderless horse with a blazed face, four white stocking feet and a saddle bearing the insignia of the U. S. Army. The horse's owner was riding inside. Only a few months earlier the Pine Hill mail coach had begun carrying passengers as part of an agreement with the Northern Georgia Transport Company.

In the center of the coach's seat, facing forward, sat the stunningly beautiful Susanna Drummond. Framing her big brown eyes and sensuous lips, her thick, dark hair cascaded in carefully styled ringlets onto the shoulders of an expensive, powder-blue dress trimmed with pale yellow lace. She had removed her bonnet and held it in her lap. Her bulky petticoats spread out against the laps and legs of two elderly women on either side of her. Susanna played coquettish eye games with the handsome army lieutenant seated across from her. For the sake of the other passengers she pretended she hardly knew him.

"You certainly look dapper in your new uniform, Lieutenant Tanner," she said flirtatiously.

The elderly mixed-blood Cherokee seated next to Peter glanced at the blue uniform and, without revealing his opinion, turned back to gaze out the window. Peter smiled. "And you, Miss Drummond..."

"Please, call me Susanna."

"It wouldn't be proper, Miss Drummond," he said, looking at the elderly women to see if they approved of his gentlemanly bearing. "But if I may be so bold, you are certainly the most beautiful young lady to ever grace this corner of the world." Again the old Cherokee glanced at Susanna to see if he agreed with Peter's compliment. He almost broke a smile before turning once again to peer out the window.

Susanna decided they had played the game long enough. She dropped the charade and fluttered her eyes, openly coy. "I've kept all the letters you wrote to me at the conservatory, Peter."

"And I still have yours I received at West Point. Every single one."

"I must inquire—could it possibly be more than mere coincidence—your showing up at the train station on this particular day to accompany the stage back to Pine Hill?" Susanna asked, very aware of his eyes fixed on her hair swaying gently with the motion of the coach.

"It's Titusville now," he corrected her. "Titus Ogilvie just about owns the whole town. Got himself elected mayor and bullied the town council into changing the name."

"I know," she bubbled energetically. "Mother told me in her letter. But it will always be Pine Hill to me. And you're just trying to change the subject."

"We escort the mail when we're expecting important documents or payroll," he explained. "I admit, however, I did request the duty for today."

Susanna smiled. It was the answer she expected to hear.

* * * * * * *

130

Charlie Swimmer, his son, *Tsu-Tsu*, thirteen, and *Tsu-Tsu's* friend, Tally, a black boy his own age, were all shoeless and bare from the waist up. They were casually herding fifteen head of cattle down the shady road toward the ferry crossing at the Conasauga River. Two mounted Cherokees, long-haired young men in their early twenties, brought a few stragglers back toward the road from the low-lying river bottom meadow plush with marsh grass. Calmly, Charlie and the boys coaxed the first of the animals onto the wide, flat barge that would carry them across. The timid yet unpredictable brutes carefully sniffed the barge's railing with bovine apprehension. A cleft hoof gingerly tested the rough board surface. The leaders smelled the alluring molasses-sweetened mixture of oats and cracked corn in a trough at the far end. Charlie and the boys knew better than to shout, poke or prod at this point. A cow boards a barge at its own pleasure, not at the beck of the ships captain nor by tail-twisting coercion from behind. But once the first two or three were aboard, the rest would follow. One had merely to remain patient.

Charlie and the boys heard the approaching six-up. In a few seconds the stagecoach arrived and pulled to a stop right behind the cattle.

"Let's go! Get out of the way!" the driver shouted down at Charlie. Peter Tanner climbed out of the coach. Susanna leaned across the elderly woman to look out the window. Appearing at the other window was the stone-faced, elderly mixed-blood man.

"What's the hold up, driver?" Peter asked before he had stepped far enough forward to see the cattle.

"They're blockin' the ferry," the driver gestured with disgust at the Indians and the animals.

Peter came even with the lead horses and assessed the situation. "Get those animals out of the way!" he barked with authority.

"We're taking them across the river," Charlie explained quietly, trying not to startle the animals still waiting to board the barge.

"Not here, you're not! Not on this ferry! You'll have to swim them across."

"The closest place to cross cattle is six miles downstream!" Charlie, equally firm, wasn't going to back down. "That would put us twelve miles from where we have to go."

Peter would brook no contradiction from some scruffy looking, half-naked aboriginal. He had seen this man before, he recalled, working from time to time for Mr. Drummond. Now he had gotten uppity and would have to be put in his place. "Don't argue with me, damn you! Just get them out of the way!"

The ferry attendant, an older full-blood with his right arm cut off just below the elbow, had watched the confrontation in silence. In Peter's mind this incompetent old man had initiated the entire incident by telling these rag-tag Indians they could cross here in the first place.

"Get those cows off the ferry! Now!" Peter demanded.

"We were here first," Charlie Swimmer said, stepping between Peter and the old ferry attendant. "You'll have to wait your turn."

"Get out of my way!" Peter yelled and shoved Charlie off the edge of the ferry into the river. Drawing his service pistol, Peter fired a shot into the air, scattering the cattle that hadn't yet stepped onto the ferry. Those already aboard were wide-eyed with terror, pressing against the loose board railings, in danger of ending up in the river themselves.

Tsu-Tsu and Tally scurried about in an attempt to contain the frightened animals. The two mounted Cherokees who had hired on for what was to have been a leisurely afternoon's work, dashed off on their horses in pursuit of three steers that sprinted along the river bank back toward the marsh grass.

Peter was about to repeat his command to the frightened ferry attendant when he was hit with a driving shoulder right in the middle of his back, launching him into the river. Peter shot up out of the waist-deep water, his soaked new blue uniform hanging heavily on his body. He clumsily tried to draw his saber. Susanna climbed down out of the coach, her parasol raised to strike Peter's attacker from behind.

"Susanna! Don't!" Peter called out, waving her away. "I'll take care of this. Get back in the coach."

Peter's attacker positioned himself directly in front of Susanna. She looked at the dark-skinned young man in traditional Cherokee clothing and knee-high, fringed boots. Her eyes burned with enmity.

"Susie?" the attacker said to her.

It took her a moment to recognize her brother. "Michael?!"

Peter Tanner slogged gracelessly up the bank, sword in hand. Michael reached down to help Charlie Swimmer out of the river.

"Drummond! I ought to cut you to pieces!" Peter was pointing the extended saber at Michael.

"And I ought to teach you some manners!"

132

"Michael, why did you do this?" his sister demanded. "Why are you even here?"

"I was only trying to get your sister home safely," Peter defended his actions. "Besides, Indians aren't supposed to use the ferry if white folks are waiting to cross. You know that!"

"Michael..." Susanna shook her head in exasperation.

"Father bought these cattle. We're taking them home," Michael refused to concede. "And we're not going six miles downstream!"

"Why do you still insist on dressing like this?" she gestured with contempt at his clothing. "When will you grow up and stop playing these foolish games?"

A familiar roan pony approached, skidding to a halt only inches from Susanna. Startled, she stepped closer to the stagecoach and looked up to see James Walker, now twenty like Michael, and dressed almost identical to her brother.

"We've got most of them," he reported on their efforts to help contain the cattle. "A few scattered into the brake over there. It might take a while."

Michael heaved a sigh. "Get back in the coach, Susanna," he said, then faced Peter. "Go ahead and cross."

"There! You see?!" Peter felt vindicated. "This entire incident could easily have been avoided."

"Shut up, Peter," Michael looked away with an effort to restrain himself. "Before I toss your worthless ass back in the river."

Peter raised his sword toward Michael, not attacking, merely gesturing with it as he spoke. "You can't talk like that to a United States Army officer."

In an instant Michael snatched the sword from Peter. With his other hand he grabbed Peter's soaked tunic and jerked him up close, the tip of the saber stuck up Peter's nose. Michael's words were heard only by the young officer.

"Shut up and get in the coach. I'm working cattle today. I don't have time for jack asses!" They stood toe-to-toe, with the taller lieutenant attempting to modulate his shallow, rapid breathing. Michael withdrew the tip of the sword from Peter's nostril, placed the handle of the saber across Peter's chest, turned the lieutenant around and pushed him toward the coach. Without a word Peter spastically wrestled the sword back into its scabbard, untied his horse from the back of the stagecoach and mounted up.

"You're a brute, Michael," Susanna scolded her brother from

the coach window. When the old woman seated beside Susanna saw Michael and James, she was convinced the stagecoach had been attacked by hostile savages. "I'm going to tell Father all about this! You're in big trouble!" Susanna warned.

Michael ignored his sister's threat just as he had ignored a million others over the years. He sprang onto Midnight and rode off with James.

* * * * * * *

William Drummond came out of the Titusville apothecary shop carrying a small, blue glass bottle. He crossed the street to his carriage parked in front of the general store which bore the recently painted sign: *Ogilvie Mercantile*. All around him were the reminders of Titus Ogilvie's take-over of Pine Hill. Beside the *Titusville* Post Office was the *Ogilvie* Assay Office, which handled all the gold brought in by miners who still believed they would grow rich from the depleted veins throughout northern Georgia. The same veins which had been abandoned by most of the gold seekers who flooded the area in 1829. And next to the general store stood the *Ogilvie* Land Office, hub of an aggressive real estate trade despite a plethora of laws prohibiting any further white settlement in Cherokee territory.

William opened the medicine bottle and handed it to Elizabeth, seated in the one-horse carriage with a blanket tucked around her legs. For the better part of an hour they had been awaiting the arrival of the stagecoach bringing Susanna home for the summer. William had missed his little girl and Elizabeth looked forward to hearing about her daughter's social life at the exclusive conservatory in Charleston.

Titus Ogilvie, whose baleen girth seemed to increase with each passing season, stepped out onto the boardwalk in front of his land office, clicked open his watch and looked up the road toward the end of town. The stagecoach was seldom right on time, but there had been a few highway robberies in recent months and Titus was a little concerned.

"Afternoon, William. Mrs. Drummond. I understand your daughter's coming in on the stage," he made polite conversation. It bothered the portly Scot no end that, while William Drummond had always been civil and polite toward him, he had never shown any interest whatsoever in becoming Titus's friend.

"It'll be getting dark soon," William said. He, like Titus,

looked up the road for any sign of the stagecoach.

"I hope everything's all right," Elizabeth repeated for the fourth or fifth time.

"Aye," Ogilvie shared her concern. "I'm expecting the latest lottery announcement. Should be some prime land changin' hands." He referred to the Georgia State Land Lottery. It was a despicable program—sponsored by the state's governor and supported by the legislature—in which Cherokee land could be arbitrarily seized by the government and assigned to whites in a drawing. The land lottery was administered by Titus's own brother-in-law, Shadrach Bogen, an Atlanta businessman whose insatiable greed had earned Titus's undying admiration. So much so that Titus had married Shadrach's termagant sister, Ariel, a veraginous spinster whose tonnage and avarice rivaled that of her new husband. William Drummond found the land lottery scheme abhorrent and couldn't resist a shot at Ogilvie's enthusiasm for such a deplorable policy.

"It doesn't bother you, Titus, stealing these peoples' farms and homes?"

"Now hold on there," the rotund Scot bristled. "I ain't stealin' nothin'! The State of Georgia says this land don't belong to the Cherokees. Rightfully b'longs to white folks. They're gettin' it fair and square through the state lottery."

A rationalization, William thought, that Ogilvie and countless others like him had embraced to pacify what shred of conscience—if any—they might still possess. But William was having none of it.

"Everyone knows Shadrach Bogen is in charge of the lottery," William refused to look at Ogilvie, which he knew irritated the merchant-mayor. "He's giving away the best land to his friends, relatives and in-laws. And you're making out like a bandit because the Cherokees around here will sell out to you for practically nothing rather than lose it all in this damned lottery."

"Nothin' wrong with that," Ogilvie defended himself. "It's a business opportunity. A man's got to earn a living. Ah...there they are," he pointed to the stagecoach coming into view at the far end of the street. Peter Tanner, his uniform still wet, rode alongside. Elizabeth took another drink from the blue medicine bottle, coughing as she forced down the bitter elixir. With William's help she stepped down from the carriage as the stagecoach rumbled to a stop in front of the general store. Peter dismounted and straightened his wet tunic—as though no one would notice—then ceremoniously opened the coach door.

The elderly mixed-blood man stepped out first, then helped

the two old ladies descend stiffly from the cramped coach. The driver passed mail bags, luggage and packages down from atop the stagecoach to several men who had appeared out of nowhere. Finally, with a grand gesture, Peter extended his hand to help Susanna down like a princess arriving at the coronation ball. The men unloading the stage stopped their work. All eyes were on her; she well knew it and wouldn't have had it any other way.

"Mother! Father!" she rushed to her parents, embracing and kissing them with a show of affection intended to impress the onlookers with her daughterly devotion. That done, she beckoned to the wet lieutenant. "Peter! Peter! Come. Come. Just look at him!"

Only then did Elizabeth and William notice the condition of Peter's uniform. "Goodness!" Elizabeth said, "What happened to you? You're soaked!"

"Father, I'm so angry!" Susanna wasted no time in fulfilling her threat to her brother. "This is all Michael's fault! He's just awful!"

"Whoa! Slow down! What are you talking about?"

"They had a bunch of cows at the ferry crossing," Peter explained.

"Yes. I bought some cattle. Michael was bringing them home." William still failed to understand the connection to Peter's wet uniform.

"They wouldn't let us cross!" Susanna whined. "Michael pushed Peter into the river. He's an absolute heathen!"

Elizabeth took her husband's arm, not hiding her distress at the endless bickering. "You aren't even home yet, and already you're fighting with your brother! I don't think I can stand it!"

Susanna ignored her mother's protest. She was determined to exact retribution for Michael's outrageous behavior. "Father, I want you to punish him!"

"Michael's a grown man," William preferred to sidestep the issue. "He's responsible for his own behavior."

"Well, there was nothing responsible about his behavior today!" Susanna countered. "And if you won't do anything about it, I will!"

"Susanna, please....your mother..." William knew his plea was futile. Though he loved his daughter dearly, he was already looking forward to the end of summer when she would go back to school.

"Fine. I'm sorry, Mother," she lied. "I'll take it up with Michael. Let's go home."

Peter lifted Susanna's bags into the back of the Drummond's carriage. William was about to climb into the driver's seat when his attention was drawn to a ruckus in front of the Ogilvie Land Office. Titus Ogilvie was grappling with a Cherokee man who had ripped down the newly posted land lottery list. Alton Ogilvie, Titus's younger son, rushed out of the land office. At the same time, his older brother, Cephus, came from the general store. It took them only seconds to subdue the much smaller Cherokee man. Titus retrieved the lottery listing and ironed it flat against his massive stomach before impaling it once more on the nails driven into the wall.

"You're not taking my land!" the Cherokee man struggled in vain against the iron grip of the two younger, larger Ogilvie boys. "This is *Tsa-la-gi* land! All of it! Even this town!"

"Not any more! That's the law!" Titus growled in the man's face. "Alton, shoot the next man touches this list!"

Alton, whose intelligence, it had often been said, only slightly exceeded that of a blacksmith's anvil, took his father's every word literally. He pulled from his belt an old, poorly kept pistol and took up his position beside the posted list. Peter Tanner stepped up onto the rough wooden walkway, pushing aside the other Cherokees who were pressing forward to see the list. With an air of authority, Peter positioned himself between Titus and the indignant *Tsa-la-gi* man, addressing all the Indians who had gathered around.

"Go on! Get out of here! All of you!" Peter ordered.

With quiet, dark bitterness, the Cherokees began to disperse. Titus once more smoothed and patted the restored list. William had witnessed it all and couldn't resist a parting shot. "Just another business opportunity, eh, Ogilvie?"

Titus moved to the edge of the boardwalk near the Drummond's carriage. "I don't know what your problem is, Drummond, but you'd better get your allegiances in the right place. 'Tis a costly mistake to do otherwise in these times!"

William snapped the buggy whip and the carriage lurched into motion. Peter stepped out into the street, calling after them. "I'll be seeing you, Susanna!" She gave him an enticing wave from the retreating carriage.

* * * * * * *

"How dare you, Michael!" Susanna screamed. Her rage had not abated in the least. "It's absolutely unforgivable!" She snatched some of her things away from Reba, who was helping her unpack, and propelled them furiously into the bottom of the large, oak armoire.

"Peter Tanner is a pretentious ass! Always has been. Always will be," Michael leaned against the doorway, not at all intimidated by Susanna's wrath. He winked at Reba, who, he knew, was delighted to see Miss Susie worked into a state. And Michael, thumbs hooked rakishly in the top of his trousers, admittedly enjoyed torturing his older sister.

"Peter is an officer and a gentleman," she corrected him.

"Pretentious ass! A menace to mankind!"

"Watch what you say," Susanna switched from fury to threats. She smoothed out a dress on the bed and flicked her hair. "He just might become your brother-in-law." She knew that would rankle her odious brother.

"He asked you to marry him?" Michael was stunned.

"Well...not yet," she admitted. "But he will."

Michael's expression became sober and dark. He went to his sister and took her by the shoulders. "You're serious about this, aren't you?"

She was moved by his unexpected ingenuousness. "Yes. I am." He kissed her gently on the forehead. Reba was herself astounded by Michael's display of kindness and affection. "Why, Michael! I don't know what to say," Susanna's voice was ripe with emotion.

"It grieves me," he said with genuine sadness, "to know my sister will become such a young widow."

Susanna looked at Reba, who shared her confusion. Michael gently touched Susanna's cheek before stepping back to the doorway. His lips curled uncontrollably into a mischievous smile and he added, "Because that fool is destined for an early grave!" From a safe distance he broke into a full grin.

"You're a disgusting creature! Get out!" Susanna roared with renewed fury. She threw an empty valise at him. He ducked out the door and down the hallway, his hearty laugh echoing back to them. From somewhere in the house came their mother's familiar plea.

"Children...please don't fight..."

* * * * * * *

The long shadows from the morning sun painted large black

patches across the road where a heavy overnight dew had formed a settling blanket over the dusty highway. A long legged, red-shouldered hawk lifted itself against a cerulean sky, hung motionless for a time then circled wide and perched in the dead top of a distant tree. Michael Drummond urged Midnight to a brisk gallop, slowing to a trot just before he cut off onto a trail leading into the woods. Fifteen minutes later he pulled the horse to a stop in front of the Walker cabin and sprang from the saddle.

Annie appeared at the door with her mother right behind her and made no attempt to conceal her excitement at seeing Michael, whose lingering look mirrored her own.

"Good morning, Annie. Mrs. Walker," he said with a slight bow. "Where's James? I thought we'd go riding this morning."

"James and Father went into town," Annie informed him.

"They took three shoats to trade for supplies," *Tse-ni-si* explained. "I thought James told you."

"Oh, well...it must have slipped my mind," Michael sounded disappointed.

"I guess I could go for a ride," Annie offered.

"That's all right. You don't have to..." he lied, hoping she would persist. And she did.

"I don't mind. You came all the way over..."

"Well...I suppose we could..." Michael's transparent nonchalance prompted a smile from Mrs. Walker. Annie and Michael looked to her for final approval of their brilliant impromptu resolution to the riding dilemma.

"I'm sure James wouldn't mind if you rode *U-no-le*," she said. Before Janice had finished speaking, Annie was already trotting out to the sapling-pole corral with Michael close behind. Janice watched them with an approving smile, then went back inside the cabin.

* * * * * * *

Michael lay on his back in the middle of the sun-warmed carpet of soft, tender grass deep in a wooded glade. Annie sat on her knees beside him. His hand rested on the ball of her shoulder, their arms touching. Both were still, listening to the serene concert of the birds high in the pines, accompanied by the music of the running creek that skirted the edge of the clearing only a few yards away.

When Annie shifted her arm to remove a twig from Michael's sleeve, his hand slipped down, coming into contact with her breast. Both froze, their eyes connecting, but he didn't move his hand nor did she adjust to move it for him. It was, in his mind, a perfect breast. Firm, yet indescribably soft and divinely shaped in one of nature's consummate creations. He stared, unblinking, as the nipple grew erect, pressing lightly against the palm of his hand. It stirred him and he felt himself beginning to engorge. Annie placed her hand over his, pressing lightly as a signal for him to gently squeeze her. Still their eyes remained locked.

With her other hand, Annie pulled the delicate leather string, untying the top of her shirt. When the two sides parted, she placed Michael's hand inside on her bare breast and held it there. With her free hand she brushed back a lock of hair from his face, then traced lightly down across his chest, over his rock-rippled abdomen and past his waist until she encountered his full erection. Her fingers encircled him and squeezed lightly, launching a searing flame up his back, through his neck and into his eyes. Throat dry. Nostrils flared. Eyes wide. A smile of recognition played across Annie's sensuous mouth. She bent over him and their lips met, gently at first, then pressing with passion.

The kiss lingered and recycled itself several times until Annie sat up straight, looking down at Michael. He couldn't read her expression and wondered if he had allowed things to go too far. As though she had read his mind, she answered by removing her shirt and dropping it to the grass beside them. Michael drank in the incredible beauty before him. He knew that he loved Annie Walker. He had loved her since they were children. He had loved her when he pulled her hair and when he pushed her down in the mud. He had loved her when he and James had swum naked with her and had pretended they were going to drown her. Before she had breasts and before he knew what an erection was for. He had loved her every Christmas when he took a bag of gifts to the Walker cabin and always pretended he had forgotten her present and made her search him until she found it. He had loved her since the first time he noticed how she moved with a lightness of being that whispered of secret connections to another world. And he loved her now as she untied his trousers and drew forth his hardened sex, stroking it gently with her fingers.

She took his hand away from her breast and guided it down to her skirt. Shifting a little to part her knees, she started his hand up the inside of her thigh. It needed no further guidance. She bent down to kiss him again and he felt her tremble slightly when his fingers found her soft, down-like hair. His own arousal increased immeasurably as he discovered the wetness of her anticipation. It was the smoothest, softest thing he had ever felt. His excitement was so intense he feared his heart might stop its pounding and cease altogether.

This wasn't the first sexual encounter for Michael. At fifteen, while attending a council meeting with their fathers, he and James had been drawn off into the woods by two mixed-blood Cherokee girls—or women; they were at least nineteen or twenty. It had been startlingly swift and explosive, finished before either boy had fully understood what was happening. Then at the university Michael and two schoolmates had engaged the favors of some prostitutes brought up from Savannah by the wealthy father of a fellow student. But this, too, had a detached quality, full of animal passion but void of any genuine emotion. Nothing could have prepared him for the beauty of this moment and the woman who with a look and a touch had possessed his soul.

Annie gently pushed his hand away just long enough to lift her knee up and over to sit astride him. She shifted her weight forward on one arm, her breasts near his face. With her other hand she positioned him so she could gradually settle her weight onto his hardness. She emitted a tiny, involuntary cry at the sweet breaking pain of first penetration, then took him completely inside her. Painful at first, the discomfort soon yielded to a warm sensation of fullness that spread up through her heart, into her throat, engulfing her mind, encompassing her entire being.

Michael touched her cheek, drawing her down close to him. Her hair fell against his face as their lips met. She smelled herself on his fingertips just before his hands glided down her back to cup her firm, round bottom. His tongue pressed between her lips, coaxing her to open her mouth and receive him there as she had below. He timed his breathing so that each time she exhaled he inhaled the sweetness of her breath, drinking in her spirit. She gasped with pleasure when he matched the thrusts of his tongue with the exact rhythm of her movement on him. He felt her gripping warmth as she flexed each time she had him fully inside her. Finally, she settled firmly on him and, with a slow circling motion, brought him to the point of explosion.

For Michael, it felt as though time had stopped. Annie, on the other hand, might have said time had launched her forward a thousand years. Perhaps a million. To a place beyond time and space where this would be the feeling of eternity. She stopped moving. A slight tremor rippled through her body. She pushed up on her arms, away from his face so she could look at him. This feeling was new, but then this entire experience was a first for her. Was this all just a part of it? her eyes asked him. His own breathing had grown heavier. He didn't want her to stop. His hands moved down from her breasts, along her slender waist to grasp her hips and restart her gentle movement. That was all it took for both of them. What had begun in Annie as a distant, tickling sensation gripped her in a burst of ecstasy that flamed its way through her loins and coiled itself tightly around him deep inside her. She released a half-moan, half-squeal and threw her head back, allowing Michael's strong hands to move her back and forth on him. His buttocks tightened as he thrust upward, almost unseating her. He exhaled with a delirious groan. Annie felt the force, the warmth, the wetness of his eruption inside her. She leaned down to him again and he encircled her with his powerful arms, holding her close as though he feared she might vanish from atop him. And there was in that moment the fleeting tickle of a sweet and wonderfully sad thought. No matter how many times or how passionately they might make love in the future; no matter how many years beyond one hundred they both might endure, there would never be another moment quite like this, their first.

Neither was aware of how long they lay entwined in each other. At some point Annie had stretched out beside him, pressing her body against his. They gazed up through the branches of the pines, sweetgum and hickory. He rolled onto his side and traced his fingers across her flat stomach, climbed her breasts and proceeded along her delicate throat until he cradled her face.

"I love you, Annie," he said softly.

"*Gŭ-ge-yu-i*," she repeated in Cherokee.

"*Gŭ-ge-yu-i, wa-le-la*," he called her his hummingbird. "I wonder what Father and Mother will say."

"About what?"

"When I tell them we're going to be married."

"And who said I would marry you?" she asked, her face serious, without the slightest hint she might be joking. But he knew her. Well enough to know she would make a point of jockeying for position in their relationship. "You know, a Cherokee woman decides who she will marry. It is her decision. Hers alone."

Michael propped up on one elbow and gazed into her beautiful hazel eyes. "And what *is* her decision?"

The teasing was over. Annie saw the love in his face. She ran a finger along the pouty curve of his lower lip. "Her decision is....yes." She twirled a lock of his long hair around her finger and

142

pulled him down toward her. Their kiss was tender yet filled with passion. When she decided they had kissed long enough, she pushed him away and sat up, stretching her arms, arching her back, her bare breasts bathed in the warm sunlight. "And....it is the Cherokee woman who decides when it's over," the teasing resumed. "If you don't treat me right, you'll come home one night and find all your things thrown outside the door. It's our custom."

"You wouldn't do that to me," Michael challenged with a smile.

"You don't think so?"

"Then who'd help you take care of all the children we're going to have?" he argued. She pushed him over on his back and playfully climbed on top of him. He took her hair in his hand and pulled her face down to his. As they kissed, he rolled her on her back and was on top of her, their passion swelling once more.

* * * * * * *

The Drummond family were nearing the end of their dinner. Reba began removing some of the large serving dishes and tureens from the sideboard adjacent to the table back into the kitchen.

"A delicious meal, Reba. As usual," William said. He never failed to compliment Reba's cooking and to thank her for her efforts on behalf of his family.

"Thank you, Mistah William," Reba responded. It had become a routine exchange between them, but each knew it was true gratitude on his part and genuine appreciation on hers.

"That's what I missed so much," Susanna chirped. "Reba's cooking."

"Mmm-hmm," Reba didn't believe her for a second. "Missed my cookin' 'bout like you missed yo' baby brother."

"That's enough, Reba," William said with a smile. He wasn't in the mood for one of their familiar bickering battles that could run on for the remainder of the evening. Snipping back and forth, neither willing to give an inch or allow the other the final word. With a cackle Reba moved her huge frame toward the kitchen. William wiped his mouth and pushed back his plate. "Lieutenant Tanner stopped me at the post office in town today," he said flatly to no one in particular.

"Peter? Stopped to talk to you?" Susanna was excited.

"Asked if he might come calling," William answered without revealing his feelings on the subject. He paused for effect, then said off-handedly, "I told him I suppose it's all right, but I didn't think you were much interested."

Susanna knew her father was teasing. With a familiar toss of her hair, she shot Michael a look of prideful satisfaction. Making no attempt to disguise the genuine dislike he harbored for his sister, Michael shoved his own plate away and blurted out the revelation he'd been repeating in his mind all evening.

"Father, I have an announcement to make! I'm going to be married!" There was stone silence until Susanna's fork clattered loudly onto the china plate.

"But...son...who...?" Elizabeth was dumfounded.

"Annie," Michael answered, beaming.

"Annie?" William repeated.

"Yes. Annie Walker."

"Oh, my God!" Susanna almost choked on her food.

"But dear," his mother leaned forward, searching his young face, "do you know what you're saying? She's...she's..."

"She's what?" Michael's expression grew dark, challenging. "An Indian? A Cherokee?"

"Watch your tone with your mother," William cautioned him.

"I'm sorry, Mother," Michael apologized. "But I love her."

Elizabeth appeared genuinely pained. How could he think her capable of a pejorative comment on Annie's ethnic heritage? "I was only going to say she's so *young.*"

"She's almost twenty," Michael reminded her. "Same age as me and James. Besides, weren't you just eighteen when you and father married?" She, of course, couldn't contradict him. He was in full possession of the facts. Michael looked his father in the eye and said, "I want to ask your blessing."

"This is outrageous!" Susanna erupted. "Father, surely you wouldn't..."

William met the fiery eyes of his son. "You're going to do this, with or without my blessing, aren't you?"

"Yes."

They looked at each other for a long time. Finally William smiled. He partially rose from his chair and extended his hand across the table to Michael. They shook, man-to-man. "I've always thought Annie was a fine young lady," William said and retook his seat.

"Lady?!" Susanna couldn't believe her father would capitulate so easily. "Father, are you mad? She's nothing but a—"

Michael wheeled on his sister, his finger right in her face.

"Watch it, Susanna!" his stern voice left no doubt as to the gravity of his warning. "Choose your words carefully."

"It's all right, Michael," William waved his napkin almost like a flag of truce. "You have my blessing."

"Thank you, Father," he said, not taking his eyes off Susanna until finally he looked at Elizabeth. "And you, Mother?"

"Why...yes..." she said and smiled at William. "I've always liked little Annie..."

Michael relaxed into a broad grin. He knew they were both honestly in favor of his marriage to Annie. Susanna pushed her chair back contentiously and rose from the table, throwing her napkin down in the middle of her plate.

"I can't believe what I'm hearing!" her voice was low, but trembling with emotion. "Have you lost your mind?! Have you no pride?" She directed her expanding fury toward her brother. "And you! You selfish child! Have you given any thought to what you're doing to this family's reputation? To Father's law practice? To your own future?"

"Susanna, you're overreacting," William held out a hand to calm her, motioning for her to sit down.

"As usual..." Michael seconded his father's assessment.

"No!" Susanna was relentless. "I am *not* overreacting! If you let him go through with this, as far as I'm concerned, I have no brother." She raised her finger to Michael just as he had done to her. "I'll not speak to you, and I ask that you not speak to me. Ever again." She stormed out of the room, shoving aside Ezekiel who was just coming in. They all stared at the doorway after Susanna had gone, listening to her stomping up the stairs to her room. It had been a practiced part of her ritual of petulance since she was old enough to mount the stairs unassisted.

"Excuse me, Mistah Drummond. Someone to see you," Ezekiel spoke softly.

"Who is it, Ezekiel?" William was curious. Visitors were unusual at this late hour.

"It's Thomas Walker."

A sober look passed between William and Michael. Had Annie told her parents about their decision, and now Thomas had come to put a stop to it? William excused himself from the table and left the room. Michael moved to follow but was stopped by a gesture from his father. Elizabeth broke the awkward silence.

"Well, now," she took Michael's hand. "Tell me more about Annie. I've known her all these years, and yet, I had no idea...."

Michael smiled, appreciating the interest he knew was sincere. He felt bad for having implied that this kind and gentle woman could conceive an ill thought toward anyone he loved. He squeezed her hand and sat down to await his father's return.

* * * * * * *

William could see that the normally imperturbable Thomas was genuinely distressed but didn't believe it had anything to do with Michael and Annie.

"They're taking my land, William." The father's fears were reflected in the face of his son who held the reins of both horses. "The land lottery," Thomas explained. "We were in town today. James says our place is on Ogilvie's list."

James confirmed his father's words with a single nod.

"I'm sorry, Thomas," William placed a consoling hand on his friend's shoulder. "I've been expecting something like this. And I'm afraid it's only going to get worse. For *all* the Cherokees."

"Ridge and his Treaty Party have betrayed our people," Thomas spat the words out bitterly. "A handful of traitors have sold us out!"

Michael, unable to contain his curiosity, ventured out onto the porch. He saw the agony in Thomas's expression and heard the anguish in his voice. He caught James's eye and knew it was serious. "Father? What's the matter?"

James answered before William could speak. "They're taking our land! In their damned lottery!"

Michael descended the steps to stand near James. Out of habit, he stroked *U-no-le's* neck and patted Thomas's mount. "There must be something we can do, Father..." They all looked at William, confident that he would provide a solution.

* * * * * * *

Brigadier General John Ellis Wool was the commander of United States Armed Forces in the southeastern district. His rise in the army had been swift. He had served under Andrew Jackson and had received a field advancement to Lieutenant Colonel at age thirty. Then, at thirty-two, he had been promoted to the rank of colonel and was made Inspector General of the Army.

A tall, well-proportioned, handsome man of fifty-two, with close cut but distinctly wavy gray hair, Wool always wore his finest

146

dress uniform when on duty, even in his temporary office in Milledgeville, the burgeoning capital city of Georgia. A long, thin, chiseled nose sloped down from between eyes that were peculiarly close together, giving him the appearance of having all his features bunched too tightly in the center of his face. He had a habit—especially when under stress—of pinching the bridge of his nose, suggesting that too many repetitions of this gesture might actually have caused the convergence of his eyes. The general had ordered his heavy mahogany desk shipped down from Washington, D.C., and he seemed far more concerned about two nicks the desk had suffered in transit than in the case being pled before him by this tenacious attorney who had ridden all the way down from Titusville. The general felt unsettled beneath the piercing intensity of his visitor's eyes.

"The new treaty says the Cherokees will be compensated fairly for their land, livestock and all other assets not taken west," William stated emphatically, watching the general pick splinters from the gouged place on his desk. "So," William continued, trying to ignore the distraction, "will you please explain to me how this illegal land lottery by the State of Georgia can be allowed to continue?"

Michael, like his father, was dressed in his best suit. Thomas and James Walker were clad in traditional Cherokee clothing, including their brightly colored head wraps. The three of them sat stiffly in a perfectly aligned row of chairs across the desk from General Wool. William had heard that this life-long military man was not without compassion. Thomas didn't hold out a great deal of hope for such a meeting, but William, after much deliberation, had convinced him it was their only course. William knew he could obtain a writ of injunction from his friend, Judge Walter Barrington. But given the inclination of the Georgians to openly flaunt the law, injunctions to the contrary notwithstanding, he knew they would need the full backing of the United States Army to carry out any such court order.

The general pinched the top of his nose and closed his eyes, then straightened up in his chair and placed his forearms perfectly parallel on the top of his desk. It was as though this were the formal military position for seated address. "I thank you, Mr. Drummond, for coming this great distance on behalf of your Cherokee friends. I'm sad to say, however, your journey has been in vain."

Thomas and James exchanged a troubled look. They had placed all their faith in William; they had taken his advice to make the long trek to Milledgeville; they were convinced that, if any man on earth could, William Drummond would be able to make some satisfactory arrangement. William took a deep breath and stretched to his full height.

"But surely, General Wool, the authority of the federal government—backed by the United States Army—can prevent these Georgia hooligans from stealing these peoples' land, their gold, their homes...their dignity..." William trailed off. His words had clearly stirred the general, as evinced by Wool's compassionate look toward Thomas and James.

Again the general squeezed between his eyes and gnawed at his nether lip before replying with a tone of sadness and finality William knew didn't bode well for his Cherokee clients. "President Jackson wants the Indians removed to the west," Wool spoke softly, clearly enunciating each word. "All of them. Not just the Cherokee. Already the process is afoot. Chickasaw, Choctaw, Creek, and eventually the Seminole. All your so-called Civilized Tribes. Privately, Jackson might not approve of Georgia's tactics, but if it moves him closer to his goal..."

General Wool took a pipe from an ornately carved rack on his desk. He rose from his chair, went to the window and gazed out at the comings and goings in the town square. A mother was scolding her son for playfully veering into the path of a delivery wagon. Nervously General Wool stuffed the pipe's bowl from a wooden canister on the shelf by the window. He angled his head toward his suppliants just enough not to be rude but kept his eyes focused out on the square as he spoke. "Of all the many assignments in my long military career, I find this the most odious. Just last week I wrote to the Secretary of War, asking to be relieved of this command—something I would never have dreamed of doing before."

William saw a genuine vulnerability in the general and pressed the point, knowing it was their only chance. "Perhaps a man with the general's sense of honor and fairness is what these people need most in their struggle to keep their land."

The general spun abruptly and leaned across the huge desk toward William. "Struggle to keep their land? Have you not heard anything I've said? If you're truly a friend to these people, Mr. Drummond, you'll put that idea out of your mind for good!" He straightened up and addressed Thomas directly for the first time. "As for you, Mr. Walker—I sincerely regret your unfortunate plight. But I will be blunt. The greatest kindness I could possibly render to you—to all your people—and I would do it tomorrow if it were possible—I would send every Cherokee to the west, beyond the reach

148

of the white man!"

Thomas obviously didn't care for the words he was hearing, but he admired the general for standing up, looking them in the eye and speaking what he believed to be the truth.

"These land-hungry vultures," the commander said softly, with an urgent tone of pleading he hoped William would understand, "sit waiting to pounce on their Indian prey and strip them of everything." Wool pointed his still unlit pipe at Thomas. "You *will* go west. Make no mistake about it. It is a sweeping tide we are all powerless to stop. I urge you—all of you—gather your belongings and go quickly with money in your pockets and your heads held high. Otherwise, you will go penniless and broken...but you *will* go...and there isn't a damn thing you or I can do about it."

A long silence followed. William turned to Thomas and James. Finally he spoke with a heavy sigh, "Thomas...I'm afraid General Wool is right."

Thomas looked at William for a long time before rising from his seat. He motioned for James to stand. Thomas straightened his tunic and stood proud and dignified as he addressed this mighty general of the United States Army. "I did not think you could help us, General," Thomas began slowly. "But my friend thought it wise to try. I will *not* go west. No one will force the Cherokee to go west! John Ross, our chief, has gone to Washington. He will have this treaty struck down. *Tsa-la-gi* land will stay *Tsa-la-gi* land."

"Would to God it were so, my friends. Would to God it were so..." General Wool admired the courage of this Cherokee man. But courage, he knew, wouldn't stem the tide of continental expansion that had been declared the divinely ordained destiny of this new nation. His sad eyes met theirs...one by one.

149

CHAPTER

9

Tse-ni-si Walker expertly chopped the weeds from her garden without ever nicking a cornstalk or severing a bean vine. She paused to wipe the sweat from her face and flicked a leaf from her hair, which was rigorously woven into a dark knot against the nape of her neck. Her grandfather, The Old One, limped around the corner of the cabin with an armload of firewood which he deposited next to a large black pot where Annie was washing clothes. When the dog began to bark, Annie paused from plunging at the laundry with the wash stick. Two *yo-neg* men were riding leisurely toward them. One pointed out features of the surrounding landscape to the other—the thick stand of pines, interspersed with hickory, chestnut, birch and sweetgum to the south and the well-kept cultivated fields to the north and east.

The visitors didn't even acknowledge the existence of the cabin or its inhabitants until they stopped their horses directly across from the Walkers' garden. Annie recognized the man who had been pointing out the trees and the fields as Cephus Ogilvie. She had seen him in town on occasion. In his mid-twenties, Cephus was bearded, dirty and weighed more than three hundred pounds. His travelling companion was older—perhaps thirty—and was lean, lanky and very tall. Even from a distance Annie could see that both men's mouths and beards were brown-stained with chewing tobacco. Anxious concern fingered its way up Annie's back as she watched her great grandfather hobble out to the edge of the road.

"Howdy, grandpa," Cephus Ogilvie spat insultingly close to the old man. "We're lookin' for Thomas Walker. This the Walker place?"

The Old One grinned and shook his head. *"Tla-ya-qua-n'-ta,"* he shrugged, not understanding. He had never learned the *yo-neg* tongue.

"I don't think he knows English," the tall, lanky one said, then pointed to Annie. "But I bet *she* does." Annie's old, threadbare dress was girted at the waist with the bright red sash Michael had given her for Christmas. Her face was wet with perspiration, but her sensuous beauty could not be missed. Cephus moved his horse closer. With measured steps, Janice came from the garden and planted herself—with her hoe—in front of Ogilvie's horse.

"Who are you? What do you want?" she demanded in a firm but respectful tone.

Cephus strained and grunted as he dismounted, his huge frame towering above Annie and Janice. "I'm Cephus Ogilvie. This here's my cousin, Mister Randolph Bogen. Of Atlanta." Bogen tipped his dirty hat and unfolded off his horse. He stood uncomfortably close to Annie, leering hungrily down at her.

But Annie wouldn't let them intimidate her. "If you have business with my father, you'll have to come back later. He isn't here today."

"Oh, he ain't, huh?" Cephus said. The two men exchanged a glance and grinned at Annie, who realized she had spoken unwisely.

"Just get back on your horses and get out of here. We have work to do." Annie tried to keep her voice from betraying concern—or worse, fear.

"Sassy little thing, ain't she?" Bogen grinned at Cephus, who pulled some crumpled documents from his pocket and held them up in front of Annie.

"This here's official papers, Missy," Cephus said, shaking them in Annie's face. "Signed by the governor. Seein' as you all is Cherokee, this here land belongs to the sover'n state of Georgia."

"And I just won it," Bogen added with excitement. "Fair and square. In the state lottery."

"I don't understand," Janice didn't like what she was hearing. "You'll have to talk to my husband."

"I'm talkin' to *you*, squaw!" Cephus yelled in her face, his lip curled in a vicious snarl. "This ain't your land no more! Even a God damn stupid Injun can understand that!"

Janice's grandfather had been standing quietly by. The quarrelsome shouting—though he didn't understand the words—prompted him to step between Cephus and his granddaughter. He looked up into the fiery eyes of the smelly giant and raised a hand, motioning for Cephus to step back. With a raking sweep of his thick forearm, Cephus knocked The Old One to the ground.

"*E-du-da!*" Annie rushed to him. Janice tried to get to them, but Bogen blocked her path. Annie helped The Old One to a sitting position and began brushing dirt off his shoulder.

"This is *my* place now!" Bogen growled. "I want you outa here! All of you! You got 'til sundown tomorrow."

"We'll be back," Cephus completed the threat. "Any Injuns still here'll be shot for trespassin'!"

Again Janice tried to reach Annie and The Old One, but

Bogen roughly shoved her back. Annie jumped between Bogen and her mother.

"You can't do this," Annie screamed.

"Don't you know nothin' 'bout Georgia law, Missy?" Bogen almost laughed at her feisty behavior.

"A white man can do whatever he damn well pleases," Cephus said.

"And ain't a God damn thing a Injun can say about it!" Bogen added.

"Get out! Now!" Annie yelled. She lunged at Cephus with both hands but was unable to budge his brick-wall frame. He grabbed her and pulled her up close, groping her breasts with his large, grimy hand.

"Leave her alone!"

Annie's mother raised her garden hoe to strike Cephus. Randolph Bogen grabbed the long hickory shaft in mid-swing and back-handed Janice, knocking her to her knees. Annie fought Cephus like a wildcat, but she was clearly no match for the mountainous man. He ripped away the top of her dress, baring her breasts. Pinning her arms to her sides, he confined her in a bear hug and lifted her off the ground from behind. She could only fling her head backward, attempting to strike him in the face.

Bogen, following Cephus's lead, threw down the hoe and grabbed Janice from behind, lifting her off the ground as Cephus had done with Annie. Both women screamed and kicked, though Janice wasn't as strong as her daughter. The men laughed with brutish delight.

"Guess we're gonna have to hump us a coupla squaws, cousin Randolph!" Cephus shouted above the screaming women.

"How come you get the young one?" Bogen roared.

"'Cause I'm younger'n you! An' better lookin'!" Cephus bellowed an instant before his hat flew off and his head snapped sharply forward. His expression grew pained and confused. The Old One had struck him from behind with a large stick of firewood. But the blow only stunned Cephus for a few seconds.

Janice's grandfather raised the stick to deliver another blow. Cephus relaxed his vice-like grip on Annie, but clung to her long hair while shaking his head to clear the fog. With his free hand he pulled a single-shot, flint-lock pistol from his belt and cocked the hammer back with his fat thumb. In a move unexpectedly fluid for a man of his bulk, Cephus swung around and shot The Old One in the chest, killing him instantly.

152

Annie struggled viciously, kicking and clawing at Cephus. He dropped the smoking pistol and wrestled her to the ground. Randolph Bogen did the same with Annie's mother. The women were slammed down hard in the dirt and their clothes ripped completely off and tossed aside. They fought as hard as they could, but their every move felt encumbered by a thousand pounds, their cries refused to leave their throats. The eyes of mother and daughter found each other as their attackers began their gruesome rape.

Annie tried to scream, but the dust stuck in her throat and she could only choke and cough. She watched Bogen on top of her mother. Using the same blood-stained piece of firewood that had struck Cephus, Bogen pressed down on Janice's throat to silence her cries against his beastly violation. Annie's chest constricted in terror when she saw her mother's eyes roll back in her head.

Then her mother was ripped from view when Annie was thrown on her stomach, face down in the dirt. Cephus clutched a handful of her hair and jerked her head back. She had never known such pain was possible when his swollen member ripped into her from behind. She was unable to fight back. One arm was pinned beneath her own body and the other caught in the iron grip of the man who was driving himself savagely inside her, thrusting back and forth, shoving her face forward once more into the dirt.

Annie was determined to see her mother. She blocked the pain and humiliation from her mind long enough to drag her bloody nose and mouth through the dirt to turn her head. But immediately Annie knew it would have been better not to have looked. Through the dust and tears, she realized the only movements her mother made were from Bogen's relentless thrusting. Janice's eyes were open, looking directly toward her daughter, but the light once there had been extinguished. Annie felt abandoned in a vast and empty universe, the sacrosanct bond between mother and daughter forever shattered in this world. She had looked into the gaping maw of unfathomable evil. In the same breath with which she uttered a prayer of thanks that her mother's spirit had already departed she whispered a plea for herself because, as yet, hers had not.

Still choking and coughing, Annie wanted to cry out, but her voice had vanished with her mother's soul. The only sounds she heard were the heavy panting and grunting of the two demons who had invaded their peaceful day, along with the shriek of a lone hawk which Annie glimpsed circling the trees, losing itself against the brilliance of the sun a second before she slipped mercifully into the painless black void of unconsciousness.

* * * * * * *

The day had grown long and the sun had dipped behind the western pines. Thomas and James Walker were exhausted after the long ride home from Milledgeville following their fruitless and disappointing meeting with General Wool. They stopped their horses when two riders rounded a distant curve in the road, coming toward them. Cephus Ogilvie and Randolph Bogen stopped a few yards from Thomas and James. Thomas nodded politely and said nothing about the fresh scratches on Bogen's neck. James eyed the bright red sash showing from beneath Cephus's hat where he had wrapped it around his wounded head. Both noticed without comment the unusually dusty condition of the men's clothes. The sun was behind the two white men, and only when their horses inched past on the narrow road did James recognize the heavier man as Cephus Ogilvie.

"You Thomas Walker?" Cephus asked.

Thomas waited silently for an explanation.

"We got some papers here for you," Cephus dug the wrinkled documents from inside his coat and extended them toward Thomas, but James snatched them for a look.

"You can read that, boy?" Bogen was genuinely impressed.

"I can read it," James said, then wadded the papers up and threw them at the feet of the white man's horse.

Cephus looked down at the crumpled paper, then back up at James and Thomas with a wry grin. "Don't matter. Like the paper says—you be gone by sundown tomorrow."

"Or what?" James snapped defiantly.

Cephus casually swept his long coat back to display his pistol, though he made no move that was openly threatening.

"Or we'll shoot you for trespassin' on my property. That's what," Bogen answered. The two *yo-negs* spurred their horses and rode on. Thomas and James watched them until they were well down the road, then urged their own mounts to a brisk gallop in the direction of home.

* * * * * * *

Dazed and huddled on the floor against the wall in the darkened cabin, Annie held her dead mother in her arms. Beside them on the floor lay the body of her beloved *E-du-da*. She didn't remember regaining consciousness. She wouldn't permit herself the details of Cephus Ogilvie's savage violation of every molecule of her being. She didn't recall dragging her lifeless mother and her dead great grandfather into the cabin. All these things would eventually take on a life of their own and, in the days and nights and years to come, would swirl and mingle into one recurring nightmare.

Annie heard the thundering hoofbeats and wondered if—perhaps even hoped that—Ogilvie and Bogen had come back to end her life. And with that very thought she was forced to admit she had been lying to herself. She remembered. She remembered everything. Every grunt. Every thrust. Every blow. Every grain of sand, every drop of blood and every tear. Through the pain and the darkness she fumbled about on the floor until her fingers closed around the knife handle. She heard the footsteps on the hard-packed earth outside and raised the blade just before the door burst open. If they had come back to kill her, she would take at least one of them with her. When she finally opened her eyes, she found herself looking up into the horrified faces of her father and her twin brother, their worst fears realized.

* * * * * * *

Thomas and James pushed their weary mounts along the dusty road in the growing darkness. Somewhere ahead of them they knew Cephus Ogilvie and Randolph Bogen were probably riding along at a leisurely pace, laughing, perhaps sharing a flask of whiskey.

At the sound of the riders coming up behind them, Cephus and Randolph exchanged a troubled look and drew their pistols. They glanced nervously back at the curve in the road. Thomas and James slowed their horses to a walk when they saw Cephus and his cousin in the moonlight ahead. Steadily they moved toward the two white men. When they were about ten yards away, Cephus raised his pistol.

"Stop right there! Don't come no closer!" he warned. Thomas and James complied and sat staring at the two men. Bogen was visibly agitated.

"You don't know we done it. You cain't prove nothin'!" his voice cracked.

"Shut up," Cephus barked. "Who said we done anything? 'Sides, it don't matter what they think. They're Injuns." He glared at Thomas, his lip curling into his familiar snarl. "Ain't that right,

Walker? Injuns can't testify 'gainst a white man."

Without warning, James's hand flew out from his side and the knife was airborne. An instant later there was a gurgling cry of pain. Cephus sat motionless in the saddle, the knife embedded in the side of his throat. In a reflex spasm he discharged his pistol into the darkness, startling his horse into a spin. Bogen fired wildly at James, missing him. Cephus fell off his horse, but managed to push himself up onto his knees. Blood gushed from his mouth and nose as well as from his severed jugular. Desperately Bogen fought to control his own horse, which, like Cephus's, had been frightened by the pistol shots. Bogen kept looking down in astonishment at his cousin who was, quite literally, bleeding like a stuck pig. When his horse began to settle down, Bogen looked up to see Thomas and James staring at him. With a tiny audible gasp—almost a hiccup—he jerked the reins to one side, kicked the horse sharply and sped away into the night.

In a single look Thomas and James reached an unspoken agreement. Thomas took off in pursuit of Randolph Bogen. James dismounted *U-no-le* and approached Cephus. The wounded man, still on his knees, dabbed repeatedly at the profusion of blood and stared at his darkened hands as though at any moment it would all make sense to him. He tugged a couple of times at the knife handle, but it was too painful. When he looked up at James and opened his mouth to speak, there was only a blood-bubbling sputter. Whatever he was trying to say, James knew by the hatred in Cephus's eyes that he was neither begging for his life nor asking forgiveness for his barbaric crime. His lip curled again into a familiar sneer. He raised the pistol at James, forgetting in his confusion that he had already fired. *Click.* A tiny spark flew when the hammer struck the flint.

Cephus struggled to his feet and staggered toward the side of the road where he fell again to his knees. He crawled the rest of the way to a large pine tree and slumped to a sitting position against its massive trunk. With one final jerk, Cephus pulled the knife from his neck in a painful, howling crimson spray. James had stalked him in silence, stopping only inches from Ogilvie, who strained to focus on the man before him as the darkness closed in. Like an expiring scorpion lashing out one last time, Cephus slowly swung the knife in a wide arc. James caught his arm in mid-swing and pried his knife from the fat, blood-slick fingers. He wiped the blade clean on the back of Ogilvie's shoulder before dropping it back into its sheath at his waist.

* * * * * * *

Randolph Bogen pushed his old, long-legged nag as hard as he could. In his mind he was certain he heard the pounding of Thomas Walker's horse closing in on him. What he didn't know was that Thomas had negotiated a shortcut down a thick, brush-covered slope where he would intercept the road, cutting a full quarter mile off the pursuit.

Thomas stopped when he heard a cry of pain from somewhere in the darkness. He listened, then moved on and reconnected with the road. It was too dark to accurately read hoof prints in the road dust, but another painful groan led him down the embankment toward the creek. A few yards into the brush Thomas saw Randolph Bogen. He had apparently attempted a shortcut of his own and had been thrown from his horse. His lanky, flailing frame was caught in the branches of a tree hanging out over the creek. In the moonlight Thomas knew from the strange angle of Bogen's left leg and right arm that both limbs were broken.

With patient deliberation Thomas dismounted and slid down the steep bank to the trees where Bogen was snagged. It was clear the white man's pain was intense. He craned around when he heard Thomas approaching through the brush.

"Please. Help me," Bogen said weakly. "I didn't mean no harm. Don't hurt me. You can keep your place." Thomas, without speaking, stopped right in front of Bogen. They were almost nose to nose in the moonlight filtering down through the leaves. Bogen's eyes were riveted on the knife Thomas drew from his belt. "No...please...I'm beggin' you..." Bogen didn't prove as implacable as his cousin Cephus had been beneath the hand of judgment.

Without ever changing his expression, Thomas pulled the man's scraggly hair back with one hand and scalped him with a single stroke. Bogen screamed, the blood running down into his eyes. But the howling abruptly ceased when Thomas firmly gripped the remaining hair on the back of Bogen's head, wrenched him to one side and cleanly slit his throat.

Thomas Walker hadn't spoken a single word throughout the entire ordeal. He wiped the bloody blade on Bogen's shoulder, exactly as James had done to Cephus, slipped the knife into his belt and quietly climbed back up the creek bank to his waiting horse.

* * * * * * *

157

"No, Michael!" Susanna snapped emphatically. "For the hundredth time—No!"

Michael stood in the doorway of his sister's room. He watched her, seated at her vanity, combing out her long, beautiful hair. He was somber and subdued, clean, dressed in his only suit, his wet hair combed straight back. He would have been the perfect picture of a fine young gentleman of his day but for the knee-high, fringed leather Cherokee boots, with his trouser legs tucked inside. Susanna looked at him and for an instant—only a fleeting one—actually felt sorry for him.

"You know how I feel about funerals. And death," she tried to be as gentle as she knew how. "I just don't like it. Please, don't ask me again."

"I didn't come here to fight with you," he said softly. "I just thought you might be of some comfort to Annie."

Susanna stopped combing her hair and gave his reflection an exasperated look. "What on earth could I possibly say to that girl? It's all quite terrible—what she's been through—but..." she sighed, searching for a way out. "I'm sure you're all the comfort she needs."

Michael looked her right in the eye. Cold, piercing, unblinking. "You're right, sister. Why did I even bother? She's just an Indian." He spun around and was gone, leaving her staring at the vacant doorway.

"Michael....I didn't mean it that way..."

* * * * * * *

A light but steady rain showed no signs of letting up. The bodies of *Tse-ni-si* Walker and her grandfather, each tightly bound in linen, lay on a low, plank platform between two open graves. A wrinkled and ancient Cherokee medicine man at the head of the platform chanted a ritual burial song. Only a few feet away was Jesse Bushyhead, a mixed-blood, Cherokee Baptist minister descended from the original *Bushyhead*, Captain John Stuart. He used his black, broad-brim hat to shield the tattered, old Bible from the rain as he read the familiar passage—where Jesus raised his friend, Lazarus, from the dead—with its reassurance to the bereaved that their loved ones would be raised up in the Last Day.

Thomas and James Walker, with Annie between them, stood beside the bodies. On their left were *Tse-ni-si's* brothers, John and Andrew Sixkiller. Behind them were the rest of the extended family—the wives and children of the Sixkiller brothers and a gathering of other distant relatives. There were no mourners from the Walker side of the family. Thomas had no kin in this part of the country. Both his parents and his three siblings were gone—a brother killed in 1814 in the war, the rest had fallen victim to a wave of cholera four years later. As far as Thomas knew, his only living relative was somewhere in North Carolina. A cousin he had never seen.

To the right of Thomas, James and Annie were William and Elizabeth Drummond. William held the edge of his long coat out like a giant wing, shielding Elizabeth from the rain. As the *di-da-nŭ-wi-s-gi* chanted and Bushyhead recited scripture, Rebecca Sixkiller, Andrew's wife, began singing a Christian hymn in Cherokee. Elizabeth hummed softly to the tune she recognized as *What A Friend We Have In Jesus*.

> *S-qua-ti-ni-se-s-di, Yi-ho-wa,*
> *E-la-di, ga-i sŭ-i;*
> *Tsi-wa-na-ga-li-ya a-yŭ,*
> *Tsa-sŭ-ni-di ni-hi...*

A flash of lightning followed by a loud clap of thunder transformed the light, steady drizzle into a relentless downpour. William drew Elizabeth closer to him. Michael's eyes never left Annie. Her vacant stare troubled him. He wanted to put his arms around her, to lead her away to a warm, dry place and make all the pain go away. But it was wet. And chilled. And they weren't going anywhere for a while.

* * * * * * *

The rain lasted all afternoon, through the night and into the next day. If there remained a sun in the solar system, it had mournfully denied its warmth and light to this corner of the planet. The iron rich, red mud splattered and the water sprayed up from the pounding hooves of a Georgia Militia squad. Galloping at the head of the group were Titus Ogilvie and his only surviving son, Alton. Bringing up the rear was a patrol of six U. S. Cavalry soldiers commanded by Lieutenant Peter Tanner.

Michael and Ezekiel were replacing some poles in the corral fence out by the Drummond's barn when they heard the thunder of horses coming off the main road. Raindrops hissed angrily in the small fire just outside the barn door. Charlie Swimmer paused from hammering a new shoe on the Drummonds' work horse. They all looked up toward the porch where William had appeared with his spectacles on and some legal papers in his hand. The militiamen and the cavalry patrol slowed their horses to a walk as they neared the house.

"Good day to you, gentlemen," William greeted them. "What brings you out in such inclement weather?"

"You know damn well why we're here, Drummond," Alton Ogilvie growled.

Lieutenant Tanner brought his horse up from the rear and stopped close to William. "Good morning, sir," he touched his hat respectfully. Peter found the circumstances awkward and uncomfortable, but he was determined to get through it. "Sorry to trouble you. Truth is, we've been scouring the countryside in search of Thomas Walker." He looked at Michael, adding, "And his son, James."

The militia sergeant, a large, thick-bodied man with a thin, stringy blonde beard, scowled irritably at the army lieutenant who had so authoritatively injected himself into the proceedings. He leaned forward on his saddle and spat in the dirt.

"They murdered Mr. Ogilvie's boy, Cephus, and his nephew, Randolph Bogen out of Atlanta."

Titus Ogilvie, bitter and steel-eyed, glared at William. His voice was soft, yet undeniably cold. "I'm certain Mr. Drummond knows all about it."

William stared back, unflinching. The militia sergeant looked from one to the other, waiting for further exchange. When neither man spoke, the sergeant felt obliged to elaborate. "Seems purt' near the whole town turned out for the funeral. And everybody for miles around."

"Everybody 'cept the *Drummonds*," Alton put in with an accusing tone.

"And the Walkers," Titus added.

"Yes. Well...my sympathies, Mr. Ogilvie, on the loss of your son," William's words sounded almost sincere, but the Ogilvies weren't certain. Michael walked up from the barn, reaching the porch just as Susanna came out, her raised eyebrows a query directed at Lieutenant Tanner.

"They got what they deserved!" Michael said gruffly.

"That's enough, Michael," William cautioned him.

"Nobody deserves to die like they did!" Alton actually believed his brother and his cousin had been brutally wronged, but

160

Michael wasn't moved.

"They do if they rape innocent women and murder old men!"

Alton jabbed the muzzle of his rifle right against Michael's chest. "Watch your mouth, boy." He gave the gun a little push before withdrawing it to rest across his saddle. Michael saw the look in his father's eye and forced himself to restrain his temper.

Peter Tanner caught a glimpse of movement from the second floor window just above them. He recognized Annie Walker peering from between the curtains, but she stepped away from the window when she saw him looking at her. His eyes came back to the porch and Susanna, who knew too well what he had seen overhead. She looked down, embarrassed.

"Do you know where Walker is?" Titus finally asked William, broaching the palpable tension between them. William remained silent, wondering if his revulsion for Ogilvie was as obvious as it felt.

"If you know, Mr. Drummond—or you, Michael—it's best you tell us," Peter advised. Another silence ensued and the stare-down continued.

"I'll ask you again," Titus never took his eyes off William. "Do you know where Thomas Walker is? Or his boy?"

"I'm under no obligation to answer your questions," William said, no longer masking his disdain.

"If you're coverin' for them good-for-nothin' Injuns that killed my brother, you'll answer to me!" Alton said loudly.

William kept his eyes on Titus, but Alton didn't miss the chill in his voice. "Don't you threaten me, boy. Not on my own property."

"I'm sure you won't mind if we just look around a bit," Titus suggested.

"Do you have a search warrant, Lieutenant Tanner?" William looked at Peter.

"No, sir. Actually, we don't...."

"Hell," Titus bellowed, "you know how them Injuns are, Drummond. Sneakin' around. Hidin'. They might be right there in your own barn. Waitin' to slip in and murder you and your whole family in your sleep."

If it was difficult for William to maintain his attorney's calm and composure, no one else saw it. "Lieutenant Tanner," he said with practiced control, "escort these men off my property."

"They cut my brother's throat and scalped my cousin!" Alton protested.

"Could be the start of an Indian uprising, Mr. Drummond,"

Peter argued unconvincingly. "Can't be too careful."

"Get out," William turned to the militia sergeant. "Now. All of you."

A fleeting look passed between Peter and Susanna. She clearly expected him to take control of the situation. At the same time, she couldn't fathom anyone disobeying a direct order from her father. Grudgingly, the militiamen started back toward the main road. Titus and Alton brought their mounts uncomfortably close to William and Michael.

"We'll catch Walker," Alton sneered bitterly. "And his boy. And we'll hang 'em."

Titus leaned down toward the Drummonds to add, "And anybody caught helpin' is gonna hang right along side of 'em." Father and son spurred their horses to catch up with the militiamen.

Lieutenant Tanner tipped his hat politely to William, then to Susanna on the porch. "Only doing my duty, Mr. Drummond. I hope you understand."

"Just go, Lieutenant."

"Miss Susanna...." Peter looked toward the porch, then motioned to his men and they galloped after the others.

* * * * * * *

Annie, still in the throes of a bottomless depression, continued to look out the window of Michael's room at nothing in particular.

"You know they're going to kill James and my father," she said to Michael, watching her from the trunk at the foot of the bed. "They'll hunt them down like mad dogs."

"No they won't," Michael wished he could have sounded more convincing.

Elizabeth, passing in the hallway, paused at the open door and looked in, first at Annie then at her son, silently asking if everything was all right. She waited but no one spoke. After Elizabeth left, they heard her footsteps fading down the hallway. Annie turned from the window with a faint smile at Michael's naïveté.

"Michael, I can't stay here forever—like a prisoner. We have to get on with our lives."

Michael rose and went to the window. He put his arms around her the way he had wanted to at the funeral. She allowed herself to be folded into the warmth of his comforting embrace. "I'll

162

go and find James and your father."

"Then what?"

"I don't know," he shook his head. "Maybe we should all go west. Away from here." Annie pushed him back to arm's length and looked at him with her brows pinched in question. He had obviously been giving it some thought. "James and your father can't stay here," he answered her look. "We all know that. And I would never keep you here—away from your family." He looked at her for a long time then pulled her back into his arms. "Everything will be all right. You'll see."

She lifted her face to his and they kissed—a single, brief but tender kiss. She then rested her head against his chest. They stood there silently, their arms around each other. He breathed in the intoxicating herbal fragrance of her soft, silky hair.

* * * * * * *

Michael sat on the stool in the mud room by the back door and pulled on his knee-high Cherokee boots. He could hear his mother and sister in the kitchen speaking in low tones.

"Well, how long is she going to be here?" Susanna asked impatiently.

"Shh!" Elizabeth scolded her quietly. "As long as necessary, Susanna. And not another word from you about it!"

Michael took his fringed, doe-skin jacket from the wooden peg and grabbed his long-rifle from behind the door. He checked his Collier revolving-barrel pistol, shoved it into his belt and opened the door. He was about to step outside when he felt a gentle tug at his sleeve. His mother had come from the kitchen.

"Be careful, son," she said softly. The love and approval he saw in her eyes meant more than any words could express. He went out, letting his mother close the door behind him.

* * * * * * *

Michael walked endlessly through the hilly terrain, leading Midnight up and down the steep, rocky embankments of the Snowbird Mountains. This lower range of the Appalachians lay in the far southwest tip of North Carolina above the Hiwassee River. Michael had ridden hard all night and well into the morning. When the land started to rise and became rockier, his pace had slowed. He didn't know exactly where he was going. He and James had ridden into this hilly cave region a few times with some other Cherokee boys. One of them, Joe Drywater, had experienced a great spiritual encounter in the caves. He claimed to have met and spoken with the spirit of an ancient Shawnee medicine man who had identified himself as Red Pony. Michael, James and the other Cherokee boys had not seen Red Pony, but they certainly couldn't deny that the changes in Joe were real and intense. And he had never been the same after that. He often spoke to Red Pony with the other boys present and assured them Red Pony was speaking back to him. Joe was never boastful when relating his conversations with Red Pony. He always spoke of his spirit mentor in a quiet and reverential manner. Red Pony frequently gave Joe knowledge and advice to pass along to various members of the tribe. Many of them believed Joe because there was no other way Joe could have known some of the private, intimate information Red Pony had revealed to him. Joe died about a year later of pneumonia. After Joe's burial, there followed a brief period of anticipation among his family and friends who wondered if Red Pony would elect to reveal himself to another member of their circle. But the Shawnee spirit guide had, apparently, moved on to other places, other times.

Michael reached the top of a hill and stopped at a large outcropping of granite. He looked out across a narrow canyon with steep, wooded sides and tried to decide which way to go. Without warning, an arrow struck the trunk of the skinny pine beside him, only inches from his head. Michael dropped to one knee, drawing his Collier pistol. He looked in the direction from which the arrow had come but saw nothing. Suddenly the tip of a bow tapped him on the shoulder from behind. He dove to the side, rolling away from the contact, and came up with his pistol cocked and ready to fire.

"Some tracker you are!" James grinned down at him. Michael was instantly on his feet and they were locked in a clinging embrace. There was a time when they would have rolled and wrestled for half an hour until, exhausted, they would plunge into the soothing waters of a nearby creek or river. But those playful times lay buried far beneath the tragedy of recent days.

"It wasn't easy finding you," Michael admitted.

"That's the idea."

"How did you know I was coming?"

James didn't have to say anything. Five young Cherokee men—the youngest fifteen, the oldest not quite twenty—stepped from the very same trees where Michael had been looking and had seen nothing. A couple of these scouts were armed with

164

blowguns—ordinarily used only for hunting small game—while another had a bow and arrows like the one James had used. One carried an old pistol—which Michael doubted would even fire—and one had a rifle that most likely belonged to his father or grandfather. James led the way through the rocks and trees.

"How is Annie?"

"Almost had to tie her up to keep her from following me here," Michael answered.

* * * * * * *

A fire crackled inside a rock circle in the center of the hideout cave. Thomas Walker sat near the flames, smoking a long pipe. He was quiet. Tired and troubled. A number of Cherokee men and older boys, including Thomas Walker's brother-in-law, John Sixkiller, lined the shadowy walls of the spacious cavern. Blankets, supplies and food had been stockpiled around the hideout, which was large enough to accommodate the horses. Michael was certain he heard the running water of an underground river from somewhere deeper in the earth. He and James sat across the fire from Thomas. No one spoke for a long time. Since Michael was the new arrival, they all quietly awaited his report.

"Annie's safe," he tried to read Thomas through the smoke. "No one will bother her at my house." He waited, but still there was no reaction from Annie's father. Finally Michael added, "She misses you."

Thomas drew on the pipe a few more times and thoughtfully studied the feather hanging from the pipe's long stem. When he spoke, it was so soft Michael had to lean forward. "You will have to take care of her now," he said, then paused before adding, "...if you still want her."

Michael knew his meaning and found it embarrassingly difficult. Annie had always been a special light in her father's life. A rare gem that in the eyes of others, her father feared, would now appear tarnished. Defiled. Nothing, of course, could diminish her in his own eyes, but Thomas knew that his and James's act of revenge would not end without serious repercussions. They had killed white men. Thomas was beginning to taste the bitter reality that he might never see his precious Annie again in this life. All of this Michael read as clearly as if it had been painted in cruel pictographs on the cave walls surrounding them. He found no words to respond to Thomas's statement, so he changed the subject.

"The militia came," Michael announced while staring at the hypnotic, dancing flame. "Titus Ogilvie is out for blood. They've got the army into it. Two Cherokee cabins have been burned."

Thomas shook his head. "It's only the beginning."

"They beat Charlie Blackhorse for not telling them where you were," Michael expanded his report. "Beat him bad. I don't think he'll make it."

"You took a big risk coming here," John Sixkiller squatted near the fire and Thomas passed him the pipe.

"I promised Annie I'd talk to you."

"It's good to see you, *U-we-tsi*," Thomas said.

Michael noted this new form of address. Thomas had called him *my son*. "I think we should go west," Michael decided to share the idea he had expressed to Annie.

"Are you crazy?" James was stunned. "That's what you came here to say?!"

"Things are different now, James! Can't you see?" Michael pleaded.

"We won't leave our land!" James shouted. His angry words echoed down through the miles of networked caverns extending into the earth beneath them. He waited for his father, his uncle and the others to agree with him and wasn't prepared for his father's response.

"He's right," Thomas looked at John and some of the older men. "Things are different now."

"I won't go!" James insisted. "They'll have to kill me first!"

Michael studied the faces of each man. No more words were needed. They all knew that killing them was exactly what the militia intended to do. Thomas passed the pipe to his son, but James declined, still piqued that any of them would even consider leaving their Cherokee hills to go west. He stalked out to the mouth of the cave, standing with his back to them as a gesture of rejection. John Sixkiller handed the pipe to Michael, who smoked, then passed it back across the fire to Thomas.

* * * * * * *

Michael spent another hour and a half talking with Thomas and the others, reporting to them the latest events from Pine Hill, New Echota and some of the other Cherokee towns. When it came time to leave, Michael was troubled—and hurt—that James continued to sulk, refusing to talk to him, to even look at him.

166

Thomas came out of the cave and joined Michael who was putting the saddle back on Midnight. He took an amulet from around his neck and placed it in Michael's hand.

"Give this to Annie," he said and folded Michael's fingers around the talisman. "It is strong medicine." Michael put the necklace carefully into his jacket pocket and was about to mount up when James grabbed him, locking him in a strong embrace.

"It isn't your fault, *tso-s-da-da-nŭ*," he said in Michael's ear. Michael knew the reconciliation was sincere from the way James had called him *my brother*.

"I'll come back in a few days," Michael promised. "Maybe I'll bring Annie. I know she wants to see you." He sprang up onto Midnight and was starting back down the mountain trail when two of the young scouts came running up through the brush.

"*A-ni-ya-wi-s-gi!*" they yelled. "*Yo-ne-ga! A-ni-ya-wi-s-gi!*"

There was instant pandemonium at the announcement of approaching soldiers and militia. The Cherokees scrambled for the cave, grabbing weapons and pulling their horses back into the cavern after having taken them out for some grass and sunshine. The first shot killed one of the young scouts. Cherokees caught too far from the mouth of the hideout were forced to dive into the brush. James pushed his father back inside. Michael tossed James his Collier pistol and pulled his rifle from the saddle.

More shots were fired from the surrounding trees. One Cherokee fell and was dragged back inside the cave. Michael spun his horse around, frantically trying to locate the source of the gunfire. Another shot exploded from Michael's left. Midnight staggered sideways and fell, throwing Michael to the ground behind a large boulder. Michael, stunned by the fall, stared gape-mouthed at the horse he'd owned and loved for so many years. Down! Perhaps Midnight had only slipped on a rock or had stepped into an animal burrow, Michael tried to convince himself. He reached for the horse's bridle but drew his hand back when he saw the enormous exit wound made by what must have been a Sharps .50-caliber rifle.

From behind the big rock Michael saw the Cherokees courageously defending themselves with their ancient guns, their bows and arrows and their blowguns. Michael spotted a militiaman—one he had seen riding with Titus Ogilvie the day they came looking for Thomas and James—charge out of the brush only to be struck by an arrow in the stomach. He lay moaning and writhing in pain. The militiaman who darted out to drag him back to safety was hit with a blow dart in the eye and fell screaming on

167

top of his comrade, breaking the arrow off at the entry point and setting off a howling duet. Michael finally gathered his wits and raised up over the boulder. He lay his rifle across the top of the rock and fired at some militia movement in the thick undergrowth thirty or forty yards across the clearing. He wasn't certain if he had hit anything.

James raced from the mouth of the cave at a full run and hurled himself behind the boulder with Michael, who was reloading his rifle.

"I'm sorry, *Tsi-mi!*" Michael apologized as he rammed the rod down the barrel. "They must have followed me here!"

"No. You're too good for that. They were bound to find us."

He popped up, fired a shot from the Collier pistol, crouched down while he rotated the barrel, then back up to fire again.

They paused to listen. The momentary reload lull created a haunting silence which only heightened the ringing in their ears from the succession of gunshots. Across the clearing, little patches of buckskin brown and army blue winked among the leaves when militiamen and soldiers shifted for a better vantage point or safer cover.

"*E-hi-na-go-i!*" a voice yelled. "Come out!"

Michael thought he recognized the voice of the militia sergeant who had been at his house a few days earlier. Then he heard a voice which there was no mistaking.

"Thomas Walker! James Walker! Give yourselves up! You can not escape!"

"It's Peter Tanner! That son-of-a-bitch!"

"This is the United States Army," Peter shouted. He was playing it strictly by the book, as usual. "I can promise you protection if you surrender." He waited an appropriate length of time to allow the subjects to comply. When no capitulation was forthcoming, he repeated the next part of his textbook warning. "I cannot be responsible for your safety if you continue to resist."

Michael and James peered cautiously over the boulder, trying to locate Peter. Michael spotted him and nudged James. As soon as James had Peter in view, he jumped up and fired the pistol, and the battle erupted again with renewed intensity.

Alton Ogilvie had been circling to his left to a flanking position. He parted the thick brush and was delighted to find himself with an unobstructed view of Michael Drummond. He raised his rifle and aimed, but before he could squeeze the trigger, John Sixkiller pounced on him. The two men tumbled out through the brush and into the clearing. John came up on top, his knife raised, ready to plunge it home when a shot exploded from only a few yards away. The bullet pierced John Sixkiller's neck from behind, severing the spinal cord. Alton shoved the dead Cherokee to one side and saw his father holding the smoking pistol.

In his flanking maneuver Alton had left himself exposed and perilously close to the Cherokees' position. He wasted no time scrambling back into the bushes, still determined to get a shot at his original target. From the thick cover of the undergrowth, he fired at Michael but missed. More of the militiamen had begun circling in similar flanking moves to both sides of the cave opening. Michael and James continued the fire fight from the protection of the boulders, but their location had become more vulnerable and the militiamen were closing in.

"*Tsi-ne-na! I-da-da-nŭ-na!*" James shouted to Michael above the roaring gunfire. "Let's go! Let's get out of here!"

They stepped from the cover of the rocks and drew fire from the militia and the soldiers. Both heard the balls whistling past their heads, but none found its mark. Michael and James fired again, then reloaded on the run as they retreated toward the mouth of the hideout. By attracting attention to themselves, they had allowed some of the younger Cherokee boys and a couple of the older men to dash from the opposite flank back to the safety of the cave.

When Michael and James reached the opening, they were met by the deafening thunder of hoofbeats. The Cherokee horses exploded from the hideout, their riders crouched low against their backs. Thomas Walker and the others made a hard right, headed down a steep slope toward thicker woods that would protect them until they reached the Hiwassee River.

The soldiers rushed from concealment directly opposite the cave, firing as rapidly as they could. Thomas was the first to get hit. He was riding low against his horse's neck, his arms stretched forward, guiding and urging the animal on. The bullet struck him in the left side, inches below the armpit. Because of his riding posture, he was able to hang on for some distance before losing his grip and tumbling off when the horse jumped a fallen log.

James and Michael provided cover fire for the fleeing Cherokees. Michael thought he had seen Thomas get hit, but Thomas had remained aboard the horse long enough for Michael to convince himself Thomas was all right. Seconds later, however, they saw him fall.

The boys abandoned the safety of the rocks and were running, sliding, catapulting down the slope toward Thomas under a barrage of gunfire from the militia and the soldiers. Many shots had already been fired by the army patrol before Peter recognized Michael Drummond.

"Hold your fire! Hold your fire!" Peter shouted. He had expected to apprehend, possibly even be forced to kill a number of Indians here today, but he hadn't anticipated seeing the brother of the woman he hoped to marry. The soldiers ceased firing on command, but militiamen fired at least ten more rounds before their guns were silenced.

James and Michael finally reached Thomas. They dropped to their knees on either side of him. James cradled his dying father in his arms. Thomas looked into the eyes of both boys, then tightly gripped James's arm and pulled him down close. He struggled to speak, but the words never came. The light faded from Thomas Walker's eyes and he was gone. James gently lowered his father to the ground. Without shedding a tear, he looked at Michael.

"*Tso-s-da-da-nŭ*," he whispered sadly, "*E-to-da u-yo-hu-sŭ*." Our father is dead.

* * * * * * *

The long, single-file column of militiamen and soldiers led their captives back down the rocky, narrow trails through the Snowbirds. Lieutenant Peter Tanner headed up the procession. Michael Drummond and James Walker, their hands tied behind them, sat back-to-back atop *U-no-le*. Michael, facing the rear, was forced to view the lifeless body of his friend's father draped across the horse behind them. It was difficult to endure, but Michael was glad it was he and not James.

A few of the other captured Cherokees were riding, but most were forced to walk, hands tied behind them, each Cherokee linked to the one ahead and the one behind by a rope around his neck. Alton Ogilvie rode up from the rear, pushing roughly past other swearing militiamen and grumbling soldiers until he had come alongside Michael and James. He fixed his wrathful glare on them.

"What are you staring at, *si-qua*?!" Michael barked, knowing the pukish oaf wouldn't understand he'd been called a pig. Michael concluded the insult by spitting at Alton. With squinting deliberation Alton flipped his rifle backwards and struck Michael in the face with its butt, almost knocking him off the horse.

"We warned you, Drummond," Alton growled. "Now we're

going to hang the both of you!" Alton was himself almost unseated when his horse collided with Lieutenant Tanner's. Peter had ridden back from the head of the column and forced his mount between Alton and the captives.

"These are *my* prisoners, Ogilvie. Stay away from them," Peter warned.

Alton kept his hate-filled glare on Michael and James for a while, then rode on toward the front. Peter rode behind his prisoners, eyeing Michael's bleeding nose and split lip.

"You all right, Michael?"

Michael stared silently at Peter for a long time, then looked away, refusing to speak. Peter shrugged and moved past them.

* * * * * * *

A door had been taken from somewhere in Pine Hill—or Titusville—and a crude, hand-painted message had been scrawled across the top: *This is wat we do too murdring indains.* The bloody corpse of Thomas Walker was nailed to the door beneath the sign. Large spikes driven through his coat on either side of his neck and a spike beneath each arm held him to the door like some limp, blood-soaked rag doll, his head slumped forward on his chest. This unhinged bier had been propped against a hitching rail in front of Ogilvie's store for public viewing. It was the customary way of publicly exhibiting slain criminals. A few feet away in the alley next to the store sat a wagon loaded with the bodies of the other Cherokees killed in the apprehension of *the cutthroat Cherokee outlaw, Thomas Walker, and his murderous son, James.*

Michael Drummond could see Thomas's body on the door and the wagon in the alley. He stood on the crude, wooden cot and peered out through the tiny barred opening high on the wall of Titusville's rat-infested stockade. James waited for a turn at the window, but Michael hopped down, blocking his way. Their hands were manacled in front, with a chain running from the wrists down to their shackled feet. Dried blood from his broken nose still darkened the lower half of Michael's face, giving him the appearance, in the shadowy cell, of having a dark but closely cropped beard.

"Don't bother. Nothing to see," he lied to James, hoping to spare him the sight of his father's body on public display. Their eyes met and James understood his meaning. He took a seat on the other cot and leaned back against the damp, moldy wall. Neither spoke for a long time, each trying to ignore the foul stench from the rusted

171

bucket in the corner. This was where they were expected to urinate and defecate. The straw ticking was gone from the end of each cot, taken by former prisoners to clean themselves after squatting over the pail.

"How long before they hang us?" James mused.

"We're not going to hang," Michael answered unconvincingly. "Father has gone back to see General Wool."

James had already experienced first-hand Wool's inability to make tough decisions. He snorted his opinion of Michael's half-hearted answer.

"Tanner promised he wouldn't let anything happen until Father gets back," Michael said, needing the reassurance as much as James.

"Your father is making a lot of enemies," James said, staring blankly at the opposite wall.

"And a lot of friends, *tso-s-da-da-nŭ*," Michael answered with a faint smile.

* * * * * * *

William Drummond found himself staring once again across the expansive desk of General John Ellis Wool. This trip, it appeared, was proving more fruitful than the first. General Wool dipped the feathered quill in the ink and scratched his signature on the document before him. He carefully blotted at the name and blew on it to speed the drying.

"This will secure the release of your son," the general said, then added with a frown, "I'm afraid, there's little I can do for the Walker boy." He extended the paper across the desk.

William, stunned by the general's words, held the document in front of him without looking at it. "But General, surely—considering the brutalities committed against his family...his mother...his sister..."

General Wool pinched the bridge of his nose where it joined his face between his closely set, beady eyes. He inhaled deeply, then picked up the quill pen once more and scratched his signature on a second document. When he had finished writing, he blew the letter dry, folded it and picked up the candle, allowing drops of molten wax to fall on the paper. He retrieved a gold engraved stamp from a velvet-lined cherrywood box on his desk and pressed his seal into the soft wax. Then the general opened his desk drawer and brought forth a bottle and two glasses. He poured the drinks, pushed one across toward William and downed the other.

"I tried to warn you," Wool reminded William of their earlier meeting. "This sort of thing was bound to happen. It was just the spark they were waiting for. And now it's gotten too big." He paused to study his empty glass as though expecting it to magically refill itself, then looked again to William. "Drink up, Mr. Drummond. Good whiskey's hard to come by."

"This is an inexcusable miscarriage of justice!"

General Wool slammed his hand down hard on the desk, bolted out of his chair and leaned across toward William, much as he had done at their first meeting, but this time with more emotion.

"You still don't get it, do you?!" he strained with frustration, not so much at William's presumed ignorance as his own inability to alter the immutable course of events unfolding exactly as he had predicted. "The President of the United States wants that land! He wants those people out of there! Wake up, for God's sake! Justice doesn't have a damn thing to do with it!" He sat back down and leaned back in the plush leather chair. Their eyes locked in understanding and William knew the truth had been spoken. After a long silence, he took the glass and swallowed the whiskey in a single gulp.

General Wool was tired—a fatigue of the soul more than of the body. He rose again and handed William the second, sealed letter.

"Please, deliver this to Lieutenant Tanner," he said, then answered William's puzzled look. "I'm ordering the execution by military firing squad. Under Tanner's command."

"Sir...?"

"Less of a mob spectacle than a hanging," the general explained. "Gives the impression that things are still under control."

"I see," William said. "A good *impression*. I'm sure the Walker boy will feel much better knowing his death is making a good *impression*."

General Wool ignored the barbed reply and poured another drink. He turned to face the window, signalling an end to their meeting.

"You have a long journey ahead of you. I suggest you get started."

William was disappointed and upset, but he knew the futility of pleading further. He carefully stowed the documents in the inside pocket of his coat. The burning in his throat and the ache in the pit of his stomach were due more to his own feeling of impotence than to the whiskey or his anger at Wool's characteristic military indifference at failing to resolve a complex dilemma.

* * * * * * *

Michael balanced precariously on the cot in the stockade cell and peered out the tiny, bar covered window. James sat in his usual place—on his cot with his back against the wall. He heaved a great sigh of resignation, accepting the inevitability of his fate.

"Who's going to bury my father after they're tired of showing him off?" he asked in a hollow voice. Michael looked down at his friend. Not once had James climbed onto the cot to look out the window, but he knew. He knew. "I've seen it all before," he answered Michael's look.

"We'll bury him, James. You and me," Michael tried to sound hopeful. "Father will have us out of here first thing in the morning."

"I want you to bury him beside my mother," James said as though he hadn't heard Michael. "Bury *both* of us next to her."

"Don't talk like that," Michael snapped. They reacted to the sound of the key grating in the heavy, rusted lock. The massive door creaked open. Alton Ogilvie and two of the militiamen who had participated in their capture stepped in. They were all heavily armed. Behind them stood the bearded, dirty jailer with two metal plates of nondescript, greasy food which he dropped onto the narrow shelf beside the door. One of the militiamen pointed his rifle up at Michael standing on the cot.

"What the hell you think you're doin'?" he asked suspiciously.

"Looks like he's tryin' to bust out!" the tall, red-haired militiaman suggested. Alton grabbed the front of Michael's jacket and dragged him down off the cot. Michael tripped on his shackles and dropped to his knees, but Alton jerked him roughly to his feet and slammed him against the wall. James jumped up and with one long hop thrust himself between Alton and Michael. Alton grabbed James by the scruff of the neck and drove his face into the wall.

"I'm gonna enjoy watching you two hang," he drooled tobacco spit, wiping his chin with the back of his hand.

The red-haired militiaman took a chunk of meat from one of the plates. "Seems a waste to feed 'em if you just gonna turn right around and hang 'em," he spoke with his mouth full, launching bits of food through the air. He greedily reloaded with a handful from the other plate.

174

Alton spun James around, their noses only inches apart. "Ever seen a man hang?" Alton sneered. "It ain't purty. You shit your pants and pee all over yourself." Alton's eyes suddenly went dull at the sound of the familiar voice behind him.

"Ogilvie!" Lieutenant Peter Tanner shouted. "I told you to stay away from my prisoners!"

"Just brung 'em some food."

"Get out," Peter ordered.

The other two militiamen wasted no time. Each grabbed a dripping handful of the prisoners' food as they exited. Reluctantly, Alton released his grip on James and squeezed past the lieutenant. The jailer attempted to follow, but Peter stopped him.

"You open this door again—for anyone but me—and I'll have you horse whipped," Peter said softly. The jailer looked into the young officer's cold, unblinking eyes then hurried out. Tanner studied the two prisoners thoughtfully, then left without a word. Michael and James listened to the heavy click of the lock.

"You all right?" Michael asked.

James didn't answer. Michael sat down and James shuffled to the cot opposite him. He wiped a trickle of blood from his upper lip with his shoulder. Michael knew his friend had something to say and he waited patiently.

"You've got to promise me something, *tso-s-da-da-nŭ*," James began. Michael sensed the gravity by the way James had uttered the familiar phrase *my brother*. "When they're ready to hang me—"

"I said don't talk like that," Michael cut him off. "Father will get us out of here—"

James grabbed Michael's arm and pulled him close. "Stop dreaming, *Mi-ki*! Your father's a good man. He's done everything he can. You'll be out of here tomorrow. Me—they'll hang." James drew a deep breath and was calm personified. Michael was in awe of his stoic acceptance. "So. Here's what I want you to do...."

Michael couldn't face his lifelong friend. If he could have reached his ears, he would have covered them to block out the words. He didn't even remember moving, but when James finished speaking, Michael was standing near the far wall with his back turned.

"I can't do it, *tso-s-da-da-nŭ*," Michael whispered hoarsely.

"You have to."

"You can't ask me to do this! You have no right!"

James rose and, this time more gently, turned Michael to face him. "*Right?*" he asked. "We're not talking about *right*! Look out

175

that window! Look out there! Tell me if what you see is *right!*"

Michael pleaded, his voice choked with emotion. "James, I can't."

"You're the best shot with a long rifle I've ever seen," James remained tranquil and resigned to the brilliance of his plan. "You could hide on top of the store." Michael shook his head no, but James pressed on. "One shot. Just before they put the rope around my neck."

"James..."

James stretched his chains to their limit and by bending down was barely able to touch a fingertip just above his nose, right between the eyes. "One shot. Right here. Pow! It's finished." He grabbed Michael's arm again, waiting for an answer. Michael pulled free and staggered across the cell, but James followed relentlessly. "Michael, I'm begging you...don't give these bastards the satisfaction!"

"Father will be here in a few hours," Michael retreated to his earlier optimism. "Everything will be all right. You'll see."

"Let me die like a man!" James beseeched. "With the last shred of honor left to my family! They've taken everything else! Give me that much!"

"I won't do it! I can't!" Michael fought the tears.

James pushed him back, pinned him against the wall and got right in his face. His voice was hoarse with desperate pleading. "I'd damn sure do it for you!" They searched each other's eyes until James relaxed his grip and lowered his head, resting it on Michael's chest. "If you love me, *tso-s-da-da-nŭ,*" Michael barely heard his muffled words, "you will do this thing."

Michael leaned his head back against the cool, damp wall and bit his lower lip until he tasted the salty sweetness of his own blood. He couldn't speak. And he could no longer stay the river of tears rising from the pit of his being.

* * * * * * *

Stray shafts of moonlight fingered their way through the parted curtains and wrapped themselves softly around Annie Walker's shoulders. She sat on the edge of Michael's bed, staring into the darkness that crouched in the corner like a spiritual panther waiting to devour her. She hardly stirred when the door opened. Reba stepped in, lifting the oil lamp a little higher to spread its light.

"You jes' gon' sit here in the dark, Miss Annie?" she asked

softly. She set the lamp on the dresser and went about quietly gathering some of Michael's clothes.

"What are you doing?" Annie finally asked.

"Mistah William done rode all into the night to get back here. I ain't never seed that man so tuckered out," Reba reported, glad Annie had broken her long silence. "Gon' be in town at the crack of dawn to get Mistah Michael outa dat jail."

Annie's interest had been aroused. She shifted on the bed to follow Reba's movements.

"What about my brother?"

"Sorry, Missy," Reba rolled up a clean pair of pants and laid them on the dresser. "I don't know nothin' 'bout that. But I'm sure Mistah William gon' do what he can to help that boy."

"Reba! Reba, where are you?!" Susanna's irritated voice sounded from the hall seconds before she appeared in the doorway holding a long, partially sewn garment and sporting her well-worn mask of royal irritation. Her words came rapid fire, like a stick raked annoyingly along a picket fence. "There you are! What are you doing? You're supposed to be making my dress! It's past midnight! The Governor's Ball is in three days. I can't show up with Lt. Tanner in some old rag! Just look at this! I don't like it at all! You have to do it over!"

Reba, with a pair of boots in her hand, glared at Susanna. The black woman shook her head and looked at Annie as though asking, *Can you believe this impudent child?* Annie was speechless. Embarrassed. Reba set the boots down and opened the wardrobe to fetch a clean shirt. Susanna petulantly stamped her foot.

"Now, Reba! Now!"

Reba slammed the wardrobe door and spun around, her hands positioned defiantly on her ample hips. "You some piece o' work, Missy!" she shook her head, then picked up the clothes and began advancing toward the door, sternly rebuking Susanna with each step. "Yo' brother sittin' in da jail house, people talkin' like he gon' be hanged, and you fussy-fidgetin' 'bout yo' pretty lieutenant and the Governor's Ball! Lawd, sometimes I jes' don't know..." She reached the door and pushed roughly past Susanna. In a few seconds they could hear Reba stomping down the stairs, dropping her full weight into each step. It was Susanna's turn to look at Annie with a shrug and an expression that asked *What's wrong with her?* Annie had no answer for either of them. This sort of conflict and censure between members of a household were foreign to her.

Annie's thoughts flashed back to the tranquility of the

afternoon she had returned from making love with Michael and found her mother patting out the roll of dough she would place in the oven to become *se-lu ga-du*, her delicious cornbread. The knowing glance and subtle smile that passed between them was typical of the serenity that had always dwelt in the Walker home. And she recalled how she had blushed—and her mother had chuckled softly—when The Old One grinned up at her from his chair and said in Cherokee, *He's a good boy. He makes you happy.*

The memory vanished as swiftly as it had surfaced. Annie stared blankly at Susanna then rose from the bed and approached the door.

"Are you all right?" Susanna asked.

Annie stopped in front of Susanna, their eyes connected, only inches away from each other, yet each knew without question they were worlds apart. Annie said nothing and closed the door in Susanna's face. With her head cocked quizzically to one side, Susanna tossed her hair and dismissed Annie's act as just another peculiar example of Indian behavior. She took off in pursuit of the recalcitrant seamstress.

"Reba! You are so rude to me sometimes!"

* * * * * * *

In the mud room just off the kitchen, Reba helped Elizabeth stuff Michael's things into a leather satchel.

"Thank you, Reba," Elizabeth never failed to show her gratitude to this angel who had watched over her family for so many years. Reba, in her customary manner, patted Elizabeth's hand without speaking. William's exhaustion showed in his face when he came from the kitchen, gnawing a cold chicken leg. Elizabeth buckled the satchel's last strap and placed it beside the back door, then stepped in front of William and gripped the front of his shirt.

"You go upstairs and get a couple hours sleep, dear," she said lovingly. And then her voice grew firm, hard as a bois-d'arc post. "Then, you get yourself into town and you get my baby out of that jail. And don't you ever let anything like this happen again." She took the ravaged chicken bone and pushed him gently toward the stairs. Susanna, carrying the partially made dress, was descending just as William started up. She stopped beside her father and placed a hand on his arm.

"Perhaps all this will wake Michael up," she said. "Teach him to keep his nose out of all this Indian foolishness."

William didn't speak. He gazed sadly at his selfish, naïve daughter and then resumed his silent ascent. From the foot of the stairs Elizabeth watched her husband climb tiredly to the top. She waited until he had disappeared down the hallway before confronting her daughter with fire in her eyes.

"You shut up, young lady! Just go back to making your silly little dress!" Before Susanna could reply, Elizabeth had retreated to the kitchen, leaving her daughter stunned and speechless. A pleased Reba looked on from the mud room door. Susanna held up the dress as a reminder, but Reba was having none of it.

"Well, I sho' ain't sewin' another stitch tonight!" she said loud enough for Elizabeth to hear from the kitchen, should she be inclined to listen. "These ol' bones has had it. Zeke gon' think I done fell over the fence and the hogs ate me!" Laughing softly at her own homespun humor, Reba gave Susanna a condescending pat on the cheek, then went out the back door into the night, headed toward the little house she shared with Ezekiel.

* * * * * * *

The red-orange claws of sunrise slashed in through the tiny window of the stockade cell, painting an enlarged portal on the opposite wall, the space between the shadow bars almost large enough for a man to escape through. The jailer removed the heavy iron shackles from Michael's ankles and stepped back. William was standing just inside the cell door, flanked by the same two militiamen who had been with Alton Ogilvie the night before and behind them were the two soldiers who had appeared with Peter Tanner. Once Michael's hands were free, William gave him the satchel of fresh clothes.

"Your mother sent these," William said, keeping his eyes glued to his son. "Come on. Let's go."

Michael took the satchel but paid it no attention. He looked expectantly at his father. "What about James?"

"He ain't goin' nowhere," the tall, red-haired militiaman said with obvious satisfaction.

William dipped his tired eyes, frustrated and ashamed. "There's nothing I can do right now," he confessed.

"But you will get him out, right?" Michael wanted some assurance.

"Son...we have to go."

Michael knew this was as close as William would come to

acknowledging defeat. "If James doesn't go, I don't go," Michael handed the satchel back to William.

"We throwed you in here, we can damn well throw you out!" the other militiaman swelled with authority.

"You have to go, son," the older of the two soldiers said softly.

For the first time, William looked directly at his son's best friend. "I did everything I could, James."

James felt William's anguish. "It's all right, Mr. Drummond," he tried to ease the tension. "I know you tried. I thank you for that." He rose and gripped Michael's arm with his manacled hands. "*Mi-ki*...take good care of Annie."

The older soldier put his arm around Michael's shoulder and physically led him from the cell. Michael craned his head around, his eyes never leaving his friend. Just before the cell door closed, James stepped toward the opening.

"Remember what I ask of you, *tso-s-da-da-nŭ*."

The heavy door clanged shut and the jailer turned the key.

* * * * * * *

More than a hundred somber Cherokees had gathered to witness the execution of one of their own. Charlie Swimmer and his wife, Eva, had waited outside the stockade. They accompanied William and Michael back across the open square. A few Cherokees acknowledged William as he passed. He felt certain many of their looks carried the burning question, *Where is James Walker?* Two Cherokee medicine men chanted softly while other Cherokees took Thomas Walker's body off the display door and placed the corpse in the back of William's wagon. The bodies of the other dead Cherokees were being transferred from the alley to the carts and wagons of their families.

"Father, isn't there something you can do?" Michael asked just before they reached their own wagon. William avoided the question, devoting his attention to carefully unfolding a blanket to cover Thomas's body. "We can't let them hang James," Michael pleaded.

"They aren't going to hang him, son," William answered. He had delivered the letter from General Wool to Peter Tanner earlier that morning when he requested a couple of soldiers to accompany him in effecting Michael's release to avoid any possible trouble from the Georgia militia. Michael's fleeting moment of false hope for James's freedom was dashed by the look in his father's eyes.

180

* * * * * * *

Lieutenant Tanner studied the milling crowd from the shaded boardwalk in front of *Ogilvie Mercantile*. Titus Ogilvie, his eyes narrowed to squints of displeasure, stepped out of his store to join the young officer.

"Look at this!" he growled. "They're makin' a hero out of this murderin' Injun! A God damn hero! I thought you said this firin' squad was s'pose to keep things under control."

"Things *are* under control, Mr. Ogilvie," Peter assured him, never taking his eyes off the crowd.

"That look like control to you?" Titus snapped back. "I'm tellin' you, Lieutenant, it still ain't too late to hang his worthless Cherokee ass!"

Lt. Tanner held up a hand in a placating gesture. "I'm taking care of this." He signaled to a group of six soldiers in full dress uniform who were standing at attention, rifles balanced at a perfect angle on their shoulders.

"All right, men," Peter said. "It's time."

All eyes watched the squad of six march out in tight formation toward the stockade across the square. There were plenty of militiamen sprinkled throughout the gathering, all heavily armed, resentful and disappointed at being cheated out of their hanging. Their only consolation was in getting to make their presence known as peace keepers, enforcers and intimidators.

The firing squad reached the stockade at the same time James, squinting against the bright sunlight, was led out by the two soldiers who had earlier released Michael. Unable to get his hands high enough to shield his eyes, James strained to scan the crowd. It didn't take him long to find Michael and William. Gradually his eyes adjusted to the brightness. He kept them locked on Michael the entire time he was being escorted across the square.

The soldiers took him to a large post set in the ground in front of the blacksmith shop. Sergeant Adams, the older of the two soldiers, unlocked the shackles from James's wrists. The younger soldier pushed James gently back against the large post, brought the hands around behind and replaced the shackles. A length of rope was then wrapped twice around James's chest and arms and tied off in the rear. All the while, James's eyes never left Michael's.

The crowd parted when Lieutenant Peter Tanner marched stiffly across the square to the killing post. He stopped directly in front of James, intentionally obstructing the prisoner's view of his friend in the crowd. Since childhood they had been adversaries, if not open enemies. Peter, who had so often been the butt of their jokes, the target of their ridicule and contempt, had always sworn he would someday gain the upper hand. This was the upper hand. And it was sweet. Yet, as a United States Army officer charged with the execution of a prisoner for the capital offense of murdering a white man, he was determined that his outward deportment would be official and military, reserving his vengeful gloating for the private chambers of his own heart.

"Do you want a blindfold, James?"

"I thought they were going to hang me," James was confused.

"It's been changed," Peter realized that James had not been informed. He made a mental note to later reprimand Sergeant Adams. "Do you want a blindfold?" he repeated. James didn't answer. Again he scanned the crowd, making eye contact with many of his friends and fellow Cherokees. He found Michael and William, who had shifted so Peter was no longer blocking their line of sight. "Well, then..." Peter said with a dull finality when he saw James wasn't going to answer. He stepped back from the prisoner and motioned to Sgt. Adams who, in turn, signalled two other soldiers. There was shocked confusion when they suddenly pulled four young Cherokee boys from the crowd. One of those chosen was *Tsu-tsu* Swimmer, snatched away before Charlie or Eva could react. A murmur of concern rippled through the gathering. The four youngsters were pushed into a line fifteen paces in front of James.

Titus Ogilvie, watching the proceedings from the boardwalk in front of his store, was a step ahead of the crowd in figuring out what Lieutenant Tanner had in mind, and he liked what he saw. His confidence in the young officer had rebounded. Titus stepped off the boardwalk and plowed through the throng to stand beside Tanner.

"This should take care of that little hero problem," he complimented Peter's strategy.

They watched four of the six firing squad soldiers give their muskets to the Cherokee boys, who handled the weapons clumsily. The remaining two firing squad soldiers trained their rifles on the boys. The four men who had relinquished their rifles drew their pistols, aiming at the heads of the newly appointed firing squad. Once the Cherokees realized that these young boys were being forced to execute one of their own, several—including Charlie Swimmer—attempted to intervene but were kept at bay by the heavily armed Georgia militiamen who would have liked nothing better than to add to the day's bloody spectacle.

"Gotta hand it to you, Tanner," Titus continued his praise. "I'm impressed. Didn't think you had it in you."

"If these boys execute Walker," Peter spoke to the man beside him but kept his eyes on the proceedings, "it'll be difficult for the Cherokees to run around making him into a legend."

James's eyes widened in horror when the realization of Tanner's plan began to sink in. But there was no time.

"Squad!....Ready arms!..." Sergeant Adams belted out the order. The boys seemed confused. They were unsure of what was expected of them and had no idea what *squad...ready arms* meant. The soldiers surrounding them prodded the boys with rifles and pistols, gesturing toward James until the boys finally understood. "Take aim!..." Sergeant Adams continued the command sequence. With more prodding and threatening the boys finally raised the rifles into what passed for an aiming position. Time was running out.

"*Ka! Ka, tso-s-da-da-nŭ!*" James yelled. "Now, my brother! Don't let them do this to these children!"

The militiamen looked nervously around, puzzled by his words, fearful that it was some secret signal meant to trigger a disruption of the execution.

But Michael knew exactly what James meant. His eyes cut rapidly back and forth between James and the young boys who were being compelled to execute him. His throat burned with emotion. Fire shot up the back of his neck.

"Do it, *tso-s-da-da-nŭ*! Now!" James repeated, his voice thick with desperation.

Michael burst from the crowd and ran straight for the firing squad with a piercing yell. He caught them all by surprise, knocking one of the soldiers off his feet and grabbing the rifle from *Tsu-Tsu* Swimmer, who was at the end of the firing line. Michael drove the butt of the rifle hard into the stomach of the second soldier who attempted to stop him, then pushed him into the path of his squad mates.

"Kill him!" the livid Titus Ogilvie shouted at no one in particular. "Shoot that son-of-a-bitch! Kill them both!"

The militia volunteers had fortified themselves with a morning's worth of liquor, hoping for an opportunity to get involved and, if they were lucky, kill an Indian or two. Now, however, they found themselves paralyzed with confusion and indecision. Things were happening too fast.

Michael knew he had only a couple of seconds, and if he

wasted even a fraction of that brief time pondering what he was about to do, he wouldn't be able to complete his mission. He brought the rifle to his shoulder and fired. A hundred pairs of eyes shot like bullets toward the killing post. The entire crowd had been stunned to instant silence—militia, military, local whites and Cherokees alike. James's head snapped sharply back against the post, then slowly tilted forward. There was a dark hole in his forehead, perfectly centered between the eyes just above the brow line.

William Drummond was numb, immobilized by the vision etched indelibly into his brain—a picture that would beleaguer his memory for the remainder of his days. Charlie and Eva Swimmer, like the other Cherokees, were in shock. Many who had witnessed the shooting and who had known of the lifelong friendship between Michael and James quietly exchanged nods of approval. They understood.

In the few seconds following the shot, the soldiers regrouped and encircled Michael with their rifles and pistols while Sergeant Adams disarmed him. By this time Michael was oblivious to them all. His attention remained fixed on the lifeless form of *tso-s-da-da-nŭ, my brother.* It took a few more seconds for Peter Tanner, followed closely by Titus Ogilvie and a handful of militiamen, to reach them.

"Are you crazy?!" Peter yelled. "What the hell's wrong with you, Michael?"

"I thought you had this thing under control, Tanner!" Titus was as upset with Peter as he was with Michael.

"Back off, Ogilvie!" Peter was irritated and embarrassed. He had lost control of what should have been a routine, if unorthodox, execution. Clean and simple. True, the prisoner had been executed, but it wasn't supposed to happen this way. "I could have you charged with murder!" he bellowed again in Michael's face.

Finally, Michael tore his tear-filled eyes from James and turned to the army lieutenant. "No, Peter. You can't do that," his voice choked with emotion. "He's just an Indian, remember? And it's no crime for a white man to kill a Cherokee!"

"There was nothing I could do, Michael," Peter softened his voice and put a hand on Michael's shoulder.

"Right," Michael's eyes were like ice. "You were just doing your duty." He shrugged Peter's hand off his shoulder and jerked free of the soldiers holding him. No one attempted to stop Michael when he pushed through the group, shoving soldiers and militiamen

184

out his way. He went to the killing post and put his arms around his friend. James's head slumped forward onto Michael's chest. Gingerly Michael lifted the head in his trembling hands. His fingertips slipped through the warm, sticky wetness from the exit wound in the back. Blood, still warm and deceptively life-like, flowed into his palms, down his wrists and along the insides of his forearms as though his own veins had been opened; as though the bleeding might never stop. Michael closed his eyes. He knew he didn't want to carry with him for the rest of his life—however brief that might be—the memory of seeing the rear portion of his friend's head gone and the pinkish-gray shreds of brain matter impaled on tiny splinters where the slug had exploded into the post.

With James's head still cradled in both hands, Michael pressed his own forehead against that of his beloved friend. He heard the soft footsteps of Charlie Swimmer and some of the other Cherokees from the crowd closing around them. They began cutting the ropes holding James to the post. Sergeant Adams handed Charlie the key to the wrist shackles and stepped away, knowing his presence there was an unwelcome intrusion on their grief.

The crowd parted quietly for William, who led the horse-drawn wagon toward the post. All he could offer was a consoling hand on his son's shoulder. With tears streaming down his face, Michael finally looked up at his father. The blood from James's wound had stuck to Michael's forehead, giving him the grotesque appearance that he, too, had been shot in the exact same place.

Titus Ogilvie had no more to say. Though he still felt cheated, there was nothing more to shout about, no one to scream at. He would swallow his anger, taking some satisfaction from knowing that the father and son—Thomas and James Walker—who had killed his own son and his nephew were now both dead. But the seeds of dislike for William Drummond and his arrogant son, Michael, had been nurtured into a full grown hatred.

C H A P T E R
10

Annie had spent most of the last several days just staring out the window of Michael's upstairs room. She saw the wagon approaching at a funereal pace from the main road. She saw William and Charlie Swimmer in the wagon's seat, their faces expressionless, tired. She saw Michael, facing away from her, riding in the back of the wagon with its blanket-draped load. And she didn't have to ask what—or who—lay beneath the blankets. Annie knew that the exact details of what had taken place in Titusville that day would never be told to her. Neither William nor Michael, she was convinced, would ever speak about it. But, in light of the special gift she had possessed since childhood, she knew much of it would eventually be revealed to her—in bits and pieces. These revelations would take the form of vivid and terrifying images that would leap out at her from the recesses of her mind, shattering the tranquility of a rainy summer afternoon or stealing their way into her troubled dreams on a dark, cold winter's night. And what Michael would never mention—but she might nevertheless at some point divine—was how on the ride home he had found matted hair and tiny shards of skull bone stuck to his hands, and, beneath his fingernails, fleshy particles he knew to be brain matter. How he had jumped from the wagon and vomited in the middle of the road, the retching spasms offering a welcome disguise for the great sobs that racked his body. How, when he finally felt completely empty—of stomach, of emotion, of thought and spirit—he had walked stoically back to the wagon where his father had stopped and climbed out without a word, waiting with his arm draped patiently across the wagon's wheel. How in silence Michael had ridden the rest of the way home, his hand resting on James's leg as his vacant eyes became lost in the dust swirling up behind the wagon.

Annie saw *U-no-le*, her brother's roan pony, tied to the back of the wagon along with Clancey, William's big, dappled gray. She heard the door open and close below. Seconds later she saw Elizabeth going out to greet them. Walking beside the wagon, Elizabeth reached up to touch her son's arm. He didn't blink, and appeared not to even notice her. Finally, Annie closed the curtain and left the room.

William stopped the wagon near the barn. Ezekiel appeared carrying a pitch fork, and Reba came out from the kitchen and hurried to join them. When Michael climbed stiffly down from the

186

rear of the wagon, Elizabeth was all over him, touching, examining, inspecting, yet she could find no wound. Half his face was still black with dried blood from the captive march back from the caves in North Carolina. But part of his face and half his body were soaked with fresh blood. There had to be a wound, Elizabeth was convinced and renewed her search.

While his mother fussed over him, Michael looked up to see Annie walking down from the house. Behind her, keeping a safe distance as usual, was Susanna, who, Michael knew, had come more out of curiosity than concern.

Michael disengaged himself from his mother, leaving Elizabeth and William clinging to each other. He stepped out to meet Annie. Quietly he put his arms around her. Hugging. Clinging. She looked at his blood covered body, then at the wagon.

"They're all gone," she whispered sadly. "I have no one left now."

"You have us, *U-we-tsi ge-yŭ*," William said, calling her *daughter*. She answered with a weak smile, fully understanding his use of the Cherokee term.

"You were a good friend to my brother," she said and touched Michael's face.

Ezekiel stepped back inside the barn and reappeared with some shovels which he placed in the back of the wagon with the bodies. He untied *U-no-le* and Clancey from the tailgate.

"We ready, Mistah William."

"Thank you, Ezekiel," William started to climb back up to the wagon seat, but Reba stopped him.

"You all ain't goin' nowhere 'til Mistah William and Mistah Michael gets cleaned up and has somethin' to eat," she said with a quiet authority that would brook no challenge. "You, too, Charlie Swimmer."

"She's right, William," Elizabeth agreed. "Come inside."

"You take care of the livin', Miz 'Liz'beth. Reba'll take care of the dead," she said in a way only another woman would fully understand. "Draw me some water, Zeke. I got to clean these mens up for proper buryin'." Reba clutched the reins beneath the horse's chin and led the wagon into the barn. Elizabeth put her arm around William's waist and steered him toward the house. Annie and Michael followed, with Charlie Swimmer a few steps behind.

* * * * * * *

The cemetery was a secluded clearing nestled among towering pines interspersed with blackjack oaks and a few birch. Michael, Ezekiel, William and Charlie had dug the two graves which, like all the others, lay in the traditional east-west alignment. The soil was still fresh on the resting place of Janice Walker and, a few feet beyond, the grave of her grandfather, The Old One.

The Drummond-Walker party were not alone in the Cherokee cemetery. Across the way, Andrew Sixkiller and members of his family had come to bury his brother, John. The members of each group mingled, sharing their grief and offering condolences. Scattered throughout the grounds were the families and friends of the other Cherokees who, like John Sixkiller, had been slain in the capture of the notorious outlaw-murderer, Thomas Walker.

They got what they deserved, had been the judgement whispered in numerous conversations by the civilized white folks, not only in Titusville but throughout the surrounding counties. *They had it comin'*.

* * * * * * *

Michael and Ezekiel worked all the next day sawing logs and splitting wood in front of the barn. The short pieces for the fireplace and the cooking stove were in one pile. Longer pieces for posts and fence railing made up another. Ezekiel, the first to see her, let go of his end of the huge, two-man saw. Michael almost fell backwards but managed to keep his footing. Annie was coming toward them from the corral, leading *U-no-le*, James's roan pony. Tied to the horse's hair and hanging down just behind its ears were three feathers. Michael was speechless. Annie stopped right in front of him. Without a word she kissed Michael gently on the cheek and placed the reins in his hand.

Michael realized he had officially been given his best friend's horse. He patted the side of *U-no-le's* head and watched Annie walk back up toward the house. He knew he loved her more than he could possibly express. He wanted to make love to her again as they had done that day in the meadow a thousand years ago. But he understood she needed more time. He admired and respected her more than he had ever admired or respected anyone else in his life, with the possible exception of her late twin brother.

* * * * * * *

The sun wouldn't be up for another half hour. The back door slammed shut when Reba came in to begin preparing breakfast. She stopped in the doorway of the mud room and grinned at what she saw. Reba's young Cherokee friend already had a robust fire going in the stove. There was a big pot of bubbling oil on top where Annie was cooking Indian fry bread.

"I couldn't sleep," she confessed with a smile.

"Me either," Reba chuckled. "I was layin' there all night wishin' I had me some of that fry bread." Annie's smile broadened and the two women went to work preparing the morning meal for the rest of the family.

* * * * * * *

Michael and Annie finally rode to the place in the woods where their union had first been made complete. But this time there was no fiery passion, no hungry groping, no lingering kisses. They sat side by side, facing opposite directions, arms wrapped around knees bent up in front of them. For a long time they remained silent, absorbing the sun's comforting warmth. Michael knew he had to do this. He took a deep breath before releasing the words he feared might give her reason to despise him.

"*A-s-da-wa-dŭ i-ya-dŭ-ne-di,*" he said softly, staring down between his knees at the grass. There. He had said it. He had admitted to the woman he loved that he, in fact, had pulled the trigger that had ended her brother's life.

Annie said nothing at first. She studied a squirrel scurrying across the far side of the clearing. She watched it leap onto the trunk of a pine and vanish from view to the other side, reappearing thirty feet up, perched on a branch whose green needles twitched delicately in the light breeze.

"He begged me to do it," Michael added, then felt foolish. It sounded like some feeble excuse or a hollow explanation that would somehow ameliorate the gravity of what he had done.

"*A-qua-n'-ta,*" she said with ancient understanding. She knew. Michael wondered how she knew. Who had told her? Perhaps no one had told her. She just knew. "It must have been very hard for you," she said with compassionate understatement, looking at him for the first time since they sat down. Then Annie got up. Michael rose and followed her down to the creek. Neither of them spoke again, their minds filled with memories. Of James. Of the three of them as children. As young adults. Michael took

189

from his pocket the amulet her father had given to him in the cave just minutes before he died. It was a tiny leather pouch barely larger than the ball of his thumb.

Pulling the top open, Michael emptied the contents into his palm: two animal teeth—one a fang, the other a molar—and a tuft of fur. Wolf, he thought. They were *A-ni-wa-ya*, the Wolf Clan. He placed the items back into the small bag and tightened the string, then slipped it over Annie's head and adjusted it to hang centered from her neck. Again, words were unnecessary. Annie recognized the fetish as her father's. And she knew his giving it to Michael to pass on to her was Thomas's way of saying good-bye. In his final communication he had blessed their union.

CHAPTER

11

Michael rode *U-no-le*, the roan that had once belonged to James. Beside him rode Annie on *Ga-tsa-nu-la*—Fast—her father's sturdy black mare. The same one Thomas was riding when he got shot and the same one that had carried his body back from the cave in the Snowbirds. They had gotten word from Charlie Swimmer who heard it from Angus Drywater, a mixed-blood Cherokee-Scot, father of James's and Michael's mystic childhood friend, Joe Drywater. Michael had wasted no time saddling the horses.

They reached the Sixkiller's cabin just as Uncle Andrew was piling the last of his family's belongings high atop the overloaded wagon. Rebecca waited in the seat with their youngest daughter, Nancy. Tiana and Timothy, the middle children, had found places among the well-tied cargo. Mark, as the oldest son, would ride the pony his Uncle John had given him for his thirteenth birthday.

"The river is rising fast, *U-we-tsi*," Andrew had always called Michael *son*, just as Thomas Walker had. "It's time for us to go," he finished tying off the final rope before facing Michael. "Take good care of our little Annie."

Annie inched her mount close to the wagon when Andrew took his seat. She leaned over and hugged her uncle and clung to her aunt's outstretched hand.

"*Do-da-da-go-hŭ-i*," she said good-bye, softly touching Nancy's cheek before they pulled away. Michael and Annie watched the rickety wagon find its way out to the trail leading to the main road. Once Andrew and Rebecca had said their good-byes they never looked back. Only Timothy and Tiana waved from the rear of the wagon.

* * * * * * *

Annie was up early the next morning, slipping downstairs and out the back door. She gathered armloads of wood and had a robust fire crackling beneath the large black cauldron by the time Reba joined her for the weekly laundering of the Drummonds' clothes and bedding. Reba had mentioned it in passing the day before, but she hadn't expected this after Annie had launched into a wistful recounting of her days helping her mother do the wash. When Reba stepped out the back door carrying a basket of laundry, she was met with a broad smile from Annie, gesturing palms up as if to say, *What*

191

took you so long? We have washing to do!

They were both still hard at work hours later, the morning sun proving unpleasantly warm for laboring near the boiling pot. Annie was bent over a large tub, scrubbing up and down on the washboard. She paused when, beneath her own armpit, she glimpsed the pair of shoes behind her. She lowered the shirt back into the soapy water, stood erect and leisurely thumbed a few strands of hair out of her eyes before acknowledging her visitor.

"Susanna...."

"I'll get right to it, Annie," Susanna looked her up and down with her typical open contempt for a mere washwoman. A *Cherokee* washwoman. "I think you should be going."

"Going where?" Annie asked innocently, though she knew quite well the purpose of Susanna's visit.

"I don't know," Susanna said with candied kindness. "You could go live with some of your relatives."

"Do I frighten you that much, Susanna?"

"Frighten me?" Susanna's laugh was as rehearsed as her kindness. "Not in the least. I just think you'd be happier with....with your own people."

"I'm happy being with Michael," Annie said flatly. Susanna had no reply. She hadn't expected the conversation to get this far before Annie capitulated. Annie repeated for clarification. "I will stay with Michael."

Susanna scrutinized the sweaty Cherokee girl before her. A single step closed the distance between them. Susanna had never failed to intimidate when intimidation was her objective. She gave her long, curled locks a familiar toss, then said, "Don't turn this into a struggle between you and me, Annie. I promise—you can't win."

"You always get what you want, don't you?"

"Yes. Yes, I do."

"Then we'll just have to see, won't we?" Annie would not yield an inch. She turned her back to Susanna and resumed her work. Susanna's eyebrows raised in surprise at the strength of this Indian girl's resolve. *How dare she! She's asking for it!* Susanna tossed her hair again and stomped back up toward the house.

Reba had heard the entire exchange. She straightened up, pressed a hand against her lower back and looked at Annie, who glanced up with a little smile. Reba broke into a broad grin and went back to work.

"Lawd, Chil'. Could it be? Has Missy Thang done met her match?"

"We'll just have to see, won't we?" Annie repeated the words she had spoken to Susanna.

* * * * * * *

The luxurious four-horse carriage swung off the main road and onto the lane leading up to the Drummond house. The elegantly clad black driver expertly handled the team and the equally dapper footman sat rigid and formal in his seat atop the rear of the coach. They moved at a leisurely pace up the winding drive, coming to a stop beneath the house's carriage cover.

Ezekiel paused from his yard work and sauntered over to admire the fancy rig, watching the footman as he sprang down from his lofty perch and opened the carriage door for the finely dressed, handsomely groomed Lieutenant Peter Tanner.

Elizabeth Drummond wore a long, beautiful pale-orange-and-black gown that flowed like lava down the conical shape from her tiny waist. She carried two large hat boxes to be opened only when they had arrived at the governor's ball.

"Good afternoon, Mrs Drummond," Peter made a sweeping bow. "Hope I'm not too early."

"Heavens no, Peter!" Elizabeth was more animated than he had seen her in a long time. "I think we're running a bit late. Susanna will be along shortly."

Reba came out carrying two large bags. She looked around impatiently and spotted Ezekiel stroking the horses and chatting with the carriage driver and footman.

"Zeke! You gon' kiss that horse, or you gon' get yo' raggedy butt in there and get the rest of these folks's things?"

Ezekiel shot her the glare he usually displayed when she scolded him in front of others, especially strangers, then hurried obediently inside. He slipped past Susanna's familiar sigh of exasperation as she rushed out onto the front porch, all enthused about the imminent journey to Atlanta.

"Reba! Be careful with my dress! And don't crush those hat boxes! Mother, you can't put them there! Oh, Peter, you certainly look dashing this afternoon! Isn't it exciting?!" Before Peter could respond, Susanna was yelling back in through the door. "Hurry, Father! We have to get there in time to get our rooms at the hotel and freshen up before the ball!"

She rushed back inside as William appeared at the door, himself impressively dressed and ready to travel. Ezekiel hurried out right behind him with the bags. He and the footman stored them in the back of the carriage under the strict supervision and critical scrutiny of Reba and Elizabeth.

Michael leaned against the barn door holding the hay fork, casually watching the hubbub surrounding the stylish carriage. After observing the flurry of activity for a while, his eyes drifted to the upstairs window. Annie was peering down at an angle, trying to get a glimpse of the activity below. She glanced out to the barn, caught Michael watching her and flashed him a smile. He returned the smile, but when he looked back to the carriage, his expression darkened. William and Elizabeth were settling into their seats. Peter, his hand extended like some foppish courtier to assist Susanna into the coach, happened to look down toward the barn. He locked eyes with Michael for a moment before climbing inside to join the others.

The footman carefully closed the door and barely made it up to his perch before the driver popped his whip, snapping the four white horses to a trot. As soon as the carriage had reached the main road and disappeared from view, Michael sprang into action.

"Zeke! Hitch up the buggy!" he called out as he raced for the house. "Reba! Is everything ready?"

"Ready as it's gon' get, Mistah Michael! Ready as it's gon' get!" Reba cackled enthusiastically. This was the moment she'd been waiting for. She hustled back into the house, calling loudly, "Miss Annie! Hurry up, Chil'!"

Reba carried a bag under each arm and shepherded Annie, clad in a plain, print dress, along the downstairs hallway in front of her. Just as they passed the stairs, Michael came bounding down in a new shirt and freshly cleaned, fringed leather boots.

"Move it, girl!" Reba's excitement hadn't abated. "You got a long ride ahead of you!"

Ezekiel hitched William's fastest harness horse to the open buggy and had it waiting beside the front porch. He made a point of standing erect and proper beside the animal, exactly as the footman and driver had done earlier. It wasn't a four-up luxury coach, but it would get them where they wanted to go. Annie came out the front door, literally pushed by the ebullient Reba, with Michael right behind her, awkwardly attempting to install his cufflinks. Reba set the bags on the edge of the porch and took one of Michael's sleeves.

"I can't believe you made Annie's dress in just two days, Reba. I don't know how to thank you!" He tried to give her a hug, but she pushed him away and grabbed his other arm to reset the first cufflink which he had improperly attached.

"Makin' the dress was joyful easy!" the black fairy-godmother chuckled. "Slippin' 'round behind Miss Susie to do it was the hard part!"

"Michael, are you sure about this?" Annie clung to the porch column. Reba looked at her, raising a gentle hand to Annie's cheek.

"Honey, you gon' be the prettiest thang at that ball!" Reba assured her. "An' Mistah Michael gon' be the handsomest man! Lawd, y'all gon' sho' nuff turn some heads! Now get in! Go!" She took Annie by the arm and guided her down the steps.

"I'm just afraid we'll turn heads for the wrong reasons," Annie's apprehension was real. Michael came around to help her into the carriage, offering his arm as a gentlemen to the finest lady in the land.

"The future Mrs. Michael Drummond doesn't have to be afraid of anything," he said, looking into her eyes. "Especially not of being beautiful." She smiled and leaned back down to meet his lips in a hurried kiss then took her seat. "Now, let's go!" Michael said, bolting around to the other side.

* * * * * * *

The luxurious four-horse carriage moved along the main road to Atlanta at a comfortable clip. The gentle rocking motion had almost put William to sleep. He opened his eyes to study Elizabeth when she began to cough. She looked tired, he thought. Not at all well. He had expressed his concern earlier in the day, but she was not to be denied her evening at the governor's ball.

Elizabeth looked across to the other seat. Susanna clung lovingly to Peter's arm and they spoke in whispers. Elizabeth could see they were very much in love. She took William's arm and smiled up at him, but he was already asleep.

* * * * * * *

Michael pushed the horse as fast as he felt the animal could go. They had, by design, gotten a late start, and there was a lot of ground to make up. He glanced at Annie and caught her gripping the side of the seat. He knew she wasn't concerned about the speed of the carriage. She loved to go fast and had often proven she could easily beat any man in a race, given equal horses. Michael flashed his winning smile and kissed her on the side of the head.

"Relax," he said, squeezing her hand. "It's time you had some fun."

"I don't know, Michael," she didn't share his confidence. "I'm sure they don't want any Cherokees at the Governor's Ball."

"I'll bet half the people there have Indian blood somewhere in their past—if they'd admit it. Don't worry. You'll be fine."

"I just don't want to embarrass you," she tried another angle. "You know I can't dance."

"Someone as beautiful as you doesn't have to dance," he countered. It was apparent he would accept no excuses. They were going to the Governor's Ball. Annie slipped her arm through his and kissed him on the cheek then laid her head against his shoulder. A *yo-neg* cotillion was not her idea of a good time, but she knew it meant a lot to Michael. And, she had to admit, it did her self image no harm to know he was so proud of her and so determined to show her off. She only hoped she wouldn't disappoint him.

* * * * * * *

Nightfall had caught many travellers still on the road, hurrying to reach their destination. Torches and oil lamps lined the expansive lawn surrounding the long, U-shaped drive of the enormous mansion that played host to this annual extravaganza. Carriages and coaches of all makes and sizes were jammed together up and down the drive, with horses tethered on the perimeter. A gaggle of black boys ten to fourteen years old darted back and forth, each determined to outdo the other in seriously fulfilling his valet responsibilities. Greeting new arrivals. Helping ladies and feeble old men from their carriages. Unhitching horses and tying matching colored ribbons to the carriage shaft and the horses' harness so teams and coaches would be properly reunited when it came time to depart.

The warm glow of the brilliant ballroom light and the fluid strains of the waltz being played by the state orchestra spilled out into the darkness, enticing the late arrivals to hurry inside lest they miss a single minute of the festivities. Through the full length french doors and windows burst a kaleidoscope of colors from the swirling gowns, accented intermittently with flashes of blue uniforms and black coats and tails spinning by.

Elizabeth and William had positioned themselves near an open window. He relished the fresh air and, though he had never

196

openly admitted it, felt somewhat claustrophobic in large crowds. Elizabeth centered her attention for the most part on Susanna and Peter. They had participated in every waltz as though they were the only couple on the dance floor. So much in love, Elizabeth thought, recalling the wonderful memories of her own courtship years ago.

William acknowledged General John Ellis Wool with a single nod but refused to return his smile. The commander chatted amiably with recently elected Governor William Schley amid a crowd of hangers-on, lobbyists, land speculators and favor-seekers, each clamoring desperately to be heard, begging for a slice of the governor's precious time.

Elizabeth thought this ball was more elegant than any she could remember in recent years and felt it boded well to have such a refined gentleman in power in Milledgeville.

"I'll give it two years," William had told her. "He's not passionate enough, not cruel enough in his hatred of Cherokees. For what Jackson wants—and Georgia—they'll have to get someone like Lumpkin back in office. Or worse, they might re-elect George Gilmer."

Among those pressing in on Governor Schley, William noticed, and bordering on sartorial embarrassment in his too-tight long coat and knickers that were noticeably frayed at the knees, was Titus Ogilvie. Slithering. Pushing. Jockeying for position. One man shifted and Titus made his move. One less obstacle between himself and the governor. Titus was plotting his next maneuver when he caught a glimpse of William. The two made passing eye contact but neither spoke nor made any gesture to acknowledge the other. Finally, the last man between Titus and the governor was pulled away by a friend and the door was open. It even appeared that the governor was about to address Titus when a tall, thin man with a large, hooked nose and recessed, dark eyes spun Titus around.

"Mr. Ogilvie? Titus Ogilvie!" the newcomer bubbled. Titus didn't recognize him and made no effort to mask his irritation at losing his shot at the governor. "Silas Green," the tall man reminded Ogilvie. "From Savannah. You sold me a hundred loads of corn when you were working out of Charleston."

Titus politely feigned recollection. "Yes, Mr. Green. Nice to see you again." He had turned halfway back to the governor when Green tugged at him annoyingly. Their conversation, it appeared, was far from over.

"Dreadfully sorry to hear about your son and your nephew," Silas shook his head with just the right amount of grief and bewilderment at life's unfair measure. "I know your brother-in-law, Shadrach Bogen. Fine feller. Tragic. You both losin' your boys. Something's really gotta be done about these Indians," Green concluded safely.

"Yes. Yes it must," Titus grumbled. "Excuse me..." When he resumed his pursuit of Governor Schley, Titus once more made eye contact with William who was close enough to have overheard the entire conversation with Green. There was only ice in the look of each man. Both were relieved when their line of sight was obstructed by the ever-shifting traffic and the swirling dancers.

At the end of the waltz, Peter and Susanna found themselves near the french doors that opened out onto the veranda. Amid the flutter of polite applause, Peter took her elbow and leaned close, his lips at her ear.

"Let's step outside for some air."

"Yes. Some fresh air would be nice," Susanna agreed. Peter was performing right on cue, as though he had read her thoughts. They had arrived from the hotel after the ballroom was full—but not overcrowded—so their entrance had received the maximum attention, and they had participated in every waltz so far. Both were excellent dancers and both knew it. It was proving to be as perfect and magical an evening as Susanna had dreamed it would be. And now Peter was luring her—or so he believed—out onto the veranda *for some air.*

The brightest stars hovered just above the trees that flanked the mansion on either side and lined the long drive. It was a night for young lovers. Susanna noticed another couple had come out for air. They were spaced an acceptable distance farther down the veranda. Soft laughter floated to them from two more couples sharing a private conversation and a bottle of raspberry *eaux-de-vie* in the gazebo near the center of the sprawling lawn.

Susanna looked up at the full moon. Peter was behind her. He leaned close to smell in her hair the sprig of jasmine she had plucked with carefully planned spontaneity from beside the door as they stepped out. She tilted her head back to rest against his chest.

"Marry me, Susanna," Peter felt bold enough to slip his arms around her waist. Susanna remained motionless, not even breathing. He waited. Nothing. He let his hands drop to his side. "I've offended you. It's too sudden," he recognized his error.

"Yes."

"I knew it. You need more time. It was improper of me—"

"Yes, I'll marry you," she interrupted and turned to face him.

198

His eyes welled up, reflecting the emotions churning in his chest. "I've been hoping you would ask," she smiled up at him.

"Susanna, I love you so very much! You've made me so happy! Is it all right if I speak to your father? It would be perfect—to announce our betrothal here tonight!"

"That would be wonderful, Peter! Yes, let's make the announcement," she was delighted with the idea. It would make them the absolute center of attention. She would, indeed, be the belle of the ball.

"I'll go speak with your father!" Peter started back inside.

"No!" She grabbed his sleeve. "Let's surprise them! Just make the announcement!" She knew her father's reserved nature and didn't want to risk his advising Peter against the plan and, worse, Peter accepting his advice.

"Susanna, dearest...." Peter hesitated. He knew the danger of arguing with Susanna, but there was protocol. "I don't think that would show the proper respect."

"Make the announcement, Peter," she said with a soft firmness. "I'll take care of Father. He knows you respect him. I'll just attribute it to the magic of the evening."

Peter was getting excited again. She had explained it all so well. More importantly, she had taken responsibility for the breach of manners they were about to commit.

"Yes! All right, then. If you're sure."

"I'm always sure, Peter," she smiled and patted his cheek. "Always."

* * * * * * *

The orchestra ended their brief pause and settled into another waltz. The polished hardwood dance floor was now occupied mostly by the middle-aged and older couples. After their traditional opening dance, Elizabeth and William didn't budge from their staked-out territory near the window. Scanning the room, Elizabeth finally located Susanna, who was surrounded by a bevy of excited young ladies. Many of them had been her classmates at the conservatory. They all turned to look where Susanna pointed across the dance floor. Elizabeth followed their line of sight through the dancers to the opposite side of the room where Lieutenant Tanner and General Wool pressed through the crowd to reach Governor Schley. The general spoke with the governor in an animated fashion, gesturing occasionally to his young charge. Elizabeth looked back to Susanna who was the focal point of all the chirping young ladies.

"Susanna is certainly enjoying herself," Elizabeth observed. William had been watching the exchange involving Peter, General Wool and Governor Schley.

"Something's going on," he said. No sooner had William spoken than the governor whispered to Peter who immediately began scanning the crowd, pointing when he spotted William and Elizabeth. Schley beckoned for the Drummonds to join him, indicating they should circumnavigate the dancers as quickly as possible. When the waltz ended, the governor clinked his gold ring loudly against his wine glass and held up a hand to silence the orchestra. Peter, at the governor's side, was beaming.

"Ladies and gentlemen!" Schley said, then repeated louder, "Ladies and gentlemen! May I have your attention, please!" The buzz of conversation finally subsided and the governor once more located William and Elizabeth. "Mr. Drummond. Mrs. Drummond. I think you'll want to join me here...."

William had begun to suspect the gist of it all, but Elizabeth, still puzzled, looked back at her radiant daughter. She and William made their way around the dance floor toward the state's highest political official.

"Ladies and gentlemen, this is indeed a great honor," Governor Schley resumed as William and Elizabeth drew near. "On behalf of United States Army First Lieutenant Peter Tanner, a fine young man in the service of his country, I would like to announce his betrothal to Susanna—the lovely daughter of Mr. and Mrs. William Drummond." He lifted his wine glass, gesturing across the floor. "Miss Susanna Drummond."

William wasn't really surprised, but Elizabeth gasped and looked to her daughter. "Susanna?" she said, excited and at the same time a little disappointed at learning of her first-born's marriage engagement in this manner. But Elizabeth knew she couldn't remain upset when she saw the blissful smile on Susanna's face. And Peter's look of worshipful adulation when he took her hand. Elizabeth felt her own tears of happiness welling up.

Susanna's luminous expression withered suddenly to a look of stark terror. A hush fell over the crowd and everyone could easily hear Susanna, though her voice came barely more than a whisper.

"Oh, my sweet Lord!"

Framed in the main ballroom doorway was her brother, Michael. He would, indeed, have been the handsomest young man at the ball in his fine new suit—were it not for the out-of-place, knee-high, fringed Cherokee boots. But even more shocking to Susanna was the presence of Annie Walker at his side. An audible gasp rippled around the room in a scintillating Cinderella moment. Everyone viewed this stunning beauty in the new ball gown Reba Campbell had made for her. Annie felt embarrassed and Michael wondered why their entrance had created such a stir. He had figured they would slip in unnoticed and just mingle for a while. Sort of ease into the situation.

"Sorry we're late," he apologized nervously.

Peter leaned down to Susanna and whispered, "How could he stand to be near her? To touch her? After what happened..."

"I know..." Susanna breathed back with utter revulsion, then called loudly to her brother, her voice a cannon volley of rage fired from across the room. "How dare you! How dare you bring her here!"

"And why not, dear sister?" Michael's humility vanished, his anger flaring to match her own. "She's going to be my wife."

The confused crowd looked from William and Elizabeth...to Susanna and Peter...to Michael and Annie.

Titus Ogilvie pushed between Silas Green and another man to plant himself in the center of the vacated dance floor. Ever the opportunistic sycophant, he felt confident he could securely ingratiate himself to the governor once and for all by taking a firm stand against this Indian-loving white trash and his squaw woman who had so inconsiderately intruded upon this esteemed and select company. With a condescending air he responded to Michael's proclamation.

"And a fine wife she'll be, I'm sure," he said, making a point of looking Annie up and down. "The face of an angel..." he paused for effect before adding, "...and the hands of a wash woman."

Annie dropped her hands to her side and sought to hide them in the folds of her dress. Michael, whatever he was feeling inside, became an iceberg to those looking on.

"Be careful what you say, Mr. Ogilvie. This isn't the streets of Pine Hill."

"Titusville," Ogilvie corrected him with pride.

"This isn't Pine Hill," Michael repeated. "I demand you apologize to this young lady."

"You *demand*?" Titus sneered, playing loudly to the crowd. "And if I refuse?"

Michael took one step toward his tormentor, his hands clasped casually behind his back, his voice low but intense. "Then

I'll gut you where you stand, like the stinking pig that you are."

William Drummond knew his son. He knew the chilled exterior they were all seeing was but a thin mantle that overlay a seething volcano. He took Michael's elbow.

"Michael, could we talk? Outside?"

William attempted to steer Michael toward the door and reached for Annie at the same time. If only he could get them alone for a few minutes. But Michael held his ground and extended his arm between his father and Annie, refusing to let her move.

"No, Father. Not until he apologizes."

"Michael," Annie pleaded in a low voice, her eyes begging William for help. "Please. It's all right."

"It's *not* all right!" Michael yelled. The entire gathering remained frozen like powder-wigged figures in a Gibson Stuart painting. Motionless. Silent.

"Michael..." Annie dipped her head, afraid to risk meeting anyone else's eyes.

"Mister Ogilvie...she's waiting..." Michael repeated.

Governor Schley approached with General Wool at his side. Their heels clicked loudly on the hardwood floor. The governor had donned his painted political smile, intent on regaining control of the situation. He stepped between Michael and Ogilvie, addressing his words to Titus.

"Sir, have you offended this young lady?"

Titus found himself in a quandary. His spur-of-the-moment plan to ensure himself a position of favor with Schley now threatened to blow up in his face. The delicious taste of government supply contracts that had him drooling minutes earlier had suddenly soured into a bitter pudding of chagrin. The last thing he wanted was to embarrass the governor. Or to embarrass himself in front of the governor. But there were limits to what any self-respecting white man should have to endure. He lowered his voice in hopes his words would reach only Schley's ears.

"Governor, I thought this affair was by invitation only. Restricted to the citizens of the State of Georgia. I didn't know it was open to the likes of—" he trailed off with a little gesture toward Michael and Annie.

"Mister...?" the governor inquired after his name.

"Ogilvie. Titus Ogilvie," the weak reply reflected his disappointment that the governor hadn't a clue who he was.

"Well, Mr. Ogilvie," Governor Schley went on, placing a patronizing hand on Titus's shoulder, "she certainly looks like a lovely young lady to me. I suggest you apologize for your ill-advised remarks and we'll all get on with the evening's festivities."

Every man has his limit, Titus thought, and he had just reached his. The attempt to curry favor with Georgia's head of state had crumbled, so what did he have to lose? He gazed straight into Michael Drummond's eyes and, though he addressed the governor, he made sure it was loud enough for all to hear.

"You know, Governor, you can put a queen's robe on a bitch dog, but when she comes in heat and howls at the moon, she's still just a bitch dog."

There was another, even more audible gasp from the crowd, followed by a blistering silence. Michael wore a strange expression many might have thought was a smile. With hands still clasped behind him, he casually stepped closer to Governor Schley and Titus Ogilvie. Then with flashing speed, Michael's hand came from behind him and punched Ogilvie full in the face.

"Michael!" the word erupted from William, Elizabeth and Susanna in unison. The response from the crowd escalated from gasps to bitten cries of shock, followed by a wave of murmurs and whispers.

Susanna gradually made her way across the dance floor and stepped up to her brother. "I knew the minute I saw you two at the door you'd find a way to ruin my evening!"

Michael ignored his sister, his fierce scowl still locked on Ogilvie.

"Am I to take this as a challenge to a duel?" Titus asked, dabbing with his sleeve at the trickle from his bleeding lip.

"I didn't come here to fight," Michael said flatly, "but you may take it however you wish."

"At sunrise then?"

"What's wrong with right now?" Michael saw no reason to waste the remainder of the evening just waiting for dawn.

"Michael! That's enough!" William's commanding voice resonated through the vast hall. Still Michael never took his eyes off Ogilvie's.

"Stay out of it, Father!" Michael had the utmost respect for William, but he would not be stayed on this point. "This is between Mister Ogilvie and me!"

"I take it, then, you are prepared?" Ogilvie felt obligated to meet the challenge of this brash upstart. In answer, Michael pulled back one side of his coat to reveal James Walker's knife in its Cherokee sheath attached to his belt. "I should have expected as

203

much..." Ogilvie sneered, looking around to make sure others heard the rest of his insult, "...from one who traffics with heathen savages. An Indian knife!"

"Not *just* a knife," Michael's voice remained cold. "The knife that slit your son's throat." Titus's eyes widened with rage, his lip curled with intense hatred. He drew a small pistol from his coat pocket, cocked it and pushed it toward Michael, but before he could fire, Michael grabbed his wrist, forcing the weapon down. With his other hand, Michael whipped out his knife and plunged it into Ogilvie's bulging stomach.

It all happened in an instant before any of the men, including William, could rush in to separate the combatants. When they finally made a move, their advance was halted when the pistol went off, striking Ogilvie in the knee. The report from the small gun echoed through the cavernous ballroom. The crowd that had surged forward as one body toward the two grappling men ebbed back, like a pulsating man-of-war in the shallow ocean surf. When Ogilvie's massive body slumped forward, Michael instinctively caught him under the arms, but he was unable to hold the larger man up. Ogilvie landed on his side. There was a grotesquely audible slurping sound when Michael withdrew the knife from the wounded man's stomach. Only after Michael had stepped back did the others rush to Ogilvie, who lay motionless, bleeding profusely all over the lovely polished floor.

"You've killed him!" the merchant Silas Green cried out.

Governor Schley stepped out of the crowd with General Wool at his side. "Get my surgeon!" the governor barked with authority. "Doctor Beckman!"

A tall, thin man of considerably more than sixty years, with thick, bushy muttonchops, pushed through the crowd to join them. He grasped the arm of the black serving boy closest to him.

"Go to my carriage and fetch my bag! Hurry!"

"Yes, suh!" the boy bolted for the door on his critical mission. Behind him the crowd pressed in, offering a rapid volley of accusation and defense.

"He's murdered the man," one said.

"It was a duel!" another defended Michael. "You heard them!"

"That was no duel!"

"I might have done the same," someone sympathized.

"My God, man! Over a Cherokee woman?"

Governor Schley looked up at Michael who was holding the

204

bloody knife and staring down at Ogilvie. The governor spoke softly aside to General Wool. "John, have one of your officers place this man under arrest."

General Wool glanced around in search of uniform blue. The closest to him was Peter. "Lieutenant Tanner, take this man into custody," the general ordered. Peter's and Michael's eyes met across the bleeding leviathan on the floor between them. Susanna looked in astonishment from one to the other.

"Don't even think about it," Michael said, shaking his head.

"I've been given an order from my commanding officer," Peter knew he had no choice in the matter. "It's my duty."

Michael had heard the *it's my duty* speech before. "Not this time, Peter," he said firmly.

Peter stepped around the body of Titus Ogilvie and found himself between Michael and William. "It's just a formality, Mr. Drummond," Peter explained, embarrassed at having to arrest Michael. He pleaded with his future brother-in-law, "Don't make it worse, Michael."

"Maybe you should go with him, son." William hoped to spare Elizabeth the unpleasant possibility of seeing Michael subdued by force.

Taking this remark as William's tacit approval, Peter put a hand on Michael's shoulder to lead him away. Michael knocked the hand away and brought the bloody knife up to the side of Peter's neck, the point pressing the skin just beneath his left ear.

"If you ever touch me again," Michael said in a hoarse whisper, "I'll consider it my *duty* to slit you from here..." he moved the knife to the other ear, "...to here."

Michael lowered the knife to Peter's chest and with a flick of the blade sent one of the shiny brass uniform buttons clattering loudly across the wooden floor. It came to rest directly between Titus Ogilvie's sprawled feet. Before leaving, Michael wiped the bloody blade on Peter's uniform. When Michael turned toward the door, he received the full force of Susanna's slap in the face. As soon as she hit him, she stepped back. It was impossible to know whether her action was because she couldn't believe what she had just done or because she feared her brother's reaction. He was, without question, deranged. And she had struck him quite hard.

But Michael only looked at her with great sadness. "Goodbye, sister," were his final words. He reached out to touch her cheek, but she recoiled, with tears in her eyes. He looked to his mother and father with an even sadder expression. "I love you,

Mother," he said to Elizabeth, infinitely remorseful that he had been the author of the anguish he read in her face. His eyes met William's. "Good-bye, Father."

"Michael...." the pain pressed hard into Elizabeth's heart. And William had no words. Michael strode briskly to the door. He took Annie's hand and they were gone, almost crashing into the serving boy returning with Doctor Beckman's bag.

The assailant had gone! The killer was escaping! All eyes were on the governor and the general to see what they would do. Even General Wool awaited the governor's word.

"Have him apprehended tomorrow," Schley said. "We don't need any more bloodshed tonight." He looked kindly at Elizabeth and William and received the gratitude of their eyes. "Play something!" Governor Schley called loudly to the orchestra leader. He looked down at the motionless mass before him and said to no one in particular but with full expectation that his order would be promptly obeyed, "Remove Mister Ogilvie and clean up this mess."

Instantly a swarm of servants, assisted by men from the crowd, began lifting the bloody, inert form, their motions connecting in strange synchronicity with the rhythm of the waltz.

* * * * * * *

Michael helped Annie into their carriage and the young black valet handed him the reins.

"Thank you," Michael said calmly.

"Good luck, sir."

The young man's look of admiration puzzled Michael, who had no idea how rapidly the account of the incident had spread from the lips of the serving boy sent to fetch the doctor's bag.

Annie had not spoken a word since leaving the ballroom. Michael thought he saw anger in her eyes. But there was also fear. And perhaps humiliation. He wasn't sure. He chided himself for having thrust her directly into exactly the sort of confrontational nightmare she had feared—and which he had assured her wouldn't happen.

"So, this is what it's like to go to the Governor's Ball," she finally spoke. "What an honor!"

"I'm sorry," his apology was sincere. "I didn't mean for it to be this way."

She handed him the buggy whip and leaned over, pulled his chin around with her finger and gave him a gentle and meaningful

206

kiss. "Well, at least I didn't have to dance," she smiled. "So....where do we go from here?"

"I love you, Annie Walker," Michael said. He was truly in awe of her ability to put the most unpleasant experience behind her and move on with her life. He had seen this quality in her for years, but never so much as regarding the events that had befallen her in the past few weeks. He popped the whip above the horse and their carriage rolled away into the night. They never looked back. Had they done so, they would have seen Michael's mother and father standing in the doorway of the beautiful mansion, and, a step apart from them, his sister. But they wouldn't have heard the words Susanna spoke.

"I hate him. I hope I never see him again!"

"Where are they going?" Elizabeth wondered aloud. She knew they would go immediately back to the Drummond house. That wasn't what she had meant. She was certain they would already be gone by the time she, William and Susanna arrived back home. And not knowing Michael's whereabouts would eat at her every day until she knew that he and Annie were safe.

William was speechless. He shook his head and gazed out into the darkness. The sound of the horse's hoofbeats grew fainter until they were drowned by the music from within.

* * * * * * *

William Drummond pressed the loose shreds of tobacco carefully into the bowl of his pipe with his forefinger, but his eyes were riveted on the buttons of the army uniform on the other side of his desk. His raccoon hollow eyes ached for the sleep he had been denied throughout the night and all the next day. But most of all his head throbbed from having to listen to the droning voice of Peter Tanner, standing before him with his hands clasped behind his back and feet planted wide in the military at-ease stance.

"I felt I owed you an explanation—perhaps even an apology—for the impulsive way in which we announced our engagement," Peter fumbled for the words. "...I suppose we got caught up in the magic of the evening..."

William exhaled a long, burdened sigh. "I assure you, Lieutenant Tanner, right now your engagement to Susanna is the least of my concerns."

"Yes, sir," Peter agreed. "In light of the ensuing events, I'm sure that's true." He knew he had made an even bigger mess of

207

things and was glad for the interruption when he heard boots loudly descending the stairs. William looked up at the young soldier who appeared in the doorway.

"No sign of him, sir," the soldier spoke to Peter. William recognized him as one of the six who had been part of James Walker's firing squad and the one who had held a gun to *Tsu-Tsu* Swimmer's head to force him to shoot at James.

"Thank you, Corporal," Peter acknowledged the report and dismissed the soldier. Now Peter was faced with finishing his apology and then excusing himself to resume the search for his future father-in-law's only son. William rescued himself when he called out to Reba passing in the hallway.

"Yes, Mistah Drummond?" Reba stepped into the study.

"How is Elizabeth?"

"She ain't well," Reba caught the look in his eye. Years of experience had taught her the role that was expected of her. "Ain't well 'tall. Caught herself a nasty chill, y'all comin' back in the night like that. She needs lots of rest." Her words were true enough, though their hidden intent was really to rid William of his unwanted guest. She scowled at the young lieutenant. "Ain't easy, with these soldier boys clompin' all through the house!"

"We'll be gone shortly," Peter assured them both.

"Mmm-hmm," Reba, hands on hips, frowned at him.

"Sir..." Peter wanted to look directly at William but his eyes kept coming back to Reba. "...if...if you...this is most awkward..."

"If I knew where Michael was, Lieutenant, I would tell you." William knew his intended snub had succeeded. Peter blinked nervously when called by his rank rather than by his name. "I'd like to get this cleared up. For Michael's sake. And for his mother's peace of mind."

"Thank you, sir, for understanding." Peter was calculating his escape route past Reba when Susanna entered carrying a tray with two cups of coffee. She set the tray on the corner of William's desk and placed one steaming cup in front of her father, offering the other to Peter. Serving coffee was well beneath her, but it was a gesture calculated to bridge the gap that had widened between Peter and her father. All the fault, of course, of her hated brother.

"Since he's taken up with that Indian girl," Susanna volunteered her analysis, "my guess is he's run away out west somewhere." She pretended not to notice William's critical look—a look she knew was accusing her of collaborating with the enemy.

"Yes. Out west. Perhaps it's best that way," Peter didn't

know how else to respond.

"Out of sight, out of mind, I always say," Susanna concluded, then politely offered, "Some molasses for your coffee, Peter?"

* * * * * * *

Michael and Annie rode double on *U-no-le*. *Ga-tsa-nu-la* was piled high with blankets and what clothing and utensils they had been able to throw together for their journey west. They had returned from Atlanta to the Drummond house in the wee hours of the morning. A groggy Ezekiel had built a fire while Reba listened in amazement to their story. She and Ezekiel had agreed there was little Michael and Annie could do but leave Georgia. Clothing, food and supplies had been hurriedly assembled, and it was determined they would spend the rest of the night in the woods at a place where Michael, Annie and James had often gone camping. They would hide out and rest during the day, then leave late in the afternoon, travelling by dark until they were well out of the area where they might be recognized.

They stopped the horses in reaction to a sound in the underbrush just ahead. Michael drew his pistol but slipped it back into his belt when they saw Martha and *Tsu-Tsu* Swimmer emerge from the brush out onto the trail.

"*Ma-di! Tsu-tsu!*" Annie was excited to see them.

"We brought this for you," Martha said. Much like Annie, she was a strikingly beautiful Cherokee girl who almost seemed embarrassed by her own comeliness. She nudged her younger brother forward, "*Tsu-tsu....*"

"You might get hungry on the road," *Tsu-tsu* handed them a bag of food and Martha gave them an extra quilt.

"Mother says it's going to be a hard winter."

"*Wa-do*," Michael leaned down and shook *Tsu-tsu's* hand like he would an adult.

"Say good-bye to your mother and father for us," Annie squeezed Martha's hand and affectionately mussed *Tsu-tsu's* hair.

"Be careful," *Ma-di* didn't know what else to say. She and her brother watched the friends they had known all their lives disappear into the trees.

* * * * * * *

The forest went on forever, opening a door here, a crack

there, swallowing them up in a way that would frighten most travellers but offered these freedom and sanctuary.

"I know it was hard, leaving without even telling your mother and father," Annie said. She nibbled a piece of cold fry bread as they rode along, reaching around Michael to push a piece into his mouth.

"I had no choice," Michael said, chewing the bread. "I killed Titus Ogilvie."

* * * * * * *

The shadows lengthened beneath a cool wind that greeted them from the north. Michael had been walking for the last ten or twelve miles, giving *U-no-le* a rest. Annie drew the quilt *Ma-di* and *Tsu-tsu* had given them around her shoulders. For the last two hours Michael had been spouting a rambling discourse peppered with regret, enumerating all the different ways he could have handled the situation with Titus Ogilvie that wouldn't have driven them from their home.

"He pulled a gun," Annie argued simply. "What else could you do?"

"I should have just walked away," Michael said convincingly, then shifted back to his initial position. "But I couldn't let him say those things to you."

Now Annie contradicted his self-contradiction. She had been toying with him in this manner for the better part of an hour, trying not to let him see her smile. Every time he flip-flopped his position she did the same, taking an opposing view.

"After what I've been through, you think his stupid words could hurt me?" she countered.

* * * * * * *

Michael no longer recognized any of the territory around them. He had never been this far west. He wasn't sure if they were still in Alabama or if they had crossed north into Tennessee. Most of his travels with James, Uncle Andrew and Uncle John had been up into eastern Tennessee and western North Carolina. Annie thought she recognized a spot beside the river they had crossed a few miles back where her great grandfather, The Old One, had once taken her and James camping and fishing when they were about ten. She wasn't sure. It looked like it. But maybe it wasn't. They were a long way from home.

210

They both walked, leading *U-no-le* and *Ga-tsa-nu-la* through a thick growth of oaks that ended abruptly, dumping them onto a wide, heavily travelled road. They saw three wagons go by loaded with assorted goods on their way west. *It was going to be big business when all the Injuns got run out of the States, and there were decent, enterprising white folks who stood to make an admirable living from these circumstances.* The diligent ones had seen the wisdom of getting an early start. Michael and Annie watched until the wagons rolled out of sight before they crossed the road into the woods beyond. Annie sprang back onto *U-no-le* and held out her hand to Michael, helping him up behind her.

"There comes a time, Annie, when you have to stop and say *No more!*" Michael continued his one-man debate. "That's what your father and James did. They said *No more!*"

"And they're dead," Annie reminded him.

"All men die," he answered. "Not all men die with honor."

"Maybe you're right," Annie softened, admitting, "I did feel something special when you stood up for me." She rested her hand on his leg.

* * * * * * *

Susanna Drummond and Peter Tanner sat in the swing at the far end of the Drummonds' front porch. The chilled breeze that had greeted Michael and Annie on their journey earlier in the day had found it's way into northwestern Georgia, bringing with it an unseasonably cool evening. Susanna had made Peter sit there while she got her shawl and now she was making him sit there while she got her way.

"Mother's health has always been poor. It will always be poor. I don't want to wait," she said emphatically and studied Peter to assess the impact of her words. Sometimes he wasn't easy to read, so she added, "After all that's happened, I deserve some happiness in my life."

"You know I only want to make you happy, Susanna, dearest," he smiled and took her hand. She was pleased. He had said exactly the right words.

* * * * * * *

Susanna, balanced on the chair in the center of the parlor, held her hair up behind her neck with one hand and pressed the neckline against her cleavage at what she deemed the appropriately revealing level. Reba, a spray of fish-bone pins clenched between her teeth, tugged and adjusted, fluffed and straightened the fabric of what was to become Susanna's wedding gown. She pinned two places at the bottom to mark the length in front and back. "Don't make it too short," Susanna scolded. "You always make it too short." Reba straightened up and pulled at the fabric around the midsection, cinching it tightly around Susanna's petite waist. Another pin was pushed firmly through the material until it found its mark.

"Ow!" Susanna yelped. "You did that on purpose!"

"Naw, Miss Susie," Reba kept maneuvering so Susanna couldn't see her smiling. "Reba's hands jes' gettin' old."

"Liar," Susanna pouted, let go of her hair and slapped behind her where she thought Reba might be.

* * * * * * *

The days flew by. There was never enough time. Susanna hosted an exquisite tea for a flock of young ladies to plan her wedding. More accurately, they had tea so the other young ladies might have the opportunity to agree and express their utter delight with Susanna's plans.

Susanna spent as much time with Peter as propriety and his schedule would allow. She would tell him all about her plans and how enthusiastically they had been received by all the other young ladies who would participate in the ceremony. Peter listened patiently and smiled, thinking all the while of what he might say or do to ingratiate himself further with William and Elizabeth. Since the incident involving the execution of James Walker, followed by the nasty confrontation with Michael at the governor's ball and the subsequent order to search the Drummond property, Peter suspected a chilled distance had grown between them.

Ezekiel, with the help of Charlie Swimmer and two other Cherokee men, constructed a raised platform for the wedding out on the broad expanse of lawn between the house and the drive leading down to the main road. All four men shuddered—inwardly, at least—each time they saw Susanna, who knew absolutely nothing about construction, charging down from the house to suggest a modification here, an addition there. They would all listen politely and grunt in agreement, then, when she had left, continued building the gazebo platform according to their original plans.

* * * * * * *

Michael and Annie crowded onto the overloaded ferry barge that would take them, along with a few white passengers, Indians from various tribes and a family of freed blacks across the Mississippi River into Arkansas just north of Helena. There was scarcely room to move amidst the wagons, horses, carts, cows, pigs and chickens. It was a cold, sunny day with a stiff wind that blew river spray into the faces of the travelers, but no one complained. They were moving. Going somewhere. Not all of them were certain of their destination, but in the mind of each man, woman and child, it was to better circumstances and a better place than the life they were leaving behind.

Michael pulled the quilt tighter around Annie, more as a gesture of affection than to protect her from the chill. "Arkansas Territory is pretty big. How will we find Uncle Andrew?" he wondered out loud. They had decided they would attempt to locate Annie's relatives who had recently travelled west following the tragedy that had devastated their family.

"He'll probably find us before we find him," Annie said with a little laugh, recalling the tales she had heard as a child of her uncle's prowess at tracking and hunting. "How much longer?"

"If the weather stays good—another week. Ten days, maybe." It was just a guess. He really didn't know.

"And we'll build our own cabin?" Annie was already looking to the future.

"Yes, *wa-le-la*." He slipped his arms around her waist. "And start our family." She always liked it when he called her *hummingbird*. No matter what they had been through or what might lie ahead, she never lost her burning need to be near him. To touch him. She felt her breasts lying against his forearms. And she felt his growing arousal pressing against her from behind. Annie faced him and opened the quilt, drawing him inside its warmth. She took one of his hands and guided it down to rest on her stomach. Leaving his hand there, she allowed hers to glide down and grip his erection through his trousers. She leaned her forehead against his chest and said softly, "That part has already been done."

Michael gently lifted her chin to look up into his face. "*A-ta-gu te-nŭ-hi?*" he whispered in astonishment.

Yes. She was pregnant. He took her face in his hands and kissed her gently, then raised up with pride to his full height and thrust his chin into the stiff breeze. Things happened in life. Some

213

bad. Some good. Mostly good, it seemed to him at that moment.

* * * * * * *

Susanna continued to direct all the decorating and final preparations for her wedding down to the tiniest detail. Everything, she was determined, would be perfect. Because a perfect wedding would bode well for the beginning of a journey that would be as near perfect as one was allowed to have in this earthly life.

On the appointed day all the important guests arrived on time. Those guests she had been expected to invite out of professional courtesy to her father or out of social courtesy to her mother had mysteriously failed to appear. Elizabeth even expressed concern as to whether Susanna had remembered to post those invitations, but Susanna assured her it had all been handled properly. Susanna had seen to it herself.

The minister waited on the platform which had been draped with powder blue banners and bright yellow flowers. With him were Lieutenant Peter Tanner and Lieutenant Weldon Stokes, the best man, a young officer Peter had befriended at West Point. Weldon had travelled all the way from Richmond for the wedding. Susanna disapproved of him. His breath was most foul and he blinked his eyes too rapidly and too often. She found it dreadfully annoying. Though she had said nothing to Peter, she made a mental note to be sure their lives didn't intertwine too closely with Mr. Stokes in the future.

The signal was given and the orchestra began to play. All eyes were on William and Susanna during the procession, measured in tiny steps up the grassy aisle between the two sections of pews borrowed from the Moravian church. Even through her veil, William marveled at the beauty of his daughter, his eyes revealing what was, for him, an uncharacteristic degree of emotionally induced dampness.

Susanna whispered "Thank you, Father," and watched him step off the platform to join her mother seated in the front row. Elizabeth's health, exactly as Susanna had predicted to Peter, had remained poor. William was concerned about her continued loss of weight, but the doctors who had seen her hadn't been able to clearly diagnose the problem. Based on the symptoms, they speculated, it could be some precursory condition that, if not properly monitored, might lead to consumption. On this day, however, despite a light but naggingly incessant cough, Elizabeth was determined to be happy and that her fragile state should in no way interfere with the

214

greatest day of her daughter's life.

The ceremony went exactly as Susanna had planned it. No one missed a cue. Everyone remembered where to stand, what to say and when to say it. Vows and rings were exchanged, the veil was lifted and the bride was kissed. In the receiving line the newlyweds giddily absorbed the gushing and effusive praises of their distinguished guests. Governor Schley was there and asked Susanna to reserve a dance for him. General Wool congratulated Peter and predicted a brilliant military career for this rising young star. Reba, Ezekiel and the additional helpers hired for the occasion served huge amounts of wonderfully prepared food and bottles of imported French wine delivered in a special wagon all the way from Charleston, South Carolina.

By the end of the day William was quite tired and knew Elizabeth must be near exhaustion. Even before the last of the guests had departed, the bride's parents had retired for the evening. Most of the work had been done. The church pews had been loaded onto the wagon and had long since departed for Titusville. Much of the leftover food had, at Elizabeth's insistence, been taken by the helpers back to their families who would enjoy the feast. Reba and Ezekiel stored away the rest—breads, pies, cakes, yams and baked ham—which the family would consume over the next few days.

Darkness found Susanna sitting on the edge of the wedding platform Ezekiel and his Indian friend would disassemble the next day and store behind the barn for future lumber needs. Susanna looked up when Peter joined her. He slipped a light blanket around her shoulders. The only thing she might have planned differently, she realized once it was all over, was a flamboyant exit in a royal, white coach. But they had been forced to forego an official wedding trip until Peter could arrange time off from his increasing military duties. Susanna's husband sat down beside her and she took his hand, giving him a congratulatory pat. The gesture communicated a true sense of accomplishment, but, Peter couldn't help notice with hidden disappointment, no real passion. Perhaps that was how married life was supposed to be. Or so Susanna apparently thought.

* * * * * * *

The last glowing embers of the campfire cast a golden warmth on Michael and Annie as they settled in for another night on the trail. They had found a small clearing in a thick stand of live oaks on a high spot just north of a creek. At a narrow point they constructed a stone weir and caught three good-sized perch. Not a large fish, but with a clean, delicious, almost sweet flavor when roasted over an open fire. Michael lay on his back with Annie almost on top of him beneath the blankets. She kissed him and tickled him gently. Their soft words clung to the flicking cat's tail of smoke climbing up the night's starry cope. Annie froze at the sound of a blood-chilling shriek somewhere off in the darkness.

"An owl. *U-gu-gu*. Relax," Michael cupped his hand onto her shapely bottom. She gripped his arm and shook her head no. Her fear was infectious, sending Michael rolling toward the fire. He scooped dirt onto the red coals to extinguish their faint light. Long ago he had learned not to question a reaction of this intensity from Annie. He was up in a crouch, nudging Annie into the shadows, her back molded to the trunk of a live oak. He drew from beneath their saddle his Collier revolving pistol, cocked it quietly and handed it to her, then pulled out his knife and disappeared into the darkness. *U-no-le* and *Ga-tsa-nu-la*, tethered a few feet away, snorted and offered half whinnies of warning. Michael listened, straining to see into the surrounding blackness, wondering if the horses' reaction had been to his own movement or to whatever else might be out there.

Her anxiety heightened by her experiences of weeks past, Annie pressed against the tree, listening intently to every sound. She heard it! A cracking noise in the woods. It was close. Very close. It might have been Michael. Or perhaps an intruder. She held the Collier against her chest, watching, listening.

Michael kept low and close to the thickest part of the coppice, gradually widening his circle, moving stealthily, pausing, listening, moving on. He caught a glimpse of what he thought had been movement off to his left only a few yards away. A moon shadow from a bird taking flight? The owl they had heard? But there had been no sound of flapping wings. Was it the outline of a man or just a gnarled, misshapen tree trunk he saw before him? Michael crept in measured steps, angling toward another clump of trees in an attempt to come up behind the intruder.

Annie caught a glimpse of Michael's movement. She inched around the base of the tree, keeping the gun poised. Michael closed steadily on the intruder, whose back and legs were like dark, deformed extensions of the tree itself. It appeared the visitor had his left arm wrapped around the trunk and was leaning around the other side. Before making his move, Michael listened closely, in case there were accomplices lurking nearby. Satisfied the intruder was alone, Michael held his breath until he was virtually right on top of the shadowy figure. In a single graceful motion Michael hooked his foot between the intruder's legs, pinned the arm against the trunk and leaned around the tree, placing the razor point of his knife against the man's neck.

"Move and I'll cut your throat," Michael spoke softly, still concerned about the possible presence of cohorts.

"*A-yŭ u-wo-hi-yu*, I believe you!"

Michael was startled to hear the man speak Cherokee. "*Hi-tsa-la-gi-s-go?*" he asked.

"I've taught you well," the man answered.

Stunned by the familiar voice, Michael pulled his captive around for a better look. "Uncle Andrew!" His death grip relaxed into a warm embrace for his adopted uncle. "Annie said you would find us!" He recounted her earlier prediction as the two men moved back toward the tree where Michael had left her.

Annie heard them approaching before they appeared out of the darkness. When she saw Michael smiling, she relaxed and lowered the pistol, breaking into a broad grin at the sight of her uncle. Michael scraped the dirt off the coals, added some kindling and blew the fire back to a robust blaze. He and Annie were both surprised when they were joined by two other Cherokee men. Michael didn't know their names, but he had seen them with Annie's father at the caves on the day Thomas and his brother-in-law, John Sixkiller, had died and again in Titusville at the execution of his blood-brother and best friend, James. If they were with Andrew, Michael knew they could be trusted.

"*Si-yo, 'Tsu-ts'*," Michael greeted the one nearest him.

"*To-hi-tsu?*" the Cherokee asked politely, and Michael responded with the familiar Cherokee grunt, indicating he was well. Andrew introduced the two men as *Tsa-tsi* (George) Starr and *Ne-di* (Ned) Proctor. They were men of few words, but offered Annie mumbled condolences on the loss of her father and brother. Following this polite exchange the two stepped back where they remained motionless in the shadows at the edge of the fire's glow.

After embracing his niece, Andrew held Annie at arm's length and looked down at her stomach, which was still flat at this early stage of her pregnancy. "Has the journey been good to your son?" he asked casually.

"*U-we-tsi?*" she asked. He said it was a son! Andrew Sixkiller was widely known to possess certain psychic abilities. He always knew when a woman was pregnant, often before she herself was aware. And in all his years he had never once been wrong in

217

predicting the sex of the child. His declarations in these matters had come to be accepted as indisputable. Annie's mother had often attributed Annie's own prescient abilities to Andrew, so, despite the fact that Cherokee uncles were traditionally much closer to their nephews, there had developed a special bond between Andrew and his niece.

"How did you find us?" Michael asked, amazed that in this vast wilderness Andrew had come to this very spot on this very night.

"He saw you in the smoke of the medicine fire," the one called *Tsa-tsi* said with the thick accent of a full-blood who seldom spoke English. "We've been waiting for you," he added, explaining that they hadn't crept up on Michael and Annie but had, in fact, been there for some time.

Ne-di explained how they had held back, allowing Michael and Annie time to finish their meal and rest from their journey. They laughed softly in the characteristic Cherokee way when relating how Andrew had wanted to see if he could sneak up on them. He had bragged to them about Michael's cunning and expertise as a woodsman, and Andrew was proud Michael hadn't disappointed him. Michael felt he had been accepted, by these few at least, as a genuine *Tsa-la-gi*.

"Did you hear, Michael?!" Annie pulled at his sleeve with quiet excitement. "We're going to have a son!" Michael looked eagerly to Uncle Andrew whose smile was confirmation.

"The crickets and the wrens are sad," he said. It was an old Cherokee saying. *Tsa-la-gi* boys grew up stalking crickets and hunting small birds with their little bows and arrows and their tiny blowguns.

Grinning broadly, Michael beckoned his visitors to sit and join them. Annie unrolled their pack and shared with the three men the remainder of the fish and some rabbit Michael had killed and cooked around noon. Life could sometimes be bad, Michael thought, but sometimes it could be very good.

C H A P T E R

12

3 Months Later

In the cavernous, musty basement of the Milledgeville courthouse, Jernigan, the bespectacled, ferret-faced, bureaucratically zealous court clerk, moved carefully through the endless stacks of dust-laden record ledgers. A few stray shafts of late autumn sunlight came sneaking through the dirty, ground-level windows high along the dank, mold-covered walls. The oil lamp Jernigan carried creaked against its wire hoop handle. The clerk showed no signs of impatience even though he frequently had to stop and wait for his visitor to catch up. *Click-and-shuffle. Click-and-shuffle.* It would have been difficult for a man the size of his caller to navigate between the stacks even without the use of a walking cane. Jernigan guessed his ailment might have been a war wound from 1814, or simply a bad case of gout. He would never know because it wasn't his job to inquire after such matters. Finally they came upon the object of their search.

"Yes, sir!" Jernigan beamed with professional pride. "The 1790 Federal Census. First year the government took to counting everybody," he said, patting the dusty binders. There would be no charge for the additional information. Encouraged by what he interpreted as a grunt of satisfaction, Jernigan droned on while he sought a specific binder. "Everybody and everything. People, hogs, mules, slaves. You name it. And what for? Look at this!" he gestured at the cluttered shelves bulging with countless identical volumes. "Forty...fifty years of records just sitting here gathering dust. I'm telling you, the day's a comin' when the United States government's gonna drown in its own paperwork...and go thousands of dollars in debt just trying to keep up with it all....let's see....here we are...." He stretched to his full height of five-feet-three-inches and brushed the dust from an ancient ledger. "Yep...*D*...1790..."

Jernigan carried the musty volume to a long wooden table, blowing a thick shroud of dust off the book and table before opening the ledger and pulling the lamp up close. He then folded his hands behind him, awaiting any further request. Finally realizing his presence was no longer required, Jernigan cleared his throat and shuffled with embarrassment.

"Yes...well...I'll just...I'll be upstairs if you need anything."

When Jernigan rounded the end of the stack and headed for

219

the staircase, he cast one glimpse back. The large man had already opened the ledger book and, bending over the table, was eagerly scanning the brittle pages.

The steps of the little clerk could still be heard ticking up the cellar stairs when the curious visitor found what he was searching for. "Drummond, Henry / b. 1761," he read aloud. A stubby finger traced down the page, scanning more of the census information. The visitor mumbled on with growing excitement and anticipation.

> Wife - Nancy (n. Sheffield) b. 1763
> Children - Matthew. Male, b. 1783.
> Katherine. Female, b. 1785.
> William. Male, b. 1790.
> Other:
> Franklin Sheffield. Male, b. 1733.
> (Fthr of Nancy)
> Rebeka Fields. Fem, b. 1708 (Grndmthr of Henry
> Drmd. - 1/2 Cherakie)

The fat finger stopped at the reference to Henry Drummond's grandmother, Rebeka, then traced back up the page, stopping at the name of William Drummond, born 1790. The finger left the page and crooked slightly so the knuckle lightly stroked the underside of Titus Ogilvie's moustache. His face was gaunt and had aged significantly during the months of his recovery.

"Well, well, well," his voice dripped with satisfaction. "Life is certainly full of little surprises, Mr. Drummond. Mr. *Cherokee* William Drummond..." His droopy eyes narrowed to slits of perverse contentment and the corner of his mouth curled up into a familiar sneer.

CHAPTER

13

Ross's Landing
Tennessee River
March 3, 1837

Eleven flatboat barges were docked along the east bank of the Tennessee River at Ross's Landing, just northeast of the juncture of the Georgia, Alabama and Tennessee state lines. Connected to the first flatboat was the steamer that would pull them all down the river. The late winter rains had raised the water line higher than it had been in years. This meant there would be less chance of running aground and would allow them to travel longer hours each day, since they weren't concerned with keeping a visual watch for sand bars.

The landing itself could accommodate only three barges at a time for loading the possessions of the 450-plus travellers about to embark for the west. It was a peaceful gathering, a mixture of affluent pro-treaty mixed-bloods and full-bloods, including Major Ridge, *Se-ho-ya*, and their entire family, son John and his wife, and Ridge's nephew, Elias Boudinot. There were many families of lesser means, but everyone—rich or poor—appeared eager to get started. Given their choice, every man, woman and child would have remained in their homeland. But, as Major Ridge had expressed so eloquently at council meetings and assemblies up and down the rivers and throughout the hills of *Tsa-la-gi* territory, the river of the *yo-neg's* greed was rising, threatening to drown them all in their own blood.

The departure operation was under the supervision of a U. S. Army detail commanded by Peter Tanner, recently promoted to captain. By order of Commanding General John Ellis Wool, Tanner's squad was to be assisted by a detachment of Tennessee Volunteers. Despite the peaceful demeanor of those Cherokees gathered to begin their westward journey, the very size of the group, the bulk of their many possessions and the hustle-and-bustle commotion of getting them loaded onto the flatboat barges made the entire landing area a roaring swarm of noise and activity. Orders were barked and minor accidents occurred. Crates were dropped and carts overturned. Pets escaped and children pursued them, darting dangerously in and out among moving horses and wagon wheels.

The Army supply officer and his clerks oversaw the loading

221

of large amounts of foodstuffs for the entire party onto every third barge.

"One hundred fifty bushels of cornmeal...twelve thousand pounds of bacon...seventy-eight barrels of flour..." the supply clerk read from his bill of laden and pointed officiously to the stockpile of each item, not really knowing—or caring—whether the contractors had furnished the agreed amount or not. Once the Indians were on their way, it really wasn't his problem.

Peter Tanner guided his prancing horse through the shifting sea of slaves and soldiers hard at work moving supplies and loading cargo. A handsome young corporal had paused from his labor to lean against a stack of wooden crates. He wiped the sweat from his face and played eye games with an attractive mixed-blood girl waiting to board.

"Let's go, Private Franklin!" Peter barked. "This is no picnic! We have five more barges to load!"

"Yes, sir!" the private winked at the young lady and went back to his work. He made a point of displaying his well defined biceps when he grasped a large crate, knowing he was impressing a certain pair of hazel-brown eyes as he carried the weighty burden toward the flatboat.

Peter moved on through the crowd, stopping his mount beside a flock of young Cherokee women, mostly mixed-bloods, dressed as well as any white southern belles out for a Sunday afternoon excursion. Aided by their young slave girls—who behaved and were treated more like friends than attendants—the young ladies transported their personal baggage from their carriages down toward the landing. Peter stared at them without expression, but they were convinced the handsome young captain was admiring them from a gentlemanly distance. Two of them flirtatiously acknowledged his presence, but their smiles faded when they realized he was staring right through them as though they didn't exist. He waited for them to pass and then rode on toward an old full-blood man with a small wagon. With him were his daughter and grandson, who carried a baby goat in his arms.

"You can't take the wagon on the boat," Peter said flatly. "No wagons. And no animals," he looked sternly down at the young boy. "All animals go on the lead boat. To be cooked for meals." The boy's mother scowled up at Peter for his insensitivity but said nothing as she pulled her son and his pet goat close to her.

"Fine," Peter said with disdain. "Starve for all I care." He jerked the reins and rode away.

Peter stopped his horse and waited for two soldiers carrying a strong-box filled with money to pass in front of him. They delivered their heavy load to a table guarded by two other soldiers where a federal agent was doling out allotment money to a long line of Cherokees. He counted out coins and shoved them grudgingly across the table as though the funds were being taken from his personal coffers. What a foolish waste, he thought, giving good money to a bunch of Indians. The agent disbursed the money and his assistant wrote down each recipient's name in a ledger.

"There you are. Fifty-three dollars," the agent growled impatiently. "Next! Move it! Next!"

The Cherokee scooped up the money, trusting that it was, in fact, fifty-three dollars. He disappeared into the crowd and the next man moved into position.

"Name?" the assistant queried without looking up.

"Sam Dreadfulwater," the middle-aged Cherokee answered softly, watching the assistant scribble his name in the ledger. The agent pushed the money across the table and motioned him along.

"Come on, you people! We ain't got all day!"

The next Cherokee in line, a one-eyed full-blood about forty, stepped up to receive his allotment. "Yellow Bird," he announced his name loudly even before the assistant asked.

"Oh, no you don't!" the allotment agent snapped emphatically. "You've been through the line! You tryin' to double up on your allotment? Get movin'! Next!"

"No! This is my first time," Yellow Bird stood his ground.

"You callin' me a liar?!" the agent reddened with anger.

"I need my allotment," Yellow Bird insisted. He pointed emphatically to the open ledger in front of the assistant. "Look in your book. Thomas Yellow Bird. My name is not there. Look."

"Don't you tell me what to do! I said move it!" The agent shot up from his seat and leaned threateningly across the table.

"Here it is," the assistant announced, pointing to his book. "Right here! Yellow Bird. You've already been paid. Now git!"

The agent sneered with satisfaction, but Yellow Bird refused to budge. "You are lying! That says Yellow *Hand*. I can read. James Yellow *Hand*. Not Yellow *Bird*."

The allotment agent motioned to the nearest army guard. Corporal Charles DeKalb, a square-jawed New Yorker of Scottish descent, rough looking with a pitted complexion and a broken front tooth, obviously enjoyed his role as enforcer. He dragged Yellow Bird away from the table and shoved him roughly in the direction of the loading dock.

"You heard him! Don't make no trouble," DeKalb said with an air of racial superiority. "Move along now!"

While most of those around the table were focusing on Corporal DeKalb and Yellow Bird, the agent slipped Yellow Bird's allotment money into his coat pocket. That should have been the end of it. He had worked his little game to perfection at least ten times already by mid afternoon, taking in more than five hundred dollars. But this Yellow Bird refused to go quietly like the others. He spun away from the grasp of Corporal DeKalb and charged back toward the table. Private Stevens, DeKalb's fellow guard, intercepted the irate Cherokee. They struggled briefly, and Stevens was attempting to draw his pistol when Captain Tanner intervened.

"That's enough!" Peter shouted with authority. He had moved his horse close enough to place the tip of his saber right between the faces of the two combatants. Peter threw his leg forward across the neck of his horse and slid to the ground, keeping the sword in position between Stevens and Yellow Bird. "Step back. Both of you."

"But Cap'n, he tried goin' through the line twice!" the agent informed Peter. "He's a thievin' Injun!"

"Yes," Peter said. "I saw the whole thing."

"He's lying!" Yellow Bird pointed accusingly.

The agent drew a pistol from his waistband. "Ain't no God damn Injun gonna call me a—" Before he could finish, Peter had whipped the blade across the table, pressing the point against the base of the agent's throat. Peter lowered the steel tip down the front of the agent's coat until it caught the edge of his pocket. A single flick slit the fabric and the coins clattered to the ground, drawing the eyes of everyone within view.

"Take your money," Peter told Yellow Bird, then brought his sword back up. "Corporal, place this man under arrest," he instructed DeKalb. Keeping the saber's point against the agent's chest, Peter guided the exposed thief out from behind the table. The agent was about to protest, but Peter shook his head, communicating the unequivocal folly of speaking at this point.

Yellow Bird expressed his gratitude to the *yo-neg* army captain and bent down to retrieve only the fifty-three dollars due him, leaving the rest on the ground. As DeKalb led the agent away, Peter's sword came back across the table and tapped the ledger book.

"You're in charge here now," he informed the assistant.

"Yes, sir," the frightened bureaucrat nervously slid along the bench to assume his position in front of the money box.

"You do know how to count?"

"Yes, sir," the assistant answered, fully understanding the captain's implied warning not to *mis*count.

"And I'd advise you to sew your pockets shut," Peter added. The newly appointed agent smoothed his coat as though to symbolically seal shut the pockets and, with trembling fingers, began stacking the coins. Peter slipped his sword back into it's scabbard and left the table. He hadn't expected to find his father-in-law standing only a few feet away. "Mr. Drummond! Didn't think I'd see you here today."

"That was a decent thing you did," William complimented Peter as the two men shook hands.

"With all due respect, sir, decency had nothing to do with it. You know how I feel about these people. But orders are orders. The law's the law. That agent was stealing."

"Well, the results were honorable, if not the intentions," William quipped.

"Sir?"

"Never mind," William dismissed the subject. "Have you seen Major Ridge and his party? I need to speak with him."

"Near the front," Peter recalled having seen the renowned leader and his entourage. "They've already boarded. They'll be leaving soon."

"Thank you," William said and hurried off through the crowd. Peter, still a little puzzled by their exchange, mounted his horse.

* * * * * * *

Major Ridge and his wife were settling in on the flatboat barge. With them was their eight-year-old mentally retarded granddaughter, Clarinda, an adorable, innocent child with large, loving brown eyes and a smile for everyone she met. Servants and other members of the party were boarding and making sure their trunks and crates were all accounted for and secured on deck. When William reached the loading area, a Tennessee Volunteer blocked his approach to the barge.

"No more! This boat's full!" the Volunteer stepped in front of William, pointing to the next boat. "You'll have to board over there."

"I have to talk to Major Ridge."

"I said you'll have to go over there!" the Volunteer repeated loudly. A deep, resonant voice boomed from the boat behind them. "Let him through," commanded Major Ridge, leaning against the boat's railing. Reluctantly the Volunteer allowed William to pass. At the edge of the creosoted dock William shook hands with the white-haired, sixty-six-year-old leader, assaulted by the fiends of age, yet still alert and proud.

"*Si-yo*, Ridge!"

"*Si-yo, Wi-li* Drummond." The Ridge gripped his hand strongly. "It was good of you to come."

"I couldn't let my friends leave without saying good-bye," William said, repeating his practiced Cherokee, "*Do-na-da-go-hŭ-i*."

Pushing past the Volunteer who had assumed a *what-the-hell-let-them-all-through* attitude, John Ridge, the Major's son, joined them at boatside. He shook William's hand, genuinely glad to see him, despite their history of political differences over Cherokee policy.

"*Si-yo*, Mister Drummond. Decent of you to come down today."

"We shall miss you," The Major added. "You've been a good friend to the *Tsa-la-gi*."

"The *Tsa-la-gi* have many *yo-neg* friends," William reminded them.

"But more enemies," Major Ridge countered, then looked out to the sprawling activity before them where army soldiers, Tennessee Volunteers and government agents watched, herded and, whenever possible, took advantage of his people. William knew the truth of his words and there was nothing to be added. He looked at John Ridge.

"You aren't travelling in the same boat with your father?"

"Sarah and I won't be going this trip," John answered, speaking of his beautiful *yo-neg* wife from New England. "We have a lot of loose ends to tie up. A couple of the children are ill. Next time. Only the Light One is going with them now," he waved to Clarinda who had joined her grandfather at the rail and was beaming with joy at the sight of her father.

"It looks to be going smoothly," William scanned the loading area. "Better than I had expected, actually."

"Be not deceived, my friend," John responded. "The government wants it to go well with us—just like the six hundred who went in January. We've been paid generously for our property. Our needs are being well met. We're merely bait—to persuade Ross and his followers to stop resisting the treaty and follow us west. *Look!* the government is saying, *how comfortably they travel! How well they are provided for!"*

"You have an astute political eye, John," William laughed at the insightful polemic. "You'll make a good chief some day."

"Or governor," John smiled.

"Or governor," William agreed.

They were interrupted when Captain Tanner called out loudly from atop his horse, only a few feet away from them. "Boats four, five and six! Prepare to cast off!" A white crewman came to the boat's railing beside Major Ridge. He braced a long pole against a stump on the bank while a shoreman untied the mooring rope. Loud bells clanged aboard the three barges. William dug a letter from his pocket and passed it across to Major Ridge. John Ridge balanced himself on the boat rail, hugged his retarded daughter and bade her a loving farewell. Friends, relatives and well-wishers crowded to the edge of the boat for a last word, a final hug, a handshake, a touch.

"Please! Give this letter to my son, Michael," William shouted above the din, "if you see him. I believe he might be with your people in the west."

"I'll see he gets it," The Ridge promised, barely grasping the letter before the crewman nudged him out of the way and pushed again on the pole. The gap between the barge and the shore began to widen. Finally John Ridge sprang from the edge of the boat, barely making it back to solid ground near William. The two of them moved along the bank parallel to the flatboat, trying to keep up until the barge caught the current and moved too swiftly. John stopped, shading his eyes as he watched them go. William ran on a few steps then slowed, waving to his departing friends.

"*Gŭ-wa-ga-ti dŭ-ga-le-ni-s-ga!*" William called out.

"*Do-da-da-go-hŭ-i!*" came the shouts from the boat. While friends and relatives watched the loaded barge pull away, Peter yelled once more from atop his horse.

"Boats seven! Eight! Nine! Into position! Let's go!"

The number four, five and six boats were towed about a quarter mile down stream where they would be moored to the opposite bank. It took another two and a half hours to load the remaining five barges. William circulated among the crowd, chatting with Cherokees he had known for years and others he had met only recently. Many had been his clients in suits against the state of Georgia, against some county in northeast Alabama or perhaps a town in southern Tennessee.

By the time the last flatboat had been loaded and the steamer came back around to attach its cables to the first barge, the hubbub on shore had abated. The paddle-wheeler emitted a shrill blast and huge billows of black smoke clawed their way skyward. The barges, swollen with their load of displaced humanity, crept along the golden, glassy surface of the Tennessee River, heading westward straight into the giant fireball of the setting sun.

"May God protect you, my friends," William said softly.

"Amen to that, sir," Peter Tanner added from a few feet away. William reacted to the unexpected sentiment echoed by his son-in-law. "Perhaps this whole thing will turn out all right after all," Peter said.

"I'm sure we'd all like to believe so," William agreed, but he wasn't convinced it would. Life's realities, William had learned, had a way of seldom conforming to one's plans, dreams, desires, hopes and wishes.

14

A new split-rail fence encircled the verdant meadow, plush from the ample spring rains that had drenched the Indian Territory. At the field's edge sat a half-built cabin. Logs had been cut from the surrounding woods and enough stones to finish the chimney had been hauled from the adjacent creek flowing southward toward Fort Coffee. The rafters were in place, but the roof wasn't yet complete. A canvas stretched across the opening flapped gently in the breeze, it's rhythmic pop perfectly synchronized with the scraping of a wood-plane.

Michael Drummond had tanned to a dark brown from all his outdoor work. His rippling muscles glistened in the sunlight and his shoulder-length hair hung from beneath the Cherokee turban. Sweat dripped from his face as he labored to shape the eight-foot beam that would become the fireplace mantle. From a cool spot of bare earth, his devoted dog, *Gŭ-li*, head resting on paws, had been observing Michael's toil with canine indifference for most of the day. He shifted his position with a plaintive whine.

Gŭ-li—or raccoon—had appeared on the trail behind Michael and Annie early one morning on their way back from an overnight stay with Uncle Andrew and Aunt Rebecca. Annie had been the first to notice him and they didn't know how long he had been following them. They had seen no farms and no other travellers on the road since they left the Sixkiller cabin just before sunrise. The dog followed them all the way home and patiently waited for whatever scrap of food Michael and Annie chose to throw him. He was a leggy, sharp-boned, floppy-eared, grayish-brown mixture of different hound breeds. His newly adopted family had named him *Gŭ-li* because of the odd stripe of black coloration that spanned both eyes like a raccoon.

"You'd rather be hunting, wouldn't you, boy?" Michael paused from his work. "Yeah. Me, too. But you won't be whining this winter when you're stretched out in front of a big warm fire." He examined his handiwork, spotted an uneven place and shaved a bit here and there. Suddenly the air was rent by a piercing scream.

"Michael! Come here!"

"Annie! Oh, God!" Michael dropped his tools and dashed toward the other side of the cabin. "It's time! The baby!"

Annie had grown more beautiful with each passing month, Michael thought, though he hadn't yet unravelled the conundrum of the pregnant female's unpredictable mood changes. All just a part of the greater mystery, he told himself.

"Michael! *E-he-na!*" she yelled again.

"I'm coming! Hold on!" Michael shouted back. He envisioned her lying in the midst of her tomato plants, gripping their stalks while she gave birth to their son. Great was his relief when he saw her standing there in the garden, leaning against the hoe, one hand pressed against her lower back. He raced toward her, not sure what to do. In an instant he forgot everything they had discussed about his course of action when the time came. "It's time! The baby's coming!" he skidded to a halt at the edge of the garden. "What do we do? Inside! Come on! Get inside! Lie down!"

"Stop it!" she swatted at him as she would at an annoying fly. "Do I look like I'm having a baby? Every time I twitch, you think I'm having the baby!"

"But you screamed..." Michael pleaded, perplexed.

Annie pointed toward the center of the garden. Amidst trampled sprouts stood their cow, calmly chewing the young, tender shoots of corn. In a delayed reaction to the commotion of Michael's arrival, the animal swung her head around with her dumb, beastly stare, blinked at the couple and went back to eating. Beyond the cow Michael and Annie saw the section of rail fence pushed out of position to gain access to the garden's succulent treasures.

"Not again," Michael groaned. "Come on, boy," he called the dog. This was the fifth time and Michael was determined it would be the last. He and *Gŭ-li* chased the cow back and forth along the fence, but she refused to go through the opening. Annie looked on, amused, enjoying the antics of her husband and the two animals. After nearly half an hour Michael succeeded in spooking the cow back through the fence. By that time Annie was laughing so hard her eyes were filled with tears. She rested on a stump and watched Michael bind the fence rails with fresh rawhide strips. Since it was almost sundown, they decided to abandoned their work for the day.

Inside the cabin, in the gray light of dusk, Michael muscled the large mantlepiece into place. He stepped back and wiped his brow, admiring his handiwork. Annie lit a pair of candles against the growing darkness, setting them at opposite ends of the cabin's newest addition. She moved up close behind Michael and pressed her swollen abdomen against him, then gently turned him around and took his sweaty face in her hands. Her fingers slipped along the sides of his head until she gripped handfuls of his thick locks, pulling his face to hers for a passionate kiss.

230

CHAPTER

15

Summer 1837

So far it had promised to be another beautiful Georgia summer day. The cavalry sergeant riding beside the team of horses pulling the large, new carriage kept his eyes straight ahead. The sun was warm and comforting on his back and it made him sleepy. He shook himself awake and glanced at the corporal who kept pace on the opposite side. A third army horse, belonging to the driver, trotted behind the coach. Bringing up the rear was a fourth U. S. cavalry soldier. Each man knew the harsh penalties awaiting them should they stumble in their duty to guard their precious cargo.

Susanna Drummond Tanner rode alone, with barely room to move inside the carriage amid her bags and trunks. She leaned across a strapped leather case and stuck her head out.

"Sergeant!" she called out, waiting for a response that never came. "Sergeant! I'm talking to you! Stop pretending you don't hear me!"

The sergeant rolled his eyes in exasperation and looked back over his shoulder at this woman who, he had come to understand, possessed an uncanny ability to sour an otherwise wonderful day. He refused to say anything, waiting for her newest complaint.

"Could you please ride on the other side? Your dust is blowing in the window and getting all over me. It's very annoying."

The sergeant looked down at the ground whipping past beneath his horse. He was hard pressed to see any dust at all, but he knew exactly what he was expected to say. "Yes, Mrs. Tanner. Sorry you were annoyed, Ma'am." He slowed his horse and waited for the carriage to pass then circled behind to join the corporal on the other side. The trailing rear guard couldn't suppress a smile. "As you were, soldier," the sergeant warned.

"Sir!" the trailing rider snapped obediently. The sergeant galloped to catch up and rode even with the corporal.

"There," Susanna voiced her approval from the carriage. "That's much better."

* * * * * * *

From the veranda of the Drummond home Susanna and her mother watched Ezekiel and the soldiers unload her luggage and

231

carefully stack everything at the edge of the raised porch. Reba came out carrying a tray loaded with clinking glasses and a pitcher of freshly made peach nectar. She set the tray on a table near the steps and went back inside.

"I'm glad you had these soldier boys to see you home." Elizabeth remarked. She hoped the nice young soldiers would realize she was genuinely grateful.

"I do love travelling with a military escort," Susanna admitted with pride. "It's so necessary these days, you know, what with all the renegades and rowdies causing so much trouble." She held out her chin and stirred a little air with the hand-made fan that matched her ensemble, adding, "Besides, it's only fitting for the wife of a United States Army *Major.*"

"Major?! You don't mean it!" Elizabeth reacted.

"I do, indeed!" Susanna squealed. "Peter's promotion came through! Isn't it wonderful?"

"But you didn't say anything in your letter!"

"I wanted it to be a surprise!"

Reba was coming back out with a tray of sweetcakes and jam. "Well, you just all full of surprises, ain't you, Missy," she said with the familiar snide tone she reserved almost exclusively for Susanna.

"You have no idea, Miss Reba," Susanna tossed her hair.

Reba stepped past them to set the second tray on the table beside the first. "Ain't nothin' you do surprise me," she mumbled.

"We were concerned to hear that Peter has gone off on a campaign to Florida," Elizabeth intercepted the friction.

"Oh, I know it," Susanna agreed. "Chasing around in the swamps after those troublesome Seminole Indians. Peter says they're worse than these Cherokees and Choctaws."

Elizabeth had little first hand knowledge of such unpleasant matters and preferred to keep it that way. "Well, we're thrilled you've decided to come stay with us while he's away."

"Where's Father?" Susanna asked. "I want to tell him about Peter's promotion!" Her brow furrowed when she noticed the troubled expression on her mother's face at the mention of William.

"He's off in New Echota," Elizabeth sighed heavily.

"That little Indian town? What on earth!?" Susanna had never been able to fathom some of the things her father did. Was it because he was an attorney? Or simply that he was a man? And why, in God's name, had he always been so interested in the affairs of these dreadful Indians?

"Every day he's either there or he's running into Titusville, hoping for a letter from Michael," Elizabeth complained. "It's grieving him something awful. I just wish we'd get some word..."

It was a subject Susanna would have chosen to completely avoid. "Well, that's not likely to happen, if you ask me," she said abruptly.

"Didn't hear nobody ask you," Reba mumbled from behind them. If Susanna heard it, she didn't react, perhaps pleased she was forcing Reba to keep her thoughts mostly to herself.

"If I know my little brother," Susanna went on, "after taking up with that Indian girl, I'm sure he's quite the full-feathered heathen by now."

"Susanna! How can you say such a thing?!" Elizabeth came to her son's defense.

"I mean it!" Susanna gave no ground. "Wherever he is, he's probably running about the countryside murdering and scalping decent white folks!" This scathing indictment, she knew, was certain to get a rise out of both her mother and Reba.

"You hush yo' mouth, girl!" Reba leaned past Elizabeth and wagged her thick finger right under Susanna's nose. "I mean it! Don't nobody talk 'bout Mistah Michael that'a way!"

"Mother!" Susanna greatly exaggerated her shock, hoping to enlist Elizabeth's sympathy against this dreadful busybody. "Did you hear how she spoke to me!"

"Reba's right!" Elizabeth snapped. "Don't you ever say such a spiteful thing in my house again! Do you understand?" She glowered at her daughter, who was, in a rare moment, stunned speechless. "Lord, I'm just glad your father didn't have to hear this," Elizabeth shook her head in dismay.

When the soldiers had finished unloading the carriage, they retreated a polite distance before wiping the perspiration from their faces and necks. The sergeant waited by the veranda for Elizabeth to finish before he spoke.

"I can have the men take your things inside, if you like, Mrs. Tanner."

"Yes, Sergeant," Susanna welcomed the interruption. "That would be wonderful. Reba will show you." She made sure everyone present understood she was issuing a direct order to the black woman. "Reba, show the Sergeant and his men where to put my things. Upstairs in my room."

Reba could not be intimidated. "Yes, Miz Susie," she flashed an artificial smile and added with thinly veiled sarcasm, "It's so good to have you back home." Reba watched two of the soldiers struggle with some of the bags. She squinted her patented evil eye at the sergeant who, like her, had been observing his men. "Well," she rolled her head and challenged him, "you jes' gon' stand there and watch?" The sergeant grabbed two pieces of luggage. The soldiers, loaded with bags, looked at her, expecting her to lead the way. But Reba possessed the qualities of a born leader and knew how to delegate. "Zeke! Show these mens where to put Miz Susie's b'longin's," she ordered and narrowed her eyes with a flick of her head toward the door, gestures which Ezekiel knew meant she wouldn't budge from the veranda because she didn't want to miss a word of the gossip. "I'll have y'all some nectar when you get back," she announced to the soldiers and continued to fuss with the tray. "An' some sweetcakes." The men disappeared into the house single file behind Ezekiel. Reba ever so slowly poured the peach nectar, hanging close to Elizabeth and Susanna.

"Well, whatever glorious adventure my dear brother Michael is making of his life," Susanna said in quiet defiance for the scolding she had received, "there's one thing I'm sure of. He won't be presenting you with your first grandchild!"

Her desired effect had been achieved. Elizabeth was shocked. Even Reba couldn't prevent the glass pitcher from clinking loudly against the goblets.

"You mean...?" Elizabeth's hand covered her mouth.

"Yes!" Susanna grinned. She was once more in command of the conversation. "We just found out last week. Isn't it wonderful? I'm going to have a baby!"

Elizabeth covered her mouth with both hands and her eyes filled with tears. Reba regained her composure and finished pouring the peach juice. "Sweet Jesus!" she clucked in amazement. "Jes' what we need 'round here...another little Miss Susie-britches!"

"Why, thank you, Reba!" Susanna replied with sarcasm. "I knew you'd be pleased." She took her mother's hands and pulled them away from her mouth, gripping them with excitement. "If it's a boy, we're going to name him William. After Father. Peter's certain it's a boy."

"Well...I...I just don't know what to say!" Elizabeth was genuinely astonished. "Your father's going to be so happy for you..." Gradually the news began to sink in. Elizabeth took her daughter by the shoulders, looking her up and down. "My little girl...having a baby..."

They hugged and Elizabeth wept and laughed at the same time. Zeke and the soldiers came back outside and sensed an

234

emotional exchange had taken place, but they knew it didn't concern them. The soldiers waited beside their horses for further orders. Reba kept her promise and carried the tray of nectar and sweetcakes down the steps, mumbling as she went, "Lawd, lawd. The mysteries of this world..."

"What is it?" Ezekiel asked softly.

"Hush," she snapped good-naturedly. "Ain't nobody said nothin' to you! Nosey men. Always gettin up in other folks's bidness. Here..." she handed him a glass then pushed past him with the tray. "These mens need some 'freshments fo' they has to git on back to soldierin'."

16

Ft. Smith — Arkansas Territory

Boats of all kinds were docked up and down the southern bank of the Arkansas River just east of the border separating Indian Territory and Arkansas Territory. There were steamers, barges and flatboats, ferries, dories, several canoes and a few rafts. The rain-muddied streets of the bustling town were teeming with Indians, whites and mixed-bloods. There were new immigrant Cherokees from the east mixing with Old Settlers—Cherokees who had journeyed west years ago, many as early as 1805. There were Creeks, Choctaws and Chickasaws—tribes which, along with the Cherokee and Seminoles, had patronizingly been designated by the whites as the *Five Civilized Tribes*. They had also been driven from their homelands in the southeast in recent years. Aside from Indians, there were merchants, gamblers, whiskey peddlers, charlatans and mountebanks, prostitutes and Indian agents. And soldiers. There were many, many soldiers.

Michael Drummond drove his two-horse wagon up the street, navigating the maze of carts, wheelbarrows and pedestrians. Beside him sat Andrew Sixkiller, who eyed the soldiers with mistrust. Michael threaded the wagon toward the large, newly constructed establishment that occupied almost an entire block. Nailed atop the unpainted wooden structure, a crude sign announced the *Genaral Store*. Michael eased into line behind another wagon at the loading dock, a chest-high platform made of rough-cut eight-by-eight timbers spaced an inch apart. Not one to sit idle, Michael leaped onto the loading dock to help a young Cherokee man in his early twenties. Handsome and muscular, there was something about the way he moved that reminded Michael of his beloved *tso-s-da-da-nŭ*, James Walker. The young man flashed a smile of appreciation, but neither spoke until the wagon was loaded.

"*Wa-do*," the young man thanked his helper in Cherokee, then introduced himself and asked Michael's name. "*Da-qua-to-a Johnny Fields. Ga-to-no de-tsa-to-a?*"

Michael finished dusting himself off and shook hands. "Michael. *Mi-ki*." He indicated Andrew, still seated in the wagon. "*E-du-tsi* Andrew Sixkiller."

"*Si-yo*," the taciturn uncle said.

Johnny led his mule-drawn wagon away from the platform to

make way for Michael's rig. "Thanks for helping out," he said. "Can I return the favor?"

"We can handle it," Michael answered, not wanting to delay Johnny from getting home.

"You Old Settlers?" Johnny asked leisurely. He was in no hurry.

"Not really. Been here since late last year," Michael answered.

"I came out about a year ago. From Georgia," Johnny offered.

"We're from Georgia! Is your family here?"

Johnny's expression darkened with recollection and he shook his head no. "My mother's dead. Last year, I decided I didn't want to be a stupid farmer in Georgia like my father."

"He's still back there?" Michael asked, visions of his own lawyer-farmer father filling his thoughts. Johnny nodded. "So, you headed west..." Michael peeked into Johnny's wagon, reviewing the supplies they had just loaded, "...to become a stupid farmer in Arkansas."

Johnny stared soberly at Michael, who was afraid he had offended his new friend until Johnny broke into a broad grin. "Looks that way!" he laughed. Even the normally laconic Uncle Andrew smiled. Johnny climbed up into his own wagon and took the reins. "Guess I'll see you down at the allotment depot," he said.

"We don't get an allotment," Michael shook his head. "We didn't come out under the treaty. Besides," Michael shrugged, "I'm not *Tsa-la-gi*."

"Choctaw?" Johnny asked, thinking he'd guessed the wrong tribe.

"*U-ne-gŭ*," Michael used the formal Cherokee word for white. "*Yo-neg*. Plain ol' white man." He slapped Johnny's mule on the rump and the wagon lurched into motion. Johnny couldn't help looking back at Michael with a puzzled expression. He would have figured Michael for at least half, maybe three-quarter *Tsa-la-gi*. Not Cherokee? Not even Indian? A *yo-neg*? Johnny waved once more before heading up the side street toward the allotment depot. Andrew clucked the horses forward, easing the wagon into position. Michael began tossing the hundred-pound bags of grain into the back.

They finished loading and pulled out into the busy thoroughfare, maneuvering through the shifting mass of mud, wood, metal, animals and people. Uncle Andrew found himself reaching for the reins on several occasions when he felt Michael was going too fast, was headed for a disastrous collision or was about to run down a pedestrian. Each time, in anticipation of Andrew's move, Michael shifted the reins out of reach. And each time Andrew pretended he had merely been stretching. He never saw the hint of a smile on Michael's face.

"With these new steel plowshares, I'll have forty acres turned in no time." Michael was looking forward to getting his homestead under cultivation.

"If they stay sharp," Andrew reminded him. "Tonight we'll make medicine for them."

Michael didn't consider himself a superstitious man, but he had been around Andrew Sixkiller long enough to know that Cherokee medicine was not to be taken lightly. Too many times he had seen Andrew's predictions come true. Back in Georgia, seeds Andrew and John had *fixed* with medicine had yielded crops three, four, even five times the harvest of identical seeds in the same soil and the same climate. He would ask Andrew not only to *fix* the plowshares but the seeds as well. And there was one more special medicine request.

"And for my son who will soon be born."

"And for your son," Andrew repeated.

From the side street taking them back to the riverside road they heard a loud and bitter argument. The road sloped down toward a string of warehouses backed up against wooden piers strung along the river, each with a loading dock facing the street. One of these warehouses sported a large, stencil-painted sign: *U S GOVT DEPOT / INDIAN ALLOTMENTS*. More than thirty Indians were gathered to draw their monthly allowance of supplies and provisions promised them by the many treaties their tribes had agreed to over the years. Each man hoped that, for once, he might receive his full and proper portion so he and his family could survive until the crops were ready to be harvested. There were also a few single women driving their own wagons. These were either widows or the wives of husbands too ill or too busy to make the trip to Ft. Smith. As they approached, Michael and Andrew saw Johnny Fields on the loading dock engaged in a heated argument with a pair of allotment agents.

"That's it, Injun! Now git on outa here!" one of the agents—a heavy, bearded slob named Callow—yelled at Johnny. Callow's associate, Wilby, was a thin, pock-marked weasel with a darkly discolored, fist-sized goiter on his neck.

238

"They's other folks waitin'," Wilby pointed at the long line of wagons.

"I'm not taking this!" Johnny protested loudly. "It's rotten!"

A gruff and sweaty army sergeant with an overhanging stomach perched atop spindly legs comfortably finished urinating off the far end of the platform. Shaking his head with irritated dismay, he clomped back toward the argument.

"What's the trouble here?" demanded Wakefield, the depot sergeant.

Callow's upper lip rolled into a sneer and he pointed to Johnny. "Damned snot-nosed Injun whinin' 'bout his allotment."

"It's all ruined!" Johnny pleaded his case to Sergeant Wakefield. "Rotten! Look for yourself!" He dragged one of the heavy wooden boxes from the tailgate of his wagon back onto the dock. With his bare hands he ripped off the nailed lid, peeled back the stained, heavy duck-cloth and held up a large slab of meat right under the noses of Callow and the sergeant. They recoiled from the foul odor that flew up at them, stabbing its way into the very membrane of their nostrils. "It wasn't cured proper!" Johnny said emphatically and tossed the meat down in front of a sad-eyed hound lying on the cool dirt of the dock's shadow. The dog merely sniffed the rancid gift and shifted his position. "See?! Even the dog won't touch it!"

"That's all we got," the grimy agent shrugged with practiced indifference. "Take it or leave it."

"You expect me to eat this?" Johnny shoved the open box toward Wilby with his foot. Many of the Cherokees—even those who had already loaded their wagons and carts and had pulled away from the dock—began checking their allotment rations. One old Cherokee man pried the lid off a box with a new ax handle and held up another slab of putrefaction.

"Mine's rotten, too!" he called out for all to hear.

"So is mine!" shouted another mixed-blood from the other side of the crowd. Both men threw the meat onto the ground next to the dog exactly as Johnny had done. The poor hound, thinking itself under attack, tucked its tail and retreated farther beneath the warehouse.

"This cornmeal is full of weevils," a middle-aged full-blood Cherokee woman said with newfound boldness.

"And rats!" Johnny added, pulling a dead rodent from his box of allotment meal. Others in the crowd took courage, daring to be heard.

"We can't feed this to our children," a young, mixed-blood mother objected.

Michael and Andrew had watched the entire drama unfold before them. As the crowd grew increasingly belligerent, Andrew nudged Michael, indicating they should move on past the warehouse and head for home. But Michael couldn't take his eyes off Johnny Fields. He knew Johnny had to be fully aware of the consequences of openly defying the government agents, yet obviously his sense of outrage at this bureaucratic abuse wouldn't allow him to be silent. Michael had found a kindred spirit.

"Get him out of here, Sergeant Wakefield!" Wilby pointed at Johnny. "He's nothing but a trouble maker!"

"He's disturbin' the peace!" Callow added.

"Move it along, son. There's nothing we can do," the sergeant couldn't argue with the evidence Johnny and the others had presented, but he also didn't want any trouble, for the simple reason that he would have to get involved, call in some of his men and, at the end of the day, deliver a written report to the duty officer. Life would be much easier if this problem would just go away. "All of you!" he called out in a tone not unfriendly. "Move along now!"

The blubbery Callow, spurred by Wakefield's apparent endorsement of his and Wilby's position, pushed the box of rotten meat back toward Johnny. Without hesitation, Johnny threw the dead rat at Callow, who cringed and jumped back when the decaying little carcass bounced off his gibraltar stomach.

"You son of a bitch!" the agent yelled. "Sergeant! Did you see what he done?!"

The ferret-faced Wilby, convinced he had the full backing of the United States Army, lunged boldly at Johnny, who easily side-stepped and drove him hard into the warehouse wall.

"I want decent cornmeal!" Johnny shouted at Callow. "And meat that ain't rotten! I'm not leaving 'til I get it!"

Wilby gathered himself and pushed off the wall, driving Johnny right into Callow's bear-hug. Johnny's foot shot up and kicked the weasel man in the groin, knocking him flat on his back. But struggle as he might, Johnny couldn't free himself from Callow's vice-like grip. Sergeant Wakefield stepped cautiously up from the side and grabbed a fistful of Johnny's shirt.

"I ain't tellin' you again, boy! Take your allotment and git on outa here!"

Johnny went limp as though acquiescing to the sergeant's warning. When he felt Callow relax his grip, Johnny twisted to one

240

side within the confines of Callow's massive arms and kicked Wakefield on the side of his leg. Instantly the sergeant back-handed Johnny in the face and drew his pistol, shoving it under Johnny's nose.

"There's gonna be some fresh dead meat in that box, all right!" Wakefield growled.

Wilby, gulping shallow, rapid breaths, pulled himself back to his feet. From beneath his coat he pulled a pistol and started toward Johnny.

Michael didn't wait. He sprang from his wagon, drawing his knife before he hit the ground. It took him only seconds to sprint through the crowd and leap into Johnny's wagon and from there to the dock just as Wilby reached Johnny. With the point of his knife against Wilby's neck, Michael grabbed his gun hand. The pistol fired. Splinters flew from the post right beside Sergeant Wakefield's head. The shot immediately brought soldiers running around the corner from the nearest tavern. Automatically they trained their rifles on Michael and Johnny. They were Indians, by all appearances, and therefore presumed the instigators of whatever trouble was afoot.

Wakefield released his hold on Johnny Fields to confront the intruder, jamming his pistol in Michael's face and taking away the knife. The two *trouble makers*, both held at gunpoint, were pushed roughly against the wall by Callow, Wilby and the first of the soldiers to arrive. Michael and Johnny held their hands high and offered no resistance. They had been outraged. They had been indignant. They had been courageous. But they would not be stupid.

"You could'a killed somebody, boy!" Sergeant Wakefield screamed at Michael.

"They started it!" Michael lowered one hand just enough to point at Callow and Wilby. "I want them charged with assault!"

"It's all right!" Johnny knew that to push further could prove fatal. "It was just a misunderstanding."

"It's not all right!" Michael refused to give in. "They have to make full restitution for these defective commodities!"

They all looked strangely at Michael, but it was Wakefield who voiced their puzzlement. "*Restitution? Defective commodities?* Them's high-falutin' words for an Injun, boy."

"I'm not Indian," Michael corrected his captor. "And I'm not a boy"!

This brought forth a gut shaking guffaw from the behemoth Callow.

"Drummond! Forget it! Let's go!" Johnny urged.

"You hear that?!" Callow howled. "He ain't no Injun!"

"My name's Michael Drummond. I'm as white as you are!"

The soldiers joined in the hearty laughter at Michael's claim. Wilby stepped forward to contribute to the jeering. "If it looks like a duck, walks like a duck, quacks like a duck—must be a duck!" he paused, then added, "A *Injun* duck!" Wilby duck-waddled along the dock, basking in the wave of derision from Callow and the soldiers.

Sergeant Wakefield led Michael and Johnny to the edge of the platform. He returned Michael's knife and placed an arm around his shoulder, drawing him close for a fatherly word of advice. "I don't know what your game is, son, but you better get on outa here before you get into some serious trouble."

"Yes, sir. We're leaving," Johnny was anxious to defuse the situation and the best way to do that was to disappear. He tugged at Michael's sleeve. "Let's go."

"Not until they give you some decent goods," Michael jerked his arm away. He had launched himself into the fray on Johnny's behalf, but now the incident had escalated to a matter of greater principle. "All of you!" Michael shouted to the crowd.

Johnny grabbed Michael's sleeve again, and this time he didn't let go. He glared at Michael and growled, "You've done enough for one day, *yo-neg*."

"Yeah, white boy," Wilby sneered.

Using a ploy he had seen Johnny resort to earlier with Callow, Michael dropped his eyes and relaxed just long enough for Johnny to loosen his grip. Michael then sprang from the dock into the back of the nearest wagon. The old Cherokee couple in the wagon's seat looked on with curiosity, wondering, as were many others, what this crazy young warrior—who claimed he wasn't even *Tsa-la-gi*—would do next. Their apprehension that he might cause more trouble was mixed with a quiet admiration of his willingness to fight. With unblinking defiance, Michael shoved a box out of the wagon with his foot. The wooden crate split open, spilling its tainted contents into the mud.

Michael looked at Johnny, who understood for the first time the depth of his new *yo-neg* friend's commitment. He bounded into the back of another wagon and repeated Michael's act, pushing a box out with his foot. Immediately Michael tossed out a second box. Johnny launched another. Then the young mixed-blood mother dragged a box from her wagon. Soon more than half the Cherokees were dumping their spoiled allotment goods into the muddy street.

242

Again Michael met Johnny's look. This time Johnny's expression was one of respect and gratitude. Michael looked down at the growing pile of boxes and crates. He saw the broken containers with their spoiled meat, some of it almost as green as the letters of the boxes' painted logo, *Glasgow & Harrison*. Then he froze when he saw the writing on some of the spilled boxes of cornmeal. *Ogilvie Mercantile / Titusville, Georgia, U.S.A. - Gov't Contractor*. Michael saw Uncle Andrew staring at the same thing.

"Like father, like son," Michael said with disgust. He hopped back into the seat beside Andrew. "I guess Alton picked right up where Titus left off." He grabbed the reins and popped them against the horses' rumps. They pulled away from the warehouse, picking their way through the Cherokees dumping their defective goods. The soldiers and the agents looked on helplessly from the dock.

When they headed west along the river road that would take them back into Indian Territory, Michael and Uncle Andrew paid little attention to the steamboat rounding the bend in the Arkansas River behind them to the east. Nor did they notice the eleven flatboat barges strung out behind the mid-wheeler with their cargo of immigrant Cherokees.

Michael and Andrew had ridden for almost an hour without speaking when Andrew—trying to keep a straight face—said, "*Ka-wo-nu-s-di*. Little Duck. It's a good name."

"Forget it," Michael said. "It's a stupid name."

"No, I like it," Andrew insisted. "If it looks like a . duck...walks like a duck...quacks like a duck... I like it. *Ka-wo-nu-s-di*." Michael elbowed his wife's uncle good naturedly, knowing Andrew would enjoy telling this story for a long time to come.

* * * * * * *

Gŭ-li ran to greet them and trotted beside the wagon until they pulled up to Michael's temporary barn. Because they were losing the daylight, the men decided to immediately unload the supplies and the new farm implements. The wagon was almost emptied when they heard a loud crashing sound from the cabin.

"Annie!" Michael reacted with panic. How could he have been so stupid? So forgetful? So selfish? He should have rushed right in to check on her the instant they arrived. What if she were lying in there right now, giving birth to their son? What if the baby had come while he was away? He never should have gone to Ft. Smith in the first place!

Michael raced to the cabin, slamming to a halt in the doorway. The inside of the cabin was in shambles. Chairs were overturned. The table was tilted against the wall. Pots and pans were scattered about the floor. Annie was in the corner by the stove, one hand on her hip in a way he had seen her countless times when casually cooking dinner.

"Annie?" Michael said softly, waiting patiently for the response that never came. "Are you all right?" he ventured.

She spun and threw an iron stove lid at him. He ducked just in time. Splinters flew when the stove lid hit the door facing. "*Si-qua!*" she yelled. "This is all your fault!"

"What's wrong?" he was genuinely puzzled. Why had she called him a pig?

"*U-tso-n-ti!*" she hissed the name *snake*. "You did this to me! I hate you!"

Michael's eyes went to the huge puddle at her feet. Annie's water had broken. She bent over, clutching her swollen belly, gripped by another contraction.

"Oh, my God!" Michael whispered hoarsely.

"Michael...help me!" Annie's agonizing scream was laced with genuine fear.

He spun in the doorway and shouted toward the barn, "Andrew! She's having the baby!" Her uncle dropped the heavy bag from his shoulder and sprang up into the wagon seat. Michael was glad they hadn't unhitched the horses yet. He rushed to Annie. She clung to him, talking fast between rapid, shallow breaths.

"I'm so glad you're here! I was afraid you wouldn't get back in time. Why didn't you come in to see about me? I didn't want to be all alone..."

"You're right. I'm so sorry. It's gonna be all right," he tried to calm her. "Here. Let's get you to the bed." He led her across the room.

"*Gŭ-ge-yu-i, Mi-ki. Gŭ-ge-yu-i,*" Annie's voice was shaky.

"Shh. I know," he said soothingly. "I love you, too, *wa-le-la.*"

"I'm no *wa-le-la,*" she was about to cry. "*Ga-li-tso-hi-da wa-ga!*" she lamented.

"You're not a fat cow," he reassured her, almost laughing. "You're beautiful!" He sat her on the edge of the bed and was lifting her feet when the next contraction came. She grabbed the knife from his belt and pushed him away, her tears vanquished by a snarl. Michael took a step toward her but stopped when she brandished the knife.

244

"Stay away from me, *ga-da-ha gi-li!*" she growled, now calling him the filthy dog that he was.

"It's all right, Annie," he forced himself to remain calm. "It's supposed to be this way." He took another step toward her and she waved the knife menacingly.

"What the hell do you know about how it's *supposed to be*? Have you ever had a baby?" she spat through grinding teeth and lips tightened with pain. "Stay away!" she threatened when he came a tiny step closer.

"I just want to help," his trembling words lost some of their sincerity as he studied the knife pointed directly at his crotch.

"Another step and I swear I'll cut it off!" she thrust the knife in his direction, emphasizing her threat. "So you can never do this to me again!"

"Just...just calm down, *wa-le-la,*" he made a placating, soothing gesture, adding, "Andrew's gone to get *We-gi.*" He hoped to shift her attention to the anticipation of Aunt Rebecca's imminent arrival.

"Good," she sank back on the bed, her breathing heavy with exhaustion. "Because you're pretty damned useless!" When he took another step, Annie raised up and threw the knife at him. He looked down at the quivering handle stuck in the back of the rawhide-covered chair right beside his leg. Dead even with his crotch.

A short time later Michael was seated on the edge of the bed, holding his beloved Annie, who was about to give birth to their son. She clung to him, kissing him, clutching his hand. Then she had another contraction and went into a rage, holding him at bay with his own pistol, threatening to make him feel the pain in his gut that she felt in hers. The contraction subsided and once more she cried out for him, begging him to hug her. Hold her. Kiss her. Anything to comfort her.

Annie's contractions increased in frequency and intensity. In her last *hug me, comfort me* mode, Michael had failed to remove the pistol from her reach. With the onset of the next contraction he found himself once again staring down the muzzle of his own gun. Feeling fairly certain she wouldn't actually shoot him, Michael ventured a step closer to the bed. He proved himself right about her not shooting him, but there was nothing to prevent her from thrashing him with the slender brass rod she had wrenched loose from the bed frame. Michael wisely backed away. He would wait.

Soon she was once more crying out for him, clinging to him, sobbing heavily against his chest, breathing rapidly, near exhaustion from the pain of her labor. This time he made sure to remove both the brass bed rod and his pistol. While Annie rested, Michael leaned against the wall across the room and gazed placidly out the window. The welcomed tranquility proved to be but the eye of the storm. In a few seconds a clay bowl crashed through the window right next to him. By this time, such a mediocre display didn't even warrant a flinch. He glanced casually down at the shattered window, then back over his shoulder at Annie. She was sitting up on the side of the bed, leaning with one arm on the wash stand. Her hair was mussed, her eyes ablaze. In her hand she held a water pitcher, poised for the launch.

"Thank God!" Michael muttered. Through the shattered window he saw the wagon burst free from the shadowy woods across the meadow, headed toward the cabin at full speed. Andrew was whipping the horses. Rebecca gripped the edge of the seat with one hand, holding her bonnet on with the other. Michael dashed for the door just as the water pitcher smashed into the wall where his head had been only a second before.

* * * * * * *

The afternoon summer sun, pregnant with its own redness, crept down the sky. Andrew and Michael had gladly withdrawn to the barn, relinquishing the midwifery duties to Rebecca. Andrew rested against the new bags of seed and grain stacked beneath the shed. He was smoking his pipe and softly muttering some incantation. Michael sat on the ground and kept himself occupied attaching one of the new steel plow shares to the wooden plow stock. He ran his thumb along the sharp blade and glanced appreciatively up at Andrew.

"If you're making medicine, see if you can make that woman not be so damn mean."

Andrew stopped chanting and looked down at Michael. "I'm only studying to be a *di-da-nŭ-wi-s-gi*," he chuckled. "A medicine man. I'm not *God!*"

They were interrupted by a shout from the cabin. "*Mi-ki!* Michael!" Rebecca, bloody to her elbows, beckoned enthusiastically from the cabin doorway. "Come on! See your son!"

Michael scrambled up and ran to the cabin, stopping in the doorway to peer quietly—and cautiously—from across the room. The warm, molasses light of the fading sun stuck to the walls, dripping down onto Annie and the tiny, twitching wad of blood-covered flesh

246

that was their son, lying on his mother's stomach. It was a sight Michael knew he would carry in his heart for the remainder of his life. As though approaching a holy shrine, he reverently crossed the room, his eyes darting from Annie's face to the child and back to Annie. He lay down—boots and all—on the blood-soaked bed beside them and stared in damp-eyed amazement. Finally he mustered the courage to touch his newborn son, his large hand covering the child's entire back. Michael's heart swelled with emotion when, responding to his touch, the baby boy made a peaceful, cooing sound. The proud new father looked up at his wife. Annie's hand rose to touch Michael's lips. He kissed her fingers and lifted his hand from the baby to gently touch her cheek.

"What shall we call him?" Annie asked softly.

Michael looked back down at their son, still amazed at the living miracle before him.

"James," he said. "We'll call him James."

Annie stroked the baby's tiny head with the back of one finger. "James Drummond," she spoke their son's name for the first time.

Michael smiled. His own finger followed hers across the soft dark hair.

"His *Tsa-la-gi* name will come later," Annie said, her voice tired but content. She looked back up into Michael's eyes and whispered, "This is our son."

Michael leaned over, mindful of the fragile treasure between them, and kissed his beautiful Annie.

17

William and Susanna strolled leisurely along the eastern bank of the Conasauga River that angled across the northwest corner of the Drummond property. The late afternoon sun was hidden behind the thick growth of hickory, sweetgums and pines that lined the opposite bank. Susanna's belly had grown quite large and William had aged more than was warranted by the intervening months since Michael's departure. There were more wrinkles, and what had once been a light peppering at the temples had spread to large swatches of gray combed back over his ears. But more than added wrinkles and gray hair, there was a permanently troubled countenance, a sadness that intermittent lighter moments could never completely erase. William stopped beside the pool formed by a natural rock dam in the river.

"This is where I taught them to swim," he reminisced. "Your brother... James and Annie Walker. They were only six years old." He pointed downstream and continued his wistful reverie. "And over there...at that narrow spot just before the bend...that's where we caught some fish. John Sixkiller and his brother, Andrew came with us. We showed the boys how to build a weir from stones..." Absently he pantomimed the wedge shape of the familiar, old fashioned fish trap, then continued with a soft chuckle, "We tried not to laugh...those boys standing there at the opening with their little nets, trying to capture the fish as they came through...going after one that got away and letting three more go through in the meantime....But they caught seven fish that day. Perch and redhorse. John and Andrew told them they were lucky. Seven is very lucky for the Cherokees..."

Susanna caught up and slipped her arm through his. "I miss Peter," she said, hoping to change the subject. It seemed all her father ever talked about was Michael. Or Michael and his friend, James. Michael as a little boy. Michael as a young man with tremendous promise. Michael and that dreadful girl, Annie. Let's talk about me for a while, she thought. Me and Peter. Michael and that girl are runaways. Outlaws. Peter and I are a family. "I did so want him to be here when his son is born. He'll be such a wonderful father."

William gazed westward beyond the pool toward the setting sun, as though by some chance he might glimpse a vision of Michael through the trees. "I can't help wondering if perhaps I already have a grandchild out there somewhere...that I might never see."

Susanna bit her tongue. She found it incredible that he could twist absolutely anything she said into a comment about Michael. But she had learned it was a subject around which she must tread lightly.

"Well," she said with a painted smile and a tug at his arm that passed for affection, "*I'm* going to give you a grandson. And soon!" That should take his mind off Michael for a while. But the best was yet to come. "Peter and I have decided," she added, lowering her voice to a conspiratorial whisper, "we're going to name him William. William Drummond Tanner. And you can see him whenever you want!"

They both looked down at her enormous, ripe belly. "I heard Reba telling your mother it's going to be a *girl*," William said.

"Then it's definitely a boy," Susanna countered. "Reba never knows what she's talking about."

William put on one of those smiles Susanna always had difficulty reading. He tossed a pebble into the water, watching the expanding concentric ripples relentlessly seeking the edges of the pool. "I'd always hoped I could teach my grandchildren to swim here," he mused. "*All* of them."

She pulled away and crossed her arms petulantly, the corners of her mouth turned down in a familiar sulk. That was it. She could bear it no longer. She knew better than to directly address the issue, but enough was enough!

"If Michael cared anything about you and Mother, he'd never have run off like that!"

"He did what he thought was best," William's defense of his son was well rehearsed, but she wasn't going to back down this time.

"Best for Michael," she argued. "Obviously, he'd rather be *Indian* than *white*. Rather be *her husband* than *your son*." William looked at his daughter with a mixture of sadness and reproach. "Now I've upset you," she pouted.

Again William stared into the trees across the river, and it appeared to his daughter that he was listening for something. For what? she thought. A sign? A message whispered on the breeze? Susanna knew she had only further alienated him, but at this point, she told herself, she didn't care. She spun peevishly and headed back along the trail toward the house. "Damn you, Michael Drummond!" she mumbled but made certain it was loud enough for him to hear, should he care to listen to anything she had to say. "You're not even here and I hate you!"

* * * * * * *

December 5, 1837

The weather had grown bitter in the following week, bringing a freezing December rain driven by an unforgiving, icy wind. The sky remained such a thick, lifeless gray for the entire day that the only way to know the hour was to look at a time piece. A hawk sat perched on the gnarled, uppermost branch of a towering, leafless tree, facing directly into the torturous elements. With a penetrating shriek, the bird lifted itself unenthusiastically into the dismal sky and struggled resolutely to gain altitude. Far below, thundering along the road, a lone rider kept himself bent low in the saddle against the stinging sleet. Major Peter Tanner, his army issue riding slicker pulled tightly around his uniform, whipped his lathered mount to top speed. The steam puffed from their mouths and nostrils like angry bulls.

The cry of the newborn echoed throughout the Drummond house and could even be heard outside where the doctor's one-horse buggy was parked beneath the carriage cover. Ezekiel Campbell, cringing against the cutting wind, draped an old blanket over the doctor's sway-back nag. He patted the animal sympathetically and listened with curiosity to the hoofbeats approaching from the main road. Peter pulled up sharply, leaping from the saddle before his horse had come to a complete stop. He tossed the reins to Ezekiel.

"Where are they?! Where's Susanna?!" Peter demanded.

"Well, they ain't in the barn!" Ezekiel said. White people could be really stupid sometimes, he thought. Peter sprang up onto the long veranda, leaving Ezekiel to control the horses.

Reba carried two large, half-empty water pots carefully down the stairs. William, pipe in hand, stood comfortably in the doorway of his study below. He and Reba heard Peter's pounding steps on the porch outside.

"Look like the General done got here...finally," she observed when Peter exploded through the door, out of breath.

"I came as soon as I could! Where are they? Are they all right?"

William looked toward Reba, then responded with an amused smile. "Well hello, Peter. Nice to see you, too."

"Sorry, sir. I was—I just—"

"Relax son," William chuckled. "Everything's fine."

Peter bounded up the stairs, taking two or three at a time.

He almost knocked Reba down, causing water to slosh everywhere.

"Sorry, Reba," he apologized but didn't stop. "I want to see my son!"

"Ain't no *son*, Major," Reba said with distinct satisfaction. "You got yo'self a plump little *daughter*!"

Peter, still a few steps from the top, halted dead in his tracks and looked back down. William grinned up in confirmation as he puffed on his pipe. Peter slowly climbed the remaining steps one at a time until he reached the landing with a leaden thud and slouched down the hallway. Reba gathered herself and regained control of the water pots, then continued on down the stairs.

"Yep. A girl," Reba mumbled with self-congratulations. "Jes' like Reba done told 'em. Reckon now they'll listen to Reba. Reba knows thangs."

"Did you say something, Reba?" William asked when she passed him on her way to the kitchen.

"Naw, Mistah D. Reba ain't say nothin'."

Just as Peter reached Susanna's room, the door opened from within. Elizabeth, looking more frail and gaunt than he remembered, came out, followed closely by old Dr. Hamilton, a white-haired man well past sixty, with a stooped walk, a long beard and kind blue eyes streaked with red from lack of sleep. Elizabeth kept her mouth covered with a handkerchief, only removing it when she looked up and saw her son-in-law.

"Oh! Peter! Goodness! You gave me a start!"

"Hello, Mother," he spoke in a loud whisper and nodded a greeting to Hamilton. "Doctor?" Peter's eyes darted from one to the other, awaiting a report.

"They're fine, Peter," Elizabeth patted his arm reassuringly.

"Mother and baby resting well," the doctor made it official.

"Is it true?" Peter asked reluctantly. "Reba said it's—"

"—a girl," Elizabeth finished for him. "And she's beautiful."

Peter was visibly disappointed. He turned to follow his mother-in-law and the elderly doctor back downstairs. Dr. Hamilton looked back at Peter with a puzzled expression. "It's all right, son," the old physician gestured toward the bedroom door. "You can go in."

"She's anxious to see you," Elizabeth added.

Embarrassed, Peter sheepishly opened the door and stepped inside. After the door closed, Elizabeth and the doctor exchanged a glance, but neither would bend the rules of politeness enough to comment. They slipped quietly down the hallway toward the stairs.

With the heavy curtains drawn and the miserable storm raging outside, the shadow-filled room felt murky, though there were officially a couple of hours of daylight remaining. Peter waited just inside the door, allowing his eyes to adjust to the darkness. Susanna, he could see, was propped up against a mound of pillows.

On the bed beside her lay a blanket-wrapped clump which he assumed was the child. The infant stirred, fretting as though she might begin to cry. Susanna gently placed a hand on the baby and there was immediate quiet.

"I'm so glad you're here," she said softly.

"How are you feeling?" he asked, remaining beside the door.

"Weak. Very tired," she mustered a faint smile. "But happy." There was a discomfiting quiet. "I heard you ride up."

"I left as soon as I got word," Peter offered what could have been either idle conversation or an impotent excuse for his tardiness. But Susanna didn't care to pursue it. An awkward stillness followed until Susanna finally spoke.

"Don't you want to see your daughter?" she asked, beginning to feel uneasy with his distant silence.

"Daughter...yes...Reba told me," he forced the words from his throat.

"Reba's a blabber-mouth." Susanna's smile wasn't real.

"I was—we were—so sure it was..." he made no attempt to mask his disappointment.

"Going to be a boy?" she finished for him. "Looks like we were wrong." There was another long pause, pregnant with tension and embarrassment. "Well? Don't you want to see her?" Susanna repeated, aware that it sounded more like a command this time.

"Oh...of course..." Peter lied. Slowly he approached the bed. Susanna looked up at him, anxious to gauge his reaction. Perhaps she had read into his voice a discontent that wasn't really there. She was glad when he looked her right in the eye, but she soon became uncomfortably aware that his eyes never left hers. Without once looking at the child, Peter bent down to plant a perfunctory kiss on his wife's forehead and said with a feeble smile, "We can always try again..."

He left the bed and moved quietly to the window, parting the curtain a tiny space with his finger. Susanna watched him, stunned, hurt.

"I've disappointed you."

"No," he lied again, refusing to face her. "It's just...well, I had my heart set on a fine son as the best Christmas present you

252

could've given me..."

"And a daughter isn't a wonderful gift?" her voice was pained.

"You know what I mean."

"No, Peter. I don't."

He kept his attention glued to the crack in the curtain. In the swirling sleet below he saw Dr. Hamilton climb into his old buggy and wave good-bye to Ezekiel. After the buggy pulled away, the black man plodded down toward the barn leading Peter's mount. Finally Peter released the curtain and looked at Susanna. He nervously cleared his throat.

"It's freezing out there. I'd better see to my horse."

Perhaps it was her imagination, Susanna told herself. No man could be so cold. So rejecting. She forced a cheerful note and asked, "What do you think we should name her?"

Peter ignored the question and walked to the door. He opened it, pausing there without looking back toward the bed. "You must be exhausted. Get some rest."

Susanna watched him go. Had he glanced back, Peter might have seen the light from the doorway glistening on the tears which only she felt; tears which she was determined no one else would ever see. The door closed, leaving her in darkness.

* * * * * * *

In the Drummond barn Ezekiel had already given Peter's horse a good rubdown. He draped a second blanket over the withers and wrapped it around the underside of the animal's neck, then paused to look across the horse's back to the next stall. Major Tanner leaned against the chest-high stall divider, staring blankly at the wall. He lifted the whiskey bottle to his lips and, with obvious affection, drained its contents. *Hurry, sweet oblivion,* he prayed with each gulp.

CHAPTER
18

Near Lewisburg on the Arkansas River
February 1838

Seven young Cherokee men—ages seventeen to twenty-five—occupied two logs on opposite sides of a roaring fire, warming themselves against the night's slicing cold. Each one barely got the whiskey to his lips before the one beside him tugged insistently at the bottle, eager for his share of the lethean potion that would help him forget. Forget the hunger. Forget the biting chill and the loneliness. And most of all forget the humiliation and the deep sense of loss at having been driven from the homeland that had always been an intrinsic part of his very being.

Behind the log pews three ratty whore tents had been erected just inside a semi-circle of whiskey wagons. The mules and oxen were tethered at the edge of the clearing on a little rise overlooking the meandering Arkansas. Four white whiskey peddlers surveyed their Cherokee customers with satisfaction. These men weren't normal merchants and businessmen. Dirty, greasy, tangle-bearded, scarred and treacherous, they were most of all cunning and greedy. Their leader was an Irishman named McGinnis. Most of his beard was missing on the left side of his face, which was purple and knotted with burn scars. He pulled a full bottle from a wooden crate stacked on the ground beside one of the wagons, popped it open and passed it to the young Cherokee at the end of the nearest log.

"Here y'are, boys! Drink up! Best whiskey west of the Mississippi!"

Just beyond the log seats two dandy gamblers were enthroned behind a makeshift table of rough planks supported on each end by large, wooden barrels. These men were a little cleaner and slightly better dressed, but no less greedy than their booze-peddling, skinker associates. Across from the gamblers sat two Cherokee men, each between thirty-five and forty years old. Both were very drunk. The heftier of the two gamblers was a man called Claymore, whose fat, stubby fingers performed the old shell-and-pea game with remarkable dexterity. His partner, a younger, thinner man known simply as Black Jack, dealt the cards for the game whose name he shared. Several older Cherokee men clustered tightly around to watch the games and to place numerous side bets among themselves. The gamblers didn't mind the off-table bets, figuring those who won

254

the side wagers would feel lucky and would be willing to bet even more when they got their chance at the table. Claymore finished a round of shell-and-pea and, to his well-rehearsed astonishment, the Cherokee had won.

"Well! I can see you've done this before, Chief!" he said with a hustler's practiced worry. "Keep this up and I'll be broke! Have to get a real job and earn an honest living!" Claymore clucked and grimaced at his own misfortune as though his financial future faced imminent collapse. The Cherokee man shoved his entire pile of money back out onto the plank table. His companions reached around him to lay their bets down beside his. As the money piled up and the anticipation mounted, one of the whiskey peddlers strategically plopped a fresh bottle down on the table. A Cherokee hand quickly encircled it and it disappeared into the tightly packed huddle. A couple more Cherokee fists found their way to the table and laid their money down.

"Take it easy, gents! Not everybody at once," Claymore lied with orchestrated concern, his thin cigar clenched between his teeth, eyes squinting against the curl of smoke that danced up into his face. He deftly shifted the walnut shells around and back and in between. His slitted eyes cut to the black jack game in progress beside him, scanning the growing pile of bills before his partner. "If the chief here wins again," Claymore lamented, "I might have to borrow right smart to pay these boys off."

Black Jack grimaced as though the suggestion called for serious consideration. The shells continued sliding and scraping. The whiskey continued to disappear and the Cherokee player continued to keep his watchful eye on the winning shell that concealed the tiny pea. Finally Claymore stopped and drew back his hands.

"All right, Chief, pick a winner." The Cherokee reached out and confidently tapped the middle shell. "You sure?" Claymore baited.

"Yes. Sure."

Claymore flipped the empty shell and began scooping up his winnings. He shrugged innocently at the moans and groans that rose up from the bettors. He pointed with feigned commiseration to the shell on his left, allowing the Cherokee to tip it over, exposing the pea.

"Black Jack! You and Claymore save some of that money for us!" croaked Rosie, the river whore. She steadied the drunk young Cherokee who was trying to get his trousers the rest of the way up as she guided him back to the log bench. Rosie was twenty-four-going-on-fifty, overworked, overweight and—as revealed in her dark, sunken eyes—tired to the pits of her soul. Her nose was clearly out of alignment, attributable to a history of angry confrontations with the likes of McGinnis and Claymore.

Another whore came from the tent next to Rosie's. Alice was thinner than Rosie and a couple of centuries older. Her latest lover was so staggering drunk that the jostling of Alice's hand busily mining his pockets for his last few coins was mistaken for meretricious affection.

"Relax, Rosie," Black Jack laughed while shuffling the cards. "There's plenty of this treaty allotment cash for everybody. Right, boys?" A general hubbub of agreement emanated from the Cherokees, and more whiskey was shoved at them by their newfound friends and comrades. Rosie lowered her Cherokee lover to the ground at the end of the log where he reclined in a grinning, sleepy-eyed stupor. His fellow Cherokees laughed heartily, prodding at him with their feet. Oblivious to their teasing, he curled up on the ground and passed out. Alice deposited her gentleman caller beside Rosie's and pulled a 20-year-old from the log.

"Some of these boys have been on the trail for weeks," Claymore elaborated on their purposeful enterprise. "Others come in on the river. They're entitled to a little relaxation. Gentlemen's entertainment."

"And some fine whiskey," McGinnis added.

"Jes' you make damn sure we get our cut this time, McGinnis!" Alice complained bitterly, not sharing the men's congenial attitude. "You're a thievin' bastard, and ye know it!"

In a flash of anger, one of the whiskey peddlers—a large, stained Irishman known only as Murph, with half an ear missing—grabbed Alice and shoved his pistol hard against her stomach. "You shet yer face, or you'll be so bloody fulla holes this lad won't know which one to stick his pecker in!"

Alice pushed the gun away and scowled at Murph, knowing he wouldn't shoot his major source of income. She led her newest lover toward her tent. Rosie pulled the handsome 17-year-old toward her temple of love while his Cherokee companions hooted and howled.

"Come on, pretty boy," Rosie touched his smooth, olive complexion with admiring envy. "You do have your money, don'tcha? Or should I be talkin' to yer daddy?" His hand slid off her shoulder and down her back to fondle her huge, wiggling derriere.

"I have money," he said with a thick tongue, eliciting even more laughter.

The whores and their gentlemen had just disappeared inside the tents when the whiskey peddlers and gamblers drew their guns at the same instant, reacting to the sound of movement in the underbrush. They were all relieved when the bushes parted and Jenkins, a fellow whiskey peddler, stepped into the firelight's circle.

"Take it easy, boys," Jenkins said through the gap of his missing upper teeth. "Look here what I done found!" He moved aside to introduce a new string of Cherokees—young men and boys—directing them to the logs bracketing the fire. Bringing up the rear was VanZandt, another whiskey peddler.

"Some more Injuns comin' up the river made camp 'bout a quarter mile downstream below that first bunch," he informed his colleagues.

"Welcome, boys. Welcome," Black Jack greeted the new arrivals. "Travel weary and ready for some fun, no doubt."

"McGinnis!" Claymore yelled good-naturedly to the whiskey peddler, "get these boys some refreshment!"

The whiskey flowed freely and the new Cherokee arrivals quietly exchanged greetings with those already present. Gradually the party grew more lively, or perhaps just louder. Hours later the fire was still blazing. Black Jack and Claymore were still raking in the allotment money. Rosie and Alice were still whoring. Cherokees were still passed out on the ground, and those who remained conscious were drunker than ever. After losing all their money and satisfying their animal urges, many had begun drifting back toward their camps, only to stumble somewhere along the trail, curling into a ball next to a stump or leaning back against the nearest tree and falling into a deep sleep. Meanwhile, new faces continued to trickle into the clearing for an evening of whiskey, whores and gambling.

The Cherokee seated across from Black Jack rolled his hole card to show a total of twenty. Black Jack flipped his own hole card to show a total of fifteen. In accordance with the rules, he dealt himself another card. Six.

"I win," the drunk Cherokee said and began pulling the money toward his side of the plank table. Jack laughed good-naturedly and put his hand on top of the Cherokee's.

"Don't think so, Chief. See—you've got twenty. I've got twenty-one. I win," Black Jack explained in a firm but friendly tone. He shoved a fresh bottle in front of the Cherokee. "Have another drink," Black Jack suggested, and the Cherokee did just that while the gambler collected his winnings. After a long, gurgling drink the Cherokee lowered the bottle, shook his head and attempted to focus on something he had seen—or thought he had seen—in the brush beyond the crackling fire. He blinked three times and looked again. There it was. A man hiding in the brush, the lower half of his face covered with a bandanna, the area around his eyes darkened with soot. Two feathers hung from a thin hair braid beneath his hat. The drunk Cherokee somehow sensed this was a fellow *Tsa-la-gi*, but it wasn't an overland traveller nor a river immigrant like himself. The man in the brush put a gloved finger to his bandanna-covered lips, signalling for silence. The drunk Cherokee stared blankly, unable to interpret the image before him.

"Play it again?" Black Jack asked as he shuffled the cards.

"What?" the confused Cherokee man's attention shifted back to the gambling table. "Oh—yes. Play again. This time I will win."

"That's the spirit, Chief!" Black Jack encouraged his mark. "Hey, who knows, you might get lucky!" When the drunk Cherokee looked back to the brush beyond the fire, the apparition had disappeared. McGinnis pulled more whiskey bottles from a wooden crate. Murph passed them out to the Cherokees and collected their money. A gunshot split the night and the bottle exploded in Murph's hand, showering the Cherokees with whiskey and shards of glass. Instantly, all the whiskey peddlers and the gamblers pulled their guns, scanning the party crowd, thinking one of the drunk Cherokees had shot at them. But the Indians were merely confused, curious or too drunk to comprehend.

Realizing none of their guests had fired a gun, the peddlers and gamblers turned to the brush and darkness that surrounded them.

"All right! Who's out there?!" McGinnis demanded.

A twig snapped and McGinnis fired blindly into the bushes. A pistol flashed from the darkness and McGinnis fell dead, shot through the heart. Murph and Jenkins spun and fired where they had seen the flash, then hurriedly began reloading their single shot pistols. Though they were drunk, most of the Cherokees—all of them unarmed—had the presence of mind to crouch down behind the logs. A few merely sat still, too stupefied to understand what was happening. Murph had almost finished reloading when he suddenly dropped his pistol and clutched frantically at the six-inch dart stuck in the side of his neck.

"God damn it! What the hell?!" Murph's voice was a mixture

of puzzlement and terror. He plucked the dart from his neck and held it out, showing it to Jenkins and VanZandt. When Murph bent to retrieve his pistol, he toppled over dead from the dart's fast-acting poison. The rest of the whites panicked and began shooting blindly into the night. Rosie and Alice bolted from their tents, followed by their confused and staggering Cherokee customers.

On the opposite side of the clearing, the soot-faced, ghostly Cherokee stepped out of the darkness and into the glow of the campfire. On either side stood two more just like him, complete with bandannas and soot-smeared faces. The first raider walked steadily toward Claymore, the gambler. Black Jack made a move. He could have been going for his gun or merely ducking for safety behind the barrels. It made no difference. The leader of the intruders spun with eye-blink quickness and fired, killing Black Jack instantly. When the raider looked back to Claymore, the gambler's pistol was being raised for a point blank shot.

One of the other raiders threw a knife, piercing Claymore's wrist. The gambler howled and dropped his gun, which discharged into the night sky when it hit the ground. From the cover of their whiskey wagons, Jenkins and VanZandt fired at the first two raiders. They missed their intended targets but had given away their own position. Before Jenkins could duck behind the wagon, he was struck in the stomach by an arrow. VanZandt knelt over him, uncertain what to do. He started to pull the arrow out, then thought better of it and retreated behind the wagon. Thinking himself safe for the moment, he quickly reloaded and cocked his pistol.

"Psst!" the sound came from off to his left. VanZandt looked down the side of the wagon and saw the eyes framed in black soot. He saw them blink once. He saw a glint of light from the campfire reflecting off the pistol's barrel. He saw the flash belch from the gaping muzzle. But he never heard the shot and he never saw the bullet that exploded into his face.

Jenkins lay on the ground, moaning and writhing. His hands, covered in his own blood, were wrapped around the shaft of the arrow in his gut. Three more raiders with their bows and arrows and smoking pistols emerged from the darkness and towered over Jenkins, watching him squirm, his face contorted with excruciating pain. His eyes met those of the raider with a doeskin quiver hanging across his chest. The feathered ends of the arrows were painted with three narrow blue bands, just like the one protruding from his own stomach. The three raiders just looked at him and walked away. Jenkins closed his eyes tightly. At first he was thankful, then immediately he realized they had left him there because they were certain he would soon be dead. Otherwise they would have shot him, stabbed him or slit his throat. They knew leaving him like this would be more painful.

From the moment the first of the five raiders had stepped from the brush until it was all over had taken less than thirty seconds. The lone surviving white man was Claymore. He lay against one of the logs near the fire, gripping the handle of the knife that stuck through his wrist and came out the other side. He was bleeding profusely, convinced that significant arteries had been severed. But he couldn't pull the knife out. With his good hand Claymore dug a pistol from his coat pocket and got to his knees. His plan was to peer up over the log, pick out the closest target among these thieving bastards and put a bullet through his skull. If he was a dead man, Claymore figured, at least he would die with the satisfaction of having taken one of these sons-of-bitches with him! But the instant Claymore popped up from behind the log, he got kicked in the face. He landed on his butt and the pistol went flying.

Lying on his back, Claymore found himself staring up past fringed Cherokee boots at the masked face of the raiders' leader. The raider knelt beside him, grabbed the front of Claymore's shirt and pulled him up for an eye-to-eye. With a gloved hand, the raider pulled down his bandanna mask to reveal the handsome Cherokee features of Johnny Fields.

"These men need their allotment money to get set up out here in the west—to get their new farms going," he said in a flat, matter-of-fact tone.

"We was just having some fun," Claymore whispered.

The second raider stepped across the body of Black Jack, braced his boot against Claymore's arm and pulled his knife from the gambler's wrist. Claymore's painful scream dwindled to a whimper when his terror filled eyes watched the raider wipe the bloody blade on the white lace ruffles of his fancy gambler's shirt. He then knelt beside Johnny and examined Claymore's badly bleeding arm. His eyes were intense, but Michael Drummond's voice was calm and to the point.

"You're cheating and stealing," Michael looked him right in the eye while he tied a leather tourniquet just below Claymore's elbow. "And the only reason we're letting you live is so you can go tell the other whiskey peddlers and gamblers what's going to happen if we catch them."

"Yeah. All right," the gambler said, bleeding and frightened,

260

at the same time ecstatic at the realization he was being spared. "I'll tell 'em! I'll tell 'em all!"

Johnny and Michael rose when two of the other raiders, *Ne-di* Proctor and *Tsa-tsi* Starr, both masked, brought a strongbox from the third tent—the one not used by the whores.

"We found it!" *Ne-di* said.

They dropped the box and stepped back while the fifth raider, *Do-tsu-wa* (Redbird), shot the lock off. *Ne-di* flipped the lid open to reveal a treasure of coins and crumpled bills. The Cherokee men and boys had gotten up and gathered around Johnny, Michael and the others. Johnny grabbed the closest Cherokee immigrant who looked sober enough to understand what he was about to say.

"Take this money back to your camp," Johnny told the young *Tsa-la-gi*. With a sweeping gesture he indicated the other Cherokees staring drunkenly at them. "Once they've sobered up, give them their money back. Split up the rest amongst you."

"You're gonna need it," Michael interjected. "Life's not easy out here."

"What about us?" Rosie asked timorously. The two frightened prostitutes were huddled together in the shadow of Alice's tent. Michael took a handful of bills and coins from the box and strode over to them.

"Hitch up your wagons and be out of here by sunrise," he said, handing them the money.

"Don't let us catch you whorin' around out here again," Johnny called from the money box. Then, at his signal, the raiders disappeared as quickly as they had come. Rosie and Alice remained crouched by the tent, afraid, listening to the disappearing hoofbeats. They dropped the coins and nervously stuffed the bills into their bosoms and anyplace else they could find, concerned the drunk Cherokees might turn on them and rob them. You couldn't trust anyone out here. Still in their scanty attire, they quickly brought two mules from the tether area and tried to hitch them to one of the wagons.

"This goes over there..." Rosie said without certainty.

"No, it hooks onto that thing," Alice was positive she'd seen it done.

"No, it don't..."

"Damn sure does!"

"Just hurry and hitch it up! It's too damn cold to argue!" Rosie conceded, glancing nervously back toward the Cherokees who were still milling in confusion around the money box near the fire.

* * * * * * *

Annie sat in the rocking chair Uncle Andrew had made for her. Little James, just over six months old, squirmed and fretted in her lap. She patted him gently until he drifted back to sleep and was herself about to doze off when she snapped awake at the distant rumble of an approaching horse. *Gŭ-li* pricked up his ears and emitted a low growl, followed by a soft whine. Calmly Annie reached for the Collier repeating pistol on the table beside her. She heard the horse stop outside. Near the barn and corral, she thought. In a couple of minutes she heard the footsteps on the cabin porch. She assumed it was Michael, but the pistol would remain cocked and pointed at the door until she was certain. The hinges creaked a little as the door swung open. Framed in the doorway in his fringed Cherokee jacket stood Michael.

"Where the hell have you been all night?" her voice was soft yet filled with acrimony.

"With the Lighthorse," Michael was puzzled why she would ask such a question. "We had business. I told you, I might be late."

"You said *late*! You didn't say *tomorrow!*"

"Well, I'm back. Everything's fine," he took off his hat with its hand-crafted, silver-studded band and hung it on the peg near the door, then went to Annie. The baby was awake and squealing with delight at the sight of his father. Michael tickled James's tummy.

"Did you take good care of *u-ni-tsi*?" he asked. Whenever he left, he always told little James to take care of his Momma. When he leaned closer to kiss Annie, he suddenly felt the barrel of the pistol pressing up against his chin.

"What if you'd gotten yourself killed?" Behind her anger was a quivering thread of genuine concern.

"I didn't," he said, kissing her on the nose.

"You could have."

He kissed her again. His finger traced up the side of her face and he felt her tears of relief. His lips came close to the ear of his she-panther, his voice low and sexy. "*Tlŭ-da-tsi*...I face more danger every time I step inside that door and get close enough to kiss you than I'll ever face out there."

He pushed the gun barrel away from his chin and their lips met in a passionate kiss. She bit him—hard enough to draw blood. It might have seemed like punishment at first, but the depth of her passion soon convinced him otherwise. James tugged at the fringe on his father's jacket, then at the front of his mother's dress.

Michael and Annie drew apart long enough to play with *Tsi-mi* for a few minutes before carrying him to his crib where he quickly fell asleep. Annie guided Michael to the edge of the bed and sat him down, climbing on top of him with a fire not to be denied.

19

New Echota, Georgia
Cherokee National Capital (East)
May - 1838

The streets of the capital city swarmed with scrambling pedestrians, horses and riders and even a few *yo-neg* carriages and buggies. Many bartered the contents of one wagon for those of another. People stopped to chat and gossip while others scurried to complete some errand or chore. The only difference between New Echota and any town in New England was that these citizens were predominantly *Tsa-la-gi*.

In the center of the main street, a band of citizens—some on foot, some on horseback, others in wagons—had surrounded a group of *yo-negs*. Rough men, most with beards, dirty, mean and sneering. Their two wagons contained some old surveying equipment in various stages of disrepair. Standing on the tailgate of one wagon was Titus Ogilvie. His son, Alton, leaned idly against the wagon while his father addressed the Cherokees. Titus's lack of respect for the *Tsa-la-gi* and his consuming greed were not missed by any in his audience.

"Listen to me, people! This is your last chance! I'm here to help you!"

"This is *Tsa-la-gi* land!" shouted Charlie Swimmer. "We don't want to hear you. Our ears are closed!" He walked away, followed by a couple of his friends.

"That's your problem," Titus shook his finger at their backs. "Your ears are closed! Your eyes are closed!"

"They're stupid Injuns, Pa," Alton squinted up at his father. "What'd ya expect?" He ducked the quick, short swipe at his head that Titus made with his cane.

"Shut up, boy," Ogilvie hissed. Alton spat nonchalantly, watching the dust envelop his gift to the earth, then resumed his whittling. "You people signed a treaty with the United States government," Titus reminded the Cherokees. "A treaty that says you have to move away from here."

"That treaty's no good!" came a shout from the crowd. "It's a phantom treaty. Everyone knows it. Signed by a handful of traitors!"

Ogilvie patiently allowed the murmurs to subside, refusing to be distracted. "That treaty was ratified by the United States Senate on May 23, 1836," he reminded them. "You were given a grace period of two years to dispose of your property, conclude your affairs and be on your way west. In a couple of weeks your grace period is up!"

"Chief Ross says the treaty will be overturned," another Cherokee yelled. "We will stay here and keep our land!"

"Chief Ross has been saying that for years! But the treaty is still on the books!" Titus pounded his fist with evangelical fervor.

* * * * * * *

In the small, rectangular frame building that served as the tribal headquarters and the chief's office, John Ross, assistant chief George Lowrey and two other tribal advisors were holding a strategy meeting. William Drummond had been asked to join them as legal counsel. The atmosphere of the meeting was grim. Chief Ross, a brilliant political strategist, was running out of flanking maneuvers and evasion tactics. He spoke with disappointment of his latest journey to Washington.

"As you all know, President Van Buren was receptive to my latest proposal for a two year extension to the deadline. That would have given us more time to get the treaty revoked." Lowrey and the others looked at him, awaiting the bad news. Ross was silent.

"However...?" William prodded.

"However," Ross ran his finger along the curve of the table top's wood grain, "Van Buren has left the final decision to Governor Gilmer and the State of Georgia."

The others responded with low grumbles that echoed the chief's own disillusionment. The Cherokees had watched with great apprehension when, exactly as William Drummond had predicted, William Schley had been replaced in the Georgia state house after a single term. George Gilmer, who served as governor before Wilson Lumpkin, had once again been chosen by the voting white citizens of Georgia. He was committed to Indian removal and had proven himself eager to serve the special interests of those influential whites who stood to profit most by getting these damned Indians out of their way.

"I have just received a copy of Gilmer's reply," Ross pushed the folded paper out to the center of the table, but no one touched it. "It says, in effect, he's ready to plunge Georgia into a bloody war if the United States interferes with the *rights of the true owners of the soil.* And he isn't talking about the *Tsa-la-gi.*"

"Then you don't have much time, Chief Ross," William, like the others, was all too aware of the soon-to-expire grace period.

"We'll have to go back to Washington to lobby for more votes in the Senate," he looked first at George Lowrey, then at the other sub-chiefs and advisors, and finally at their legal counsel. "William, we need you to get court orders, stays, injunctions—every legal maneuver at your disposal—from state and local judges sympathetic to our cause. Buy us some time. You should go first to your friend, Judge Barrington."

"Walter will do whatever he can to help," William was confident, recalling the writ the Judge had so willingly given when Chief Ross had been illegally imprisoned by the Georgia Militia. Before Chief Ross could continue, there came a pounding at the door. Charlie Swimmer burst into the room.

"*Gu-wi-s-gu-wi!* He's back!"

"Who?" Ross asked.

"Titus Ogilvie. With his land-stealers," Charlie used the descriptive Cherokee term for surveying transits. "He's offering us money to sell out and go west." They rose in unison and followed Charlie out the door.

Ogilvie continued to preach his gospel of give-it-up-and-go-away. Sell-cheap-and-hit-the-trail. The Cherokees assembled before him weren't interested in what he had to say. Their only reason for staying there was to prevent the whites from spreading out from New Echota with their land-stealers, but Titus exhorted them as any cleric would a group of sinners in need of conversion.

"In two weeks it'll be too late. The army will come and drive you away. The government might give you a little money for your land and livestock, but then again, they might *not.* I'm here *today* to offer you fair market value for your property, before it gets taken away and redistributed through the lottery. And I have to tell you, once the army moves in, I can't guarantee I'll be able to pay as much. You could wind up with *nothing!*" He opened a tattered leather case and pulled out a handful of papers. "Now, who'll be the first intelligent individual to sign an agreement that'll make your life much better in the long run?"

"We're tired of signing *yo-neg* papers!" someone grumbled from the crowd.

"Nobody's going to sign your agreement, Titus," William Drummond challenged.

Ogilvie hadn't seen William and the Cherokee chiefs

266

approaching from the side street. He looked down at them from his perch on the wagon's tailgate. Alton bristled at their intrusion, glaring at each man. Chief Ross recognized a pair of Ogilvie's surveying crew, Brantley and Solmes, as two of the men who had burst into his cabin late in the night, had beaten his guest, John Howard Payne, and had hauled them both off to jail. They sneered their recollection of that evening. Their swagger and posture suggested that events might repeat themselves if and when the opportunity arose.

"Ah, Mister Drummond," Titus said more with disgust and disdain than with feigned politeness. "I should've expected as much."

"'Nother God damn Injun lover," Alton snorted and added to the muddy expectoration collecting at his feet.

Ross stepped up and calmly but firmly informed Titus he was in violation of town policy. "You have no authority to conduct business in New Echota, Mister Ogilvie. This is a Cherokee town."

"You people just don't get it, do you?" Titus shook his head in disbelief at the chiefs. "These are the men who have pissed away the two most critical years of your lives!" he raised his arms to the crowd.

George Lowrey put a hand on the side of the wagon and gave it a little shake to get Ogilvie's attention. "Take your wagons and your men and go."

Titus ignored the assistant chief and continued to address the larger group. "Are you all stupid? Or just too damn stubborn to listen to good advice? Well, I'm here to tell you, the *age of generosity* is over, my friends. The *age of enforcement* is hard upon you!"

"You won't be enforcing anything in New Echota, Mr. Ogilvie," Chief Ross repeated his earlier admonition.

"Maybe I won't. But there's an army on the way, in case you didn't know!"

"Of course they know that," William said.

"Nothing happens in *Tsa-la-gi* territory that we don't know about, Mister Ogilvie," Ross forced himself to remain civil.

"Then you have to know, *Gu-wi-s-gu-wi*," Ogilvie bent down toward the chief with all the false sincerity he could muster, "the end is near for you. For New Echota. This will be a ghost town soon. You can sell to me *now* and walk away with money in your pocket..." He paused for effect.

"Or...?" Lowrey challenged.

"Or, in a few days—a few weeks at the most—the army'll kick

you outa here and I'll *still* get what I came for!" Ogilvie faced the crowd. "And *you* will end up with nothing!"

When George Lowrey shook his head, the silver and bone decorative adornments hanging from his nose clinked together. "Not if we get court orders to stop the army. And stop you!" he swelled to his full height in defiance of this arrogant, Indian-hating white man.

"Let me tell you about your ridiculous court orders—" Ogilvie was about to explain the realities of Georgia's strategy to take all of their land when they were interrupted by the shouts of two young Cherokee boys running the length of the town's main street, yelling as they came.

"They're coming!" shouted *Tsu-Tsu* Swimmer.

"*A-ni-ya-wi-s-gi!*" his companion yelled. "Many soldiers!"

The words were hardly out of their mouths before the sound of hoofbeats and the *thud-shuffle* of countless marching feet reached them from the other end of town. All those present—white and Indian alike—were awestruck as the full regiment of United States Cavalry rounded the turn in the road just where it entered New Echota. At the head of the parade rode a stately, distinguished man of fifty-two. The hair showing beneath his feathered hat was white and his thick muttonchops were salt-and-pepper. The six-foot-four-inch, three hundred pound army commander rode tall and erect in the saddle.

"My God, it's General Winfield Scott!" William said.

"Yes. I met him a few months ago. In Washington," *Gu-wi-s-gu-wi* recalled.

"*Old Fuss and Feathers* himself," William spoke softly with respect.

"I believe him to be a good and fair man," Ross's words sprang more from what he prayed would prove true than what he knew to be fact.

"Don't get your hopes up, John," William cautioned. "He's here to follow orders. And we all know what those orders are."

Behind the cavalry appeared the mule-drawn caissons of the artillery, and after them flowed an endless blue river of marching infantry. More Cherokees came out of houses, shops and side streets, gathering along the main thoroughfare to watch the parade of *yo-neg* soldiers, the *a-ni-ya-wi-s-gi*. As they approached, William, like so many others, was drawn to the imposing figure of General Scott. When a Cherokee boy's dog ran across the road in front of the advancing army, the General's horse skittered to the side and

268

William caught a glimpse of the staff officers riding behind the general. Among them was none other than his own son-in-law, Major Peter Tanner.

General Scott stopped his horse a few feet from the Cherokee leaders. Major Tanner made a slight nod to his father-in-law, then glanced at Titus Ogilvie, whose expression, with the advent of the army, had waxed smug. He had proven himself the prophet of the hour. His chest swelled with *I-told-you-so* superiority.

The exchange between Chief Ross and General Scott was polite, though somewhat awkward. Two adversaries with mutual respect who, under different circumstances, might well have become the closest of friends. Ross stepped out from the group.

"*U-li-he-li-s-di*, General Scott. Welcome to New Echota."

"Good to see you again, *Gu-wi-s-gu-wi*," Scott said with a genuine, if seldom seen smile. "I won't deceive myself into thinking, by any stretch of the imagination, that my arrival comes as a surprise to you."

"We knew you were coming," the chief said. "We didn't expect you here *today*."

The General shifted his massive weight forward, leaning with his hands on the pommel of his saddle. "I'll be establishing my headquarters here," he said as he looked around the town. "I'll need some of these buildings as offices and barracks."

William stepped out beside Chief Ross to greet Scott. "General, I don't suppose we could prevail upon you and your men to bivouac on the outskirts of town?"

"And you are...?" the General raised his eyebrows.

"William Drummond, sir. Attorney at law. A friend to the Cherokee."

"And a burr under the saddle of the United States Government!" Ogilvie chirped. He stepped to the front of his wagon and extended his hand. "How'd'ya do, General? Titus Ogilvie. Merchant. Businessman. Loyal United States citizen."

General Scott ignored the offered hand. His eyes remained locked on William. "These buildings will do nicely, Mr. Drummond." Scott exhaled loudly and pivoted in the saddle toward his officers. "Major, conduct a reconnaissance of the available buildings and begin setting up headquarters."

"Yes, General," Peter Tanner answered sharply. He glanced quickly at William before motioning a couple of junior officers and sergeants to accompany him. They pulled their horses out of ranks and rode away to fulfill their orders.

It wasn't the first time someone had refused to shake Titus Ogilvie's hand and, he was certain, it wouldn't be the last, leaving him completely undaunted by the rejection. His primary and immediate goal was to make a good impression on a very powerful and influential man.

"I'm here to be of service in any way possible, General," he reassured the commander, then pointed to Ross and his group. "I can tell you right off, these men are up to no good. They're gonna bribe some local judges for court orders to block what you and your men are here to do. You oughta just throw every last one of 'em in jail right now. Make life a lot easier for all of us!"

Scott winced at Ogilvie's magpie chatter and ingratiating manner. He kept his eyes on William, Ross and the other leaders while he answered. "I have neither the authority nor the inclination to countermand the ruling of any state or local magistrate..." he said, pausing for just the right effect, then adding, "...*provided* that ruling doesn't conflict with the terms of the treaty I've been sent here to enforce."

Titus straightened with a smirk. Once again, his earlier words had proven uncannily prophetic. The price he would now pay for prime Cherokee land had just been slashed by at least two-thirds.

General Scott faced Ogilvie directly for the first time. He made no attempt to hide the fact that he didn't like the oily, obsequious merchant in the wagon.

"And you are, I presume, that same Titus Ogilvie whose supply contract I intend to cancel as my first order of business?"

Titus had hoped to bond with the general. They were, after all, decent, self-respecting white men with a common goal—to rid these United States of the heathen aboriginals who stood in the way of civilized progress. A little enterprising commerce conducted in the course of that worthwhile endeavor couldn't be a bad thing. Not shaking his hand was one thing, but the general had insulted him before a bunch of Indians. This concerned him.

"I—well, yes, I'm a government contractor—"

"Not any longer. As of today," the general said bluntly.

"But—I don't understand..." Ogilvie whimpered.

"I've received word from General Arbuckle in the Arkansas Territory that the allotment supplies you shipped out west for the Cherokees who've already moved are rotten and worthless."

"General..." Ogilvie paused and clasped his hands together prayerfully, shaking them, studying them, making sure he chose exactly the right words. "I'm sure there's been some misunderstanding..."

"That will be all, Mr. Ogilvie," General Scott cut short the grovelling. "You and your men are free to go. I don't want to see you in New Echota again." That was all the general had to say to the merchant whose tainted reputation had reached all the way to Arkansas Territory and back. Scott addressed the Cherokee chief and the other tribal leaders. "Chief Ross, I want you to call an emergency national council meeting for one week from today. That will give your people time to assemble. It's important that as many Cherokees as possible hear what I have to say."

"That can be arranged," the chief said. "But I must tell you, General, it won't be without opposition."

"I'm not unsympathetic to your situation, Chief Ross. But I have my orders."

"Excuse me, General!" Titus Ogilvie called from the wagon, refusing to go quietly. "Look, I'm sure we can clear this whole thing up! If I could have a word with you...in private..."

General Scott had been annoyed earlier. Now he was fully irritated by Ogilvie's implication. "I don't take bribes, Mr. Ogilvie. You may go. That's my final word on the matter." And it was. General Scott rode off in the direction taken earlier by Major Tanner and the junior officers. The artillery teams wheeled around and were soon followed by the foot soldiers under the marching command of the infantry sergeant.

William looked up at Titus in the wagon. "You heard him, Ogilvie. His final word."

Titus glared down at William, then finally signalled to his surveyor-thugs who began climbing into the wagons or onto their horses. Titus bitterly took his seat and grabbed the reins. His eyes narrowed to their familiar, hate-filled squint, and he leaned one last time toward William. "We shall see, Mr. Drummond, who has the *final word*. We shall see, indeed."

He slapped the reins against the horses' rumps and his two wagons pulled away, followed by the rest of his men on horseback. They skirted the edge of the street counter to the flow of the marching army, leaving William Drummond and the Cherokee leaders behind in the street.

"I think I should delay my trip to see Judge Barrington until after we hear what General Scott has to say," William advised the chiefs.

"We can't afford to lose a whole week," George Lowrey voiced concern.

"But we'll need specifics for court orders and injunctions," William argued logically. "Specifics we won't know until after he speaks."

"William's right," Ross agreed. "We have to wait."

Lowrey, as always, would support the chief's decision. There was nothing left for the head men of the *Tsa-la-gi* nation to do but stand back and watch the blue river of soldiers streaming past. Each man knew that the signing of the removal treaty on a cold, rainy December night in New Echota two-and-a-half years earlier had marked the beginning of the end. The arrival of an army that would soon glut their capital represented the harsh and immutable reality of that end. And, ironically, they sensed to a man that New Echota, along with all the other Cherokee towns and villages up and down the waterways and perched on hillsides throughout their beloved land, would soon lie fallow, languishing in a vacuous solitude, aching for the sounds of feet, hooves, wheels, laughter, threats, political bombast, the cries of joyful birth, the anguished grief of passing, the whispered secrets of love—sounds which would never again be heard on their streets, alleys and forested byways.

* * * * * * *

From the trail running along the edge of a thickly wooded hill overlooking New Echota, Titus Ogilvie and his son, Alton, were also observing the phalanx of soldiers pouring into the Cherokee capital. Titus leaned forward, his hands propped against the wagon's footboard. His voice quivered slightly with the rage he fought to keep inside. He could have screamed. He could have hit something. Or someone. But he liked to keep it inside where it festered and intensified the hatred, for *that* was the feeling on which he thrived.

"I don't need the blessing of Winfield Scott to win this war!" he growled. "Titus Ogilvie always gets what he wants!"

"What do you want, Paw?" his less-than-astute son asked. Titus rolled his eyes and shook his head without answering. Alton spat, took off his hat and scratched his head. He examined the findings beneath his nails and pressed his father, "What do we do now? We ain't got no more gov'ment contract."

"Shut up, stupid! Can't you see I'm tryin' to think?"

Alton—whom even his own father considered a paragon of hebetude—looked genuinely hurt, like a child trying desperately to please, only to be harshly scolded by an adored parent.

"What'd I say?" he whined.

CHAPTER
20

The lone horse ambled down the center of the dirt road, clopping up little clouds of dust. A single rein dangled erratically in the dirt, scribbling the illegible signature of the rider's state of mind. Peter Tanner, his uniform mussed and unkempt, his hat dangling by its chin strap on his back, was unaware he had lost his means of controlling the horse. Hanging loosely in his hand was a nearly empty whiskey bottle. He raised it to his lips, drained the last drop, then studied the glass before hurling it into the roadside bushes. For the first time he noticed the dragging rein. He reached for it, almost tumbling from the saddle in his attempt to recover the lost strap. The horse kept walking, paying no attention to the shifting, squirming burden on its back.

* * * * * * *

Susanna Drummond Tanner sat gently rocking her daughter on the veranda of her parents' home. Margaret Elizabeth—Meg, they had begun calling her—bore the name of both her grandmothers. At six months old, she was lively and alert, a happy, evenly dispositioned child who hadn't yet shown signs of having inherited her mother's demanding temperament. Susanna had, in fact, lost some of her own fire in recent months. The pendulum motion and rhythmic creaking of the wooden rocker clicked off the wasted heartbeats of wasted days which Susanna feared was proving to be a wasted life. She gazed vapidly out toward her father's barn with an expression of vacant surrender.

William rode Clancey, his big gray, ahead of the wagon driven by Ezekiel. In the back sat Charlie Swimmer and three other Cherokee men hired by her father. When they reached the barn, William dismounted. Charlie jumped from the wagon and took Clancey's reins. William strode up toward the house. Meg had begun to stir, and Susanna was cooing softly to her when William reached them and stepped up onto the veranda. He studied his daughter and granddaughter as he wiped the perspiration from his face and ran the handkerchief around the inside of his hat band. He was worried about Susanna. After the baby was born she had lost all her pregnancy weight and, William and Elizabeth agreed, another twenty pounds too many. She had always looked healthy and full, but now her eyes were sunken and dark, her arms like brittle twigs of kindling.

"How's your mother?" William asked. He was equally concerned about his wife. Elizabeth, whose constitution had never been hale, had steadily declined during the past six months. Susanna dabbed a bit of spittle from the baby's mouth without answering. "Susie? I said, how's your mother?"

"Reba thinks she's getting worse," Susanna said flatly. "I can't really tell."

William searched for words to express the thought that hadn't quite taken shape in his mind. He squatted beside the rocking chair, tracing a finger back and forth across the baby's cheek, tickling her nose. Meg laughed and smiled up at her grandfather. "Well, come on in. Get ready for dinner," his words rang hollow, void of the enthusiasm he had tried to impart.

"I'm not hungry. I'll just sit here a while."

"You say that every day. You need to eat," William said. In an uncharacteristic display of affection, he touched her cheek with the back of his hand. Susanna looked into her father's eyes, then looked away. He rose and started for the door.

"Father...." she said hesitantly. William stopped. "Are you sure it was Peter you saw the other day in New Echota?" she finally gave voice to the question that had been plaguing her. She knew the answer and knew she didn't want to know the answer.

"He's probably very busy," William responded to her real question: *Why hadn't he been by to see his wife and daughter?* "I'm sure he'll be around as soon as—" he broke off in mid-sentence.

They both heard the sound of the horse coming up the lane from the main road. Cantering toward them was Peter, straightening himself in the saddle, trying to position his hat properly on his head. He adjusted his tunic and brushed away some dust as he rode up to the edge of the veranda. His eyes, glassy and distant, looked first to Susanna, then at William.

"Peter," William's greeting was cool.

"Mr. Drummond," he said, taking off his hat. He made a grand, sweeping gesture toward his wife. "Susanna...." She kept her focus on the child, refusing to look up at her husband. Their mutual silence appeared to trouble William more than it did either of them.

"Well....you're probably hungry. We'll be having supper shortly," William extended a perfunctory invitation.

"Thank you, sir," Peter's voice dripped with the excessive gratitude of inebriation. "I had a little something at the post."

William went inside, leaving them alone. Peter stepped his

horse over in front of Susanna. In a soft falsetto steeped in drunken sarcasm, he said, "'Oh, Peter, my darling! I'm so glad to see you. I've missed you terribly!'"

Susanna looked directly at him for the first time. "You're drunk."

"I am not drunk," he stiffened with self-righteousness. "I've had some whiskey, but I'm not drunk."

"Father said he saw you three days ago," her voice went beyond accusation. "In New Echota."

"Things are very busy right now." Peter stiffly dismounted, making sure to maintain his equilibrium. "I came as soon as I could." He stepped up onto the edge of the veranda and looked back down toward the barn where Ezekiel was unhitching the horse from the wagon while Charlie and the other Cherokee men unloaded the freshly cut sapling fence posts and stacked them in a neat pile. "What's your father going to do for hired help once all these Indians are gone? I keep telling him he oughta buy himself a few slaves. Lord knows, he can afford it. Uh-oh. I forgot. You're the Queen of Abolition around here, aren't you?"

While he had been rambling idly, avoiding the real issue, Susanna had risen from the rocker. When he looked back to get her reaction to his barbed remark, Peter was startled to find her standing right beside him. She ignored his abolitionist taunt, lifting Margaret Elizabeth toward him.

"Here. Don't you want to hold your daughter?"

Reflexively he took a step back. "I—I'm all dirty. From the road."

"It's all right. She won't mind. She wants her Poppa," Susanna was intent on forcing the point. Peter remained frozen, staring at her, refusing to make eye contact with his own child. "Never mind, Peter," Susanna pulled Meg away. Her words addressed to the baby were clearly meant for the father. "He's never held you, has he? You're almost six months old and your father has never held you. Not once. Why should he hold you now?"

"Susanna, don't start."

"But then again, in six months he hasn't touched me either," she continued. He knew she was just getting warmed up. "Why do you suppose that is, little Meg? Why won't your father hold you? Or make love to me? Do you think it's too much road dust?"

Peter turned away from her again and leaned against the porch post. "When I was in Florida Territory, I saw some land."

"*This* land will be ours someday," she reminded him.

"Michael's gone. Dead, for all we know. So I guess it'll pass to me. To us. And there's your father's property across the river. Why would we want to go to Florida?"

"I was thinking of getting a little place. Starting a family," he said, still gazing out across the lawn, determined to ignore Susanna who was nuzzling the baby.

"I thought we'd already started a family," she said, wishing it didn't hurt so much. As usual, she masked her pain in bitter sarcasm. "Or perhaps what you're saying is: *We'll go live in Florida. See if you can bear me a son. Maybe next time you can get it right.*"

"No," Peter said flatly. "That's not what I meant."

"Of course it is, Peter. You hate this child because she's not a boy," Susanna was relentless. "And you hate me for having her!"

"Fine, Susanna. Whatever you say," he refused to be drawn into her little self-pitying melodrama.

"Don't you take that patronizing air with me, Peter Tanner! I'll not have it!"

Still he refused to face her and was determined not to look at the child who had begun to fret. "I'm going to be extremely busy for some time to come," he enunciated each word carefully. "I don't know when I might see you again."

It was a long time before she spoke. "Does this mean you're leaving us, Peter?" He refused to answer. She waited, then finally vented her contempt for his cowardice. "Look at me, Peter Tanner! If you've come to say you're leaving me, for God's sake, be a man! Look me right in the eye and tell me you're abandoning your wife and daughter!"

Finally he faced her, but still he couldn't bring himself to look at the baby, which had begun to cry. "This isn't easy for me, Susanna," he said as though he deserved her sympathy, not realizing he had actually rekindled some of her old fire.

"Oh, it isn't *easy*?!" she was incredulous. "Well, I'm sorry I've made things so terribly difficult for you, Peter! Go! Go back to your post! Go to Florida! Go straight to hell!" Susanna's outburst had set Meg to screaming, and still Peter couldn't look at the child.

"You're upsetting the baby," he said.

Susanna lifted Meg onto her shoulder and patted her gently. The crying stopped almost instantly, and Susanna made a concerted effort to lower her voice. "*The baby* has a name, Peter! Her name is Margaret Elizabeth. After your mother and mine."

For the first time Peter forced himself to look at his daughter. Susanna studied Peter's face, hoping to see him melt with love for this tiny bundle of innocence. But his expression was as inscrutable as his heart.

"Say good-bye to your father, sweetheart," she cooed. "This could be the last time you ever see him." Peter continued to stare at Meg, transfixed. He raised a hand to touch her, but Susanna pulled the child away. It was too late. He'd had his chance and he'd let it slip away. She walked to the door, pausing only to say, "It's getting dark. You'd better get back to your post." Mother and daughter disappeared inside the house, letting the door slam behind them.

Peter's eyes caught the shiny reflection of the fading afternoon light. It could have been tears. Or merely the glassy-eyed residue of cheap whiskey.

The road leading into New Echota was packed with Cherokee travellers. Young, old and in between. Full-bloods, mixed-bloods. Some on horseback, others in wagons, most on foot. All along the road U. S. soldiers—both infantry and cavalry—watched quietly. Some were curious, others merely bored. Their presence on the main thoroughfare into the Cherokee capital was replicated on other roads and trails throughout *Tsa-la-gi* territory. They had been sent out to post themselves along every highway and trail, not to interfere, not to enforce any ruling or policy, not to interact any more than necessary with the Cherokees. Their purpose was both to observe and to ensure the safe passage of the Cherokee people to New Echota to hear the address of the great American general, Winfield Scott. Every Cherokee knew the subject of the talk. Many chose not to go to New Echota for that very reason, preferring to stay at home in their wooded cabins. A few others had even packed their belongings and fled to the caves in the mountains of western North Carolina. They had no intention of leaving their homeland, so what good would it do to listen to the words of a *yo-neg* war chief?

Many of the soldiers—especially the younger ones—were even more uneasy than the Cherokees they had been sent to observe. Some of the recruits had tried to relate in an open and friendly manner, but the reception had been chilled at best. History had taught the *Tsa-la-gi* there was little reason to trust the *a-ni-ya-wi-s-gi*, the white soldiers. And Cherokee parents had passed on to their young the costly lessons they had so painfully learned over the generations.

The afternoon proved an exceptionally warm one, with a sticky humidity that hinted of coming rain. The area around the council house in New Echota was packed with the hundreds of Cherokees who had begun arriving shortly after sunrise. Despite the huge turnout, a somber quiet hung over the crowd, in marked contrast to the swarm of activity, the music and laughter that usually accompanied such gatherings of this good-natured and humor-loving people.

At the appointed hour the Cherokees assembled at the council house. The enormous crowd spilled out the structure's seven open sides and flowed down the hill. Many of those outside in the blistering sun couldn't even see the featured speaker, General Winfield Scott, standing in full dress uniform before a seated row of his senior officers. Across from them sat principal chief John Ross, along with his assistant chiefs and a few lesser chiefs and tribal dignitaries. The full-blood woman who would translate the words of the *yo-negs* into *Tsa-la-gi* waited patiently, hands folded in her lap. Formal introductions had been made, official amenities exchanged. It was time to talk. General Scott looked to the interpreter. She indicated that she was ready.

"Cherokees! The President of the United States has sent me here with a mighty army." The general's booming voice carried well throughout the crowd. His officers were a little startled when the interpreter spoke, the tiny woman's voice almost as forceful as Scott's. "In obedience to the Treaty of 1835," he continued, "you must now go to join those Cherokees already established in prosperity beyond the Mississippi. Under the treaty, you were given two years in which to make this move. Unfortunately, the two years have expired. I can not, I *will* not, grant you any further delay. Before another full moon passes, every Cherokee man, woman and child must be in motion to join your brothers in the west. My friends! This is no sudden decision on the part of the president. For two years you have been warned that the treaty would be enforced. I am here to enforce it..." Scott paused, allowing the interpreter to catch up. He savored the two dippers of sweet spring water he drank from the bucket at the end of the officer's bench. A huge man, Scott didn't like warm weather, and he found the clinging humidity insufferable. All this, added to the heat of the ceremonial fire that always burned—winter or summer—for any council session, promised the general a long afternoon.

Reaction to Scott's opening remarks rippled through the crowd. Some Cherokees understood the inevitability of their fate. Others felt *Gu-wi-s-gu-wi* would be able to stall for another two years, and then another two after that, delaying indefinitely their removal. There were whites visiting to hear the general, some to divine a way to profit from coming events, others to learn the fate of their Cherokee friends. Many of the young soldiers were curious and somewhat apprehensive about what lay ahead. They felt a moral and ethical conflict about forcing a peaceful people out of their homeland. Other soldiers of a less sensitive nature were seedling thugs, eager for an excuse to dominate and, given the opportunity, to abuse anyone weaker, more vulnerable than themselves. The seasoned veterans, for the most part, allowed themselves no emotional involvement one way or the other. They would follow orders as they had always done. It was the way of the professional soldier.

General Scott dabbed at the corners of his mouth, cleared his throat and resumed. "Many of my troops now occupy positions throughout your country. And thousands more are on the way. You will not be able to resist. You will not be able to escape. But all these troops—regulars and militia—are your friends. They are as kind-hearted as they are brave. It is the desire of every one of us to carry out this painful duty with mercy."

There were whites and Cherokees alike in the crowd who knew the promise of friendship and kindness was but an obligatory statement of official policy. Few, if any, were naïve enough to trust in its fulfillment. Humanitarian treatment would be on an individual basis. Brutality would be no stranger, the words of the esteemed General Winfield Scott to the contrary notwithstanding.

The general shifted to partially face John Ross and the row of chiefs to address an issue he knew was coursing through the minds of many listening to his words. "Chiefs, head men and warriors! It would be most unwise to resist, compelling us to resort to arms. Or to take flight, forcing us to hunt you down. Resistance or flight means conflict. Conflict means bloodshed. Once blood is shed—on either side—it will be well nigh impossible to prevent war and carnage. I, too, am an old warrior. I have seen far too much slaughter. Spare me—and yourselves—the horror of witnessing the destruction of the Cherokees."

Scott paused again, wiping the perspiration from his face. He ran his fingers back through his damp, gray hair and stepped closer to the edge of the council house. Perhaps it was to observe the simple Cherokees gathered outside the building, or perhaps just to get farther from the heat of the fire in search of a whispered breeze. The general made eye contact with some of the full-bloods and mixed-bloods and continued, "I beg you: don't wait for the soldiers to appear at your door. Settle your affairs and proceed with all haste to Ross's Landing, to Gunter's Landing, or to the Cherokee Agency on the Hiwassee River, where you will be received in kindness by officers selected for the purpose. There will be food for all and clothing for the destitute. You will then be transported, at your ease and in comfort, to your new homes. Those who don't come in voluntarily will be rounded up and escorted by U. S. Army and volunteer militia to special temporary holding camps. These stockade compounds are under construction even as I speak. There you will be housed until travel arrangements can be made for you."

To bring his address to a close, General Scott planted himself directly in front of Ross and the other chiefs. His voice was lowered for the desired dramatic effect. The general knew his statement would be translated loud enough for all to hear. "These are the words of a warrior to warriors. May God prosper both the Americans and the Cherokees and keep us long in peace and friendship."

Scott ended his speech with a sincere, respectful salute to his distinguished hosts. He heard the buzz spreading through the crowd as the Cherokees—along with soldiers and visiting whites—began analyzing his remarks. Beginning with the least of the chiefs, the general shook each man's hand until he came to their principal leader.

"Chief Ross, as soon as this meeting is adjourned, this building will be cleared and converted into a barracks. I'll have many more men arriving in the next few days." Without waiting for a reply—or an argument—General Winfield Scott left the council house, followed by his officers.

William Drummond, who had been seated behind the row of chiefs, joined *Gu-wi-s-gu-wi* and the others to assess the impact of Scott's message. Whatever their individual opinion, to a man they knew it was a pivotal point in the history of the *Tsa-la-gi*. Just how things would unfold for the Cherokee nation from this point forward would be a topic for debate, but no one doubted things would never be the same.

The detail of six U. S. Cavalry soldiers galloped briskly in double column through the pre-dawn gray. They rode silently and with purpose. The sergeant in charge made a simple hand signal to turn them off the main road and up a winding trail that clung to the side of a hill. The farther they rode the rougher the terrain and the thicker the woods became.

Michael Drummond, barefoot and wearing only his trousers, stepped out onto the porch of his cabin, stretched comfortably and drank deeply of the fresh morning air. A few chickens scattered in a squawking flurry when *Gŭ-li* chased an escaped piglet through the flock. Michael leaned lazily against the post and pulled on one boot. He took a couple of sips of water from the gourd dipper, then poured the rest ceremoniously over his head and shook out his long hair. After slipping his foot into the other boot, he grabbed a shirt from the nail by the door and headed for the barn and corral where *U-no-le* whinnied an enthusiastic greeting. With his shirt half on, Michael stopped between the cabin and the corral, his attention drawn toward the narrow road that ran along the edge of the valley before twisting up and around the hills to the east of his farm. He listened carefully, confirming his first impression of approaching horses. *Gŭ-li* gave up his swinely pursuit to join his master, ears pricked and alert, his nose held high, interpreting the message of the breeze. A low growl preceded a string of intermittent barks.

The mounted soldiers broke into view around the side of the hill and began their descent into the valley. Once off the grade, the cavalry squad quickened their pace to a steady gallop, riding straight toward Michael. He finished pulling on his shirt and took a couple of steps back toward the cabin. But when the soldiers drew near, the sergeant flicked another subtle signal and one column of three split off, blocking Michael's retreat. When the other column pulled up in front of him, Michael recognized their leader as Wakefield, the same sergeant he and Johnny Fields had encountered at the government Indian allotment depot in Ft. Smith. And many of the soldiers were the same who had come running to break up the altercation with the crooked agents, Callow and Wilby. Annie, holding baby James, appeared with sleepy-eyed concern at the cabin door.

"Michael? What is it?"

"What can I do for you?" Michael asked the sergeant.

"I reckon you know why I'm here, don'tcha?" Wakefield said,

looking down at Michael, who didn't answer. The veteran sergeant saw Michael's darting eyes sizing up the situation. Weighing his options. Looking Left. Right. Back toward the woman and child at the cabin door. "You're under arrest," he informed Michael, not doubting for an instant that flight was a distinct possibility. He looked toward the cabin when Annie stepped out onto the porch with fire in her eyes.

"What for?!" she demanded. "He hasn't done anything!"

"Best stay inside, ma'am," the soldier closest to Annie advised. "You don't want that young'un gettin' hurt."

Michael took a couple of steps toward the house, ready to make a break, but the soldiers closed ranks, cutting him off. At another nearly imperceptible signal from Wakefield, those with pistols drew them and the others aimed their rifles at Michael.

"You can come peaceful or slung over the back of a horse. Don't make no difference to me," the sergeant said in a flat, businesslike tone.

Michael would do nothing to endanger Annie and the baby. He started toward the corral. Annie tried to follow but was blocked by another soldier, who dismounted and stood right beside her.

"Michael!" Annie's voice was fraught with apprehension.

"It's all right, Annie," he tried to instill his own voice with reassurance. "I'll be back before noon."

"Don't bet on it," the soldier standing with Annie snorted and flashed a tobacco-stained grin. He spit on the ground in front of her, drawing a defiant glare.

"*U-tso-n'-ti*!" she snarled, calling him a rattlesnake.

"Feisty little thang, ain't she?" he joked with the nearest mounted soldier, who grinned down from his horse. Neither of them saw the rapid flutter of her eyes or the tension in her face as she forced back into inky forgetfulness the vision of Cephus Ogilvie and Randolph Bogen that had flashed across the tapestry of her consciousness. And neither of them saw her hand slip behind her to feel for the knife she had concealed in the sash tied around her waist. And neither of them knew that, had they come a step closer or said anything else to her, one of them, perhaps both, would have felt the icy blade between their ribs.

Michael rode bareback on *U-no-le* from the corral, directing the horse between Annie and her tormenters, bumping the soldier away from her to make his point.

"Take care of *Tsi-mi*. I'll be back," he said softly, hoping to reassure her, then told her in Cherokee to find Johnny and tell him to be careful.

"No Injun talk," Wakefield said. He leaned from his saddle and began tying Michael's hands.

"Where are you taking him?" Annie asked.

"Fort Smith," the sergeant answered. The soldier nearest Annie mounted up and the seven rode back toward the trail. Wakefield led the way, with the other six completely encircling Michael and *U-no-le*.

* * * * * * *

The thick wooden door of the Ft. Smith stockade burst open and Michael was shoved roughly into the darkened room. He stopped just inside the doorway. A second push propelled him across the cell where he slammed into the shadowy forms of two other prisoners. The hinges creaked and the door clanged shut behind him.

"Sorry..." Michael apologized and stepped away from the man he had bumped hardest. He didn't know who was in the cell with him and, until his eyes adjusted to the darkness, he felt vulnerable and disadvantaged should there be trouble. He could hear the others breathing—it sounded like three, maybe four. One of them chuckled, he thought. The man Michael had accidentally struck grabbed his arm and pulled him toward the high window. Michael was poised to strike when the man's face came into the narrow shaft of light. It was Johnny Fields.

"*Tsa-ni!*" Michael was stunned.

"You all right, *'Tsu-ts'*?" Johnny asked.

"Yeah. You?"

"I didn't tell 'em nothin'. None of us did."

At the reference to the others, Michael looked around. The faces of the rest of their raider gang took shape in the ring of light. "*Tsa-tsi. Ne-di.* That you, *Do-tsu-wa?*" Michael greeted them, reaching out to touch each one. "They got any proof?" he asked Johnny.

"They don't need *proof, Mi-ki,*" Johnny reminded him. "We're *Injuns*. All they have to do is *say* we done it."

Michael's serious expression cracked with a hint of a smile. "Yeah. Well, we done it, didn't we?" No one laughed aloud, and there were no grins or broad smiles, only that defiant glint in their eyes that Michael had come to love and respect.

* * * * * * *

At noon the five manacled prisoners squinted against the brilliance of the Arkansas sun. Before them stood Sergeant Wakefield, along with a Major Tyler, assistant to the post commander. Tyler was a middle-aged man who had kept himself in good physical condition. The immaculate uniform, mirror-like boot shine and neatly trimmed hair displayed the man's vanity. To the Major's left was the army legal officer, Captain Stanley, a thin, bespectacled man whose uniform hung loose and ill-fitting. A full guard detail flanked the officers and prisoners on both sides. Positioned safely between Tyler and Stanley was Claymore, the river gambler. He closely studied each prisoner and grew quite agitated when he came to Johnny.

"That's him!" Claymore pointed. "That's the murderin' bastard!" And, standing beside Johnny, Michael was singled out next. "And that one! I'd know those eyes anywhere! He's the one stuck me with a bear knife! Crippled me!" He raised his stiff arm, already showing signs of atrophy, the fingers curled downward from the severed nerves and tendons.

"All right, Mr. Claymore, settle down. You'll get your say at the trial," Major Tyler liked everything and everyone to be under complete control at all times. But the gambler had seen all his friends and associates killed and had waited too long for this face off. He had no intention of *settling down!*

"Trial?!" Claymore exploded. "You oughta just go ahead and hang the bunch of 'em! Right now!"

"What about the others, Mr. Claymore?" Stanley, the army lawyer, asked. "Can you identify these men?"

"Yeah, that's them, all right. The whole gang," Claymore sounded less than convincing and had shown no sign of recognition when he first viewed Ned, George and Redbird.

"You gonna tell us what we're being charged with here?" Michael demanded of Captain Stanley.

"Charges are armed robbery and murder." He read from a paper for all to hear. "*The savage massacre of an innocent gathering of businessmen encamped along the Arkansas River near Lewisburg on the night of May Tenth last.*"

"Based solely on the word of this man?" Michael challenged.

"Don't make no difference," Sergeant Wakefield interjected. "You all guilty and you all gonna hang."

"How do you plead?" the army lawyer asked.

Michael looked at him incredulously. "Is this supposed to be a formal arraignment? And we don't even have representing counsel?"

"Jesus! What we got here? A Injun lawyer?" Wakefield said, taking a step toward Michael. "I warned you once about them highfalutin' words, boy!"

"That's enough, Sergeant!" Major Tyler called Wakefield off and stepped closer to Michael. He scrutinized this intelligent young firebrand with heightened interest. "What's your name?" he asked softly. Michael straightened to his full height, met the Major's eye and refused to speak. "I said, what is your name?" Tyler repeated, his voice controlled but firm.

"Drummond. Michael Drummond."

"And where are you from, Michael Drummond?"

Michael was somewhat perplexed by the commander's gentle approach. The Major waited patiently, studied the ground for a while, then looked back into Michael's eyes.

"Pine Hill, Georgia," Michael said.

"Pine Hill, Georgia, *sir*," Tyler corrected him. Michael understood. It wasn't about information. It was about control. Domination. Who was going to emerge the victor in this little struggle. The two men stood almost nose to nose in a soft-spoken but intense duel of wills. Michael refused to bend. He would never address this man as *sir*.

"They call it Titusville now," Michael offered the information in a friendly enough way, defusing his failure to comply with the major's demand.

"And you've come all this way from Pine Hill....or Titusville...just to rob and murder the good citizens of my territory?" Tyler asked with a twisted smile.

"I have a farm. West of here. Near Fort Coffee," Michael said in monotone, like a prisoner of war giving only the required information.

"A farm," Major Tyler pretended he was impressed and somewhat confused. "And how is it, Mr. Drummond, that a simple Cherokee farmer knows so much about the legal proceedings of the United States judicial system?"

"My father is an attorney." Michael was determined the Major would be the first to blink.

"An attorney. A Cherokee attorney. Intriguing," Tyler smirked.

"We're not Cherokee."

"Oh? Chickasaw? Choctaw?" the Major pretended he really wanted to know.

"I'm as white as you are, Major."

"Really?" Major Tyler took a step back to get a better look at Michael. He continued, almost with a sneer, "I doubt it. But what I *don't* doubt is that you're a liar. A thief. And a murderer. I don't believe your father is an attorney. In fact, based on what I'm hearing, I'm convinced this isn't the first time you've run afoul of the law. Furthermore, your obvious knowledge of legal terms and procedures stem, I'm certain, from being brought to account for previous crimes. This trial you're about to receive—it isn't your first, is it?" Michael refused to acknowledge such lunacy with an answer. Tyler leaned a bit closer and, in a whispered chuckle, added, "But I promise you, it *will* be your last." A long, fierce glare hung between the two men. The major didn't like having his authority contested. His will challenged. And Michael Drummond liked nothing better than being the challenger.

"You refuse to let us see the post commander?" Michael asked.

"The commander is a busy man. He doesn't have time to waste on murdering, thieving trash like you," Tyler said, determined to intimidate this upstart Cherokee. Finally, he beckoned to Wakefield. "Sergeant, take these men back to their cell. Enter a plea of guilty, Captain Stanley. For all of them," he instructed the legal officer with a flick of his hand that registered his disgust with the lot.

"This is a joke!" Michael shouted as the soldiers moved in to escort them back to the stockade. He refused to move, planting his feet, preparing for a struggle.

"Michael...no...," Johnny urged, bumping his friend with a shoulder to move him along. "It's not good."

Michael stepped back and refused to go on. "They can't get away with this!" A soldier's rifle butt to the middle of his back knocked Michael to his knees, taking away his breath. Two other soldiers jerked him to his feet and dragged him past the grinning Wakefield.

"You don't learn too good, do you, boy?" the sergeant taunted. He was taken completely by surprise when Michael spun free from the soldiers and head-butted him in the face, breaking his nose. Michael then lunged for Tyler, not sure what he would accomplish with his hands bound behind him,but he never reached his target. The next blow from a rifle butt was to his stomach.

When he finally regained his breath and shook his vision into focus, all Michael saw were the barrels of the rifles and pistols pointed at his face.

"Michael! Let it go!" Johnny yelled.

"We can't just let it go, Johnny!" Michael spoke to his friend but kept his eyes on the gun barrels. "They aim to kill us! I know! I've been through this before!"

"You'll get a fair trial," Major Tyler assured them with his half-smile.

"Yeah. And *then* we'll hang ya," Sergeant Wakefield laughed from behind a blood-soaked handkerchief.

"Sergeant!" Tyler scolded without conviction, then waved them on, "Get them out of here." With one final glare of victory at Michael, Major Tyler marched off in the direction of his office, accompanied by Captain Stanley. With Michael and Johnny in the lead and the others crowded close behind them, the prisoners were shoved, prodded and herded back toward the stockade.

* * * * * * *

It wasn't unusual for a group of Cherokee leaders to ride together down an Arkansas road. Major Ridge, his son, John, and nephew Elias Boudinot had settled into their new, temporary homes in the west since moving out in the spring and summer of 1837. Once they were settled in and had their business ventures well established, they all anticipated building large new houses for their families that would rival or surpass the homes they had left behind in the east. Riding with them were Stand Watie, The Ridge's nephew and older brother of Elias Boudinot, whose given name was *Ga-la-gi-na*, or Buck Watie. Another Cherokee leader, Assistant Western Chief, John Rogers, accompanied them. What was unusual was their destination, their purpose, and that in their company rode two young women, Annie Drummond and *E-gi-ni* (Agnes), the sister of Michael's friend and fellow raider, Redbird. No one spoke during the final miles before they reached Ft. Smith. They all knew where they were going and why.

* * * * * * *

Major Tyler looked Annie up and down. His upper lip quivered slightly, threatening to convert his polite smile into the openly lustful leer he strained to conceal. The group had stopped at

Annie's insistence about a mile from Ft. Smith. She had walked into the woods, emerging minutes later in the nicer of the only two dresses she owned, hoping to make a good impression in her plea to free her husband. The simple cotton print garment clung to her, accentuating her full, firm breasts, slim waist and shapely legs.

"Well, I can see why Mr. Drummond, who *claims* he's white, is so enchanted with your people," Major Tyler could barely keep his tongue in his mouth.

Chief Rogers saw the fire in Annie's eyes and made a little gesture, hoping to silence her impending response. Annie bit her lip and concentrated on the wall behind the post's administrative officer and second in command. *E-gi-ni* lowered her eyes, hurt at being ignored and more than a little jealous at the fuss made over Annie's beauty. She was shorter and thicker than Annie, though not unattractive by most standards. But she wasn't Annie, and she knew it.

"*Do-tsu-wa* is my brother," she explained her presence. "He's a good man."

The major's tone was blatantly condescending, "I'm sure he's a good Indian." Sergeant Wakefield and the two sentries by the door exchanged smirks, which Tyler couldn't openly acknowledge, but clearly it pleased him. The Ridge stepped toward Tyler's desk.

"Major Tyler, I'm sure you're aware that the proliferation of whiskey, gambling and prostitution during the removal has reached unacceptable proportions. And nowhere has it been worse than along the Arkansas River, from here all the way to Lewisburg and beyond," Major Ridge said.

Though Tyler obviously had no respect for the Cherokees—or any other Indians—he couldn't help being impressed by the eloquence of this distinguished, silver-haired tribal leader.

Encouraged by Major Tyler's attention to The Ridge's words, Chief Rogers ventured an addition. "It has caused untold misery among our Chickasaw, Choctaw and Creek brothers as well. It threatens the livelihood—the very moral fiber of our young Cherokee men."

"But we're talking about robbery and murder here, Chief...?" Tyler had already forgotten the name from the introductions only minutes earlier.

"Rogers," the chief said respectfully.

"Chief Rogers. Yes. Well, this isn't just some little scrape where we can look the other way," he said, expecting them to beg.

"You can release these men to us, Major," The Ridge assured

him. "We have our own court system. Our own police."

Tyler chortled with his familiar half-sneer. "Oh, I'm certain justice would be well served, *Major* Ridge," his voice oozed sarcasm. "And punishment swiftly and fairly meted." As he finished, Tyler's hungry eyes drifted back to Annie. "Tell you what I'm going to do," he leaned back in his chair, rolling a coin deftly between his fingers. "As a personal favor to the lovely Mrs. Drummond here, I'm going to release these men to you." He ogled her ravenously, awaiting an expression of her gratitude.

"Thank you, Major Tyler," she forced the words out with great effort.

"Thank you. *Wa-do*," Agnes echoed.

"My pleasure, Mrs. Drummond," Tyler's eyes stayed on Annie, completely ignoring *E-gi-ni*, as well as the outpouring of *Wa-do's* and thank-you's from Major Ridge and the other Cherokees. And now that he had them all licking his boots, Tyler sprang on them his one condition. "However!" he began, pausing until they were all quiet and attentive. "The one called Fields has to stay."

"Why Fields?" Stand Watie asked.

"Because I have an eye witness who's identified him for murder," Tyler looked from one leader to the next. "He's already pleaded guilty. I can't let him go."

"If we guaranteed his appearance for trial?" Chief Rogers offered.

Major Tyler was becoming irritated. They weren't supposed to negotiate. They were Indians. Hadn't they come here to grovel and beg? Was this constant maneuvering and bargaining a show of disrespect toward him, or was it merely the innate sneaky nature of Indians?

"I suggest you take what you've been given and leave, Chief Rogers," Tyler made no attempt to mask his vexation, adding, with another leer at Annie, "While I'm still in a generous mood."

Annie's eyes burned with hatred, but she bit off any response that might jeopardize the freedom of her husband.

* * * * * * *

The afternoon skies had grown dark with the distant rumblings of a thunderstorm rolling down on them from Missouri. By the time they reached the ferry to cross the Arkansas River, a steady rain was falling. The Cherokee leaders all had slickers or blankets to ward off the downpour. A couple of extra blankets had been found for Annie and *E-gi-ni*. Though drenched, *Tsa-tsi*, *Ne-di* and *Do-tsu-wa* regarded the rain as a welcomed cleansing of stockade stench. They helped the ferryman pull on the ropes to propel the barge across the river. *E-gi-ni*, her blanket drawn tightly about her shoulders, sat alone at the rear of the boat looking wistfully back in the direction of Ft. Smith. Michael, also soaked, stood with Annie and Major Ridge at the ferry's bow.

"The *Tsa-la-gi* have enough problems, Michael," The Ridge lectured the young man he had always liked and whose spirit he and the others regarded as Cherokee, even if Michael's blood was not. "These things reflect on all of us," the sage leader reminded the fiery young warrior.

"I'm sorry, Major Ridge," Michael's apology was sincere. The *Tsa-la-gi* statesman was convinced Michael was truly remorseful.

"Your father is a good friend to the *Tsa-la-gi*," The Ridge continued, staring out across the river. "I don't think he'd like to see you causing trouble for our people. And I know he wouldn't want to see you in jail."

"We were trying to help," Michael said, offering an explanation, not an excuse. "These whiskey peddlers and their whores are stealing the *Tsa-la-gi's* allotment money, leaving them penniless when they reach the west. Then they have to sell their soul just for simple tools to dig a garden or build a cabin."

The Ridge had to smile a little at the young man's fervor. "Promise me something, Michael," he said. His eyes never left the face of his young charge.

"Yes, *E-to-da*," Michael called him father as a term of respect.

"Promise me you'll stay out of Cherokee affairs. Go back to your farm. Raise your crops. Raise your son. In peace."

For the first time Michael felt the sting of rejection. Never in his life had he been able to stand by and watch others being abused. His dearest friend, his *tso-s-da-da-nŭ*, James Walker, had been *Tsa-la-gi*. No one would ever know the pain Michael carried in his heart for having put a bullet through his head. And his beloved Annie, his wife, his very soul. Could he turn his back on her people? The people of his son?

"If there's no peace," he tried to keep a calm and respectful tone with The Ridge, "it's because of *them*, not *us*."

"Son, you *are* them," The Ridge reminded him gently. "Help us make it work."

"All right," Michael held up his hands, conceding the point. "I promise, I'll try to stay out of trouble."

Major Ridge smiled, fully aware of the *I'll try* loophole Michael had left himself. He reached beneath his slicker and produced the tattered letter William Drummond had shoved into his hand as the barge was pulling away from Ross's Landing long ago.

"This is for you," The Ridge handed Michael the letter. "Your father gave it to me the day I left. I was to give it to you if I ever saw you," he explained, adding with a smile, "I have seen you."

Annie joined Michael with increased interest. Michael looked at her in disbelief, shielding the letter from the rain.

"Annie! It's from my father!"

Annie slipped her arm through his, leaning her head against his shoulder while he opened the letter. She held the top of the blanket out to shield the fragile paper while Michael read.

"Well? What does it say?"

"Things are fine at home....Father and Ezekiel have their hands full....Mother isn't well, but then, she never is...." he read on for a while, then shook his head. "It figures."

"What? What?" Annie tugged at him.

"Susanna married Peter Tanner."

"Well, that's really no surprise," she said. They would have been shocked to learn otherwise. Michael's eyes widened and his mouth dropped open. "Michael! What is it?"

"Titus Ogilvie's alive!" Michael was almost breathless. "I didn't kill him!" Annie gripped his arm tighter, grateful for the unburdening she knew Michael had been carrying, even though Ogilvie had been a loathsome beast. "I saw some boxes in Ft. Smith with his name on them, but I figured it was his son! Father says we can come home!"

"*Mi-ki*," she said with a half-hurt, half-confused expression, "our home is here."

"He knows that," Michael excused his father's letter. "That's just his way." He looked out at the west bank of the Arkansas creeping closer to them. Annie studied his troubled face.

"You really miss him, don't you?"

He looked at her with a smile of appreciation and knew again how profoundly he loved this woman. She had lost her own father, her mother and her brother and had endured nightmares few imagined existed in hell, much less in Georgia.

"No more than you miss your father," he said, pulling her closer to him.

* * * * * * *

The rain had stopped but the sky's thick, dark underbelly threatened an imminent deluge like judgement held over them by a wrathful god. Michael helped Rebecca up into the seat of Uncle Andrew's wagon. Annie held one-year-old *Tsi-mi* who was fretting and reaching for his great aunt.

"*Wa-do, E-lo-gi,*" Annie squeezed Rebecca's arm with affection. "Thanks for looking after Jimmy. I don't know what we'd do without you."

"*Tsi-mi* has *da-lo-ni,*" Rebecca, as she frequently did, spoke a mixture of English and Cherokee. She attributed the child's fretting to stomach ache and prescribed some spicewood tea. "Give him *no-da-tsi a-di-ta-s-di.*"

"Yes. We will. I'm sure he'll be all right."

Before climbing up to join his wife, Uncle Andrew offered Michael a word of caution. "They'll be watching you close. Be careful."

Michael whispered, "I've got to get Johnny out."

"You're determined to make me a widow. And your son an orphan," Annie said with a scowl. She hadn't heard what he said, but she could read his moves and, he was convinced, his mind as well.

"We've been here before, Annie," Michael knew he didn't need to remind her, but he hoped to leverage her memories into tacit approval. "We both know exactly what's going to happen to Johnny if I don't get him out."

"He's right, Annie." Contrary to his conservative nature, Andrew sided with Michael.

"I know," Annie admitted. "That's what scares me."

"*Wa-do,*" Michael said. Andrew climbed up into the wagon and clucked the old horse into motion. As the Sixkillers drove away, Michael pulled Annie to him and put his arms around his wife and son.

"You promised The Ridge you'd stay out of trouble," she reminded him.

"I said I'd *try.* All that means is, I don't intend to get caught!"

"*U-lŭ-no-ti-s-gi,*" she told her husband he was crazy.

"The whole world's going crazy," he agreed. They watched the wagon climb the trail that wrapped itself around the hills across the meadow.

23

New Echota, Georgia

The entire town looked more like a U. S. Army post with a few Cherokees hanging around than the capital of the *Tsa-la-gi* nation. Every street and alley had become an artery flowing thick with soldiers, army horses and wagons loaded with incoming provisions or with lumber and building supplies. Mule skinners directed their log-laden teams to one construction site or another. More soldiers arrived every hour of every day. A host of thugs and criminals had rushed to enlist as Georgia Guard, Tennessee Volunteers or North Carolina Militia to *help with the Cherokee problem.*

On the grade leading up to the council house scores of army troops stood in formation while others darted and scurried around and through them, hurrying to find their own units and get into position. General Winfield Scott conferred with his staff officers on the speakers' platform of freshly hewn planks that had been erected adjacent to the open-sided council house. Interspersed among the blocks of soldiers and loosely formed clusters of volunteers and militiamen were Cherokees who had come to hear what new things the great *yo-neg* general would say that would dictate their future.

By the time General Scott checked his watch, motioned to his officers to be seated and stepped to the rail at the edge of the platform, even more soldiers had formed up and more Cherokees had crowded in among them. It was another sweltering summer day with only an occasional light breeze as an ephemeral respite from the oppressive heat. A hush fell over the entire gathering. Somewhere in the distance two dogs barked their canine message. The chanting of an old Cherokee *di-da-nŭ-wi-s-gi* floated in from the outskirts of the crowd. Scott waved off a fly buzzing around his face, cleared his throat and began addressing the soldiers. He spoke of the Cherokees as though they weren't present, yet he fully intended his instructions to the troops be heard and understood as both threat and assurance by those same *Tsa-la-gi.*

"The Cherokees, by the advances they have made in Christianity and civilization, are by far the most interesting tribe of Indians in the territorial limits of the United States. More than 15,000 Cherokees are now about to be removed. We know that four out of five of them are *opposed* to distant relocation. You men will have to cover the entire country they inhabit. You will be forced to make prisoners of many of them. You will march them or transport them in wagons to the nearest detention facility—some of which have now been completed; others are in the final stages of construction. You must show them every possible kindness. And if, among your ranks, some despicable individual inflicts wanton injury or insult on any Cherokee—man, woman or child—you are hereby ordered to seize and arrest the guilty wretch! And I promise you, that man *will* receive the severest penalty of the law! You will, with all human kindness, provide for the care of the sick, the feeble, lunatics, infants, women and the aged—any Cherokee in a helpless condition—and through your consistent acts of kindness, no doubt the Cherokees will soon place their confidence in the army. Instead of fleeing into the mountains and forests, they will flock to us for food and clothing. Naturally, a few of them will be unduly afraid and will try to hide. You will pursue them and offer them a chance to surrender. Don't fire upon them unless they attack you. Even then, try to negotiate before resorting to violence. If you get control of the women and children first, the men will follow. Or, if you can capture the men first, the rest of their family will readily come in when assured of forgiveness and kind treatment. Do not separate families. If you take food and supplies from the Cherokees for army consumption, you must give them a voucher, clearly stating what you have taken so the owners can be repaid. These are a noble people. Treat them as such."

When the general finished his speech, the sea of faces before him were completely silent for some time. Each man—soldier, white civilian, state militiaman and Cherokee—had heard described what, in a perfect world, they would be expected to perform, individually and collectively. But each knew, for better or for worse, it wasn't a perfect world. Were it so, the entire scenario unfolding on what was by all divine and cosmic rights a *Tsa-la-gi* stage would never even have been written.

General Scott stiffly descended the platform followed by his officers. Sergeants barked dismissal orders to the soldiers. They broke formation and moved off toward the bivouac encampments that surrounded the council house, cascading throughout the entire town and overflowing into the wooded areas around New Echota. Scott stopped for some much needed relief in the shade of the sheltering pines. He surveyed the pulsating, amorphous ebb and flow before him while loading his favorite pipe from a Cherokee tobacco pouch. It had been presented to him as a gift from an old warrior who knew he would soon be starting a journey he had no expectation of completing. There were dark days ahead. This the general knew. How *many* dark days even the cynical Winfield Scott could not have foreseen.

* * * * * * *

Campfires and army tents heavily dotted the night. Hundreds of soldiers milled around, tending to their evening duties. Many wrote letters by the light of their lanterns or campfires. Others cleaned their guns or honed the razor-sharp blades of their army sabers. Still more oiled their saddles or cleaned their boots. The variant behavior of individuals found its way into the expanded expression of the group. Low-keyed individuals grouped together quietly. Rowdy soldiers found each other, forming unruly parties. In one such boisterous cluster, a couple of young soldiers jostled and wrestled with each other. Two more cleaned their rifles. One stood with his back to his comrades and urinated against a pine tree. Corporal Charles DeKalb entertained his mates by slipping up behind the urinating soldier and pretending to take his scalp with his saber.

By contrast, the group adjacent to them, consisting mostly of raw recruits on their first duty assignment, sat quietly. One cleaned a pistol; another repaired his saddle. Robert Barton, a handsome corporal from Springfield, Massachusetts, penned a letter by the campfire's flickering light. Barton signed his name, blew on the brittle paper and mumbled to himself in rereading his words.

"...and I must tell you, dear Mother, though I feel it my patriotic duty to serve this great country, to defend her to the death against her enemies, yet I am now filled with a grave concern that, with the morning light, I shall be compelled to herd decent folk around like a bunch of cattle. Folk who are no more my enemy than any of the good citizens of our beloved Springfield. And it puzzles me no end why so many of my comrades seem to relish the thought of subjecting a defenseless and innocent people to unspeakable indignities."

Barton finished, made a couple of minor corrections and folded the letter, sealing it with a piece of wax heated over the fire. He sat with his knees drawn up in front of him and absently watched the shadows and forms moving past in the night. Tents

296

stirred now and then in a light breeze or bobbed like white canvas ghosts when a soldier tripped against a rope. Horses clopped tiredly with their flubbering exhalations as they were led to the remuda. Supply wagons streamed in endlessly from all directions late into the night.

Barton studied one encampment of what could only be described as a horde of civilian carpenters, identified by their liquored loudness and their fifteen wagons filled with tools, lumber and building supplies. These wagons encircled the largest campfire in the area. Recalling the words of the revered General Scott, Barton knew these men were there to erect the prison camps, which were being euphemistically referred to as *temporary holding facilities*, where the Cherokees would be incarcerated while awaiting transport to the west. Corporal Robert Barton stayed awake a long time, sitting quietly in the dark, smelling the odors, listening to the sounds, enjoying the coolness brought on the evening breeze, until one by one the lanterns and campfires were extinguished and all was quiet around the Cherokee national council house.

* * * * * * *

Dawn found the fog-draped hillsides surrounding New Echota sprinkled with thin strands of smoke swirling skyward from the morning fires of the Cherokees. They had camped overnight to keep an eye on their capital. But as the mist climbed lazily out of the valley, New Echota revealed itself to be little more than a tent-city ghost town. The last few army patrols—both mounted and on foot—disappeared up the road at the end of town. Some angled off onto trails through the woods, others kept to the main road until they vanished over a hill or around a bend. And moving out from the opposite end of town were the carpenters' wagons. The rough, dirty workers clung to the piles of lumber and supplies. The huge vessels moved with such chelonian sluggishness that the foot soldiers jokingly scolded them for not keeping up.

* * * * * * *

Corporal DeKalb's squad consisted of himself and five other soldiers. They were among the first mustered out before sunup and wasted no time in rounding up their first Cherokee family—a young man and his wife, the wife's elderly parents, and three small children. DeKalb watched with bored disinterest as the Cherokee wife and her father helped the aged mother up into the rickety old wagon. Two of the children perched atop the family's loosely packed possessions watched their younger brother chasing a baby goat near their cabin.

"Better get that other young'un loaded," DeKalb barked at the young Cherokee wife.

"He wants to take the *tsu-s-qua-ne-gi-dŭ,*" she said, pointing to the baby goat. "It's his pet."

DeKalb chewed impatiently on a pine needle and shook his head in disgust. "Bad enough I got to spend all day bringin' you people in. Ain't haulin' no goats, hogs or chickens."

"*Wi-li! E-he-na!*" the woman called to her son. But the boy ignored her and continued chasing the animal. In one smooth motion, Private Stevens, one of DeKalb's thick-bodied thug-soldiers, drew his pistol and shot the goat. The Cherokee boy stopped in his tracks, staring down at the bleeding pet at his feet. He looked up at his mother, his face twisted with emotion, but he never made a sound. The gunshot brought the child's father charging from the cabin. In one hand he carried pots and pans tied together with a leather strip. In the other he held his old hunting rifle. With one look he assessed the situation.

"You could have killed my son!" he yelled.

"Yeah. I missed," Stevens said sarcastically. "I'll shoot better next time."

While the other soldiers shared a good laugh, the father leaned against the wagon and bit hard into his own arm to keep from going after Private Stevens, an act he knew would have left his family widowed and orphaned. He tossed the pots and pans into the back of the wagon and handed the rifle up to his father-in-law. DeKalb moved his horse in close and grabbed the rifle from the old man.

"I'll take that," he said. Without uttering a word, the young Cherokee father clung to the stock with an iron grip and wouldn't let go. "It's orders. No guns," DeKalb reminded him.

Still the Cherokee man refused to give up his hunting rifle. He jerked it from DeKalb's grasp and handed it back to the old man for the second time. The other soldiers drew their pistols and aimed their rifles at the Cherokee. DeKalb drew his saber and held it to the man's throat. He dismounted and back-handed the Cherokee in the face, then snatched the rifle from the old man and tossed it to the nearest soldier.

"Oh, I forgot," DeKalb sneered. "I'm supposed to be *gentle.*"

"I need my rifle for hunting," the Cherokee man said, wiping the blood from his lip with the back of his forearm. "It's the only way I'll be able to feed my family."

DeKalb lowered his saber, satisfied he had taken the fight out of this upstart Indian. "Right. Tell you what I'm gonna do," he said and called to Stevens. "Private! Get out that paper and ink." Laughing, DeKalb scribbled something on the paper and blew until it was dry. He then rolled it into a tiny scroll and handed it to the young Cherokee man. "When you get to your new home out west—wherever the hell it is we're sending you people!—" he paused to allow his men to respond with the anticipated laughter, "—you give this to the first army officer you see. And that officer will make sure you get what's due you. Understand?"

The Cherokee man looked at the rolled up paper and traced his thumb thoughtfully along its feathered edge. Stevens placed a hand on the man's shoulder.

"You read any English?"

The Cherokee man shook his head no.

"Well, you just do like I said," DeKalb concluded. "Now, let's go. We got about forty more Injuns waitin' up at the crossing. You can join up with them."

The Cherokee man, still suspicious of these *yo-negs* who had rousted him and his family out only minutes past sunrise, eyed his rifle. A sharp prod from the butt of a soldier's musket put him in motion. Grudgingly he took the harness of the single horse hitched to the wagon and moved toward the road, followed by all the soldiers except DeKalb and Stevens.

"What'd you write on that paper?" Stevens asked the squad leader.

"*If this Indian asks you for his rifle, give him ten lashes with a whip and send him packing!*" DeKalb couldn't even finish before he and Stevens burst out laughing. They mounted up and followed the procession. Hearing the two soldiers howling behind them, the young Cherokee father knew he had been the butt of their humor. Sad, frustrated and feeling helpless, he let the rolled up paper slip from his hand where it lay unnoticed until one of the soldiers unwittingly trampled it in the dust.

* * * * * * *

Two Cherokee men and a teenage boy were hard at work chopping weeds in their corn field. The tender green stalks had

299

responded well to the ample rains of late spring. Like many other Cherokees, these men and their families had listened to all the speeches and were aware of the army's arrival and all the political maneuvering that had already taken place. All this would no doubt continue. But they felt it had little to do with weeding their crops.

The trio paused from their work when they saw Corporal Robert Barton and his five soldiers emerge from the woods on the north side of their field. The Cherokees leaned on their hoes and watched the *a-ni-ya-wi-s-gi* come toward them. They noticed that Barton and his men stepped their horses carefully between the stalks in crossing each row so as not to trample a single plant. No resistance was offered when Corporal Barton asked them to accompany him and his men. They were instructed to unhitch the horse from their wagon and bring the animal along. They could ride if they wished. Nor did the soldiers interfere when the two older Cherokees picked up their rifles that were leaning against a fallen tree at the edge of the field. One of the soldiers offered the young Cherokee boy water from his canteen. The boy politely declined and thanked the soldier, who looked on admiringly when the shoeless lad sprang lightly up onto the horse's back.

* * * * * * *

A barefoot young full-blood, grimacing with determination, his face dripping perspiration, looked anxiously behind him as he ran frantically down the dirt road. Once he had successfully broken visual contact with his pursuers, he disappeared into the woods. Seconds later, Corporal DeKalb and his patrol rounded the bend at a sporting gallop as though leisurely pursuing the fox at some distant Lancashire estate. They had no problem following the fleeing man's footprints in the dirt. DeKalb motioned to Stevens and another soldier to race ahead while he and the rest cut through the woods. DeKalb laughed with delight at the morning's entertainment and spurred his horse into the trees.

Ten minutes later Stevens emerged from the woods back onto the road. He was turned in the saddle, grinning back to where Corporal DeKalb led the captured young Cherokee with a rope around his neck and his hands tied behind him. When the prisoner stumbled, DeKalb spurred his horse ahead, pulling the rope tighter, making it virtually impossible for the Cherokee to regain his footing. Bringing up the rear, doubled over their horses with laughter, were the rest of DeKalb's detail.

* * * * * * *

The old Cherokee woman worked methodically at her spinning wheel, basking in the warmth of the afternoon sun slanting in through the open cabin window. Her shriveled fingers moved swiftly and accurately, schooled over seventy-plus summers. From the thread she spun she intended to weave a blanket for her granddaughter, soon to marry a handsome young warrior from the Panther, or Blue Clan.

A shadow fell across the spinning wheel. Her wrinkled, squinting eyes drifted up to the window. She actually smelled him before she saw the dirty, bearded Georgia guardsman framed in the opening. She didn't know this big lout of a man sneering down at her, but she knew why he was there. The fear of dislocation that had always been there, simmering beneath the surface of their simple, *Tsa-la-gi* lives ever since the white man first began appearing in numbers, had boiled up into their collective consciousness once again.

The old woman looked away from the window and toward the cabin door where her daughter stood with an expression of muted fear, a second guardsman holding her by the arm.

* * * * * * *

The family of six were escorted away from their cabin on the side of a hill by three U. S. Army infantrymen and a single, mounted cavalry soldier. Each member of the Cherokee family carried hastily assembled items tied up in blankets, dresses or pants with their legs knotted at the end. As much as possible had been strapped onto the back of their single horse. They had gone no more than a few yards from the cabin before a family of *yo-neg* rabble swarmed in from the trees like coprophagous green flies on fresh manure, looting the possessions the Cherokees had been forced to leave behind. Silently the departing family watched the shoeless, dirty white woman untie their milk cow from a tree behind the cabin. *Perhaps they have children who need the milk,* the Cherokee mother thought. *What will my own children do now for milk?* she wondered. She saw her two oldest run out to lovingly touch the sprawling oak in and beneath which they had played their entire lives. Their new climbing rope still hung from the high limb where their father had attached it only last summer.

* * * * * * *

Throughout the day, as General Scott had promised, Cherokees were driven from their homes. Sons and fathers—even mothers and daughters—were taken straight from the fields, given only a few minutes to dash back and fetch what they could. Anyone going back into a cabin did so under escort of a U. S. Army soldier, a Georgia state guardsman, a North Carolina militiaman or a Tennessee volunteer.

"Don't trust any of 'em," was the standing order of the day for the *yo-negs*. "That old woman could get a gun and gut-shoot ya right out from under that wad of blankets!"

Word of the roundup had spread far and wide. Whites were often lined up at the edge of a clearing like sprinters at the starting line. As soon as the last Cherokee was prodded out of the cabin and herded along with the rest of the family, the race was on. Anything left worth taking—furniture, food, livestock—was greedily seized. Frequently the pillage was well under way even as the Cherokee family looked back for one last glimpse of their simple but beloved home.

Cherokee heirlooms handed down through generations were dragged from their places of respectful display, piled in front of the cabin and set afire by the whites.

The cabin had to be cleaned out and made ready so the thirteen-year-old daughter who'd got herself knocked up by that half-witted boy from the next holler would have a home. A place to start. Later they could add on or go find a larger cabin someplace. Or by then her grandma and grandpa'd like as not be dead and the young couple could move back in with ma and pa, leastwise 'til their young'uns was too big. But by the time the youngest one had quit shittin' his britches and taken to cobbin' like the grown ups, his older sister'd be in the family way, ma and pa'd like as not be gone and the cycle would repeat itself. It was their destiny. The White Man's Burden. To conquer and civilize the continent. And to do whatever it took to drive out the heathen savages. Send them packing out west. It was God's will.

It was a taking in the twinkling of an eye, but it was a far cry from the Biblical rapture. Loaves of steaming hot bread were left on the hearth, still warm when snatched up by greedy white hands. Smoked hams, turkeys and sides of bacon suspended from rafter poles in tiny, dark smokehouses were cut down and tossed into pots and pans that had been left hanging on cabin walls, forgotten in a

302

hasty exit. A hand-woven mesh bag filled with roots and herbs was thrown in for good measure. A gourd dipper spun idly in a half-filled water bucket at the well. Stuck into the bark of a spreading blackjack oak with an old knife, a cracked piece of parchment bore the Cherokee symbols spelling out *u-ni-gi-sŭ u-tsa-ti-na*. Gone far away.

* * * * * * *

At sundown of the first day, last minute construction continued on the Hiwassee concentration camp, even while the Cherokees were being herded in by the hundreds. This was only one of many such *detention facilities* thrown up throughout Cherokee territory stretching across portions of four states—Georgia, Tennessee, Alabama and North Carolina. It was all that remained of the *Tsa-la-gi* territory that once covered eight states.

The Cherokees came on foot, carrying as many possessions as they had been granted time to grab, not stopping to pick up what was dropped along the way for fear of a sharp jab with a stick or a rifle butt. They came in overloaded wagons from which things fell—a string of pots, a wad of blankets, parts of a disassembled spinning wheel, a three-year-old child. They came with horses laden with the very old and the very young, sometimes almost hidden beneath the baggage piled high around them. Some captives were escorted into the camp with patience, kindness and respect. Others received harsh pokes and prods and even harsher words. The most brutal of the official and quasi-official escorts were the Georgia guardsmen, followed by the older soldiers who carried anti-Indian sentiments from a career of Indian skirmishes, battles and wars in years past, though many of these seasoned veterans were encountering Cherokees for the first time.

* * * * * * *

Outside the front gates of the camp stood the Camp Hiwassee headquarters building. New Echota had been established as the official army command post for Cherokee removal, but Hiwassee, to the north, was to occupy a considerable portion of General Winfield Scott's time. An army dispatch rider raced up and skidded his pony to a halt.

Inside, General Scott paced back and forth behind his desk in a familiar pensive posture, his chin impaled on his right thumb, the index finger resting thoughtfully against the tip of his nose. The commander finally stopped at the desk and stared down at the pile of ledger books and loose paper. Throughout the day his staff and their subordinates had been trying in vain to compile a log of all the Cherokees brought into the camp. The dispatch rider received a sour look from the sentry when he entered without first knocking and waiting to be announced, but the young soldier apparently didn't care. He strode confidently up to Corporal Edward Mears, the general's *aide de camp*, and slapped the message pouch into his hand. Edward, a young, immaculately groomed, by-the-numbers military man, returned a similar pouch. The dispatcher crisply saluted General Scott and was out the door. With a click of his heels, Edward pivoted with a military flourish and formally delivered the message.

Scott read the report and tossed it on the desk. He went to the window and looked out on the river of humanity streaming past in the fading light. Edward, standing close to the desk, rapidly scanned the report without being so presumptuous as to pick it up.

"There's too much violence," Scott said, his back to the room. "Only the first day, and already eleven people have been killed."

"Surely, General, you didn't expect this to come off without bloodshed," Edward attempted to remove any undue burden of concern from his commander's shoulders.

"I want the Georgia Guard and the North Carolina Militia dismissed as soon as it's feasible. I don't trust them," Scott concluded.

Edward now took the liberty of picking up the report and reviewing it. "They do appear to be involved in most of the violence. Probably taking revenge for *Indian atrocities* against their forefathers."

"Real or imagined," Scott added. "Others, I'm convinced, are merely grabbing the opportunity for unchecked brutality. The Tennessee boys seem to be all right, but let's keep an eye on them, too." He continued staring out the window while he loaded his favorite pipe. "Look at them. Many appear to be sick. Some look half starved, yet the reports say they refuse to eat the food."

"They're afraid we're trying to poison them," Edward had already heard the unofficial word whispered by those trafficking in and out of headquarters all day.

"*We* are the ones who've been poisoned, Edward. Make no mistake," the general exhaled laboriously. There was a heavy silence, marked only by the soft crackling of the general's pipe and the muffled sounds of shuffling feet, creaking wheels and the hooves of horses, mules and oxen from outside.

"Have my horse ready at sunrise. I'm going to Ross's Landing," Scott said.

"Yes, General," Edward noted the order in his log book. Scott continued to peer out the window at the river of prisoners flowing by. He knew this was only the beginning. It would go on for many more days, and it would only get worse, not better.

* * * * * * *

On the morning of the second day, there was an air of solemnity as the Swimmer family sat down to breakfast. Charlie and *Tsu-tsu*, now fifteen, occupied opposite ends of the table. The men of the family. Eva served chunks of boiled salt-pork to each plate. Six-year-old Sally kept her threadbare, satin rag doll tucked safely under one arm while she served each a piece of bread, starting with Grandma Nancy Ward Swimmer, Charlie's mother. Buck, just a year older than his little sister, and Martha, the oldest at seventeen, waited patiently. Everyone hesitated when the dog barked outside. Looks of apprehension went around the room, but no one spoke. Charlie and *Tsu-tsu* glanced toward the two rifles leaning against the wall. Buck took a blowgun from his lap and laid it on the table. Grandma Nancy looked at him and smiled.

"What're you going to shoot with that, *Ga-la-gi-na?*" Martha asked him.

"Put that away, Buck. Eat your food," Eva pointed her finger at him.

"If the soldiers come, I'm going to help *E-to-da* and *Tsu-tsu* fight them," he said with quiet defiance. "I'm not afraid," he wanted to make that point very clear.

"Me, too," Sally chimed in as she sat down. To everyone's astonishment she placed a knife on the table beside Buck's blowgun, then carefully positioned the rag doll next to the knife.

"You'll do no such thing!" Eva said.

Martha took the knife and blowgun and handed them across the table to their mother who deposited them on the sideboard. Outside, the dog barked again.

"*Gi-li. A-ni-ya-wi-s-gi,*" Nancy pointed to the door with an arthritic finger, announcing the arrival of the white soldiers.

"We know, *E-li-si,*" Martha patted her grandmother's arm.

"*Hi-ga.* Eat," Charlie said calmly. During the night a

number of visitors had dropped by to check on the Swimmers and to report what they had heard or seen regarding the first day's round up. Charlie and his family knew it was only a matter of time before the *yo-negs* came. And now they were here. Charlie wondered if it was Georgia Guard or U. S. Army. *When they come, you'd better pray it's army*, their visitors had whispered in the night as though their captors were waiting just outside the cabin. The rumors—far too many of them true—had spread like thistledown on the wind. *Would they be treated with dignity or like animals?* These thoughts had been with Charlie and Eva all night. In a few seconds they would know.

Coming up the trail toward the cabin were two U. S. Army round up squads, one detail commanded by Corporal Robert Barton, the other led by Corporal Charles DeKalb. This was their first activity of the morning. Later they would split up to cover more territory. Corporal DeKalb held up his hand, signalling them all to stop.

"Spread out. Surround the cabin. We'll sneak up on 'em."

"Don't be stupid," Corporal Barton resented DeKalb's attitude, both toward the Cherokees and for presuming to take command of the combined squads. "They know we're here. You don't *sneak up* on these people."

"Well, what do *you* suggest, Corporal Barton?" DeKalb made no attempt to mask his dislike for this sensitive young man from Massachusetts. He considered Barton a cowardly weakling.

"Knock on the door and tell them they have to come with us," Barton said, his tone suggesting it was the obvious course. DeKalb snorted his contempt and motioned for the others to go ahead and surround the cabin.

"I want a man at every window. And cover the back," he ordered. Barton motioned for his own men to follow him. They would ride straight up to the cabin. DeKalb rode along with them, watching the progress of his own squad circling around to either side. When they reached the Swimmer's cabin, neither Barton nor any of his men made any special attempt to be quiet in compliance with DeKalb's *sneak up* plan. DeKalb gave each of them a dirty look and kept his hand on his saber to reduce the noise as he dismounted.

Corporal Barton raised his gloved hand, but before he could knock, the cabin door disappeared from in front of him. DeKalb had stepped up beside him and, with a single kick, blasted the door inward off its hinges. The flying door struck Charlie Swimmer on the back before clattering to the floor. Charlie withstood the blow and, though thrown forward against the edge of the table, managed to keep his seat. Martha stifled a scream. She looked up at the doorway into the face of Corporal Barton. Instinctively, Sally grabbed her beloved rag doll.

With a smirk of satisfaction at Barton, DeKalb strode past him into the room. He casually drew his army pistol and cocked it in a gesture of intimidation. Eva started around the table, but Charlie held up a hand to signal he was all right.

"Don't even think of trying to escape," DeKalb bellowed. His eyes went from the window on one side to the one opposite. At each opening stood one of DeKalb's men with a musket to which he had attached a bayonet. "You know why we're here," DeKalb said in a loud voice. Eva glared defiantly at him, prompting a distorted grin from DeKalb. "Stevens!" he called to the private standing in the doorway. "Get those rifles."

In order to retrieve Charlie's and *Tsu-tsu's* rifles from against the wall, Stevens needed to get past Eva, but she refused to move. "Get out of my way, squaw," Stevens told her. Eva said nothing and refused to budge. Without hesitation, Stevens pushed her roughly aside and went for the rifles.

"*E-tsi!*" Martha screamed. Bolting from her chair, she grabbed the knife from the sideboard and lunged at Stevens. Only Barton's alert reaction intercepted her and prevented her from driving the knife into Stevens's chest. Her eyes burned with hatred for the man who had touched her mother. Charlie sprang to his feet, but the guns of two more soldiers were instantly in his face, forcing him back into his chair.

Corporal Barton spoke to the beautiful young girl he suddenly found in his arms, his voice firm but not unkind. "You don't want to do that." He pried the knife from her hand and tossed it back onto the sideboard. Despite the strained circumstance, he couldn't help notice Martha's beauty, the sweet aroma of her herb-washed hair as it brushed his face, the stirring combination of firmness and softness of the body his arm encircled. But one doesn't spend too much time admiring the beauty of a wildcat one is holding in one's arms. Martha jerked an arm free and slashed at Barton's face, leaving a trail of four parallel scratches down his cheek. He recaptured her free hand, this time holding her wrist firmly. And in that fleeting instant she couldn't help notice, despite her counterattack and the wound she had inflicted, there was a gentleness in his eyes quite different from the others. She found it most disconcerting. Barton's kind expression was broken by a flash of outrage directed at DeKalb. "There's no need pushing these people around. They've done nothing!"

DeKalb shrugged with a confused, almost amused look. "Why do you keep callin' 'em *people*? They're God damn Indians, for Chrissake!"

Charlie bowed his head and began reciting, "*Ga-du-si wi-di-ga-ga-ni na-hna, tsŭ-di-da-le-hŭ-s-ga a-qua-li-ni-go—*"

"What the hell's he doing?" DeKalb's man at the window asked.

"Some Cherokee gibberish," Stevens dismissed it with a wave of the hand. "Probably puttin' a curse on us. Shut up!" He jabbed Charlie sharply in the back with the butt of his rifle. Sally put a consoling hand on her father's arm.

At the other end of the table, *Tsu-tsu* picked it up in English. "I will lift up mine eyes unto the hills, from whence cometh my help. My help cometh from the Lord, which made Heaven and Earth."

"It's the Hundred-twenty-first Psalm!" Barton was astonished. When he relaxed his grip on Martha, she broke free and bolted for the back door, but Private Evans, another of DeKalb's soldier-thugs, knocked her away from the door and pinned her hard against the wall, his rifle barrel pressed across her chest. Corporal Barton interceded, pushing the rifle away and placing his hands on Martha's shoulders. He looked into her eyes with pleading, "Listen to me! Please! You're much better off staying with your family. Under our protection." She tried to claw his face again, but he caught her wrists in mid-swing. "You're only making things worse! Now stop it!" His voice was taut with frustration at not being able to make her understand.

"*Ma-di!*" Charlie called to his daughter.

"*Tle-s-di a-la-s-di!*" Eva urged her not to fight.

"Please....please," Barton's voice softened. She didn't resist when he led her to the window to look out. At the edge of the meadow, some whites were already driving the Swimmer's cattle into the woods. A teenage boy chased one of their pigs with a stick, while two others tried to get a rope on one of Charlie's horses.

"*E-to-da!* They're stealing the animals!" Martha turned to her father with a shocked expression.

"Get out there and stop them! Move!" Barton snapped to Private Baker, one of his own men.

DeKalb held out a hand, delaying Baker just long enough to amend the order. "Tell them to leave the horses. And the wagon," he said, then pushed the private on out the door. DeKalb shrugged at Barton, justifying his directive, "They're gonna take everything after we're gone anyway." Enough talk. It was time to get moving. "Grab what you can carry," DeKalb told the Swimmers. "You've got a long way to go and we have to move a lot of Injuns today."

"*Ma-di, E-li-si,*" Eva called to her daughter and her mother-in-law, "get everything you can. Tie it up in the blankets. Sally, you help. You, too, Buck." She knew they couldn't stay, and they had clearly been shown the futility of resistance. The Swimmers knew what they had to do and knew they must do it quickly and efficiently.

Charlie motioned to his older son. "*Tsu-tsu,* come with me to hitch up the wagon."

DeKalb motioned for one of his men to go with them. "Keep an eye on them two. I don't trust 'em."

Charlie and *Tsu-tsu* stepped over the fallen door and were followed outside by Private Thorpe, one of DeKalb's men. Grandma Nancy picked up a large pan of shelled corn and sorghum grain from the sideboard and moved toward the back door. Private Miles Franklin, of Barton's detail, stepped in her path and looked to Barton for instruction. Before the squad leader could reply, the withered old woman gently nudged Franklin aside and opened the back door. She motioned DeKalb's man with the bayonet musket out of her way. The soldiers looked quietly at the chickens flocking to her. Nancy tossed the feed out to her babies, one trembling handful at a time.

It took only a few minutes for Charlie and *Tsu-tsu* to hitch up the horses and load the wagon. Charlie wrestled a small anvil into the rear along with the rest of his smithing tools. Martha, *Tsu-tsu* and Buck carefully helped Grandma Nancy up into the wagon seat. Buck was sobbing quietly, trying not to let it show. Sally, clinging to her rag doll, sat perched high atop their possessions. The soldiers stood around waiting. Only DeKalb paced anxiously back and forth between the wagon and the cabin.

"Let's go! Let's go!" he urged impatiently.

Eva pushed and shifted bundles to make more space where additional items might be carried. "I'd like to get a few more things, if it's all right," she asked politely, aware that DeKalb was the one she had to entreat.

"Come on! We don't have all day!" he kicked peevishly at the dirt.

"Please..." Eva begged. When DeKalb directed his man Evans to accompany her, she looked with mistrust at the soldier. Evans looked back to DeKalb and shrugged.

"She might have a gun hid in there somewhere," DeKalb motioned irritably for Evans to do as he had been told. Corporal Barton cut the soldier off.

"I'll go," Barton said.

"Thank you," Eva said. She didn't trust any of these *yo-neg* soldiers, but Barton had shown himself to possess at least a thread of compassion in the way he had handled Eva's daughter. Inside the cabin, Eva tied up the corners of a blanket she had quickly filled. "May I get a few more pots and pans?" she asked the young corporal.

"Sure, ma'am," Barton answered, drawing a flash of amazement from Eva. He had addressed her as *ma'am*. "You're gonna need everything you can carry," Barton added off-handedly as though making idle conversation. She spread out another blanket and began gathering more items. Barton glanced around, waiting patiently. He spied a beautiful, hand-carved wooden rocking horse at one end of the room. Squatting beside it, he admired its intricate handiwork, an example of true craftsmanship. Eva paused to look at him.

"It was my son's. Buck," she explained. "That's why he was crying. Leaving it behind. His grandfather made it for him."

"It's beautiful," Barton ran his fingers over the smooth wood.

"You may have it if you like," Eva said softly.

"Are you sure?"

"We certainly can't take it with us."

"I hope to have a son...someday," he said, continuing to examine the rocking horse.

"Are you married?" Eva asked. She found it strange, actually having a civil conversation with a white soldier. She almost smiled when the young man shook his head with obvious embarrassment. "You have a girl?" she ventured. Again, he shook his head, avoiding a verbal response.

"Perhaps I could disassemble it and have it shipped back to Massachusetts," he proposed.

"Disassemble it?" Eva cocked her head, puzzled.

"You know. To ship it. So it doesn't get broken."

"You can't take it apart," she told him.

He tilted it toward the light and examined it more closely. His eyes widened with astonishment. "My God! It's all one piece!" his voice was almost a whisper.

Eva tried to carry too much at once and dropped a pan. With the clattering interruption Barton abandoned the hand-carved horse

310

and helped her recapture her things.

Grandma Nancy and all the children were situated in the wagon. Charlie stood by the horses. He forced himself to remain motionless while watching the white rabble in pursuit of the last of his livestock. Two of his best cows were being herded up the trail in the distance behind the cabin, the opposite direction they would be taking. Other whites waited near the tree line as though they were somehow showing respect and consideration by allowing the cabin's inhabitants to depart before swarming down to ravage whatever was left. Vultures waiting to descend and devour.

Eva emerged from the cabin carrying a piece of her weaving loom and balancing the load with the four blanket corners gripped tightly in her fist. Corporal Barton carried the pots and pans and immediately came under the scornful eye of Corporal DeKalb and his men.

"Damn, Barton," DeKalb said with unrestrained contempt, "you're here to round 'em up, not haul their shit for 'em!"

Barton ignored the insult and deposited the load onto the overflowing wagon. On the other side, Charlie did the same with the things Eva had brought. The couple then climbed up beside Grandma Nancy and the wagon pulled out. The horses strained visibly against the load.

The wagon had gone little more than a hundred yards when Buck and Sally, facing the rear, cried out. *"Ha-ga-ta! A-tsi-lŭ!"*

Charlie halted the wagon. He and Eva stood up and looked back. The whites had swarmed down as expected, ransacking the cabin for whatever had been left behind. Corporal Barton felt a twinge of jealous anger toward the seedy white man making off with the hand-carved rocking horse. Upset that the *damned Injuns* had been allowed to take most of their belongings, the would-be looters had torched the cabin to express their frustration and disappointment. It took only seconds for the flames to lap up through the windows and ignite the thatched roof.

The Swimmers watched in silence as fire engulfed their home. Corporal Barton, Private Franklin and the other soldiers of their squad shook their heads, appalled at the wanton destruction. Martha looked at Barton with great loathing. He was *yo-neg.* The people destroying the only home she had ever known were *yo-neg.* In her eyes, the only difference was the uniform. Barton recognized the connection she had made in her mind. He felt ashamed and could only look away.

"This is a disgrace," he complained to DeKalb. "This whole

311

thing will be a dark stain on our nation's honor."

"Nobly put, Corporal Barton," DeKalb chuckled sarcastically. "All I can say is: I'm glad I'm a soldier and not a Cherokee."

"You call this soldiering!?" Barton's outrage was mounting. "Herding people around like cattle?! Destroying their homes?!"

"I keep tellin' you—" Stevens interrupted, "they ain't *people*, they're Indians."

"Jes' shut up and get 'em on down the God damn road," DeKalb had heard enough talk. He slapped the nearest wagon horse on the rump. When the wagon lurched forward, Sally's ragged little satin doll toppled out unnoticed. Like so many other insignificant treasures of a displaced people, in a few seconds it had been trampled into the dirt by the unwitting foot soldiers bringing up the rear.

* * * * * * *

For the Swimmers, the rest of the morning was spent inching along the road or sitting in the scorching sun. Move a little, then wait. Wait while the soldiers rousted more Cherokee families from their cabins or chased down a recalcitrant young Cherokee man, adding to their ever increasing number bound for the nearest *detention facility*.

Eva whispered her concern to Charlie when she saw two Cherokee children—a boy and a girl about seven years old, possibly twins—in the custody of a rowdy group of Georgia guardsmen who had joined them around midday. The children looked terrified and helpless. Eva anxiously surveyed the group of captives but saw no one who might be the children's parents. Then she began looking around for Corporal Barton. She wasn't sure why. If she could get his ear, perhaps he would persuade the Georgians to let the children ride on the Swimmer wagon with Sally and Buck. But Corporal Barton was nowhere to be seen. He and his patrol had gone off down a side road to fetch the two families Eva knew lived there. He would probably join them later down the road where the trail came out near Raven Creek.

Then Eva noticed a very old full-blood man who had grown tired, unable to keep up the pace. He angled toward a fallen log beside the road and sat down. Eva was relieved when one of the guardsmen who had been hanging a little too close to the two young children left them to go and retrieve the old man. He nudged the ancient one, gently at first with the butt of his musket, but when the old man refused to move, the next prod was more forceful. Still the old man didn't stir. Without hesitation and before anyone could react to stop him, the guardsman calmly drew his pistol and shot the old man in the head. Casually the guardsman began reloading his pistol while strolling up the road to rejoin the others. Eva stood up in the wagon. Her hand covered her mouth and her eyes filled with tears. Charlie, as outraged and shocked as his wife, pulled her back down beside him. Eva's simple, honest reaction had already drawn suspicious looks from other Georgia guardsmen.

Eva was still wrestling with the horror of what she had witnessed when they passed a familiar Cherokee cemetery on a gentle, grassy slope adjacent to the road. At first they thought a funeral was in progress and looked to see if they recognized any of the mourners. Perhaps it was someone they had known. They might be able to convey the news to friends and loved ones they would later encounter. They quickly realized, however, all the people in the cemetery were white. And, despite the numerous mounds of freshly dug earth, there was no funeral. Graves—some no more than a few days old—had been reopened. One of the *yo-negs* shifted, allowing Charlie and Eva an unobstructed view. A skinny white man was down in one of the graves on his knees, straddling the decaying corpse, pulling at the silver pendants draped around the dead *Tsa-la-gi's* neck. Another white, on his knees in the dirt beside a second grave reached down into the hole to retrieve a set of silver spurs and a small, silver urn. Grandma Nancy Ward Swimmer in her seventy-odd years had seen many things, but never anything like the desecration going on before her while the wagons creaked past. She caught the look of hopelessness—and helplessness—in her son's eyes. There was nothing any of them could do. And they all knew they dare not even open their mouths in protest.

* * * * * * *

By noon Corporal DeKalb's squad and Corporal Barton's detachment had gathered a dozen more Cherokee families in addition to the Swimmers. Combined with the captives of the Georgia Guard who, uninvited, had attached themselves to the army-led party, there was a long string of wagons and pedestrians. As the train approached a young black family sitting beside the road, Eva recognized the pregnant black woman, her husband and their two children.

A few of the Cherokees in the area owned slaves—usually one or two at the most. But, unlike the whites, the *Tsa-la-gi* often worked right alongside their people and, as a rule, treated them more like family members than objects or possessions. When the removal began, most blacks preferred to face the unknown with their Cherokee *family* rather than endure what they knew could befall them under a harsh white owner. For the most part, the *Tsa-la-gi* did not consider slaves as property—like livestock, barns and orchards—to be disposed of prior to the removal.

Eva jostled Charlie from his dazed depression. "Look! It's Jane and Solomon. Tom Rogers's people."

Charlie stopped the wagon beside the black couple. Stevens trotted up, irritated at the unauthorized delay.

"Move along! You don't stop 'less we tell you!" he yelled at Charlie.

"We know these people," Eva explained as though it would make a difference to Stevens. She and Charlie were already climbing down from the wagon when DeKalb and Barton rode up from the rear. The halted Swimmer wagon had set off a chain reaction stoppage all the way back down the line.

"What's the problem?" Barton asked.

Solomon stepped into the road between his wife and the soldiers, as much to protect Jane as to explain the situation. "We was goin' with Mistah Tom Rogers, but Jane here cain't go so fast. The soldiers jes' left us here. Said catch up later, but Jane don't feel so good. It's 'bout her time," he said, searching among the soldiers for a compassionate face.

"If she can't walk, just wait here for the next group," DeKalb answered impatiently. He hated delays. They had to get moving.

"Put her in our wagon," Charlie said to Solomon.

"Your wagon is full," DeKalb interrupted. "Leave 'em and let's get moving!"

"We're not leaving her here like this." Eva stepped around Solomon and helped Jane to her feet.

"We're here to round up Indians," Stevens protested. "They didn't tell us nothin' about haulin' no niggers."

"*Tsu-tsu* and I'll walk," Charlie offered. "My wife can drive."

"Let's get her in the wagon then. Hurry it up," Corporal Barton encouraged them without rancor. He knew DeKalb would soon resort to his usual bullying tactics to get the assembly moving again. Solomon and Jane understood the order and flashed Barton a look of gratitude. With Charlie's and Eva's help, Jane managed to get up into the wagon and take a seat beside Nancy. Barton remained with them while DeKalb and Stevens, rolling their eyes and snorting their well known disdain for Barton's humanity, rode back down the line to get the others started.

While Eva climbed into the driver's seat beside Jane, Corporal Barton drank from his canteen. He looked out across the flask and caught Martha watching him from the corner of her eye. He wiped the mouth of the canteen with his sleeve and offered it to her.

"Would you like a drink?"

They stared at one another, then Martha turned her eyes from his without answering. Gradually the wagon wheels creaked into motion. A loud clap of thunder was followed by the onset of a gentle shower that pelted the dry, dusty earth.

24

A light drizzle had been falling since mid-morning, dampening the travellers going to and from Georgia's capital city. William Drummond kept his slicker drawn around him and his hat pulled down over his face. He eased Clancey to the side of the Milledgeville road when he noticed a wagon coming from town. From the black coat and stove-pipe beaver hat of the lanky, beak-nosed undertaker riding beside the driver, William knew it was a funeral hearse. When the wagon drew near, the black driver politely touched the brim of his hat to acknowledge those who, like William, had moved aside out of respect. The coffin on the hearse was sparsely draped with a few wilted, rain-beaten flowers. Behind them, a hollow-eyed fourteen-year-old boy—a son, William thought, or a grandson—walked unblinking in the rain, leading a horse on which the black-clad widow rode side-saddle.

As the woman passed, William removed his hat. She turned her head slightly and appeared to be looking directly at him, but William couldn't make out her features through the dense weave of the veil. Nevertheless, it gave him a chilled feeling that went beyond the effects of a long ride in the rain. When the cortége had passed, William donned his hat and rode on, urging Clancey to a trot, hoping to make up some time.

* * * * * * *

William knocked at the office on the second floor of the courthouse. He had been there numerous times to speak with the man whose name was engraved on the polished plate: *Chambers - Hon. Walter M. Barrington.* After waiting almost a full minute without hearing any response, William knocked again. This time he was aware of how loudly the rapping echoed down the long corridor with its dark walls and highly polished hardwood floors. He was about to knock a third time when Jernigan, the bespectacled court clerk, peeked out of a doorway down the hall like a squirrel in a tree investigating the annoying presence of a woodpecker.

"I'm here to see Judge Barrington," William smiled, hoping to be remembered from their previous encounters. What had begun as a polite smile from the clerk instantly darkened to a twitch of fear. Jernigan ducked back into the file room. William heard the door latch click. He turned to find himself facing a tall, slender, pock-faced man, skeletal and sinewy in his long black coat. While certain he'd never met this man, William had the overwhelming feeling he seemed strangely familiar. Then William recalled the undertaker from the funeral procession he had passed on the way into Milledgeville. The similarity was so uncanny William was convinced the two men must be brothers. William knew he was facing the local sheriff by the large, shiny badge pinned to the long, black frock.

"Hello," William greeted him. "I'm looking for Judge Walter Barrington."

"I heard." The sheriff chewed on a wooden splinter clenched between rotted teeth. He appeared intent on preventing his paper-thin lips from touching the wood as he spoke.

"Where can I find him?" William asked.

"You ain't from 'round here," the sheriff looked the newcomer up and down.

"No. William Drummond. From Titusville." He extended his hand, but the sheriff ignored it.

"James Pryne," he said, never blinking. "*Sheriff* James Pryne."

"Sheriff, can you tell me where I might find—"

"Come in on the old Pine Hill road, did ya?" Pryne cut him off.

"Yes."

Pryne pulled a gold pocket watch from his vest and studied it. "Just now?"

"Yes," William said, confusion creeping into his voice.

"You must'a passed him then."

"I don't think so," William tried to sound polite. "I would have seen him."

Pryne's nose crinkled up and his over-bite flashed an archtoidean grin. "Ain't likely. Less'n they had his coffin open."

"Coffin?" William was starting to make the connection. "You mean that was—?"

"The Honorable Walt Barrington. Deceased," Pryne was pleased to make the official announcement.

"But how?"

Pryne touched his neck with the wooden splinter. "Slug through the throat, near as we could tell."

"Murdered?!"

"Didn't say that," Pryne said flatly.

"You're saying it was an accident?"

"Didn't say that neither," Pryne shook his head.

"I don't believe the man would take his own life."

"Could'a been feeling guilty," Pryne was content to go in that direction. "Guilt's a powerful thang."

"Guilty of what?" William found it incomprehensible.

"Sympathizin'. Bein' a Injun Lover," Pryne suggested. "Drove him mad."

"That's absurd! I don't believe you!" William shook his head emphatically. He had known Walter Barrington for too many years. William didn't miss Pryne's implied meaning when the sheriff eased his long coat back and rested the heel of his hand on the pistol butt.

"You say you're a good friend of his?" Pryne asked with menacing insinuation.

"Didn't say that," William parodied the sheriff's earlier tone.

"You here on court business?"

"Didn't say that neither," William openly mocked the sheriff's drawl. Pryne flashed his murine grin once more. William stepped around him and headed for the stairs, his footsteps echoing loudly down the hallway. The question darted through his mind, *How had this specter of a man come up behind him so silently?* Jernigan poked his head out for a second, but found himself staring right into the beady eyes of the sheriff and disappeared back inside his room like a frightened rodent.

* * * * * * *

Ezekiel closed the barn door. It had rained off and on all day, but the work had continued. Exhausted, Ezekiel made his way up toward the Drummond house. Halfway there he paused, looking out toward the main road where he heard the clopping of hooves and the rattle of an approaching wagon. Reba stepped out onto the porch that wrapped itself around the front and side of the house. She dried her hands on her apron and watched the newcomers with equal curiosity.

A rickety old wagon pulled by two mules wobbled toward them. Reba's darting eyes counted thirteen people in the wagon, not including the black man riding one of the draft mules. Another black man was driving the wagon. On the seat beside him were two white women. In the back of the wagon sat five white children, two black women and three black children. Ezekiel had never learned proper ciphering, but he knew a wagon load of folks when he saw one. They were all poorly dressed—blacks and whites alike—and

318

squirmed constantly, competing for space. Their tattered, rope-bound possessions that included a few odd pieces of furniture had been piled so high that each time the load shifted the wagon looked in danger of tilting over.

Beside the wagon two white men rode double on a large plow horse. The man in front was in his early thirty's, tall, with a beard. He was a larger, younger version of the man hanging on behind him. They were obviously father and son, the elder sporting more gray hair and considerably fewer teeth. On the other side of the wagon two adolescent white boys were on a skin-and-bones nag with only a folded blanket for a saddle. But what was even more puzzling to Reba and Ezekiel were the three U. S. soldiers trailing behind them.

Ezekiel reached the house and shrugged in answer to Reba's questioning look. Silently they waited until the wagon creaked to a stop near the porch. Reba noticed that the soldiers halted several yards behind, keeping the same distance they had maintained on the road. And considering the foul odor of unclean bodies and children's soiled undergarments wafting her way, Reba understood why. No one spoke for some time. The wagon's occupants gazed all around, surveying the house, the barn and the surrounding fields. They were visibly impressed. The younger of the two black women in the back of the wagon eyed the Drummond's house.

"Mmm-hmm. I'm gon' like takin' care of this house," she said emphatically. Reba and Ezekiel exchanged another look.

"Somethin' we can do for you folks today?" Reba asked, smoothing out her apron.

"We're movin' in," announced the older of the two adolescent white boys atop the skinny nag.

"Hush up, Leonard," snapped the younger of the father-son duo on the big plow horse.

"This is our new home," explained Ellen, the younger white woman in the wagon seat. Reba figured her for the wife of the younger man on the plow horse and mother of most—if not all—these smelly children. The white ones, anyway. Reba looked in amazement from one to the other. She had seen people like this once as a young slave girl, before Ezekiel purchased her freedom. She had gone on a trip with her owner back up into the hills of eastern Tennessee to buy what was supposed to have been a prized pregnant brood sow, but it aborted thirteen piglets and then died of hog cholera two days after they got her home.

"Beggin' your pardon, ma'am," Ezekiel said politely, "I think y'all must'a took a wrong turn somewhere."

"Is this the Drummond house?" one of the soldiers eased his horse forward.

"Yes, it is," Reba placed her hands disapprovingly on her hips, not at all pleased with where this seemed to be going.

"We drawed this place in the Georgia Land Lottery," the large, bearded man grinned, showing he was well on the way to duplicating his father's dental forfeitures.

"We got papers," the older white woman asserted. Papers always made things official.

"Well, I can tell you what you can use dem papers for..." Reba dipped her chin, looking at them from the tops of her large brown eyes.

The old man studied Reba and Ezekiel then tugged at his son's sleeve. "Tom Junior, you reckon them niggers comes with the property?"

The old man's son didn't answer directly but glared sternly at the black woman who had just come nigh to sassin' a white man. "Is your master at home?" he squinted at Reba. "You'd best git him on out here."

Inside the Drummond's library Susanna was re-setting a comb in the long, beautiful locks of little Margaret Elizabeth. Her attention had been drawn to the muffled conversation outside. She looked toward the door when Elizabeth came down the stairs and stepped into the library.

"What's all the fuss out there?" Elizabeth inquired.

"I don't know," Susanna adjusted the comb again. "Some people in a wagon."

"They have soldiers with them," there was apprehension in Elizabeth's voice. "I saw from the window."

"I wish Father would get home. With all the unrest these days..." Susanna complained. Both she and the child jumped when the front door flew open and the large, bearded man strode confidently in, looking around. He flicked the brim of his tattered hat as a polite greeting to Susanna and Elizabeth.

"Ladies. Thomas Mason, Junior," the man introduced himself. Instinctively, Susanna drew Meg closer. Elizabeth looked for an explanation from Reba who had stepped in right behind Mason.

"Sorry, Miz 'Liz'beth. This man sayin' he owns this place. Say's he's got some papers," Reba's voice betrayed her genuine concern.

Without even looking at Elizabeth, Mason, Jr. shoved the

320

papers at her and continued running his other hand along the finely crafted interior woodwork trim.

"State Land Lottery," Mason, Jr. repeated. "All signed and proper. This here's some fine work. Yessir!"

Elizabeth had no choice but to take the papers thrust right in her face, but she didn't read them. She watched Ellen and two of the smaller children from the wagon crowd in behind Reba and immediately begin exploring. A dirty-faced, large-eared boy about ten reached for a crystal vase on a sideboard in the hallway. The vessel slipped from his grasp and shattered on the floor. His mother flashed a grin of embarrassment and feebly scolded the boy.

"Eugene, you be careful with them thangs."

Mason, Jr., in a conditioned reflex, cuffed Eugene on the back of the head. The boy cringed in anticipation of a second blow, then grinned, genuinely pleased when it wasn't forthcoming. Elizabeth didn't understand any of what they were telling her, but she'd had quite enough of this intrusion.

"Please! Would you leave? Just get out of our house!"

Mason gestured with his large, calloused finger at the papers Elizabeth still held. "Ain't yours no more. Read them papers."

"I don't care what your papers say!" Elizabeth thrust the documents back at him, but he ignored her and continued his examination of the woodwork and the fine furniture.

"You're lying!" Susanna said boldly. She guided Meg around to a position safely behind her. "I know for a fact the only property redistributed through the lottery is land taken from the Cherokees!"

Mason, Jr. grinned at the feisty young woman. A string of tobacco spittle dribbled down from the corner of his mouth and spread its brownness through his beard. "You know that *fer a fact* do you, Missy?"

"When my father gets home, he'll prove these documents are forgeries. Completely illegitimate," Susanna thrust her chin out in defiance.

"The papers are legitimate, ma'am," said the soldier. None of them had noticed him slip quietly in and position himself beside the door. "All signed and official. State seal and everything."

"This is ridiculous!" Susanna bellowed. "Do you know who I am, Corporal?"

"Ma'am?" the soldier cocked his head, puzzled.

"Do you know Major Peter Tanner? My husband?"

"Major Tanner? Yes, ma'am, I know who he is. But my orders were to escort Mr. Mason here to take possession of his property."

"This is *not* his property!" Susanna had to force herself to keep from screaming at the confused young soldier. She made sweeping gestures toward the front door. "I want you out of this house. Now! All of you!" She moved forward, hoping to herd the intruders in front of her. Meg clutched at her mother's dress and began to cry.

Mason, Jr. calmly wiped his mouth with the back of his hand and towered over Susanna, his voice menacing. "No, ma'am. I want *you* out of *my* house. Best git your niggers busy loadin' yer goods," he paused to let his words sink in, then added, "You got 'til dark to git off *my* property!"

Concerned about the yelling they had heard from outside, the other two soldiers—young privates—stepped just inside the front door and made eye contact with their company leader. The corporal signalled that everything was under control. He spoke firmly but politely to Elizabeth.

"I really wouldn't waste any time if I were you, folks. Travellin' by night ain't always safe in these times."

"Where do you expect us to go?" Elizabeth asked, still incredulous.

"I don't know, ma'am," the corporal answered innocently.

"Shouldn't we take 'em to the camps?" one of the privates whispered.

The corporal leaned toward his men, lowering his voice. "You want to be the one to herd Major Tanner's family into one of those filthy places?" This silenced the private's concern but did nothing to ease the looks of genuine fear from Elizabeth, Susanna and Reba. Meg continued to fret and whimper, sensing her mother's and grandmother's distress.

Thomas Mason, Jr. looked at the women with a hint of a smile. "Well, I don't give a damn where y'all go. Jes' get goin'," he said with an eerie lilt that almost sounded like he was teasing, but everyone in the room knew he wasn't. His boots made a hollow echo in the hallway as he resumed the exploration of his lovely new home.

* * * * * * *

The sky remained dark and heavily overcast, though the rain had ceased almost an hour earlier. The last rays of the setting sun painted the fluffy underbelly of the black clouds with broad, feathered splashes of gold and red-orange. On the high ground overlooking the entrance of the Ft. Coosawattee concentration camp stood principal chief John Ross, his journalist friend, John Howard Payne, Assistant Chief George Lowrey, former Principal Chief Charles Hicks, and other Cherokee leaders, including Lewis Ross, the chief's brother, Thomas Foreman, Hair Conrad, and the ancient chiefs, Going Snake and *Tsunaluska*. The tribal authorities watched their people streaming into the camp under military escort, some even at bayonet point. Wagons overtook walkers, pulling into a long line of other wagons to begin unloading.

The chief's attention was drawn to a lone rider angling up toward them from the main trail below. When the newcomer drew closer, the Cherokees recognized their *yo-neg* friend, William Drummond. Chief Ross noted a sadness and a lack of resolution in William's expression he hadn't seen before.

"I judge by your expression the news isn't good."

Before answering, William took time to acknowledge each man there, calling them by name, exchanging the familiar Cherokee greeting. He shook hands with Payne, the journalist.

"I take it you were unable to secure a court injunction," Payne concluded.

"Walter Barrington is dead," William reported. "Murdered, I suspect. For his Cherokee sympathies. And I'm afraid there are no more like him to be found. Not in the state of Georgia."

The Cherokee leaders grunted their agreement. Charles Hicks added, "And all the doors in Washington appear to be sealed shut. Our most outspoken friends—Henry Clay, Daniel Webster, Ed Everett—all seem powerless to help us."

The disillusionment was contagious. The sentiments expressed came as nothing new to any man there, but for the first time they found themselves collectively forced to acknowledge the harsh reality. George Lowrey's low-pitched voice was soft and tinged with sorrow. "I'm afraid, gentlemen, very afraid...that we're not going to defeat this treaty."

Old Chief Going Snake made a sweeping gesture toward the sea of activity below them. "And this...this is not the answer..."

Hair Conrad's eyes appeared fixed on some distant, unseen point, as though experiencing a vision far worse than what lay before them. "It has only just begun, and already there are deaths in the camps. Dysentery. Consumption. Cholera."

"And it will only get worse," Hicks said with foreboding.

"It's hardest on the children and the old ones," Lowrey's words carried a deathly prophetic ring.

"I must go back to Washington," Ross finally said with renewed determination.

Tsunaluska shook his head no. He had seen too many winters, too much *yo-neg* greed and hatred, too many battles, too many trips to Washington and too many broken promises that always left his people wanting and suffering. "It is too late for that, *Gu-wi-s-gu-wi*," the old one warned.

"I have to try," Ross said, searching for a shred of hope. "When I tell them what's happening here, they'll have to listen."

"John, they haven't listened before," the journalist advised his friend. "*Tsunaluska* is right. Look what they've already done to the Chickasaw. The Choctaw. And the Creek."

"I know," Ross had heard it all before. "But I have to try. One more time."

No one spoke for a long time. They looked down the hill at the continuous flow of Cherokees being herded into the camp. Finally, with a somber expression, George Lowrey addressed Ross. "Then you'd better leave tonight. We're running out of time."

It was decided. Not always brilliant in the face of a problem that demanded an immediate *solution*, Ross had proven himself again and again unsurpassed in coming up with a *plan*. "They've granted tribal leaders temporary amnesty, so at least you're free to move about. Do whatever you can. Try to find more *yo-neg* doctors willing to come to the camps. See if we can get better food," he wanted to leave them with a full slate for as long as the whites were willing to allow them any latitude whatsoever. "Tell our people not to fight. It will only make things worse. There are plenty of these Georgia hooligans itching for a chance to kill a Cherokee." He knew disease, accidents, even depression and suicide, would take a large enough toll in the coming days. It was essential they do everything possible to minimize the loss of life among their people. He faced Lowrey, his trusted friend and assistant. "George is chief until I return." Finally, he thanked his friend and counsel. "*Wi-li*, again, *wa-do*."

"I'll come with you," John Howard Payne said. Together the two rode away from the camp. The others watched until Payne and Ross had disappeared into the trees.

"You're a true friend to the *Tsa-la-gi*, *Wi-li* Drummond," acting chief Lowrey said. "Go home. Have a nice, quiet evening with your family."

William smiled. That was exactly what he intended to do. They all mounted their horses. William rode off in one direction and the Cherokee leaders in another.

* * * * * * *

The highway was still wet and packed from the day's rain. William, tired after the long—and fruitless—journey to Milledgeville and back, was grateful for the refreshing cool breeze the night offered, and he appreciated the absence of the choking dust normally kicked up on the heavily-travelled road. He was looking forward to the rest of the evening. After a hot bath he would sit in the study with Elizabeth and read a good book, prop his feet up and sip a glass of his best whiskey. Clancey jerked his head up and danced to one side at the sound of gunshots in the distance. William soothed the startled animal and quickened their pace. The shots, William was certain, had come from the direction of his own house. When William turned off the main road, his concern heightened. Another round of gunshots had undoubtedly come from his house. William pounded the sides of the big gray, urging Clancey to speeds he hadn't known in years.

The situation at the Drummond house had deteriorated and was completely out of control. The wagon and mules of Thomas Mason, Jr. and his family were still there, but they had been joined shortly before sundown by a second group of whites—the Wilkersons—with three wagon loads of belongings and relatives. The new claimants had arrived under the escort of none other than Colonel Absalom Bishop and his Georgia Militia.

The Wilkersons, along with the three soldiers who had originally escorted the Masons, had taken cover behind the Wilkersons' wagons. As William rode up, he saw that their attention was directed toward the second story bedroom. There was a bright flash from the window and the loud report of a rifle, followed by a sharp ping as the slug ricocheted off a steel wagon wheel rim. From behind their cover, the Wilkersons and the Georgia militiamen opened fire, pelting the exterior of the house all around the shattered upstairs window.

William had no way of knowing that Elizabeth, Susanna and baby Margaret, along with Reba and Ezekiel, had taken refuge in the library. Reacting to the shots, Susanna clutched the baby tighter, almost crushing her. Reba instinctively stretched a protective arm in front of Elizabeth. They looked up at the ceiling, listening to the shooting and stomping directly above them.

With his pistol drawn, William leaped down from Clancey

near the militia leader and the three federal soldiers. "What's this all about, Bishop?! Where's my wife?! My daughter?!"

Another rifle shot from the window struck the wagon only inches from William, showering him with splinters. Again, the Georgia militiamen shot back. Under the barrage of cover fire, three or four of the Wilkerson clan ran down toward the barn.

"Stop shooting at my house!" William yelled and pushed the closest militia guns up into the air. He headed for the house, but more shots from the window struck the wagon and the ground around his feet, driving him back to protective cover.

William had heard in the latest flurry of shots a yelp that didn't sound human. When he looked back toward the house, he saw Poke, the family dog, lying on his side. The animal had recognized his master, and when William started for the house, Poke charged from beneath one of the Wilkerson wagons to join him. The whimpering continued, and William watched the poor beast inching toward him, pulling with only his front feet. Another shot flashed from behind William. Poke emitted a single cry then lay silent and still. William was about to berate the soldier who had fired, but a glance back at Poke revealed that the first shot had ripped open the dog's stomach. His intestines were strung out behind him in the dirt. The angry outburst poised on William's lips changed to a soft, hasty *thank you* to the young trooper before William turned his wrath on the Georgia Militia commander and his men.

"What's going on here?!" William yelled for someone, anyone, to explain this insanity.

Colonel Bishop offered an answer. "'Pears to be some disagreement about who this property belongs to."

"What are you talking about? This is *my* property!"

"Not no more, it ain't," the leader of the Wilkersons shouted while reloading his pistol.

"Who the hell are you?" William demanded, then turned on Bishop before Wilkerson could answer. "What's he talking about?"

"That there's my brother-in-law, Theo Wilkerson," Bishop's answer was intended to pass for an introduction.

"This here's *my* place now," Wilkerson said proudly. "I got it in the state land lottery."

"Problem is," Bishop explained as though he expected William to sympathize with their dilemma, "a bunch of white trash showed up earlier today claiming it's theirs."

The army corporal, crouching low to remain protected by the wagon, ducked over to join them. He felt obligated to defend his official position. "Mr. Mason's papers are all in order, I assure you, Colonel Bishop."

The militia commander ignored the soldier and finished his explanation. "Mason and his bunch has barricaded themselves upstairs. Won't come out."

William was speechless. He started once more for the house. A couple of shots were fired, hitting the ground inches to the left of William's foot. That was it. With the errant bullets flying past him, William calmly cocked his pistol, took careful aim and fired at the upstairs window.

The young corporal yelled at him from behind the wagon. "You don't want to do that, Mr. Drummond. You kill somebody, you'll hang," he warned. "Rightfully speaking, you're trespassing, sir!"

No one was hit, but William's shot came close enough to drive the Masons—Junior, Senior and Leonard, the oldest boy—away from the window, allowing William time to make a run for the house.

The women and Ezekiel were still huddled in the library, terrified by this latest outburst of gunfire.

"Elizabeth! Susanna!" William called out. His booming voice was a welcome sound to them all.

"We in here, Mistah D! In the lib'ary!" Reba screamed, drawing a scowl from Ezekiel whose ear was only inches from her trumpeting lips. He pulled the heavy desk away while William forced the door open from the other side. Elizabeth and Susanna, with Meg in her arms, rushed to him.

"Are you all right? Anyone hurt?" he was at once relieved and concerned.

"Everybody's mostly jes' skeered," Ezekiel told him.

Susanna fought back the tide of hysteria. "Father! I'm so glad you're home!"

"What's happening, William? What are these people doing here?" Elizabeth's voice was shaky. She still didn't fully comprehend what it was all about.

"They movin' in, that's what they doin'!" Reba characteristically reduced things to their simplest terms.

"They showed up this afternoon sayin' this is all they land now!" Ezekiel filled William in.

"There were soldiers!" Elizabeth said excitedly, as though the presence of the military lent some special meaning.

"Then, next thing you know," Reba added, "another bunch shows up sayin' it's *theirs*."

"Father!" Susanna tugged at his sleeve, "you have to straighten this out!"

"I want these people out of our house, William!" Elizabeth said with finality. She had told William what she wanted him to do and now everything would be set right. "I just don't understand any of this!"

"Father! Look!" Susanna screamed and pointed to the window. William spun around to discover that the Wilkersons who had earlier run to the barn had subsequently made their way up to the side of the house and had started a fire right outside the library. The curious flames leaped up to explore the window sill. A piece of firewood wrapped in burning rags crashed through the window. As soon as the glass shattered, the arsonists ran around toward the front of the house. William and Ezekiel immediately began stamping out the burning missile.

Through the front door, which William had left open, they saw the arsonists attempting to ignite a second blaze right on the front porch. Everyone—William and his family as well as the Wilkerson arsonists out front—reacted to the fresh volley of gunfire from the second floor window, followed by pounding footsteps racing down the stairs.

William left the fire-stomping to Ezekiel and rotated the cylinder of his Collier repeating pistol. He motioned to Elizabeth, Susanna and Reba.

"We've got to get out of here! Come on!"

Thomas Mason, Jr. came charging down the stairs just as William stepped from the library out into the hallway. In a panic, Mason fired an errant shot from his old flintlock pistol. Like a man possessed, he kept charging, oblivious to William's gun pointed right at him.

"They're settin' fire to my house!" Mason cried with all the sincere anguish of a life-long home owner. William, incredulous, kept the pistol aimed at Mason but didn't fire. He held his other arm up to block the library door, protecting his loved ones. Close behind Mason, Jr. came Leonard, the oldest boy, followed stiffly by Mason, Sr. Leonard carried a rifle, which his father grabbed and aimed at the intruders outside on the veranda where the second blaze was in full bloom.

William sprang from the darkness and cracked Mason, Jr. on the back of the head with the Collier, knocking him to the floor. Mason, Sr. yelled and lunged at William, but Ezekiel emerged from the library door and hit the old man with a lowered shoulder, laying him out next to his son.

"Pa! Grandpa!" the frightened Leonard cried out.

Mason, Jr. had risen to his knees and was rubbing the back of his head. He pivoted from his low position and tackled William around the legs. Seven men burst through the front door—two of the federal soldiers, two Georgia militiamen and two of the non-arsonist Wilkersons followed by Colonel Absalom Bishop. The soldiers immediately began pulling William and Mason, Jr. apart. As soon as William was free from Mason's grasp, he turned his attention to the spreading fire.

"Get some buckets! Get water!"

Ezekiel and the two soldiers raced out. Reba emerged coughing and choking from the smoke-filled library with Susanna and Elizabeth close behind her. Meg screamed in terror and clung desperately to her grandmother's neck with one arm and her mother's sleeve with the other hand.

"They set fire to my house! I'll kill 'em," a heartbroken Mason, Jr. cried out. He slipped while trying to get up and crashed to the floor again.

"Shut up!" Colonel Bishop barked. "You ain't gonna kill nobody!"

"It's mine! I got it fair and square!" Mason, Jr.'s protest was somewhere between a whimper and groan. "I was here first! You can't run me off my own property! I'll shoot the next son of a bitch I see tryin' to start a fire! I ain't givin' it up!"

Old Theo Wilkerson had arrived at the door just in time to hear Mason, Jr.'s threat. "Ain't your'n to give up or hold on to, you worthless piece o' hog dung!" With his mouth twisted in a snarl, the aged patriarch raised his pistol right at Mason's face and squeezed the trigger, but Colonel Bishop knocked the pistol into the air, causing it to fire only inches above the heads of Elizabeth and her granddaughter. William had almost reached the door but spun around when he heard the shot. At the same time, Ezekiel and the soldiers returned with buckets of water and began dousing the fire lapping up the front porch post.

With the shooting apparently over, members of the Wilkerson group—men, women and children—rushed forward to join the fire brigade. They carried water in buckets, wash pans and cooking pots to both fires, the one on the front porch and the other by the library window. William worked feverishly at both locations until he was certain both blazes had been extinguished.

Sweat drenched and exhausted, William went back inside to

check on his family. There appeared to be even more people than before, he thought. White women, black women, black men, whimpering children—black and white—seeped endlessly in from the kitchen and dining room where they had taken shelter during the gun battle. William pushed through the milling throng to reach Elizabeth and Susanna. Satisfied they were all right, his frustration and anger finally erupted.

"Out!" he screamed. His booming voice startled everyone. "I want you all out of my house! Now!" Uncharacteristically, this man who had embraced tranquility, reason and composure as a way of life abruptly pointed his own pistol at the ceiling and fired. "I mean it! Get out of my house! Leave my property! Now!"

A chill went through William and the hair stood up on the back of his neck. The voice he heard behind him elicited in the pit of his stomach a bilious and revolting irritation.

"I'm afraid that's no longer an option, Mr. Drummond."

It was only the utmost self restraint that prevented William from wheeling and firing. All eyes were on the door where Titus Ogilvie limped from the darkness into the faint light from the lantern someone had left sitting on the stairs. He was followed by his dim-witted son, Alton. As much as William felt compelled to go straight for Ogilvie's throat, he found himself second in line behind the irate, stiff-jointed old Theo Wilkerson.

"You double-dealin' son of a bitch! You told me this was *my* property!" Theo drew back a quivering fist and went for Titus, but he was intercepted by two of the soldiers.

"That's right, Ogilvie," Colonel Bishop put a grimy finger in Titus's face. "You sure 'nough did! You made me look like a fool!"

Thomas Mason, Jr., however, wasn't about to surrender his own legal claim to the Drummond estate. "I got papers!" he whined, pushing up against the backs of the soldiers. "Signed by the governor! They're legitimate!"

"Like hell they are!" William bellowed again, waving the pistol at both Mason and Wilkerson.

"Oh, they're legitimate, all right, Mr. Mason," Titus Ogilvie said with immeasurable satisfaction, relishing every word, every syllable, every phoneme. "As legitimate as *these*," he added, holding up another set of papers.

"Mr. Ogilvie! What's the meaning of all this?" Elizabeth demanded of the man she had always known simply as the owner of the general store and most of the other businesses in town. The man who had gotten himself elected mayor and bullied the town council into changing the name from Pine Hill to Titusville.

"It pains me something awful to tell you this, Mrs. Drummond," his voice dripped with feigned compassion. "I'm sure your husband has deceived you just as he has the rest of us."

"William, what's he talking about?" It was all madness to Elizabeth.

Susanna stepped out to challenge Ogilvie. "My father's an honest man! He would never deceive anyone."

"What are you up to now, Ogilvie," William scowled.

With great ceremony, Ogilvie unfolded the papers. He made a wide, sweeping flourish and held them out in front of him, staring with hate-filled, sneering satisfaction hard into William's eyes. "These census documents—the Year of Our Lord 1790—prove indisputably, Mrs. Drummond, that your husband is the direct descendent of a Cherokee Indian woman by the name of..." Titus paused, holding the paper toward the lantern light, looking down his nose to read, "...Rebeka Fields...grandmother of one Henry Drummond." He found immense gratification in every wrinkle, every hint of painful realization in the face of William Drummond, his long-time nemesis. "Henry, if I'm not mistaken, would be your father." With a slight bow as though explaining to a child, he added for Susanna's benefit, "And your *grand*father. The woman in question was *his* grandmother."

All eyes shifted to William.

"Father?" Susanna's voice trailed off.

William took the papers from Ogilvie. The room remained hushed but for a scuffling boot or a nervous cough while William stepped closer to the lantern and read silently. When he had finished, William kept his eyes lowered as though ashamed to meet the questioning looks of his family.

"William?" Elizabeth echoed her daughters earlier request for an explanation.

"Tell them it isn't true, Father," Susanna's plea had the ring of a command. All William had to do was say the word, put an end to this foolishness and restore order to their world. "Tell them to get out," Susanna continued. "Make them leave us alone."

William was silent. His eyes remained interminably fixed on the papers until his gaze finally drifted down to the floor, as though seeking a crack in which to take refuge.

"What about me, Ogilvie?!" demanded Theo Wilkerson. It came as no surprise to him that this man Drummond was part Cherokee. Hell, that's why he and his family were there in the first place. "You told me this property would be mine!"

Colonel Bishop was equally perturbed, rekindling his earlier anger at Titus. "I promised you protection by the Georgia Militia if my brother-in-law here got this place! We had us a deal! I cain't be responsible for your safety if you was to go back on it!"

Ogilvie's long and eagerly anticipated gloating at the costly turn of fate for William Drummond had been cut short. Titus knew he had better resolve the situation before it got any uglier.

"Gentlemen! Gentlemen!" he smiled with a placating gesture toward Wilkerson, Colonel Bishop and the irate Thomas Mason, Jr. "There's been a misunderstanding. An honest mistake! I'm sure I can straighten it all out."

"Ain't nothin' to straighten out!" barked Mason. "This here's *my* place!"

"Take it easy, Mister Mason," Titus made the soothing hand gesture again—to both Mason and Wilkerson. "Let's just call it a clerical error. Actually, what I had in mind for you, Mr. Wilkerson, wasn't the *Drum*mond place, but the *Ham*mond farm up on Timber Creek. About ten miles from here. It's actually better than this place."

"Yeah?" Theo Wilkerson showed interest. Lust for bigger and better can often serve as a miracle remedy for jilted greed.

"More cleared acreage," Ogilvie bubbled enthusiastically. "Richer creek bottom land. Fruit orchards. More cattle."

"Then why didn't you tell *me* about that one?" Mason, who only moments earlier had been prepared to kill for his claim to William's land, now sounded injured and disappointed. "How's come I got stuck with this place?" Loss of bigger and better can often plunge the greedy into depths of despondency.

"Father? What is all this madness?" Susanna demanded. "Is it true? About this...this Cherokee woman?" Why would no one explain this whole thing to her? It was inconceivable that her father—that she herself!—could be part Indian. Never mind how small that part might be. It ran contrary to everything she had ever believed about herself. About her father. Her family. And it certainly put an unacceptable spin on the disdainful air of superiority she had felt toward the Indians that had always surrounded them.

Elizabeth tried to sum it all up as though it would make things clear in her own mind. "You're taking our land because my husband's *great grandmother* was *part* Cherokee? You can't be serious!"

Ogilvie bowed slightly, continuing his false concern. "And all this time it has been kept from you. Out of the profoundest sense of shame, no doubt."

William, normally stoic and in control of any situation, had earlier reached his limits when he fired a pistol into the ceiling of his own house. Now he lashed out and struck Ogilvie in the face with that same pistol, knocking him backwards into the arms of his son, Alton. Immediately William was seized by a Georgia militiaman and one of the soldiers. While they held William's arms, Colonel Bishop wrestled the pistol from his hand.

"This right here's why Indians ain't s'posed to have guns!" Bishop said with an instructing tone to his guardsman and the soldier. "Get him out of here. Go on!" He included Elizabeth and Susanna with a sweeping gesture of the pistol. "All of you. You'd best go now." Lastly, he said to Ezekiel, "Get 'em a wagon hitched up. Go on. Move!"

William was half-led, half-dragged away by the soldier and militiaman, with Ezekiel hustling after them. Considerably larger than either of his escorts, William twisted loose and yelled back at Titus. "You won't get away with this, Ogilvie!"

With the help of Alton, his son, and Theo Wilkerson, Titus got back on his feet. Rattled but exhilarated, he dabbed at his bleeding lip with a handkerchief. *Won't get away with it?* Was that what the once high and mighty Mr. William Drummond, Esquire, had uttered? *Won't get away with it?*

"Oh, I already have, Mr. Drummond. I should think that would be painfully evident at this point," he said, then added, "And I'll tell you this—I'd rather be *dead* than be a God damn Indian!"

"Father!" Susanna cried out.

"William!" Elizabeth called after her husband. She handed Meg back to Susanna and, clinging to Reba's arm, followed William and Ezekiel out into the night.

Colonel Bishop watched them go, then shook his head in disbelief at what he had just learned. "Cherokee! A God damn Indian!" he said incredulously. "I can't believe he come into my office one time actin' just like a white man....I even give him some of my best whiskey to drink..." he clucked at the deception and the shame of it all.

25

Arkansas Territory

The steel-rimmed wheels moved along crisply behind two horses, kicking up a rooster-tail of road dust. In the Arkansas moonlight it created the appearance of a turbulent phantom pursuing and attempting to wedge itself beneath the carriage. The coachman was a middle-aged black man named Jacob. His lone passenger was Territorial Judge Franklin Harvey, a bearded man of fifty-five whose planetary girth quivered visibly with every little jerk and roll of the vehicle. From his perch up front, Jacob sneaked a glance behind him where the behemoth was nodding off with a near-empty flask about to slip from his grasp. The judge woke himself with a loud belch, gripping the container an instant before it fell.

"How much fu'ther, Jacob?" he slurred.

"Be there d'rectly, Jedge," Jacob popped the carriage whip to demonstrate he was coaxing maximum speed from the old horses. "Four—maybe five mile."

"Damn, you're slow, boy!" the irascible old jurist snapped from habit. "Reckon I'm just gonna have to git me a new nigger."

Jacob popped the whip again, but there was no increase in speed. Through the years he had grown accustomed to this treatment and his response was as familiar as the judge's complaint. "Jacob ain't pullin' the carriage, Jedge. You need to be gettin' you some new *horses*."

"Don't mouth me, boy. Jes' get me to Fort Smith before Christmas!" The judge, as always, had the final word. He grunted mightily, drained the flask, coughed, leaned back and closed his eyes. Jacob glanced back again, his expression registering the disgust of countless years enduring his master's drunken coarseness.

* * * * * * *

It had been an uneventful night for the military compound and the surrounding town of Ft. Smith, Arkansas Territory. The sentry on duty at the post's main gate stole a sip from a skin flask which he quickly tucked beneath his tunic when he heard the approaching hoofbeats. He adjusted his rifle on his shoulder and stepped out into the road as the carriage eased to a stop.

"Judge Franklin Harvey. Here for the trial," Jacob

announced.

"Evenin', Judge," the soldier greeted the jurist with familiarity. He pointed Jacob toward a building off to one side in the compound. "Take him on to the officers' quarters."

"I want to see the prisoner first," Judge Harvey wagged a finger toward the stockade.

"Tonight, sir?"

The judge shifted to the side, his massive weight straining the leaf springs and tilting the carriage. Glassy-eyed, he leaned out toward the sentry and spoke in a conspiratorial whisper. "Always let the prisoner look into the eyes of the man who's gonna send him to Hell," he said, adding with a diabolical chuckle, "Gives him somethin' to think about all night."

The guard shrugged. He was neither prisoner, judge nor executioner, so it made no difference to him one way or the other. "You know where it's at," he said to Jacob and thumbed over his shoulder toward the stockade. Jacob popped the reins and clucked the tired old horses forward.

* * * * * * *

Still glassy-eyed and wobbly, the rotund judge peered through the cell bars, displeased. On the judge's left stood the man in charge of the stockade, Sergeant Alexander Bolton. On Harvey's right was the jailer. A young corporal was stationed just inside the door.

"Well, I'll be damned," Judge Harvey grumbled. "He's Indian."

"Yes, sir. Cherokee," Bolton confirmed. A compact little man of about forty with an admitted thirst for brutality, Bolton, unlike most noncommissioned officers often relegated to stockade duty as an unofficial form of demotion, had actually volunteered for the post. Soldiers who might have served an evening or two under Bolton's roof vowed never to return. And many a civilian prisoner had never had to worry about a second visit—they didn't survive the first. Bolton demanded only two things of his prisoners: they must display an attitude of cravenly submissiveness, and they were strictly forbidden under any circumstances or for any reason, to ever—ever!—look him directly in the eye. To do so invited immediate punishment, usually in the form of a merciless beating, often resulting in death. Appropriate charges and explanations were always available by the time Bolton was required to report to his superiors on the death of a prisoner. As long as it sounded plausible,

Bolton had learned, the higher-ups really didn't much care.

Johnny Fields sat on the bunk in his cell, his back to the wall, knees drawn up in front of him. He stared back at the fat, old judge who had come to condemn him to death. As far as Johnny was concerned, there was nothing to say. He was determined not to give Harvey the satisfaction of seeing him the least bit troubled by his imminent execution. He had learned to survive under Bolton's rules, keeping his eyes down and his mouth shut, but he knew Harvey was here for one reason—to see that Johnny was hanged. And that was a game Johnny refused to play.

"The messenger didn't say nothin' about it being no God damn Indian," Harvey tried to rotate to face Sergeant Bolton, almost losing his balance in the process. "I drove all night to get here. And my gout's killin' me. Hell, anybody can hang an Indian. Don't need an important judge like myself for that."

"Sorry, sir." Bolton didn't know how else to respond.

"Well...no matter," Harvey waved it off. "You guilty, boy?" he asked the prisoner with a chuckle. Johnny remained silent. "No, of course not," the judge's belly shook with silent laughter. He looked to Bolton with a wink. "I've never hung a guilty one yet, Sergeant."

"Sir?"

"They *all* swore they was innocent. All hundred an' thirty-six of 'em." He gripped a cell bar with one hand and pointed between the bars at Johnny with the other. "But don't worry, you'll get a fair trial tomorrow...and a speedy hangin' next day. You'll be number one-thirty-seven." He waited for some sign of fear in Johnny's unblinking, inscrutable eyes. The judge shrugged. "See you in court, Chief."

"Corporal, show the judge to his quarters," Sergeant Bolton said.

"Yes, sir," the soldier held the door wide open for the huge man who, unsteady from drink, managed to bang both sides in passing through. Once outside, the sentry walked slowly in front of the toddling Harvey after he had been harshly scolded for trying to *run off and leave* the judge.

"You'll fetch me some whiskey over to my quarters, young man?"

"Sir?"

"A bottle of Major Tyler's best," Harvey put his fat, heavy hand on the corporal's shoulder to steady his progress. "Medicinal purposes, y'understand. For my gout."

336

"Yes, sir."

As they continued toward the officers' quarters, neither noticed the darkly clad figure pressed motionless against the wall in the narrow alley between two buildings opposite the jail. As soon as they had passed, Michael Drummond darted across to the stockade. He waited patiently for Bolton to leave for the night. The door opened and Bolton's boots clomped on the narrow boardwalk that ran the length of the building. He rounded the corner, heading toward his own quarters.

As soon as the judge and Sergeant Bolton had gone, the jailer resumed his familiar nighttime position—leaning back in his chair with his feet propped up on the desk. He gnawed a fowl drumstick and waved a tattered hand-fan in search of relief from the sweltering heat. Never once did he look at Johnny Fields who lay motionless on his bunk. Hands clasped behind his head, Johnny studied the squirrel-shaped cluster of knots in the pine rafters above.

"*Tsa-ni,*" the whisper came from outside. Johnny glanced at the jailer, who had heard nothing. Without moving, Johnny looked up toward the high window of his cell. The end of a black stick protruded a couple of inches inside, tapping lightly against one of the bars. Johnny faked a cough to mask the sound and glanced back at the jailer whose mind was fully occupied with ravaging the turkey leg. Johnny rose casually to a sitting position. He kept a watchful eye on the feeding jailer as he reached up for the stick.

Outside in the shadows Michael stretched up to drop a tiny, leather pouch through the window. Johnny caught it and brought it immediately down to his lap, keeping one foot up on the bunk so his leg blocked the jailer's view. He unwrapped the parcel to discover a single blow dart and a small, glass vial. With one hand Johnny adeptly removed the stopper and immersed the tip of the dart in its dark contents. He then slipped the dart into one end of the slender blowgun. In a fluid, graceful motion Johnny eased the blow gun up to his lips as he rose from the bunk. The vial that had been left on Johnny's lap clattered loudly to the floor, immediately drawing the jailer's attention. His face registered puzzlement when he saw Johnny with the blow gun pressed to his mouth. The jailer lowered the drumstick to the table and stood up.

"What the hell you think you're doin'?" he growled. His only answer was the soft *pffftt* which he heard a fraction of a second before the tiny dart pierced the fleshy side of his sweaty neck. His eyes widened with the painful sting. He pulled the tiny feathered projectile from his neck, examined it with seeping recognition, then looked back to Johnny. "You lousy, no-good sumbitch!" he snarled and reached for the rifle leaning against the table. But he never made it. His knees buckled beneath him. He grabbed the chair for support, slumped sideways and crashed to the floor.

From outside Michael heard the jailer fall. He slipped in and went straight to Johnny's cell. They spoke in whispers so as not to disturb the other two prisoners sleeping soundly in the other cell.

"Where are the keys?" Michael asked.

"On his belt!"

Michael rolled the limp, heavy jailer over and recovered the keys. "What took you so long?" Johnny whispered sharply. "I was starting to think you'd forgotten about me!"

Michael fumbled nervously with the keys. But despite the urgency he couldn't resist a lighter response. "I figured you needed time to ponder the evil of your ways." Johnny reached through the bars and cuffed him good-naturedly on the head. Finally, the lock clicked and the two of them stepped over the jailer and slipped out the door.

Once outside they were forced to drop to the ground, pressing themselves against the edge of the boardwalk in front of the stockade when a cluster of soldiers walked by only a few feet away. Michael and Johnny smelled the liquor on the soldiers who talked and joked among themselves. They weren't disorderly, but the two escapees were thankful they also weren't very alert. Once the soldiers had passed, Michael and Johnny dashed behind them across the open quadrangle to the shadows of the livery stable.

Catlike, the two men moved down the darker side of the building then darted along the back until they found the plank door and slipped inside. At the front of the stable a young soldier leaned nonchalantly against a support post, his rifle propped beside him. He heard nothing and suspected nothing, then suddenly his feet were taken out from under him. When his head struck the post, his startled yelp trailed off into a soft groan as he slipped into the inky lake of unconsciousness.

"Where's your horse?" Johnny whispered, creeping along the row of stalls.

"In the trees. To the north," Michael answered. He came to a bay mare. "Here. Take this one."

Both of them froze at the scratchy voice that rumbled up from the darkness. "Hell, *I* can run faster'n *that* nag." They spun around to see Jacob's shadowy form raise up on one elbow from his bedroll beneath Judge Harvey's carriage. "That one there's the best in the barn," he pointed to a buckskin with black mane and tail.

Michael and Johnny looked at one another, each silently asking, *What do we do about him?* Jacob answered for them. "You'd best get on outa here. I ain't seen nothin'. Slept through da whole thang."

"*Wa-do,*" Michael and Johnny said in unison. "Thanks. Whoever you are." They moved swiftly to the horse Jacob had pointed out. With a soft chuckle the black man lay back down, rolled over and settled back to sleep.

Michael and Johnny led the stolen horse in the shadows along the livery stable. When they came to the front corner, Johnny peered out across the quadrangle. It looked clear to go. But just as he motioned to Michael, Sergeant Bolton burst out of the stockade.

"Escaped prisoner! Sound the alarm! Escaped prisoner!"

Michael was first on the buckskin and Johnny sprang up behind him. Michael pointed the spinning horse in the direction of the gate and kicked him into action. Bolton spotted them immediately and ran across the quadrangle, drawing his pistol and positioning himself to block their escape. The sergeant knew they would have to run right past him—or over him! With the buckskin charging at full speed, Bolton planted his feet firmly and raised his pistol, aiming point blank at Michael's chest. Michael bent forward, lying low against the horse's neck, exposing Johnny. Bolton didn't care. He knew he would get one of them. And, in fact, he preferred it be his fleeing prisoner. No one had, after all, ever escaped from his custody. He had a reputation to uphold.

But Michael hadn't ducked to avoid the soldier's fire; he had bent down for another reason. With a masterful flick, the knife pulled from his boot went flying and found its mark, burying itself in the sergeant's chest. Bolton staggered backward and fell in a seated position. He heard—and felt—the buckskin's hooves thunder past him. The mortally wounded stockade sergeant stared down at the knife handle, squandering his final thought with the trivial curiosity of how far in the blade had gone. His eyes shifted to the tips of his boots, then dulled in death and he fell backwards in the dust.

Michael jerked the buckskin to a sliding halt in the grove of trees just north of Ft. Smith and jumped off. Johnny slid forward on the horse and watched Michael beat his fist furiously against a tree.

"Damn! Damn, damn, damn!"

"You had to do it, *'Tsu-ts',*" Johnny consoled his liberator, thinking Michael was disturbed about killing the stockade sergeant.

"He'd have gotten one of us for sure."

Michael hurried to the tightly clustered stand of live oaks to get *U-no-le*. He untied the horse and looked up at Johnny. "I know," he said, "but my name was on the handle of that knife." Johnny understood Michael's concern. But there was no chance of them going back. What was done was done. Michael bolted up onto the roan, gave Johnny a shrug of fatalistic resignation, spun *U-no-le* around and they disappeared into the woods.

CHAPTER
26

The Drummonds had been cast out into the night with no place to go. Ezekiel had wisely suggested to William that they take refuge in the old, abandoned Walker cabin. It was a familiar place and they knew the way easily in the darkness. The men had filled the carriage and wagon with whatever they could assemble in a very short time, all under the close scrutiny of Thomas Mason, Jr., making sure they didn't take any of *his* new property.

William languorously unhitched the last of the horses and tethered the animal with the others while Ezekiel carried a load of bedding from the wagon into the cabin. Elizabeth, physically and emotionally drained, collapsed onto a wooden bench beside the open window. She coughed. It was the kind of gripping cough that stabs and denies the treasured breath the lungs cry out for. Reba dipped a cloth in the bucket of well water Ezekiel had brought in when they first arrived and bathed Elizabeth's forehead.

Susanna sat in the corner nursing Margaret Elizabeth. Daughter whimpered and fretted, her routine disturbed by the night's events. Mother sulked and refused to look at any one. It was an outrage. The wife of a United States Army major thrown out of her own home in the middle of the night.

Ezekiel entered with the bedding and deposited the load on the lone bed frame, only to have it collapse at his feet.

"I said *make* the bed, Zeke, not *break* it!" Reba snapped.

"It's all right, Reba," Elizabeth finally got her breath. "Just put something together on the floor."

Susanna spoke for the first time since leaving the Drummond house. "On the floor, Mother? You can't be serious!"

"I don't see that we have much choice," Elizabeth answered. Meg had finally drifted off to sleep and Susanna laid her on a makeshift pallet atop the wooden table. Reba herded Ezekiel back toward the door. There was much yet to be done and she saw signs of him slowing down. If he ever stopped to catch his breath, Reba knew he'd not move again until morning.

"Zeke, fetch some wood," she instructed him. "We'll need a little fire first thing in the morning to knock the chill off Miz 'Liz'beth an' the baby."

Zeke paused by the door and looked at his employer's wife. He had heard folks cough. He'd been around those who'd taken ill and walked in the valley of the Shadow. And those who didn't come

341

out the other side. Reba knew his thoughts and shooshed him on out the door. Susanna dug into the pile of things Zeke had placed in the corner. Finally she came up with a small, blue medicine bottle.

"Here. You'd better take some more laudanum," she told her mother and handed the medicine to Reba. Between coughing attacks, Elizabeth managed to force down a large gulp of the bitter liquid.

"Reba," she said weakly, "I think you and Ezekiel should leave us."

"Don't worry, Miz 'Liz'beth," Reba picked up the blanket that had slipped and fallen to the bench and tucked it snugly around Elizabeth's shoulders. "Zeke and me gon' sleep out under the wagon."

Elizabeth rapped her dear friend affectionately on the hand. "You know that's not what I meant. I recall hearing you say once that Ezekiel has people up in Illinois."

"Yes'm. A brother and some cousins," Reba said flatly. She knew what was coming and didn't like it. Didn't like it at all.

"I want you to leave tomorrow. It's best," Elizabeth said with all the determination she could muster. But Reba was having none of it.

"Hush, now. That medicine done got you talkin' crazy," she scolded lovingly. "Reba ain't goin' nowhere."

Elizabeth yielded to another coughing spell just as William came in. Reba hovered over her employer and dear friend. She answered William's troubled look with a shake of her head that told him it wasn't going well. Susanna stood in front of her mother feeling frustrated and helpless. Unable to bear seeing her like this, Susanna crossed to the other side of the room. On the wall was the old stuffed wolf's head, hanging in the same place she had seen it on her one previous visit. She looked to the table when Meg began to stir, awakened by her grandmother's coughing. Susanna watched the baby closely and was grateful when Meg settled back to sleep. She was drawn back to the wall. Near the wolf's head was an old shield. A leather quiver with some arrows. A bow.

"We came here once," she remembered. "It was years ago."

"Yes," William said softly, staring with her at the wall. In light of the day's genealogical revelations, these objects had taken on a new meaning, a greater significance. "We had dinner with the Walkers. Then went to the council meeting." To William it seemed a thousand years ago.

"A disgusting rabbit stew. I remember," the evening was

reborn in Susanna's memory. "I despised those people then. I despise them even more now."

"*Those people?*" Reba cocked her head to one side. "Missy, you *is* those people."

"Shut up, Reba! I have nothing to do with the Cherokees and they have nothing to do with me!" Susanna stormed out of the cabin in a huff, almost knocking the load of firewood out of Ezekiel's arms as he squeezed in the door. Reba had put up with Susanna's petulant, self-centered fractiousness for years and was running out of patience.

"Umm-hmm. You ain't got nothin' to do with 'em. An' that's why you restin' all peaceful like up in yo' four poster feather bed right now," Reba fired her sarcasm at the open door. Miss Susie probably didn't hear it, but it needed to be said.

"That's enough, Reba!" William followed his daughter outside. He found Susanna leaning against the wheel of the carriage, arms crossed, her face drawn in a familiar sulk. "Reba's right, Susanna. Things have changed." He knew if they were to survive she would have to accept the reality, no matter how harsh, of their present situation. But he was about to discover Susanna was neither ready nor willing to accept any such thing.

"No, Father!" she shook her head vehemently. "*You* might be part Indian. And I'm sure, if he were here, Michael would be absolutely thrilled. But not me! And not Margaret Elizabeth. I don't give a tinker's damn what somebody scribbled on a silly piece of paper almost fifty years ago! I'm the same person I was yesterday. Last month. Last year! And always will be!" She spun away and walked out toward the well. William followed her. Though she knew he was close behind her, she kept her arms crossed and her back to him.

"Susanna...I'm sorry..." he struggled to find the words.

"Tomorrow I'm going to find Peter," she cut his apology off.

It was a long time before William finally responded. "I don't think Peter is going to be much help."

"Of course he will," Susanna's little laugh was strained, unconvincing. "He's going to straighten all this out."

"Peter's one of *them*, Susanna," her father said with a pained sadness she had never heard from him. "He's on the other side now."

"He's still my husband. The father of our child."

William was tired. Not just the tiredness of a day that's been too long. It was the tiredness of betrayal. Of disillusionment. The exhaustion of lost faith. The dull pain of the death of hope. The last thing he needed on this night was to argue with his only daughter, no matter how selfish, how stubborn, how wrong she might be.

"Well. Try to get some rest. It'll be dawn soon."

"You don't really expect me to sleep in that....pig sty!" she gestured with disgust at the Walker cabin. "God knows what kind of vermin we're already infested with, just being here!"

"As you wish," he said, defeated. "I'm tired. I'll see you in the morning." He started back toward the cabin and she called to him, this time in a gentler tone. He looked back, waiting for her question.

"Did you know about her? The Cherokee woman?"

"My great grandmother? No. I never knew her. I was born the year of that census. 1790. She must've died shortly after. I vaguely recall my father talking about her once or twice when I was a child, but, no, I never knew her," he shrugged and shook his head, as stymied as Susanna herself by the irony of their fate.

"I suppose you just conveniently *forgot* about it," she didn't know if she believed him, but she was quite certain she hadn't forgiven him. "And who could blame you? It's something *I'd* sure want to forget." She turned abruptly, signalling she had nothing more to say. Downcast and dejected, William trudged heavily back toward the cabin.

Susanna lifted her eyes to the heavens, not so much praying as interrogating and chiding. With a bitter *amen* she was about to go inside but stopped sharply. She was stunned, confused, doubting her own eyes. Questioning her own sanity. In an old cowhide-covered chair just outside the cabin door sat the ancient, withered little Cherokee man she remembered as The Old One, James and Annie Walker's great grandfather. She recalled he had been killed when Annie and her mother were raped and Mrs. Walker murdered. Susanna was frightened, yet entranced when The Old One looked directly at her, smiled and extended his hand, beckoning to her.

Drawn by some strange force outside herself, Susanna inched closer. The Old One's eyes remained on her, and though his lips barely moved, she heard him mumbling softly in what she assumed was Cherokee. As she drew near, he opened his outstretched hand to reveal a tiny, leather draw-string pouch. Susanna took the small bag. The instant she touched it she heard the wolf howl from the woods, but she couldn't take her eyes off the pouch until The Old One pointed, directing her toward the forest. Like a dream in which time and motion are mired in a thick molasses, Susanna saw the glowing eyes of the wolf staring at her from the tree line. She didn't know how long her eyes remained locked with those of the beast. It was an experience out of time. When she finally freed herself from the wolf's hypnotic stare, she found the chair before her empty. The Old One had disappeared. She looked back to the tree line, but the wolf, too, had vanished.

Susanna sat down in the cowhide chair and inspected the pouch cradled in her hands. She slowly loosened the draw string and dumped the contents out into her palm. A silver ring with a delicately carved wolf's head caught a shimmer of moonlight. Still dazed, Susanna put the ring back in the pouch and let the tiny bag drop to the dirt at her feet. She leaned her head way back against the rough cabin logs and closed her eyes. Heaving a great sigh, she felt the tears trickle down the side of her head and into her ear. If it was a real wolf she had seen, let him come and devour her. She was too tired to care. If it was only an hallucination born of exhaustion, she would probably encounter him again in her nightmares.

* * * * * * *

The sun had risen after a couple of hours, bathing Susanna's face with a comforting warmth as she slept outside in the cowhide chair. She did not sense the shadow moving up her body to block her face, but the sound of a saber being unsheathed woke her with a start. Despite her stiff neck she felt relieved to find herself looking up at her husband, barely recognizable in dark silhouette against the brilliance of the sun directly behind him. Still half asleep, she extended a tired hand.

"Peter! I knew you'd come! I'm so thankful you're here!" When the soldier shifted to one side, Susanna saw it was not, in fact, her husband, but rather Private Stevens of the round up patrol headed by Corporal Charles DeKalb. Stevens leered down at her. His face registered a lascivious delight at the way she had greeted him.

"Maybe we should go around behind the cabin and you can show me how thankful you *really* are."

Susanna looked at the tip of the saber resting against her breast. She was wide awake. And enraged. She slapped the saber blade away with the back of her hand.

"You watch your mouth, soldier! Or I'll have you whipped

345

and thrown in the stockade!"

The roar of laughter from Stevens and the others woke Reba and Ezekiel from a rigid sleep. They lay on the hard ground beneath the wagon pulled up against the side of the cabin. Gravel-eyed, they blinked with rising concern at the scene before them. William, sleepily rubbing his face, appeared in the cabin doorway, staring at the soldiers. He knew they weren't there to rescue the Drummonds from their desperate situation. They had come for another reason altogether.

* * * * * * *

The wagon had been quickly reloaded to overflowing. Reba held the baby while Susanna and William helped the rapidly deteriorating Elizabeth from the cabin.

"Put her in the wagon," Corporal DeKalb barked when he saw them headed for the buggy.

"She'll ride easier in the carriage," William explained.

DeKalb, intolerant of any serious challenge to his authority, roughly put his horse between them and the vehicle, almost knocking Elizabeth down. "You ain't gonna need no damn carriage where you're goin'. Now put her in the wagon!" he yelled at William. "Unhitch the horse and leave the carriage," he growled at Ezekiel.

"You needn't treat us like animals!" Susanna snapped as she helped steady her mother.

"We're as white as you are!" Elizabeth added, "and obviously a great deal more civilized!"

DeKalb leaned forward in the saddle, exasperated with this whole bunch, but he didn't feel threatened by this wisp of a sick old woman. "Lady, a good quarter of the folks we been rounding up and shovin' into these camps'd pass for being whiter than me. But that ain't my problem, now, is it? Let's go. Git movin'."

Ezekiel tied the carriage horse to the back of the wagon. Reba handed Meg up to Susanna, then started climbing up into the wagon beside them. From atop his horse, Stevens reached out and kicked the side of the wagon to get Reba's attention. "Slaves have to walk. Only Cherokees ride."

"I'll have you know," she glared fiercely at him, "I ain't no slave!"

"And I'm not Cherokee," Elizabeth added.

"Leave 'em be," DeKalb dismissed it all with a wave of disgust. "Let's just git movin'!"

346

Ezekiel walked beside the wagon which was driven by William. DeKalb rode in front, Stevens behind. The rest of the patrol, on foot, were equally distributed front and back. Elizabeth tried unsuccessfully to ward off another coughing fit.

"Maybe it'll rain again and settle the dust," was all William could offer to mask his growing concern for her weakening condition.

"Shut up! No talkin'!" Stevens yelled from the rear.

They pulled away from the cabin. Susanna's eyes drifted back to the old cowhide chair, then shifted to the tree line where only hours before she had seen the wolf. Above the trees the dark clouds were forming in the east. A flash of lightning fingered its way earthward, announced seconds later by a peal of thunder.

CHAPTER

27

Indian Territory

The dew-laden morning silence of Michael and Annie Drummond's farm was gently stirred by the rooster's crowing from the fencepost, the pig's single grunt from the pen behind the barn and the hungry calf's plaintive cry. The tranquility gradually yielded, however, to a faint rumble that grew steadily stronger until it had become a thunderous din. The detachment of twenty U. S. Cavalry soldiers galloped as fast as the narrow road would allow, winding their way around the hills and through the hollows. At the head of the column rode Major Tyler, second in command at Ft. Smith. They had left in the pre-dawn darkness to cross into Indian Territory and reach the Drummond farm as early as possible. The element of surprise, Tyler thought, was always important when attempting to apprehend the innately sneaky and treacherous Indians.

A cat scurried to the safety of the barn and chickens scattered in a flurry when the mounted soldiers rode into the clearing in front of the cabin. Each man had been carefully instructed as to his specific duties once they arrived. The cabin door exploded inward, breaking off its hinges. Three soldiers rushed in, two with pistols drawn, the third with his saber. Theirs were the faces of men bent on blood. But snarls of vengeance melted to looks of frustration and disappointment when they discovered the cabin was empty. Two soldiers jerked the barn door open wide for the others who rushed in with pistols and muskets. A thorough search produced only the milk cow and her calf, a plow mule lazily munching hay in his stall and the rafters filled with wrens that fluttered out through the loft opening. The soldiers returned from the cabin and the barn and assembled before their leader in the center of the clearing.

"Well, I'm not surprised," Tyler grimaced. "They're crafty, these Cherokees."

"All Injuns is sneaky, Major. It's their nature," one of the cabin soldiers interjected.

Tyler stroked his neatly trimmed goatee, pondering his next move. "Yes...well,..all right then! Let's circle back to the creek. See if we can pick up their trail." But before they left there was one or two more things the Major had planned.

The commander's horse jumped slightly. The shot was

instantly followed by a single squeal from the hog. The soldier appeared from behind the barn, his pistol still smoking. Three other solders emerged from the barn with bundles of straw tied up to form torches. They stopped where a fourth soldier squatted before a pile of kindling he had just ignited. The three fagots were soon ablaze. Two were tossed back into the barn and the third sailed through the open door of the cabin.

Tyler had correctly guessed that he and his troops were being watched by the man they had come to arrest. No doubt the outlaw and his squaw had shared a laugh at the army's expense when their place had been found deserted. Well, thought Tyler, keep watching. The show was just getting started.

From their vantage point in the thick grove of live oaks covering a neighboring hill, Michael and Annie saw the puff of smoke from the gun and saw their cow drop to her knees even before the sound of the shot had reached the hilltop. Then they saw *Gŭ-li*, their dog, dash out from the barn, driven before the hungry fire. One of the soldiers dropped the animal on the run. They saw their beloved pet tumble forward with his own momentum, and a split second later they heard the shot, followed immediately by a sharp yelp. Michael reached for his rifle against the saddle beneath his leg. The soldiers were so tightly clustered he was certain he could get at least one of them. But from *Ga-tsa-nu-la*, Annie stuck her foot out and put it against the weapon. At the same time, she held little Jimmy firmly in front of her and blocked his view. He had been excited about the early morning adventure and didn't understand what was happening in the valley below. Michael and Annie hoped he hadn't seen *Gŭ-li's* brutal slaying. Though he said nothing, *Tsi-mi* was quiet from that point forward. His lower lip rolled out and quivered as though he might cry. But he never did.

In pained silence Michael and Annie watched the soldiers mount up and thunder away from the blazing cabin and barn, headed for the creek that lay to the west. Michael and Annie, their sad faces tinged with anger, looked away from the wanton destruction below. Their eyes found each other. Michael knew this was the home Annie had always wanted. The cabin she had painted for him on the ferry one cold and rainy day when she first told him she was pregnant. And now it was being destroyed because of his own actions. And though he knew she would never say a word to blame him, he would feel the pain of her loss for as long as they lived.

"I'm sorry, *wa-le-la*," he said with emotion. "For bringing this on you."

"You did what you had to do," she said, not with approval, but with forgiveness born of a deep love for a man with deep convictions. She knew there was a place inside himself where he went to make decisions. A place she knew she could not—and, in truth, didn't want to—follow. But she also knew there was courage there. The burn to be right. To do what was right. She knew it was from this secret place he emerged when he had lunged from the crowd, seized a rifle from a fourteen-year-old Cherokee boy and put a bullet through the head of her twin brother, his best friend. She knew beyond a doubt there was courage in this hidden place of his. Courage and demons. And she knew she could do nothing to daunt the former and dared not challenge the latter.

"I never meant for it to come to this," he caressed his son whose tiny hands tightly gripped the horse's mane. Annie placed her hand on Michael's and continued to look at him.

"Do you wish you were back east? Safe at home with your family?"

"My home...my family...is wherever you and *Tsi-mi* are," he answered honestly. It was the answer she wanted—needed—to hear. Michael leaned over and kissed her. They rode their horses back down the other side of the hill, away from the direction taken by the soldiers. Away from their blazing cabin and barn.

350

Northwest Georgia

A steady rain had begun to fall shortly after they left the Walker cabin, and by mid morning the Drummonds had been joined by four more wagons filled with Cherokee families and their belongings. The early drops, like forward scouts, had explored the dry dust before sending a silent message summoning more to follow, until the rain beat against the faces and ran off the hair and down the backs of the Cherokees. A few murmured with hushed gratitude; the rest plodded silently onward, eyes cast down at the mud beginning to squish up around their moccasins and between the toes of the shoeless.

Ezekiel walked beside the Drummond wagon, watching the rain drop off the hat brim that hung low, concealing his apprehension and uncertainty. Up on the wagon seat, Reba was seething. Her harsh, defiant glare at Corporal DeKalb brought a scowling response.

"Don't be givin' me no evil-eye, Nigger," DeKalb snarled. "You'll be down walkin' in the mud with him," he added, pointing at Ezekiel.

William said nothing. All day he had been battling an overwhelming sense of defeat. What could he possibly have said that would make any difference? he thought. His chief concern was for Elizabeth and her rapidly deteriorating health. He glanced at her, seated between himself and Susanna. From beneath the blanket pulled up over her head, he heard the rattling cough. His attention drifted to his daughter, who, like himself, had been monitoring her mother with concern. Baby Meg leaned close, fussing and soaked, but secure in her mother's arms. William glanced past Susanna to the wagon filled with Cherokees rolling along beside the Drummonds. The young Cherokee woman's glazed eyes attached themselves to nothing in particular. Her child nursed fretfully at her breast. Behind her in the wagon, her son, perhaps ten, looked at his father as though waiting for the once-proud warrior to do something. William empathized with the Cherokee father. Feeling powerless and ashamed, the man avoided his son's gaze and kept his eyes straight ahead.

When they approached a crossroads, they saw coming up to join them from the road on their right another collection of wagons filled with more displaced Cherokees and a few blacks. The new group was escorted by Corporal Robert Barton's detachment. On reaching the intersection, Barton came abreast of the lead driver and ordered them to fall in behind the DeKalb wagons.

As the Drummonds moved through the intersection, William noticed the first of Barton's wagons carried the widow of John Sixkiller, James and Annie Walker's late uncle. With her were her four children and her mother-in-law, the seventy-five year old mother of the Sixkiller brothers and their sister, the late Janice Walker. William flicked a wave of greeting. Tom, the oldest boy at sixteen, nodded back. Like the rest of his family, he was astonished by the sight of the esteemed *yo-neg* attorney, Mr. William Drummond, driving a wagon in this parade of captured Cherokees.

By noon the rain had stopped, but the clinging humidity weighed heavy in the stifling heat. The train of captives was forced to halt at a swollen creek. Cherokee men and a few of the blacks assessed the situation with Corporal Barton and a couple of his men. The draft animals were unhitched and led to the water's edge for a much needed drink.

"Let's go!" Corporal DeKalb shouted impatiently. "Ain't nothin' to talk about here! Just get the hell on across!"

"Come on! Move it!" Stevens echoed his squad leader.

Corporal Barton, standing with William, Ezekiel and a few other Cherokees, pointed to a spot a few yards downstream. "I think if you angle across down there, you'll be all right."

"That current looks pretty strong," William countered respectfully. "The animals are tired. And most of these wagons are overloaded."

Barton, like many of the others, was puzzled by the presence of this tall, likeable, obviously well-educated man in the midst of these captives, but it wasn't his place to question such things. His job was to bring them all to the holding camps. And, much as he disliked Corporal DeKalb's harsh attitude, he knew they were already well behind schedule for the day.

"We really don't have much choice, Mr. Drummond," he said. "We'd better get moving." They all knew the young corporal was right and headed back toward their wagons.

Just as William had predicted, the first wagon that attempted to cross overturned in the middle of the raging stream, resulting in the loss of the Cherokee family's entire load of possessions. Ironically, however, the wagon, sacrificed on its side lengthwise across the creek, served as a partial dam, diverting the stronger part

352

of the current and making it easier for those who followed.

Grandmother Sixkiller had taken a seat on a fallen log at the side of the road. She staunchly refused the pleas of her daughter-in-law and grandchildren to get back into the wagon. Like many other Cherokees, she superstitiously believed that unfamiliar waters were the domain of unknown—and perhaps unfriendly—spirits. Spirits which, in light of the hardships they found themselves facing, she was unwilling to challenge. When Corporal Barton saw Private Stevens headed in her direction with his familiar scornful impatience, he hurried to cut him off.

"Go ahead, Stevens. I'll take care of her."

Stevens looked back with disdain and moved on to join the others. Barton casually took a seat beside the old woman and wiped his brow with his sleeve. The old woman stared straight ahead, ignoring the young soldier.

"It's getting hot," Barton noted nonchalantly. "Gonna be a long day." She didn't answer, but he was patient, as though he hadn't really expected a reply. He fanned himself with his hat, then asked, "Are you tired? Need some water?" He opened his canteen and extended it toward her. For the first time, she looked at him, puzzled by his genuine compassion. She shook her head no. Barton took a sip, then closed the canteen. "We have to get moving, you know," he said in a friendly tone, sharing his concern. "I'd hate to see you get left behind. Look..." he gestured toward the Sixkiller wagon, "...the children are worried about you."

The smaller ones stood in the rear of the wagon staring at their grandmother. "*E-li-si! Tsi-ne-na!*" the youngest girl, about ten, called out. "Let's go!"

Corporal Barton repositioned his hat, then rose and held out his hand to her. He waited patiently until she finally placed her hand on his forearm and pulled herself up. He took a step, intending to escort her back to the wagon, but she stopped and reached for his canteen. With a faint smile he left it with her and walked on ahead toward the other wagons waiting to cross.

* * * * * * *

In a large clearing carved out among the towering pines loomed the sixteen-foot high wall. The logs had been cut from the very trees felled to create space for Fort Coosawattee. Each log was buried in the ground like a post, with the top sharpened to a point. The *fort*—another government euphemism for what was, in reality, a concentration camp—was a vast square covering many acres. A few barracks for the soldiers and a couple of administrative buildings, including the Fort's headquarters, had been erected just outside the front gate. Inside, long, narrow, open-sided buildings with thatched roofs and dirt floors had been constructed as shelters for the *detainees*. Angling across the northeast corner of the enclosure was a narrow creek from which the entire population was expected to draw their drinking and cooking water. Bathing was among the luxuries first to be sacrificed. Many of the incarcerated Cherokees, now numbering in the hundreds, were huddled beneath the army-built sheds while others chose to construct their own shelters and lean-to's adjacent to or abutting the perimeter walls.

U. S. soldiers, Georgia militiamen, and volunteers from North Carolina and Tennessee came and went, ushering in the constant stream of despondent humanity. Many of these volunteers bartered with the Cherokees, exchanging family heirlooms of gold and silver for a few dollars or a bottle of contraband whiskey. Others merely stopped wagons on the trail or at the front gate and took whatever struck their fancy. The Cherokees subjected to such thievery and abuse often pleaded in vain with the army troops for assistance or protection, but most of the young soldiers were intimidated by the older, rougher guardsmen and volunteer militia.

Soldiers assisted the civilian supply contractors in passing out the government supplies provided for the Cherokees awaiting removal to the west. Arguments frequently escalated to shouting matches when a soldier or a contractor attempted to explain to an irate captive about the rationing. One pound of flour and one-half pound of bacon per day for each Cherokee. The entire operation was a chaotic swarm. Cherokee families continued to stream in faster than they could be assigned a location and get settled in. Most of them still didn't understand—or had simply refused to accept—what was happening to them. Many of the younger soldiers made every effort to adhere strictly to General Scott's adjuration to treat their charges with kindness and compassion. But there was too much confusion and too many older soldiers, militiamen and volunteers who relished the idea of bullying these defenseless people and cheating them out of personal possessions or their allotted share of government commodities.

* * * * * * *

"I told you, the rations is for Cherokees."

354

"All right. I'm Cherokee."

"You just told me you was white. But you're hungry, so now all of a sudden you're Cherokee?"

"Just give us our rations. The children are starving."

"Them two there look sick."

"You would, too, if you'd marched all day and half the night in the rain."

"Half pound of bacon? That's all we get?"

"This flour is full of weevils."

"Take it or leave it."

"No vegetables? No fruit?"

"Take it or leave it."

For days the endless river of uprooted and displaced families had poured in through the gates of Ft. Coosawattee from just after sun up until well into the night.

"Please! I need to go back and get some bedding. We can't sleep out on the bare ground."

"The rest of 'em are. You can, too."

"We need pots and pans. We didn't get the pots and pans."

"Should'a thought of that. You have to stay here. It's for your own protection."

"Protection! From what?! This is a prison!"

"Lady, I'm just following orders."

"You don't have to call 'em *Lady*. They're Injuns, fer Chrissakes!"

"She looks a lot like my sister..."

"Jake says she *humps* a lot like your sister!"

"Go to hell!"

"Gimme that bottle o' whiskey."

"Can we get a doctor? My son is very sick."

"This place is full of sick folk. Had three die last night. Ain't but one doctor for the lot."

* * * * * * *

By mid-afternoon the DeKalb-Barton train of captives finally arrived. A group of drunken Georgia guardsmen lounging near the main gate eyed Susanna and the other younger women hungrily. They didn't care who heard their lusty remarks and raucous laughter as they wrestled and jostled playfully over the whiskey jugs being passed around.

Inside the gate, soldiers pointed the wagons loaded with

arriving captives first in one direction, then another, alternating the lines in an attempt to alleviate the congested scramble for shelter space. As the Drummond wagon made its way into the camp, William quietly noticed a number of white men riding in and out of the gate at will. Some appeared to be supply contractors. Militiamen and volunteers. Others merely white trash making last minute efforts to bargain the Cherokees out of family valuables which, they warned, would be confiscated anyway before the Indians' removal journey began.

"Contractors over there!" a soldier yelled at William and pointed off to his left.

"Hell, he ain't no contractor," Private Stevens shouted back from across the wagon. "He's a God damn Cherokee."

"Hard to tell sometimes," the soldier laughed, redirecting William to a different path alongside the shelter building farthest from the gate. "Over there. Go on down as far as you can and pick a spot."

William tugged at the reins to turn the horses then pulled back sharply, bringing the wagon to a rattling halt. A few yards to his right they saw four Cherokees—two men, a woman and a teenage boy—whose hands were tied to metal rings nailed to the thick log poles high above their heads. Their shirts had been ripped off and they were being whipped on their bare backs by two Georgia militiamen. Two U. S. soldiers guarded the proceedings.

"William! Do something!" Elizabeth gasped in shock.

He stood up in the wagon and cupped his hands to his mouth. "Stop! Stop it!" This strange and unexpected interruption did, in fact, temporarily interrupt the flogging. The Georgians looked at William. Corporal DeKalb rode briskly up to the Drummond wagon.

"Keep moving! This ain't none of your business!"

"What have these people done to deserve this?" William demanded.

One of the soldiers guarding the punishment detail volunteered an explanation to William, who once again had been mistaken for a white man. "They tried to run away. Had to teach 'em a lesson. Fifty lashes each."

"Oh, my God!" Elizabeth looked away.

"Same as you'll get if you're caught tryin' to escape," DeKalb used the incident to make a point.

"This is outrageous!" William snapped at the corporal. "These people aren't criminals!"

The soldier, realizing his error in thinking William a white man, joined in the scolding of this brazen, upstart Cherokee. "Maybe you want a little taste of this yourself?" William didn't answer. "That's what I thought," the soldier said. He rejoined the guardsmen and motioned for them to resume the beating.

"Come on! Get movin'!" DeKalb shouted and slapped the rump of the Drummonds' horse, which lurched forward, almost toppling William from the wagon before he regained his balance and grabbed the reins. He was the only one who ventured a look back at the beating as they rumbled deeper into the camp.

* * * * * * *

Charlie and Eva Swimmer, their children and Charlie's mother, Grandma Nancy, had been in the camp for a couple of days—long enough to establish their territory beneath the long shelter. Blankets had been hung over ropes strung between the shed's support posts to define *private* areas. Once the other bundles had been placed beneath the hanging blankets to complete the *wall* and the bed rolls had been laid out, there was little else to do.

Long, steamy stretches of humid boredom alternated with fits of lip-biting apprehension and hand-wringing anxiety over what lay in store for them. As the hours and days began to fold around them, the Cherokees realized General Scott's words had been greatly lacking in detail. *You will be removed from your homes.* He had said nothing about the invading white rabble, the fires, the curses of the soldiers and the sharp prods of their musket butts and bayonets. *You will be taken to temporary holding facilities.* He had failed to mention the thirty mile march in the driving rain and clutching mud. And now that they were here, how long would they stay? Where would they go next? When? *Do not resist.* Most of them had not resisted, and still there had been floggings, even killings. And there was the unspoken concern that brought terror to the hearts and minds of so many—*disease.* Too well the Cherokees knew the devastation that could be visited upon them by the white man's ailments. Small pox. Measles. Cholera. Dysentery. Colic. Consumption. When would it begin? How far would it spread? How many would die? Eventually these horrifying questions became too burdensome and burrowed themselves beneath an insulating lethargy.

Eva and some of the other women in the area stood just outside the shelter conversing in soft tones. During the day the heat was so intense, the humidity so thick that extended periods beneath the shed proved unbearable. Martha tried to get her grandmother to eat, but Nancy refused. Charlie was outside, demonstrating to *Tsu-tsu* and Buck how to use a crude shovel which he had fashioned from a piece of board. Once *Tsu-tsu* grasped the concept, Charlie directed him toward a spot out near the high log fence to dig a toilet trench.

"Dig it about so deep..." Charlie measured twelve inches between his hands. "Over there. The breeze has been mostly that direction. It'll be down wind. Buck, you help." *Tsu-tsu* and Buck took off with the makeshift shovel. They passed a frustrated Martha who had come out to join her father.

"She won't eat!" she gestured helplessly, showing him a plate of food that had hardly been touched. "She thinks they're trying to poison her."

Charlie looked at the disgusting piece of boiled salt-pork on the plate. "Maybe she's right, *Ma-di*," he tried to lighten his daughter's concern.

"*E-to-da*, she has to eat, or she'll—" Martha stopped short in mid-sentence. Her mouth dropped open in shock. Charlie turned to look at the approaching wagon and saw William Drummond and his family. Charlie's forehead crinkled with genuine confusion.

William was glad to see a familiar face. He pulled his wagon out of line and stopped beside Charlie. Eva interrupted her conversation with the other Cherokee women and, as incredulous as her daughter and husband, walked out toward the Drummond's wagon.

"I don't believe my eyes," Charlie said softly.

"Charlie! It's good to see you!" William's voice was warm and sincere though fraught with stress. A long silence followed. Other Cherokees—and a few blacks—stopped what they were doing to look on. Susanna glowered down at Eva and Martha.

"Well, you needn't stare!"

"Susanna!" William's tone was sharp. "These are our friends."

"They're *your* friends, Father. Not mine," she said, continuing to scowl down at Eva and Martha.

William was painfully embarrassed by his daughter's rudeness, but Charlie understood. He smiled and spoke to Susanna in a gentle tone. "In the days to come, Miss Susie, you're going to need all the friends you can get!"

"She doesn't need friends, *E-to-da*," Martha said mockingly. "She's been to *finishing school*."

"That's enough, *Ma-di*," Eva said, then welcomed the other women in the wagon. "It's good to see you, Miz Elizabeth. Reba."

Martha glared defiantly up at Susanna before marching back to her grandmother. Elizabeth, like William, was glad to see a friendly face.

"Hello, Eva. I suppose we've all seen better times."

"How utterly and absurdly self-evident, Mother!" Susanna rolled her eyes at these feeble attempts at polite greetings and civilities. It troubled her not a whit that she had merely made a difficult situation more awkward for them all. Eva was the first to get beyond it.

"Well, you might as well get unloaded," she said. "You can set up here next to us, if you like."

Ezekiel helped Reba stiffly descend from the rear of the wagon. His eyes widened when Reba's weight shifted to his support, aware he might be crushed should she fall. William climbed down, answering Charlie's puzzled expression.

"It came as quite a surprise to us, as well, Charlie. Turns out my father's grandmother was *Tsa-la-gi*."

"Well, it's no surprise to *me*," Charlie answered with an understanding smile. "Your heart has always been *Tsa-la-gi*."

William clamped a grateful hand on his friend's shoulder and surveyed the camp setup. They saw the glut of humanity continuing to pour in through the main gate. The aged, the young, the infirm, the frightened, the infuriated, the depressed and the dying. Cherokees. Blacks belonging to or inseparable friends of Cherokees. Whites married to Cherokees. Blacks, like Reba and Ezekiel, who had been assumed to be slaves because of their relationship with a Cherokee family. William's attention came back to his friend.

"We got here a couple of days ago," Charlie told him. Then there was a long silence before he asked, "What's going to happen, Mr. Drummond?"

"William, please. Or *Wi-li*." William knew he would no longer be *Mr. William Drummond* to anyone. He was in a prison camp, but he wasn't beaten. Not yet. He had fought to overcome his earlier feelings of defeat and helplessness. Too many depended on his leadership. Already he was planning his next move. "Maybe they'll let me go to New Echota to talk to General Scott."

"Last I heard," Charlie offered, "he's up on the Hiwassee. They've got a camp just like this one at the Cherokee Agency."

* * * * * * *

By the time the Drummonds finished unloading, it was evident they had brought with them more than any of the other families in the immediate area. Reba pulled two bags and slid Susanna's huge steamer trunk to the tailgate of the wagon. When she tried to lift the trunk, it slipped from her grasp and fell into the mud. Immediately, Susanna charged out from the shelter with Margaret Elizabeth on her hip.

"Must you be so clumsy, Reba!" she shrieked. "I saw that, and I do declare, I believe you dropped my trunk on purpose!"

Reba rolled her eyes and shook her head. "Oh, that's right, Missy. Reba got nothin' better to do than throw yo' stuff 'round jes' for spite."

"Don't you take a surly tone with me!"

Reba moved away from Susanna to keep from uttering something she might later regret. She found herself looking right into the eyes of Jane, the pregnant black woman the Swimmers had picked up alongside the road. Reba left the large trunk sitting in the mud and picked up the two smaller parcels. "Fine. Haul yo' own damn trunk!"

Susanna followed Reba back into the shelter, continuing her tirade. "Reba! You come back here and apologize! I will *not* have you talk to me that way!"

"That's fine, too, Missy!" Reba said and kept walking. "Reba jes' won't talk to you at *all*! Never 'gain." She deposited the bags beside the huge pile of their belongings near the cot set up for Elizabeth.

"Mother, I've had it with this woman!" Susanna whined. "I demand you release Reba this instant! After all I've endured, I will not have her speak to me this way!"

"All right, Susanna," Elizabeth's voice was weak. Her condition had continued to worsen. "Reba just said she wouldn't talk to you any more."

"No! I'm serious! I want her sent away!" Susanna insisted.

"Believe me, Chil'! If it weren't for yo' Momma an' that sweet baby, Reba done been long gone 'way from that mouth o' yours," Reba pushed past Susanna and went back to the wagon.

Jane was still there, her mouth hanging open, stunned by the exchange she had just overheard. She inched closer to Reba. "You mean you ain't no slave?" she asked. "And you been bucklin' to that uppity mouth? When you ain't *gots* to?!" Reba heard the astonishment in Jane's voice, and Jane, reading Reba's expression, knew Susanna was standing right behind her. Jane glanced back for

360

A Cherokee Odyssey

confirmation, then ducked her eyes and stepped back to her own area.

"That's right," Susanna called. "Reba's not a slave. We don't believe in slavery. We're Abolitionists," she announced proudly. "Reba's free to go....at any time," she added with a glare at Reba, then stalked back inside the shed to her mother.

"Umm-hmm," Jane said when Susanna had gone. "I reckon we *all* Abolitionists, honey. That's why we all gon' jes' pick up and march on outa here!"

"Excuse me?" Susanna came storming back, venting her fury on Jane. "Did you have something to add to this conversation?" Jane didn't back down, but she had nothing more to say. "No? I thought not! When I want your opinion, I'll ask for it. Until then, you're free to go!"

Reba and Jane exchanged a look of mutual support, then Jane answered with a smirk, "You better stop dreamin', Chil', and look around you!" Before Susanna could respond, Jane swaggered off, making sure hers would be the last word. For once Susanna was speechless. She glared first at Jane, then at Reba, and finally retreated back inside the shelter.

"Susanna," Elizabeth's voice was even fainter than before, "please fetch my laudanum..."

"They're dreadful, Mother. All these people. They're absolutely dreadful," she whimpered, expecting consolation and sympathy. She hadn't anticipated the firmness of Elizabeth's response.

"Susanna, dear....shut up!" Taken aback by her mother's bluntness, Susanna pouted and searched for the medicine. Elizabeth studied her daughter, knowing much of her petulance sprang from her distress. "Why won't you just *try* to find Peter?" Elizabeth's question came in a much kinder tone. "Ask some of the soldiers. They must know him."

Susanna, as she had done for some time, declined to respond to any reference to Peter. At the Walker cabin she had told her father she would find Peter, but she knew even then it was a hollow assertion. He had abandoned them. Her pride wouldn't allow it. Elizabeth accepted her daughter's silence, took the bottle of medicine Susanna shoved at her and said no more.

* * * * * * *

The greasy, dirty Georgia militiamen who had assisted in

capturing Cherokees continued to hang around the main gate of the Ft. Coosawattee compound, drinking, joking and watching civilian whites barter with and steal from the unending influx of captives. By some invisible sign that mysteriously signalled the end of their revelry, the drunken Georgians mounted their horses. They leaned this way and that in the saddle, passing around a pottery jug.

A hand went out and the jug was extended to a man in a fringed leather jacket with his wide-brimmed Georgia hat pulled down over his eyes. His big gray horse soon lost itself among the others—jostling and bumping. Lifting the jug to his lips as though to drink, William Drummond tilted his head back just enough to gauge the distance to the gate and the positioning of the soldiers there. With several days growth of beard and no bath in longer than he could remember, William fit right in with the rest of the guardsmen.

"Hey! Leave that jug here with us!" one of the Georgians on the ground shouted, bringing laughter from the others. William handed the jug down to a grimy, groping hand and swung Clancey around, making sure he stayed in the middle of the pack. He cut a glance from beneath the wide brimmed hat toward the shadowy side of the supply shed opposite the gate. There, silent and motionless, Charlie Swimmer watched his friend. No one challenged the rowdy militiamen ambling their mounts leisurely out of the camp. William slowly exhaled, realizing he'd been holding his breath for at least two full minutes. But he tensed once more when a guard stepped out toward them. William recognized the same soldier who had earlier mistaken him for a supply contractor. If the guard recalled him from the flogging protest, William knew he might easily find himself lashed to the wall for a taste of the whip.

"Hey!" the gate soldier shouted. William pretended he didn't hear. "You! On the spotted gray!" the guard repeated. William stopped and turned slightly in the saddle, hoping to keep his face shaded by his hat. He could see back through the gate that Charlie Swimmer had left the safety of the supply shed. Now, seeing William stopped, Charlie pressed himself back against the building, sliding unseen into the shadows.

A couple more soldiers stepped out behind the first and approached William's horse. The first gate guard put his hand on William's leg, keeping it there while the other soldiers crowded up behind him. Then he looked around cautiously before he said in a low voice, "How's about you bring *us* a coupla them jugs when you come back this way!"

362

William hoped they didn't hear the depth of relief in his long exhalation. "Sure thing, boys," he said, then urged Clancey to catch up with the others. But William had gone only a few feet when yet another soldier—a baby-faced private—darted out and walked beside Clancey. William had seen Miles Franklin with Corporal Barton's patrol.

"You know, you really don't look like some of these other guardsmen," the private said.

William shrugged indifferently, but his hand on the opposite side of the horse slid down to a knife hidden between his leg and the saddle. At the same time, from the shadows of the hat, his eyes measured the distance to the woods and counted the number of soldiers who could get a clear shot at him before he reached the safety of the trees.

The private glanced around then back to William and whispered his request. "See if you can find a couple more doctors willing to come in here and help these people. Some of 'em don't look so good. They're gonna start droppin' like flies..."

William was moved by the young soldier's humanity. He relaxed his grip on the knife.

Private Franklin stepped back, slapped the spotted gray on the rump and yelled out for the other soldiers to hear. "And don't forget that whiskey, dammit!"

William waved and spurred his horse away from the gate.

* * * * * * *

The widow of John Sixkiller was seated on a wooden box surrounded by a flock of children transfixed by her story. While mothers, fathers and older siblings were busy setting up their areas in the shelter or scrounging for slivers of firewood or scraps of food, grandmothers and grandfathers, or merely old Cherokees with no family but who still had something to contribute, gathered the little ones and led them on adventures of the imagination. Not only did it keep them out of mischief and out of harms way, it took them, if but for a short time, on the soaring wings of brother eagle or for a plodding but exciting race on the back of Mother Turtle.

Just outside the shelter area taken by the Drummonds, Susanna sat on a chair Ezekiel had loaded the night they left their home. She held Meg in her lap, fanning herself and the baby in search of relief from the relentless heat and the sickening stench which combined to form the deeply felt but unseen soul of

Coosawattee. The same spiritual oppression was echoed throughout the other camps sprinkled all across Cherokee territory. Occasionally Susanna glanced at the Widow Sixkiller and the children gathered at her feet. She found it all too ridiculous and, for the most part, annoying.

"In the very beginning, the People say," Widow Sixkiller spoke with an air of mystery and looked around, drawing each child personally into the story, "Dog was king of the mountain, and it was Wolf who stayed in the village by the fire. When winter came, Dog decided he did not like the cold, so he went down to the village and drove Wolf from the fire. Wolf ran to the mountains where he prospered and did very well. He and his brother wolves ventured down to the village where they killed some animals. The People chased them back into the mountains and killed many of the wolves. Then Wolf and his brothers came back to the village and took such revenge that ever since, the People do not like to hurt a wolf."

Like a true master story teller, when the tale ended, Widow Sixkiller leaned forward but remained silent, allowing the children an opportunity to react. Some sat wide-eyed and silent while others bared their *fangs* like wolf cubs. A few of the older boys growled and tickled the smaller children, eliciting squeals of delighted fright. Susanna stood up with Meg and stepped toward the story circle.

"That's terrible! Is this what you teach your children?" her voice was thick with scornful revulsion. "All this violence and revenge? It's absolutely disgusting!" Widow Sixkiller and the children stared at the strange young woman who was so full of rage. And so clearly more *yo-neg* than *Tsa-la-gi*.

* * * * * * *

Inside the shelter, Elizabeth lay helpless in the choking grip of another coughing seizure. She waved off the attention of Reba and Susanna, who had just entered with Meg on her hip. For the hundredth time Reba rearranged the myriad of boxes and baggage to further define the *territory* they had claimed. She simply didn't know what else to do but felt she ought to be doing something. Susanna dipped a cloth into a pan of water and wiped Meg all over, hoping to cool and soothe the fretful baby. The lingering tension between Susie and Reba was made more palpable by having to move around each other in such cramped quarters.

"I think Meg is getting a fever," Susanna informed her mother, knowing how much it hurt Reba to be excluded from the

364

care of the child she so completely adored.

"I'm sure it's this dreadful heat..." Elizabeth spoke softly and slowly to avoid triggering another round of coughing.

"It's *everything* here, Mother! It's *all* dreadful," Susanna complained in her familiar whine. "The heat. This putrid stench! The rubbish they give us for food. All the sick people."

"Like me." Elizabeth felt she had in some way contributed to her daughter's disgust and discomfort.

"You know that's not what I meant," Susanna vocalized a pronounced sigh.

"Susanna...come here..." Elizabeth's weak, almost death-bed tone grabbed Susanna's attention. Without being asked, Reba took over bathing the baby. Elizabeth patted the cot beside her, signalling Susanna to sit, then finished folding and tying up an old leather letter pouch. With great ceremony, she took the candle and dripped wax all up and down the flap for a secure seal.

"I want you to give this to your brother."

"Michael?" Susanna was puzzled. With determined purpose Elizabeth placed the packet in Susanna's hands. "Surely, you don't really believe we'll ever see Michael again!"

"I'm certain *I* won't," Elizabeth closed Susanna's fingers around the pouch. "But I'm hoping that *you* will. And when you do, give him this."

"What's in here?" Susanna examined the packet.

"Promise me you won't open it."

"Mother..."

"Promise me. Only Michael is to open it. Promise me."

"Yes. All right. I promise," Susanna gave in, convinced the reunion with her brother was nothing more than a fantasy in her mother's fevered mind and would never happen.

"Put it in a safe place," Elizabeth released her daughter's hands and the letter pouch.

"All right, Mother! I said I would!" Susanna got up with her familiar exasperation. "I'll put it in my—" she stopped short with a gasp. On her knees in front of Susanna's precious steamer trunk—the one she had accused Reba of deliberately dropping in the mud—Sally Swimmer had pulled Susanna's satin wedding dress out onto the ground. She pressed the delicate fabric gently to her cheeks. Susanna emitted a piercing shriek. "Get away from there! You savage little devil!" She roughly pushed Sally away from the trunk, then snatched the wedding dress and examined the tiny hand prints all over it. Terrified, Sally began to cry under the onslaught of Susanna's continued tirade. "You've ruined it! You little wretch! That's my wedding dress! Go on! Get out of here!" She made little kicking motions, herding the half-crawling, half-stumbling, petrified little girl before her. "Go back to where you belong!"

Sally finally regained her footing and started to run but had only taken a couple of steps before she crashed into the legs of her older sister, Martha.

"She didn't mean to harm it," Martha glared at Susanna.

"Well, she *did* harm it! Just look! She's ruined it!" Susanna held the dirty dress up for Martha to see. "I can't believe she did this!"

"She had a little doll. Made from the same material," Martha tried to explain her little sister's infatuation with the wedding dress. "Father brought it from Charleston."

"Well, this is obviously not her doll, now is it?!" Though she frequently demanded apologies, Susanna seldom accepted them—and never graciously.

"No," Martha tried to remain calm. "It isn't. Her's was lost somewhere on the way to this place. She loved it more than anything."

Susanna felt she might have reacted a little too harshly—but only a little! She softened the tone of her scolding—but only a little. "Well...I didn't mean to frighten the child. But if her doll was so precious, she should have been more careful. She'll just have to find something else to *love*. And someplace else to play. She shouldn't be here. In our area."

Sally peered out timidly from behind her big sister's legs at the evil witch who had screamed at her. Martha recalled Michael Drummond and Annie Walker and how much she had liked them. She remembered with fondness the handsome young man who was so well liked by her people and who had so romantically carried his *Tsa-la-gi* bride off into the sunset, fleeing the *yo-negs'* justice for an act committed in the defense of his woman's honor. How could this possibly be that man's blood sister?

Sally's attention soon drifted to Margaret Elizabeth. A delightful pixie, but not worth venturing out for a closer look, Sally thought, or, God forbid, perhaps to touch. Martha continued staring at Susanna who didn't know what to make of it.

"What? What is it you want?" Susanna demanded impatiently.

"I came to ask your help..." Martha said, wondering if she hadn't made a foolish mistake.

"*My* help? How on earth could I possibly help you?"

"Some of the men who just arrived killed a deer along the way. A large buck," Martha hesitated. It would probably be best to just leave right now, she thought.

"What does that have to do with me?"

"We need help skinning it. Preparing it to cook," Martha was embarrassed. "You could have some…"

"A nice piece of venison would be wonderful!" Elizabeth had sat up on the edge of her cot and was listening to Martha. "I can't eat this spoiled salt pork. It gives my stomach a terrible turn."

"Mother!" Susanna flashed her usual irritation. "I'm not going to bloody my hands on any animal. I can't believe you'd suggest such a thing. Father will bring us back something to eat. We're having nothing to do with these Indians."

In an instant, Martha's embarrassment switched to quiet rage. "*These Indians?* Who do you think you are?! You're afraid some *thieving Indian* is going to come in here and steal your precious things?"

"Most of which are damned worthless, under the circumstances!" Elizabeth snapped. Neither Martha nor Susanna had seen her approaching with an armload of Susanna's belongings taken from the trunk. She pushed past them and headed for a growing pile accumulating just outside the shelter. It was a collection from other families of excessive, frivolous and otherwise useless items grabbed up in their emotionally traumatic eviction. "I can't believe some of the things you brought along!"

"Mother! What are you doing?!" Susanna had already forgotten about Martha Swimmer and her foolish butcher's request. She was appalled at the sight of Elizabeth tossing perfectly lovely items onto the rubbish pile. Susanna had seen her mother truly angry no more than once or twice her entire life. Elizabeth stormed back and pushed right up in Susanna's face.

"I am sick to death of your whining, moaning self-pity! Do you hear me? Sick of it! Enough is enough!"

Susanna was completely embarrassed. Her mother had scolded her like a recalcitrant child. And in front of an Indian! Determined to regain control, she took a condescending tone.

"Mother, dear. This is just your fever talking." She attempted to guide Elizabeth back to the cot, but the frail, sickly woman pulled free.

"Take your hands off me, young lady! You're going to listen to what I have to say!" Elizabeth snapped and went about gathering up another armload. "You think I'm just some weak, mindless, babbling old woman because I'm eaten up with this damned disease? For most of your life all I've had the strength to say is *mind your manners* and *please don't fight with your brother!* Well I'm *not* just some feeble old hag! I am your mother! Show me some respect! Stop your infernal belly-aching, get up off your lazy behind and *do* something! I don't care if it's nothing more than shovelling manure! Do something! Make yourself useful because, little girl, I'm here to tell you we are at a crossroads! Things—and people!—that are of no use will be left behind! Do I make myself clear?!"

She tossed the second load outside with the rest. Exhausted from the work and the tirade, Elizabeth made her way weakly back to the cot. Susanna—and all the others who had gathered—were in a state of shock. Even Ezekiel had come in from outside and stood gaping in amazement. Susanna looked to Reba—an unlikely source of support—pleading for sympathy. Reba avoided her eyes, trying to hide the hint of a smile tugging at the corners of her mouth. Ezekiel had endured years of Susanna's petty rebukes and reprimands. Other than that, she had never engaged him in any civil exchange he could recall. Strange she should now look to him for solace. He astounded even himself by speaking.

"You heard what yo' Momma said." He handed her a shovel and walked away. In the awkward silence that followed, everyone else began drifting back to their own areas, leaving Martha and Susanna.

"I'm sorry," Martha said softly. "I didn't mean to cause trouble."

Sally parroted her sister, "Sorry. I didn't mean trouble."

Unable to meet Martha's eyes, Susanna looked down at the wedding dress she still held. It symbolized her marriage, her wedding day—the most beautiful of her young life—and her eternal union with Peter. How dare a dirty little Indian urchin touch it! She leaned Ezekiel's shovel against the nearest shelter pole and brushed idly at the tiny, smudged hand prints. Ignoring Martha, she folded the sacred raiment and placed it back into the trunk. Susanna bit her lip. Despite her tears she was determined not to make a sound. Elizabeth coughed. Having somewhat regained her composure, Susanna stood erect and dabbed at the tell-tale tears with her sleeve.

"Excuse me," Susanna said coldly, looking past Martha, not at her. "I have to see to my mother."

"Tell Mrs. Drummond I'll bring her some venison stew,"

Martha said. Susanna cocked her head defiantly and moved past Martha and Sally without a word.

"Was she crying?" Sally asked softly.

"I doubt it," her sister answered. "People like her don't cry. Come on, we have work to do." Quietly they slipped from the Drummonds' area.

29

The fire-red reflections from the sun coming off the Hiwassee River stretched into the distance. Just like at Coosawattee, an endless train of Cherokee wagons and overloaded horses, escorted by U. S. cavalry and infantry, militiamen of the Georgia State Guard and volunteers from Tennessee and North Carolina, streamed into the concentration camp. The captives were led, prodded and driven through the gates of the sixteen-foot high walls, identical in every respect to Coosawattee and all the other camps scattered throughout Cherokee territory. One difference was the greater number of Indian Agency buildings and a much larger contingency of military tents outside the Hiwassee camp. One of the agency buildings had been requisitioned by General Winfield Scott. He had allowed the Cherokee capital of New Echota to remain the center of military operations for the roundup of *Tsa-la-gi* captives but found himself spending much of his time farther north at Hiwassee. Tied to the hitching post in front of the headquarters building stood Clancey, the spotted gray horse belonging to William Drummond.

Inside, the golden glow of the setting sun bathed the room with an artificial warmth. A large map of Cherokee territory covered one wall. General Scott was seated at an expansive oak desk where he poured over the papers and reports being shoved under his nose one after another by a swarm of *aides de camp*. The general paused occasionally, leaning to receive whispered messages from Corporal Edward Mears, his chief administrative assistant. Dispatch riders hustled in with news and status reports and departed with freshly issued orders bound for one sector or another. A private in shirtsleeves constantly erased and rewrote figures scratched on a large slate board opposite the map, updating the population figures of the various camps—a difficult statistic to accurately maintain, because the Indians were being very uncooperative in the role taking and head counts. Many had escaped, heading into the hills and mountains of North Carolina and eastern Tennessee.

William Drummond waited patiently to one side, out of the traffic. His hands were folded behind him. A messenger dashed in and spoke in a low voice to General Scott. The general's brow furrowed with displeasure. From across the room William couldn't hear the murmured exchange nor could he read the scribbled note before the messenger dashed out. Eventually the traffic thinned. General Scott rummaged through the clutter on his desk for a cup into which he drained the last drops from a bottle.

"It's getting out of control, Mr. Drummond! This whole unpleasant mess is threatening to blow up in our faces." Scott searched patiently for a fresh supply of distilled relief.

"Sir?" William ventured a deferential step forward.

"That last messenger—" the general gestured toward the door. "We're getting reports of U. S. soldiers being attacked by renegade Cherokees. Two of my men were killed yesterday. There are rumors of an Indian uprising. Too many are dying. On both sides."

"I'm certain it's just an isolated incident," William said, but he really wasn't *certain* of anything any more.

"Nevertheless! It fuels the fear that stands ready to bolt the restraints of reason and burn a destructive path across this entire part of the nation," Scott said, making a wide sweep with one hand while with the other he continued shifting papers or opening drawers in search of more whiskey.

"I can speak to the tribal leaders," William offered. "I'm sure it won't happen again."

"Hell," the general said with the fatalistic resignation of a man faced with an impossible task, "for all we know, Drummond, the soldiers provoked it." He looked in a wooden box on the floor beside his desk, then kicked it aside. "The fact remains: the camps *will* be completed. The Cherokees *will* be gathered into them and, if there remains a shred of sanity among the leaders on both sides of this poisoned issue, they *will* be transported with God's speed to the west. Anything less, I assure you, will result in tragedy for all concerned." With mounting frustration, he ransacked the final drawer and was pleasantly surprised to actually find a bottle. He opened it with a vengeance and sniffed it before trickling the amber treasure into his cup. "I must say, Mr. Drummond, when we first met in New Echota, I had no idea you were Cherokee."

"To tell you the truth, General Scott, it came as news to us all..."

Scott, uncertain of William's meaning, glanced up, then back to his pouring. "Yes. Well. As you know, we're granting temporary amnesty to key men of the tribe. We feel they can be of assistance in getting everyone rounded up as calmly as possible. Prevent a panic. Which seems bent on giving birth to itself nonetheless," he paused and took a tiny sip from the cup, then another. "At any rate...I would certainly think you qualify as one of the tribe's key men."

"Thank you, General. My wife is quite ill, and, truth be told, this will give me time to make other arrangements," William tried not to sound overly emotional in his gratitude. Some leaders, he knew, lose respect for a suppliant who appears too needy.

A second searching expedition of much shorter duration produced another cup. Scott poured from the bottle and shoved the drink across the desk toward William. "In a few days I'll begin shipping Cherokees to the west," he said, then looked up at William with genuine concern. "Where the hell is Chief Ross with all this going on?"

"*Gu-wi-s-gu-wi* is in Washington. Looking after the interest of his people," William recited the official party line, which earned him a sidelong glance and a raised eyebrow from Scott. The general exhaled heavily and pushed his huge frame up out of the chair. He went to the maps on the wall and began tracing from point to point with his finger.

"His people—*your* people—are being rounded up like cattle!" The commander's thick finger danced around the area of North Carolina, "Ft. Lindsay, Ft. Hembric, Ft. Delaney..." The finger moved down to Georgia, "...Ft. Scudder, Ft. Gilmer, Coosawattee, Talking-Rock, Buffington..." Back up and over to Tennessee the finger glided, "...Ft. Case..." Scott slapped the map in frustration. "*This* is where the interest of his people lies! What in God's name does the man think he's going to accomplish talking to politicians in Washington?!"

"Overturn the treaty," William repeated all the reasons he'd heard the tribal leaders discuss so many times. "Forestall the expulsion of his people. The loss of their—*our* homeland."

Scott stepped across the room to refill William's cup before returning to his desk.

"His intentions are good," William added. A feeble and transparent attempt to justify Ross's absence, he thought.

"God save us all from well-intentioned people," Scott said with a cynical snort. He lifted his cup and drank.

"God save us all...period," William concluded what almost sounded like an informal toast to their future.

Scott lowered himself back into the chair, found a piece of paper and dipped his quill pen in the tiny bottle of ink. "Indeed. Well, enough polemics for one day. It was nice to see you again. I mean it. I wish you and your family well in the west." The scratching of the pen on the brittle paper sounded excessively loud to William, even with the clerks and *aides* bustling about in the

372

performance of their duties. He glanced at Edward who, during this entire exchange, had remained frozen beside the door.

"You know, I have a son. I believe he's in the west," William said for no reason and to no one in particular. Scott stopped writing and looked up, puzzled, but genuinely interested. "It's ironic," William now felt obligated to elaborate. "He doesn't even know he's Cherokee. Yet, all his life he's acted like he was."

The general paused to dip the quill pen and said, "I can think of far worse things to be, Mr. Drummond, I assure you." He looked at William with compassion and respect, then resumed his writing. The personal interest he had shown—whether genuine or merely out of politeness—further encouraged William to express things carried in his heart. Things which, under ordinary circumstances, he would never have voiced to this man. But these weren't ordinary circumstances.

"He has a wife," William went on. "A lovely Cherokee girl. We haven't seen them for almost two years. It's driven his poor mother to distraction. Perhaps things won't be so bad, after all. I might even have a grandson out there somewhere.... But I'm babbling on. Forgive me."

"Not at all," the general said. He blotted the paper, blew on it and extended it toward William. "Take this to the commander at Coosawattee. I wish I could tell you it will make life easier. In truth, all it will do is buy you a little time."

William rolled the document carefully as though it were some sacred scroll, then leaned across the desk and firmly shook the general's hand. As William retreated toward the door, Winfield Scott took another drink and, with a sad expression, watched his guest depart.

* * * * * * *

The western horizon clung desperately to the dying redness of the sunset. Silhouette figures hustled back and forth past the headquarters building going in and out of the camp. William closed the door behind him and placed the tightly rolled document into his leather brief pouch for protection, tucking it securely inside his jacket. He moved aside for another dispatch rider who hurried in with more news for General Scott.

William stepped out toward the hitching post and looked up for the first time. Clancey was gone! William quickly scanned the area around the headquarters building. Finally, through the criss-cross of pedestrians and riders he spotted his horse being led away by what, from behind, appeared to be two of the white rabble who had been hanging around the camps to barter or steal whatever they could from the Cherokees. The men wore the dirty, fringed leather jackets and leggings similar to those worn by many of the whites helping the army with the round up. William figured them to be local Tennessee volunteers. Seated in the saddle was a five-year-old boy, apparently the son of one of the men.

"Hey! Hey, you!" William yelled and ran after them, dodging and darting through the crowd. "Stop! That's my horse!" By the time he caught up, they had already gone some distance from the camp. The road was still crowded with Cherokees marching in under military escort. "This is my horse!" William panted, out of breath from the pursuit. He took the reins from the boy and immediately incurred a snarling challenge from the taller of the two men.

"Like hell it is! I just bought this horse!"

"That's impossible! This is my horse," William argued. "My name is Drummond. William Drummond. I'm an attorney. I was just inside speaking with General Scott." William would lay it out clearly for them. He had all the facts. It was his horse. This they would have to understand.

"And I'm the President of the United States!" the shorter Tennesseean sneered, looking William up and down—the scruffy beard stubble, the wrinkled, road-soiled clothing, the old, rain-battered wide-brim hat. This wasn't the appearance of an attorney. Not even a Tennessee frontier lawyer.

"Hell, he's just another drunk Injun! You can smell it all over him," the first volunteer said through a rainbow of yellow, brown and black teeth.

"I had a drink with the general," William explained, smoothing out his shirt. His words brought howls of laughter from the two Tennessee men and the dozen others who had stopped to witness the confrontation.

"Yeah!" the smaller man played to the crowd, "and we just had tea with young Queen Victoria!"

The tall man pushed William on the chest and attempted to snatch the reins back, but William held fast.

"You can't take my horse!"

"I got a bill of sale right here. I paid the man twenty dollars!" the tall Tennesseean dug a tattered shred of paper from his pocket.

"What man?" William shook his head at the insanity of it all.

374

"It wasn't his horse to sell!" He reached up to help the little boy down off the horse.

"Poppa! Help! Git him off me!" the frightened child cried out.

"You keep your God damn hands off my boy!"

The father lunged at William. They hit the ground, rolling around in the mud. William's hat flew off and the leather brief pouch slipped undetected from his inside coat pocket.

William had always abhorred violence as a means of resolving disagreements, but he had reached his limit. The two men, both large and strong, struggled, kicked, choked, poked and pounded, cheered on by the crowd that doubled in size almost instantly when the fight broke out. Both men soon tired from battling the strength of the other and began rolling over and over in the sludge until they came to rest against a pair of military boots.

With their arms around each other—William clutching a fistful of beard and the Tennesseean gripping William's throat—the two men found themselves looking up into the weathered, battle-scarred face of a U. S. Army sergeant. He kicked each of the mud-caked Titans hard in the ribs, then motioned for two of his men to separate them. The Cherokee prisoners being escorted into camp by this sergeant and his patrol stood silently by. The soldiers kicked and pulled until they finally dragged the two combatants apart and jerked them roughly to their feet. William's nose was bleeding and the other man sported a badly cut lip.

"These men stole my horse!" William protested.

"He's lyin'," came the immediate denial from the shorter, non-fighting Tennesseean. "We paid twenty dollars for this horse. Got a bill of sale. Bought it off a Cherokee goin' into the camp."

"You're the one that's lying!" Despite William's near physical exhaustion, his outrage had not abated. He reached across the shoulder of the young trooper restraining him and took another swing at the tall Tennesseean. Six of the soldiers had their hands full holding back the large, enraged man who was convinced he had been wronged.

"Crazy son of a bitch claims he's a friend of General Scott!" said the Tennessee fighter. He wiped his bloody mouth on the back of his hand and studied it as though expecting to divine some mystic message there.

The soldiers laughed at the idea of this frantic, mud-covered, babbling fool who reeked of whiskey being the general's friend. Even the other Cherokee captives had to smile. William, still breathing

375

hard, looked around at the crowd but met only the eyes of disbelief, scorn and pity.

"Come on," the sergeant grabbed William by the arm. "Let's go see the general." Soon the soldiers were on the march again, moving their collection of Cherokee prisoners toward the Hiwassee concentration camp. William looked back to see the two men hoisting the little boy back up onto Clancey and receiving the congratulations of the onlookers.

"What about my horse?"

"I'm sure the general will sort it out," the sergeant patted William reassuringly on his muddy back. "Then I'll send someone to fetch your horse."

"Thank you, sergeant. Thank you." William breathed easier, believing all would soon be well and he would be on his way back to his family in Georgia. He saw neither the smirks of the soldiers nor the amused glances from the Cherokees at his naïve self-deception.

Night was full upon them by the time they reached the camp gate. William, in his expectation of getting the whole incident straightened out by General Scott, angled toward the headquarters building. One of the escort patrol gave him a rough shove to keep him in line with the others.

"Where you think you're going?" the soldier asked gruffly.

"The sergeant said I could see the general. I have to get my horse back," William reminded him. His only reply came in the form of derisive laughter from the rest of the soldiers. And finally William understood. He had been the butt of their joke. He would not see General Scott. The situation would not be resolved. And he would never see Clancey again.

"You lied!" William bellowed to the leather-faced old sergeant whose long moustache twitched slightly, no doubt with humor at William's gullibility. "You don't believe me! I demand to see General Scott!"

"Keep moving!" the younger soldier barked then dealt William a hard blow to the kidneys with the butt of his musket. William painfully staggered onward with the others. Feeling embarrassed and foolish, he glanced back toward the headquarters building. One old Cherokee man ventured within speaking distance.

"You really aren't *Tsa-la-gi*, are you?"

"Well...no...actually, yes...I am..." William stammered, still trying to stabilize his breath from the blow to his back. The old Cherokee managed a smile and shook his head.

"No. You're not."

376

A second Cherokee picked up his pace to come even with William on his other side. "You *must* be *yo-neg*. You're acting too stupid to be *Tsa-la-gi*."

As they entered the Indian Agency concentration camp on the banks of the Hiwassee River, William looked back one last time at General Scott's headquarters. In the glow of torches and bivouac camp fires he saw Scott exit the building and exchange a few words with some of his staff while Edward, his *aide*, led the general's horse around from the side of the building.

The group of captives stopped a few yards inside the gate. William continued to watch the general. He saw two soldiers help the massive commander onto his horse. When the sixteen-foot tall gates began swinging shut, creaking on their giant hinges, William realized he had been brought in with the last captured group of the day. Stunned by the turn of events, he continued staring numbly at the closing gates. He was oblivious to the barking of orders, the jostling and the bumping when he and his fellow Cherokee prisoners were roughly herded into lines where mud-splattered, resentful bureaucrats would log them into the camp's register.

PART II

Eastern Oklahoma
Present Time

I stood in Grandma Mary's doorway and stared out through the old screen door. The long shadows created by the late afternoon sun dipping behind the trees stretched across the clearing. I envied the simple life of the chickens scratching idly in the dirt around an old, abandoned refrigerator. *Icebox*, Grandma would call it. There was a tranquil solitude in being there that I recalled from the few times I had visited when I was a child. A feeling of being safe. As though the world outside the Cherokee hills of eastern Oklahoma was a completely different world. In many ways, I supposed, it was.

Boomer, the old hound dog, rested his head lazily on his outstretched paws and gazed up at me with curious, doleful eyes. I knew, despite my determined intentions before I arrived, I wouldn't be leaving Grandma's today. But at this point I didn't care. I had heard Grandma rummaging around in the kitchen for a while. The shuffle-flop of her threadbare, terry-cloth slippers on the patchy, black-rimmed remnants of linoleum announced her return. I felt her eyes on me and heard the constant, rhythmic creaking of the floorboards beneath her rocking chair. For the past hour—since she had interrupted her story to go to the bathroom—I couldn't get out of my mind the rich fabric of the incredible tale she had been weaving. They were people I didn't know, had never even heard of—outside the names of Ross and Ridge—and had never had a reason to care about. But now they were alive in my mind.

"Where do you fit into all this, Grandma Mary?" I asked, still gazing down at the dog. I knew she had stopped rocking when the boards ceased their creaking.

"I don't tell you these things so you know who *I* am. I tell you so you will know who *you* are."

From the door I watched her pour from a small jug into two cups. "What's that?"

"Blackberry wine," she said, trying to steady the jug. "I make it every year. From berries I pick in the woods."

"Maybe I'll just have some water," I said. I didn't want to hurt her feelings, but the idea of an old woman's homemade brew didn't strike my fancy.

"Try the wine," she urged. "Then, if you still want *a-ma*, we'll get you *a-ma*." I slipped my hand from my pocket and tried to sneak a peek at my watch before I remembered Grandma had

378

confiscated it earlier. I saw the smile flicker across her face.

"It's getting late," she said. "Maybe you're right. No wine. You'd better go. It's a long drive to Austin."

I walked back to the table. "Oh, no! You're not getting rid of me now! I want to know what happened to the Drummonds. William and Elizabeth. Susanna. Michael and Annie. To Reba and Ezekiel. I want to hear it all!"

"But it's such a long story," she said with an exaggerated sigh.

"I don't care, I'm not leaving!" I knew from the twinkle in her eyes I had said exactly what she wanted to hear. But it was true. I wanted to know and I wasn't leaving until I had learned more.

"Then, maybe we should order some pizza," she suggested.

"You're kidding! Right?"

"It's OK," she said. "They deliver."

"Pizza? You order pizza?" Somehow, the images just didn't work together.

She chuckled softly and pressed the cork back into the neck of the little jug. "Haven't you heard anything I've been telling you?" she asked, looking up at me. "That's how the *Tsa-la-gi* have survived. Adapting to the *yo-neg* ways. The number's there on the side of the icebox."

It took a while—almost two hours—for the delivery boy to find us, but with the sound of the Mazda pickup fading away down the dirt road, I inhaled the aroma of the deep-dish, thick-crust pizza supreme. It smelled better than any I'd ever had and would, I was convinced, exceed all previous contenders in taste as well. Grandma motioned me back to my seat across the table from her. Despite an insatiable appetite, my thoughts kept returning to the long discourse that had taken up most of the afternoon.

"Grandma, why don't more people know about this? The things that happened to the Cherokees. To the Creeks and the Choctaws—and the others. Why don't they teach this in school?"

She finished chewing a bite of pizza, her eyes squinted closed in quiet delight. She wiped her fingers on a paper towel before she finally answered in a solemn tone.

"History books are written by the conquerors, *'ge-yu-ts'*. Always. They create their heroes and set them on thrones of courage and honor. Then they forget that these pretty thrones rest on the bones and spirits of the people they crushed. They only want to remember what makes them look good. And feel good about what they did. The truth gets left in the dust."

I stared at her for a long time, in awe of the profound wisdom of this small, shriveled old woman. When she was satisfied her fingers were clean, she reached across the table and touched the tattered rag doll. Then it came back to me.

"Wait a minute!" I said. "I thought that little girl—Sally Swimmer—lost her doll. The soldiers trampled it in the mud."

"Goodness!" she looked at me, her tired old eyes widened in what I knew was feigned astonishment. "You really *were* listening, weren't you? Well, the story isn't finished, dear. Not quite yet." She took another bite of pizza and just looked at me. It was like a game of checkers. She had made her play and now it was my move.

"So, go on," I said. "What happened after they threw William Drummond into the Hiwassee concentration camp?"

CHAPTER
30

The sunlight had long since disappeared, but the day's heat refused to come out from under the long sheds of the Ft. Coosawattee camp like a frightened cat hiding beneath the bed. Dr. James Hamilton slouched along with the burden of his sixty-plus years. It was the end of another exhausting day in this prison which the politicians and the military euphemistically called a *fort*, a *camp* or a *detention center*. He led the horse hitched to a rickety wagon loaded with clothing, pots, pans and a rapidly dwindling stock of medical supplies. The doctor's long, black coat was soaked through with perspiration. Walking beside him was Quatie Ross, wife of the principal chief. They stopped at an entry of the long shelter and grabbed an armload of clothing and utensils from the wagon.

"Mrs. Ross! *A-ni-da-we-hi!*" a young Cherokee woman rushed out to meet the one they called *the angel*. Quatie's compassion for her people was legend. She had already been in some of the other camps, spreading hope and encouragement while trying to meet the pragmatic needs of food, supplies and medical treatment. It had taken little more than a woeful look to persuade her longtime friend, Dr. Hamilton, to accompany her to the camps to treat those whose condition had become critical. They both knew if the removal didn't get under way soon, it was only a matter of time before they were beset with a host of dreaded diseases—typhoid, consumption, cholera, measles—any one of which, by itself, could sweep through all the camps leaving more death in their wake than any invading army. And should these dreaded enemies come one after another—or, God forbid, at once—the entire tribe faced certain annihilation.

Dr. Hamilton began examining a sick child covered with open sores. The Cherokees had learned of the doctor's presence in the camp and had been waiting patiently for hours. The Cherokee woman tugged at Quatie, trying to lead her deeper inside the shelter.

"Please, Quatie! My sister is dying!"

"Doctor Hamilton is doing everything he can," Quatie's soft voice had an immediate soothing effect on the distraught woman. "I'm trying to find more doctors."

Other Cherokees appeared out of the darkness and began unloading the food and supplies in a peaceful, orderly manner. Despite the growing desperation and concern that the camp was bulging far beyond its intended capacity, there was no pushing or shoving or hoarding of goods among the *Tsa-la-gi*.

* * * * * * *

In another area of the shelter, Susanna Drummond Tanner shook out an old blanket and folded it in half. She looked down at the old woman on the bed in front of her.

"I think all the travelling and the rain has given you a chill," she said, trying to sound, if not kind, at least not so very harsh. "Maybe the doctor will come soon. In the mean time, you should eat some stew."

Susanna bent down and tucked the blanket around her patient, Grandma Nancy Ward Swimmer, whose expression of gratitude was laced with suspicion. The old woman looked across the congested living space to her granddaughter, Martha.

"She's right, *E-li-si*. You need to eat," Martha confirmed Susanna's advice.

Without so much as a glance of acknowledgment to Martha, Susanna went back around to the other side of the hanging blanket divider to the Drummonds' area. Frail and pallid, Elizabeth sat on the edge of her cot and ate the tasty venison stew Eva had brought her as promised.

"It's delicious," Elizabeth managed a weak smile. "Better than my own."

Eva smiled and squeezed Elizabeth's hand. She rose with a glance at Susanna but didn't speak before disappearing back around the blanket wall, leaving mother and daughter alone. Susanna made a half-hearted pass at straightening up, then fluffed the ratty pillows behind Elizabeth.

"Whatever it is, just say it!" Elizabeth's eyes had been following Susanna.

After a prolonged silence Susanna finally spoke. "It's...well, it's just...I can't believe you spoke to me that way!" She couldn't forget the humiliating public scolding her mother had given her. Never in her life would she have imagined such a thing possible. She was a Drummond! She had been to finishing school!

"I can't believe I *had* to!" Elizabeth fired back. "I'm sorry if I embarrassed you."

Susanna took the empty metal plate away and wiped Elizabeth's mouth. Elizabeth coughed, fighting hard not to let it develop into another uncontrollable spasm. Susanna pushed her gently back to recline on the cot and tucked a blanket around her. It was commonly believed best—despite the heat—to keep the sick warmly wrapped to sweat through the fevers and, hopefully, break the hold of whatever it was that gripped them.

"Have those soldier boys located Peter yet?" Elizabeth asked. Her breathing was rapid and shallow. She feared a larger taste of the acrid air would only induce another cough.

"Mother, as far as these soldiers are concerned, we're nothing but Cherokee Indians," Susanna said. She blotted a drop of spittle from the corner of Elizabeth's mouth.

"Peter could help us, Susanna. Swallow your pride, girl."

"Peter has made his position perfectly clear. He obviously doesn't need Meg and me. We don't need him. Father will get us out of this."

Elizabeth voiced the concern they had both been feeling. "He should have been here by now."

From Susanna's *room* in the Drummond area Meg began to cry, adding to the endless chorus of fevered babies who shrieked inconsolably.

"I'll be back to check on you. Try to rest," Susanna told her mother. Reba had picked up the crying baby. She watched Susanna and Elizabeth from the edge of the blanket wall. "What are you staring at?" Susanna snapped.

"Sorry, Missy," the black woman's apology was sincere. "Reba didn't mean nothin' by it." Susanna gently rubbed the fretting child's feet.

"I think she still has a fever," she said softly.

"She's toler'ble warm, for sure," Reba agreed.

"It seems all she does is cry," Susanna's voice was charged with maternal concern. She took Meg into her arms. "Get some rags. Dip them in the water bucket."

Reba's eyes abruptly widened in shock. "Get away from there!" she yelled. "What you think you doin'?"

Her shout intensified Meg's crying and prompted Susanna to look. Even Elizabeth sat up on her cot, drawing the blanket around her. Susanna and Reba rushed to the edge of the shelter where two soldiers were scooping up armloads of the Drummonds' possessions.

"Those are our things! Put them down!" Susanna shouted.

"I'm sorry, but you have to get rid of most of this stuff," one of the soldiers said.

"You and everybody else. Brought too much," his companion added.

By the light of the campfires and lanterns, Susanna and Reba saw other soldiers hauling goods out of the government sheds and even from the tents and lean-to's scattered along the compound walls. Corporal Robert Barton strolled between the shelter buildings monitoring the house cleaning. He chatted with two friends from his squad, Privates Virgil Johnson and Miles Franklin.

"Where are you taking our things?" Susanna called out to Barton.

"There's a big bonfire," he answered politely.

Elizabeth appeared beside Reba and Susanna, small and fragile in her raspy fury. "Put them down! This instant!" she ordered the young soldiers. "You can't burn our things! I'll not have it!"

Private Johnson stepped toward them but kept a respectful distance. "Look, there just ain't enough room in the camp," he explained. "More Cherokees comin' in every day. Besides, there sure won't be enough room for all this junk on the boats and wagons when you people leave here."

"*You people!?*" Elizabeth took the phrase as an insult. "*You people!?*"

"He meant no disrespect, Ma'am," Corporal Barton hastened to defuse the situation. "But he's right. You can't possibly take all these things with you."

Corporal DeKalb, also monitoring the reduction of baggage and possessions, sauntered up to investigate the disturbance.

"What's the problem here, Barton?"

"They've got too much stuff, Corporal. Like most all the others," Private Franklin inserted. The commotion had brought Eva and Martha Swimmer from their area, each carrying an armload of their own belongings.

Corporal DeKalb, uninvited, took charge. Posturing officiously, he spoke in a loud voice to attract as much attention as possible. "All of you. Pick out what you can carry. Sell whatever you can to the white folks hanging around outside the camp. They ain't offerin' much. But it's better'n nothin'. What ain't sold gets burned."

Again Elizabeth took umbrage at the soldier's tone and choice of words. "*White folks?* Who do you think you're talking to?"

DeKalb, who normally tolerated no arguments from Cherokees, found this feisty little woman amusing, recalling her spirited belligerence from rounding them up at the old Walker Cabin. He eyed her up and down and answered with a smirk, "Cherokee Injuns, if I was guessin'."

Susanna shifted Meg to the hip farthest from DeKalb. "By *white folks* I take it you refer to that riffraff loitering about the gate

384

when we arrived?"

"Call 'em what you want," DeKalb shrugged. "Fact is, they're stayin' and you're goin'."

With the blanket still drawn around her, Indian style, Elizabeth stepped out beside her daughter. "I demand to see your commanding officer! This very minute!"

"That ain't gonna happen neither," DeKalb shook his head.

"And why not?" Susanna insisted.

"Cause he's busy. And so are we!" DeKalb was tired of being challenged. He no longer found the brash little woman amusing. "So you better start pickin' what you wanna keep or it'll all get thrown—" he stopped and snapped to attention, his eyes directed beyond Susanna and Elizabeth. "Major, Sir!" DeKalb acknowledged his commanding officer with a crisp salute.

Elizabeth, Susanna and Reba were amazed to find Peter standing behind them. His bafflement mirrored their own. Peter's uniform was disheveled, he hadn't shaved for days and even from a distance they could smell the mixture of liquor and stale body odors. The soldiers, though ignorant of the relationships involved, were fully aware of the palpable chill and sensed an emotional involvement that went beyond their understanding. The women, stunned by Peter's sudden and unexpected appearance and thrown off by his unkempt aspect, still hadn't grasped the fact that he was, indeed, the commandant of the Ft. Coosawattee concentration camp. In their minds it was simply a matter of a negligent husband and father who had taken far too long to find his wife and child. Susanna glared at him without speaking, but Elizabeth saw it as an answer to prayer.

"Peter! Oh, God! We're so glad to see you, Peter!" she started toward him but Susanna grabbed the blanket, holding her back.

"You know these people, Major Tanner?" DeKalb asked with fawning obeisance, unnecessarily concerned that he might face some sort of reprimand. Peter stared back at his wife until finally she spoke.

"I am *Mrs.* Tanner," she said with a burning softness, shifting Meg back to the other hip, "and this is the Major's daughter."

DeKalb and the other soldiers were paralyzed. "I'm—I'm sorry, sir. I—uh—there's been a terrible mistake, sir."

"It would appear so," Peter answered, then motioned to Miles Franklin. "Get their things, Private." Peter's eyes—glazed but unblinking—remained on Elizabeth and Susanna. "Come with me," he said.

"Thank God!" Elizabeth was energized by the thought of leaving this awful place. She immediately began pointing out to the young soldiers the things she wanted to take.

Peter took a step closer to Susanna. Clinging protectively to Meg, she stepped back from him. He felt her distance.

"No! Leave those things where they are!" she barked emphatically.

Everyone, including Elizabeth, looked at Susanna, baffled by her jolting proclamation. DeKalb, Barton and the other soldiers looked from Susanna to Peter, uncertain what to do. Elizabeth gripped her daughter's arm.

"Susanna. This is our chance to get out of here!"

"You can go, Mother. By rights, you shouldn't even be here. You're not Cherokee," Susanna charged the word with all the bitterness she could muster, then put her hand against her mother's cheek, both as a loving gesture and to gauge her fever. "Besides, you need to get to a doctor."

Peter inched closer. He preferred not to air his family problems in front of his subordinates. "Susanna, don't do this. Come on. Let's go."

"We don't need you!" She made her voice louder to compound his embarrassment. "Father has gone to see General Scott. So just go somewhere and have yourself another drink. Everything's all right."

"Susanna, don't be a fool!" Elizabeth said. "Yes, Peter. Thank you so much." She coughed lightly but was able to control it. "If only we could speak with the commander of this god-forsaken place..." Elizabeth's words asked. Her eyes begged.

Again, all the soldiers looked at her, perplexed. Finally Corporal Barton stated the obvious. "Ma'am...Major Tanner *is* the commander of Fort Coosawattee."

It was the women's turn to be numbed to silence. "Take their things to my tent," Peter instructed the soldiers. He faced Elizabeth and Susanna once more and tried to keep his voice low. "I'll get the doctor. We'll get you something decent to eat. I can explain everything."

"There's nothing to explain, Peter," Susanna refused to go quietly. "The situation speaks for itself. Meg and I—we're staying right here." She sat down on her large trunk against the shelter post and refused to budge. The stare-down between her and Peter continued.

386

"Fine," Peter gave her a dismissing flick of his hand. "Have it your way, Susanna. You always do. Mrs. Drummond," he turned to Elizabeth, "you may come with me. Corporal, find Dr. Lassater and have him report to my tent."

"Yes, sir," DeKalb saluted sharply and was about to depart.

"No!" Elizabeth stopped him. "Don't bother. I'm staying here."

She walked in little steps to the trunk—struggling to stifle another cough—and sat down beside Susanna and Meg. Susanna put her arm around her mother and glared defiantly at Peter. The dumbfounded soldiers looked at their commander. Peter took a deep breath and chewed his lower lip as though considering his options. As though he actually had options to consider.

"As you wish," he finally said in a flat, polite tone one would use in addressing complete strangers. "You know where you can find me." He tore his eyes from them and turned to Barton. "See that they get extra rations of milk, Corporal." Peter pivoted with a scorching look back at Susanna. "That is, if Mrs. Tanner has no objection."

She wished more than anything to find some way to hurt him. And she found it. "I never thought I'd say this, but in one point I must agree with something my brother once said."

"And what might that be?" Peter instantly regretted asking.

"You are, indeed, a pretentious ass!" Susanna immediately turned away and concentrated on Margaret Elizabeth, letting Peter know unequivocally the conversation had ended.

"Carry on," Peter growled at the soldiers.

"Yes, sir," they all snapped their salutes.

The major and his men began to move away. Elizabeth called out to Peter. He stopped and looked back. "I do have one request," she asked as calmly and politely as she could, glancing at Reba and Ezekiel. "Our friends...the Campbells. They don't belong here. As commander of this...this *place*...I'm asking you to provide them with a wagon and to vouch for their free status, should they wish to leave."

"Consider it done."

"Thank you. That's all." Elizabeth had nothing more to say.

Susanna waited until Peter and the soldiers had gone. "You don't have to stay here, Mother. This is between Peter and me. You should see the doctor."

Elizabeth focused on Meg and changed the subject. "Tomorrow we must find some berries or some fresh fruit for this child..." She was gripped by another coughing fit. Through sheer force of will she overcame it, then began sorting through their possessions, tossing unessential items onto the sell-or-burn pile.

* * * * * * *

Corporal Robert Barton and his men, Privates Miles Franklin and Virgil Johnson, had been the last to leave. They moved along the side of the shelter building where they passed Martha Swimmer standing just outside her family's area, her arms loaded with things to be discarded. Corporal Barton caught her eye and stopped. He remembered, as she obviously did, their first encounter when he and his men, in conjunction with DeKalb's unit, had taken the Swimmers captive. He was drawn to the incomparable beauty of her face but found himself equally unsettled by the cold judgement in her eyes.

"Not all of us are like Corporal DeKalb," he offered clumsily. "Or even like the Major, for that matter."

"One *i-na-dŭ* is pretty much like the next," she raised one eyebrow.

"*I-na-dŭ*. That means snake, doesn't it?" Martha was impressed he had bothered to learn even one *Tsa-la-gi* word. She couldn't resist a hint of a smile. Barton caught it and stepped closer, speaking in a friendly, confidential tone. "What's the story with those two? This woman and the major?"

Martha studied him briefly and reaffirmed what she had noticed the first time she saw him—that his eyes possessed an uncommon gentleness. She recalled the day at the cabin when he had grabbed her and wrestled the knife away. Even then he had acted without malice. Still, he was *yo-neg* and not to be trusted. But it wouldn't hurt to provide the information he sought.

"Turns out she's *Tsa-la-gi* and never knew it. She thinks it's wrong for her to be here."

Barton surveyed the entire camp before answering. "If you ask me, it's wrong for *any* of us to be here..." It wasn't the response she had expected. He finally looked back to her and their eyes met in a fleeting moment of understanding. Finally, Barton bashfully touched his hat and excused himself. "Corporal Robert Barton, at your service, Miss....?"

"Martha Swimmer."

"At your service, Miss Martha Swimmer." He hurried off to catch up with Franklin and Johnson. She stared after him, a little puzzled, a little interested, and still more than a little suspicious.

* * * * * * *

Hours later, Elizabeth Drummond sat outside the shelter in the old chair that so far had survived the property purge. Shadows danced all around her. The glimmering orange and yellow glow from the bonfires burning all over the camp played across her drawn and sallow face. She tilted the tiny blue vial to her lips and with a customary grimace swallowed the final bittersweet drops from her last bottle of laudanum. She watched Ezekiel stacking and rearranging their remaining boxes and trunks to maximize the available space in the overcrowded shelter.

Even at this late hour, Coosawattee was a beehive. As far as one could see up and down the corridors between the shelters, armloads of goods were being heaved onto raging fires. Local whites, who in the beginning had confined their aggression to the area near the main gate, had brazenly made their way deep into the camp, bartering, even begging for the discarded goods of Coosawattee's captives. One Cherokee family, when offered an insultingly paltry amount, proudly refused and tossed a beautifully hand-carved jewelry box with gold and silver inlay into the white-hot center of the fire. The same was done at virtually every conflagration throughout the camp—here a fine secretary of intricate design; there a delicately handcrafted table; somewhere else a mixed-blood family's collection of Robert Burns volumes and other books they wouldn't be needing. Elizabeth heard the disappointed groans of the whites, followed by their anguished but too-late assurances that they would have paid more. It was only their opening offer.

Soldiers, Georgia militiamen and volunteers from Tennessee and North Carolina lounged around. They watched, drank and engaged in loud, boisterous conversation. Many were raucous and insensitive. Some openly made peccant jokes about the plight of the Cherokees while others leered lasciviously at the Cherokee women and girls. A few of the volunteers and a number of the younger soldiers were more sympathetic, even kind, and didn't hide their dislike for their present assignment.

Reba came out of the shelter and put a blanket around Elizabeth's shoulders. When Reba started back inside, Elizabeth took her wrist and held it tightly. "Reba, listen to me. You are not slaves. Ezekiel is a freedman. You're a freedman's legal wife. I want you to go. You and Ezekiel."

Reba gave Elizabeth an affectionate slap on the back of her hand. "Now, Miz 'Liz'beth, you know me and Miss Susie been carryin' on with one 'nother since the day that little gal first talked. Reba don't mean nothin' by it. An' I s'pect Missy don't mean it, neither."

"No, Reba," Elizabeth shook her head. "It has nothing to do with Susanna. We're in a desperate situation. There's no reason for you and Ezekiel to even be here."

"Hush!" Reba said, fussing to make her friend more comfortable. "You done got crazy with the fevers again."

"No. I mean it," Elizabeth tugged at Reba's arm. "Get as far away from this place as you can. There's death here, Reba. I can feel it."

"I just can't leave you, Miz 'Liz'beth. Not in yo' condition."

"Nonsense!" Elizabeth knew her plan would be difficult to sell. "All other things being equal, you know good and well you wouldn't freely choose to be here. No one would. So go."

"Mmm-hmm," Reba gave her familiar response that appeared to be in agreement but left little doubt of her true feelings. "You jes' be quiet now. Eva over there's boilin' up some herb tea. For you and Mister Charlie's momma."

"Reba, don't make me get nasty with you," Elizabeth knew she could never truly be upset with this woman, but she was determined this time to have her way. "I'm ordering you to go. And I want you to take most of our things."

Reba took a seat on Susanna's trunk next to Elizabeth's chair. She took Elizabeth's frail hands in her large, bony ones. "Miz Liz'beth, Zeke an' me, we can't do that. No..."

Elizabeth jerked her hands away and wagged her finger in Reba's face, trying to sound firm, even acrimonious. "Like hell you can't!" she said as loudly as her weakened condition would allow. "You'd rather let this thieving Georgia riff-raff take our things?"

"I know what you tryin' to do, Miz Liz'beth," Reba dipped her eyes with uncharacteristic vulnerability, "but I—we—you and me—been together so long—"

"I'm thinkin' she might be right, Reba," she was interrupted by the soft voice of Ezekiel who had appeared out of the darkness to stand behind his wife. "Maybe we oughta head on up north. Go see my brother, Jedediah."

"Shut yo' mouth, Zeke," Reba fired back over her shoulder. "You ain't goin' no place."

"No, listen to him, Reba," Elizabeth seized on the two-against-one advantage. "He's making sense. Nothing else around here makes sense, but...just do it. Go. I beg you." With tears welling up in her large, doe-like brown eyes, Reba looked from Ezekiel to Elizabeth and couldn't speak.

* * * * * * *

By an hour after sunrise Reba and Ezekiel had filled the wagon Major Peter Tanner had arranged for them with a few of their own things and other items Elizabeth had persuaded them to take along. Elizabeth also insisted they take one of the old mules—the same ones Ezekiel had worked for years pulling logs, clearing stumps, even birthing a stubborn calf or two. Ezekiel heaved one final bundle up with the rest, threw a rope over the top and began lashing it to the wagon staves. Elizabeth, with the blanket still wrapped around her shoulders—now a permanent part of her wardrobe—stared out in the direction of Coosawattee's main gate. For the last half hour Reba had been smothering Meg with kisses, hugs, pats, cuddles and strokes. With great and evident pain, she finally relinquished the child to Susanna. The two women looked into each others eyes. Reba forced a crackled little laugh.

"Always knew they'd be tears of joy in yo' eyes if you ever seen Reba's big ol' butt goin' off down the road."

"Reba..." Susanna struggled to find the words. "I was always so wicked to you..."

Reba wiped the tears from Susanna's cheeks. "That you was, Chil'. That you was."

"Thank you," Susanna gripped the black woman's arm. "For everything you've done for us. Especially for my mother."

"An angel if ever they was one," Reba's voice was an emotionally choked whisper. With a final squeeze of hands, Reba left Susanna and went out to stand beside her employer and dear friend of so many years. She knew Elizabeth had riveted her eyes on the gate for no other reason than to keep from having to watch her and Ezekiel preparing to leave. She also knew Elizabeth was deeply concerned about William, who had gone away early the day before, promising to return by nightfall. "Mistah William gon' be all right. He'll be here d'rectly. Reba feels it. Best he didn't try comin' back at night, no how. Too dangerous."

"I hope you're right, Reba."

"Reba always right. Folks jes' don't listen to Reba."

"Be careful," was all Elizabeth said. Reba tried to turn Elizabeth to face her, but Elizabeth resisted with unexpected strength. "Don't make me look at you," she said, "or I won't be able to let you leave. Just get on out of here."

Reba understood. She patted her friend affectionately on the shoulder. "We gon' miss you somethin' awful...you say our good-bye's to Mistah William..."

Elizabeth held her hand up as if to say *No more. Just go.* Reba pulled the blanket snugly around Elizabeth from behind, a loving hand lingering on the sick woman's shoulder.

* * * * * * *

By mid morning a new wave of captives was streaming in under military escort through the large main gate. Ft. Coosawattee crouched like a giant beast with a gluttonous appetite for Cherokees, willing to devour the flesh in pursuit of its true delight, that elusive morsel, the *Tsa-la-gi* spirit.

Ezekiel navigated the mule-drawn wagon against the tide of newly arriving prisoners. The guards waved them on through. Peter had honored his promise to Elizabeth, vouching for Reba's and Ezekiel's departure. The soldiers, feeling they had stretched their luck far enough by imprisoning the commandant's wife and daughter, weren't about to risk another mistake of such magnitude.

Once the wagon was outside Ft. Coosawattee, a crowd of whites swarmed them. "You gonna sell that stuff?" a man with one eye and only slightly more teeth yelled. "What you got?"

"Nothin's fo' sale. We jes' leavin'," Ezekiel waved them off.

"Y'all jes' git on out da way," Reba scolded. A second white man grabbed the mule's harness, stopping the wagon.

"If you don't sell it to us, we might jes' take it anyhow!" he said loudly, looking to the rest of the whites for support. A third man stepped up onto the wheel hub and looked inside the wagon.

"Likely they stole it," he called down to the others. "Ain't no nigger ever had stuff this good!"

"Get down off the wagon!" the voice startled them all, including Reba and Ezekiel. A rifle barrel was laid across the chest of the white man holding the harness, pushing him away from the mule. Corporal Robert Barton made a wide swing around the front, clearing the vultures from his path. He walked up to Ezekiel's side of the wagon and handed the rifle, three tins of powder and two bags of shot up to the puzzled—but relieved—black man.

"Here's your rifle and ammunition."

"Naw, suh. That ain't my rifle," Ezekiel corrected him. But Barton looked him squarely in the eye, waiting for him to take the items.

"Yes. It is," he said firmly. "The same one you checked in when I brought you into this camp."

Reba elbowed Ezekiel sharply in the ribs. "Fool! Don't know yo' own rifle when you sees it?" She took the gun, powder and shot from Barton. "Thank you, sir." Gradually it sank in for Ezekiel.

"Oh. Yeah. My rifle," he said unconvincingly. Reba looked at Barton and rolled her eyes. She nudged Ezekiel again.

"Well? You gon' stop and play checkers wit' dese gen'l'mens, or we goin' to Iller-noise?" Ezekiel slapped the reins against the mules' rump and the wagon creaked forward.

"Have a safe trip," Corporal Barton called after them. As the wagon pulled away, Barton defiantly met the irritated looks of the ignorant white trash who felt they had just been bamboozled but weren't quite certain how. The corporal pushed his way through and marched back toward the camp gate.

* * * * * * *

The rains of a few weeks earlier were but a distant memory. With so much traffic up and down the crowded lanes between the shelter buildings, a choking cloud of dust hung thick in the air day and night. Martha Swimmer carried two baskets and Susanna Drummond had two cloth sacks draped over her shoulder. Tentatively they approached the camp's main gate. Meg was cradled in Susanna's arms. She had fallen asleep almost instantly after they left the shelter. Martha and Susanna exchanged a concerned look, but neither had the courage to speak of what they saw. A few yards away travelling parallel with them, a Cherokee family transported the blanket-wrapped corpse of a loved one out of the shelter and toward the gate. The children with them cried softly, as much from fear as from grief. The expression on the faces of the adults remained inscrutable.

The two young women forced their attention away from the death bearers. "I appreciate you doing this, Martha." Susanna was sincere. "Meg and my mother could both use some berries and fresh fruit."

"And my grandmother," Martha added. "She refuses to eat the food from the army. She thinks it's poisoned."

They stopped short of the gate. "You're sure you know where to go?" Susanna asked.

"I saw a grove of peach trees half a mile back up the road

when we came in, and the creek bank was covered with berries,"
Martha recalled. She eased the two cloth sacks from beneath Meg's
head and off Susanna's shoulder, then slipped them through her
waist sash. "I shouldn't be more than a couple of hours," she said.

"Be careful," Susanna urged quietly.

Martha took a deep breath of determination and headed for
the gate. With practiced meekness she approached the soldier on
duty. Martha recognized Private Thorpe, one of Corporal DeKalb's
patrol who had taken the Swimmer family captive. She hoped he
wouldn't recognize her or remember her attempt with the knife.

"I need to go out," she said softly, head dipped, eyes
respectfully on the ground.

"Oh, you do, huh?" Thorpe swelled in his dominant position.
"You need to go out?"

"To get some fruit. And berries," Martha said in an
entreating tone. Out of the corner of her eye she saw a couple of
Georgia militiamen and some white rabble strolling toward the gate
with their usual leers and sneers.

"Ain't nothing within miles of here," Thorpe informed her.

"There's peaches a half mile back down the road. And berries
along the creek," she said, careful not to make it appear she was
contradicting him.

"And you think I'm gonna let you sashay right on outa here?
Just like that?" Thorpe winked at the Georgians and the other
whites.

"I'll be glad to escort this purty little thing down to the
creek," one of the Georgians offered lustfully. "Yes, sir....yes, sir."

"We could have us a fine little picnic..." one of the local
whites grinned, absently picking his nose. The militiaman shoved
him good naturedly.

"Who the hell invited you?"

The other militiamen laughed and passed around one of their
ever-present jugs. It was getting interesting, a much needed livening
of an otherwise dull morning. Finally, Thorpe shook his head and
motioned Martha back into the camp.

"We been havin' a lot of escapes. From all the camps. Can't
let you go out," he said, taking great pleasure in denying her what
she sought, at the same time laying the blame back at the feet of her
own people.

"I promise I'll come back."

"You *promise?*" Thorpe laughed. "Hear that, boys? This
Injun princess made me a promise!"

394

Susanna patted Meg and bounced rhythmically to keep her asleep. She moved closer to the gate to hear the developing complications and to offer support. "We need the food," Susanna explained. "For the babies and the old folks."

"And who the hell are you?" Thorpe challenged with an amused smirk.

"She's Major Tanner's wife," Martha answered promptly, drawing a dark look from Susanna.

"No! Don't say that!" she shook her head. Thorpe gave the woman and child a closer look. Rumors of the encounter the night before between the camp's commander and the woman purported to be his wife had raced through the enlisted men's bivouac. Thorpe hadn't been present and wasn't sure. He remembered Susanna from when DeKalb's unit rounded them up at the old Walker cabin, but he recalled nothing about any connection to an army officer. He didn't want to incur the wrath of Major Tanner, but he had never seen Mrs. Tanner and didn't want to be duped by a clever Cherokee trying to escape from protective custody. Not on his watch!

"You can't go," the voice came from behind them. It was Corporal Robert Barton. Martha's first reaction was a harsh glare that said *I knew I couldn't trust you!* Barton pointed to Susanna. "You go," he said.

"Me?"

"What the hell are you doing?" Thorpe snarled, peeved at having his order countermanded. His protest was echoed by a chorus of objection from the militiamen and the other whites.

"You know you can't trust no Injun!"

"You done gone crazy!"

"What makes you think she'd come back?"

"They been sneakin' out since they got here!"

"Give the baby to her," Barton pointed to Martha. "You take the child."

Martha didn't know what to make of his calling her by name. Was he trying to be friendly? Or was it merely a condescending familiarity? She took Meg, who awoke and began to fret. Barton joined them. He gently stroked Meg's cheek with the back of his finger.

"This is a beautiful little girl," he smiled at Susanna, then faced Thorpe. "That's how I know she'll be back."

"Damn, Barton," Thorpe sneered. "You done gone soft in the head!"

Barton motioned Susanna toward the gate, then addressed

the militiamen and whites, speaking loud enough for Thorpe to hear as well. "And, in case any of you didn't know, this lady is, in fact, Major Tanner's wife." This startling confirmation melted their leers and smirks into looks of confused apprehension. Barton watched until Susanna had cleared the gate and was well on her way toward the creek before he turned to Martha. "You'd best get the baby out of the sun. Feels like she's already got a fever," he cautioned, then tipped his hat politely as he had done the night before and walked away. Martha never took her eyes off him until he disappeared behind one of the army buildings inside the main gate.

CHAPTER

31

Lewis Ross, the stocky, younger brother of *Gu-wi-s-gu-wi*, principal chief of the Cherokees, rode up to the headquarters building just outside the Hiwassee concentration camp. He led a saddled but riderless, beautiful blaze-faced roan. They drew glares of suspicion from the lingering white civilians, militiamen and soldiers, but no one stopped them. Lewis boldly returned their stares as he dismounted and tied the horses securely to the hitching rail. He refused to avert his eyes—a gesture of intimidated deference many whites had come to expect, almost demand, from all Indians. He stepped past the sentry and rapped on the door.

Soon after Lewis Ross had gone into General Scott's office, a messenger darted out and disappeared into the camp. A few minutes later William Drummond, wrists manacled, ankles shackled and with a soldier on each side, was escorted from the tiny stockade building to the general's office. The same militiamen and local whites who had laughed at William the evening before were there to witness his return.

"Well! Looka here!" one of the *yo-negs* cackled. "It's the general's drinkin' buddy! Back for more whiskey?" The soldiers, militiamen and civilians all roared. William held his head high and was ushered inside.

* * * * * * *

Minutes later, William, unfettered and accompanied by Lewis Ross, exited the Hiwassee headquarters to curious looks from both soldiers and civilians. William completely ignored them. He paused on the steps to fold a new set of documents and tuck them safely inside his jacket.

"Take care of those papers," Lewis Ross cautioned. "You're now an official member of the Tribal Council."

"I'll guard them with my life!" William assured him. Lewis untied the horses and handed William the reins of the blaze-faced roan.

"I'm sorry about your horse, William. This one belongs to *Gu-wi-s-gu-wi*. It's yours for as long as you need it."

"I can't thank you enough, Lewis," William wanted to forget the events of the previous day and the horrors of the night spent in Hiwassee's cramped, bug-infested single cell. Lewis dismissed his

397

gratitude with a wave.

"I remember a time when you came in the middle of the night to get my brother out of jail," Lewis recalled with a smile. "And you didn't even know you were *Tsa-la-gi* at the time!"

"That seems like decades ago," William said and mounted the roan. "So much has happened."

"It's only fitting, in my brother's absence, that I should repay the kindness," Lewis said. They rode away from the Hiwassee concentration camp, against the unending flow of Cherokees headed for incarceration. Both men looked at the influx of recent roundups, speaking first to one, then to another, lending words of hope and encouragement. When they reached the first intersection, the two men reined up and moved aside for another group of Cherokees being herded by an army patrol.

"Have you heard from your brother?" William asked.

Lewis shook his head, his expression troubled. "We've sent John many letters asking him to come home immediately. At this point, most of us feel he's wasting his time in Washington. It's too late to renegotiate the treaty. General Scott just told me he plans to ship eight hundred of our people out of Ross's Landing tomorrow. I'm on my way there now."

"Perhaps I should go with you," William felt obligated to offer but hoped his services wouldn't be required.

"Right now, you should see to your family. They need you," Lewis gave him the answer he wanted to hear.

"Perhaps I'll ride over tomorrow."

"As soon as *Gu-wi-s-gu-wi* gets back from Washington, there'll be a meeting of the National Council," Lewis informed him.

"We're running out of time, Lewis."

"The river is rising, *Wi-li*. It's rising fast."

"Good-bye, Lewis," William said solemnly.

"*Do-na-da-go-hŭ-i, Wi-li*." Lewis watched him ride off south toward Coosawattee. When William had disappeared around the bend in the road, Lewis rode west toward Ross's Landing.

32

Susanna found the orchard described by Martha Swimmer, although going the half mile from the Coosawattee camp gate had felt more like traversing a continent. She had never liked exercise—other than swimming, which she had excelled at only to compete with Michael for their father's approval. And she had never bothered to learn any of the forest lore or navigational skills that had so intrigued her spiteful, want-to-be-Cherokee brother all his life. On one or two occasions while searching for the orchard she found herself wishing Michael were there to help her. But as soon as she spied the first peach tree beyond the stand of birch and sweetgum lining the road, she dismissed all thoughts of her brother and repainted the images of her daughter and her ailing mother on the canvas of her mind.

She picked hurriedly through the orchard, filling her basket with the best peaches, including a few that were still green. They would ripen with time, extending the period for them to enjoy the fresh fruit. She assumed the owners of this orchard were Cherokees taken captive and might even be imprisoned at Coosawattee. No signs were posted and no one came to warn her off the property. Many peaches had already fallen and begun to rot, filling the air with their fruity, sweet fragrance of decay.

Carrying the basket carefully so as not to drop or bruise a single peach, Susanna started back toward the camp. In the confusion at the gate, she had failed to get the two cloth sacks from Martha, so she was saving the smaller basket for berries. Angling off the road through the thick brush, Susanna followed the babbling sound to the creek. At the water's edge she pushed aside the heavy undergrowth of vines and ferns to find herself facing a riot of plump, juicy blackberries and mayberries blanketing the steep slope of the opposite bank. She negotiated her way down the incline and found a large, flat rock that formed a promontory out into the shallow stream. There she set the basket of peaches. Taking the empty basket, Susanna lifted her skirts and waded across, pausing in the middle to enjoy the cool water swirling around her ankles. She untied the large blue bandanna from her waist and dipped it into the creek. When she reached the other side, she wrung out the excess water and tied the sash around her head, grateful for its soothing coolness.

A mere month ago, she thought, the idea of her roaming

through the forest, wading across a creek, tying a wet rag around her head and picking berries would have been absurdly remote. Now it was the most exquisite moment she had known in days. She hungrily filled her mouth with berries, savoring their divine sweetness and recalling the taste of the jellies, jams and cobblers Reba used to make. There were far more berries here than she could carry back to camp, so she would eat as many as she could while picking her basket full. Her greatest desire was, of course, to be gone from the hell of Coosawattee as soon as possible, but should they be forced to remain for a while, she would try to find this same spot in a few days. She noted an abundance of red unripe berries that would soon be black, fat and juicy, and the ample spray of hard, little green buds that would grow larger and turn red on their journey to ripeness. She must remember exactly how she got here, she thought.

In twenty minutes the berry basket was nearly filled, Susanna's fingers were purple stained with berry juice and her forearms bore countless tiny scratches from the thorny vines. She was stretching to capture a pair of huge, fat berries that enticed her from high up against the bank when she froze at the clamor of baying hounds. Seconds later she heard the splashing of someone running through the shallow stream. Susanna crouched among the vines behind a thick myrtle bush. She had barely pulled the basket of berries close to her before three Cherokee men exploded around the bend, running right down the center of the creek. Instinctively Susanna knew they weren't Cherokees eluding the round up patrols, but rather men who had escaped from Ft. Coosawattee. All three men looked directly at her when they ran past. Her throat constricted with terror, preventing her from crying out. She recognized the older man in the middle from the camp, though she had never spoken to him and didn't know his name. The one in the lead seemed to know his way, and the teen in the rear greatly resembled the older one in the middle. Susanna assumed they were father and son. She found it strange that her fear of them had vanished. Somehow she knew they meant her no harm. Their fleeting looks even carried a trace of greeting and were charged with a silent warning to secret herself from what would follow.

The hounds rapidly closed the distance. Susanna pressed back against the bank when the dogs appeared along the opposite side, sniffing and whining. They were having difficulty picking up the scent of the three Cherokees. A few seconds later, three soldiers rode up behind the dogs. Susanna remembered Stevens and Higgins

400

from Corporal DeKalb's unit—the ones who had driven them from the Walker cabin. The third soldier she didn't recognize. They sat on their horses, watching the dogs. Terror gripped Susanna tenfold. She knew the slightest movement in the dried leaves would be heard by the dogs, possibly even by the soldiers. She felt a slight breeze blowing from across the creek and knew she was downwind from them, a point in her favor. There was a flash of self-congratulation for even having thought of the direction of the wind, though she knew it was a matter of pure luck that would turn on her should they cross to her side.

The soldiers looked behind them at the sound of a fourth rider making his way more awkwardly through the thick brush. Stevens shifted his horse to one side to reveal Major Peter Tanner—dirty, unshaven, his uniform tunic partly unbuttoned and a whiskey bottle hanging loosely in one hand. From the unsteady way he sat his horse, Susanna knew that her husband was quite drunk.

The hounds suddenly picked up a scent or heard a noise and were off. Their loud baying echoed back down through the creek bed. The three soldiers dashed off in pursuit with Peter following at a slower pace. Shortly Susanna heard the hounds change from the loping bay of the chase to the frenzied, high-pitched barking at their cornered prey. Almost immediately they were joined by shouts from the soldiers.

"Halt!"

"Stop, or we'll shoot!"

"They're getting away!"

"Not this one! I got him!"

Susanna knew by the exchange that the three Cherokee men must have stopped running shortly after passing her and had found a place to hide. Discovered by the dogs, they had resumed their flight, but one of them had not escaped. She wondered which one it might be. Peter took another drink and tossed the empty bottle down, then drew his pistol and spurred his horse in the direction of the shouts.

Emerging from her brushy hiding place, Susanna followed, crouching low and staying against the creek bank. She didn't know what insanity prompted her to do such a foolish thing and thought perhaps the fact that it was Peter had momentarily given her a false sense of security. Though she couldn't see what was happening from her position down in the creek bed, Susanna recognized her husband's irate voice.

"Where's the rest of your bunch of runaway cowards?" he shouted at the captured Cherokee, who apparently refused to answer. "Talk to me, God damn it!" Peter yelled in a thick-tongued slur.

Susanna crossed the creek where the water—barely an inch or two deep—raced over a bed of rocks. She worked her way up to the base of a mighty oak whose gnarled and twisted roots were exposed like giant, arthritic fingers clinging desperately to the eroded creek bank. The swirling root system formed a tiny grotto, offering seclusion. She leaned out and stretched up just enough to peek—from ground level—around the edge of the tree. In the clearing Higgins and the other soldier held the older Cherokee's arms while the hounds nipped savagely at his legs and feet, undeterred by the Cherokee's defensive kicks. After a few minutes of this baiting sport, Stevens pulled the dogs away. Peter's back was to Susanna. With his pistol hanging loosely at his side, he stopped a few paces from the Cherokee.

"I'm asking you one more time," Peter slurred. "Where did they go?"

"*Tla-ya-qua-n-ta*," the frightened *Tsa-la-gi* answered.

"Like hell you don't know!" Higgins jerked at his arm.

"Every Indian I ever knew was nothin' but a God damned liar," Peter said. Then with a little wave of his pistol he added, "Let him go."

"Sir?" Higgins gave Peter a confused look.

"I said let him go! I don't feel like taking him all the way back to the camp."

Higgins and the other soldier released their prisoner. The Cherokee backed up a few paces, eyeing the soldiers suspiciously before turning to run. He had gone no more than three or four steps before Peter raised his pistol and fired, hitting the Cherokee in the back, just left of center, straight through the heart. Only the echoing report of the shot kept them from hearing the sharp cry of horror that escaped Susanna's lips.

"Good shot, Major! Damn good shot!" Higgins congratulated his commanding officer. He would now have an exciting tale to spin around the campfire that would make him the center of attention for many nights to come.

Peter dug a fresh bottle from his saddle pouch, opened it and took a long drink. When he lowered the bottle, he was looking across the back of his horse directly into Susanna's eyes.

She ducked down, her pounding heart ready to explode. Susanna knew he had seen her. What she didn't realize was that, in

402

his drunken state and with her uncharacteristic wearing of the blue bandanna around her head, Peter hadn't recognized his own wife. In his mind it was just another escaped Cherokee and he was pretty certain it was a woman. He pointed toward the tree.

"Private Stevens—there's somebody over there!"

All three of the soldiers looked toward the tree. "I don't see nothin', sir," Stevens reported.

"I'm telling you, I saw someone!" Peter said emphatically. "A woman!"

"A woman, sir?"

"Yes, a woman! Get the dogs over there!"

"If there's a woman, we don't need no damn dogs!" Higgins joked. He and the other soldiers started for the tree. Stevens released the dogs, but instead of going toward the creek they raced over to sniff the dead Cherokee. Higgins and the other soldier leaned out on either side of the large oak and looked up and down the creek bed but saw nothing. Had Higgins looked more closely, in the distance he would have seen the basket of peaches still perched on the promontory rock jutting out into the creek. But a basket of peaches wasn't what Major Tanner had reported, so there was no reason for Higgins to notice one. He leaned around the tree and said to the other soldier in a low tone, "Maybe he jes' *thought* he seen something...through the bottom of that bottle."

"I reckon," the other soldier chuckled. They left the large oak and rejoined Stevens and the major. Susanna could finally exhale—slowly, quietly. They had been only inches above her, but she had pressed herself back among the roots against the cool dirt of the bank and hadn't breathed. Now she held her hand over her mouth and listened to the sounds of Peter and his death squad mounting their horses and moving off through the woods.

"Come on," she heard Peter say. "Let's go find the rest of those sorry bastards."

Susanna waited. She was afraid to move. What if they came back, she thought. Perhaps to continue their pursuit of the two Cherokees who had escaped. What if the hounds circled back and discovered her scent. She waited. The woods were dank and black with shadow, the forest floor pungent with the rot of its own castings—leaves, twigs, cones, seeds and bark that would decay and become the earth itself, as would, if not discovered, the lifeless corpse of the Cherokee man her husband had murdered in cold blood.

* * * * * * *

Susanna didn't know how long she remained cradled in the roots of the great oak before she finally emerged and dashed back up the creek to recover her baskets of peaches and berries. No matter what, she told herself, she was determined to make it back to camp with the fruit she had gathered for Meg and her mother. She kept to the main road leading to Fort Coosawattee. Her emotions were in turmoil. Had the greater shock come from witnessing the murder of an innocent Cherokee man or from the fact that the executioner had been her husband, the father of her precious daughter? So deeply was Susanna immersed in her own thoughts she didn't hear the galloping hoofbeats from behind until the rider was almost upon her. Shocked back into awareness, she instinctively darted toward the woods.

"Wait! Don't run away!" the voice's familiarity pried its way into her consciousness.

Peering cautiously back around the tree, Susanna was flooded with a sense of relief. She stepped back out onto the road, set the baskets down and ran to meet her father, clinging to his leg, sobbing, unable to speak.

"Susanna! I thought that was you!" William said, as mystified as Susanna at their chance encounter. "What are you doing out here? Are you all right?" Still she couldn't answer. He dismounted and took her in his arms, feeling her entire body racked with gasping sobs of release. "It's all right, Susie," he stroked her head and held her close. "Shh. It's all right."

John Ross
Principal Chief, Cherokee Nation
(McKenney & Hall)
From the Collection of Gilcrease Museum, Tulsa

Major Ridge
Treaty Party Leader
(McKenney & Hall)
From the Collection of Gilcrease Museum, Tulsa

John Ridge
Son of Major Ridge
(McKenney & Hall)
From the Collection of Gilcrease Museum, Tulsa

Stand Watie
Treaty Party Leader (Nephew of Major Ridge)
(Unknown photographer)
From the Collection of Gilcrease Museum, Tulsa

George Lowry (also: Lowrey)
Assistant Chief to John Ross
Attributed to George Catlin (1796-1872)
From the Collection of Gilcrease Museum, Tulsa

Major Gen. John Ellis Wool
Army Commander in Cherokee Territory
(Unknown photographer)
From the Collection of Gilcrease Museum, Tulsa

General Winfield Scott
Commander during Cherokee Removal
(Unknown Artist)
From the Collection of Gilcrease Museum, Tulsa

John Jolly
Chief of "Old Settlers" in the West
Attributed to George Catlin (1796-1872)
From the Collection of Gilcrease Museum, Tulsa

33

Ross's Landing
Tennessee River
June 6, 1838

An aura of manic purpose infused the hundreds of Cherokees amassed at Ross's Landing. The *Tsa-la-gi* had known their lives would be transformed from the moment the river of more than seven thousand U. S. Army troops began flooding into their forested hills. In truth, many had known since they first learned the removal treaty had been signed on that cold, wet December night in New Echota two and a half years earlier. Regardless of when the immutable truth of their removal had hit them, they all realized the dreaded and irreversible transformation had begun.

A string of double-decker keelboats were docked along the east side of the Tennessee River. Each barge measured one hundred thirty feet in length and had a two-story *house* that took up almost the entire deck. These house-like structures measured twenty feet wide by one hundred feet long, with a rail around the top which, in effect, created a third level. Strategically located around the upper deck were five stone-and-metal hearths for cooking. The floor inside each house was divided into two equal rooms, twenty by fifty feet, for a total of four large rooms per boat. At the head of the line was a one hundred ton steamer that would pull its load of human cargo along a perilous water trail west.

The army, assisted by the usual array of Georgia militiamen and volunteers from Tennessee and North Carolina, had begun marching Cherokees out of the camps at first light. By the time they reached Ross's Landing, many were seeking the shade of the surrounding trees against the rising heat. It promised to be another in a week-long string of unusually scorching days.

Government agents scrambled to get the required census information on all Cherokees being shipped west. But the usual bureaucratic inefficiency was compounded by the impossibility of organizing such a large and constant flow of people. Once they arrived, they were continually shifting around in quiet but emotional reunions or trying to align themselves with friends or relatives in hopes of being assigned to the same boat. In addition, many of the Cherokees were simply uncooperative, either out of fear or resentment.

Lurking at every turn of the road and at every entry point into the staging area were the ubiquitous white scavengers, always looking to bargain away from the Cherokees that last piece of family jewelry or to illegally sell them whiskey for their last dollar of government allotment money. Provisions for the trip were being loaded onto the keelboats from contract supplier wagons lined up along the river bank. As soon as empty wagons rolled out, full ones moved in to take their place.

From atop a hill overlooking the swarming departure scene, General Winfield Scott, in full military dress complete with plumed hat and clanking saber, sat on his horse observing the operation. With him were his *aide de camp*, Corporal Edward Mears, three junior officers and a dispatcher, poised to dash off with orders or messages to the officers working the crowd below. Also present were many of the Cherokee tribal leaders—Lewis Ross, Charles Hicks, George Lowrey, Hair Conrad, Thomas Foreman, Going Snake and *Tsunaluska*—along with the journalist, John Howard Payne. William Drummond rode up the slope to join them. With a troubled expression he glanced frequently back down the hill.

"Mr. Drummond," General Scott greeted the tall attorney he had grown quite fond of.

"*Si-yo*," William greeted the Cherokee leaders, then made a request of Scott. "General, can you do something about these damned whiskey peddlers?"

"I've ordered them to leave," the general replied.

William pointed to a distant line of trees. Scott and a couple of his officers extended their telescoping spy glasses to have a look. Through their magnifying pieces they saw the whiskey peddlers darting in and out of the crowd, hawking their wares while keeping a watchful eye out for patrolling soldiers, then retreating to the safety of the trees to restock for another run. In addition to the whiskey peddlers, other white mountebanks and bargain seekers moved greedily among the emigrants.

"And these white hustlers—trying to take every last dollar from these people!" William added, just in case they were concentrating only on the whiskey sellers. But he needn't have worried. With a dark scowl General Scott growled to the nearest junior officer while pointing down the hill.

"Lieutenant, put the word out to every officer down there," he said forcefully, leaving no doubt as to the degree of his vexation. "Any white man not married to a Cherokee or not working directly for a contract supplier is to be arrested and imprisoned on the spot.

406

Any whiskey peddler found within a mile of this landing will be summarily shot!"

The young lieutenant rode down the hill toward the river bank. The dispatcher angled toward the other side of the landing, passing a new messenger arriving with a note for General Scott.

William kept his spyglass trained on the whiskey peddlers below, observing their covert sorties, sallying back and forth from the trees at the far end of the landing. Furious but not surprised, William discovered Titus Ogilvie, his son, Alton, and a number of their men in a shady grove at the edge of the crowd. Through the glass William watched Scott's young lieutenant ride up to them. There was a heated exchange in which Titus and his son gesticulated bitterly before riding away. They disappeared into the trees for a while, but William shifted his spyglass along what he knew to be the path back to the main road. When they emerged from the trees, Titus looked angrily up toward the men gathered on the hill before riding on.

The tribal leaders observed with great concern the loading of Cherokees onto the keelboats. "Five of our people died yesterday at Ft. Gilmer," Lewis Ross gave the casualty report, just in case the general didn't know.

"And six at Coosawattee," Scott fired back, demonstrating his awareness of Ross's intent, and letting them all know he was in full possession of the latest statistics. He recited the rest of the report, "Six at Talking Rock. Three each at Buffington and Ft. Case."

"This entire exercise becomes more tragic with each day," William put in.

Scott continued to view the activity down the hill. "The real tragedy, Mr. Drummond, is that you people have sat around for two years hoping the treaty and this removal would somehow magically go away. Sympathetic as I am to your situation, you have only yourselves to blame for much of your present misery. Meanwhile, your chief insists on wasting his time in Washington talking to politicians."

"My brother will be back soon," Lewis Ross inserted.

"There'll be a National Council meeting," Hair Conrad added.

More meetings and more talk. Scott wasn't impressed. He lowered his spyglass and looked from one tribal leader to another. "Ten days from now, another six hundred Cherokees will depart by boat and a thousand more by land. If your chief wants to be a part of the fate of his people, he should forget what's going on in Washington, forget about council meetings, and get involved in what's happening *here!*" Scott's genuine concern for the Cherokees was seasoned by his frustration at their stubbornness and delay, particularly on the part of John Ross. The commander watched the proceedings below.

Payne, the journalist, looked at the Cherokees, expecting one of them to offer a rebuttal, but, each man's face acknowledged the bitter kernel of truth in the general's words.

* * * * * * *

William sat on the edge of the cot in the darkened Drummond area of the long Coosawattee shelter building. His elbows rested on his knees; his forehead was propped on the heels of his cupped hands. The night had lowered the temperature only a few degrees, certainly not enough to bring relief from the stultifying atmosphere created by the relentless, insufferable heat. Elizabeth, propped up on pillows and blankets beside him, endured another coughing seizure, which had been steadily increasing both in frequency and intensity. When the coughing subsided, she lay back, near exhaustion, her hand resting affectionately against her husband's back.

"How many dead today?" her question came soft and faint. Lately she had taken a preternatural interest in the fatality count of the concentration camps.

"More than twenty," William answered in a dull monotone without looking up.

"Nancy Swimmer has cholera," Elizabeth informed him.

"It's spreading. Through all the camps."

"I watched them carry out six people this morning," Elizabeth said with a heavy sense of foreboding. He heard in her voice a profound sadness. It was shaded with the same fearful yet unutterable concern he felt for their own granddaughter. "William, some of them were children."

He knew her pellucid, though unspoken, meaning. So far, Meg had survived. William, like everyone else, prayed daily it would remain so. But he knew there wasn't a damned thing he could do to prevent her being stricken or, worse, taken from them.

"Eight hundred left from Ross's Landing today," he gave her another statistic. "On keel boats. Pulled by steamships. Maybe I should try to get us in the next group."

Elizabeth shook her head weakly. "I couldn't make the trip now. I keep thinking I'll get stronger. Perhaps in a few weeks."

"I don't want to sit here and watch you die."

She took his hand. "You're a good man, William Drummond. We've had a decent life."

"Until now," he said with self-recrimination. "And it's my fault."

"Don't blame yourself, dearest," she consoled him. "I'm determined to get better. Before I go from this earth, I intend to see my son. To have my family all together again."

They looked out at Susanna and Margaret Elizabeth, seated on Elizabeth's old chair outside the edge of the shelter. Mother and child were bathed in the glow of a fire burning a few feet up the way. Susanna lovingly fed Meg slices of peach and a few berries from a wooden bowl.

"What happened out there, William?" Elizabeth asked. "She won't talk to me about it."

"In time, dear. You need to rest." William avoided the issue and pushed her gently back on the cot, adjusting the pillows.

Susanna had taken refuge from the horrors of the day in this intimate moment with her precious child. Feeding her. Caressing her. Watching her every move. Martha Swimmer, with Sally in tow, approached quietly and took a seat on an old wooden box. Sally was still afraid of Susanna and stayed on the safe side of her big sister. She buried her face in Martha's dress when Susanna extended the bowl toward her. Martha took a couple of berries and gave them to Sally.

"*E-li-si*—my grandmother—said to tell you she really liked the peaches," Martha was genuine in her gratitude to this woman she had never liked. "It's the first she's smiled in a long time."

"Good. That's good."

"*Wa-do*," Martha added.

"Excuse me?"

"*Wa-do*," Martha repeated. "It means *thank you*."

Susanna smiled. Martha waited until Sally had finished the berries and then they left. Susanna resumed feeding Meg. She didn't hear the footsteps approaching, but, sensing a presence—or perhaps smelling the whiskey breath—she looked up into the face of Peter Tanner. Startled at first, her expression clouded with a mixture of fear and revulsion.

"Is it all right if I see my daughter?" he asked.

"You're in charge here," she retreated to the insulation of her long-practiced sarcasm. "I suppose you can do as you wish."

"I didn't come here to argue," Peter played his humility card.

"Why *did* you come?" Susanna tried to appear disinterested. "I told you...to see my daughter."

"You never gave a fig or a feather for Meg before. Why now?"

Peter didn't answer. Instead, he reached down and picked Meg up. She was neither frightened of him nor glad to see him. Complete indifference would best describe her reaction. "I'm not a beast, you know," Peter announced in a low, husband-and-wife-arguing-civilly-in-front-of-the-child tone.

"That's comforting to hear."

"I'm concerned." Obviously unaccustomed to handling children, he tried clumsily to adjust the baby to a comfortable position. "A lot of these Indians are going to die."

Susanna pivoted on her chair, turning sharply away from him. She dipped the blue bandanna in the bucket of water at her feet and wiped her face and neck before tying the cloth around her head just as she had done earlier at the creek.

"You should know, Peter," she said over her shoulder.

"Susanna, I can get you and Meg out of here," he said quietly, making what he thought was a magnanimous offer. "I can tell them it was all a mistake. You're no more Cherokee than I am!"

She faced him with a burning glare. "Yes. I suppose if you thought I really *were* Cherokee, you'd have to hunt me down and shoot me in the back." She rose from the chair and took Meg from him. There was a flash of recognition in Peter's eyes and he noticed the berries and peaches for the first time. Susanna had calculated her words carefully. She studied his face for any revelation. His reaction told her he had figured it out. Her fear had subsided, but the revulsion had only increased. "I've been asking myself for some time now...how you could have changed so much. From the man I fell in love with. The man I married. But you haven't changed at all, Peter. I just didn't see it. Or, if I saw, it didn't matter, because—it pains me to say—I was just like you."

This loathing, rejecting tone from the woman he had married twisted Peter's lip into an embryonic sneer. "But now all of a sudden it matters?"

She looked around the camp, up and down the crowded strip between the long, open-sided sheds. "What do you think, Peter?"

"I think you have a chance to save yourself and your child. But you'd rather be unreasonable. Prideful. Even if it costs you your lives. You're becoming more like that brother of yours every day."

Susanna thought about his intended barb, then fired back,

"Thank you. I'll take that as a compliment."

Peter, seeing he was rapidly losing ground, reverted to his initial entreating approach. "Susanna...please...just...please listen to me."

"Don't beg, Peter. Hang on to your last shred of dignity as a man," she shook her head at the pathetic drunk before her. "I have to see about Mother now." She shifted Meg to the other hip and started back inside the shelter where she knew he wouldn't follow.

"It isn't over, Susanna," Peter called after her.

Susanna stopped and looked back. "It never is with you, Peter." She disappeared into the darkness of the shelter, leaving him staring after them.

"I'm telling you...this is only the beginning!" His words drew looks from Cherokees in the vicinity. From somewhere inside the shelter he thought he heard her say *Good-bye, Peter*, but he wasn't certain. Ignoring the curiosity of these Cherokee prisoners he so bitterly despised, Peter swelled to his full height and marched back toward the main gate. How dare she humiliate him in front of a bunch of ignorant Indians! Well, he would show her a thing or two. This little finishing school princess who had always prided herself on having the last word.

* * * * * * *

A steady rain had fallen for most of the night. Despite a heavier than normal spring rainfall, this would be the last precipitation the region would see for months. It would turn out to be one of the driest summers the area had ever known. When the rain stopped by mid-morning, the day was draped with a weighted quiet. The humidity and sweltering heat became a burden all their own.

Peter Tanner's bloodshot eyes scanned the woods. With sweat rolling down his face, he took a drink and swatted idly at the myriad insects that filled the air. He motioned to a group of soldiers in the trees off to his left to move forward, then signalled to his right for three Georgia militiamen to advance. Peter eased his horse steadily forward, closing in on a tightly bunched clump of trees. A young Cherokee man about twenty broke from the trees and darted across the clearing toward a narrow trail leading into the shadowy forest. Peter calmly took aim. Just before the Cherokee reached the trail, he dropped the fugitive with a single shot, then guzzled a celebratory drink. Two of the militiamen rode out through the trees, laughing, shaking their heads in amazement, truly impressed with Peter's marksmanship. Seldom had they seen a man stone cold sober shoot so well. Such an accomplishment by a drunkard they found astonishing. The stuff of legends. With laughter and good-natured compliments, they handed a wad of bills to the major, winner of their friendly wager. Peter pocketed the money and rode away, another profitable Cherokee hunt behind him.

* * * * * * *

An unarmed Cherokee man, about twenty, like the last victim of Peter Tanner's hunting party, ran swiftly along the forest path. He ducked behind the thick trunk of a pine tree and looked back down the trail. The first rider appeared in the distance. Peter Tanner led the pack consisting of his usual companions: Privates Stevens and Higgins, two young officers—first and second lieutenants—and the three Georgia militiamen Peter kept around because they always bet against him, always lost, and so far had always paid. The runaway Cherokee darted back out onto the trail, running as fast as he could. Higgins was the first to spot him.

"There he goes!"

The hunters surged after him like one murderous, galloping amoeba, thundering through the woods, down a steep embankment and across a creek. Horses collided when the riders halted in the restricted flat space on the other side. They were alarmed by what they saw. Standing atop a large rock formation directly in front of them was the runaway Cherokee they had been pursuing. He glared down at them defiantly and cocked the rifle he was holding.

"Where the hell did he get a gun?!" one of the Georgia militiamen yelled.

"I don't like it," Peter looked around swiftly. Despite his drunken state, his ingrained military training seeped through enough to recognize they had been lured into a dangerously vulnerable position. The others sensed it as well. They looked around at the cliffs on either flank and at the steep bank they had just descended before crossing the creek.

"Ambush!" Private Stevens yelled.

Twelve Cherokee warriors had materialized in the rocks and trees above and to either side of the soldiers and militiamen. They were all heavily armed with rifles, bows and arrows and the traditional Cherokee war ax.

412

"Jesus! They're Chickamaugans!" Higgins screamed, his voice thick with fear. The Chickamaugans were the fiercest and most resistant band of Cherokee renegades. Their faces were painted red and black and their braided hair decorated with war feathers.

The soldiers and militiamen had scarcely drawn their weapons before a barrage of bullets, arrows and war axes rained down upon them. The second lieutenant and two of the militiamen were killed instantly. The survivors frantically returned fire while trying to retreat, but there was really no place for them to go. Horses, wild-eyed and panic-stricken, thrashed about in the creek and attempted to struggle back up the steep embankment, making themselves and their riders defenseless targets. It was impossible for the men to reload a rifle or a pistol while trying to control the darting, spinning mounts.

Stevens and Higgins were the first to make it back up the steep creek bank, followed shortly by the lone surviving militiaman. Peter had sobered instantly. He managed to grab the rifle from the second lieutenant's riderless horse, spinning aimlessly in the middle of the creek. Steadying his own mount just long enough to squeeze off a shot, Peter killed one of the ambushing Cherokees, then furiously spurred his horse up the slippery, muddy embankment.

The young Cherokee who had baited the hunters into their death trap had reloaded his rifle. He kneeled on the large granite boulder and fired. Peter had almost reached the top of the opposite bank when the rifle ball struck him in the right shoulder. At first he was thrown forward by the bullet's impact, but when his horse made its final lunge, Peter flipped backwards and slid all the way back down the bank into the water. One of the Chickamaugans drew his knife and another grabbed a war ax, both intent on climbing down from the rocks and finishing off the wounded major, despite the covering fire from Stevens, Higgins, the first lieutenant and the militiaman from the trees along the opposite bank. The other Chickamaugans fired a final volley of bullets and arrows—killing Private Higgins and the lieutenant—before melting into the rocks or fading into the woods beyond.

*   *   *   *   *   *   *

Susanna Tanner and Eva Swimmer had brought their laundry to the creek that angled through the northeast corner of the Coosawattee compound. There they joined other women hard at work scrubbing clothes against boards. Unlike the others, Susanna was clearly unskilled and clumsy, her knuckles soon scraped raw. Eva and the others tried to be subtle, but Susanna caught them watching her.

"What?!" she asked in frustration. "What are you gawking at?"

"I'm sorry, Susanna," Eva apologized.

Susanna examined her hands. "Is it that obvious?"

"Look," Eva's voice was gentle, "use a stone..." She revealed a flat, rounded stone held with her fingertips against the heel of her hand. Susanna took the stone and attempted to use it as Eva had demonstrated. Though still awkward and inept, her efforts earned the approving looks of Eva and the other women. Susanna knew what they were doing and was grateful for their kindness.

"How's your mother-in-law?" Susanna inquired.

"She won't last much longer," Eva answered. She understood that Susanna was at least trying to relate socially to her and the other women. It was more than any of them would have expected. "And your mother?" Eva asked.

Susanna looked down at the bloodstained garment on the board before her and couldn't answer. For the past couple of nights Susanna had lain awake listening to her mother lapse into deep, painful bouts of coughing which had resulted in her spitting up blood. Susanna and her father knew—but each had refused to acknowledge—that the end couldn't be far off. Eva stood up to stretch her back and looked out at the camp.

"There are too many dying. Cholera. Consumption. God knows what else," she said. The other women grunted in agreement. Eva shaded her eyes as she observed the area around the main gate. "This doesn't look good," she said, her tone drawing the others' attention.

The endless stream of captive Cherokees trudging into the camp was nothing new. They had been watching it for days. Their eyes were on the horses being led in with dead soldiers and dead Georgia militiamen draped across their backs. When Susanna raised up to look, she emitted a sharp gasp and stepped up out of the creek.

"That's...that's Peter's horse..." she wiped her hands absently on her dress and started for the gate.

Susanna tried to get a glimpse of the men leading the horses, but they were all on the other side of the animals, blocked from view. Despite the gulf that had opened between her and Peter, he was the first man she had loved, the first man—the only man—to ever be inside her, the father of Margaret Elizabeth. She hated what he had

414

become. But there was still some love, even if only in the form of a memory, for what he had once been—or at least for what she had once perceived him to be.

The corpse patrol finally reached the camp's headquarters building. Susanna's attention remained on Peter's horse. The body was untied and lowered to the ground on the other side. The horses were finally led away, revealing the three survivors—Private Stevens, a Georgia militiaman and Major Peter Tanner. Peter was shirtless. A crude, dirty bandage around his shoulder kept his arm pinned to his side.

Susanna's initial relief at seeing Peter was promptly replaced by a renewed wave of revulsion. She didn't have to ask what he'd been doing or how he had come to be wounded. Not only had his drunken, murderous lust nearly gotten him killed, it had cost the lives of other men as well. In the midst of giving orders while his wounds were being tended, Peter's attention was inexplicably drawn in her direction and their eyes met. Susanna was the first to look away. Without once looking back at him, she returned to the creek and resumed her work. Eva and the other women saw the tears rolling down Susanna's cheeks, but none of them spoke.

* * * * * * *

The temporary headquarters of Winfield Scott at the Hiwassee Indian Agency was crowded as usual, but the only sound was the general's heavy, scratchy breathing as he unblinkingly held captive the eyes of Major Peter Tanner, who had presented himself all cleaned up and properly bandaged. He had ridden all the way up from Coosawattee to personally deliver his official report: *he and his men had suffered a brutal ambush attack at the hands of an estimated one hundred savage, bloodthirsty Chickamaugan warriors while apprehending indigenous Cherokees who had escaped from the Coosawattee detention facility where they were being held prior to their removal west.*

When Peter concluded his carefully rehearsed narrative, General Scott drew a long breath, drummed a finger on his desk and looked at Peter with a raised eyebrow.

"A hundred warriors?! Indeed. It's amazing any of you survived, Major Tanner."

"It was quite a battle, sir," Peter cleared his throat and thought it wise to remind the general of the ferocious reputation of the enemy. "Chickamaugans, sir."

Scott studied some papers on his desk and loaded his pipe. "Ah. Chickamaugans." The general recalled a few choice phrases from Peter's account. "The fiercest of all Cherokee bands. Renegades. A bloodthirsty lot."

Peter shifted uncomfortably, sensing that his story hadn't been received with complete credulity. "The men with me...they fought bravely."

"I'm sure they did," Scott pushed the papers back. "Major Tanner, I've had reports that a number of Cherokee corpses have been discovered in the woods near your camp. None of them were Chickamaugans. All of them, however, had been shot in the back."

"There's been bloodshed on both sides, General. In times like these, it's inevitable."

"Inevitable....And what, Major Tanner, can you tell me about beatings in your camp?" Scott shifted from the ambush issue. He had been receiving these reports for some time, but had told himself that he was too busy to pursue it, that this whole unpleasant business would end soon or that the reports themselves had been exaggerated.

"Beatings, sir?" Peter shrugged innocently. "Only those caught trying to escape."

"And who ordered these beatings?"

"Why...I did, sir. As camp commander," Peter was confused.

"You're lucky I don't have *you* beaten!" the general growled in disgust.

"Sir, if we don't make an example of these people—"

Scott pounded the desk with his massive fist, shouting at Peter, "*These people*—as you call them—are having their very world ripped out from under them, Major! What the hell would you expect them to do?!"

"But sir—" this reaction from his commanding officer had completely bewildered the young major.

"Shut up!" Scott snapped, then took a deep breath and gathered himself. "I'm relieving you of your command," he said, then pushed his three hundred pounds up out of the chair, picked up the candle from the bookshelf by the window and lit his pipe. "I'd truly love to send you completely away from this country, but, as you know, I have a shortage of officers. So I'm going to transfer you. To the quartermaster. You'll be in charge of procurement."

Peter had come here expecting a commendation at the very least. Perhaps even a field promotion to Lieutenant Colonel. The idea of a harsh reprimand—and in the presence of subordinates—had

416

never entered his mind. And what amounted to a career-ending reassignment was inconceivable. He looked at Edward, the general's *aide*, to see if he could detect any sign this might be a practical joke the general had concocted for one of his brilliant young officers. But Corporal Mears wasn't smiling. And neither was General Scott.

"But, sir, that's—that's nothing more than—" Peter trailed off, unable to verbalize the abhorent thought.

"A *grocery clerk?*" Scott finished for him. "Exactly! See if you can do the job without a whiskey bottle. And without killing any more Cherokees...or soldiers! That's all, Major. You're dismissed."

This was, indeed, a summary order of execution for Peter's career. The shining star of West Point. "General, with all due respect, sir—"

"Dismissed, Major!" Scott cut him off firmly. There was no doubt the general's mind was set. Unable to salute because of his wounded shoulder, Peter spun on his heel and stomped out of the office. He needed a drink.

Three-fourths of the enlisted men's bivouac tents at Ft. Coosawattee were set up outside the gate in the space where the trees had been cleared to build the walls of the camp itself. The remainder were located inside the compound just behind the handful of administrative buildings fashioned from a combination of logs and roughly hewn boards. The tents were all empty. Their inhabitants remained outside in hopes of catching a breeze to bring some relief from the warm, humid night. The crickets and night toads voiced their sympathy in a chorus from the surrounding woods. From beyond the high wooden fence came the plaintive brattle of a lonesome dog which had become separated from its Cherokee family.

Corporal Robert Barton sat writing a letter by the light of a tiny fire in front of the tent he shared with his closest friends and members of his platoon. A few feet away Private Virgil Johnson mended a pair of pants and Private Miles Franklin leaned against a stump and cleaned his musket. None of them spoke. All three, despite their youth, appreciated a moment of silence and solitude when it was to be had, declining the raucous revelry of many of their fellow soldiers. On this night, however, their revered tranquility was short lived. Frequent waves of bawdy laughter and outbursts of profanity drifted their way from two tents over where Corporal Charles DeKalb and his men, Stevens, Evans, Thorpe, Whitaker and a handful more just like them, openly drank whiskey, which was forbidden inside the camp—for either soldier or Cherokee. After one such interruption Barton watched DeKalb wander away from the group and over to the creek that ran through their corner of the camp. He opened his trousers and began to urinate.

"DeKalb!" Barton called out. "Why can't you go outside in the woods like the rest of us. These people have to drink that water."

"Yeah. I know," DeKalb laughed and finished pissing, then staggered back toward his friends.

Robert shook his head in disgust and went back to his letter. After penning a few more words, he heard soft padding footsteps in the darkness and looked up. Martha Swimmer was bringing some animal skin water bags to the creek.

"*Si-yo*, Miss Swimmer," he smiled.

"Corporal Barton," she responded shyly.

"Robert."

"We need water," she explained the purpose for her late night excursion.

"*A-ma.*"

"Yes. *A-ma,*" she smiled and started toward the very spot where DeKalb had just relieved himself.

"Wait!" Robert said sharply. He set his letter down, jumped up and trotted toward her. "You don't want to get your water here."

DeKalb and his men were looking in their direction, grinning in hopes that the joke would find its conclusion at Martha's expense when either she or Barton filled her bags with urine-tainted creek water. Martha understood what had happened.

"You want water from farther upstream," Robert said softly. Martha looked toward the creek. *Farther upstream* meant going outside the walls. Barton knew she didn't want to endure another lengthy exchange with the gate guards or subject herself to their lustful insults—or worse. "You wait here," he said, taking the skin bags. "I'll get the *a-ma* for you."

Martha watched him hurry off toward the gate, then went to wait by his little fire. She didn't have to look to feel the chilling leers of DeKalb and his men. Johnson and Franklin smiled at her but politely made a point not to gawk. She sat down beside the fire, pulled her knees up in front of her and wrapped her arms around her legs. Soon her eyes drifted down to Robert's letter on the ground. She glanced at Private Johnson and then at Franklin. Neither one was watching her. She picked up the letter.

"My dearest Mother. I hope to see you again at the end of what has proven a most unpleasant summer. God willing, I will be in Massachusetts before the first leaf turns gold. In the course of just over a month, my duties have gone from rounding up Cherokees to acting as their jailer. We have literally driven these noble people like animals from their forest homes, their mountain sanctuaries, their streams and rivers. I have seen Cherokee estates burned to the ground that would stand the equal of any in Boston or New York. And now, guilty of no crime but having Cherokee blood in their veins, they languish in these stockades — which we bravely call forts — packed with Indian humanity, bewildered children, brokenhearted wives and mothers, stunned warriors, ancient and resigned chiefs. Here they are forced to endure unspeakable privation.

Disease threatens to devour us all, white and Indian alike. Cholera, consumption and dysentery claim more lives each day. And the saddest of all is to look into their eyes and see the spirit dying before the body. In the name of civilization we have become barbarians, and those deemed savages shall, I fear, be the only ones to emerge from this ordeal with their humanity unsinged..."

Martha was interrupted when a drop of water splattered on the brittle, parchment-like paper. She looked up to see Robert Barton standing over her holding the fattened skin bags.

"Your water," he smiled down at her.

She was embarrassed at having been caught reading his letter. "I'm sorry. I didn't mean to..."

"You can read English?" he asked. She could tell he was genuinely curious and in no way meant the remark as a slight to her intelligence.

"I studied a little at the Brainard Mission, up by Ross's Landing." She rose and took the water bags. "It's a wonderful letter," she added.

He smiled his appreciation. "I was just about to tell my mother about the beautiful Cherokee girls I've seen here." Robert saw she was pleased, but it was equally apparent he had further embarrassed her. He put a hand gently on her shoulder. Martha glanced at Johnson and Franklin and, although they weren't looking, she twisted her shoulder from beneath Robert's touch. "I didn't mean to embarrass you," he apologized.

"You'll be home with your mother by the end of summer," Martha said. It was clear to Barton that, in choosing to deal with neither the embarrassment nor his apology, she had simply changed the subject. But her eyes burned into his in a way that made him realize embarrassment had nothing to do with her reaction. He had touched her. Breached the wall of familiarity. He found himself attracted to her, yet—and this he clearly understood—from her perspective they were from two entirely different worlds. Worlds which, based on the events of recent days, would not—could not—be bridged.

"And you..." he said, the excitement drained from his voice.

"I'll either be dead or somewhere in the west," she put it bluntly.

"So, why bother making a friend. Is that it?"

She saw the hurt in his eyes and regretted her words. "You've been very kind to me and my family. We won't forget you."

"Like I told you once before, we're not all alike." He glanced at DeKalb's group, then back into her eyes. She placed her hand on his forearm.

"Finish your letter, Robert," she said softly. There was an intimacy in the way she spoke his name that gripped his heart. Their eyes lingered for some time before Martha walked away. After a few steps, she looked back, her smile visible in the fire's soft glow. "*Wa-do.* Thank you for getting the water," she said just loud enough for him to hear.

"Good night, Martha," he said, unable to completely hide the longing.

"*Ma-di,*" she said. "In *Tsa-la-gi*, Martha is *Ma-di*. Good night, Robert Barton." She walked off into the night. He watched her, silhouetted by the fires scattered back down the long lane between the shelters until she had disappeared from view.

"Good night, *Ma-di* Swimmer," he whispered.

CHAPTER
35

June 18, 1838

From low in the east the rising sun breathed through the moisture in the northern Georgia skies, splashing the heavens with a brilliant red-orange glow. Every Coosawattee inhabitant—captives and captors alike—hoped it augured rain which would bring them welcome relief from the overbearing heat and dust.

Corporal Robert Barton and the men of his patrol were preparing to ride out for another day of rounding up Cherokees. By now, most of the *Tsa-la-gi* had been incarcerated in the many concentration camps spread throughout the territory that had once belonged exclusively to them. Each day's grim harvest became smaller as distances to remote cabins in the outlying areas increased. Corporal Barton had just stowed his kit bag in his tent and was about to retrieve his horse from the remuda near the north wall when he saw them—a burial detail consisting of Charlie Swimmer and three more Cherokees, accompanied by a few black men. They were hauling out the bodies of those who had perished during the night. Robert made a quick count. There were at least six corpses. Two in a wheel barrow, one on a two-wheel push-cart and three more on a drag sled pulled by two Cherokees and a black man. The others carried shovels and a couple of picks, useful tools for burying the dead but not considered weapons by the army.

Miles Franklin and Virgil Johnson joined Barton. All three looked on with genuine compassion for the personal loss this procession represented for numerous families. One old Cherokee man, his white hair flowing from beneath his blue traditional turban, kept a firm grip on the leg of his dead grandson lying on the two-wheel cart. In his other hand he carried a shovel. Near the gate, the old man had difficulty keeping up but was determined not to let go of the dead boy's leg. He lost his balance and began to stumble. In an instant, Robert was there to catch him by the arm just before he went down.

"Let me take that," Barton said, relieving the old man of the shovel. He motioned for the men pulling the cart to stop while he helped the ancient one up to sit beside the dead boy. A call from Robert brought Virgil and Miles as additional escorts to usher the funeral cortége out the main gate past the guards.

They exited Ft. Coosawattee and headed for a clearing on a

gentle slope just north of the camp. It had been designated the camp's cemetery. No one paid any attention to the lone rider coming up the road and entering the camp. Titus Ogilvie tipped his hat politely and rode past the gate guards, stopping his horse in front of a large, tattered tent. He smiled at the sign posted in front: *U.S. Army Quartermaster*.

Major Peter Tanner sat behind a table cluttered with ledger books and papers. A tin plate of fly-covered, half-eaten, watery eggs had been pushed aside in favor of a cup containing only enough coffee to darken the whiskey. Peter looked with heavy eyes at the man standing across from him.

"We're *not* old friends, Ogilvie. And just because we go back a long way doesn't mean a damn thing," he said and took a drink from his cup.

"Call me Titus. Please..." Ogilvie flashed his most ingratiating smile.

"I've never even *liked* you, Titus," Peter set the cup down and wiped his mouth with the back of his hand. "Why in hell would I want to become your *partner*."

"I'm not asking you to marry me, Tanner," Ogilvie chuckled. "I'm offering to make you a rich man. Think it over. Let me know if you come to your senses. This is where you can find me." He dug a piece of paper from his pocket and laid it on the edge of the table. Peter refused to look at it and forced his eyes to remain on his visitor.

"Get out of my office, Ogilvie."

Titus looked around the cluttered, dirty tent, then back to Peter. With a soft and confident sarcasm he said, "And a fine office it is, Major Tanner." Their eyes met in silence. Ogilvie had played this game often enough to know he had his man, even if Peter couldn't see it yet.

"Get out."

"Yes. Of course," Ogilvie said, stifling a smirk. "Well, then, you can just set fire to that little piece of paper," he gestured to the burning candle on the corner of the major's table. Titus donned his hat and left the tent.

As he slipped the reins from the hitching post, Titus knew full well that Major Tanner was, at that very moment, contemplating the little piece of paper on the corner of his desk. The one Titus had advised him to burn. And Titus was equally certain he didn't smell any smoke.

On the Arkansas River

A serious drought had parched the area for more than two years with only the occasional shower that granted no lasting relief. The Arkansas River had dropped to an unusually low level, even for this time of year. The engine of the steamer pulling the keelboats hissed loudly and the giant paddle wheel locked up and kicked out of gear. Cherokees and soldiers watched with curiosity and concern. Many of those on the middle and trailing barges leaned out over the upper rail to get a better view of the bustling activity aboard the steamer. Boat hands dashed to the foredeck with their sounding poles to measure the water's depth.

"That's it, Cap'n," the foremost deck hand shouted after examining his line. "We're hittin' twenty-six to twenty-eight inches. These keelboats draw a good forty-two."

On the upper deck the captain twisted his mouth in frustration and looked around. It was already late afternoon. Clouds had been building on the southeast horizon. He'd been up and down this river often enough to know that if they were in danger of running aground here, there would be even less water—and more problems—barely three miles upstream.

"We'll pull in over there," he pointed from the upper deck. "Make camp for the night...and pray for rain to help get this river up."

* * * * * * *

The tortuous Arkansas River meandered from one side to the other of a flat, narrow valley lying between opposing ranges of rolling hills. From a heavily wooded ridge overlooking the river, a ragged band of eight outlaws watched the steamer and keelboats in the distance. The leader of the gang was Tom Carver, a tall, evil man of forty, with a stringy moustache that hung down far below his jawline and was usually encrusted either with food particles that didn't make it all the way in or some phlegmatic expulsion that had failed to make it all the way out. A thick scar ran from the outer edge of his left eye down the middle of his cheek. It pulled the outer corner of the eye down, giving him the appearance at first glance of being very sad. But sadness it was not, for sadness is an emotion, usually suggesting some degree of feeling or vulnerability. And Tom Carver possessed neither. Cross him or provoke him and death was sudden, as many men and numerous women had learned but hadn't lived to benefit from their discovery. Carver collapsed his spyglass, slipped it into the side pocket of his long coat and moved out, followed by his men.

By dusk the Cherokees had disembarked and set up their camps. Fires twinkled up and down the river bank like fireflies in the settling darkness. Mixed with an occasional shout or the chopping of firewood was the ever-present sound of coughing. Somewhere in the fading light a medicine man chanted to the rhythmic beat of a ceremonial drum. A few of the Cherokee men and older boys returned from brief hunting excursions. They tossed their bows, arrows and blowguns down beside empty hunting sacks before the vacant looks of disappointed wives and daughters, sisters and mothers.

The soldiers—quiet, watchful, bored and generally despising their assignment—had, as usual, set up their own campsite some distance removed from the Cherokees. They had been sent along, according to the government agents, to protect the emigrants from marauders, whiskey peddlers, gamblers and prostitutes. In reality, the Cherokees knew the army was there to prevent them from escaping, at least until they were far enough west that a fugitive would be running right to Indian Territory anyway.

* * * * * * *

A young Cherokee boy carried an armload of limbs and twigs from the woods back toward his family's campsite at the edge of the river. He didn't know he was being watched from the thick stand of live oaks and blackjack. Tom Carver and his seven bandits—the youngest at seventeen, the oldest forty-five—hungrily contemplated their unsuspecting prey.

"Ripe for the pickin', Tom. Let's go," one of the robbers twitched eagerly.

Carver held up a hand to silence him. "Hold on. It'll be dark soon." He stretched his spyglass out to its full length and aimed it at the soldiers' camp. The troops, mostly young enlisted men commanded by a crusty old sergeant, were milling around, cooking their supper, pitching tents, cleaning and re-cleaning the guns they'd cleaned every night since leaving Ross's Landing and had never fired. Scanning across to the nearest Cherokee camps, Carver estimated the distance the soldiers would have to travel. In his mind he expertly calculated the amount of time it would take the soldiers to realize something was wrong, then to decide what—if anything—to do about it and, finally, how long it would take them to reach the Cherokee camps where he and his men would strike.

"Scare 'em," Carver spoke of their intended victims, "but don't shoot 'less you have to. The longer we can work 'em 'fore them soldiers come stickin' their noses in, the more loot we get."

Two of the robbers loaded their pistols. Another calmed a restless horse. Some of the men pulled bandannas over their faces and looked out at the camps strung up and down the river bank for almost a mile.

"Hell!" said one robber with no upper front teeth, "we can work our way right along the river!"

Carver pointed to the cluster of Cherokees nearest them. "We'll start here and work our way back upstream. Away from the soldiers." He collapsed the spyglass and dropped it in his pocket, then glanced up at the sky which was steadily blackening with its emerging mantle of stars. "Let's go." Those not yet wearing their bandanna masks concealed their faces and they all mounted up.

* * * * * * *

Two white doctors who had journeyed with the Cherokees all the way from Ross's Landing examined a group of sick and weary travellers—focusing mostly on the very young and the very old. Near the medicine tent two Cherokee women pried the lid off a wooden box labelled *U. S. Gov't - Salt Pork* before a hungry, waiting crowd. The men, women and children standing closest retreated a step from the fetid odor that assaulted their nostrils. The quivering gray mass was alive with maggots.

Hungry eyes passed through shock and revulsion to arrive at anger. Other eyes merely sagged in hollow defeat, lost in an overwhelming hopelessness. A Cherokee father of three bitterly dumped the entire contents onto the fire and tossed the greasy box on top. The sizzling and crackling of the burning pork gave way to the sound of pistols being cocked.

"Everybody jes' stay put now!" Tom Carver's deep, scratchy voice came from the darkness just beyond the fire's glow. Carver and his gang stepped cautiously forward into the light. The Cherokees looked at the robbers and then at each other. A few glanced in the direction of the soldiers' camp. The faint rise and fall of conversation and occasional laughter drifted toward them on the breeze, and they knew there would be no help from the distant fires of the *a-ni-ya-wi-s-gi*.

"Awright!" the youngest robber announced excitedly. "You all know what we're here for!"

"We don't have anything," one woman responded, puzzled why anyone would even bother to rob a bunch of destitute Cherokees.

"We're on our way to Indian Territory," her husband took a protective half step in front of her. "The river's too low for the boats to pass."

"We know who you are and where you're goin'," the oldest outlaw snapped.

"And we know you got money," Carver added. "Gov'ment money from sellin' your land and livestock."

"I'm telling you," the *Tsa-la-gi* who had dumped the pork on the fire insisted, "we don't have any money."

Carver lashed out and back-handed the man in the face, knocking him to the ground. The outlaw leader cocked his pistol and straddled the fallen Cherokee, pointing the gun down at his face. Wise enough to know he shouldn't move, the prone *Tsa-la-gi* nevertheless glowered up at Carver, unblinking and unafraid. Carver calmly stepped away from the Cherokee as though he considered the incident finished and it meant nothing to him. Suddenly he grabbed the woman he guessed to be the Cherokee's wife and roughly threw her face down on the ground. He dropped on her with one knee pressed into her back, then uncocked his pistol, shoved it into his belt and drew a huge knife. With his free hand Carver grabbed a handful of the woman's hair, pulled her head back and held the blade to her throat. The woman's ten-year-old son and eight-year-old daughter stepped toward their mother but were intercepted by two of Carver's men.

"All right! All right!" their father cried out. "We'll give you the money!" He got to his feet and kept a watchful eye on the knife pressed against his wife's neck. With a sweeping gesture to the other Cherokees, he said, "Give them the money!"

The Cherokees looked at each other. A few had begun reaching for bags or trunks to dig out what little money they might still have when the words came strong and sharp from the darkness.

"No! Don't give 'em nothing!"

Everyone—robbers and Cherokees alike—turned toward the voice. Vague forms outlined by the glow of the fires stepped closer until their faces were revealed. The one who had spoken was slightly ahead of the others. It was Johnny Fields. Behind and flanking him on either side were Michael Drummond, Ned Proctor, *Tsa-tsi* Starr and Redbird, the one called *Do-tsu-wa*. They no longer wore masks or darkened their faces with soot.

Tom Carver figured them for another gang of outlaws. By his own count it appeared he and his men had the intruders outnumbered. Unless there were more gunmen hiding out in the brush. And though Carver would kill a man at the slightest provocation—or even without, if it suited him—a gunfight right now wasn't what he wanted. He had come for money. Gunshots would only bring the soldiers. Possibly before he and his men had collected enough to make it worth the effort.

"We're already workin' this camp," Carver snarled at Johnny who, by his forward position, was assumed to be the leader. "We was here first!"

The Cherokee travellers were initially as wary of the new intruders as they had been of Carver's gang until Johnny, ignoring Carver, addressed the Cherokee man in his native tongue, asking if he was all right and if anyone had been hurt. The man's eyes cut to his wife, who was still at the mercy of Carver's blade.

Hearing the newcomers speak Cherokee, Tom Carver and his men took a closer look. "They ain't here for the money..." the youngest outlaw deduced brilliantly.

"We've been tracking you for a day and a half," Michael said, stepping up beside Johnny.

"We figured this is what you were up to," Johnny added. His eyes never left Carver's knife at the woman's throat.

"Who the hell are you?!" Carver demanded.

"Your judge and executioner, if you don't put down that knife," Johnny said with calm, confident firmness.

The oldest robber, his hand still tightly gripping the neck of the 8-year-old girl, yelled at Johnny. "You know who you're talkin' to, Mister? This here's Tom Carver. We're the Carver Gang."

"Well, Mr. Carver's a dead man if he don't drop that knife," Johnny repeated. Carver moved the knife away from the Cherokee woman's throat and laid it down beside the fire. With his other hand—shielded by his body—he slipped the pistol from his belt. Still in a crouch, Carver twisted and brought the hidden pistol up, aiming it at Johnny. *Do-tsu-wa* reacted instantly.

"*Tsa-ni!*" Redbird yelled and lunged, shoving Johnny out of the way. The leader of the raiders had been saved, but *Do-tsu-wa*

428

took the bullet in his chest. Michael fired instantly, wounding Tom Carver in the right side. The Cherokee emigrants scrambled for cover when the rest of Carver's gang began firing wildly. The Cherokee pork-burner fell, shot in the leg. Johnny and the rest of his men opened fire. The oldest outlaw let go of the young girl and staggered backward. A stream of blood arched out into space from the side of his neck where the bullet had passed through and ruptured his jugular. His hand started for his pistol but never made it. He fell backwards beside the campfire.

* * * * * * *

A quarter of a mile away, Annie Drummond sat on *Ga-tsa-nu-la* with little James in front of her. She held *U-no-le's* reins. A few feet away, Betty Jo Proctor, Ned's wife, sat on her horse with their daughter, Janie, in front of her. Betty Jo held the reins of both her husband's and *Tsa-tsi's* horses. Her son, Jack, sat quietly on *Ne-di's* horse. Betty Jo possessed a simple beauty with honest eyes that penetrated when she spoke—which was seldom—and absorbed with genuine interest when she listened. Annie had grown very fond of Betty Jo and both her children, who adored little *Tsi-mi*.

No one spoke, but apprehensive glances went around at the distant sound of gunfire. This had been their lives since the day the army had ridden out from Ft. Smith and burned their cabins. A life on the run, eating berries and wild fruit and game the men killed. Living in abandoned cabins, in caves or in lean-to's thrown up for the night. Always on the run.

Annie and Betty Jo looked at the other rider, *E-gi-ni*, Redbird's sister, who held the reins of *Do-tsu-wa's* and Johnny's horses. She turned toward the gunshots as though by sheer force of will she would be able to see the events taking place. She didn't know that only a few feet away Annie closed her eyes tightly and saw even more. Annie's eyes opened and she looked sadly at *E-gi-ni*, who had just lost her brother.

* * * * * * *

The gun battle raged on at the Cherokee camp. The raiders killed four of the Carver Gang. The three surviving bandits managed to grab their wounded leader and vanish into the darkness. The gunfire had set off a chain of shouts from others up and down the river, including the soldiers.

The Cherokees stepped over the bodies of the slain robbers to express their gratitude to the *Tsa-la-gi* vigilantes who had appeared out of the night to save them. Others, including the two white doctors, tended to the wounded Cherokee's shattered leg and to *Do-tsu-wa*. Johnny, Michael, *Ne-di* and *Tsa-tsi* hovered over them, waiting for their friend to get up so they could get back to their women and children waiting in the woods nearby. One of the doctors placed a hand on Redbird's face and closed his eyes, then looked up at Johnny and Michael and shook his head. The raiders surrounded *Do-tsu-wa*, but before they could pick up their friend's body, they heard the shouts of the soldiers thrashing through the brush coming toward them.

Johnny hurriedly removed Redbird's gun belt, then grabbed the arm of the closest Cherokee man. "Will you bury our friend?" he asked.

"He is our friend as well," the *Tsa-la-gi* answered. "Go."

"Do you have any food?" Michael asked. The Cherokee man pointed to the fire where the remains of the maggot infested pork still sizzled.

"It's all rotten. I'm sorry."

The man's wife stepped forward and offered Johnny a basket of berries picked along the river just before dark, but he refused. A little girl brought two blankets and extended them up to Michael.

"*Wa-do*," Michael touched her cheek. "We need blankets." They all heard the rustling leaves and cracking twigs as the soldiers approached.

"*Mi-ki! Tsi-ne-na!* Let's go!" Johnny whisper-shouted. Michael snatched the blankets and the four raiders disappeared into the night only seconds before ten soldiers came crashing through the brush, pistols drawn and rifles ready. Most of them wore only their boots and trousers. Some had suspenders pulled up over cotton undergarments, others with bare chests glistening with sweat. Their noses crinkled at the smell of scorched hair and burning flesh. One of them kicked the hand and arm of Carver's man out of the fire.

The sergeant, overweight and huffing from the jog over to the Cherokee camp, looked around at the four dead outlaws, the body of *Do-tsu-wa* and the wounded Cherokee having his leg tended. There was no reason for him to think Redbird was anything other than an unfortunate Cherokee emigrant who had fallen victim to this plundering band of white scoundrels. His main concern, however, was whether there were guns hidden among the Cherokees.

"Who shot these men?" the sergeant asked, pointing to the

corpses of Carver's men. He looked around and, as he had anticipated, was met by a wall of inscrutable expressions. The sergeant knew their game of silence. He looked again at Redbird's body and the Cherokee who grimaced from the pain of his leg wound. "Doc?" the sergeant inquired of the tired, hollow-eyed physician.

"We were in the next camp," the old doctor lied. "It was over by the time we got here."

The sergeant looked at him for a long time. He knew the doctor was lying, but why? Why protect a bunch of Indians? The sergeant studied the Cherokee man who had agreed to bury *Do-tsu-wa.*

"Are there guns in this camp?" he asked, knowing full well he wouldn't get an answer. "Who has a gun?" Still no response. "Were these men trying to rob you?" A few Cherokees responded with a single nod. "Who stopped them?" was the next logical question, to which there was still no answer. "I suppose they got greedy over all your money and argued amongst themselves?" the sergeant mused, knowing they would completely miss his sarcasm. "All right," he concluded, pointing to a cluster of soldiers. "You four get these bodies out of here. The rest of you, check the other camps." He tried to look into the eyes of the nearest Cherokee, but the *Tsa-la-gi* avoided him, watching the four soldiers grab the dead outlaws and drag them away.

* * * * * * *

The women all breathed easier when the men appeared out of the darkness. There was still the get-away ride ahead of them, but they knew the area well. As usual, with each mile they had travelled to get here they had mentally mapped out a variety of possible escape routes in case of an emergency.

E-gi-ni dismounted and rushed to meet Johnny, but her joy shifted to concern when her brother failed to appear. With dread of the obvious in her eyes, she dropped the reins and started to run back toward the Cherokee camp. Michael intercepted her, holding her tightly, his voice compassionate but urgent.

"I'm sorry, Agnes! There's nothing we can do! He's gone."

"*Do-tsu-wa! Tso-s-da-da-nŭ!*" she screamed into the night for her lost brother. Michael clamped his hand over her mouth and lifted her into the saddle. *Tsa-tsi* and *Ne-di* flanked her horse tightly on either side as they rode into the night. The distant shouts of the soldiers and the Cherokees from other camps up and down the river were soon drowned out by their pounding hoofbeats.

* * * * * * *

Michael, Johnny, *Ne-di* and *Tsa-tsi* sat in silence around the crackling fire. Annie leaned against Michael. Her hand rested on *Tsi-mi*, asleep on the ground beside her. Betty Jo sat near the sleeping Janie and Jack. No one had spoken for a long time. Their thoughts were on *E-gi-ni* at the edge of the clearing nestled in the middle of a sycamore grove. She gazed out across the valley below, her back to the group and the fire. The soft tones of her high-pitched chanting carried on the night.

Johnny was the first to speak. "I feel really bad for her," he said in a low tone. His knees were drawn up under his chin and he stared into the dancing flames. "*Do-tsu-wa* took a bullet meant for me."

"It all happened so fast," Michael said.

They listened to the mournful chant in the darkness for a while longer. Then Johnny rose and picked up Redbird's gun belt. *E-gi-ni* stopped the song when she heard Johnny's footsteps behind her, but she didn't turn. He put a consoling arm around her shoulder and handed her the gun belt.

"*Do-tsu-wa* was a good friend. He saved my life."

E-gi-ni absently examined the gun belt's intricate leather work. Feeling awkward, Johnny let his arm slip from her shoulder and started back toward the campfire. *E-gi-ni* grabbed his arm and pulled him to her. She dropped the gun belt at her side and with both hands pulled his face down to hers and kissed him. A long and passionate kiss. There was no mistaking her burning desire for this man who had been the secret keeper of her heart for as long as she had known him. But it all came as quite a shock to Johnny. His eyes widened. He couldn't match the passion of her kiss, yet neither did he push her away.

* * * * * * *

Annie tossed a couple of twigs onto the fire and looked up at Michael.

"Did you get any food?"

"They had nothing," his answer was hollow with disappointment. He tucked one of the blankets given to him by the little Cherokee girl closer around their sleeping son. Annie gripped his arm firmly.

"This has to stop, *Mi-ki*." Her voice was low but left no doubt about the depth of her determination. "Living like wild animals on the run!"

"I know, *Wa-le-la*. There's nothing else we can do right now. We have no place to go," he looked away, his own heart heavy with the shame of dragging his family around like a pack of stalking wolves. And he felt frustrated at being unable to change the situation. He was glad for the distraction when Johnny rejoined them—alone. Without speaking, Johnny rolled himself up in his blanket in the shadows across the clearing.

An hour later, Michael and Annie lay still beneath their shared blanket. Michael and *Tsi-mi* were sound asleep, but Annie lay propped on one elbow, mesmerized by the glowing embers of the campfire. *Ne-di* and Betty Jo Proctor were asleep on the same side of the fire, with Jack and Janie between them. *Tsa-tsi*, from his chosen spot near the tethered horses, snorted a couple of times in his sleep and resumed his soft, rhythmic snoring. Annie remained perfectly still when she heard *E-gi-ni* return to camp. She watched the grieving woman go quietly to Johnny's blanket and slip beneath it. Annie looked in their direction for a while, then lay down and closed her eyes.

Under Johnny's blanket, Agnes spooned herself against his back. His eyes opened, staring straight ahead. Without stirring, he closed his eyes and pretended to be asleep. He felt her hand on the back of his neck, lingering there as though waiting for him to react. Then her fingers traced their way lightly over his broad shoulders, down his arm and onto his waist. His eyes popped wide open when her hand glided below his waist and around to the front. She knew he was awake and was fully aware of her. She began nibbling on his ear as her fingers encircled his expanding maleness.

CHAPTER

37

U. S. Army Command Post
New Echota, Georgia

The sentry paced back and forth in front of General Winfield Scott's headquarters, a rectangular building sixteen by thirty-two feet, anchored at the foot of the slope leading up to the Cherokee national council house which, for the duration of the removal, had been converted into an open-sided barracks. New Echota was the general's center of operations, though he frequently rode north to the Indian Agency on the Hiwassee River where he would remain for days at a time.

The Cherokees certainly owned some fine animals, the sentry thought, admiring the horses hitched to the rail in front of the command post. It was evident they were well fed and well cared for. The crafting of the saddles—the designs carved in the leather, the inlaid silver—reflected a level of craftsmanship and artisan expertise he had never seen in the north. Whatever they were doing in there, it must be important, he concluded, else General Scott wouldn't have personally summoned him from his usual job of hauling water up from the spring to fill the barrels on the platform erected behind the general's quarters. The sentry swelled with importance and saluted briskly when a captain and a lieutenant rode past.

The Cherokee tribal leaders inside the New Echota command post all wore somber expressions. John Ross's trip to Washington, D.C. had proven no more successful than any of his countless previous journeys. With him were his brother, Lewis Ross, along with the usual assemblage of reliable leaders—Charles Hicks, Assistant Chief George Lowrey, Hair Conrad, Thomas Foreman and the ancient ones, Going Snake and *Tsunaluska*. Joining them for this important meeting at the request of both *Gu-wi-s-gu-wi* and General Scott was William Drummond.

Scott unbuttoned his tunic in search of relief from the sweltering heat, then relit his pipe and stared out the window. Seated on a bench against the wall, exhausted and near collapse, Dr. Hamilton and Dr. Springfield sipped their whiskey near the end of what seemed to them another endless day. The general's ever present *aide*, Corporal Edward Mears, stood erect and silent in the corner, his uniform immaculate as always, whether hot or cold, humid or dry.

434

Mixed with the sound of the general's scratchy breathing they all heard the crackling of the tiny fire in the bowl each time Scott drew on his pipe. John Ross had just related a detailed account of his most recent narrowly-failed-almost-successful trip. The general felt Ross had heavily laced his narrative with a subtle plea. And Ross knew Scott despised the politicians who had rejected the Cherokees' petitions. He knew the only hope for—indeed, the ultimate fate of—the *Tsa-la-gi* now lay in the general's benevolent hands.

This man, the general thought, is himself a master politician worthy of any accolades bestowed upon the most seasoned veteran in the hallowed halls of the United States Congress. And, just as Scott had suspected during Ross's delivery, the chief had been setting him up for the big request: to delay indefinitely any further removal of Cherokees from their home land.

Scott took his time pondering the chief's proposal—analyzing every aspect and potential consequence. He would not allow himself to be pressured for a hasty answer. As was his custom, the general had listened attentively to Ross's eloquent discourse without interruption. And now the chief and his entourage could wait quietly while he deliberated and formulated his response. The Cherokees sat motionless and patient until the great *yo-neg* commander finally spoke.

"Chief Ross, I am here to enforce the New Echota Treaty of 1835, not to rewrite it. Not to throw it out. Not to postpone it." He faced them from the window, pausing to run the already soaked handkerchief beneath the collar of his tunic and around the back of his neck. "The Supreme Court has ruled that your people are *not* a separate nation. And the treaty dictates that you shall be removed to the west. Hopefully with as much haste as decency and discretion will allow."

William couldn't resist the temptation to inject an editorial comment. "If decency and discretion held sway in this matter, General, we wouldn't be having this discussion!"

Scott betrayed a hint of a smile. He liked William. Had liked him from the first time they met. He recognized in the attorney a man of genuine integrity, sincerity and compassion, qualities he hadn't often associated with the legal profession.

"Indeed," he said in agreement. "The fact remains, gentlemen, you have wasted two years when you could have been preparing for this."

The tribal leaders shifted nervously. They had given their

allegiance to *Gu-wi-s-gu-wi* who had promised them the treaty would be overturned. Their lack of preparation hadn't been from laziness or indifference. Like most Cherokees, they were convinced that, if they showed signs of preparing to remove to the west, it would be viewed as tacit approval of the Treaty of New Echota and would significantly weaken their position in the fight to have the treaty thrown out. They watched Scott zero in on their principal chief, pointing at Ross with the stem of his pipe.

"And you! Pissing away precious time with those idiots in Washington! And now you have the nerve to ask me to halt the removal?!"

"There's too much sickness among our people, General. We need a delay."

"Nearly three thousand have already gone west in the past month," Scott's brow was furrowed with a portentous distaste for the idea. "Do you want your people strung out clear across the country?"

"We want our people *alive*, General," Ross pleaded. "Whatever it takes."

The general poured himself another whiskey and stepped across the room to replenish the glasses of the physicians he had summoned to this meeting. "Gentlemen? Your thoughts?"

Hamilton ran his fingers through his snow white hair and leaned his head back against the wall, closing his eyes. His voice was flat but convincing. "Sanitation has become a major problem in all the camps."

Dr. Springfield, tall, balding, his skin tanned and leathery, leaned forward, elbows propped on his knees. He studied the treasured contents of his cup. "The water is stagnant," he confirmed Hamilton's diagnosis. "Polluted. Unfit for animals—much less humans."

General Scott chewed his lip, considering their words as he walked back to look out the window. "So, the sooner we get these people out of here, the better?" he asked, remolding the doctors' negative assessments into support for his own argument: to continue the removal uninterrupted.

"Ordinarily, that would be true," Springfield said. "But there's a lot of sickness. Cholera could wipe us all out. And each day we have more cases of dysentery. The flux. Consumption."

Dr. Hamilton opened his tired eyes and looked across the room at the general. "And measles are now rampant among the children. Travel with any of these ailments would mean certain death for so many."

George Lowrey, who seldom spoke in the presence of a white man, though his voice was well known among his own people, stepped out from the others to address General Scott. "If we could get fresh water...and wait for cooler weather..."

Lowrey's words encouraged *Tsunaluska* to add his opinion. "Besides, the drought in the west has the rivers so low the boats can't pass. That's the word we've been getting."

"And the food rations for the travellers are rotten," William added to the list. There followed a long silence. Then General Scott heaved a thunderous sigh and faced his visitors once again.

"I've always firmly believed a military decision should be made with the head, never with the heart. That's why I'm certain I'll live to regret what I'm about to say." He paused, perhaps for effect, or perhaps just to run it through his mind for one last chance to be the tough, unfeeling commander he had been sent to be. But he knew, no matter what the politicians in Georgia, Tennessee, North Carolina, Alabama or Washington, D.C. might think, his decision was the right one. True, there was a chance it could blow up in his face. But it was the chance he would have to take, because he knew it was the right thing to do. He looked from one leader to the other before he finally announced his decision. "Further removal will be delayed until September tenth."

"God will reward you, sir," Charles Hicks said, his voice uncharacteristically thick with emotion for a man of normally impermeable restraint.

General Scott chuckled softly, "And President Van Buren will probably have my commission."

George Lowrey tugged at the large silver ring in his ear before speaking. "General. There is one other thing. Some of the ministers among our people would like to hold services..."

Scott's eyes took on a sad expression. Lowrey's request brought home once more the point that these were no heathen savages he had been charged with capturing and driving from their homeland.

"By all means," Scott replied. "Edward, draw up the permits."

"Yes, sir," the *aide* snapped and immediately set about his assignment with quill, ink and paper at the secretary desk in the corner.

"God knows," the general added, once again looking each of his guests directly in the eye, "we need all the prayers we can get.

437

Chief Ross...gentlemen..." Scott returned to the work on his desk, signalling an end to the meeting.

* * * * * * *

Ft. Coosawattee Concentration Camp

The night had denied its usual surcease from the day's oppressive heat. Fires were kept small, used only for light and for a little cooking, if, indeed, enough food was available to warrant it. Many of the camp's inhabitants lay prostrate, exhausted from endless days and sweat-drenched nights of incessant coughing, clinched bellies, vomiting and diarrhea. The ubiquitous chanting of medicine men sifted throughout the entire compound. Cherokees came and went, gliding by silently in the night like spiritless manifestations. Steeped in a leaden somnolence, others sat around their fires, back far enough to elude the unwelcome heat. Here and there a sympathetic soldier manned his guard post, musing to himself what a waste of time it was to guard these poor, pathetic people who had been physically weakened and spiritually depleted to the point of posing no threat. Or, if differently disposed, a sentry might harbor resentment for these same people as the cause of his discomfort and abject misfortune at having to serve on this wretched assignment. Why couldn't they have simply packed up and gone when asked? After all, hadn't the request come from the highest levels of the United States government?

Inside the long, open sided shelter, Elizabeth Drummond, Eva Swimmer and Quatie Ross helped a young Cherokee mother care for her children of two and four, both spotted with measles. Eva had brought a fresh pan of water from the creek. Elizabeth and Quatie dipped rags and waved them back and forth to increase their evaporative cooling effect before laying them on the fever-baked bodies and faces of the fretful children.

Eva and Quatie took over when Elizabeth had to step away, gripped by a rattling cough. Susanna stood in the entry way holding the eight-month-old Meg, hoping, praying for even a whisper of a breeze. When she heard the familiar sound, Susanna looked inside just as Elizabeth stepped—or staggered—around the blanket divider.

"Mother!" she scolded without harshness, "get back to your bed!"

"Get that baby away from here!" Elizabeth wheezed painfully, more concerned for Meg than for herself. "These children have measles!"

"And you want to give them consumption to go with it?!" Susanna tried to be gentle but was serious in her reprimand. She knew of her mother's great love for the children, but clearly Elizabeth hadn't exercised good judgment.

"Go on," Quatie had overheard them and stepped around the blanket divider to officially relieve Elizabeth of her duty. "We'll take care of them."

"Are you sure?" Elizabeth asked, not wanting to shirk what she felt was her responsibility, yet knowing her own well-being had been seriously compromised since entering this wretched place.

"Go," they heard Eva say softly but firmly from beyond the blanket walls.

* * * * * * *

Elizabeth lay exhausted on her cot, a forearm across her brow. "You must take better care of yourself, Mother," Susanna repeated.

"I can't bear to see these children dying," Elizabeth's voice was barely more than a whisper.

"I know. I know."

"How's my little Meggie?"

"I can't get her to eat," Susanna tried not to sound overly alarmed.

"Maybe it's just the heat." Elizabeth, like her daughter, evaded a more serious prognosis.

After a long silence, metered only by her mother's raspy breathing, Susanna finally said, "I wish Reba were here. She'd know what to do."

Despite her discomfort, Elizabeth couldn't resist a weak smile.

"Susanna..." the voice came from just outside the shelter. Susanna looked to the opening. Elizabeth raised her head. Framed in what served as their doorway was Peter, his arm still in a sling. He was sober, clean and well groomed.

"Hello, Peter," Elizabeth greeted him with genuine surprise.

"How are you, Mrs. Drummond?" Peter asked politely.

"I have my moments, dear."

Susanna, however, was having no part in such civilities. "She's dying in here, Peter. We all are."

"Don't listen to her. How is your arm?" Elizabeth struggled to a sitting position on the edge of the cot.

"Yes, how is your arm?" Susanna's question dripped with her sarcasm of old.

Peter made a feeble attempt to respond in kind. "So very nice of you to inquire, dearest wife. It would appear that my war wounds have compelled me to relinquish my field command in lieu of a less prestigious administrative position."

"You're looking well," Susanna eyed him up and down, noting his vastly improved appearance.

"Thank you. And feeling well." Peter stepped closer and held out his hand toward Meg, who shrank from him. He made a point of not taking it as rejection. "Hello, Meg. Can't you come see your Poppa?" His wait for a response lengthened into an awkward silence. Finally he cleared his throat, straightened his uniform and abandoned his perfunctory attempt to connect with the child. "Susanna, I could still arrange for you and Margaret...and your mother, of course...to—"

"This is the first time I've seen you sober in some time," she interrupted, hoping to avoid the anguish of the obligatory offer she knew was forthcoming.

"Yes. No more whiskey. I suppose I really have only myself to blame for..."

"For your demotion?" she jumped in again.

"I've been reassigned, not demoted," he corrected her and pointed to the major's insignia that still adorned his uniform. "But, yes," he confessed, "the drinking had become a problem. I'll admit it."

"Well, I'm so glad it didn't have anything to do with shooting defenseless Cherokees in the back...just because they wanted their freedom."

"They were escaping!" Peter was genuinely frustrated that she couldn't understand this made them fair game.

"Escaping from what?!"

"I refuse to be drawn into this argument," he held his hand out to stop the exchange, then spoke deliberately, almost haltingly, "I came to see you in hopes...perhaps we could...mend our situation."

Susanna's voice was a pained whisper. "How do you simply *mend* what has been shattered beyond recognition?"

Peter exhaled a prolonged sigh and stared blankly into the black depths of the shelter. "I can't believe you would choose this, when I'm offering you a way out."

"No one in this God forsaken stink hole *chose* to be here, Peter," her voice was low but intense. "Is that so difficult to understand?"

"I'm a soldier, Susanna. I follow orders."

"Just go, Peter," she said, realizing she would never get through to him. "Go, and by all means, follow your orders." Susanna turned her back as she had always done to signal an end to a conversation. Peter looked once more at Meg, then walked away without another word.

* * * * * * *

Major Tanner marched briskly toward his quartermaster tent behind the Coosawattee camp headquarters, then veered sharply, headed for the main gate. Peter raised his right arm slightly in its sling and flicked his hand as a return salute to the guards, which included Corporal Robert Barton and his friend, Private Virgil Johnson. They watched the major walk directly to the wagon of some white peddlers camped outside. Barton and Johnson exchanged a knowing glance before pacing back to the other side of the gate. None of the other soldiers on duty noticed or cared, one way or the other.

Robert retrieved his canteen from a peg near the gate. Both the young soldiers were burning with fever, their complexions pasty, eyes tired and blood-shot. Barton drank unquenchably, spilling down his chin and onto his uniform.

"Take it easy, Robert," Virgil implored.

"I can't get enough to drink, Virgil," he said, lowering the canteen.

"I know. I'm the same way."

"They say that's a bad sign," Robert allowed the apprehension they both felt to creep into his voice. Every day for the past few weeks they had seen the bodies carried out—the very young, the very old and everything in between. And the bodies had not all been Cherokee. A corporal from Kentucky and a sergeant out of Connecticut had died the night before. And they had heard more than a dozen soldiers at the other camps throughout Cherokee territory had succumbed to one disease or another. But it was a subject never directly addressed in conversation, as though by avoiding the topic they somehow improved their chances of eluding the diseases themselves. Barton and Johnson mutually felt too much had already been said. They dropped the matter and looked back out toward the whiskey wagon.

The outline of Major Tanner was rimmed by the glow of the

peddler's fire. Voices carried across the forty-odd yards separating them from Coosawattee's main gate.

"Go on, Major! Your money's no good here!" one of the whiskey peddlers grinned up at Peter. They remembered appreciatively how, during his former tenure as camp commander, he had accommodated them by looking the other way while, against specific orders from General Winfield Scott, they had plied their profitable trade. And there was still plenty of money to be made from both sides. They had furnished potent libation to the soldiers and whites to ease their troubles and to put them in the proper mood to take advantage of their unfortunate captives. At the same time they had illegally sold whiskey to the Cherokees to ease their troubles and to put them in a distorted frame of mind, making them easier prey for the soldiers, militiamen and civilian whites.

"Much obliged, gentlemen," Peter thanked them for the jug. "Make yourselves scarce before sun up."

"Always do, Major. Always do," the squatting peddler chuckled. "G'night."

Corporal Barton and Private Johnson exchanged another glance and made a point to be looking the other way when Peter started back in their direction. Again, they tilted their canteens and drank unquenchably. Neither was aware of the young Cherokee girl watching them from the shadows of the long shelter nearest the gate.

Martha Swimmer was especially interested in Corporal Barton. She had noticed, when they had passed each other during the past few days, his increasingly pallid appearance and a clouding of the eyes. She picked up the basket at her feet and was about to approach but withdrew sharply into the darkness when Major Tanner stalked back through the gate with his jug. He ignored the guards and headed for his quartermaster's tent. Robert and Virgil returned their canteens to the peg in the wall. They were both startled when Martha appeared out of the shadows beside them.

"*Ma-di!*" Robert smiled weakly. This was her first opportunity in a while to examine him at close range. She was visibly distressed by what she saw.

"You're ill, Robert. It looks bad," she said frankly, not intending to alarm them.

"No worse than lots of others," Barton reinforced his own ignore-it-and-it-will-go-away attitude. But Martha was having none of it. She gently pushed him to a seat on the large stump just behind them. From her basket she took a pot of steaming herbal tea, removed the clay lid and held it to his lips. Without resistance,

442

Robert drank, then passed it to his companion.

"Here, Virgil. You need it more than me." Johnson drank, grimacing at the bitter taste, but he knew it was good for him. Martha reached into her basket and produced a small wooden bowl containing a poultice.

"Open your shirt," she commanded softly. Robert put his hand on his tunic and looked at Virgil with modest embarrassment. "Open your shirt," Martha repeated. "Plaster this on your chest." He took the bowl, recoiling at the terrible smell. "Go ahead. It's good for you. My grandmother made it."

"How is she doing?" Robert asked, eyeing the rancid paste.

"Not well," Martha answered, then gestured at the bowl. "Go on..."

"Open your shirt, Virgil," Robert pulled rank.

Equally embarrassed, Private Johnson sat down on the stump and unbuttoned his tunic. Robert scooped out a handful of the sinapism and began smearing it onto Virgil's fevered chest.

"Thank you, Miss." Decency prevented Johnson from looking her directly in the eye—not with his shirt hanging open!—but his gratitude was sincere.

"*Ma-di*," Robert said to his friend while looking at Martha. "Her name's *Ma-di*. It means Martha."

"Thank you, *Ma-di*," Virgil glanced up at her, then looked away. He lifted the pot to his lips and finished the bitter tea. Martha put her hands into the bowl at the same time as Robert, their fingers touching. Their eyes met for an instant, then both involved themselves studiously in applying the plaster to Virgil's chest. They were almost finished when Robert stopped, his hand poised above the bowl. Martha turned in the direction he was looking. Slipping out the gate, unseen by the other soldiers, was Charlie Swimmer.

"Isn't that your father?" Robert asked. Martha nodded and continued spreading the smelly concoction onto Johnson's chest. Barton caught her wrist, stopping her. "Were you sent here as a decoy? To distract us?" His voice reflected a feeling of betrayal. Martha jerked her hand free. She was visibly hurt by his suspicious allegation.

Private Johnson watched Charlie heading for the peddlers' wagon. "Look. I think he's just going for whiskey."

Barton looked sheepishly back to Martha. "I'm sorry, *Ma-di*. It was wrong of me to doubt you." She continued to pout, but expressed her forgiveness by digging out a finger full of the malodorous goop and smearing it onto his cheek, then painting a dab right under his nose. She broke into a broad grin when Robert winced at the foul smell.

* * * * * * *

Charlie Swimmer carefully unfolded the bandanna to display a collection of finely crafted silver jewelry—bracelets, belt buckles, a silver hat band—which he had brought to barter for a jug of whiskey. The squatting peddler raked his fingers backwards through the pile, spreading the items for a better view. He cut a glance up to his partner, who was bending over the display, hands propped on his knees. They masked their greed in pursuit of greater booty. If this was the first the Indian was willing to reveal, they thought, he must be hiding the really good stuff.

"This ought to be worth a couple bottles of good scotch whiskey," Charlie pressed.

"Well...I don't know, chief..." Squatting Peddler whined, shaking his head.

Charlie forced himself to ignore their condescending manner of calling all Cherokee men *chief*. "Please. I need it. For my wife," Charlie said, instantly feeling he'd made a mistake by sounding needful.

"Of course you do," Bending Peddler flashed a gap-toothed, patronizing grin. "Good medicine, right?"

Charlie glanced toward the camp gate. He was anxious to get back before attracting the soldiers' attention. "Come on. It's pure silver!" he insisted.

"Yeah," Squatting Peddler feigned concern. "See, that's the problem. We'd rather have some *gold*."

"Gold? What gold?"

"Hell, everybody knows the Cherokees struck gold 'round here nigh on ten years ago," Bending Peddler slapped Charlie on the shoulder.

"I don't have any gold," Charlie answered flatly.

"Come on, Chief," Squatter tapped the nearest jug with grimy fingers. "I give you some *amber*, you give me some *gold*."

"I never had gold," Charlie shook his head. "And those who did—the white man stole it years ago." He folded up the corners of the bandanna, rose and walked indignantly back toward the gate.

"Hey, Chief!" Bending Peddler straightened up and shouted in a whisper. "All right! The silver's good! We can work with the silver!"

"The bastard's lyin'," Squatting Peddler growled up at his cohort. "You know damn well he's got gold."

* * * * * * *

Charlie reentered the Coosawattee gate with his head down, disappointed, headed back toward his shelter. "*E-to-da!*" Martha called to her father. Charlie looked up, surprised to see his daughter standing with two *yo-neg* soldiers. He approached them, at first concerned that Martha might be in trouble. He saw Martha wipe her hands on her dress and noticed Private Johnson's open tunic where the plaster had been applied to his chest. Charlie flashed a suspicious look at the soldiers.

"They're sick," Martha explained. "I brought them medicine."

She picked up her basket to accompany her father. Openly showing his displeasure, Charlie tugged sharply at her arm, pulling her toward the shelter.

"Mr. Swimmer!" Corporal Barton called. Charlie and Martha stopped. "You need whiskey? For medicine?" Robert asked. Charlie's eyes were cold and mistrustful. Barton motioned to Private Johnson. Virgil pulled a thin flask from beneath his uniform. "*E-ti-ŭ-s-di,*" Barton said in Cherokee, hoping to put Charlie at ease. "Give it to him," he translated for Johnson. Virgil passed the flask to Robert who handed it to Charlie.

"*Wa-do*, Robert," Martha said.

"*Wa-do*," Charlie repeated softly.

"Good night, Mr. Swimmer. Good night, *Ma-di*. Maybe I'll see you tomorrow," Corporal Barton said. Martha dipped her eyes coyly and walked away with her father, leaving Robert staring after them.

* * * * * * *

Neither Charlie nor Martha spoke during the walk back. Past the fires, past the curious looks, they marched in step with the distant chanting and moaning that emanated from every corner of the camp. Charlie kept his daughter a few steps in front.

"Stay away from him," Charlie finally said when they reached their area of the shelter.

Martha stopped abruptly and spun around, pained by his disapproval. "He's been very good to me, *E-to-da*."

"He's *yo-neg!*" Charlie made what he felt was the only argument necessary. "He wants only one thing from a young *Tsa-la-gi 'ge-yu-ts'*."

"The same thing the *Tsa-la-gi* boys want?!"

"He doesn't drink from the same river, *Ma-di*," Charlie said in a softer tone, aware of the attention they were attracting.

"You don't know anything about him!" Martha said loudly.

"*Ma-di*. He's here to drive us from our land. That's all we need to know about him."

"He doesn't like being here any more than we do!" she said, holding back the tears. She pointed to the flask in her father's hand. "And he needed that just as much as you and Mother did! Maybe more!"

She left him and hurried inside. Charlie bobbed the flask a few times in his hand, then followed. Somewhere in the darkness he could hear a Cherokee fiddle scratching out a mournful tune of Scottish origin.

38

The bright Sunday morning had given birth to yet another blistering day in northern Georgia. A slow rendering of *What A Friend We Have In Jesus* on fiddle and bagpipe accompanied the steady stream of Cherokees, whites and blacks flowing solemnly out through the gates of the Ft. Coosawattee concentration camp. Troops who had drawn assignment were stationed along the path. Off-duty soldiers joined the crowd on their way to attend the worship services sanctioned by General Scott. Among them were William and Elizabeth Drummond. They kept a slow pace so as not to aggravate Elizabeth's sensitive respiratory condition. Susanna walked behind them carrying Meg on her hip. William had spotted the entire Swimmer family—Charlie, Eva, Martha, *Tsu-tsu*, Buck and Sally—a few yards back. When they passed through the main gate, Martha looked around, hoping for a glimpse of Robert and Virgil. But they were nowhere in view and the crowd was pressing her on.

The temporary church—which had been constructed on a flat piece of ground opposite the sloping cemetery—was, in typical Cherokee fashion, open sided with a thatched roof. Benches had been made from split logs, and a crude pulpit was positioned at the eastern end of the structure. A young Cherokee woman and a middle-aged black man, each playing fiddle, sat near the pulpit. Malcolm Stewart, an octogenarian Scot who had married a full-blood of the Wild Potato Clan more than sixty years hence, sat on the bench just behind them. He played the bagpipes he had so lovingly maintained through the years. Flanking him on either side were two old Cherokee men who softly tapped their ceremonial drums in time with the music. This unusual *ensemble* continued to play softly while the church filled up.

The Drummond family took a bench a few rows back from the pulpit and studied with interest the two middle-aged Cherokee preachers, well known and highly regarded men of God among both the Cherokees and the whites in their local communities. They sat with heads bowed in prayerful contemplation before the services. William leaned to Elizabeth and pointed out the preachers, speaking in a hushed tone.

"John Wickliffe. They call him *Ka-ni-da*," he said of the taller, thinner man, then indicated the other. "And *O-ga-na-ya*. They've come over from Camp Butler." He looked around at the crowd pouring in from every side. "Baptists. Methodists. Moravian.

Everybody's here."

Elizabeth was almost tearful in her relief at being even a few feet outside the hated Coosawattee camp. "It's so nice to be in church again. It's been so long."

"Do they preach in English or in Cherokee?" Susanna wondered out loud.

"Both," William whispered.

Malcolm, the superannuated piper, and the fiddlers ended the first song. They looked at each other and, on a nod, began a mournful rendition of *Amazing Grace*. William craned around and finally spotted Charlie Swimmer and his family. The two men exchanged a nod of greeting. Most of the soldiers, William noted, were positioned around the outer edges of the open-sided shelter. It was a simple matter to distinguish the guards from the off-duty men who had come to worship. The guards were the only ones with weapons. A few soldiers—even a couple who were supposed to be on guard duty—had taken a seat on the outer end of the long benches and appeared more interested in worshipping than in overseeing the conduct of their prisoners.

In a strangely melodious blend, the gathering worshippers began singing simultaneously in English and Cherokee.

> Amazing grace, how sweet the sound
> That saved a wretch like me...
> I once was lost, but now am found;
> Was blind, but now I see...
>
> *U-di-la-nŭ-hi u-we-tsi*
> *I-ga-gu-yŭ-he-i*
> *Hna-quo tso-e wi-u-lo-se*
> *I-ga-gu-yŭ-ho-nŭ*

During the singing, Martha Swimmer tried to sneak glimpses at the soldiers, still hoping she might see Robert Barton. When she caught her father watching her, she gave him a defiant scowl and continued her search. But Robert Barton was nowhere to be seen. Eva was fully aware of the silent battle being waged between her husband and their daughter and had noted *Ma-di's* grave concern.

The services weren't as orderly and organized as might have occurred within the chapel walls of the various denominations represented. The preachers were emotional, exhorting, gesticulating, praying fervently. The congregation was a blend of full-bloods,

448

mixed-bloods, whites intermarried with Cherokees, soldiers, and a few scattered blacks who had chosen to remain in the camps with their Cherokee owners who were, in many cases, also their closest friends. After a couple of hours, many of the soldiers who were supposed to be guarding prisoners leaned their guns against trees or held them casually across the back of the neck with arms dangling over them in a posture eerily reminiscent of a crucifix. Meg Tanner, like so many little ones, lay asleep across her mother's lap; other children dozed leaning against a grandparent or an older sibling.

Later in the day—after hours of preaching—*Ka-ni-da* and *O-ga-na-ya* baptized the day's converts, immersing them in a pool formed by the same creek that flowed through a corner of Ft. Coosawattee. Amid long afternoon shadows the setting sun bathed the worshippers in a soft, golden glow that rendered a false sense of richness and peace. Mindful that they were still prisoners, the Coosawattee inmates gradually began returning to the camp. Elizabeth Drummond, like so many others in the crowd who were gravely ill, showed signs of fatigue and exhaustion, yet her expression registered a heretofore unseen energy born of spiritual renewal.

The Drummonds had gravitated toward the Swimmers at the end of the day. The families chatted on their march back toward Coosawattee. Martha Swimmer made a point of positioning herself on the outside edge where she would be afforded a better view on their approach to the main gate. Once inside the camp, she drifted out of the flow and gradually worked her way back toward the spot where she had been with Robert and Virgil the previous evening.

Disappointed at not finding them, Martha was about to rejoin the stream of captives when she suddenly stopped. She looked through the flow of church goers toward an area behind the camp's headquarters. Dr. Hamilton was down on one knee, bending over someone. Martha's view was further obstructed by the soldiers flanking the doctor on either side. A chill ran through her when Hamilton unfurled a blanket to cover the soldier who had just expired in his care.

Panic stricken, Martha fought her way through the current and raced to the group hovering over the lifeless soldier. She arrived just in time to glimpse the face of Private Virgil Johnson. A soldier held her back. In silent anguish Martha watched the other soldiers pick up the body and carry it away.

From a few feet away she heard what sounded like a mixture of coughing and sobbing. Robert Barton, himself near death, sat on the same stump as the night before. With quivering body he mourned the loss of his friend while battling for his own life. He had walked away after Dr. Hamilton closed Virgil's vacant eyes and hadn't seen Martha approaching. She gently put her arms around him from behind and kissed him on the top of his head. Robert didn't have to look. He knew who had embraced him. When Dr. Hamilton joined them, a soldier took Martha's elbow and gently pulled her away so the doctor could examine Corporal Barton. Robert smiled weakly.

"Please save him, Doctor," Martha entreated.

"We're doing all we can, young lady," Hamilton mouthed the words he'd uttered so often. He glanced up for the first time and recognized her as one of the many young Cherokee women who had given so much of their time and energy assisting him and Dr. Springfield in recent weeks. He smiled and added, "I think he's going to be all right."

With this shred of encouragement Martha allowed herself to be steered back toward the parade of Cherokees returning from the church services. With every third or fourth step she looked back, hoping for one more glimpse of Robert. From the corner of the shelter Charlie Swimmer watched his daughter. She spotted him and was initially prepared to see a scowl—at least a frown—then realized his inscrutable expression was neither approving nor disapproving.

* * * * * * *

By the middle of the week Robert had begun to show signs of improvement. Martha caught a glimpse of him now and then but hadn't been allowed to visit. She kept to herself the feelings that had been coursing through her. Who was there to share them with? She had no real friends in the camp. All she knew was she would die soon if she didn't get to see him, touch him, hear his voice, look into his gentle eyes. From her post at the end of the long shed closest to the main gate—and nearest the soldiers' bivouac area—Martha watched through the torrential downpour that painted everything in dreary shades of dull brown, gray and black. An ancient Cherokee man stood in the rain, his hands raised and his face uplifted to the cleansing waters. A Cherokee woman, soaked to the skin, stood on the bank of the tributary flowing through the compound. The creek that had recently dwindled to a polluted, unpotable trickle was now a raging flood of muddy red water—equally useless to the prisoners of Coosawattee. All throughout the camp women and children had spent the entire day setting out buckets, pans, dishes—anything in which to capture the clean rainwater.

Despite the welcome relief of the storm, the day drew to a close around the usual suffering and dying. Martha watched a young Cherokee man, his face tightly drawn in grief, walk out into the rain carrying the body of his dead six-year-old son. And through the rhythmic patter of the downpour she heard the chanting of medicine men and medicine women, the wailing of mourners, the cries of the survivors and the groans of those whose hours were numbered.

* * * * * * *

As night settled in, Meg Tanner sat on the ground beside her grandmother's cot. Elizabeth fought off another coughing seizure while Meg studied with infantile fascination the dog that had come along outside the shelter, sniffing, hoping to find a scrap of food. When the coughing subsided, Elizabeth, near exhaustion, reached down and stroked the child's head. Susanna punched up the pile of clothing and blankets that served as her mother's pillow. Gently she tried to persuade Elizabeth to lie back down.

"You need to rest, Mother."

"I'm feeling much better today. Really," Elizabeth answered and beckoned to Meg. "Come here, little precious. Come see your grandma." Weakly she lifted Meg up onto the cot and held her close, then instantly called out. "Susie! This child is burning up!"

Susanna felt Meg's forehead and mirrored her mother's anxiety. She lifted the child off the cot and placed her on another bed across the crowded, blanket-walled cubicle. Meg whimpered when Susanna stretched her out.

"I wish your father were here," Elizabeth said listlessly.

Susanna made no effort to hide her resentment. "He's never here any more, Mother. He's forever going off with all those Cherokee men. And where has it gotten us?" She came back and gently pushed Elizabeth down on the cot. "They have their meetings. They smoke their pipes. And we have no decent food. Everyone is sick or dying."

Elizabeth folded her arm across her eyes. "Don't scold your father," she said weakly. "He's doing all he can for us."

"He's doing *nothing*, Mother, because there's nothing he can do!" Susanna said in a matter-of-fact tone, void of anger. "It's impossible to find the doctor. And even if we find him, he has no medicine to give you."

"Susanna..." the voice came from the opening between the blankets. Eva Swimmer was standing in the doorway. Sally, still fearful of Susanna, peered cautiously from behind her mother's legs. Susanna had detected the quiet urgency in Eva's voice. Elizabeth uncovered her eyes and looked up at their visitor.

"Eva. So good of you to stop by. Have you brought more of your delicious stew?" Elizabeth asked, building a sincere compliment into the request.

"I'm sorry, Mrs. Drummond," Eva's eyes were downcast. "There's no stew."

"I know, Eva. It's all right," Elizabeth said, mistaking the reason for Eva's sadness.

"Susanna..." Eva repeated with a beckoning gesture.

"I'll be back as soon as I can, Mother," Susanna said and checked on Meg who had fallen asleep on the other bed. Elizabeth dismissed them with a little wave before repositioning her arm across her eyes.

Eva bent down to Sally and said softly, "Go find *Ma-di*. Stay with her." Sally looked at Susanna and clung even tighter to her mother's leg. "Go on, *Sa-li*," Eva urged, sending the reluctant child off toward the Swimmer's area of the shelter. A distant rumble of thunder rolled over them as Eva and Susanna left the Drummonds' quarters.

* * * * * * *

In another cubicle bordered by tattered blankets and patches of cloth stitched and tied together, Eva and Susanna once more attended the two Cherokee children stricken with measles. The situation had become more complicated after the young mother contracted cholera. Hollow-eyed and delirious from fever, she appeared on the verge of succumbing to her malady. Susanna sat on the edge of the mother's bed, which was nothing more than a pile of blankets on top of three uneven wooden boxes shoved together. She put cool rags on the woman's burning face and neck while holding the little girl at the same time.

Eva brought in two fresh pans of rainwater. She stopped in front of Susanna, who had been trying to get the young mother to drink some water. Susanna looked up and noticed Eva staring at the child she was holding. For the first time in several minutes, Susanna looked down. The little girl had gone completely limp in her arms. Dead. Susanna lifted her eyes to Eva. Her mouth formed a scream, but so deep was the pain that no sound escaped Susanna's throat.

* * * * * * *

Meg had left her own bed to crawl up and lie across the foot of Elizabeth's cot. She studied the lines and callouses on her grandmother's foot, then touched it lightly with her fingers. She thought she might initiate a game of tickle. Meg waited for Grandma to wiggle her toes. That was the game. Meg tickle. Grandma wiggle. When Elizabeth didn't move, Meg crawled along the edge of the cot until she reached her grandmother's side. She tugged lightly at Elizabeth's arm which slid off her stomach and flopped over the edge of the cot. Meg poked lightly at Elizabeth's shoulder, not understanding that her grandmother was dead. Finally the child began to cry because there was no one to play with her.

* * * * * * *

Indian Territory

Michael and Annie were still on the run with Johnny, Ned and George. The weather had been fair and there had been no need to find a cave or an abandoned cabin or even to construct a lean-to. They made camp beneath a clear sky and slept soundly with *Tsi-mi* between them. The night was cool and the warmth from the campfire's glowing embers felt good. Annie sat up and looked around in the darkness. She clearly felt the presence of someone new in the camp. But there was no one to be seen. She touched her child, then looked down at Michael who was sound asleep. With a sad expression, Annie touched his face with the back of her hand. She had sensed death. But she hadn't received a clear impression of whose death it was. It had something to do with Michael, and she wondered if it might have been a premonition of his own passing, or, God forbid, *Tsi-mi's*. Michael stirred at her touch but did not waken. Annie sat with her knees drawn up and gazed into the coals for a long time. Finally she lay down and begged to receive the oblivion of sleep which she knew wouldn't come.

* * * * * * *

Ft. Coosawattee Burial Ground

The day was dimmed by the continuing light drizzle. Graveside services were conducted by the well known Cherokee preacher, the Reverend Jesse Bushyhead, a mixed-blood descendent of the curly-haired Scot, Captain John Stuart, one of the earliest prominent European traders to marry into the Cherokee tribe.

Elizabeth's coffin was a patchwork of gray, weathered wagon boards and freshly hewn pine, its only adornment a few hastily gathered wild flowers and Elizabeth's beloved, tattered old leather-bound Bible. William sat motionless on the wooden bench. His shoulders were drooped, his normally erect posture crushed beneath the weight of his grief. Susanna looked equally dazed and felt completely lost. The entire Swimmer family were in attendance, standing quietly in the rain a respectful distance away on the opposite side of the coffin. Reverend Bushyhead preached from the Gospel of John, recounting Christ's resurrection of Lazarus, quoting His familiar words to Martha, sister of the dead man of Bethany. *I am the resurrection and the life; he that believeth in me, though he were dead, yet shall he live. And whosoever liveth and believeth in me shall never die...*

Up the slope beyond the Drummond funeral, simultaneous interments of other Coosawattee captives who hadn't made it through the night were taking place. These included the young Cherokee mother stricken down by cholera and her daughter who had died in Susanna Drummond's arms. At the edge of the burial ground sat the black fiddler and old Malcolm Stewart with his bagpipes. They were playing for no one group in particular.

Reverend Bushyhead concluded the funeral with the familiar *...ashes to ashes, dust to dust...* litany. But in truth William had heard little of the burial service. He wouldn't allow the minister's words to intrude upon his own rigorous and recriminatory self-examination. Could he have prolonged the life of his beloved Elizabeth? Had his extensive involvement in Cherokee tribal affairs been but a cloak of cowardly avoidance on his part? Afraid to confront the reality of his wife's terminal illness? Fearful of his own mortality? Had he sought excuses to take him away because he couldn't face her in his shame for having brought them here in the first place? Was it a basic flaw in his character? A compulsion to deny a truth whose distasteful consequence would be more than he could bear? Is that what he'd done over the years, conveniently forgetting about his half-Cherokee great grandmother? Since that night not so long ago when Titus Ogilvie had flooded his home with intruders and resurrected his Cherokee heritage, William had been haunted by images of a dried up crone, but he had never been certain whether these were actual memories grounded in experience or nightmarish visitations to torment him for the cruel misfortune he had brought upon his family. Wherever the elusive truth might lie—and whatever that truth might be—William Drummond was convinced he and he alone stood accused, indicted, tried and convicted of being responsible for all the evils that had befallen those he so dearly loved.

Having pronounced himself guilty, William thought it appropriate to recall a few of the more endearing memories of this woman who had possessed his soul from the moment he first met her at the home of a friend in Savannah. They had been together for more than a quarter of a century. She had given him two wonderful children. Together they had built a home and a family. But strangely William was unable to summon forth a single, detailed memory of his life with Elizabeth Ann Sheffield Drummond. It troubled him greatly. Would he ever be able to remember? All he could think of in one of those insane flashes of insurmountable grief was how his precious Elizabeth, lying lifeless in the box before him, couldn't even smell the new pine boards that made up a portion of her coffin. It was an aroma she had always loved. A fragrance she had treasured above flowers or exotic perfumes. It had been her one positive comment when they first arrived at Coosawattee. *I love the smell of the freshly cut pine logs,* she had said the first day while unpacking their possessions. But it didn't take long for that rich smell to be overwhelmed by the malodorous stench of vomit, rotten food, disease, diarrhea and death.

Susanna gently placed a loving hand on her father's back. He blinked in recognition, but his eyes remain fixed on the rustic box that would be his beloved Elizabeth's final resting place.

* * * * * * *

The rain had finally stopped by the time they trudged back into the Coosawattee camp. William Drummond walked with his head down, appearing older and more defeated than his daughter had ever seen him.

Susanna's eyes drifted aimlessly, looking around at nothing in particular. Then she saw him. William, unaware that she had stopped, kept moving toward their shelter area. Susanna stared across the river of plodding mourners at her husband. Peter Tanner stood outside the quartermaster tent, which, she had learned, also served as his living quarters. Even from this distance she could tell he'd been drinking again. She noted, however, that he appeared genuinely sympathetic, as though he wanted to talk to her. If he had something to say, she thought, let him make the effort to come to her and say it. She waited but Peter didn't move. Susanna glared at him, then hurried to catch up to her father. Only after she had gone did Peter take a couple of steps in her direction, but no more. He didn't follow. Even if he could have found the words to say, it was probably too late. What would be the point?

Upon entering the shelter, Susanna went immediately to check on Meg. The widow of John Sixkiller had been sitting with the sick child. Susanna's eyes widened with horror when she touched Meg's burning face where red measle blotches had appeared.

"Oh, God..." the words slipped from her lips with a heavy breath.

"*U-ne-yo-ti-s-gi*," the old woman pronounced her diagnosis of the obvious.

William had been staring statue-like at Elizabeth's empty bed. "Meg has the measles," Susanna broke through his wall. As she had done since she was a little girl, she looked to her father for a solution. This time, however, William's only answer was a lost expression. With the glassy-eyed fatigue of a man twice his years, William sat down on Elizabeth's cot. He reached underneath, pulled out a small jug of whiskey and took a stiff drink. Then he reached under again, this time bringing out a hammer.

"What are you doing?" Susanna asked.

William took another drink before answering in a flat voice, "Granny Swimmer just died. I have to help Charlie and *Tsu-tsu* make a coffin."

Susanna watched her father push himself up from the cot and walk out into the mist. She knelt beside Meg and gently stroked the fretful child's fevered head. Quietly Susanna buried her face in the blankets at her daughter's side, her body twitching, racked with deep, silent sobs. She had never felt so alone.

* * * * * * *

The relief of the isolated rainstorm was only temporary. In a couple of days everything had turned hot, dry and dusty once more. Susanna used an old ax handle to beat the dust from a blanket

456

hanging outside on a rope strung between two shelter poles. Her hair had grown longer than she had ever worn it before—now braided on either side and twisted up around her head, much as she had seen Eva Swimmer do on numerous occasions while sitting outside the shelter at night, waiting for the air to grow cool enough to sleep.

Eva approached carrying a basket of berries. With a wary eye, Sally kept her mother as a shield between herself and Susanna. Eva shook out a portion of berries into a dented old pie tin. Susanna stopped pounding the blanket.

"Hello, Sally," Susanna leaned past Eva with a smile. Sally ducked to safety behind her mother.

"Each day we have to go farther and farther just to find a few berries," Eva voiced concern. "They're almost gone. And only a couple of the *a-ni-ya-wi-s-gi* will let us go out at all." She handed the pan to Susanna. "Here. Give these to Meg when she wakes up. How is she doing?"

"Better. Much better," Susanna said, feasting on a single berry. "I was so afraid we would lose her."

"We were lucky. Sally had the measles three years ago."

"*U-ne-ti-s-gi,*" Susanna tried to pronounce the Cherokee word for the disease.

"*U-ne-YO-ti-s-gi,*" Eva corrected her.

"*U-ne-yo-ti-s-gi.* Measles," Susanna said, pronouncing it perfectly.

"Very good," Eva smiled.

"It's not at all like French," Susanna remarked. It was a veiled apology for insensitive remarks she remembered having once made about her accomplishments at finishing school. Eva's smile broadened to a grin. She hadn't missed the subtle message. The women chatted idly for a few more minutes like neighbors across a backyard fence on a breezy April afternoon.

After Eva and Sally moved on, Susanna went back inside the shelter where she found Meg asleep on the make-shift cot. Her complexion was finally free of red blemishes. Susanna sat on the edge of the bed and gently awakened her daughter. Meg opened her eyes, stretched, rubbed her face and managed a smile—the first Susanna had seen in a long time.

"Let's go see if we can find Grandpa," Susanna suggested and kissed Meg on the tummy. "You can share these berries with him."

Meg sat up, pulled the pan into her little lap and briskly devoured all but three of the berries, saving those for her grandfather. Susanna playfully shook the child's foot, immensely grateful to have her daughter brought back from the precipice.

*   *   *   *   *   *   *

Near the creek in the corner of Ft. Coosawattee, William Drummond sat on an earthen berm that afforded him a view looking out through the camp's main gate. Susanna sat down beside him. Neither spoke. It was as though his job was to watch the gate and hers was to watch Meg, Sally Swimmer and her brother, Buck, playing with a raccoon they had adopted and which no one had yet thought to kill and eat. From their vantage point, William and Susanna could see at an angle through the gate to the burial ground outside the camp. What they saw there had by now become a distressingly familiar scene. Two separate funerals were in progress. In grim anticipation, three new graves were being dug only a few feet away.

Susanna had never seen her father looking so sad and helpless. In perfect synch with the distant lamentations of the graveside mourners, he lifted the whiskey jug to his lips. She studied him for some time before speaking gently, without scolding.

"I've never seen you drink so much."

"I never *needed* it so much," he wiped his lips with the back of his hand, an unrefined gesture they both knew he would never have made prior to the events of the past months.

"It won't bring Mother back," Susanna said softly.

"I should have been there, Susie. With her," he said, his voice heavy with self-condemnation. His eyes never left the cemetery. "We should have gotten her out of here when we had the chance."

"What chance?" she challenged. "From Peter? I told her to go, but she insisted on staying. I was proud of her."

"I should have made her leave," he repeated in his dull, guilt-ridden tone. "She might be alive today."

"We don't know that. What we *do* know is she would never have allowed the family to break up," Susanna said, continuing her attempts to console him. William took another drink. She watched him in silence, but when he started to lift the jug again, she gently took it from him. "I know it isn't easy for you, Poppa."

For the first time he looked directly at her with a sad smile. "*Poppa.* You haven't called me Poppa since you were a little girl." His eyes drifted back out to the burial ground as though trying to locate his wife's resting place. "So much is happening, and I have no control. I've always been in control. I'm frightened, Susie. I feel so helpless."

She studied the twists of dry grass at their feet, then finally looked up at him and said, "But you're *not* helpless."

William was puzzled. He was trying to tell her he had run out of answers. What was she saying? Still holding the whiskey jug, Susanna got up and took a few steps toward the children, keeping her eye on them. Then she spun around to face her father, her voice charged with newfound excitement.

"Why can't you and Chief Ross and the rest of your so-called tribal leaders just go and tell General Scott you want to be in charge of getting us out of this place?! These people—no, *we, our* people—don't trust the army. And these state militia hooligans! My God!"

"It isn't that simple," he said, failing to embrace her enthusiasm. But his daughter would not be denied.

"Who said anything about *simple*?! Nothing in our lives has been simple for a long time now! But I am sick to my very soul of this wretched place. They've taken our home—there's nothing we can do about that now. So let's get on the road! A few of us will die! And that's tragic. But we're dying in here every day. By the dozens! By the score! What will it take? A hundred dead a day? In each camp? 'Til there's no one left? For God's sake, let's get going!"

Was this his Susanna? William wondered. Sophisticated, sybarite Susanna of the Charleston Ladies Conservatory finishing school? Debutante Susanna of the governor's ball? Intolerant Susanna who her entire life had despised any and all things having to do with Cherokees? He was taken aback by her passionate outburst. Even the children had stopped their play to gape at her, as had other Cherokees in the vicinity. Realizing she had created a stir, Susanna quietly rejoined her father. She handed him the whiskey jug and bent close to him, her voice a coarse whisper, the tears flowing from a face twisted in anguish.

"Poppa...we *must* get out of here!" she squeezed his arm, then scooped her daughter up and marched back toward the shelter.

* * * * * * *

In the growing darkness a fourteen-year-old Cherokee watched the horses tied to the trees surrounding Chief John Ross's cabin, located near Red Clay, Tennessee, just across the Georgia state line. The boy's attention drifted frequently to the twitching silhouettes on the window covering, back lit by the glow of lanterns and the flames from the fireplace.

The mood inside the cabin was somber. *Gu-wi-s-gu-wi* delicately lowered a handful of brittle old papers into a wooden box lined with a heavy, black, water-proof wax cloth. Those who watched him could see the flowery, swirling script of pages penned in English and many others written in the symbols of the Cherokee language introduced two decades earlier by Sequoyah.

Helping the chief pack the Cherokee Nation's valuable documents for transport were his wife, Quatie, his long-time friend and assistant chief, George Lowrey, the Hicks brothers, Charles—Ross's predecessor as principal chief—and Elijah, and tribal elder statesman, the arthritic but proud Going Snake. William Drummond still thought of himself as a *yo-neg*, though his very life had crumbled because he was, in fact, part *Tsa-la-gi*. The only true white man there was Chief Ross's actor-turned-journalist friend, John Howard Payne, who shared William's background of formal education and a fascination for Cherokee history. Ross paused to watch the two men pouring over one of the documents with great interest.

"In nearly all the treaties the *Tsa-la-gi* have made with the *yo-negs* down through the years, the *yo-negs* always say two things," *Gu-wi-s-gu-wi* held up one finger. "*We have to take your land. There is no other way.*" Then he held up another finger and said, "*But this is it. This is the last time we will take Cherokee land. This is all we want. We will be satisfied....*"

"The first part is always true," Going Snake said, his long, white hair dancing each time he nodded with emphasis. "But the second part is the lie. They are never satisfied. And they never stop taking."

John Ross knew the old man spoke wisely. "The land we go to in the west is good land. I've seen it. But you mark my word: they'll find a way to take it from us."

Quatie finished wrapping the last of their china place settings handed down from John's grandmother on his Scottish father's side. "We have to go there and become strong again," she said, then looked across the box she was packing straight at William. "*Wi-li* speaks true. We must go soon. Before we all die here in these stinking prison camps."

William seized the opportunity to underscore the suggestion he had brought them following Susanna's impassioned plea.

460

"Initially, we thought a delay in the hottest part of summer would help," he acknowledged his involvement in their previous strategy to which General Scott had agreed. "But it's only gotten worse. If we don't go soon, everyone will be too weak. Too sick to travel."

William was glad when the taciturn George Lowrey spoke in favor of his new position. "And there is much work—hard work—to be done at the end of the journey. To prepare for winter," the assistant chief said. All those present looked at each other, each realizing they had arrived at a key turning point in the fate of the *Tsa-la-gi* people.

CHAPTER
39

Two horses bearing the brand of the U. S. Army were tied up in the grove of sycamores with a group of others whose tack identified them as Cherokee. A couple nibbled idly at the flaking, peeling sycamore summer bark. Their ears flitted back and forth, listening to the rustle of leaves and snapping of twigs that pinpointed the location of their riders walking through the woods on this bright, warm summer day.

General Winfield Scott was accompanied, as always, by his *aide de camp*, Corporal Edward Mears, stiff and proper, his leather bound log book tucked firmly beneath one arm, always exactly four paces behind the general. Not so close as to crowd the commander, yet always within ear shot and ready to jot down an order, a reminder or merely something worth remembering. Scott had loosened the collar of his tunic for this stroll in the forest and was enjoying the huge cigar John Ross had presented him. The Cherokee chief, along with the Hicks brothers, George Lowrey, Hair Conrad and William Drummond walked with the general. Trailing the others by a few steps—amusing themselves by making Edward uneasy in their subtle Cherokee way—were the tribe's elder chiefs, Going Snake, White Path and *Tsunaluska*.

The men moved at a leisurely pace among the trees adjacent to a pool formed in the creek by a natural earth and rock dam. General Scott drew a long drink from the fat cigar and studied it with appreciation as he blew the smoke out in a thin jet. He stopped near the widest part of the pool and cast a sidelong look at the Cherokee leaders.

"I already know about your meeting at the Aquohee camp, gentlemen," he said. Scott wanted to impress upon them that he was aware of their movements, their meetings, their planning and plotting.

"A meeting of the National Council," Lowrey explained.

"Not much happens in these camps that I don't know about," Scott said and lowered his three-hundred-plus pounds onto a fallen log adjacent to the creek. "Edward. Pull off my boots," he barked at his *aide*. Immediately the corporal sprang into action. He carefully laid his leather pouch on the log beside Scott and began tugging at one of the general's boots.

"If you know all this, General, then you know why we are here," Chief Ross said.

"To tell you the truth," Scott chuckled, "I haven't the slightest idea, Chief. Why don't you tell me. To complain about the camps, I suspect. I know *I* certainly would." He exhaled with great satisfaction when the second boot finally came off. "Ahhh, that feels good."

"Conditions in the camps are insufferable, General," William didn't want that point to go begging. "And they're getting worse every day." Scott looked up at William and offered his sincere condolences.

"I was sorry to hear about the passing of your wife, Mr. Drummond."

"Thank you, General. Many families have suffered great loss."

"I know. I know," Scott motioned with the cigar to his *aide*. "What are the latest figures, Edward?"

The corporal scrambled to flip open his leather pouch and whipped out the requested report. "August 31st - fourteenth week of incarceration at the Cherokee Indian Agency encampment. Population: approximately 3200—close to 4,000 counting Negroes. Remittent fever: 11. Flux: 60. Dysentery: 100. Wounds: 25. Measles: 63. Whooping cough: 40. Dead: 6." He stopped reading and there was a painful silence. Finally he asked, "Do you want figures from the other camps, sir?"

"That's enough, Edward. That's enough." Scott shook his head, then gestured at the Cherokees with his cigar. "So....make your point, gentlemen. Whatever it is." He pushed his mammoth frame up off the log and, to the astonishment of the others, pulled his trouser legs up tightly around his fat knees. John Ross spoke his piece as formally as though they were standing before Scott's desk back at his New Echota headquarters.

"General, we realize the delay you granted is about to expire. We understand that final removal is imminent."

"Yes, Chief. It is. Get to it," Scott urged, then walked a couple of steps out into the cool creek, the water rising halfway up to his knees. "Ooohh. Damn, that feels good!"

The older Cherokee leaders watched him, exchanging wry glances. This simple act by the aging military commander had elevated him in their eyes. "Good things happen when a chief goes to the water," White Path pronounced.

William felt compelled to make their point but didn't want to risk irritating the man who controlled their fate. "General, we'd like you to consider—just consider—putting us in charge of the removal."

This unusual request did, indeed, grab the general's attention. "By *us* you mean...?"

"The Cherokee National Council," Lowrey said, then glanced at John Ross. "Under the direct leadership of *Gu-wi-s-gu-wi*. Chief Ross."

"Fully empowered by the tribal council to negotiate all contracts, distribute the allotments, make travel arrangements," William elaborated.

General Scott balanced on one foot—remarkably well for a man of his girth—and swished the other foot back and forth in the cool waters. "Interesting...." he said, taking another puff on the cigar, then pointing the wet end of the tobacco log at Ross. "This better not be just another one of your stalling tactics."

"Not at all, General," the chief reassured him. "We need to get going. Bodies are dying, true. But worse than that, their spirit, their hope is dying."

Scott waded out farther into the pool. The water came up just above his knees, soaking his trousers. He heaved another pleasurable sigh and the end of the cigar glowed red-orange. His *aide's* eyes were wide with disbelief, but the corporal said nothing. Scott noted Edward's reaction. It was evident the general greatly enjoyed making the young man uncomfortable. "Does this bother you, Corporal Mears? Me getting in the water?"

"Sir! No, sir!"

"You're a damn liar, Edward," Scott chuckled softly, then looked *Gu-wi-s-gu-wi* in the eye. "You know, a lot of your people placed their hope in *you*. Hope that you would defeat this treaty. Now that you've lost that battle, will they still follow you?"

"*Gu-wi-s-gu-wi* is chief of the *Tsa-la-gi*. Nothing has changed that. The people will follow," George Lowrey ascribed to the rest of the tribe his own allegiance to his chief.

Scott pursed his lips and continued to ponder the proposal. The Cherokee leaders grew more encouraged. He could easily have refused by now. The more questions he asked, the more time he took to consider, the better their chances, they felt.

"And I suppose you'd assign the procurement and provision contracts to that brother of yours?" Scott asked.

"Lewis," Chief Ross mentioned his brother by name. "Would that be a problem, General?"

"No! On the contrary!" the general shook his head vigorously. "I've been told the two of you run a good business. Some of the contractors we've had to deal with...." he trailed off,

464

recalling his run-ins with the likes of Titus Ogilvie. Taking another draft on the cigar, Scott looked around and spotted a large submersed rock. Impulsively, he sat down on the boulder, the water rising up to his chest. "This is the best I've felt since I came here!" he announced and glanced up at Edward who couldn't hide his shock at this transgression of proper military protocol. "You breathe a word of this, Corporal Mears, and I'll have you court-martialed and shot."

"Yes, sir!"

With his leather pouch gripped tightly under one arm, Edward snapped to attention and focused on the trees beyond the general. Scott took the cigar out of his mouth, careful not to get it in the water. "Come here, Corporal," he ordered with a twisted smile.

"Sir?" Edward's brow furrowed.

"I said come here! Are you deaf?"

"No, sir...I...there?...over there?" Edward was completely bewildered.

"Right here," Scott pointed to another rock in the water beside him. Edward didn't move. "Right here, damn it! Is that so hard to understand?"

In a good natured way the Cherokees were being thoroughly entertained watching the general toy with his *aide*. Edward was a military man. And a military man follows orders. His face registered his discomposure, but he obeyed and walked out into the water—boots and all—until he was standing waist deep and at attention in front of the general.

"Sit down, Edward."

"Sir?"

"Sit," Scott repeated, pointing to the rock beside him. "Right here." Edward kept his back stiff and erect. His eyes drifted down to the general, then to the rock just beneath the surface. "Now, Corporal! Sit!" Scott roared. Edward lowered himself stiffly into the water, holding his leather pouch high in the air with both hands like a sacred scroll. "There! Doesn't that feel good?"

"If—if you say so, sir," the corporal stammered.

"Damn right, I say so!" General Scott grinned with the big cigar held firmly between his teeth. "All right. Where were we?" he asked. "Oh, yes, I believe we were turning the removal over to the Cherokees," he squinted, weighing the proposition. "Actually, it's a damn good idea." These were more positive words than any of the tribal leaders had expected. John Ross flashed a look of renewed hope to his companions. General Scott methodically continued with all the reasons why he thought it a good plan, as though to more firmly convince himself and to prepare the rationalization he might be forced to present to a military court martial when this thing turned sour. "Your people don't trust the army. Hell, who can blame them? They refuse to eat. They won't answer roll call. Won't cooperate in any way. Maybe they'll listen to you. Of course, you'll have a military escort. For your own protection."

"We would insist on it, General" Chief Ross assured him.

"And then I can send most of these boys home," Scott played out the scenario in his mind.

Ross wanted absolute confirmation the removal was being transferred to his people. "So, you'll agree to let us take over?"

The general paused and squinted up at Ross, his forehead wrinkled. "Are you sure you and your brother can handle the arrangements? For twelve...thirteen thousand people?"

"Yes, General. We can handle it," Ross was already ahead in the planning.

"Good," Scott pointed at him with the soggy end of his cigar, "I can get rid of these thievin' white bastards with their government contracts." The general beckoned to some of the other Cherokees. "Gentlemen...if you could give me a hand..." Hair Conrad and the Hicks brothers waded out into the water and helped pull the portly commander to his feet. Corporal Mears rose and snapped to attention. "I'll have Edward draft the order...soon as his britches are dry. Right, Edward?"

"Sir! Yes, sir!" the young man appeared to stiffen even more, if that were possible.

The general smiled and nodded, imminently pleased with his decision and the prospects of its ultimate fallout. He splashed toward land and chuckled, "Damn! This'll give ol' Andy Jackson an apoplectic fit! I'd give anything to see his face."

When they reached the water's edge, the Cherokees on the bank extended their hands to help pull the uniformed leviathan to shore. Old chief Going Snake repeated White Path's earlier words. "Good things happen when chiefs go to water."

With his feet planted firmly on land once more, his dripping uniform sagging heavily on his massive body, General Winfield Scott shook the hand of each Cherokee leader there, men to the last one whom he had come to appreciate and respect.

* * * * * * *

The shadows of the Ft. Coosawattee headquarters offered a cool respite from the late afternoon sun—an ideal place for off-duty Corporal Robert Barton to curry his horse. Barton, in his military boots and trousers but no shirt, had his suspenders pulled up on his well-muscled, sweat-glistening shoulders. He paused to douse himself with a dipper from the bucket sitting on a stump, shook his head vigorously to shed the excess water and froze when he spotted Martha Swimmer watching him from a few yards away.

"*Ma-di!*" he said excitedly, grabbing his shirt off the saddle slung across the hitching rail.

"How are you feeling?"

"Better. Much better, thank you. I go back on duty tomorrow."

"I was so worried. That you might die."

She had shortened the distance between them while he was putting on his shirt and he went the rest of the way to meet her. She didn't resist when he took her hand and pulled her close. "You got me through it," he said, his gratitude sincere.

"I'm sorry about Virgil."

"I wrote to his family," Robert said. "I told them how much you had helped."

Martha was astonished—but pleased—that he would mention her in his letter to the family of a *yo-neg* soldier. Her hands slipped inside his open shirt, tracing up his broad, muscular chest until they emerged above his collar and found his face. Their lips met in a long, sensual but gentle kiss. His chest was pounding and he felt the stirring of his own passion. It was an inner fullness he had never experienced before and, at the same time, an incredible emptiness he knew only she could fill. Then as impulsively as they had connected, she placed her hands on his chest and pushed back.

"What is it? I'm sorry. Did I do something wrong?" he pleaded.

"No," she said, looking up into his eyes with a longing as deep as his own. "But I have to keep reminding myself—you'll be leaving soon. A lot of the soldiers have already started back to their homes. I'm sure you'll get your orders any day now."

"*Ma-di*. Please, don't be sad," Robert whispered. He couldn't bear the thought of her being unhappy. Or of not being with her. Yet reality had been pounding at his consciousness for several days. It was a picture in which he hadn't been able to reconcile the life of an American soldier from Massachusetts with a young Cherokee girl who would soon be forced to ride a river barge or to march overland to Indian Territory. Barton would not, could not open that door. He pulled her back to him, but this time they didn't kiss. They simply stood quietly, their arms around each other, staring off in different directions.

CHAPTER

40

For the first time in weeks the stir of activity within the walls of Ft. Coosawattee wasn't due to a fight, a fire out of control in one of the shelters, the pursuit and punishment of an escaping Cherokee or the wailing and mourning that inevitably accompanied the bearing out of a dead child or grandmother. Cherokees, soldiers, wagons—both old and new—horses, mules and oxen hustled in all directions in preparation for their imminent departure. Trunks, baskets, boxes and blanket-wrapped bales were loaded onto wagons, carts and beasts of burden—including cows, goats and a thin but sturdy pig, in addition to the usual draft horses and mules. The doctors continued their efforts to help the sick and to ease the suffering of the dying. But the cries of the survivors and the incessant chanting of medicine men and medicine women proclaimed the dismal failure rate of the *yo-neg* medicine which, the government had assured the Cherokees, was vastly superior to their own primitive, archaic treatments. While the living prepared to depart for the west, many of their loved ones were carried out to the burial ground on litters, in boxes or merely wrapped in their own disease-infested blankets to be planted in the earth, facing east, to begin a final journey of their own.

The Drummond's area of the shelter was no different from any other. William and Susanna were busy packing. Boxes and trunks sat open. Clothes, blankets and other items lay inside, outside and in between. William had intended to pack quickly, but each item that found its way into his fingers was gently rolled, weighed and examined, conjuring up memories of Elizabeth—memories he felt compelled to indulge, lest they slip into forgetfulness as they had on the day of her funeral. And it was these treasured vestiges of their past, William knew, that would carry him through the days ahead.

Going hurriedly through her prized steamer trunk, Susanna examined a number of things which she had once insisted on keeping, shook her head wondering why and tossed them onto a growing pile to be burned or left behind. Meg helped by indiscriminately pulling one item after another out of a trunk or box and dragging it to the discard heap. Susanna watched Meg, thought about scolding her, then decided it made little difference what was taken, what wasn't.

"So what happens now?" Susanna looked up at her father.

469

"Everyone will be moved from the camps to the nearest departure point. For us, that'll be Ross's Landing," William welcomed the interruption from his reverie.

"We're all going by boat?"

William shook his head no and resumed packing. "Some will go by river," he answered. "But there aren't enough boats for everyone. Most will go by land."

"What about us? Are we going by boat or by land?" Susanna asked, not that it made any difference.

"We won't know until it's time to leave. Did you have a preference?" he wondered. Susanna didn't answer. William looked around at her. She was seated on the edge of her cot, holding her satin wedding dress. Then he noticed her attention wasn't on the dress but on an old leather letter pouch.

"I used to carry briefs in that years ago when I first began practicing law," he said. "You must have been about Meg's age."

"Mother gave it to me before she died," her voice cracked with emotion. "She made me promise to find Michael and give it to him." Susanna clutched the letter pouch tightly to her breast and looked up at her father, the tears welling up in her eyes. "Do you think we'll ever see Michael again?"

"Of course we will...of course we will," William said, his words hollow and unconvincing, his eyes glazed with a distant look. Susanna took his hand with an affectionate squeeze.

"I'm so very proud of you, Father. You've been good for the Cherokees."

William broke out of his daydream and smiled down at his daughter. "You're turning out to be a pretty decent *Tsa-la-gi* yourself."

Meg was sitting in front of a box which she had almost completely unpacked for the second or third time when the men appeared at the opening of the Drummond's shelter area. The precocious little girl grinned up at Going Snake, White Path and *Tsunaluska*.

"*Wi-li! Tsi-ne-na!* Let's go!" Going Snake called and made a face that delighted Meg.

"There's a council meeting," *Tsunaluska* added. "*Gu-wi-s-gu-wi* wants you there."

"I'll finish packing," Susanna said, rising from the cot. She wrapped the letter pouch in one of Elizabeth's old shawls and placed it back into the trunk. William dug through the pile on the other cot and found his hat. He turned to join his Cherokee friends but

470

stopped short, staring at the entry way.

The Cherokee elder statesmen had stepped inside to wait and had been replaced in the entrance by Peter Tanner. He was in civilian clothes and his arm was no longer in a sling, though he held it cocked in front of him, a result of its never having healed properly. The old Cherokee men's faces remained frozen. Their eyes didn't hide their intense dislike of this universally despised *yo-neg a-ya-wi-s-gi*. William, too, openly scowled his displeasure.

"Afternoon, sir," Peter said politely.

"Peter..." William's voice was chilled. Susanna spun around at the sound of Peter's voice.

"What are you doing here?"

Peter evaded the blunt challenge and forced a playful greeting for his daughter. "Hello there, little Meggie!"

Margaret Elizabeth looked quizzically at her mother, then busied herself again with the box she was packing. Or unpacking. White Path caught William's eye and beckoned to him. They needed to be going. William checked with Susanna to see if she needed him to stay.

"Go ahead, Father. I'll be all right," she told him. William adjusted his hat and left with White Path, Going Snake and *Tsunaluska*. Susanna squeezed the wedding dress in her hands, keenly aware of the irony it represented with Peter suddenly standing before her. She set the dress aside and began picking out articles of clothing and other mementos of Peter's, including an oil painting they had commissioned shortly after the marriage. Peter had posed tall and proud in his uniform; Susanna so lovely in the very dress she had just rediscovered.

Peter picked up the beautiful gown, running his fingers back and forth across the smooth fabric. Still seated on the cot, Susanna snatched the garment from him and tossed it back into the box where Meg sat playing. She then shoved the oil painting into Peter's hands, and jumped up, energized by the brilliance of the idea that had struck her. Susanna gathered up all Peter's things heaped on the bed. When she had an armload, she marched to the opening and tossed everything onto the ground outside.

"What are you doing?" he asked.

"I'm divorcing you," she answered with undeniable satisfaction.

"You're what?!"

"I've learned it's the custom of my people," she said. "The Cherokee woman decides when the marriage has ended."

"Are you having fevers? You're no Cherokee woman! You're no more one of these dirty savages than I am!" he said, completely perplexed by her behavior.

"Oh, but I must be, Peter," she snipped. "Why else would I be here? All I have to do is put your things outside the door," she said as she dropped the last item and flamboyantly brushed her hands. "There. It's done. We are no longer man and wife."

Peter looked down at the pile, then up at his wife—his *former* wife—and shook his head at her apparent dementia. Finally he spoke. "I came to tell you I've resigned my commission."

Susanna concentrated on her packing, making it obvious his presence was unimportant to her. "Are congratulations in order?"

"The shoulder and the arm have refused to heal properly."

"And that must make it very painful to swing your saber or to shoot defenseless Cherokees in the back," she jabbed. "The tragic end of a brilliant military career. I'm so sorry."

"I'm not here for your sympathy. Or your sarcasm. I'm going into business for myself," he informed her.

"How enterprising of you."

"I don't think we shall see each other again."

"Proving once again," she quipped, "that God, in His infinite grace, does answer prayer."

Peter bent down and picked up Meg. She neither resisted nor embraced this man who was a complete stranger to her. He studied her as though she were some mysterious elfin creature.

"I suppose you must think sarcasm becomes you, Susanna. Well, in your prayers, ask God if perhaps this little girl might still have a grandma if you had taken your mother out of here when you had the chance."

Susanna glowered at him, her face rigid with anger. "I might be sarcastic, Peter, but you are cruel. I'd like you to leave now."

"I intend to take Meg with me," he said.

Susanna's nostrils flared. She stepped toward him, fighting the urge to snatch Meg away.

"This is no place for her," he continued. "I can give her a good life. Culture. Education. Things she won't have where you're going."

Susanna took Meg and shifted her to the hip farthest from Peter. Her voice was soft but intense. "I don't know what false sense of guilt or obligation has filled your head with such foolishness, but you will never—*never!*—have this child. You've ignored her since the day she was born. You've shunned us both because she wasn't

472

the son you'd always dreamed of. You don't love Meg. You're only doing this to spite me."

"And you'd rather drag her into the wilderness with a bunch of savages just to prove your point!" Peter barked his exasperation, then forced himself to be calm. "If necessary, I'm prepared to ask General Scott to issue an official mandate granting me custody of Margaret Elizabeth."

Susanna deposited Meg on the cot and then stepped close to Peter. Her voice was a mixture of trembling desperation and burning anger of an intensity he had never known her to possess. "You listen to me and you listen good, Peter Tanner. If you ever so much as come near this child, I will rip your heart out and feed it to the ravens! Do you understand me?" She ended her declaration with a sharp breath, as shocked as Peter at the image she had painted. Where had such words come from? she wondered.

"Perhaps you've become a bit more the savage than I thought," his lip twitched the way she had seen it do many times when he couldn't decide whether or not to let it snap up into a sneer.

"Get out!" she growled. "And don't ever come back."

They glared at each other for a long time before Peter finally stepped to the entry way and, with a little flourish, tossed the oil painting onto the mound of his things she had thrown outside. He looked back at Meg one last time, then marched away.

Susanna sat down on the wooden box by her trunk and pulled out the dried, wilted bridal bouquet she had so carefully packed and transported through the gates of Hell. She tossed it out the entry way where it landed on the portrait of her and Peter. She picked up the wedding dress and embraced it in a flood of emotion. Then, with teeth-gritting determination, she began ripping the dress apart.

* * * * * * *

Three rough-hewn boards had been nailed up between two pine posts outside the Ft. Coosawattee headquarters. In the early morning coolness it was the focal point for several companies of soldiers when new duty rosters, detail sheets and, more importantly, release notices were posted. Word had begun circulating the day before that a big change was in the offing regarding the removal of the Cherokees. The enlisted men knew little or nothing about the administrative and logistical realignments involved, but included in the rapidly spreading rumors had been hints of early releases. Most of the soldiers couldn't have cared less where the Cherokees went so long as it meant they—the soldiers—were going home. Among those pressing forward with anticipation were Corporal Robert Barton and his friend, Private Miles Franklin.

A short distance away—unnoticed by Barton or Franklin—Martha Swimmer dumped an armload of possessions reclassified as rubbish onto a huge bonfire fed continuously by the Cherokees since it was ignited the previous afternoon. Martha had just started back toward the elongated shelter when she spotted Robert and Miles. She observed them at a safe distance from the shadow of one of the few trees left standing inside the camp. A smile played at the corner of her lips. She enjoyed watching Robert and his friend talking and shifting from one foot to the other with nervous anticipation. She wished she were close enough to hear their words.

A gruff duty sergeant with a long but neatly kept moustache swaggered out to the posting board and tacked up a new set of papers with the butt of his pistol. When finished, he roughly pushed the nearest soldiers back a couple of steps.

"All right! Quiet!" he yelled, then hooked his thumbs into his belt. "If your name is on this list, you will march to New Echota at sunrise tomorrow. There you will either be discharged from the army or reassigned to your next duty post." His words were met by a roar from the assembled troops. Even the normally dour sergeant was in a good mood. "Unless, of course, you wish to volunteer to escort Injuns out west!" he joked, eliciting hoots and laughter from the men. The sergeant then added a sober note. "Seriously, men—if your name ain't on this list, you'll be serving extended duty and will assist in the removal of these Cherokees to the territories."

The sergeant ducked beneath the posting board and headed back toward headquarters. Immediately the men surged forward, crushing each other to get to the list. In a few seconds the first group of soldiers had found their names and burst exuberantly through the crowd.

"We're getting out of here!"

"We're going home! We're going home!"

"Boston, here I come!"

"It's Richmond for me!"

Once the first wave of soon-to-be-liberated soldiers had vacated the area immediately in front of the board, others, including Robert and Miles, pushed closer to search for their own names. Robert ran his finger down the list to the "B's". It was there! *Barton, Robert Corp.* A hop to the next column and down until he found *Franklin, Miles Pvt.* And just as the others had done, Robert and Miles exploded jubilantly back out through their pressing comrades.

"I'll bet you can't wait to get as far away from this hell hole as your horse will take you!" Miles said, brimming with excitement.

Robert laughed in agreement. "I'll tell you, Miles, after what we've been through, a million miles would still be too close to this place!" When they came to a stop, Robert was stunned to find himself looking into the face of Martha Swimmer standing less than fifteen feet away. His heart exploded in his chest with the most searing anguish he had ever known when he saw the pain his overheard words had etched into her face. *"Ma-di..."* he said softly. He reached out to her but she hurried away before he could get closer. *"Ma-di*! Wait!"

She quickened her pace, losing herself among the bustling throng of Cherokees, and he knew it was useless to go after her.

*   *   *   *   *   *   *

The Cherokees busily packed their wagons and carts. Grown men strained beneath the load of huge bundles which they leveraged up onto the backs of horses and mules. The atmosphere wasn't so much one of exhilaration as of sheer relief at finally getting out of Coosawattee. The Cherokees' haste was born more of an urgency to go before the authorities changed their mind than of any real anticipation of the journey ahead of them. Many who had been herded into the camp weeks earlier had already departed, but their journey had taken them only as far as the sloping burial ground outside the main gate. The hundreds who had survived were preparing to go forth in their own corpse-like condition, beaten down by time, fatigue, disease and depression.

In contrast to the mental, physical and spiritual burdens born by every adult prisoner every minute of every day, an occasional burst of laughter erupted from the younger children—the healthy ones at least. In and out they darted among the adults and the animals, between wagon wheels or under the belly of a harnessed mule, ignoring parental caution to stay near the family, only to scurry back to mother or father when a *yo-neg* soldier strolled through the area, watching, patrolling, keeping order or hurrying things along.

Eva and Charlie Swimmer piled their belongings onto their large wagon. Like many other wagons throughout the camp, many of Charlie's sideboards were missing. They had been requisitioned to build coffins, in some instances for the very *Tsa-la-gi* who had leaned against those same boards on their ride into Coosawattee. After positioning the parcel and lodging it firmly between two others, Charlie Swimmer looked across his wagon into the sneering faces of newly promoted Sergeant Charles DeKalb and two of his men, Corporals Stevens and Thorpe.

"So. Guess the cholera didn't get you, huh, Chief?" DeKalb said. Charlie remembered with an icy glare the men who had driven him and his family from their home. He hadn't liked them then and he didn't like them now.

"It's a good thing, I reckon," Stevens joined in. "Guess they need him around to protect this purty little thing..."

Martha came out of the shelter and tossed a pack atop a large, two-wheel cart hitched to a scrawny ox. She glowered coldly at the soldiers who were ogling her.

"Leave us alone," she hissed defiantly.

"It's gonna be a long trip, Missy," DeKalb raised an eyebrow. "We liable to become close friends...*real* close..." Stevens and Thorpe joined DeKalb in a lusty laugh before moving on. Martha continued to glare at them until they had disappeared into the throng, then looked back in the direction from which they had come. She was searching for something. Or someone. But the clouds of dust from the tramping of feet—animal and human—and the spinning wheels of the wagons and carts had reduced visibility to only a few yards in the crowded lanes between the long sheds and in the open area around the main gate.

"Forget it, *u-we-tsi 'ge-yŭ*," Charlie Swimmer told his daughter. "You'll never see him again."

"I know," she murmured sadly and lowered her eyes. Disappointed, she went back inside the shelter.

Charlie readjusted the same carton he had already firmly seated three times and said to his wife in a low voice, "I tried to tell her, all *yo-neg* soldiers are no good."

Eva pushed his hands away and situated things the way she wanted them. "She's not interested in *all* of them. Only one."

"Still. It's no good."

"Have you forgotten, *Tsa-li*?" she caught his arm, "how we were at that age? How my father was against you?"

"That was different," he refused to meet her eyes.

"Different time. Different place," she said and touched her own chest. "But in here, it's the same."

476

"But he's *yo-neg*," Charlie insisted. "I'm glad he's gone. He didn't even say good-bye to her. What does *that* tell you?" That was all he wanted to say on the matter and all he wanted to hear. Charlie started back into the shelter and was met by his youngest, Sally, who ran out to him crying. She raced to the tiny cart to which she had hitched *Tsu-s-qua-ne-gi-dŭ*, her pet goat. Charging out right behind her were her brothers, *Tsu-tsu* and Buck.

"No! I won't let you! No!" Sally cried.

"*Tsu-tsu!*" Eva grabbed her older son by the arm as he ran past. "What have you been telling her?"

"They said you're going to kill *Tsu-s-qua-ne-gi-dŭ!*" Sally answered before the boys could speak. "That we have to eat him, or we'll die!"

"It's true! It's true!" Buck continued to tease his sister.

"Hush, Buck!" Eva snapped. "*Tsu-tsu*, she's only a child! You're old enough to know better!"

Sally took a defensive stance in front of the goat and pointed at her brothers. "We'll kill you instead!" she yelled. "That'll be two less to feed! Then we'll have plenty for everybody!"

"Come here, *Sa-li*," Eva beckoned. "It's all right. No one's going to kill *Tsu-s-qua-ne-gi-dŭ*."

"Not yet, anyway," Charlie chuckled under his breath.

"Charlie Swimmer!" Eva poked him in the ribs. Charlie gave *Tsu-tsu* and Buck an affectionate cuff on the back of their heads and pushed them toward the shelter.

"Get back to work, you two," he said and followed them inside.

"Come here, *Sa-li*," Eva called again. Satisfied that *Tsu-s-qua-ne-gi-dŭ* was safe, Sally joined her mother and together they headed toward the Drummonds' area.

Meg sat on the blanket near the shelter opening and watched her mother loading the wagon. Eva arrived and picked up one of Susanna's bags, muscling it up beside the others.

"Thank you, Eva," Susanna said, breathing heavily, spent from the labor. She looked past Eva at the little girl who was still frightened of her. "Hello, Sally!" As usual, the child hid shyly behind her mother, confused by Susanna's soft and gentle tone. "Please don't be afraid, Sally. I'd like you to come here. I have something for you. Something special."

Eva, sharing Sally's curiosity, gently pulled her daughter from behind her. With her hands on Sally's shoulders, she inched the child closer to Susanna. Sally approached with trepidation, frequently looking up at her mother. Susanna squatted to Sally's level and unwrapped a tattered piece of an old blanket to reveal a beautiful, hand-made doll, much like the one Sally had lost on the morning the soldiers came and drove them from their cabin. Sally's eyes widened in amazement at the wonderful creation fashioned from Susanna's wedding dress. Eva was as stunned as her daughter. Sally looked up and Eva nodded, indicating it was all right to accept the marvelous gift. Sally took the doll and cradled it in her arms as though it were her own living child. For the first time she found a warm smile for Susanna.

"What do you say, *Sa-li?*" Eva prompted gently.

"*Wa-do*...thank you," Sally dipped her eyes shyly. Susanna rose and saw the gratitude in Eva's face.

"That was your wedding dress," Eva whispered.

"Maybe she'll get better use from it than I did," Susanna said, sharing a knowing look with Eva before they went back to work.

* * * * * * *

By late afternoon the exodus from Ft. Coosawattee had begun. Wagons creaked, overloaded with possessions and riders—primarily the very old and the very young. There was an acute shortage of wagons. Much of what the Cherokees had brought in was left behind and a lot more had been burned, but in the past few months many of the wagons had been dismantled for coffins or for replacement parts to make other wagons fit for the journey. Anyone able to walk was required to do so. But undeniably there were more riders than before—the weak and infirm who hadn't recovered from the many diseases that continued to plague the *Tsa-la-gi.*

What had earlier been an irritating haze of dust grew into a tangible, choking cloud, thickened by the smoke of the bonfires, many of which were still shooting flames twenty to thirty feet in the air. Most of the shacks and lean-to's around the perimeter walls were torn down and set ablaze, along with a couple of the long shelter buildings themselves. Ragged and dirty whites with sores on their faces and greed in their eyes unabashedly entered the camp and scurried about like rats. Some even attempted to rescue items from the fire. The *Tsa-la-gi* gathered what they thought they could carry and the Devil take the rest. Into the flames. Finally, wagons began rolling and feet plodding toward the main gate. The normally stoic expressions of the Coosawattee inmates became portraits of dismay, terror, fear, confusion, anger and, for many, a tragic resignation.

Susanna and Meg were seated beside William in the Drummond wagon. Meg twisted around and waved her own doll—a little different in appearance from Sally's, but made from the same wedding gown. Immediately behind the Drummonds was the Swimmers' wagon. Eva was at the reins. Martha and Sally rode with her. This time Sally clung tightly to her new doll. Each time she saw a blue-uniformed *yo-neg* soldier she shifted her *baby* protectively to the other side and gripped Eva's skirt a little tighter. In her mind she attributed the tragic loss of her first doll directly to these demon creatures who had forced them from their home. Unaware that she had dropped the doll on the morning they were taken captive, Sally, in her sleep on many nights since, had relived the nightmare in which the soldiers came in the darkness to steal her baby. And had Sally not flattened herself beneath the covers, held her breath and made herself invisible, they surely would have taken her, too. Now she was determined they would have neither.

Beside the Swimmers' larger wagon Charlie walked with the two-wheel cart, rhythmically slapping the old ox with a cane switch. Fulfilling his embarrassing punitive assignment, *Tsu-tsu* followed behind them. He zig-zagged, keeping Sally's beloved goat, *Tsu-s-qua-ne-gi-dŭ*, and its tiny cart on course. Buck cracked a slender reed switch above the goat, mimicking his father's actions with the ox. From the wagon, Sally gloated down at *Tsu-tsu* with a victorious smirk.

Soldiers were everywhere. More than usual, it appeared to William, Charlie and many others. Some were mounted, others on foot. They moved up and down the line, making certain the able-bodied Cherokee men and boys stayed with the group and didn't attempt to break away. Martha Swimmer's eyes followed first one cluster of soldiers, then another. It was difficult to make out their faces in the thick smoke and dust until they were only feet away, and then they often disappeared before she could get a good look. Hope would rise, only to be dashed when a soldier turned and it wasn't Robert Barton.

The Swimmer wagon, like so many others, was forced to stop near the gate where the traffic bottle-necked at the narrow opening. There they noticed many soldiers who didn't appear at all concerned with the departing Cherokees. They were preparing to leave Coosawattee and march to New Echota where they would be reassigned or discharged.

"Corporal?" Martha boldly called out to a soldier on foot,

leading his horse near the Swimmer wagon. He apparently didn't hear her. "Corporal!" she said louder. Miles Franklin finally responded with an apologetic smile.

"Sorry. I was a private for so long. I just got promoted," he announced proudly. Stepping closer to the wagon, squinting against the dust and smoke, he finally recognized Martha. "Oh...hello, Miss Swimmer."

"Have you seen Corporal Barton?"

"Corporal Barton?" he shook his head no and smiled. "Don't know any Corporal Barton, ma'am. You might ask my sergeant." He looked past her. The newly promoted *Sergeant* Robert Barton rode up beside the wagon. To everyone's astonishment, Martha leaped right into his arms and clung tightly to him. Robert was at once pleased and touched—and more than a little embarrassed. He put his arms around her and finally managed to pry her face from his chest, forcing her to look up at him.

"I knew you wouldn't leave me," she said softly. "I knew it."

"I volunteered," Robert explained his presence in the escort patrol. "Miles and me both. I wanted to find you and tell you immediately, but they kept us at New Echota for briefing."

Impulsively, she reached up and kissed him.

"Hey..." he teased, "we were told not to fraternize with the *Tsa-la-gi*." She kissed him quickly once more as though specifically to break the rule. He glanced around, then with a what-the-hell shrug he kissed her, long and passionately.

Charlie stopped the ox cart on the other side and stood next to Eva seated in the wagon. She looked down at him with a raised *I-told-you-so* eyebrow. Seeing his daughter so happy, even Charlie couldn't entirely suppress a smile. But it was of short duration, disappearing the instant the other soldiers trotted into view out of the dust cloud.

"Let's go, Barton!" DeKalb barked. "You know the rule about mixin' with the Injuns." With him were his usual cronies—Stevens, Thorpe, Whitaker and Evans—all of whom, like Miles Franklin, had been promoted as an inducement to serve as volunteers escorting the Cherokees to the west. Robert regarded DeKalb with every bit as much antipathy as did Charlie Swimmer. "Go on. Put her down," DeKalb said, then added with his familiar sneer, "Unless you gonna just give her your army mount to ride!" He pulled close enough to slap Robert's horse on the rump with his reins, spooking the animal and almost dumping Martha in the dirt. Robert regained control and safely deposited Martha back onto the wagon. The normally placid young sergeant then spun his horse around and pulled up close to DeKalb, leaning right into his face.

"Someday, DeKalb...someday, you're going to push too far."

"Yeah?" DeKalb grinned at the challenge. "And what'll you do, Sergeant Barton? You learnin' some good Injun tricks? You gonna scalp me?" The grin faded when Robert continued to glare at him with an intensity that unnerved even DeKalb. Without answering, Robert spun away, tipped his hat to Martha and trotted out through the gate. DeKalb shrugged off the confrontation and spurred his horse, almost knocking both Charlie and Corporal Franklin down. He galloped back down the line, followed by Stevens and the others.

Eva gave Martha an approving pat on the leg. "I'm glad he's going," she said confidentially. "He's a good man." Martha appreciated her mother's support and looked down at her father. Charlie pretended to be busy coaxing the reluctant ox to get started. Martha smiled. She knew her father well.

The congestion of wagons eventually creaked into motion and began rolling out through the main gate. Occasionally a Cherokee glanced back at Coosawattee, much of which was engulfed in flames. The homesick expressions they had worn when rounded up and forced from their cabins were gone, replaced by a different kind of sadness. And while many refused to look back at the filth, disease and humiliation they were leaving within the walls of Coosawattee, there wasn't a single eye—even of the blind—that didn't seek out the piece of ground outside the camp that symbolized the journey's end for so many of their friends and loved ones.

41

Rattlesnake Springs, Tennessee

More than six hundred wagons hitched to horses, mules and oxen—in teams of two, four and six—sat motionless, strung out along the undulating road over the gentle hills as far as the eye could see, disappearing into the forest. Carts and wagons were piled high with the belongings of emigrants who were weary before the journey had even begun. Clumps of people gathered around each wagon, shaking hands and saying good-bye to sick friends and relatives who would remain behind for a time, hoping to gain strength and come along with a later group. A somber stillness lay heavy on the whispering masses, betraying a universal and permeating sadness of the heart.

The *yo-neg* doctors who had given so freely of their time and their love in caring for the Cherokees—Butler, Springfield, Hamilton and many others like them—dispensed the last of their paltry supply of pharmaceuticals and closely checked the younger children and the very elderly who were about to depart.

Lone widows and unmarried or widowed old men attached themselves to whatever family would have them, grateful to be accepted and gratefully received. In many cases they substituted for grandparents who had perished in the camps. A bony knee to sit on or a soft if sagging breast to lie against, a refuge of solace for a young Cherokee boy or girl. Like so many of the adults, most of the children still couldn't fully comprehend what was happening to them.

Quatie Ross was among those angelic souls who scurried about, caring for the young, giving herbs and medicinal concoctions to mothers and lending encouragement to the aged.

Barton, Franklin, Baker, DeKalb, Stevens, Thorpe, Whitaker and Evans were among the host of soldiers—some volunteers, others by compulsory assignment—moving casually up and down the line. Many, like Barton and Franklin, were friendly toward the *Tsa-la-gi*, even when they received only blank looks or sidelong glances of cold mistrust for their kindness. Others, like DeKalb and his men, donned their masks of practiced disdain and had few civil words for their aboriginal charges.

The Drummond's wagon wasn't in this line, but the Swimmer wagon and ox cart were. It had been decided by the tribe's leadership that William and his family would remain behind for a short time and then go by river. They would camp near Ross's Landing for a few days—under military guard, of course. But Susanna and Meg had come out to Rattlesnake Springs to say good-bye to the Swimmers. Sally hugged little Margaret Elizabeth.

"Bye-bye, Meg," she said. Each child loosened her tight hold on her new doll just long enough to press them together in a parting embrace.

"I wish you were going with us, *Su-si*," Eva said.

"Chief Ross wants my father to go on the river," Susanna explained. "Keep yourself safe, Eva. We'll see you when we get there." It was a phrase uttered hundreds of times on this day, more as a prayer of hope than as a prediction or a promise. She hugged Eva and Martha, then held Martha at arm's length with a warm word of encouragement. "I hope your soldier turns out better than mine did, *Ma-di*."

"Robert is different," Martha said, recalling his own words. Susanna gave Martha's hands a loving squeeze.

"I know. Don't let him get away."

Martha clung to Susanna and pulled her aside in need of a confidant. "Susanna..."

"What is it, *Ma-di*?"

"I don't know..." Martha's voice was filled with hesitation and uncertainty. "I'm worried maybe I'm not good enough for him..."

"Nonsense!" Susanna wouldn't hear it. "Don't you talk that way! You're as good as any man alive!"

"No, I don't mean that," Martha shook her head. She looked around, her discomfort evident, and whispered, "I mean—I wish—I—well, Robert is well educated. I wish I had gone to school more."

Susanna realized her advice had been sought because of her own formal education, which struck her as ironic, given her past snobbery and her present situation. She put an arm around Martha's shoulder and took her a step or two away from the wagons.

"When we get to our new home, we'll just have to make sure the Cherokee Nation sets up a good school, proper for educating lovely young ladies like you."

"I'd like that," Martha smiled shyly.

* * * * * * *

William and Charlie stood near the front of the Swimmer wagon. *Wi-li* had come to say good-bye to his friend of so many years. He shook hands with *Tsu-tsu* and Buck. It made the boys feel important.

"It won't be easy, Charlie," William said gravely.

"For any of us," Charlie added. They clasped hands, then William put his arm around *Tsu-tsu's* shoulder. "Keep your father on the right trail, Martin," he said. "And Buck," he added, mussing the younger boy's hair, "you don't let him go near the whiskey peddlers!" *Tsu-tsu* smiled and shook William's hand again. Buck swelled with pride and viewed his assignment with the utmost sobriety.

Sergeant Barton, Corporal Miles and a couple of other soldiers approached. Robert spotted Martha, flashed her a smile, then addressed her father. "Good day, Mr. Swimmer. Everything ready to go?"

Charlie didn't answer. Barton ignored the snub and sneaked another glance at Martha. Franklin and the others moved on down the line. Barton tipped his hat to Eva, then followed his men.

"He's a good man, *Tsa-li*," William said of the young soldier.

"He's a *yo-neg*," Charlie insisted.

"So was I, at one time," William reminded him. Charlie smiled with understanding, then leaned closer to William. "I know he's a good *yo-neg*," Charlie muttered softly with a wink. He thumbed back toward Martha. "But *she* doesn't have to know I like him."

* * * * * * *

The time drew near for them to actually begin the long journey west. Anticipation ran high among the Cherokees. All up and down the line of wagons and carts, large clusters gathered to be led in prayer by their Christian spiritual leaders—Reverend Jesse Bushyhead, Reverend Evan Jones, John Wickliffe, also called *Ka-ni-da*, *O-ga-na-ya* and others. In other groups, traditional medicine men and medicine women chanted, prayed, *fixed* tobacco or smoked their pipes and entreated the Great Spirit to grant safe passage for those who were about to embark on a journey into the unknown.

Cherokees had gone west to Arkansas Territory before, and many had returned to the east on tribal business or for personal visits with stories of the verdant beauty that awaited them. Tribal leaders—including *Gu-wi-s-gu-wi*—had been there and could vouch for those descriptive accounts. But many of these Cherokees who would soon find themselves sleeping on the road and waking up each

484

morning in unfamiliar surroundings had never been more than ten miles from their rustic forest cabins. And the concept which the *yo-negs* were incapable of grasping—from the president of the United States to the lowest ranking soldier who would prod them along their way—was that for the *Tsa-la-gi* it wasn't simply a question of geographical relocation. For a people whose deepest, ingrained cultural, social, familial and religious foundations were inextricably linked to the God-given land itself, this forced removal constituted nothing less than a savage and unforgivable rape of the spirit.

The venerable, white-haired, eighty-year-old Going Snake waited beside his pony atop a knoll overlooking the meandering river of humanity extending before him. He gazed out at the western horizon, his lips scarcely moving as he earnestly pleaded the case of his people before *Ye-ho-wa*, the Great Spirit. A low area between Going Snake's hill and another adjacent to the main road formed a shallow valley where many of the tribal leaders congregated to discuss the logistics of the impending departure. William Drummond joined Lewis Ross, Charles and Elijah Hicks, Hair Conrad and Thomas Forman, along with the trail conductors selected to guide the Cherokees on the long overland route. Maps were spread on the grass as the men discussed last minute details. On the second hill General Winfield Scott stood with principal chief John Ross, *Tsunaluska*, White Path, *Situwakee* and a few more of the older leaders. Each man held the reins of his horse and surveyed the churning sea of Cherokees below. General Scott studied the men in the shallow valley between the hills.

"Some of these men are new to me, Chief Ross," he said. "Have you elected new leaders?"

"We held our final council meeting this morning," Ross explained. "These men have been selected as trail conductors. You know the Hicks, Charles and Elijah. And there's Moses Brown. Daniel Colton. James Brown. Peter Hildebrand—this is his group leaving today. That one there—John Taylor. And John Drew will bring the last group."

General Scott had transferred much of the responsibility for the removal to the Cherokees, and he had full faith in their ability to select the appropriate leaders and trail guides. "You've made all the arrangements for your supplies along the way, I trust?" he asked.

"The suppliers have been given a schedule to meet us at pre-designated locations, with instructions to wait for us if we're late," Ross explained.

"How can you be sure they'll be there?" Scott asked Ross with a raised eyebrow. "Or that they'll wait?"

"We've already paid them," Ross answered.

"That doesn't really answer my question, does it?"

"I guess we'll just have to trust them, won't we," the chief replied. General Scott's sidelong glance and subtle smile showed his appreciation of Ross's irony. The military leader looked at *Tsunaluska* sitting proudly on his horse. The old warrior had a long face.

"Chief *Tsunaluska*," Scott called to him. "I know it makes your heart sad. I hope you will find true peace in your new home."

Tsunaluska turned to the general with a dignity of bearing and a profound wisdom Winfield Scott would never forget. "It is one earth, General Scott," he delivered the words with the weight of all his years. "One mother. One father sky. We are all brothers."

"Yes, I believe that, Chief."

"Today, the white man finds it easy to kill his red brother and drive him from his home," *Tsunaluska*'s eyes burned into the *yo-neg* warrior chief with a prophecy that sent chills up the general's spine. "Before the full season of a man, the day will come when the *yo-neg* will turn and kill his own. This land you take from us today will flow with your own blood and the blood of your white brothers."

After a long silence the general spoke in a low, solemn voice. "You could well be right, Chief."

The general's *aide*, Corporal Edward Mears, rode up the hill and stopped next to Scott. Accompanying Mears was Peter Hildebrand, earlier pointed out as the leader of today's departing group. Hildebrand was a sturdily built man with an air of quiet confidence. It might not be an easy journey, but there would never be any doubt who was their leader or whether he knew what he was doing.

"Yes, Edward?" Scott greeted Mears with a wave that passed for a salute.

"Sir. Mr. Hildebrand is ready to get them under way."

Somber looks came from each man present. Atop the adjacent hill, Going Snake had mounted his snow-white pony. He raised his seven-foot-long ceremonial lance straight up in the air.

"Move on!" Going Snake shouted. He urged his pony down the hill at a steady walk. The first wagons lumbered forward, and one by one the Cherokees began their journey west. When he reached the road, Going Snake trotted toward the head of the wagon train. Peter Hildebrand caught up with the ancient chief and they were joined by other Cherokee men and women who rode behind the

486

respected old warrior in a final show of tribal pride. When they neared the front wagon they were greeted by a peal of thunder rumbling in from the west. The noise grew louder, rolling toward them with a deafening roar. Going Snake stopped his pony, triggering a halt by those riding behind him. As if by some unseen signal, all the rest—wagons, riders and those on foot—stopped in their tracks. The old chief was facing west, his white hair streaming out behind him in the stiffening wind. On the horizon they beheld an unusual climatological occurrence. Two black funnel clouds dipped out of the sky. The wind increased to mighty gusts. Horses spooked; oxen rolled their eyes with bovine apprehension.

In anxious silence the Cherokees witnessed a rare phenomenon—twin tornadoes. To a superstitious and spiritually attuned people, this was an undeniable omen. It was made even more portentous by the fact that, with the exception of this one isolated spot in the distance, the rest of the sky was sunny and bright with no sign of clouds or rain. Eventually the funnel clouds moved off to the west, marking the direction to the Cherokees' new home. And then, as suddenly as they had appeared, the double twister columns withdrew into the black underbelly of the thick clouds just before they vanished beyond the horizon.

The entire wagon train appeared frozen in time and space like a Brummet Echohawk painting until Going Snake urged his pony forward at a walk, followed by Hildebrand. Whips popped on oxen backs. Axles creaked. Horses strained in harness. Wagon wheels began turning. Boots and moccasins shuffled off through the dry, dusty soil.

High above circled *ta-wo-di*, the hawk, its shrill cry a mournful farewell to the one-time inhabitants of these forested hills. Wider and wider the majestic bird expanded its winged circumference until it disappeared from the view of the westbound *Tsa-la-gi*.

*   *   *   *   *   *   *

Ross's Landing

The scene at Ross's Landing was a marked contrast to the departure from Rattlesnake Springs two days before. This was a swarming bedlam. People milled about everywhere. Some moved with destination and purpose, others were aimlessly lost. Wagons that had carted people and their belongings from the concentration camps had been abandoned in chaotic disarray. Cherokees with full wagons attempted to thread their way down to the shore. Many *Tsa-la-gi* far back in the crowd simply left their wagons and went down to watch the loading of the keelboats. Wagons pulled as close as possible to the shore so boxes, trunks and packages of every conceivable shape and size could be passed on board by the human chain of Cherokees, black slaves, black freedmen and soldiers. A throng of Cherokees and blacks congregated near the awe inspiring steamboats that would tow the barges. They jumped fearfully each time the steam engine emitted its loud, dragon-like hiss.

Medicine men chanted to the boats to ensure the vessels would be indwelt by benevolent spirits. Soldiers yelled at curious Cherokees who had gone aboard the barges before being logged in by the clerks seated at a row of tables. Isolated pockets of men and women talked among themselves. Some cast their mistrustful glances at the boats and the soldiers, while others looked with great apprehension on the unending stream of Cherokees that continued to arrive. It felt like they would keep coming until those nearest the bank were forced into the river. Here and there a Cherokee played a mournful tune on a fiddle or on an old set of bagpipes handed down from a Scottish or Irish ancestor.

Principal chief John Ross piloted his horse carefully through the sea of confusion. He responded to greetings from his people, touching outstretched hands and offering words of encouragement to those who looked particularly fearful of the imminent departure. When not communicating with someone on the ground, Ross stretched up in the saddle, scanning the crowd as though searching for someone in particular. Finally, he spotted his target and began steering his mount toward William Drummond. Susanna was bathing Meg in a tub balanced on the tailgate of their wagon which contained only a couple of saddles and a few personal items, the rest having been unloaded near the water's edge. William had begun unharnessing the horses when Ross reached them and dismounted.

"*Si-yo, Gu-wi-s-gu-wi,*" William greeted the chief.

"*Si-yo, Wi-li. Su-si.* I was beginning to think I might not find you."

William paused to wipe his face in search of relief from the sweltering heat. They looked down toward the river. Although the Cherokees had been given control of their own removal, it appeared the army had taken over once more and were, in usual fashion, making a catastrophic mess of it all.

"It's getting out of control," William said. "I thought *we* were supposed to be in charge."

488

"I was told we are in charge of *gettin' the Injuns to the river.*
Those were the Major's words. The army, he says, will get us loaded
and on our way."

They unhitched the horses from the Drummond wagon,
glancing frequently down toward the loading area near the boats. "I
think more should be going by boat than by land," William observed.
"Especially the weaker ones. The sick. The old folks."

"Many are terrified of going by water, *Wi-li.*"

"That doesn't make sense," William said, puzzled. "I've seen
them going up and down this river all my life!"

"The Tennessee—here in the area—is familiar water. But
travelling into unfamiliar regions—by unknown waters—that's what
frightens them," the chief said. "Besides, it's important you and
some of the other leaders get there ahead of the rest. And the river
is the fastest way." They tossed the harness into the wagon and
pulled out the saddles.

"Maybe *you* should go on ahead by river," William suggested.

The chief shook his head no. "It wouldn't be right for me to
take the easier way. We'll be leaving in the morning. About two
hundred and fifty of us. We should catch up with Hildebrand's
group in a few days. The rest should all be on their way within the
next two or three weeks. In groups of a thousand or more. The
sicker ones will leave last. They need time to build up their
strength."

"Then we'd better pray for good weather, because they won't
survive a harsh winter," William warned.

"But if they left now, they'd perish on the trail for certain.
They're too weak."

"What do you want us to do when we arrive?" William was
looking ahead.

Ross thought about it while they brushed the horses and
positioned the saddle blankets. Finally he answered, "Meet with the
government agents. Make certain the allotments are arriving. Our
people will need their money to buy tools and seed to start their
farms. Try to get a feel for the mood of the military in the area.
Diplomacy will be a precious commodity."

"I don't know why we should expect it to be any different
there than it's been here," William snorted.

"You're probably right," Ross agreed. After a brief silence, he
shared his thoughts. "I'll tell you, *Wi-li*, my biggest concern is the
reunification of our people. It isn't going to be easy."

"Reunification?" William realized this was a master politician, always thinking, analyzing, planning, strategizing and, some of his critics would say, plotting and scheming. He watched the chief's blue eyes take on a glazed, far-away look.

"The white man has always counted on disagreement within the tribe to bring us down. They love to see us shed our own blood. They did it to the Shawnee. The Iroquois. All the tribes in the north that have perished."

"And you think they'll try it with us in the west?" William asked.

"They did it *here*, didn't they? Besides, our situation is ripe for it," Ross expounded. "We'll have three different factions struggling for power. The Old Settlers who've been there over thirty years. To them, we're *all* newcomers."

"And the Treaty Party. Major Ridge, John, Elias Boudinot, Stand Watie and the others," William was starting to see the picture.

"I'm sure they feel since they signed the treaty and were first to honor it by going west, they constitute the *official* tribal leadership recognized by the United States government," Ross added.

"But General Scott, the army, the government—they've all recognized *you* as chief," William argued.

"Yes. Here. Now. When it's convenient for them," Ross said. William found the chief unusually tense and frustrated. Ross continued, "When they wanted a treaty, they had no problem waiting until I was away and then recognized a more cooperative group. So, who knows what will happen in the west. This much I can tell you: unless there is peace among *all* the *Tsa-la-gi*, *none* of us will make it."

"You want me to talk to them? Ridge, Boudinot and the others?" William offered.

"It can't hurt," Ross agreed. "And it might help." He tightened the cinch on the horse he had saddled, then mounted his own. William brought the horses around and handed the reins up to Ross.

"What's this?" Ross looked confused.

William patted the blaze-faced roan on the neck and smiled up at the chief. "Well, this one's *your* horse, *Gu-wi-s-gu-wi*." Ross took a closer look at the animal he had helped William unhitch from the wagon and then brush and saddle.

"Why, so it is!"

"Lewis loaned it to me while you were in Washington," William explained. "I thought you knew. And this one..." he gave a loving slap on the neck to Stick, the long-legged black gelding he

490

had owned for so many years, a half-brother to Clancey, the big gray stolen outside the Hiwassee Indian Agency concentration camp. "I'd be obliged if you'd turn him over to Charlie Swimmer once you catch up with Hildebrand's group. Charlie'll get him to Arkansas for me. I'll need him out there to get started."

Ross took the reins and led the horses back toward the road. "I'll look for you at Ft. Gibson," he told William. "If you're not there, leave word where I can find you."

"I'll see you out west, *Gu-wi-s-gu-wi*."

"Count on it," the chief said. He circled the horses around the back of the wagon and smiled down at Meg, wrapped in a blanket and standing on the tailgate. Ross tipped his hat politely to Susanna.

"Good-bye, Chief Ross," she said. "Give our love to Quatie."

Ross lifted a hand in parting and rode away, leading the two horses.

CHAPTER

42

Despite the chaos at Ross's Landing, the barges were loaded and finally pulled away shortly after midday. By late afternoon, the smooth surface of the Tennessee River was a tortuous, shiny glass mirror snaking its way through the northeast corner of Alabama into the brilliance of the setting sun. The two smoke-belching steamers, the *Vesper* and the *George Guess*, crept steadily along, dragging the overloaded keelboats pressed almost to the water line with the weight of their human cargo and the Cherokees' possessions.

For the most part the *Tsa-la-gi* were a quiet and watchful lot. The overcrowded boats had proven in short time to be no more than floating versions of the concentration camps they had just left. As John Ross had said, many of the river travellers were burdened with an irrational fear born of superstition. The disquietude of others was grounded merely in the uncertainty of what lay ahead. But the waters were smooth and most were relieved just to be on their way. A few of the Cherokee women built fires and began preparing food at the metal fire boxes atop the house portion of the boats.

Susanna, with Meg in her arms, leaned into the welcome breeze near the front of the fifth barge tied to the *Vesper*. She knew her father was aboard the steamer, most likely on the captain's deck with their pilot, Army Lieutenant Edward Deas.

William and Lt. Deas watched the bare-chested young soldiers and blacks on the main deck below the bridge lashing down Cherokee trunks and boxes—items for which no room had been found on the keelboat barges. William glanced abaft where other soldiers and blacks gathered armloads of wood which they hauled forward to fuel the insatiable fires of the steam engine. And strung out behind the *Vesper* were the six keelboats under tow. Approximately 150 yards behind them chugged the steamer *George Guess*, piloted by Lieutenant R. H. K. Whiteley. The boat had been christened with the *yo-neg* name of the renowned Cherokee linguist and teacher, *Sequoyah*. With its chain of five Cherokee-laden keelboats, the *George Guess* was a mirror image of the lead vessel.

"Looks like we're making good progress, Lt. Deas," William observed. "I hope the rest of the trip goes as well."

Lt. Deas was young and friendly, strikingly handsome but very no-nonsense in the performance of his duties. His bearing was of a distinctive military architecture with a suggested nautical touch. He was good-hearted and more than a little sympathetic to the

Cherokees, yet he was pragmatic enough to realize there was absolutely nothing he could do, no recourse within his power to reverse the decisions which had been made in the halls of government. He couldn't overturn treaties, whether signed by legitimate council members of the Cherokee nation or, as he had heard rumored, an unsanctioned assembly who had been pressed into signing the Treaty of New Echota. What he could do was provide safe passage and humane treatment for all those in his charge.

Deas loaded his pipe, then offered his tobacco pouch to William who graciously accepted. The young lieutenant had taken an immediate liking to the tall, well-educated lawyer who, as William had often been told, seemed so markedly different from the other Cherokees. But Deas also realized many of those he was transporting had no Cherokee blood whatsoever, and others—like William Drummond and his family—such a minute portion as to make the government's entire removal policy based on fractional genealogy an embarrassment to any decent, truth-loving citizen of the United States.

"This first leg of the trip is always good," Deas studied the river ahead and gestured toward an area of darker waters. "This is the deepest part of the river. Even so, she's five, maybe six foot below normal. Look...there..." he pointed to the bank where a distinctive demarcation line ran along the soil and rocks about five or six feet above the water, indicating the normal shore line. "It's three feet lower than when I took the other groups through last June," Deas continued. "And we had trouble then. We'll be lucky to make it through *The Suck* before nightfall. After that, we'll have to stop."

"*The Suck?*"

"The first set of rapids," Lt. Deas explained.

"*The Suck.* That doesn't sound good," William's concern was evident.

"That's only the beginning," Deas chuckled, but there was a serious undertone to his voice. "Then comes *The Boiling Pot. The Frying Pan* and *The Skillet.* Each nastier than the one before. And with the water level down, it'll be a nightmare. The shallower the river, the closer you are to the rocks and the faster the water moves across them. Least it seems that way. I've been through them at night," he gestured back toward the *George Guess.* "But Lt. Whiteley, the other pilot, doesn't want to risk it. He's right, with all these people aboard."

"How much damage will the worst of these rapids do to the

keelboats?" William asked. He had already assessed the condition of the vessels and wasn't impressed with their seaworthiness.

"Speakin' true, Mr. Drummond, I doubt we'll make it that far. Just have to wait and see," Deas answered. With a sense of foreboding, William contemplated the water, then glanced back at the keelboats and at the *George Guess*. Finally his attention returned to Lt. Deas, who was intently studying the river ahead.

* * * * * * *

The Suck

The Suck was a demonic, swirling maelstrom that violently tossed dead tree trunks and other river debris like toys, shattering them against the large granite rocks that stood ready to deny all passage beyond this point of the Tennessee River. A quarter mile upstream, the steamboat *Vesper*, it's paddle wheel churning in reverse, had arrived with its load of Cherokee-laden barges to challenge the demons. And another quarter mile behind, the *George Guess* duplicated the *Vesper's* reversing maneuvers, coming gradually to a stop.

Lt. Deas scrambled from bow to stern, barking orders, overseeing the mooring of the keelboats safely to the shore and directing their alignment for their one-at-a-time escort through *The Suck*. He politely ignored William and some of the other Cherokee leaders who were trying to be helpful but were mostly in the way. Though ineffective in their efforts, Deas figured their presence and the illusion that they were contributing might allay the anxieties of the Cherokees who would certainly be feeling helpless and frightened at this point. The lieutenant stopped along the starboard rail to explain the situation to William and the others.

"We take them one at a time...through there..." he was forced to shout above the roar of the rapids as he indicated a place where the churning water was foamy white. In comparison, however, it appeared less agitated than any other spot. "Once we get a barge through, we'll tie it off downstream. Then the steamer doubles back over there—on the other side—to get the next one." He now pointed to an area along the far bank.

"Why can't we all just go through over there?" William shouted the question the others were thinking. "It looks like calmer water."

"It is," Deas agreed. "And we could, if the river was up. But

494

now it's too shallow for the keelboats. The *Vesper* draws a lot less, and she'll just barely make it."

"How long will it take?" one of the Cherokees shouted.

"Rest of the afternoon," Deas yelled. "The *George Guess* will come up and help. We'll be done by dark, if we're lucky."

"This is pretty dangerous, isn't it?" William once again voiced the obvious.

Lt. Deas answered with an ominous grin and reminded them the rapids farther downstream were even more hazardous. "This time tomorrow, you won't even remember *The Suck!*"

A young soldier trotted along the starboard side of the steamer to reach Deas. "First one's ready, Lieutenant," he reported loudly.

Deas waved. It was time to get down to business. He turned to William and the other Cherokees. "Tell all your people to get away from the edge of the boat. Stay in the middle. Make sure all fires are out and find something to hold on to! It's a rough ride!" Without further ado, the lieutenant headed for the foredeck. William and the others went aft and began shouting instructions to the Cherokees on the first keelboat. William searched the anxious faces, looking for Susanna and Meg. His concern mounted when he couldn't find them until he realized the barge that had been last in the tow line would be first to go through *The Suck*. A rapid scan of the keelboats tied up along the shore calmed him. He spotted Susanna and Meg at the rail of the barge. They waved tentatively when the *Vesper* began churning toward the rapids.

When the steamboat and its first keeler entered *The Suck*, the force of the current pushed the steamer at a sharp angle, violently jerking the tow cable and tossing the barge against the rocks. Lieutenant Deas had personally taken the helm for this perilous navigation. With intense concentration he fought the spokes of the large, wooden wheel. No one dared speak to him. William looked on with grave concern, but he had faith in this young man whom he guessed to be little more than Michael's age and who had, in a short time, earned the confidence and respect of the *Tsa-la-gi*.

The Cherokees aboard the barges still awaiting their shot at the rapids crowded the rails to watch. Some were convinced their friends were going down to certain death and their own would soon follow. Soldiers were kept busy discouraging them from grabbing what belongings they could carry and leaping ashore. The terrified passengers aboard the first keelboat to pass through *The Suck* were equally convinced they had entered their watery grave. But without exception they all did as they were told—they clung desperately to any rail, post or doorway they could dig their fingers into.

Despite the unusually rough waters—even for *The Suck*—Deas had done a masterful job of negotiating the rapids. When the *Vesper* lunged out of the swirling foam into the placid pool below, a loud cheer went up from the usually quiet Cherokee passengers and was echoed from the *Vesper's* decks by the soldiers and crew and from the Cherokees on the barges awaiting transport through the potentially deadly waters.

*   *   *   *   *   *   *

On the northern bank, high above the boiling waters of the Tennessee River, a slender, wiry Cherokee man in his mid-forties peeked out through the thick foliage with his one good eye. The left eye had been extinguished in battle with the British a quarter century earlier. From his hiding place he had watched the first keelboat being escorted—or dragged!—through *The Suck* and then anchored downstream to the north bank to wait for the others. *Tsisdu*, or Rabbit Man as he was often called, got his name from the occasional rapid twitching of the left side of his nose and upper lip, like an unconscious reflex attempt to clear and restore vision to the missing eye.

The *Vesper* circled back to the south side of the river just as the *George Guess* began bringing its first keelboat through the rapids. With the less-skilled Lieutenant Whiteley at the helm, the ride was even rougher than the *Vesper's* previous venture but was successfully completed. Throughout the afternoon the cycle repeated itself. Some of the passengers' possessions were tossed into the river, but so far there had fortunately been no casualties and no serious loss of property.

The steamers switched positions once more, the *George Guess* circling back upstream while the *Vesper* prepared to bring its next keelboat through *The Suck*. *Tsisdu* had made his way down the steep embankment—darting from bush to bush, tree to tree, a little at a time—until he was near the keelboats that had already come through the rapids. Once satisfied that virtually everyone on board was looking at the steamer and keelboat about to enter the treacherous passage, he slipped quietly down toward the water. What *Tsisdu* had not seen was the man on the *Vesper's* deck looking his way.

William Drummond had been studying the barges that had

496

already made it through for any signs of damage that would need to be repaired before continuing their journey. In his peripheral vision he glimpsed movement in the brush just above the keelboats.

"Lieutenant, may I...?" William reached for the spyglass hanging on a strap near the helm. Steadying himself against the bulkhead, he trained the glass on the shore and watched with great interest as *Tsisdu* glided through the brush along the river bank to some huge cypress and willows overhanging the water. In the shadow of the trees *Tsisdu* waded out toward the last boat that had just come through *The Suck*. William lowered the spyglass, puzzled by what he had witnessed.

Intriguing as it was, however, William had more important things to consider. The barge being towed through *The Suck*—the *Vesper's* fifth and the ninth overall for the day—carried his daughter and granddaughter. Susanna held Meg tightly in her arms and braced herself in the doorway of the keelboat's house. A young Cherokee mother beside them kept her hand firmly on the shoulder of *Me-li* (Mary), her five-year-old daughter. *Me-li* cradled a fluffy baby chick in her arms.

William grasped the rail firmly and made his way abaft along the *Vesper's* port side, seeking a better vantage point from which to keep an eye on the keelboat as they went through the rapids. He motioned with one arm to Susanna, screaming to be heard above the thundering water.

"Get inside! Completely inside!"

Susanna started back inside the house. The tow line snapped taut, jolting the barge and startling the little girl's baby chicken, which jumped free and fluttered out across the open deck. In an instant the child had slipped from her mother's grasp in pursuit of her pet. The mother cried out and bolted from the doorway after her daughter.

"*Me-li! Me-li!*" she screamed.

From the situation unfolding aboard the keelboat, William glanced ahead to the river. The *Vesper* was starting into the roughest part of the raging rapids. He waved wildly and shouted, "Get back! Go back inside! Hurry! Get away from the edge!" But his words were lost in the blaring *ka-chunk ka-chunk* of the steam engine and the angry roar of *The Suck*. Sensing impending disaster, William raced along the steamer's edge toward the rear deck. Susanna reappeared, clinging to the doorway, her face etched with horror. The young mother caught up to Mary just as the keelboat jerked violently to one side, throwing them both overboard into the unforgiving waters.

Aboard the *Vesper* hardly anyone had noticed. A couple of the white crewmen had seen, but they simply looked away, hanging on through the rough ride. It was easy to convince themselves there was nothing they could do. William looked around. He yelled forward to Lieutenant Deas, but he knew his words went no further than arm's length. And if they had, what could Deas have done? Without another thought, William drew a bead on the bobbing, floundering mother and daughter and plunged into the water.

Susanna handed Meg to another Cherokee woman who had joined her in the doorway. Clinging to anything at hand, she made her way to the edge of the keelboat. The young Cherokee mother was valiantly fighting the thrashing waters and frantically trying to locate her daughter.

"*Me-li! Me-li!*" she cried, gasping and choking.

"*E-tsi! E-tsi!*" her daughter's screams were faint and distant. Where was she? Where was she?

William pounded furiously at the water, keeping visual contact with his target while battling the current. He reached the mother first. She flailed and clawed at him, crazed with concern for her daughter, almost pulling William under.

"Stop fighting!" he yelled.

"Where is she?! Where is she?! *Me-li! Me-li!*" the mother cried, clutching at William's shirt. They both desperately scanned the water's surface while being tossed like driftwood in the churning rapids. From the deck of the keelboat, Susanna screamed as loudly as she could, pointing her father toward the child.

"There! Father! Over there!"

William could see but not hear his daughter. Following Susanna's direction, he finally spotted *Me-li* being driven farther out into the river by the swirling current.

"Get my baby! Please! Go!" the mother gasped and pushed him toward the child. William let go and began swimming hard in *Me-li's* direction. The young mother tried to follow, but she was slowed by the weight of her water-logged dress which had become entangled in the gnarled fingers of a dead tree.

As soon as the keelboat cleared the worst of the rapids, Susanna jumped overboard. She tore off most of her skirt before she began swimming with smooth, powerful strokes.

The Cherokees aboard the downstream barges had become aware of the emergency. They crowded the edges of their keelboats to watch the rescue attempt. William swam toward Mary, putting

498

more and more distance between himself and the struggling mother. But despite William's efforts the gap between himself and *Me-li* continued to widen as the current swept her swiftly away.

The onlookers reacted to a splash in the calmer waters near the keelboats where someone else had leaped into the river. They studied the surface until the one-eyed, twitching face of *Tsisdu* broke through. He got his bearings and began swimming with speed and agility toward the center of the Tennessee at an angle he hoped would intercept the little girl. He quickly covered the distance and reached *Me-li* just as she was going under. She had swallowed a great deal of water and appeared to be losing consciousness. *Tsisdu* adeptly got her in tow and started back toward the north bank.

William had become increasingly fatigued, but was still a good fifty yards away, struggling against the strong current. When *Tsisdu* reached the child, William rose as high as he could in the water and attempted to reestablish visual contact with *Me-li's* mother. He spotted Susanna and, at first, mistook her for the Cherokee woman. They swam several strokes toward each other before William realized this was his own daughter who had joined the search. They paddled in circles, anxiously surveying the swirling waters. When their eyes met the next time, each knew it was too late. The little girl's mother had perished. After treading water for some time, William clawed with weakening strokes back toward the bank. Susanna caught up with her father and swam beside him.

"We lost her!" William proclaimed the painfully obvious.

"We did all we could," Susanna saw the anguish in his face. "Are you going to make it?"

"I'll...be...all right! You...go...ahead," he said haltingly between strokes. She slowed her own pace to stay even with him. From the keelboats, Cherokees prepared to toss ropes as soon as any of the swimmers were close enough.

* * * * * * *

The night forest twinkled with campfires scattered up and down the river bank. More fires burned on the tops of the keelboat houses where many of the Cherokees had chosen to remain for the night. William Drummond sat at his campfire with a blanket drawn around him. He hoped the mug of steaming coffee cradled in his hands would brace him against the chill of the strong wind. Their camp was in a clearing close enough to the river to hear the water lapping against the sides of the barges. Susanna, in a dry, fresh dress, sat near her father. *Me-li*, or Mary, the young Cherokee girl rescued from the river, was also wrapped in a blanket. She clung to Susanna, the fear and anguish still evident in her eyes. Meg held on quietly to Mary's blanket. While neither child could fully grasp the finality of death, each appeared to sense the gravity of the ordeal. Voices from nearby campfires drifted their way, accompanied by a mournful tune from a Cherokee fiddle. From another, more distant campsite they heard a sad concertina. Mary looked continuously around the camp. William, Susanna and *Tsisdu* knew that in her little mind she expected to see her mother step out of the darkness at any moment and join them by the fire. They looked at each other, but no words could be found.

    Tsisdu poured more coffee for William, then checked on the rabbit roasting on a green stick. Satisfied it was done, he tore off a leg and offered it to Mary. Susanna reached for the meat, but *Tsisdu* pulled it back, then offered it again directly to Mary. She smiled at *Tsisdu* and took the food. *Tsisdu* tore off another leg and gave it to Susanna. She held it up before her and thought of all the years when she would have laughed—or wretched—at the idea of eating the leg of a rodent roasted on an open campfire. But on this night she bit into the seared meat with gusto, savoring its delicious juices and the pinch of salt *Tsisdu* had added. She offered a bite to Meg.

    William looked at his daughter with newfound respect and admiration. "I can't believe you just jumped into the river like that, girl," he said, shaking his head.

    "I can't either," she answered with a faint smile.

    "And you!" William turned to *Tsisdu*. "You were amazing."

    "I've always liked the water," *Tsisdu* said. "But the river can trick you."

    "*Wi-li* Drummond," William introduced himself. "*Ga-to-no de-tsa-to-a?*" he asked their guest in Cherokee.

    "*Tsisdu*," the little man answered. He paused, then added, "Rabbit."

    "Rabbit?" William repeated. *Tsisdu* grinned, his nose and lip twitching as if on cue. He poured himself some coffee. "Well, *Tsisdu*, you swim better than any rabbit I ever saw!"

    "And I make a damn good stew," *Tsisdu* threw in. William and Susanna exchanged a glance, not sure how to take the remark. *Tsisdu's* grin widened. "It's a joke! Rabbit stew! I'm Rabbit. I make a good stew!" William and Susanna looked at him then at each other, uncertain what to make of their new friend. *Tsisdu*

500

laughed softly, amused by his own brand of humor. Mary inched closer to him and held out her hand for another piece of meat.

* * * * * * *

The food had all been consumed and the fire had long since reduced itself to a bed of glowing embers. William and *Tsisdu* talked softly. Across from them Susanna lay staring up at the sky, with *Me-li* stretched out on one side of her and Meg on the other. *Tsisdu* rolled some herbs between his palms while he talked, allowing the shreddings to drop into his metal cup. He added a few more sprinklings from a bag here, a pinch or two from a medicine pouch there. William watched but did not question. *Tsisdu* glanced at Susanna and the girls.

"You're lucky, *Wi-li*, to have your family here with you," he said. William looked down and swallowed a pang of grief, a gesture not missed by the one-eyed man. "You lost someone. In the camps. Your wife?"

"Consumption," William answered, slipping momentarily into reverie before he finally asked, "What about you?"

"I wasn't in the camps," *Tsisdu* grinned. "They couldn't catch the Rabbit." His voice took on a serious tone. "My wife died many years ago, giving birth to our only child."

"I'm sorry," William offered his condolences. He wondered why a man who had successfully eluded capture by the army and most likely could have remained hidden in the hills and caves of North Carolina—as many others had done—would attach himself to a group of downtrodden Cherokees on their way west. "If they never caught you, why would you—I mean, now—?"

Tsisdu paused from preparing his concoction and looked out into the night. "I haven't seen my son for such a long time. That's why I'm going west. To find him."

"What's his name?" William asked.

Tsisdu, as William had done earlier, wandered for a time through the maze of his own reminiscence. "We called him *Sa-lo-li*. Squirrel," he explained after a long silence. "Because of the way he could climb up and disappear into a tree."

"I have a son," William said softly.

"I know," *Tsisdu's* nose twitched.

William glanced at the strange little man. How could he have known such a thing? Perhaps he didn't know but had merely said so to voice his empathy, William thought. *Tsisdu* looked at William with a nose-twitch and a smile, then dropped more grindings into the cup and added water from a pot simmering on the coals. Susanna, unable to sleep, sat up, drew her knees up in front of her and listened to her father and *Tsisdu*.

"You will see your son again," *Tsisdu* said in a mysterious tone. "You and me—we share the same dream."

Though William wasn't completely sure of *Tsisdu's* meaning, he took comfort in the little man's words. He glanced at Susanna. "What we did out there today—jumping into *The Suck* like that—could have put an end to that dream."

"Oh, no. It is meant to be," *Tsisdu* said. He swished the brew around in the cup, then poured half into another cup, handing one to William and the other to Susanna. "I saw it in the crystals. My boy. And the *Yŭ-wi-tsu-na-s-ti-ga*," he said, then added in answer to Susanna's puzzled look, "The Little People."

"Are you a medicine man?" William asked.

Tsisdu grinned. "I dabble. I dabble." He reached into his bag and pulled out a ratty old red bandanna, carefully unfolding it to reveal three long crystals shafts. He rolled them gently back and forth, staring intently, tracing over them lightly with his finger. "You will see your son..." he said in that distant, mysterious voice he had used earlier.

William found it interesting—even amusing. As a man of intellect—trained to always seek empirical evidence—he had never given credence to such things. Susanna was even more skeptical and took a hostile tone.

"Don't do this, Father," she cautioned William. "You have no right!" she snapped at *Tsisdu* indignantly.

"Michael is in trouble," *Tsisdu* stunned her to silence by speaking her brother's name. "He needs you. Both of you." William and Susanna were speechless.

"How did you know his name?" William finally asked in a near whisper.

Tsisdu ignored the question and continued gazing into the crystals. "He's in danger. The law is after him."

"That's why he ran away," William explained. "He thought he had killed a man. But the man lived."

Tsisdu shook his head and continued staring into the crystals. "No. This is different. This is now."

Susanna and William exchanged a look. She saw that her father, in his weakened state of mind, appeared ready and willing to believe whatever this man said, but she remained suspicious. It was obviously some sort of deception. A charlatan's game. This little one-eyed trickster had apparently dug up some information about them and had plotted to use it for his own gain. She predicted he would shortly ask her father for money or some favor. Yet she continued to watch with a certain undeniable fascination. The Rabbit Man continued to roll the crystals gently in his hand, then looked at her with a smile.

"Your brother has a son," he said.

"A son?! I have a grandson?" William broke in excitedly.

"He's a good boy. They call him—*Tsi-mi.* James. Jimmy."

"They named him after James," Susanna looked at her father. Something about the manner in which *Tsisdu* had spoken this last revelation struck something deep inside her. She couldn't explain why, but she knew he wasn't lying. They watched *Tsisdu* once again go inside his crystals. His expressive face with its tightly clustered features and his one beady eye registered a wealth of emotion as he appeared to experience one vision after another. They noticed the tears streaming down his cheeks from his one good eye and the withered socket. Though small—almost lithe, some might say—he was captain of an inner strength which through the years he had quietly tuned into a faculty that permitted him to peer into the lives of others. To read the secrets hidden behind their eyes. And when that window of revelation opened onto some aspect of his own life, he wasn't immune to the same emotional response often engendered in the totally uninitiated.

"It is good," he finally said in a soft, vulnerable voice. "It is good. You will find your boy."

Susanna felt a flood of compassion for the emotional little man. She still didn't understand, but she was no longer quite so ready to toss him back into the river.

"Don't worry, *Tsisdu.* You'll find your son, too," she said.

Tsisdu raised a finger to point at her. "I see you, too."

"I beg your pardon?"

"I see you in the crystals," he repeated. "With the *Yŭ-wi-tsu-na-s-ti-ga.*"

"Me? With those Little People?" Susanna was at first astonished at such an idea. He took his eyes off the crystals for the first time to smile at her. "Well, yes," she reasoned. "I suppose you would. Michael is my brother." She pointed at William. "He's my father. But I must tell you, Mr. Rabbit, ordinarily I don't hold with such foolishness."

Tsisdu folded the bandanna around the crystals and exhaled, as though the experience had both physically and spiritually exhausted him. "Someday you will believe," he said. He looked her right in the eye and added, "You have seen *wa-ya*, the wolf."

"How did you know that?" she gasped. A distinct chill fingered its way up the back of her neck.

"Rest now," *Tsisdu* said with a dismissing wave. "We have many hard days ahead." William was puzzled by the last exchange between his daughter and *Tsisdu*. He knew nothing of any wolf. Had Susie seen a wolf? She had never mentioned it to him. Not that he recalled. *Tsisdu* continued to watch her even after she turned from the fire and prepared to lie back down with the sleeping girls. "*'Ge-yu-ts'*," he said, using the familiar Cherokee form of addressing a young woman. "Don't be afraid to be who you are," he said. Then, to make sure there was no doubt about his meaning, he added, "*Tsa-la-gi*."

Susanna's eyes remained on the Rabbit Man. He tilted the pot and extinguished the coals with a loud hiss. Finally she stretched out on the ground, with Meg and Mary between her and William. Susanna could feel *Tsisdu* studying her and her father from the darkness for a while before he tossed a few remaining herbs onto the muddy ashes she was certain had been completely doused. To her amazement, however, a merlinesque flame shot four or five feet into the air and vanished. At that instant she heard from three distinct directions the cry of three separate night owls, as though they were responding to the mysterious flash of fire. Once Susanna's eyes had adjusted to the darkness, she made out *Tsisdu's* wiry frame and thought she saw him lift his face toward the thick trees surrounding their little clearing.

What Susanna had not seen were the Little People—the *Yŭ-wi-tsu-na-s-ti-ga*—perched in the treetops staring down at them. The faint light from other fires beyond the clearing flickered across their faces and shiny little bodies. Had Susanna been able to see them, she would have sworn one of them, sitting a little apart from the others, was a true-to-life miniature of *Tsisdu* himself, complete with left eye missing and the hint of a mischievous smile. What Susanna *did* see through the darkness, or so she thought, was a smile on *Tsisdu's* face. It was as though he had taken great consolation from some unseen source. He puffed one last time on his pipe before laying it aside and leaning back against the big rock. In that seated position he closed his good eye in sleep.

504

43

It had taken less than four days for John Ross and his band of 250 Cherokees—which included many of his close personal friends and relatives—to catch up with the larger Hildebrand group moving northwest across Tennessee. Throughout the day, creaking wagon wheels and tramping hooves along the wooded trail sent flocks of birds fluttering from the tree tops. The travellers welcomed the shady relief from the blistering sun and hoped the forest would remain with them for at least another couple of days. The first few nights on the road had ended on schedule at the pre-appointed campsites selected to place the travellers near creeks or springs to provide an ample water supply. In the beginning there had been an abundance of game along the way, hunted mostly by the younger boys, to supplement the government provisions. The journey, despite its tragically unfair genesis, had proven a welcome change from the confining stench and sweltering heat of the concentration camps. Because the Cherokees were still relatively close to their homelands, the army patrols had been particularly alert those first few nights, making sure no massive organized escape conspiracies ripened to fruition.

The early risers began stirring about four in the morning. The smell of coffee and fresh pork frying soon got the others up and about, and the entire group was organized and on the road well before sunrise. They had made good time for the better part of an hour when the train of wagons, strung out along the road for more than a mile, inexplicably came to a halt.

The large, rugged, hairy hand cocked the hammer of the old flintlock musket and the muzzle came up to press against the neck of *Gu-wi-s-gu-wi*. The heavily armed band of thirteen whites included some of the same Georgia militiamen who had helped round up and imprison many of these Cherokees. They had then spent the following weeks hanging around the camps, drinking, gambling and stealing whatever they coveted from the *Tsa-la-gi*. One of their leaders, and the man holding the rifle to Chief Ross's neck, was none other than Alton Ogilvie.

Ross sat calmly on his horse. There was little else he could do. He looked at Quatie sitting in the wagon. Though delicate and fragile, she was a strong woman and *Gu-wi-s-gu-wi* knew he could rely on her to have a stabilizing effect on the others. The Ross wagon was about a third of the way back in the train, so a large number of wagons had already passed before the band of whites first emerged from the woods. The forward wagons continued on for another two or three hundred yards before realizing those behind them had stopped. There were no soldiers around. *Gu-wi-s-gu-wi* figured their attackers had waited to catch a section of the wagon train unprotected by army escort. This short stretch of road lay between two sharp curves about fifty yards apart. Cherokee men began to appear on foot from up and down the line to find out the cause for the delay. Most of them had expected to find a wagon with a broken axle or a separated wheel rim. The chief looked down from his horse at the man holding him at gunpoint.

"I know you," Ross said. "You're a long way from home, Ogilvie." He looked around and thought he recognized some of the others. Two of them he remembered from years ago when Colonel Absalom Bishop and his Georgia Militia thugs had burst into his house in the middle of a rainy night and arrested him. The chief hoped a little talk would help defuse the situation. "Most of you are from Georgia. Do you intend to follow us all the way to Arkansas?"

"As far as it takes, Chief. 'Til we get what's ours," Ogilvie snarled and unburdened himself of a mouthful of tobacco spit. He cast a precautionary glance up and down the short stretch of road between the curves. "Where's your soldier boys?"

Ross spoke in a calm, almost casual tone, as though they had all been expecting this sort of interruption. "A few are scouting on ahead. Most are at the rear. Making sure the stragglers don't get too far behind. They'll be along any minute now."

"Is that right?" Alton grinned at what he thought was the Indian's feeble attempt to bluff. He spoke loud enough for the others to hear. "Then I reckon we better conclude our business and be on our way."

"And what, exactly, is your business?" Quatie demanded.

"Mr. Northridge? What, exactly, is our business?" Alton grinned at a tall, dirty, sixty-ish, bearded man who, like Ogilvie, spewed a stream of tobacco juice before answering.

"Somebody's got to pay for my corn," Northridge proclaimed. Another man who bore a notable resemblance to Northridge—but shorter, with fewer teeth and only one arm—pulled his horse closer to Alton and Ross.

"And my pigs! And my fruit orchards," the one-armed man conjured up a list of losses.

Crow Smith, one of the Cherokees who had come back around the curve from the lead wagons, challenged the claim. "The only orchard we passed in the last three days used to belong to *me*—'til you *yo-negs* stole it!"

"Well, I got papers says its mine now!" the dirty, one-armed man screeched. "So pay up!"

"Most of these people don't have anything," Chief Ross said softly, a master of soothing address in a heated situation. "They didn't get the allotment money the government promised."

"Well, now, that ain't really my problem, is it?" One-arm sneered. "I'll just be takin' this here fine lookin' horse as payment," he said, indicating Stick, William Drummond's black gelding saddled and tied to the tailgate of Charlie Swimmer's wagon a few yards ahead of the chief's. Charlie stepped around the ox cart to join Ross and Alton Ogilvie.

"That horse is worth ten times any little bit of fruit or corn that was taken," he said firmly.

"Didn't you hear?" Northridge said with a high-pitched snicker that sounded strangely diabolical coming from such a large man. "Price of corn went up yesterday."

"These debts—these claims—they're all fabricated," Ross said. "You're just trying to—"

"—to steal from us!" Charlie interrupted. "You won't get away with it!"

Without warning, one of the Georgians standing beside Charlie drove the butt of his long-rifle into Charlie's ribs, knocking Charlie to the ground beneath the feet of his own ox. Martha leaped down from the wagon and *Tsu-tsu* jumped over the double-tree to help their father. Ross held out a hand in a placating gesture toward the whites. He knew them well. Once they had a man down, they tended to become even more violent.

"Please!" he said loudly, hoping to draw attention away from Charlie. "You've driven us from our land. At least allow us to leave in peace."

Northridge moved his horse closer to the chief's and repeated his charges. "I seen a bunch of Injun and nigger young'uns stealin' corn outa my field," he barked in his shrill voice and pointed to *Tsu-tsu* and a nearby black youth. "Could'a been them two right there!"

Adding to his own list of grievances, One-arm pounded his forehead with the heel of his hand in an unorthodox gesture of emphasis. "And my pigs has been actin' peculiar ever since y'all went past my place. I think y'all got a Injun witch puttin' a hex on decent folks's hogs. I'd be plumb skeered to eat the bacon!"

Alton cockily began untying the reins of the blaze-faced roan

William Drummond had returned to *Gu-wi-s-gu-wi*. "I figure it'll take both these horses to square us even," he announced. Charlie Swimmer, back on his feet, fearlessly stepped between the *yo-neg* and the animals he was attempting to extort.

"You're not taking these horses," Charlie persisted.

"Get outa my way," Alton growled and shoved Charlie aside. He mounted the roan and hung on to the reins of Stick.

"You're not taking those horses," Martha repeated her father's words in a clear, strong voice.

The One-arm rabble spun around to see who had challenged them so confidently. "You a feisty little thang. An' purty! Ain't she purty, boys? Maybe you'd like to stay here with us..." He tosses his rifle to the nearest Georgia militiaman and reached for Martha, gripping her tightly just above the elbow. She swung her arm in a wide circle, twisting free of his grasp just as *Tsu-tsu* lashed him across the face with his father's ox whip. One-arm retreated instinctively from the whip. He stepped back near the ox cart only to receive a rapid thrashing from the stinging cane switch adeptly wielded by Buck. This drew a shower of guffaws from the other whites.

The humiliation stung worse than any blow of the whip or switch. One-arm grabbed his rifle back from the militiaman, but before he could decide what he intended to do with it, they all looked behind them. Galloping around the sharp bend in the road were Sergeant Robert Barton, his friend, Corporal Miles Franklin, and three other soldiers. They didn't know the details of the delay, but when Robert saw the Georgians, he drew his pistol, letting it hang relaxed at his side, just in case. The whites who had earlier dismounted started getting back onto their horses. They rested their rifles across their saddles in front of them. Sergeant Barton and the other soldiers reined up, eyes watchful, taking the measure of the armed intruders who clearly had the soldiers outnumbered.

"What's going on here, Chief Ross?" Barton asked.

"They're trying to take our horses."

"We just takin' fair payment for our crops and livestock," Northridge asserted.

"We never took anything from you! You're all lying!" Charlie said loudly, shaking his finger in Northridge's face. Such a pointing gesture was an incontrovertible affront from an *Injun*, and Charlie had further compounded the insult by calling them liars. Northridge and the other whites looked at Robert, waiting for him to chastise the Indian for his social transgression. Instead, Sergeant Barton turned on Alton Ogilvie.

"Get off the horse."

Alton grinned and launched another stream of tobacco juice, expertly splattering the liquid missile on the hoof of Robert's mount. At the same time, Alton shifted his rifle slightly so it pointed more toward Robert's men.

"I said get off the horse. Now," Robert repeated firmly.

Alton shrugged and lifted his leg as though to throw it forward over his horse's neck and dismount. But he was only using his knee to elevate the rifle barrel, which fired, hitting one of Barton's men in the shoulder. The startled roan reared up, unseating Ogilvie. The entire area erupted in a blazing hail of crossfire when all the whites brought their muskets up and began shooting indiscriminately. They didn't care what they might hit—soldier, Cherokee, man, woman, child, or even one of their own.

John Ross slammed his horse into Northridge and grabbed the larger man's rifle. The soldiers returned fire, taking more care than the whites not to aim in the direction of the emigrants. Cherokees and blacks ducked down in their wagons. Those on foot dove underneath, dragging small children with them. Adults caught in the open threw children to the ground and fell on top of them.

A ball from one of the whites' rifles splintered a board in the side of the Swimmers' wagon dangerously close to Sally. *Tsu-tsu* jumped against the hub of the wagon wheel, using it as a springboard to vault himself onto the back of the nearest *yo-neg's* horse. Once astride the horse's rump, *Tsu-tsu* sprang to a standing position, balancing himself behind the rider. With his hands open and cupped, *Tsu-tsu* slapped the white man hard on each side of his head, driving the compressed air painfully into the man's ears. The *yo-neg* screamed. *Tsu-tsu* reached around the man's shoulders with both hands and secured a grip on the rifle. Placing his knees against the man's spine, *Tsu-tsu* leveraged himself backwards, creating an effective choke hold with the rifle grinding into the front of the *yo-neg's* throat. In a remarkable display of balance, *Tsu-tsu* maintained his hold in this position, even with the horse spinning wildly out of control.

Tsu-tsu's daring act lasted barely five seconds. In that brief span, Robert spurred his horse toward Martha, yelling for her to get under the wagon. But instead of obeying, she pointed behind him.

"Robert! Look out!" she yelled.

He spun in the saddle and fired his pistol, hitting a Georgian square in the chest. On impact, the Georgian discharged his rifle.

The bullet struck the wagon wheel only inches from Martha. *Tsu-tsu* finally lost his balance on the back of the spinning horse, but when he came off, he brought the *yo-neg* with him. He was immediately joined by more Cherokees who rushed to his aid and began pummeling the white man.

After Alton Ogilvie had been thrown from the roan, he scrambled to his feet, drew his pistol and killed one of the Cherokees beating the *yo-neg* unhorsed by *Tsu-tsu* Swimmer. Without pausing to reload, Alton grabbed Stick's reins, then jumped back onto the roan and rode off into the woods leading the black gelding. Most of the other whites took this as their cue to leave. Some followed Alton. The rest scattered into the trees on the opposite side of the road.

Once the dust had settled and the gun smoke had cleared, Chief Ross and Sergeant Barton dismounted to assess the damages. *Tsu-tsu's* victim had been rendered unconscious. Two other *yo-neg's* lay dead in the road. One Cherokee man had been killed by Alton Ogilvie and two more were critically injured. One of Robert's men had suffered a serious shoulder wound.

Martha rushed to Robert. Neither spoke. Robert put his arm around her, greatly relieved that she and her family were unharmed.

Chief Ross knelt beside the two injured Cherokees while Quatie tended to their wounds. The chief instructed a young boy to run back down the road and fetch one of the group doctors. Quatie's face registered both sadness and frustration at not having been able to do more. She looked up at her husband and shook her head. It was too late. They were gone. Quatie rose and embraced the family members who had gathered around their fallen warriors, husbands, fathers.

"I'm sorry we didn't get here sooner," Sergeant Barton apologized.

"It's never going to stop, is it, Sergeant?" Ross said without recrimination. "The killing. The insanity." But the sergeant said nothing. Each knew the answer, and each knew there was nothing to be gained by uttering it. Barton looked around at the carnage wrought in a matter of seconds. At a time like this, words were meaningless. Robert's eyes swept the entire scene, finally coming to rest on the ironic image of a Cherokee man and one of his own soldiers standing together, each quietly recounting his perspective and recollection of the incident to the other. Barton went to check on Corporal Franklin. Miles assured him that, but for the shoulder wound to Private Conner, they had escaped unscathed.

510

"Find some shovels," Robert said softly to Miles. "Bury these men. We have to get moving if we're going to meet those supply wagons by noon tomorrow."

Miles and two other soldiers started back down the road with some of the Cherokee men. Robert and Martha joined the group beside the Swimmers' wagon where *Tsu-tsu* was quietly being congratulated for his bravery in battle. Buck hastened to remind them of the cane flogging he had courageously administered to the one-armed *yo-neg*.

CHAPTER
44

On the Tennessee River

After successfully negotiating *The Suck*, the next day the *Vesper* and the *George Guess* made it through the subsequent rapids—*The Boiling Pot, The Frying Pan* and *The Skillet*—with only minor loss of Cherokee property and no further deaths or serious injuries. One white crewman suffered a broken arm when thrown against a bulkhead, and a ten-year-old Cherokee boy's fingers were crushed between two large wooden boxes that shifted when the keelboat was tossed against the rocks. The trip after that had been uneventful until they were forced to stop just northeast of Decatur, Alabama where the Tennessee River ran almost due east and west.

Lieutenant Edward Deas, Lieutenant Whiteley, Lieutenant Barrett—a stumpy Irishman serving as Whiteley's backup on the *George Guess*—a handful of their men and a few Cherokee leaders stood to their waists in the Tennessee. Some idly studied the chain of barges strung out behind them. Others—including William Drummond—watched the water lapping lazily against the first keelboat's hull. Lieutenant Deas slapped the side of the grounded barge in frustration.

"Damn! I was afraid of this!"

"Some of the men could dig it out," Whiteley suggested. "Widen the channel a bit. If we unload the boats, they'll sit higher in the water. I think we can get through."

"It's no use," Deas shook his head. "The river's like this for miles. It's been a dry season. We'd be loading and unloading every other mile."

"What are we going to do?" William asked.

Deas wiped the sweat from his lip and forehead with his forearm and looked around. His answer to William came in the form of directions for Whiteley.

"Take some men. Go into Decatur. Round up all the wagons you can find. Tell them the government will pay them," he said, then called loudly to the rest of his troops and the civilian boat crew. "You men start unloading the boats!"

"Everything?" a soldier whined in a nasal Carolina drawl, not looking forward to the job in the scorching heat.

"Everything. Everybody," Deas answered, then laid out his plan as it unfolded in his own mind. "We'll have to go by train down to Tuscumbia. The river's deeper from there on to the Ohio. Lieutenant Whiteley, once we're on the trains, you and Lieutenant Barrett will take the boats down river. They should make it all right if they're empty. We'll meet you there. All right, men! We've got work to do! Let's go!"

The soldiers and crewmen standing in the water dispersed in different directions, some toward the shore and some back to the steamers. William climbed right up onto the keelboat in front of them.

* * * * * * *

The road to Decatur was a fine gray powder that fluffed into a choking cloud with each footstep. The grinding of wagon wheels and the pounding of feet and hooves made it impossible for man or beast to draw a clean breath. The scrawny horses and obstreperous mules secured to transport the Cherokees and their possessions strained under the burden of overloaded wagons. Even the very young and the very old were forced to walk, often requiring the help of the adults and older children. A small wagon pulled by a single horse skirted the slow moving procession. Lieutenant Deas and five of his soldiers walked briskly along handing out rifles to the Cherokee men.

William walked beside the wagon that carried the Drummond belongings along with those of several more Cherokees who had walked on ahead in search of other family members. It was a challenge to manage the two mules, and William remembered with fondness—and renewed respect—how masterfully Ezekiel Campbell had always been able to control these beasts.

Tsisdu, having attached himself to the Drummonds, waddled beneath the weight of the large bundle balanced on his back. Susanna carried a parcel only slightly smaller than *Tsisdu's*. She walked behind the men, keeping an eye on Meg and *Me-li* in the rear of the wagon. The gun cart pulled alongside them. Deas handed William a rifle and the corporal assisting him gave *Tsisdu* a pistol.

"Lieutenant! What's going on?" William was puzzled. "I thought we weren't supposed to have guns."

"We got reports of a bunch of locals not too happy about our being here," he explained.

"But we're just passing through," *Tsisdu* argued.

"Doesn't matter. They're afraid we'll bring in disease. Or steal their livestock. Who knows," Deas shrugged. William secured the rifle under one arm and popped the mules to hasten them along.

"You think they'll make trouble?" he asked the lieutenant.

"I hope not. But I won't let them massacre a bunch of unarmed Cherokees."

"You could get in trouble for this, you know," William reminded him.

"We'll take our chances," Deas said, then moved hurriedly up the line.

"He's a good man, that lieutenant," *Tsisdu* grunted, trying to balance his load with one hand while examining the pistol. "I wonder if this thing works?"

* * * * * * *

The shiny steel tracks of the *Western and Atlantic* Railroad undulated in the heat of an abnormally warm autumn day in northern Alabama. The creaking blades of the windmill rotated barely an inch or two at a time in the absence of any breeze strong enough to complete their circumference. The Cherokees examined the strange *iron road* which many were seeing for the first time. A few smelly, slat-sided box cars were strung along a short side track, but there was no locomotive. The *Tsa-la-gi* men studied these strange *wagons* with curious apprehension. *Tsisdu* chanted and sprinkled herb medicine on the rails to bring them good luck and a safe journey.

The chaotic layout of the temporary camp reflected the fatigue and discouragement of the Cherokees. Goods were piled on the ground in an uncharacteristically disorganized manner. The animals leased by the soldiers had proven cantankerous and difficult to control. The wagons and carts, in various stages of disrepair —from a little creaky to falling apart—had been abandoned in a haphazard morass of tangled tongues, wheels and harness. Lieutenant Deas, William, a few Cherokee men and a number of soldiers strolled through the camp encouraging the travellers to make some semblance of order out of the confusion.

"How long do we have to stay here like this, Lieutenant?" William asked.

"I wish I could tell you, Drummond," Deas answered. "Two locomotives were supposed to be here. I don't know what's holding them up."

William followed the lieutenant, reminding him of their critical logistical problems. "There's no food. And one tiny spring

514

won't be nearly enough water for all these people."

Deas spun around and threw up his hands in frustration. "I've sent Lt. Whiteley and some of the men to buy food. I don't know what else I can do, short of digging a well with my bare hands!"

William realized he had unintentionally been badgering the young officer who genuinely had the Cherokees' best interest at heart. "I'm sorry Lieutenant. I didn't mean—"

The sound of approaching riders and a wagon interrupted them. Lt. Whiteley and the food detail had returned. But it took only a glance to see that none of the riders had any potato bags slung across their saddles and the wagon rode too high and bouncy on the corduroy road. It was empty. Deas walked out to meet them, his palms open and outstretched asking *What happened?* The riders pulled up and the wagon rattled to a stop.

"None of the locals would sell us any livestock," Whiteley reported. "I even offered 'em double the going price."

"And n'ary a merchant in Decatur could spare so much as a single bag of corn meal," said the corporal driving the wagon.

"The bastards!" Deas slammed his hand down on top of the wagon wheel.

"It's all right, Lieutenant," William tried to settle their leader. "We can organize some hunting parties."

"No. You'd better stay in camp," Deas shook off the idea. "If they won't sell us food—knowing these people are starving—they wouldn't hesitate to shoot the first Cherokee hunters they see on their land—then claim it was a war party. We'll just have to wait." Everyone felt for the young lieutenant who was clearly feeling the pressure of his command. He pursed his lips tightly, then said, "If we have to, we'll eat their damned horses." William and the others looked around at the wormy, skin-and-bones nags hitched to the wagons or tethered about the camp area. It wasn't a tasty prospect.

* * * * * * *

Hours passed and still the rails ran empty to the eastern horizon. No sign of the delayed locomotives. Hungry, thirsty and tired, the *Tsa-la-gi* waited. Uncertain. Frustrated. One old Cherokee man, bent with the weight of his four score years, stooped to cautiously examine the parallel steel ribbons. Never before had he seen such a thing. He thought he remembered it being described to him once, but it had made no sense then and it made no sense now. Inquisitively, he tapped the rails—first one and then the other—with his carved walking cane. Two young boys in the shadow of a slatted boxcar banged rhythmically on the iron rail with a loose spike they had found. The old man rocked with the same tempo familiar to him from decades of Cherokee ceremonial drums. He sauntered past the boys, poking at the metal wheels of the boxcar with his cane and looking underneath. A rare gust of otherwise nonexistent breeze snatched the old man's tattered, flat-brim hat and mischievously rolled it beneath the boxcar. A cluster of Cherokees engaged in idle conversation a few yards away paused to watch, chuckling with amusement when the ancient one got down on his hands and knees and crawled under the boxcar. Having recovered the runaway hat, he stiffly uprighted himself and flashed a toothless grin to his audience.

"The iron wagon tried to steal my hat!" he gummed the words in Cherokee.

"It must be a *yo-neg's* wagon," one of the *Tsa-la-gi* onlookers laughed.

The old man's grin faded and the other Cherokees looked up toward the ridge where he was pointing. More than thirty mounted and heavily armed whites were stretched out against the southern sky. Without panic, the Cherokees casually checked the guns they had been issued, shifting them forward into plain view of the hilltop crowd. Yes, let the *yo-negs* see the guns, they thought. Let them think long and hard about whether or not they really want to ride down that hill and start some trouble. Lieutenant Deas, accompanied by William, *Tsisdu* and a Cherokee named Youngbird, stepped out from the shade of some live oaks to get a closer look at their visitors.

Susanna, holding Meg and with *Me-li* at her side, moved closer to a group of *Tsa-la-gi* women and children. Throughout the camp, all eyes had been drawn to the southern ridge. Anxiety and apprehension was written on every face. So far their journey westward had proven to be a trial of body, mind and spirit. The road ahead—whether dirt road, steel road or the river—offered no promise of relief. This was an added affliction they could well have done without.

"What should we do," Youngbird asked.

"Nothing," Deas said, squinting up at the whites. "Absolutely nothing."

"We're pretty exposed here, Lieutenant," William pointed out.

"That's exactly why we can't give them an excuse to start

516

shooting," Deas explained.

Tsisdu shaded his good eye until he had seen what he needed to see. He lowered his hand and turned his back in a gesture meant to dismiss as unimportant the presence of the armed Alabamans.

"They won't shoot," he proclaimed with confidence. "They just want to see what we have. What we're doing."

"I hope you're right," the lieutenant said in a low voice.

William looked eastward down the rails. "When will those engines get here?"

"It better be soon!" Deas said, finally shifting his eyes from the hill to a cluster of his own soldiers standing near the tracks. "I want all the firewood you can find stacked and ready to load the instant those locomotives arrive," he ordered. "Get some of your men to help," he told William and Youngbird.

Cherokee men and most of the adolescent boys went to work immediately gathering wood and making sure their guns remained visible to the *yo-neg* observers on the hillside. They were glad for something specific and positive to do. A feeling of dignity and a glint of the old warrior spirit had been rekindled within them—even if only temporarily—when the young army lieutenant had shown them enough trust and respect to issue them firearms. They were all fully aware that his action was in violation of official government policy.

* * * * * * *

Tsisdu had proven right in his evaluation of the armed whites gazing down at the Cherokee camp. They sat there the entire afternoon, apparently satisfied that the bunch of crazy, sick and dirty Indians scrambling around piling up firewood next to the train tracks posed no immediate threat. Still, they bore watching. By the end of the day, all but three or four of the whites had disappeared. These few had been left to sound the alarm should anything unpropitious begin to unfold. *You can never tell with Indians. They're sneaky that way.*

But it wasn't the hawks on the hill by the light of day that posed the only real threat to the *Tsa-la-gi*. In defense against a more insidious enemy, the Cherokees, beneath the light of the full moon, were lined up across the road behind a picket of their own rifle barrels. Out in front of the forty armed *Tsa-la-gi*—which included William, *Tsisdu* and a number of Cherokee women—Lieutenants Deas, Whiteley and Barrett and six soldiers blocked the road at the edge of the sprawling encampment.

Facing them were six brightly painted wagons, home and transportation for the troupe of whiskey peddlers, gamblers and prostitutes, some of whom had already snared the attention of the young Cherokee men positioned immediately behind the gun line. The whiskey peddlers sipped from jugs, making it appear irresistibly delicious. A gambler casually shuffled a deck of cards. Another juggled a pair of dice from hand to hand. The leader of this travelling carnival of debauchery was Antoine Benoit, a skeletal, oily French Arcadian from Louisiana with a curled, waxed moustache, a gold front tooth and constantly darting eyes. He fingered one of the moustache curls and nervously watched Deas. The lieutenant's feet were widely planted, his pistol held loosely at his side. The elapid Cajun in his fancy, hand-embroidered vest, spoke with what Deas suspected was an affected French accent.

"Certainly you realize, Lieutenant, the locals are most displeased with the presence of your little entourage. Rumors are rampant of a bloody Indian uprising. We can offer much to—shall we say—ease the tensions, no?"

"We don't need your whiskey or your whores, Benoit," the lieutenant said, although there were many older *Tsa-la-gi* who would argue the first point and clearly a host of the younger ones who would stand erect to gainsay the second. "And we don't need gamblers cheating these men out of what little money they might have. So just turn your wagons around and go back to Mobile or New Orleans or wherever you came from."

Benoit gestured at their surroundings with an unctuous smile. "You would send us away in the middle of the night?"

"Everyone knows wolves can see in the dark. You'll find your way." Without warning, Deas abruptly raised his pistol and fired off to his right. The clay jug exploded in the hands of the whiskey peddler just as he was passing it to three Cherokees who had slipped across the line to conduct a little business. The peddler and the Cherokees jumped back, startled and whiskey drenched. "You men get back behind the line!" the lieutenant barked to the *Tsa-la-gi*. He stared coldly at Benoit, who merely shrugged with a smirk that said *c'est la vie* and motioned for his wagons to swing around.

"A man has certain thirsts, Lieutenant," the words slipped melodiously from his tongue. "And hungers. Even a man such as yourself." The wagons circled back into the darkness. The prostitutes smiled and waved good-bye to their handsome, young and glandularly disappointed prospective customers. With a sarcastic tip of his meticulously sculpted river boat hat, Benoit sprang lightly up to the seat of the last wagon, which raced ahead to take its position at the front of the cavalcade.

* * * * * * *

Susanna tucked the blankets snugly around Meg and *Me-li*, spoke softly to the young Cherokee woman who had agreed to watch the children, then walked off into the night in the direction she had seen William take a half hour earlier. She followed the narrow trail into the thick woods until she found her father sitting on a large rock in a tiny clearing where motes of moonlight sifted down through the whispering pines. He thoughtfully smoked his pipe and raised his eyes to the brilliant night sky. Somewhere in a distant corner of the camp a melancholy Cherokee fiddle scratched out its mournful tune. It was a sound which, woeful as it was, had become a comfortingly familiar element from night to night. Through the trees drifted the cries of children and distant muffled conversations in a mixture of English and Cherokee. Susanna touched her father lightly on the shoulder as she passed by, then walked on and stopped with her back to him. William could see well enough in the moonlight to know by her sagging shoulders and fallen chin that she was tired, haggard and troubled. And he knew she would say what was on her mind only when she was ready.

"What's happening to us?" she finally spoke. By the tremble in her voice William knew it was a struggle for her to hold back the floodgates of emotion.

"This hasn't been easy for you, Susie," he said, thinking how shallow and meaningless such words must have sounded after all they had been through.

"I feel like we have no control..." she went on.

"Things are really tough right now."

"You always taught us, if we use our head to make the right choice, and if our heart is in the right place, we have the ability to shape our own destiny." She looked up as though hoping to read the answer in the stars. "But we didn't choose for Mother to die. We didn't choose for any of this to happen."

William felt the burden of Elizabeth's death on his own shoulders, and if Susanna wanted to blame him, he understood. "I'm sorry. I don't have any answers. I can understand your feeling bitter."

She finally unleashed the bilious choler she'd been choking back for so long. "It's more than that, Poppa! I feel *rage!* At the same time, I feel totally helpless!" She no longer fought back the tears. "Is this our destiny? To be robbed of everything we own? To be stripped of all human dignity and treated like animals?"

What could he possibly say to comfort her in the face of such overwhelming despair? "Maybe tomorrow will be better."

"Tomorrow? I'll tell you about tomorrow!" she made her hand into a tight fist as though preparing to strike some elusive, invisible foe. "Tomorrow we'll all be crammed into those railroad cars like pigs and cows, forced to stand in our own filth! Or maybe—if we're lucky!—those men we saw on the hill today will just ride in here and slaughter us all. That's what we can expect from tomorrow!"

"We just have to keep hoping. And praying," he offered unconvincingly.

Emotionally drained and physically exhausted, Susanna came and sat beside her father on the large rock, propping a hand on each knee and examining the ground at their feet.

"Who knows what to pray for any more, Poppa? And we're running out of hope. Nothing makes any sense."

The familiar voice came out of the darkness only a few feet away. "What you need is a vision."

Tsisdu, seated on another rock not far from them, had been partially blocked from view by the saplings at the edge of the clearing. In the moonlight they saw he was carving a talisman of some sort.

"A vision?" the disdain in Susanna's voice bordered on ridicule. "Please! Spare us your superstitious gibberish, Rabbit Man. Your visions and your herbs. Incantations. Little People. You've done absolutely nothing to help the situation." She rose from the rock, wrapped her arms around herself and walked farther into the darkness, farther from camp, farther from these two men who had offered only empty words of impotent consolation and useless suggestions of other-worldly escape.

"I'm sorry. I'm sure she didn't mean it," William apologized for his daughter's rudeness. He heard a soft chuckle from the other rock.

"No. It is good. She has strong medicine. Here," *Tsisdu* tapped his chest. "She just hasn't discovered it yet."

* * * * * * *

Susanna didn't know how deep into the woods she had gone

520

along the narrow, poorly marked trail. Having found no answers in the stars, she studied the ground before her. Perhaps the mystery might be revealed in the reading of stones and twigs or whispered by her own shadow created by the full moon high overhead. By the time Susanna stopped, there were no sounds from the camp. No distant, muffled conversations, no crying children, no doleful ditties on Cherokee fiddle, concertina or bagpipes. She became acutely aware of the ghostly quiet. The suspiration of the night breeze blended harmoniously with the shrickling of the nearby creek where the water leaped down the stones in a two-foot drop.

A large shadow fell across Susanna. She looked up, reacting to a heavy wing-flapping sound from high in the sky. Silhouetted against the moon was what appeared to be a man-sized creature—part human and part eagle. Its muscular human chest, shoulders and upper arms became lost in a feathered wing structure of tremendous span. The head was an eagle's, though human in size and proportionate to the rest of his body. The thickly feathered thighs flowed into the trim, muscular calves and feet of a man. Though the wings flapped with an awesome force, they did so at an exceedingly slow pace, giving the impression that this creature was more suspended or floating than actually flying.

Susanna looked down at the ground and shook her head vigorously. Either she was hallucinating from exhaustion and stress, she told herself, or she had completely taken leave of her senses. She was confident that when she lifted her eyes again she would be looking up into the full moon. The irony struck her that what for centuries had been considered a sign of insanity—had, indeed, gleaned its name *lunacy* from gazing at the moon—was what she now hoped for as a sign her reason was intact. But she could see on the ground that the creature's shadow continued to envelop her. Lifting her eyes once more, she noted he—it—had descended even closer. Mesmerized, she watched him float to the ground in a tiny clearing. She felt herself spellbound by the creature, yet strangely unafraid.

"Who are you?" she asked softly. "What do you want?"

The creature's head was cocked to one side with his eagle eye directly on her. The eye blinked twice with hypnotic effect. He spread his left wing out to its full length and folded it across his chest, concealing his body. He then dropped to one knee. It reminded her of the sweeping gesture of a magician's cape, like she and Michael had witnessed once as children. Their mother and father had taken them to Atlanta where they had seen a travelling

521

medicine show. The eagle-man swept his immense cape-like wing away to reveal a coffin lying on the ground in front of him.

Susanna recognized the same patchwork box of weather-grayed wagon boards mixed with freshly cut yellow pine in which her mother had been buried. She gasped, her hand going instinctively to her mouth, and took a single step toward the fascinating, mysterious image before her. She stopped abruptly when the wing passed in front of the coffin for an instant, then opened once more. This time, the coffin lid had been removed and Susanna clearly saw her mother lying in restful repose.

"Mother..." the hoarse whisper escaped Susanna's lips. Elizabeth sat up in the coffin, her face peaceful, full and beautiful, not gaunt and wasted as she had appeared in death. Susanna smiled at the loveliness of the vision through the tears that filled her eyes. Her mother held something in her left hand, clutching it to her bosom. Susanna strained to see until she recognized the leather pouch Elizabeth had given to her and had made her promise to deliver to Michael. From the bottom of the pouch a thin trickle of blood traced a crooked line down the front of Elizabeth's white dress.

Susanna, now weeping profusely, felt confused by the symbolism of the vision. Was the bleeding letter pouch her mother's way of telling her Michael was dead? Or was it saying her mother's sadness after Michael's departure had hastened her own death? Or the blood could have come from her heart rather than from the leather pouch itself. It was impossible to determine which. Susanna was about to ask, but the eagle-man drew his wing across Elizabeth and the coffin, and she kept silent. When he opened his wing again, the coffin was closed and sinking slowly into the earth. The spot where it lay was brightly illuminated by a conical shaft of moonlight coming through the trees.

Once the coffin had disappeared, the eagle-man stretched to his full height and turned his captivating eye on Susanna for some time before spreading his massive wings and rising into the air. When he had ascended to an altitude of twenty to thirty feet, the wings flapped with a great blast of wind that blew in Susanna's face. An initial flash of fear gave way to an incredibly refreshing sense of restoration. She felt herself irresistibly drawn to the place where she had seen the coffin melt into the earth. Kneeling, she placed her hand on the undisturbed grass, moving it back and forth. It felt no different in length and texture, but the spot was many degrees warmer than the exact same grass and soil surrounding it. Susanna was about to rise and dismiss the entire incident when her hand brushed against something in the shadows near her dress. She picked up and cradled in both hands a large eagle feather.

* * * * * * *

The eastern sky's twilight gray had taken on little flecks of orange and gold, announcing the dawn that would soon peek into the Cherokee camp near Decatur. Here and there a few women began to stir. They stoked ash-covered embers back to crackling flames and prepared to make fry bread, coffee—whatever they could scrape together to feed their families.

Susanna returned to the camp from the thick woods, gliding past a Cherokee sentinel who had taken his position long after she had walked out into the night. He looked at her but said nothing. At their campfire, William sat wrapped in a blanket, leaning against a stump where he had drifted off while keeping vigil for his daughter. The girls were still fast asleep across from him. Only *Tsisdu* was awake, squatting at the fire, warming his hands. He watched Susanna as she approached.

"*Si-yo, 'ge-yu-ts',*" he greeted her quietly.

"*Si-yo,* Rabbit Man."

William snapped awake, blinking his eyes repeatedly to orient himself. "Susie! Are you all right?"

"I'm all right, Father," she said. Her voice was strangely distant, her expression pensive.

"I was worried."

Even while speaking to her father, Susanna hadn't taken her eyes off *Tsisdu* since coming back to camp. "Everything's all right," she reassured William. Meg began to stir at the sound of her mother's voice. William turned his puzzled look on *Tsisdu*.

"Don't worry," the one-eyed man said. "She'll be fine. You'll see. Strong medicine, that one. Very strong."

It made no more sense to William now than it had when *Tsisdu* had uttered similar words the night before. They both watched Susanna and Meg. The child rubbed her eyes and took the eagle feather from her mother's hand, studying it with drowsy curiosity. Susanna silently brushed Meg's hair back then gently shook *Me-li* awake.

* * * * * * *

By mid morning the thirty-odd whites from Decatur had

reassembled on the southern ridge overlooking the Cherokee camp. Each man was heavily armed, stone-faced and righteously prepared to bring the situation to a head. A few of them rode down the hill to confront their unwelcome visitors. Their leader was Decatur Constable Hogan Calvert, a surly, heavy-set, middle-aged man in a long black riding coat. His face was pock marked and had his eyes been any closer together, a single skeletal orbit could easily have accommodated them both, giving the man a near cyclopean appearance. A massive double-barrel shotgun lay balanced across the pommel of his saddle.

"We was told by the gov'ment agents these Injuns comin' through here wouldn't have no guns," he roared from atop the tallest horse William and many of the other Cherokees had ever seen. Hogan wanted every *Tsa-la-gi*, to the hindmost corner of the camp, to know he was fully aware of the guns among them. Lieutenant Deas, with Lieutenant Whiteley at his side, had taken his position a few paces out in front of a line comprised of the rest of his soldiers interspersed with armed Cherokees. Calvert waited patiently for the lieutenant's answer, but Deas said nothing. The constable hadn't asked a direct question and the lieutenant offered no response to his observation. Finally Calvert leaned forward across the shotgun and asked in a softer voice, "So, how come they got guns?"

"I issued them weapons, Constable," Deas replied in a calm, matter-of-fact tone, then immediately escalated the confrontation by adding, "for protection against people like you. I'll take full responsibility."

One of Calvert's men cocked his flintlock rifle threateningly. "Damn right you will!" he snarled down at the young lieutenant.

The constable held up a hand to stay his men. He looked down the razor ridge of his long nose at Deas with a sneering smile. "You got a sassy mouth, young buck. But I'm the law 'round here. You ain't nothin'."

"Nothin' but a God damn Injun lover!" another of Calvert's posse pointed at Deas and eased his mount forward a step or two. He was a thin, nervous man in his early twenties with open sores on his neck and upper arms.

Lieutenant Whiteley rested his hand meaningfully on the butt of the pistol stuck into his belt. "Maybe you ought to just leave, Mr. Calvert, before this whole situation gets ugly," he said.

"Oh, it's *already* ugly," Calvert's sneer curled tighter. "You people're stinkin' up our town. We can smell you all the way into Decatur."

William stepped forward to join the lieutenants. Trained to seek a calmer path, a negotiated settlement, he tried to sound congenial and nonthreatening. "Please, Constable Calvert. We're pretty much at the mercy of the elements here. We never intended to cause you any anxiety—"

"Damn!" cackled the man who had cocked his rifle. "This'un talks like a God damn circuit judge!"

"I'm an attorney," William explained.

Calvert leaned down even farther toward the man standing before him, his sneer softening but his voice deadly serious. "No, sir. You're a Cherokee Indian. An' don't you forget it. An' you got no bidness in Decatur, Alabama." He had allowed the muzzle of his shotgun to swing around until it was uncomfortably close to William's face.

"Yes...well..." William stammered, "we'll be gone just as soon as—"

His statement was cut off by the shrill blast of a steam whistle from the eastern horizon. Chugging toward them were the two long-awaited locomotives, each pulling an additional six slat-sided boxcars and, at the very end, a couple of flatcars. Many of the Cherokees were awe struck, seeing a locomotive for the first time in their lives. Small children peeked shyly from behind their mothers' skirts. Older children and many adults backed up instinctively to distance themselves from the smoke-belching black iron dragons descending upon them.

* * * * * * *

A light breeze had come up, just strong enough to spindle the creaking blades of the windmill. The water pumped into its elevated wooden cistern flowed immediately out through the long spout suspended above the first locomotive's water tank. Soldiers, assisted by Cherokee men and older boys, loaded the wood car directly behind the locomotive with the firewood Lieutenant Deas had wisely ordered stockpiled. Aboard the train, the firemen stoked the boiler, throwing in as much of the split wood as the dragon's iron belly would hold.

Hitched to each locomotive were eight slat-sided boxcars followed by two flatcars. The boxcars' drop-down doors served as crude, unstable loading ramps. Hundreds of Cherokees—men, women, young and old—nervously gathered with whatever possessions they could carry. Their anxious eyes and apprehensive faces were locked on the engines and on the boxcars into whose bowels they were about to entrust their future, their loved ones, their very souls.

William, Susanna, Meg, *Me-li* and *Tsisdu* stayed close together. Susanna kept a watchful eye on her large steamer trunk and wondered how they were going to get it up the flimsy ramp and into the boxcar. Or perhaps it could be strapped onto one of the flatcars. What if it rained? But it hadn't rained since they left Ross's Landing. How would she oversee its loading and still keep a close watch on Meg and Mary?

William and *Tsisdu* joined Lieutenants Deas, Whiteley and Barrett near the end of the first train. All four men eyed with uneasy concern Calvert's armed posse who had formed a picket surrounding the Cherokees.

"Mr. Drummond," Deas greeted William.

"Lieutenant."

"By the looks of it, the sooner we get out of here, the better," Deas said.

"Most of these people have never seen a train before. Many of them are terrified," William reported.

"I hope none of them get so scared they try to make a run for it," Whiteley noted, squinting at the semi-circle of armed whites. "Calvert and his men are just itching for an excuse."

"Sergeant Haney!" Lieutenant Deas called to a tall, thin, red-haired young soldier. "Collect the guns from the Cherokees. And start loading these trains."

"Yes, sir!" Haney snapped and hurried off, joined by several more soldiers. Deas, William and the others watched Calvert and his men for a while longer before Deas set the final stages of their departure into motion.

"Lieutenant Whiteley! You and Lieutenant Barrett take your men and go back to the boats. We'll meet you downstream below Tuscumbia."

"Right," Whiteley acknowledged the order.

Deas placed a hand on Barrett's shoulder. "You all be careful." Barrett, a man of few words, flashed his familiar Irish wink—his way of saying he was ready, almost eager, for any trouble that might arise. Deas couldn't resist a smile. There was no man he'd rather have at his side or watching his back in a fight-to-the-death brawl. Barrett, along with Whiteley and their men, headed back toward the river beneath the close scrutiny of the Decatur mob.

* * * * * * *

William held both Meg and his newly adopted granddaughter, *Me-li*—one in each arm. Meg clung affectionately to her grandfather's neck. *Me-li* still hadn't fully resolved the mystery of her mother's disappearance, but from the adult conversations she had heard around the campfires, she knew it had something to do with her mother being in the river. In her child's imagination she envisioned her mother walking on the river bottom beneath the water, possibly petting the fish. It was all very strange and confusing, but *Me-li* liked her new family and felt quite certain ten-month-old Meg had been placed in her care. It was much better than having a pet chicken. William gently kissed each girl's cheek, his voice soft and reassuring to allay their mounting fear of the train.

"Be brave, girls. We'll ride the train for a while, then we'll get back on the boat."

"I'm not giving up this trunk," Susanna declared with a note of defiance in her voice. "Not after I've gotten it this far. It was Mother's."

"Don't worry. We'll get it loaded," William said and transferred the girls back to Susanna.

Tsisdu noticed the eagle feather hanging from Meg's hair at the side of her face. She fingered it gently from time to time, proudly drawing attention to her marvelous new adornment.

"You're going to be a great warrior someday, *Me-gi*," he said.

Susanna looked at him, annoyed. "Why do you say such things?"

"Don't you know what this is?" *Tsisdu* said, touching the feather.

"No. Not really," her answer was sharp and unduly irritable. "It's just a feather. I found it."

"It's a *war* feather," he corrected her. "It has great power. Strong medicine."

Their eyes met and this time she didn't ridicule or scoff at him. She sensed that he knew a part of her she herself didn't yet understand. He had somehow seen the things she had seen, but he understood them while they continued to perplex her. Two young soldiers interrupted them. It was time to load their things onto the train.

The boarding process transformed the entire staging area into one giant, amorphous organism, flowing first toward the trains, then ebbing back, then toward the boxcars once more. Rifles and pistols were dropped by the Cherokees back into the boxes on the two-wheel

527

carts. Feet shuffled with trepidation through the dry dust. Confused, uncertain. Soldiers walked up and down the length of the trains, yelling and gesturing for the *Tsa-la-gi* to begin loading, but no one was eager to get on board.

Who will go first?

Not me.

You go ahead.

No, after you.

The first foot timorously toed its way onto the shaky wooden ramp. Others followed hesitantly. The ramps creaked and sagged beneath the weight. Feet stepped back, afraid, then tried again, slow and cautious.

Susanna, like other mothers, clung to children with one hand and belongings with the other, barking to soldiers and helpful Cherokees to make certain her trunk stayed within view and got loaded onto the boxcar. And like many others, she found herself deciding at the last moment that some item would have to remain behind.

Many children cried and had to be literally dragged aboard the train. Other children were silent, too frightened even to whimper. Old Cherokees—once proud warriors, their heads now shamefully bowed in defeat—hid the terror in their eyes as they were driven into the slatted belly of the steam-hissing monster. But they couldn't hide from their own hearts the painful humiliation burned into them by the scornful eyes of Calvert and his *yo-neg* posse.

Soldiers moved up and down the line exhorting the Cherokees to speed up the loading. And the ubiquitous white jackals were hanging around the perimeter just as they had done in the hills and forests when the *Tsa-la-gi* were rounded up and driven from their cabin homes. Just as they had done when the *Tsa-la-gi* were herded into the concentration camps and again when they were marched out and put into wagons to go overland or packed onto keelboats to travel by river. Eagerly waiting to rummage through whatever the *Tsa-la-gi* might leave behind. But the Cherokees had silently agreed that any abandoned possessions would be broken up, ripped apart and tossed onto the fires started for that purpose. No matter how trivial the item, it would not fall into the greedy hands of the hate-filled, vulturous whites.

The first train's whistle screamed and the engine strained, creeping forward only enough to allow the second engine to pull in under the spout and take on water. The same old Cherokee man lost his prized hat once again and was crawling beneath the boxcar to retrieve it just as the second train began to move.

"No! Get away from there!" Lieutenant Deas saw the old man and ran toward him. "Oh, sweet Jesus!"

It was too late. Deas felt sick in the pit of his stomach and thought he might vomit. He had seen men die before, but he had never watched an innocent old man cut in half by the steel wheels of a train.

The old man apparently had no family. Only the soldiers and Cherokees in the immediate vicinity were even aware of the incident. The rest were too concerned with being prodded, poked and hurried up the ramps and into the boxcars. Deas pulled three soldiers off the line and dispatched them to take the body—in two parts—over to the abandoned campsite and, as fast as possible, dig a grave. They wouldn't leave, Deas declared, until the old one had been properly and respectfully interred.

Eyes peered out through the boxcar slats. Tired eyes. Defeated eyes. Frightened eyes. Dull eyes. Old eyes. Young eyes made old too soon. Tiny fingers slipped through the cracks, holding on.

Susanna, Meg and *Me-li* made it into one of the boxcars where they staked out a tiny piece of territory in the corner. *Me-li* stood on top of the old steamer trunk. Like so many other children completely bewildered by the mysterious chain of events, she pressed her eyes to the narrow opening between the boards. Her finger chased a bug along the horizontal slat until it escaped to the outside and she could no longer see it.

The soldiers and three Cherokee men who had witnessed the accident hurriedly dug a grave near the tracks for the old man whose severed corpse lay in a blood-soaked blanket, his fatally elusive hat lying on top of the body. A gust of wind caught the hat and carried it away, rolling it once again beneath the boxcar. But no one noticed. No one cared.

Sweat-drenched soldiers and Cherokees finished loading the second train's wood car, piling the short logs high until no more would fit. The rest they crammed into the gluttonous boiler furnace until it, too, was overflowing. The engineers and firemen tightened bolts on the iron beast, checked valves, poured animal fat from spout cans to lubricate collars, bearings and any other moving engine part they could reach.

Once each boxcar had been filled to capacity, one or two more Cherokees would inevitably be crowded in before the ramp was swung back up, sealing the human cargo inside. William, *Tsisdu*,

Youngbird and the other Cherokee men who were looked to as leaders were among the very last to board. The gun carts, the small army wagons and the remaining supplies were loaded on the two flatcars at the rear of each train. There the soldiers and the last few Cherokee men who had found no space in the boxcars would ride.

Lieutenant Deas openly glared his dislike of Constable Calvert and his posse before signalling the first train to move out. The locomotives belched black smoke. Steam hissed from beneath and all around the wheels as the massive pistons stirred to life. The rear train held back until the first had gained some distance, then repeated the same departure ritual. Lieutenant Deas was the last to jump aboard the trailing flatcar before it pulled away. He took a seat on a wooden supply box and looked back to see Calvert and his armed posse breaking ranks. Just as he and the Cherokees had predicted, the white Decatur vultures swarmed down on what was left of the Cherokee camp. A few tried to beat out the fires in hopes of salvaging something of value. Others rifled through the trunks and boxes left behind. White children ineffectually tossed rocks and hurled epithets at the receding trains. Calvert and his men solemnly congratulated each other for having once again preserved their community from destruction at the hands of uncivilized heathens.

The trains rocked gently side to side, gaining momentum until they were swallowed up in the giant red maw of the setting sun.

CHAPTER
45

Arkansas Territory

Four wagons, single file—each drawn by four mules—plodded steadily through the wind driven rain. The hills rose sharply to the east and west of the winding road that sliced through the Ouachita foothills. An armed guard sat beside the drivers of the first and fourth wagons. The lead driver raised his hand to signal a stop. He jumped down and began unrolling a heavy tarp, stretching it across his load of boxes and bags. The driver of the second wagon joined him shortly to help. They pulled the tarp down over the stencil-painted logo on the side of the wagon that read: *Tanner Overland Freight / U. S. Govt Contractor*. The drivers of the third and fourth wagons teamed up to spread tarps over their loads as well—pulling, looping, wrapping and tying them off. The first driver, a tall, leather-faced man named Tarpley, worked his way around the wagon to the second driver, a younger, stocky man they called Wilkes, with shoulder-length, prematurely gray hair.

"You see 'em?" Tarpley asked without looking up at the hills behind them.

"On the ridge to the west," Wilkes answered, pulling the rope taut.

"How many? Can you tell?"

"I seen at least four," Wilkes reported. "Walker said he counted six. What you figure they want?"

"Don't know," Tarpley shook his head. "But they're up to no good, you can bet."

"Could be Kiowa," Wilkes moved on to the next rope. "Or Comanche up from Texas. I hear they been gettin' pretty rowdy."

"Well, keep your eyes peeled," Tarpley advised, "and your powder dry." It was an old expression but ominously appropriate under the circumstances.

* * * * * * *

In the cover of the rocks and trees high above the road, Michael Drummond, Johnny Fields, Ned Proctor and *Tsa-tsi* Starr waited patiently in the rain. But Michael's and Johnny's spy glasses weren't trained on the four transport wagons stopped in the mud far below. Michael shifted his wide-brimmed black hat to better shield his face from the rain. Johnny pushed back the eagle feather tied to a small braid hanging at the side of his face. With his hand beneath his jacket he searched for a dry spot somewhere on his shirt to wipe the raindrops from the spyglass lens.

In a tight clump of trees where the road disappeared into a sharp draw ahead of the wagons, they saw Tom Carver and his gang. Three of the men were the same ones who had escaped with Carver from the first encounter with Johnny and Michael. Four new men had been recruited only a few days earlier. They were no more than dirty, crude and scurrilous replicas of the men they had replaced. A sweep of Michael's spy glass brought into view the wagons which Carver and his men had been stalking. Michael caught the *Tanner Overland Freight* sign on the side of the wagon just before the final tarp was pulled down. He lowered the spyglass and chewed at his lip. Could it be?

Johnny noticed Michael's reaction. "What is it, *Mi-ki?*"

"Nothing," Michael shook his head. "A ghost from the past. Let's move!" The four raiders scrambled toward their horses waiting in the trees down the slope behind them.

* * * * * * *

The Carver gang bunched their horses together, pulled bandannas up over their faces and made a final gun check. Carver signalled four of them to split up and move off through the trees. They would mount the assault from two angles.

The mules' feet sent spray flying from the puddles when the first wagon rounded the sharp curve in the road. The second wagon came into view with the third and fourth close behind. The drivers and the guards had seen the raiders above them in the rocks and had mistaken them for outlaws. They were expecting to be attacked from that direction. They were ready.

Michael, Johnny, Ned and George pushed their horses at full speed, expertly negotiating the steep slope down through the woods and between the rocks. Only their masterful horsemanship kept them in the saddle. Johnny, in the lead, pulled up and signalled the others to stop. They had reached a plateau that offered a view of the road below just as the last of the cargo wagons disappeared around the curve into the narrow draw. Gauging their distance and estimating the speed of the wagons, Johnny knew the Carver gang would have already struck and vanished by the time they got there.

"This way!" Michael yelled and dashed down another trail

that would get them there quicker.

* * * * * * *

Tom Carver and his three original gang members moved out to the edge of the grove and waited close to the road. Carver steadied his rifle in the crook of a branch and fired the instant he had a clear shot at the lead wagon, hitting the armed guard in the throat. The force of the rifle ball threw him completely out of the seat and back onto the tarp-covered cargo. When the mules skittered at the rifle's report, the dead guard slid off the side of the wagon and landed in the mud. Tarpley fought to control the startled animals while groping to for the guard's rifle on the tarp behind him.

Carver and his three men bolted from the trees and quickly closed on the first wagon. The four men Carver had earlier dispatched erupted from the woods and circled up from the rear, catching the wagons in their cross fire. The guard in the fourth wagon stood up and aimed his rifle at the gang riding toward them from the front. Before he could get off a shot, he was hit in the back by a bullet from the tall outlaw with no upper front teeth. The guard was thrown forward out of the wagon. He hit the rump of one of the mules and fell to the ground between the two frightened animals, his feet tangled in the traces. Had the bullet not killed him, the trampling mules certainly would have.

The gang members from the front moved swiftly down one side of the wagons. The four attacking from the rear came up the other side, putting a man on either side of each wagon. The drivers worked to control their mule teams, at the same time holding their hands high in the air to demonstrate they had no intention of resisting. From beneath his long coat Carver drew a large Bowie knive and hacked viciously at the ropes. He flipped back the tarp to reveal the spoils of their conquest—bags of flour, grain, seed, plow shares and farm tools.

"What else you got?!" Carver demanded, holding the knife point to Tarpley's throat.

"Nothin' else! This is it!" the driver answered, his frightened eyes on the blade.

"This ain't army stuff!" the toothless outlaw lisped. "Check the other wagons!" he yelled to those who had attacked with him from the rear. He spurred his horse around the front of the mule team to join Carver on the opposite side.

"We figure you're haulin' army rifles and ammunition.

Maybe even some payroll," Carver growled.

Tarpley shook his head vigorously. "This is all government contract stuff. For the Cherokees."

"He's lyin'!" Gap-tooth yelled. Led by the nervous-and-jerky youngest outlaw, four of the gang cut the rest of the ropes and ripped back the covers.

"If we was carryin' guns or money, we'd have an army escort," Wilkes called out from his seat in the second wagon.

Carver slapped Gap-tooth on the chest with the back of his hand. "You stupid ass! Ain't that just what I told you?!" He looked back toward the other wagons and read the disappointed expressions of his men. They had, indeed, ambushed a wagon train of food and farming supplies bound for Indian Territory.

"Don't matter! We'll take it anyhow." Gap-tooth refused to admit they had completely bungled the robbery.

"You get stupider every time you open your mouth!" Carver spat, hitting the rump of Gap-tooth's horse. "What the hell we gonna do with plows and plantin' seed?"

The nervous young robber rode up to join them. "We could jes' kill the drivers," he offered a plan, "and take the mules over to Ft. Gibson. Sell 'em to the army." Carver back-handed Gap-tooth on the chest again.

"See! How come you don't have good ideas like that?"

Gap-tooth's face twisted with the strain of conjuring up a defense. A shot rang out and the third and fourth fingers vanished in a spray of red from Carver's left hand. The same slug entered Gap-tooth's chest and the impact flipped him backwards off his horse. Tarpley, Wilkes and the other drivers instinctively took cover beneath their wagon seats. Carver and his men spun their horses toward the screaming Indians bearing down on them from up the road. Leaning, cursing, jerking their horses this way and that, they tried to aim for a shot at the Cherokees without hitting each other.

The raiders had overshot the spot where they had intended to reach the road. They had emerged from the trees ahead of the wagon train and were forced to double back. Johnny, in the lead, had taken off Carver's fingers and killed Gap-tooth with a single shot. He stuck the rifle back into the scabbard and reached for his pistol. Michael rode with his Collier repeater held poised and ready. *Ne-di* had a rifle in one hand and a single-shot pistol in the other, while *Tsa-tsi* kept his two pistols in his belt. He would use them only if his much preferred bow and arrow proved ineffective.

With his horse at a full run, Michael fired the Collier, striking another of Carver's men in the chest. When the outlaw fell from the saddle, his foot became entangled in the stirrup. The spooked horse galloped away, dragging the body through the mud. Both his arms and the one free leg flopped and splattered almost comically.

Tom Carver gawked incredulously at the blood pouring from his left glove where his fingers had been. He looked at his rifle and realized he wouldn't be able to reload it. The other members of his gang were firing wildly...and hitting nothing.

Tsa-tsi swung his mount out of the pack and urged him into the lead. Clinging to the horse tightly with his knees, he drew the bow and released the arrow, an art he had practiced to perfection since he was fourteen years old. The missile struck the young, nervous outlaw from the side, passing through the triceps and literally nailing his right arm to his rib cage. He screamed and dropped his pistol, staring in disbelief at the arrow while trying to remain aboard the erratically spinning horse. The young outlaw looked up at the approaching raiders with a dazed, confused expression. He saw the muzzle flash from Michael's pistol and felt the bullet hit him in the left shoulder. Somehow he managed to stay in the saddle with both arms hanging limp and useless. Unable even to hold the reins, he frantically tried to spur his horse out of its spin to take flight. His expression changed to wild-eyed panic when the animal began trotting directly toward the oncoming raiders.

Two of Carver's new gang members raced back down the road and around the curve to escape the raiders' fire. The other two new recruits aimed at the raiders, who were almost upon them. One fired and missed, then immediately disappeared into the woods. The other fired his flintlock pistol, but the rain-dampened powder only sputtered and fizzled. He followed his companion into the trees.

When the raiders reached the wagons, *Tsa-tsi* continued into the woods in pursuit of the two outlaws who had just fled the scene. Johnny and Ned both fired at Carver and missed, then raced past him after the two outlaws who had ridden back down the road. Michael brought up the rear. He found himself alone against Carver, who grabbed the dead guard's rifle off the first wagon. Hearing the pounding of Michael's horse, Carver knew he'd only have time to spin and fire from the hip.

The shot was low, missing Michael but shattering *U-no-le's* knee. The forward momentum launched the animal into a giant cartwheel, hurling Michael into the mud. His Collier pistol flew out of his hand, leaving him unarmed.

It was the second time in two years that Michael's horse had been shot out from under him—first Midnight and now *U-no-le*. Michael landed at an awkward angle on his neck, head and shoulder, rendering him almost unconscious. Dazed, he pushed himself up onto his hands and knees. He wobbled badly on his first attempt to get to his feet and fell back down. The gray clouds that had filled the sky were suddenly inside his head. Dark and foreboding. He knew the evil heart of the man bearing down on him.

Each muddy clop of Carver's horse thundered in Michael's head, an executioner's countdown. Carver rode up beside him, the reins wrapped tightly around the bloody left hand with the missing fingers, serving both as a tourniquet and to control his mount. With his right hand, the normally left-handed Carver drew his pistol, cocked it and lowered it directly into Michael's face.

Though groggy from the spill, Michael fully comprehended the situation. He thought of Annie. The mystery of her eyes. The beauty of her touch. The fire of her spirit. He thought of his precious son, *Tsi-mi*. And James, his son's namesake. Michael's beloved *tso-s-da-da-nŭ*. Annie's twin brother. He saw the face of his mother and hoped the news of his death wouldn't be more than she could bear. He wished he had told his father more often that he loved him.

Michael knew he was about to die, but, just as his friend James Walker had done, he refused to cower or beg. He glared up at the outlaw with unblinking defiance. Carver's blood-shot, demonic eyes peered down at him from the shadows of his hat and the bandanna covering his face. Like Michael, Carver didn't blink when he squeezed the trigger. The powder was just dry enough to partially ignite but damp enough to have lost most of its power. The misfired ball ricocheted off Michael's cheekbone, splitting the skin in a bloody but superficial wound. Frustrated by the thwarted robbery and bent on avenging his own disfigurement, Carver threw the pistol down and clumsily attempted to draw his large knife. Before he could bare the blade, he first heard—then saw—Johnny riding around the curve coming back toward the wagons.

The adrenalin rush of being shot in the face had actually helped clear Michael's head. Taking advantage of Carver's momentary distraction, he pulled the knife he always carried in his boot and prepared to defend himself. Carver lowered his bandanna mask and sneered down at Michael.

"You ain't seen the last of me, Injun!" he growled. With a glance back at Johnny, Carver kicked his horse hard and rode up the road a few yards before cutting into the woods. Johnny stopped beside Michael.

"You all right, *'Tsu-ts'*?"

"Yeah," Michael answered slowly, still dazed. He looked at *U-no-le*—a twisted, broken heap lying motionless in the mud—and said, "He killed my horse..."

* * * * * * *

The four wagons were ready to move out. The steady drizzle continued, soaking the blanket wrapped bodies of the two dead guards who had been lashed down on the first wagon. The three dead members of Carver's gang lay piled in the mud at the edge of the road. *Ne-di* and *Tsa-tsi* had abandoned their chase of the other bandits and returned to the wagons. Michael took one of the dead outlaw's horses and retrieved his own saddle from *U-no-le*. The horses of the other two dead men were tied behind the fourth wagon. Johnny rode up to Michael, who remained very quiet, blinking with each excruciating throb from his concussion.

"Ready?"

"Ready," Michael mumbled. He patted the neck of his new mount, figuring an animal this well cared for had most likely been recently stolen. "He's a good horse." He squinted against the rain and looked at Tarpley. The lead driver was ready to go. "Where're you headed?" Michael asked him.

"Ft. Gibson."

"We'll ride with you 'til we get near Ft. Smith," Michael flicked a glob of mud off the brim of his hat.

"We're not exactly welcome there...if you know what I mean," Johnny explained.

Tarpley nodded. "Well, you boys is welcome at my door any day!" he said sincerely, looking at each of the men who had saved their lives—the same men they had seen on the ridge above and had mistaken for outlaws.

Michael and Johnny rode out ahead of the wagons. Tarpley, Wilkes and the other drivers snapped the reins, cracked their whips and barked at the mules. The wagons strained forward against the clutching mud. *Tsa-tsi* and *Ne-di* brought up the rear. No one relaxed. They were all on the lookout for a possible revenge ambush from the Carver gang.

* * * * * * *

Betty Jo Proctor and her two children, Jack and Janie, little James Drummond and *E-gi-ni* Redbird were all huddled beneath the lean-to the men had built the night before. Water dripped in through the thatch roof, but no one noticed. *E-gi-ni* dipped porridge from a pot over the fire at the shelter's edge. She filled the clay bowls and handed one to each child. The last to receive his breakfast was two-year-old *Tsi-mi* Drummond, who took his bowl but didn't eat. He looked out through the downpour across the tiny clearing. *E-gi-ni* put the wooden spoon in the pot and crawled out into the rain.

Annie stood in the open, arms crossed, oblivious to the water running down her face. She stared unblinking into the forest. *E-gi-ni* stepped up beside her.

"Annie?" There was no reply. Not even a twitch of acknowledgement. "What's wrong? Is it *Mi-ki*? *Tsa-ni*?" Over time, *E-gi-ni* had come to know—and believe in—Annie's ability to see things, especially visions relating to danger and death.

"They're all right, *E-gi-ni*," Annie finally answered. "Now. But it was close. Too close." She pressed her hand to her forehead as though she were sharing the pain of Michael's concussion. *E-gi-ni* was relieved to learn the men were safe, but she was still concerned for Annie, who had been distant and melancholy for some time.

"Come. Eat."

Annie allowed *E-gi-ni* to lead her back to the shelter.

CHAPTER
46

Tennessee

The same storm that had drenched Arkansas stretched eastward halfway across Tennessee. A shaved pine log—three to four inches in diameter and twenty feet long—had been strapped to an old wagon wheel. Two sand-filled burlap bags tied to the short end served as a counterweight when the log was lowered to form a barricade across the road. A steady drizzle fell on the half dozen whites aligned behind the road block. The youngest was barely fourteen; the oldest, a toothless, knobby-jointed stick man of seventy-five or eighty. They were a dirty, menacing, in-bred lot, armed with ancient flintlock rifles at port arms and poorly kept pistols prominently displayed in their belts. They remained statue-like in the rain, staring patiently up the road. Earlier that morning they had spotted the Cherokees and had ridden on ahead to set up their toll blockade. And they had waited.

The first of the *Tsa-la-gi* wagons appeared like specters in the mist, rising out of the hill to the southeast. As soon as they saw the log spanning the road they knew what it was and why it was there. They had encountered a number of these sub-human, mongoloid mountain trash families determined to capitalize on the Cherokees' misery and exact a toll for allowing a bunch of *Injuns* to trample across their land—even though the Cherokees had kept strictly to the open roads.

At the head of the emigrant wagon train rode Peter Hildebrand, the trail conductor, and Chief John Ross. Just behind Ross and Hildebrand were *Tsunaluska*, Going Snake and White Path, who was wrapped in a blanket, his hollow eyes dark and sunken. Hildebrand signalled the wagons to halt about ten yards short of the pine log barricade. Sergeant Robert Barton, Corporal Miles Franklin and others from their company came up to find out why they had stopped.

"This is a public thoroughfare," Barton glared down at the whites on the other side of the log. "You have no authority to set up a toll gate and charge these people—"

The leader of the toll-mob—a bearded, big bellied man with spindly, bowed legs—raised his huge .50-caliber rifle and fired above the soldiers. A large limb blasted off a tall pine crashed to the ground just behind them. Cavalry horses and the draft animals of the front wagons bolted and had to be subdued. After their initial reaction of dodging the falling limb, the soldiers drew their weapons. The rest of the tollgate whites brought their guns up, aiming at the Cherokees.

"That there's my 'thority," their leader answered Barton. He sheltered the smoking barrel beneath his wide-brimmed hat and calmly began reloading the massive gun. His slanted eyes were squinted almost closed but darted up now and then, watchful and wary. He expertly launched a string of dark brown tobacco juice in the direction of Robert's horse. "I know fer a fact you soldier boys is jes' along fer the ride. So y'all shut up," he said, then looked at John Ross while tamping the rod down into the rifle barrel. "It's gonna be seventy-five cents apiece for wagons, thirteen cents for horses. Ox and mules five cents a head. And you're damn lucky we ain't back-chargin' you for all them dead Injuns you been leavin' up and down the road 'tween here and Nashville. Stinkin' to high heaven! Lord God A'mighty!"

"Tsa-la-gi bury their dead," *Tsunaluska* spat the words out with disgust.

"Any bodies you've found weren't Cherokee," Hildebrand said. "Or if they were, they got dug up by animals...or worse..." He glanced at the scrawny fourteen-year-old, buck-tooth boy who was trying to balance his rifle with one hand while tucking a silver Cherokee amulet back inside his shirt with the other. "It happened even before we left Georgia," Hildebrand went on. "Grave robbers. Looking for silver. Gold."

"Watch yer' filthy, lyin' mouth, Injun!" the burly tollgate leader snarled. He yanked the ramrod out of the muzzle and slid it back into its rack on the rifle's underbelly. "Cost of them wagons just went up five cents each."

"We won't pay. Get out of the road," the ancient Going Snake demanded and started walking his horse toward the toll gate. The whites all cocked their guns. Clearly they would not hesitate to shoot the old chief.

"Wait!" John Ross held up his hand. "It's not worth it, Going Snake." He rode to the lead wagon and motioned to his nephew, the slender, handsome young mixed-blood, William Shorey Coodey, the tribes treasurer. "Pay them the money, William." *Gu-wi-s-gu-wi's* declaration was met by a round of protest from all those within earshot.

"It's highway robbery!"

"*Gu-wi-s-gu-wi*! No!"

"You can't be serious!"

"Word will get around! They'll be stopping us every ten miles!"

"Just give them the money," Ross repeated his order to Coodey. He was tired of looking at these white trash. But more than that, he was tired of seeing his people die needlessly. "Let's get on down the road. Before someone else gets killed."

Coodey dragged a strong-box from midway in the wagon to the tailgate and unlocked it. The *yo-neg* leader flashed a victorious look to his kinsmen then squinted up at Ross with a smug, tobacco-drooling grin.

"The wise thing to do, Mister. Tell you the truth, you don't look like no Injun, but they oughta make you chief anyhow."

Ross glared down at the man with a quiet, intense hatred.

* * * * * * *

Kentucky

The rain that would have given the captive *Tsa-la-gi* much needed surcease from the oppressive heat and choking dust while they were in the concentration camps had cruelly been withheld. Now that they were out on the road, exposed to the elements without even a shoddy lean-to or thatched-roof shelter, the rain hounded them mercilessly for days without breaking for more than an hour or two at a time.

Through the relentless downpour the Cherokees , drenched and fatigued, pulled at the oxen, horses and mules, pushed wagons from behind or threw their weight into forcing the wheels to turn. *We have to get them on across the creek! It's rising fast! It'll be out of its banks in another hour. Two at the most!* Women and older children fought the rocky creek bed and the swirling current to get across with bundles they unloaded to make the wagons lighter. Smaller children clung to the hand of a frail grandfather or a blind and terrified grandmother. John Ross, *Tsunaluska* and a number of the Cherokee leaders rode back and forth through the creek, lending encouragement and assistance.

Charlie Swimmer and his son, *Tsu-tsu*, were waist deep in the creek, coaxing, pulling and whipping the mules. Martha was in the driver's seat. Beside her, Buck and Sally yelled and swatted at the mules with their willow switches. Eva, balanced on the tailgate, became frustrated in her attempt to re-tie the tattered piece of tarp covering their goods. Even if it stopped raining and the sun came out scorching hot in the next five minutes, it would take days for everything to dry out. Their bedrolls, blankets and clothing had taken on a rancid, sour smell. The days were getting shorter, the nights colder and already too many cases of pneumonia had been reported. An old Cherokee widow riding on the Swimmer wagon held onto a leather strapped box. She stared blankly out into the rain, calmly awaiting her imminent and inevitable watery death.

Miraculously, the mules' feet caught solid ground and the Swimmer wagon shot out of the creek to the safety of the other side. Sergeant Robert Barton rode back from the front of the wagon train.

"Let's go! Keep 'em moving!" he encouraged the Cherokees.

"The water's rising!" Charlie yelled back. "And every wagon cuts deeper into the mud!"

John Ross joined them at the creek's edge. "We have to rendezvous with the supply wagons at noon tomorrow. They'll be waiting for us."

Barton looked around in the downpour and spied what looked like a narrow, relatively shallow place farther downstream. He waved to those waiting to enter the raging water.

"Start bringing some of the wagons across down there!" he shouted. "It looks like a good place! Not too deep!"

A few of the wagons broke out of line and headed for the spot Barton had indicated. Satisfied they were once more making progress, Robert spurred his horse close to the Swimmer wagon. He looked at Martha with the reins in her hands.

"You all right?"

Martha smiled but didn't speak. She cracked the whip at the mules, demonstrating she knew what she was doing. He grinned and went back through the swirling stream to assist with the crossing.

Right behind Barton rode Chief Ross. He had spotted Dr. W. P. Rawles coming from the rear of the wagon train.

"Dr. Rawles!" *Gu-wi-s-gu-wi* called out. The chief hadn't received a status update since early the previous day.

The middle-aged physician with salt-and-pepper beard clutched the front of his black long coat to keep it closed and tugged the wide brim of his hat down tighter against the rain. He pulled the mule he was riding to an abrupt halt and appeared startled to hear his name called. Ross saw the doctor was exhausted and he deeply appreciated his dedication to the *Tsa-la-gi*.

"Chief Ross. We just lost another child. We must have medical supplies and decent food!" Rawles delivered the predictable report.

"Tomorrow, Doctor. Tomorrow." Ross knew his words sounded empty. "Can you come with me, please?" He turned his horse around and they headed back toward the front of the wagon train.

"You really must speak with Mrs. Ross," Rawles leaned toward the Chief as their mounts lunged up the other side of the creek.

"Quatie?"

"She's quite ill herself," Rawles answered. "But she refuses treatment. She insists the medicine be given to the children and the old ones."

Gu-wi-s-gu-wi looked at him sadly. "Of course, Doctor. What else would Quatie say?"

* * * * * * *

Later that same afternoon—hours, miles and a couple of swollen creeks later—Chief Ross, *Tsunaluska* and a handful of other tribal leaders hovered around Dr. Rawles while he examined White Path. Weak, road weary and trumpeting a death-rattling cough, the old warrior sat on the tailgate of a wagon beneath the sheltering sprawl of a gnarled and ancient oak whose knotted limbs reached out to encircle its spiritual brother. Rawles shifted aside to accommodate a withered old medicine woman.

"*Red Woman! Red Woman! Red Woman,*" she uttered emphatically. In the tradition of Cherokee medicine, *Red Woman* was chanted for an ailing man, *Red Man* for a sick woman. The *yo-neg* physician watched her scoop a handful of a pungent poultice from a wooden bowl and pack it onto White Path's chest. Rawles was one of a growing number of white doctors who, even before the removal, had developed an abiding respect for the healing practices of native medicine, though it had frequently cost him the esteem of his skeptical *yo-neg* colleagues.

"Pneumonia..." Rawles confirmed his suspected diagnosis with a telling look at Ross. He handed White Path a black bottle. The ancient chief squinted with one eye to peer inside. He handed it to the old medicine woman just before he was gripped by another coughing seizure. The medicine woman sniffed the bottle, squinched her nose, gave a single nod of approval to Rawles, then poured the black liquid into the wooden bowl and mixed it with her own plaster. Round and round she stirred the concoction of new and old with a knotted arthritic finger.

"Something must be done, *Gu-wi-s-gu-wi*," *Tsunaluska* spoke with his characteristic quiet simplicity. "Our people are dying."

They all stared, hypnotized by the old woman's fingers slogging rhythmically through the plaster. Softly she began to chant in a high-pitched voice.

* * * * * * *

The Cherokees had pressed on well past dark, had wasted no time making camp and had quickly fallen into the fitful sleep of exhaustion, only to be prodded awake before sunrise. Their leaders were determined to make it to the preappointed meeting with the supply contractors by noon. Chief Ross feared if they were so much as an hour late, the contractors might use it as an excuse not to wait for them. The first Cherokee wagons arrived at the designated supply drop shortly after eleven o'clock. By late afternoon, however, the supply wagons still had not appeared. The chief sent riders on ahead for miles in case there had been some confusion about the exact location of the scheduled rendezvous. The scouts later returned with long faces and nothing to report.

Eva Swimmer raked her fingers through a bowl of damp, clotted, weevil-infested corn meal. The other Cherokee women shared her frustration in their efforts to scrape together the simplest meal for their families. Eva had presented the bowl of rancid meal to Chief Ross and his nephew, W. S. Coodey, who sat with Sergeant Robert Barton and a few other soldiers out near the road, listening for hoofbeats or hoping to see supply wagons approaching. Coodey examined the meal.

"Soured by the rain," he shook his head. "Smells more like bad whiskey than cookin' meal." Sharing her disgust, he handed it back to Eva. Three hunters emerged from the tree line. Even from a distance one could see their hunting sacks were limp and flat. The nearest hunter answered Coodey's questioning look with a disappointed head shake.

"Small game has been pretty much killed off by the earlier groups," Sergeant Barton commiserated. "It'll be getting dark soon, Chief Ross."

Gu-wi-s-gu-wi stretched and pressed his fists into his lower back. "The suppliers were to meet us here at noon. They've already been paid. The next drop point is five days away."

Sergeant DeKalb sat on a stump at the side of the road,

544

scraping mud off his boot with a stick. "If they ain't here, they ain't here," he said with his customary impatience. "I say we get movin'. Maybe they'll catch up by the time we break for the night." They looked up the road to see Corporal Miles Franklin, Corporal Evans and the last two Cherokee scouts riding toward them.

"Doesn't look good," Charlie Swimmer read their faces.

"No sign of them, Sergeant," Franklin reported directly to Barton, who looked to Ross for a decision.

"It's up to you, Chief."

Ross studied the bright spot in the clouds that was the sun on its western descent. "I have to agree with Sergeant DeKalb," he said. "We'd better move on while there's still a bit of light. We'll just have to ration what we have and hope we can make it to the next supply point."

"What if they don't show up there either?" Barton asked.

"Well, I reckon we'll be mighty hungry," Ross forced a smile. "What we *won't* be is surprised. Let's get going."

Cherokees and soldiers began moving up and down the line to spread the word. There would be more miles—and little or nothing to eat—before they slept. No one paid attention when the brief dry spell ended and the rain began falling once more.

*   *   *   *   *   *   *

From a wooded hill a half mile away the entire proceeding had been witnessed. The arrival of the tired and hungry Cherokees. The gathering of the leaders. The dispatching of scouts up and down the road. The return of hunters with empty sacks and defeated, hollow stares. And finally the departure in the pelting rain for another couple of hours in the mud before darkness overcame them.

Titus Ogilvie lowered the spyglass and looked back to his son, Alton, and to Brantley and Solmes, the two scurrilous wags who were always around when Titus needed bodies. In addition, he had recruited a few other ne'er-do-wells to help drive the wagons loaded with fresh supplies.

"Gentlemen, a lesson in business," Titus grinned wickedly. "This here is what you call *compounding your profits*."

"But you already got paid for these supplies, Paw," Alton scratched his head in confusion.

Titus took off his hat and swatted at his son. "That's right, ox-brains! And we'll just camp right here for a few days and sell 'em again to the next bunch that comes along. That's the compounding part, son. Try to pay attention!"

By his expression, it was evident Alton still didn't understand, although he pretended he did. Titus shook his head and rode back toward the others. He dismounted next to one of the loaded wagons bearing the *Tanner Overland* logo.

"You understand it, don't you, partner?" Titus asked.

Peter Tanner stepped from the shadows beside the wagon. He was drunk, his beard thin and scraggly. His tattered army tunic hung open, having shed most of its brass buttons. Peter collapsed his spyglass by pressing it against his stomach and retrieved his jug of corn whiskey from the crotch of a limb.

"What you lookin' for, General?" Ogilvie teased. "That little Injun gal you was married to?"

Peter's rage simmered just beneath the surface. He took a stiff drink and glared with bloodshot eyes at Titus. "I'd've made general before I was forty. She ruined my career."

"Well, forget it," Ogilvie's massive stomach shook with suppressed laughter. "You ain't gonna be no general. But you will make a lot of money if you stay in business with me. That is, if you don't drown yourself in sour mash first."

Peter threw the jug, shattering it against the tree right beside his tormentor. Ogilvie jumped aside with unexpected agility for a man of his girth, especially considering his game leg.

"Don't take a tone with me, damn you! I own half this business!" Peter slurred his protest.

Titus pulled out a large knife and with its tip inscribed a box around the word *Tanner* on the wagon's sideboards, then buried the blade in the rough-grained wood between the two *N's*. "That, Mister Tanner, is how much of this wagon you own!" he barked at Peter. "You're here because I need your name to get government contracts! Beyond that, you're a worthless, good-for-nothing drunk!"

"Hey!" Peter pointed a shaky finger at what he was convinced was a moving target. "Don't disrespect me in front of my men!"

Titus snatched the knife from the wagon and tapped Peter lightly on the shoulder with the blade. "First off, this ain't the army, General Tanner. These are not your men. Second, what the hell would you know about respect?"

Through glazed, half-closed eyes Peter watched Ogilvie walk back to the other wagons. "Someday you'll push too far, Titus."

Ogilvie reached beneath the tarp covering, got a fresh jug of whiskey and brought it back. He popped the cork and handed the jug to Peter, then gave him a conciliatory pat on both upper arms and mockingly straightened Peter's tattered army jacket.

"You're a strong man, Peter. The pride of West Point. You can take it."

Peter lifted the jug for a drink, his eyes locked on Ogilvie's. He lowered the jug and wiped his mouth with the back of his hand. "Don't mock me," he said in a mash-fumed whisper. Titus snapped a sharp salute and walked away. After a few steps he stopped, staring at his son. Alton squatted before a pile of twigs he was attempting to ignite with his flint. Rolling his eyes, Titus limped to his son and scattered the kindling with his walking stick. He then kicked Alton sharply, landing him on his ass in the mud.

"What the hell you think you're doing!" Titus growled.

"Making a fire!" whined the pathetic son who, no matter what he did, seemed inevitably miscast in life.

The father bent down, his face close to Alton's. "Why don't you just shoot off a cannon and start yellin' to the God damn Injuns, *Hey! We're up here in the trees! And we've got all your supplies!?*"

"But Paw, I was hungry. I was gonna cook somethin'.."

Titus smacked him again with his hat. "You're *hungry*? You're *hopeless*, that's what you are!" He gimped away, shaking his head in dismay and mumbling to himself. "You got it from your Ma. You had to. Damn sure didn't get it from me. Feeble minded as a dung beetle...."

Alton scrambled up and followed his father. "Paw! Paw, wait..." He caught up with Titus, who spun around.

"What?!" he snorted impatiently.

Alton shuffled, twisting on one foot, talking out of the side of his mouth. "Paw. I don't like it when you do that in front of the others. You'll make 'em think I'm stupid or something."

"Gosh! You think?" Titus raised his brows in mock wonder.

"Well...yeah, they might. Maybe," Alton had completely missed his father's sarcasm. Titus placed a comforting hand on his son's shoulder.

"Son, nothing I could ever say is gonna make these men change their opinion of you."

"Oh. Good," Alton breathed easier and appeared satisfied. "I got some jerky in my saddle bag. I could eat that."

Titus tapped the side of his head with his finger. "Now you're thinking!"

Basking proudly in his father's praise, Alton headed for his horse to get the smoked, dry meat. Titus shook his head once more and pulled out his own pocket flask for a stiff drink of whiskey.

47

The twin *Western & Atlantic* transport trains rolled westward through northern Alabama, stopping only to take on water and firewood, which the blazing furnace and the hissing steam engine devoured with insatiable hunger and unquenchable thirst. The gentle rocking motion of the boxcars together with the stifling heat and humidity made many of the Cherokees sleepy. And no one objected to passing an hour or two here and there in sweet forgetfulness. It was always a welcome escape until reality stuck an elbow in the ribs or a fart up the nose. But seldom did one complain. Shift a little to the left to give someone else a bit of room. Roll a little to one side—put the pressure on the other hip that would soon grow numb with the circulation cut off. Then switch back. Press a face to the narrow opening between the slats in hope of catching a breath of cool, fresh air. Idly search for a place wide enough between the boards to get your fingers through. No reason. Just a fingertip's worth of freedom.

Susanna sat on her old trunk with Meg asleep in her arms. Cherokee bodies touched her on all sides. In the beginning she had found it most annoying, but as time went on, she realized that pressing against another human was more comfortable than being continuously thrown against the side slats or the end wall of the boxcar. She slipped a hand down and stroked the hair of *Me-li*, pressed against her leg in search of comfort and safety. Susanna looked at her father. He was dozing off to the rhythmic roll and *clackety-clackety* of the train.

Through half-closed eyes, glazed with exhaustion, William looked at his daughter and the two beautiful little girls, then drifted to a point just beyond Susanna where another Cherokee mother held her dead baby in her arms. He read the expression of grief and silent anguish in the woman's face. Throughout the boxcar—and from the car ahead and the one behind—he heard the coughs and groans, even above the clacking of the iron wheels on the rails. William and Susanna watched *Tsisdu* and three other Cherokees lift an old man's corpse onto a stack of boxes at the far end of their car. He would be buried in the ditch beside the rails somewhere in northern Alabama the next time they stopped to take on wood and water. The train would roll on and those who had loved him and cared about him would desperately and intensely study the surroundings, noting this tree or that rock, thinking someday they might come back and take his remains to their new home in the west. But only the youngest or the most foolish truly believed it. They simply needed something to cling to.

* * * * * * *

Tuscumbia, Alabama

The trains stopped at the eastern edge of town. Stiff and sore, the captive passengers disembarked down the wobbly ramps. Soldiers hopped off the flatcars, slapping at their bodies to rid themselves of the miles of dust and grime.

Lieutenant Deas, Sergeant Haney and their soldiers—along with the four guard dogs that had made the journey—formed a line between the huddled Cherokees and the gathering of Tuscumbia whites. A few had come to peer curiously at the Indians. Not unlike Hogan Calvert's posse in Decatur, however, others were armed to make sure there was no trouble from these treacherous heathens. Many openly expressed their disappointment that the Indians didn't appear as savage as they had expected. *And who'd'a thought there'd be this many niggers and white folks?*

The mayor of Tuscumbia—a tall, crane-like man with a long, drooping moustache and dark, cavernous eyes—stood beside Lieutenant Deas, watching the Cherokees with a wary eye.

"How long you reckon you all gonna be here, Lieutenant? In Tuscumbia?" he asked.

Deas knew exactly the kind of man he was dealing with. If not the pastor, at least a deacon in the local church, determined to keep this land clean, safe and secure for *God's people* and make certain the unchristian savages were prudently and expeditiously sent along their way. All the while maintaining, of course, a proper Christian concern for the white soldiers—these poor, unfortunate sons into whose hands had been placed the sacred responsibility of carrying out the wishes of the nation's great leaders. The United States government had decreed, by ratification of a legal treaty, that Cherokees, along with other southeastern tribes—the Creeks, Choctaws, Chickasaws and Seminoles—must be removed to the west. They were making this part of the continent safe for settlement by decent, civilized, God-fearing Christian folk. Deas looked at the mayor darkly, almost with a sneer. *How long would they be here?*

"As long as it takes to regroup and head for the river, Mayor. You needn't worry."

"But I must tell you, Lieutenant, I *am* worried," the mayor clucked with concern. "We've heard tales of bloody uprisings. Massacre of innocent white folks."

Deas faced him and was about to utter a few choice profanities. He looked at the Cherokees, then back to the mayor and heaved a great sigh of exasperation. "Do these people look to you like they're about to massacre anyone?"

"Never can tell with Indians," the mayor said, assuming the tone of the seasoned sage instructing the young neophyte. He stroked his long moustache pensively. "They're sneaky, you know. But I can't help notice, Lieutenant, a lot of these people look more like white folks."

"That's right, Mayor," Deas forced himself to remain civil. "A lot of them *are* white. Or mixed-bloods. And some of their blacks."

"Slaves? These Injuns own slaves?" the mayor found it curious.

"A few," Deas answered. "They're mostly like family. They didn't know where else to go."

The mayor shook his head in amazement. "Well, don't matter none. Injuns. Niggers. What's the difference? You know? And any white that'll take up with a Injun—well, they cain't be trusted neither. Know what I mean?"

"No, Mayor," Deas had to look away and bite his lip. "Actually, I don't." The lieutenant walked away, leaving the grallatorial mayor somewhat perplexed. Deas beckoned to a soldier carrying a tablet and pencil. "What's the news, Corporal?"

"Two children died, sir," the young man said with a note of puzzlement in his voice, not sure why or how such a tragedy could have occurred. He scanned the tablet. "One baby was born. One old man suffocated. They're buryin' him now. And lot's more have gotten sick. Some real bad, sir."

The mayor had followed Deas and overheard the corporal's report. His civic concerns had been justified. "You see, Lieutenant? That's just what I'm talkin' about. We can't afford to have these people bring some deadly plague down upon the good citizens of Tuscumbia. We've heard tales of them spreadin' diseases. Cholera. Consumption. God knows what all."

"It seems you've heard a lot of *tales*, Mayor," the young lieutenant studied the corporal's papers. "But I assure you, these people want nothing more than to get back on their boats and continue their journey."

"Good." The mayor sounded relieved. "That's good."

Deas handed the tablet back to the corporal. He knew the answer to his question before he even asked, but the lieutenant thought it worth a try. "Mayor, I don't suppose you and the good citizens of Tuscumbia might spare some medical supplies? A few blankets? Some food? We'd pay, of course."

The mayor tugged at his moustache once more and grimaced with the answer. "Sorry, Lieutenant. We'd just rather not get involved. We have nothing for you."

"You know, somehow I felt that'd be your answer," Deas said. "If you'll excuse me..."

The mayor extended his hand for a parting shake with the likeable—if somewhat naïve—young officer. But the lieutenant ignored it. He spun on his heels and marched over to a Cherokee woman and her young son who were wrestling with their belongings just tossed from the boxcar.

"I'm sorry," Lieutenant Deas said with compassion. "You'll have to pick out whatever you can carry and leave the rest behind." He glanced up to see Susanna Drummond going by with her father and the Rabbit Man. She watched the two men struggle with the steamer trunk she had fought so long to keep. When Susanna overheard the lieutenant's words, she tugged at her father's sleeve and told them to set the trunk down. She caught the lieutenant's apologetic smile before he walked on down the line.

"Open it," she said.

William and *Tsisdu* complied, then stepped back. Susanna studied the contents. Already Meg and *Me-li* were helping her choose by dragging things out into the dirt in search of something worth keeping.

* * * * * *

Feet shuffled along the dusty road. Many feet. Feet with shoes. Feet with shoes so tattered they barely stayed on. Feet with no shoes at all. Dusty feet. Mud-caked feet. Dried mud, covered with a fine, gray, chalky dust. Feet with sores. Feet bleeding from sharp rocks in the road. Big feet. Dainty feet. Children's feet. Old feet. Dog feet. Soldiers' feet. All in boots. Good, strong boots.

Mixed with the feet were the cracked rims and splintered spokes of the two-wheel carts and small wagons brought on the flatcars with the soldiers.

Some children cried. Others didn't. Medicine men and medicine women chanted. Others sang ancient songs in Cherokee.

551

Or Christian hymns in English. Or Christian hymns in Cherokee. Conversations for the most part were kept short. It was too dusty. Made one's teeth gritty and the throat scratchy. And they had found no springs or creeks between Tuscumbia and the Tennessee.

"How far is it to the river?"

"A few miles. The soldier said it's a few miles."

"*A few miles*? What does that mean? Two miles? Three miles? Ten?"

"What difference does it make? Just keep walking!"

"What if the boats aren't there?"

"The boats will be there. I just hope we get some food soon."

Feet on the march. Marching fast. Tired. But marching fast.

* * * * * * *

The mid-morning sunlight lay like a glaze on the dark, glassy surface of the Tennessee. There was no sign of a keelboat or a steamer as far as one could see in either direction. No distant whistle, no remote vibrations of a chugging steam engine or rhythmic slapping of a paddle wheel in water somewhere up around the bend to the east. No column of smoke hanging against the cerulean sky. The myriad of rail-weary, road-spent Cherokees arrived sick and exhausted at the water's edge, gaping hollow-eyed up and down the river.

From a knoll overlooking the Tennessee and the masses gathering along its banks, Lieutenant Deas, Sergeant Haney and the other soldiers surveyed the situation. In a fit of frustration, Deas took off his hat and threw it in the dirt.

"Damn them! Where the hell are they?" he roared, his voice reedy and hoarse from all the dust he had swallowed. "You gonna tell me they couldn't get two empty boats and a few barges through those little rapids and down the river by now?"

"It's been a dry year, sir," Sergeant Haney offered. "The river's down. Maybe they hit some sand bars."

Private Loven, a tall, baby-faced Swede, picked up the lieutenant's hat and handed it back to him. Deas scowled at the well-intentioned recruit, grabbed the hat and threw it down in the same spot.

"Nonsense!" Deas dismissed Haney's explanation. "I've been through here plenty of times when it was lower than this!"

Once again Private Loven retrieved the hat, dusted it off and presented it to Deas, only to be met by the same look of astonishment. Sergeant Haney leaned close to the young soldier and whispered, "He'll pick it up when he's ready, Private." Loven nervously bent down and replaced the hat on the ground.

* * * * * * *

The ranks of the Drummond family had grown to five with the addition of *Tsisdu* and *Me-li*. They were among the last to reach the banks of the Tennessee. Susanna had fashioned a traditional Cherokee back pack held in place by a wide band of cloth that came from behind and wrapped across her forehead. In this native harness she had walked the entire distance from Tuscumbia without speaking a word. *Tsisdu* had been a great help in watching the girls, for which Susanna was exceedingly grateful. She was glad the girls were so fascinated by the Rabbit Man they always wanted to be near him. No matter how far they had gone or how tired they might become, *Tsisdu* always had a smile for them and never lacked for ways to tease them and keep them entertained.

Tsisdu continued to fulfill his role as night came on. Susanna sat exhausted against a tree, a little apart from the campfire. The Rabbit Man quietly engaged Meg, *Me-li* and a gaggle of other Cherokee children with some sleight-of-hand magic tricks. He was trying—with moderate success—to keep their spirits up and their minds off the fact that they had no food. In Susanna's lap lay the leather pouch she'd promised her mother she would deliver to Michael. The same letter pouch Elizabeth had held in the haunting vision of the eagle-man creature late one night in the forest near Decatur. It was an apparition she had never been able to completely get out of her mind since seeing the human-sized eagle's head with its hypnotic, unblinking eye. She studied the cracks in the aged, worn leather. It was one of the few things she had salvaged before abandoning her trunk on the road outside Tuscumbia. Lightly her finger traced across the two tiny silver buckles and the wax seal her mother had placed there.

"I see you're still holding on to that old thing," William's voice came softly from the darkness. Susanna looked up at him with a faint, melancholy smile. He had come from a walk in the dark and was smoking his Scottish pipe. He glanced at his granddaughter with the other children. Though his fatigue was evident, William's face was more relaxed than Susanna had seen him in some time. Perhaps, she thought, his mood had been enhanced by some pleasant reminiscence triggered by the old leather pouch.

They were silent a while before she asked, "Do you know what's in it?"

"No," William shook his head. "Some of your mother's wisdom, no doubt."

"I'm tempted to open it." She looked up for his reaction and William cocked his head a little to one side, not convinced she should. She told him why. "I don't think we'll ever see Michael again."

William's pipe crackled with a long draft. He pressed a hand into his sore lower back and sought answers in the growing darkness. Never seeing his son again was a possibility he had refused to consider. An idea he had chosen to deny. Susanna saw the hurt she had caused him.

"I'm sorry, Father. I shouldn't have said that."

"I'm afraid you might be right," he admitted. "About not seeing Michael..."

She raised the leather pouch, holding it to her breast. "I won't look. She said only Michael was to open it."

"Have you had anything to eat?" William changed the subject.

Susanna had made two small cakes from the last of the corn meal she had managed to save after picking out the weevils and rat droppings. "I gave it to Meg and Mary. I wasn't hungry," she said. William looked down at her with pride, knowing she was lying. Knowing she must have been as hungry as the rest. He touched the top of her head affectionately then walked back toward the campfire.

Resting her chin on the letter pouch still held to her breast, Susanna watched her father empty his pipe and join *Tsisdu* and the children. She reacted with a start when something fell out of the end of the letter pouch and into her lap. To her amazement, it was the tiny leather draw-string bag given to her by the phantom Old One—the hallucination—she had seen at the Walker cabin the night before they were taken into captivity. She opened the little bag and dumped out into her palm the silver, intricately carved wolf's head ring. Transfixed by the amulet, Susanna slipped it onto the third finger of her left hand where her wedding band had once been. Immediately her attention was drawn to the edge of the woods. An old medicine man sat cross-legged before the red embers of a fire beside the graves of the two children who had died on the train.

This old man was no phantom. He chanted softly in Cherokee. With a carved stick about two feet long he probed at the embers, adjusting and trimming the neat, seven-sided configuration he had made of the ashes. From a pouch around his neck he

554

sprinkled tobacco onto the sacred septagon. A slight hesitation of the hand was his only reaction to Susanna approaching. She stopped with the two small graves separating them and stared down at the *di-da-nŭ-wi-s-gi* as though she were in a trance.

"*S-gi-li...S-gi-li,*" he mumbled.

"What? What does that mean? *S-gi-li?*" she asked softly.

The gap-toothed old one interrupted his incantations and squinted up at his visitor. "Witch. *S-gi-li.* Witch. The *s-gi-li* comes from the night sky..." he said with a slow, sweeping gesture. "To steal the souls of the dead..." His hand swept downward, indicating the two graves. "Especially souls of children. The *Go-la-nŭ A-ye-li-s-gi* were here. The *Raven Mockers*. But the children were already dead and buried. It was too late for them to eat the hearts of the little ones. But they were with us on the train. They stole the life of the old man. Now the *Go-la-nŭ A-ya-li-s-gi* have gone away. But the *s-gi-li* are here to steal their souls."

He sprinkled more tobacco on the embers. Susanna squatted, her arms extended and resting on her knees. She watched the shreddings burst into a spray of sparks and smoke that climbed into the darkness. "I make medicine seven years before I saw the first *s-gi-li*," he said.

His addressing her directly encouraged her to ask, "Do you always see witches when someone dies?"

The old man shook his head. "No. But I will this time. I feel it. I can hear the voices...there..." he pointed off into the darkness.

"What are they saying?"

"Five witches," the medicine man cocked his head to one side as though listening to evil whispers from another room. "They are fighting over who will get these two souls."

"How will you stop them?"

He held up a hand to silence her for a while longer, then, when the voices stopped momentarily, he answered. "I stay here until morning. Chanting. Make new tobacco. For three days."

"Three days?"

"Until the souls of the little ones reach their new home," he revealed a toothless smile and extended the tobacco pouch toward her. Susanna hesitated. At his urging she took a pinch and sprinkled it onto the embers. They were both startled by the extraordinarily bright explosion of sparks and a larger cloud of smoke than before.

"Good medicine...*wa-ya* medicine," the holy man pronounced his approval.

"*Wa-ya?*" A chill went through her. It was the same word *Tsisdu* had used in speaking of her. The old man pointed a crooked finger at the wolf ring.

"*Wa-ya.* The Wolf. Strong medicine," he repeated.

She examined the ring. Then, compelled by some unseen force, Susanna looked back toward the campfire to *Tsisdu* and the children. From across the clearing she watched her father interacting with the girls. *Tsisdu* had temporarily stopped playing and was staring right at her. She had the overwhelming sense—even from this distance—that he had heard her entire conversation with the old medicine man. She looked down at the ring, then rose and walked back toward the campfire.

* * * * * * *

Later Susanna went for a long walk in the woods along the Tennessee River's southern bank. She wondered which apparition would be waiting for her this time. Would she encounter the mysterious eagle-man? A snarling wolf? The ancient great grandfather of Annie and James Walker? Or would she see another vision of her mother? Susanna wasn't sure if the feeling in the pit of her stomach was fearful apprehension or anxious anticipation. These phantoms had never harmed her or threatened her or made her feel in any kind of danger—physical or spiritual. What they *had* done was raise many more questions than they answered. If they had appeared to deliver some message, why then the mystery? The ambiguity? What was the message?

As it happened, there were no visitations for Susanna that night. She was alone with her own thoughts of all that had happened to her in the past several months. And with her own questions for which, as yet, she had no answers. She had lost her home. She had lost her husband. She had lost her mother. And, she feared, she had lost her brother—something she had often wished for, prayed for and now regretted. And the overwhelming question racking her mind and clawing at her soul was embodied in the single word: *Why?*

When she got back to camp, Susanna sat down next to her father. She felt they needed to be close to each other, but wasn't sure who needed it most. Meg fell asleep in her mother's lap. *Me-li* sat on the ground, leaning against Susanna's legs.

"Tell a story," *Me-li* said, looking up at Susanna.

"It's late. Time to sleep."

"No. Tell a story!"

Some of the other children within hearing scampered to the fire and positioned themselves for a story.

"Maybe another time. Tomorrow perhaps," Susanna smiled at the other children. They ignored her answer, waiting patiently for the story to begin.

"I don't think they're getting the message," William said with a smile. Susanna looked from one to the other, hoping they would go away. They were waiting. Waiting for the story to begin. They were not going away. For the first time, she really studied their faces. They were beautiful faces. Some almost as fair skinned as Meg; others, the full-bloods, darkened by the summer sun. All with beautiful, trusting eyes, some dark brown, others hazel or even blue. She tried to think of a story they would like to hear. Something they could relate to. Finally she began.

"In the very beginning, the People say, Dog was king of the mountain..." she tried to recall from the first and only time she had heard the tale. It was a million miles away and a million years ago.

"*Gi-li,*" *Me-li* said.

"What?" Susanna was brought back to the campfire.

The other children repeated with *Me-li*, "*Gi-li*. Dog. Dog is *Gi-li.*"

"*Gi-li*. Yes," Susanna said. "*Gi-li*, the Dog, was king of the mountain. And it was *Wa-ya*, the Wolf, that stayed in the village by the fire. When winter came, *Gi-li*, the Dog, decided he did not like the cold, so he came down to the village and drove *Wa-ya*, the Wolf, from the fire. *Wa-ya* ran to the mountains where he prospered and did very well. He and his brother wolves ventured down to the village where they killed some animals. The People chased them back into the mountains and killed many of the wolves. Then *Wa-ya* and his brothers came back to the village..." she paused, leaning toward them with quiet intensity, "...and took such revenge that ever since, the People do not like to hurt *Wa-ya*, the Wolf."

The children were spellbound. Even William and *Tsisdu* were impressed with Susanna's story-telling ability. Once again William marveled at the transformation wrought in his daughter. *Tsisdu* leaned close to him.

"A real *wa-ya* has been born tonight," he said softly.

Susanna looked at the Rabbit Man without speaking, as though for the first time she understood his cryptic pronouncement. A long silence followed which was finally split by the distant but distinctly piercing scream of a steam whistle. When the shriek finally stopped, they heard the labored hissing and huffing of the engines.

Lieutenant Deas and Sergeant Haney instantly jumped up from their campfire and raced to the water's edge. Private Loven, out of breath, ran up to join them from the far end of the camp.

"Lieutenant! Lieutenant! I think the boats are here! They're coming!" Loven shouted with excitement. Deas, a tin cup of coffee in his hand, stared at Private Loven until the gangly, youth finally comprehended. "I...guess you heard...already..." Deas shook his head good naturedly then looked out at the river. The pin-point lights of the *Vesper* and the *George Guess* reflected in long, rippling lines on the water's ebony surface.

* * * * * * *

An hour after sunrise the keelboats were almost loaded and ready to get under way. The last of the Cherokees were boarding the barges with their possessions. On the high ground overlooking the river, Private Loven had been trying for half an hour to persuade the old medicine man to abandon the graves of the two dead children and get on the boat. But the old man refused, simply ignoring the presence of Loven and the two soldiers with him.

"*S-gi-li*. Three days. Souls of the children," the old one mumbled repeatedly. Loven shuffled with nervous frustration and saw a beleaguered Lieutenant Deas coming up the hill toward them.

"What's the matter? Why isn't he on board?" the lieutenant demanded. "We're ready to cast off. Come on! Let's move!"

"He won't budge, sir," Loven whimpered.

Deas squatted beside the old man and put a gentle hand on his shoulder. "Time to go, Old Timer. *Tsi-ne-na*."

Again, the medicine man ignored them as though they didn't even exist, focusing exclusively on his witch repelling duties.

"We could just pick him up and carry him down to the boat, sir," Loven suggested.

They watched the medicine man stir the fire with his carved stick. With his other hand he scooped up some ashes from the outer edge and, without looking up, tossed them in the direction of the witches.

"*S-gi-li*. Three days. *S-gi-li*."

"What the hell's he talking about?" Deas asked.

"He must remain here for three days," Susanna's voice came from behind them. "To protect the souls of these children."

William and Susanna, with Meg on her hip, were coming up from the river bank. Susanna had a sack of food with a round loaf of cornbread sticking out. Deas closed his eyes, pinched the bridge of his nose, then surveyed the river, the boats and the loaded barges waiting to depart.

"Great. Just what I need." Deas took his hat off and raked his fingers through his hair. "A crazy old man doing battle with witches. As if I didn't have enough problems."

"So, this is really about *your* problems, Lieutenant?" Susanna glared down at him.

Deas looked up, thrown off by her harsh tone. He had thought on more than one occasion that she was one of—no, *the*—most beautiful woman he'd ever seen. He'd lain awake by his campfire wondering how—or *if*—he should engage her in a purely social conversation. He had always dismissed it as a foolish idea. Born of a soldier's loneliness on a long and arduous assignment, far from family and friends. And besides, he told himself, she probably viewed him as a significant contributor to their present misery. That he had actually become quite fond of this gentle yet courageous and noble people was of little consequence, given their current situation. Yet still, there was a mysterious quality about her. A haunting beauty; an alluring puissance. Even when she was upset.

Deas rose, rubbing his face. "Look, General Scott agreed to put the Cherokees in charge of their own removal. I was ordered to pilot these boats and get you safely to Ft. Gibson." The lieutenant was at a loss. "Can you talk to him, Mr. Drummond? We've got to go!"

"Then let's go!" Susanna said sharply. "He's just one old Cherokee man. What do you care?"

Had it been anyone other than Susanna Drummond, he would have merely scowled and walked away. But he felt it important she understand. He bit his lip and took a deep breath before he answered. "If I didn't care, Ma'am, I'd have already left him, and we'd be two miles down river by now."

Susanna softened, realizing this man had taken better care of them than any *yo-neg* she had known since the night they were driven from their home.

"Won't there be other boats along in a few days?" she asked in a kinder voice. "I've brought him some food." She set the bag down next to the old man. He looked up at her—the first time he had acknowledged the presence of any of them—and signalled his thanks with a single wave of his hand.

"He could die here," Deas put it bluntly.

"He could die on your boat," Susanna countered.

The lieutenant's eyes met Susanna's, then they both looked down at the old medicine man, who had resumed his mumbled incantations. The *di-da-nŭ-wi-s-gi* sprinkled more tobacco and herbs on the fire.

* * * * * * *

A half hour later the *Vesper* and the *George Guess*, with their string of keelboats bulging with human cargo, pulled away from the south bank of the Tennessee River. On the hillside by the two graves the old medicine man had brought the dying embers back to a robust blaze. He interrupted his singing to look out toward the boats. Despite his near ninety years, his eyes were still keen enough to spot Susanna, holding Meg, with *Me-li* at her side. They stood at the back of the *Vesper's* last barge and looked up toward him. She lifted her hand in a final good-bye.

"*Wa-do, Wa-ya 'ge-yu-ts'*," the ancient one uttered his parting thanks to the *Wolf Woman*. He lifted his eyes to the clouds gathering in the northwestern sky. The rolling thunder trumpeted the departure of his people, some of whom he had known through four generations. The witch warrior gazed out at the boats until they were tiny dots on the river, then redirected his energy to the protection of his beloved children lying in the ground beside him.

CHAPTER
48

Near Hopkinsville, Kentucky

The storm front that had announced its imminent performance for the Cherokees aboard the *Vesper* and the *George Guess* stretched northward into western Kentucky where it promised a renewed deluge for the land travellers breaking camp in the early· light. Silently, grimly they prepared for another day's journey. Tattered wraps, threadbare coats and old shawls had been brought out against the unexpected drop in temperature.

Charlie and Eva Swimmer had almost finished packing their wagon when the thunder tumbled over them, literally causing the ground to tremble. It was a signal to speed everything up. Campfires were extinguished. Cherokee men and boys scooped feverishly to cover the slit-trench toilets. The night's only two casualties—one adult and one child—were buried. Friends and family gathered around the roadside grave to mourn, weep and pray. Cherokee mothers dug feverishly through bags and boxes in search of any rag to help keep their children warm.

Chief White Path coughed, so weakened that he could no longer stand on his own. Martha Swimmer wrapped a second blanket around the tattered, threadbare one already draped over his bony shoulders. Too feeble to mount or even sit his horse, he had been riding in the Swimmers' wagon. Sally's teeth chattered from the chilled wind. She clutched the wedding-dress doll given to her by Susanna Drummond and stared at the withered old chief across from her.

Most of the carts and wagons—the Swimmers' included—had been forced to take on more passengers who, like White Path, had become too ill to walk or even ride a horse or a mule. Others who had expected to walk all the way from Georgia to Indian Territory now found themselves too sick to keep up, forced to ride double—even triple—on horses and mules already overworked and underfed. Even the bony-backed oxen became mounts for a sick old woman, a consumptive old man or a couple of hollow-eyed children.

By mid morning what began as a light drizzle had become a stinging, peppering sleet that steadily softened the road to mush. The sick and afflicted were severely jolted and jostled about as wagons lurched through canyon-like ruts or bounced over rocks. Deeper and deeper the wheels cut into the mud until some wagons ended up buried to the axle in the pasty quagmire. Others, attempting to circumnavigate these roadblocks, found themselves stuck in the ditch.

* * * * * * *

The Swimmer wagon was buried to within a few inches of its axle. Charlie had cut two tree limbs. One was laid across the mud as a fulcrum for the other, which he placed beneath the axle. While Charlie coaxed and tugged at the mules, *Tsu-tsu* pushed up on the limb with all his strength, attempting to leverage the axle up out of the mud. Suddenly the limb snapped and the ragged, splintered end shot downward, ripping open the under side of *Tsu-tsu's* forearm. He dismissed his mother's concern, determined to finish the job. It was important, because other Cherokee men had gathered to help pull at the wheels and to give direction and encouragement. *Tsu-tsu* wanted to be viewed as a contributing adult, not as a foolish child who had been hurt while getting in the middle of a man's work. But the injury was serious and the flow of blood profuse. Only at the insistence of the other Cherokee men did *Tsu-tsu* finally slog his way out of the muck and allow his mother to apply some herbs and wrap his arm in some old rags. But as soon as the bleeding subsided, he was right back into the mud, pushing against the back of the cart, pulling on a wheel, adding his weight to help increase traction.

* * * * * * *

The already frigid temperature dropped another fifteen degrees by noon. It was the hardest freeze this early in the Fall that any of the Cherokees—even the very old ones—could remember. Chief Ross rode near the front of the creeping wagon train with guide Peter Hildebrand and Dr. Rawles, each man drawn within himself and bending into the freezing rain. Needles of sleet pricked their eyes, stabbing viciously at squinted lids. *Tsu-tsu* Swimmer jogged up to them from behind. The rags around his wounded forearm were crusted with frozen blood. The drivers of the first few wagons watched the well-liked youngster pull at Hildebrand's leg to get the trail conductor's attention. After a brief but urgent exchange, the three men turned their horses around. *Tsu-tsu* ran back down the line ahead of them. Hildebrand and Ross signalled the wagons to stop.

The old chief had gripped Sally's arm until the little girl cried out to her mother. The Swimmer wagon had stopped, blocking the road. Eva and Charlie helped White Path out of the wagon and over to the tree he had weakly pointed out. He leaned on them for support, his face only inches from the rough bark, his lips moving as though he were murmuring to the tree some mysterious secret. Then he shook free from Charlie and Eva and raised his frail arms to embrace the massive oak. By the time Dr. Rawles arrived with Chief Ross and Peter Hildebrand, White Path had turned and was leaning with his back against the tree. A long, dwindling exhalation was his last. Rawles walked up to the revered old *Tsa-la-gi* leader and looked into his blank stare, then reached up and gently closed the dead chief's eyes.

*   *   *   *   *   *   *

Cherokee faces streaked with the attenuated light of a frozen November day watched White Path's blanket-wrapped body being gently lowered into the shallow, muddy grave hacked out of the hardened ground at the road's edge. With the exception of the boys and young men tending the wagons and the animals, the entire party had assembled for the sad occasion. *Tsunaluska* tied the feather White Path had always worn in his hair to the end of a long pole. The Cherokees—from chiefs to children—ceremoniously dropped muddy clumps of earth into the grave.

Charlie Swimmer and three more Cherokees dragged a large trunk to the grave site. It was crude and simple, but it would be their beloved chief's only catafalque. Charlie glanced up at his daughter. He noted Sergeant Barton's arm, warm and protective around Martha. Their eyes met briefly, but neither man spoke. Corporal Miles Franklin and Corporal Richard Baker, another from Barton's unit, respectfully acknowledged the Cherokee men passing them with the trunk. But Sergeant DeKalb and his men—Thorpe, Whitaker and Evans—weren't as deferential.

"Just another dead Cherokee. Nothing worth freezin' for!" DeKalb grumbled, shivering beneath his long army coat. "Let's get going. We have to cover fifteen more miles today!" For his comments, DeKalb received dirty looks from Robert Barton and Martha Swimmer and the other Cherokees who had heard him. But DeKalb's smirk said clearly that he didn't care.

The grave continued to fill up, a handful at a time. Two Cherokee preachers recited—one in English, the other in Cherokee—the passage from the Christian Bible White Path had loved best. Like many others in the Cherokee nation had done for generations, the old chief had adapted. He had taken part of what the white man's Bible offered and augmented without compromise his own traditional, pre-Christian *Tsa-la-gi* beliefs.

"I will lift up mine eyes unto the hills, from whence cometh my help..."

"*Ga-du-si wi-di-ga-ga-ni na-hna tsŭ-di-da-le-hŭ-s-ga a-qua-li-ni-go hi-s-di-s-gi u-di-la-nŭ-hi....*"

"My help cometh from the Lord, Which made Heaven and Earth..."

"*A-gi-s-de-li-s-gi na-s-gi u-wo-sŭ-nŭ-hi ga-nu-la-di a-le e-lo-hi.*"

* * * * * * *

The bitter cold continued to invade the Cherokees, mercilessly prying its way into their bones. It felt as though the temperature had dropped another ten degrees by the time White Path's grave was filled. The words *White Path* were written in both English and *Tsa-la-gi* characters with lime whitewash on the sides of the trunk Charlie Swimmer and the others had brought. It was set atop the grave to discourage those necrophagous vermin who would desecrate the site—whether of the four-legged or the two-legged variety. Even before the last Cherokees had left the grave, the steady pelting of rain and sleet had already begun erasing the words in a slow, diluted trickle.

The pole *Tsunaluska* had prepared with the single feather and a white linen flag was stuck into the ground at the head of White Path's grave. Along either side of the trunk, smaller poles trailed brightly colored streamers to clearly mark the grave for those to follow.

One by one the Cherokees returned to their wagons. They paused to look with shivering curiosity when a scout galloped toward them from the front of the wagon train. Behind him two other scouts on foot ran at full speed, their vaporized breath extending before them like ghostly trumpets poised to deliver their urgent message. The dispersing funeral crowd, sensing the scouts' urgency, flowed forward to meet them.

"They're coming! They're coming this way!" the mounted one shouted.

"Who's coming?" *Gu-wi-s-gu-wi* asked.

"A mob of *yo-negs*. From Hopkinsville just up the road!"

The runners arrived, moving among the crowd, repeating the warning. "*Yo-negs*! Whites! They're coming here!"

"How many?" Hildebrand wanted to know.

"A hundred. Maybe more!" the mounted scout answered.

"More!" the runner corrected him. "*Ga-di-a ta-l'-s-go-hi-s-qua!*" he set the number at two hundred.

"What do they want?" *Tsunaluska* asked.

"You know what they want!" a Cherokee man answered.

"They want our horses. Our money. Same as all the rest!" Charlie Swimmer said loudly. Those around him grunted their agreement.

Peter Hildebrand asked Sergeants Barton and Dekalb if the army could—or would—protect them.

"Six or seven of us? A dozen at best? Against two hundred of them?" DeKalb held up his hands in a gesture meant to decline the request.

"At least you're armed!" Charlie Swimmer barked at him. "All our guns were taken away!"

"We was sent along as a token escort," DeKalb snapped back. "We ain't supposed to die for you people!"

Robert Barton left Martha and stepped out of the crowd, his disdain for DeKalb's reply evident. "Your courage in the face of danger is inspiring, Sergeant," he said. Before DeKalb could respond, Robert yelled out to the Cherokees. "Get together everything you have. Bows, arrows, your blow guns. Hell, get sticks and rocks, if you have nothing else." The Cherokees were impressed with this *yo-neg a-ya-wi-s-gi's* courage and leadership. Many of them dispersed to gather whatever weapons they could find. "Corporal Franklin, you, Baker and Evans take up a position twenty yards in front of the first wagon," he ordered in a calm but commanding voice. "Conner, you go with them," he motioned to the private with the wounded shoulder. "Thorpe, you, Stevens and Whitaker pull the first four wagons across the road to form a frontal barricade."

"What do you think you're going to do?" DeKalb sneered.

"Try to talk some sense to this mob," Barton answered. "I suggest you go to the rear and get under the last wagon. You certainly don't want to risk danger for *these people*."

* * * * * * *

Sergeant Barton stood alone out in front of his men. The barrel of his rifle rested in the crook of his arm. A pistol was tucked prominently into the belt of his uniform. One hand rested on the hilt of his army saber. His face was set with determination, oblivious to the steady assault of drizzle and sleet. A couple of steps behind him, Corporals Franklin, Baker, Conner and Evans were evenly spaced across the road. Sergeant DeKalb, sulking, leaned against a wagon wheel. Assembled a few yards farther back were John Ross, *Tsunaluska*, Peter Hildebrand, William S. Coodey and other Cherokee men, including Charlie Swimmer. Just behind them an even larger group of Cherokees filled the road. Men young and ancient, along with *Tsu-tsu* Swimmer and some of his teenage friends, as well as several women, including Eva and Martha Swimmer. Solemn Cherokee faces, darkened with concern, looked past the soldiers. They knew the barricade of wagons offered little defense against a hostile mob, but it was the best they could muster in so short a time. Their crude weapons had been assembled as Robert had ordered. From behind the wagons the remaining Cherokees—the old, the sick and the smaller children—directed their fearful apprehension up the road, into the dark trees, squinting against the freezing rain which had increased its intensity.

The distant voices, like disembodied souls, were heard before vague human forms began to take shape in the mist, coming around the sharp bend in the road. A wave of white men, their rifles hanging loosely at their sides, were out in front, followed by other men leading horses. A lot of horses. Perhaps twenty-five. And behind them were wagons, flanked on either side by legions of whites. How heavily these others might be armed was difficult to determine through the driving rain.

The first whites stopped ten yards from the soldiers and the line of crudely armed Cherokees. The rest of the *yo-negs* bunched up behind them, spreading out to either side until there were two distinct lines—*Tsa-la-gi* and white—facing each other. The Cherokees, watchful, suspicious, anticipating trouble, kept their weapons ready. The whites, however, appeared more curious than ominous and threatening. Many of them looked at each other, uncertain what was happening. The Cherokees were equally puzzled. Never before among the numerous mobs and gangs of whites that had accosted them along the route had there been so many women. There were even young children among these *yo-negs*.

As the two groups sized each other up, the long silence was marked only by the incessant patter of the cold rain. Finally, a white woman caught Quatie Ross's eye across the space separating them. Sensing a kindred spirit, the white woman was the first to

566

step forward, past the horses and between the armed men out front. She crossed the open ground and stopped in front of Quatie, unaware that she had approached the First Lady of the *Tsa-la-gi* nation.

"We're from Hopkinsville," the woman said softly, holding out an armload of blankets. "These are for your children. And the sick ones."

All eyes—Cherokee and white—were on the two women. Quatie smiled and accepted the much needed blankets. "*Wa-do*. Thank you."

The white woman removed the top blanket from the stack and wrapped it around a coughing nine-year-old Cherokee girl standing beside the chief's wife.

A white doctor was the next to step out from the Hopkinsville *mob*. He crossed the open space, going directly to *Tsu-tsu* Swimmer, who retreated a step at first. The doctor smiled and gently lifted the bloody, rag-wrapped arm.

"I'm a doctor," he said. "Let's take a look at this."

The Cherokees closest to Quatie Ross and *Tsu-tsu* Swimmer looked at each other, then back across to the whites. Their wariness hadn't completely vanished, but they were beginning to realize the benevolent intent of this visitation. All across the line of whites, men, women and older children ventured forth with armloads of clothing, shoes, boots and more blankets. Others carried food—hams, smoked turkeys, bags of grain, butter, cheese and baskets of bread and vegetables. A couple even had cloth-covered buckets of fresh milk! Looking past the first wave of whites, the Cherokees noted that many of the wagons were filled with bags of grain, flour, potatoes, pumpkins, corn and more foodstuffs, along with clothing, blankets and other essential supplies.

Gradually the realization spread among the *Tsa-la-gi* and they began moving tentatively out to meet the whites, shy at first, almost reluctant to accept the gifts. Though many of the Cherokees were near starvation, the first to receive the food ate sparingly, making sure a loaf of bread was torn into pieces and shared with others or that dippers of fresh milk went first to the children. Those who had been travelling with bare feet, even through the rain, sleet and freezing mud, gratefully accepted the boots and shoes.

Threading carefully through the mingling crowd, the local white men and older boys led teams of fresh, strong, healthy mules and oxen which they offered to help get the Cherokee wagons through the axle-deep roads and swollen creek crossings.

567

* * * * * * *

Quatie Ross, assisted by Eva and Martha Swimmer and two of the white women from Hopkinsville, spent the next two hours passing out blankets and clothing. The chief's wife continued to ignore her own worsening condition. She fought off one coughing attack after another, centering all her energy on ministering to the sick children and the old Cherokees. Eva tried to put a blanket around Quatie's shoulders, but she refused, giving the blanket instead to a shivering Cherokee boy.

Sergeant Barton accompanied one of the Hopkinsville doctors to a wagon near the middle of the train where medical attention was needed. Robert and Martha frequently passed each other, each time exchanging a look and a quick smile. She was so proud of him. True, this crowd from Hopkinsville had proven to be friendly, but Robert couldn't have known that. Yet he had been willing to stand first in the line to face what might have been, like so many of the others, a potentially murderous mob.

John Ross caught up with the women on their way to the next wagon. Eva took advantage of the opportunity to lovingly scold Quatie in hopes of enlisting *Gu-wi-s-gu-wi's* support. "Quatie, you need to take care of yourself."

"No," she repeated, coughing. "The children come first. Always the children."

"Chief Ross," Martha picked up on her mother's intention, "what are we going to do with her?"

Gu-wi-s-gu-wi smiled at his wife and took off his own coat. "I learned a long time ago, you don't *do* anything about Quatie. You just get out of her way." He tried to put his coat around his wife's shoulders, but she was stubbornly insistent.

"No, *Gu-wi-s-gu-wi*. You have to stay well. The people need you."

"I'm fine. Don't worry about me," he assured her. Finally Quatie relented, allowing the coat to hang loosely on her shoulders while she distributed blankets and clothing. Chief Ross walked along with them for a while.

"We've set up the town hall in Hopkinsville," one of the Kentucky women informed the chief.

"Of course," the other one added, "it isn't large enough to hold everyone, but we can use it as a hospital."

"If you can stay for a few days, it'd sure be good for those in really bad shape," the first woman suggested.

"Especially the children and the elderly," the second put in.

Chief Ross stopped and placed an appreciative hand on the shoulder of each woman. "As much as we need to rest, we must push on. We've already been on the road forty days and we're way behind schedule. It's turning out to be a hard winter."

He saw the disappointment in their faces and was genuinely moved by these good souls who, for the first time on the Cherokees' long journey, hadn't gathered to either rob or threaten them or, at best, to make certain they kept to the road and passed without incident through the whites' community.

The two women understood the travellers' necessity to keep moving, but each hoped that a warm fire, a properly prepared meal and the much needed shelter and medical help they offered would weigh heavily in changing the chief's mind once they reached Hopkinsville.

* * * * * * *

At the Swimmer wagon, Charlie and an old, bent farmer in his late sixties who had introduced himself in a thick Scottish brogue as Angus Reid, had just replaced Charlie's two skin-and-bone mules with a fresh team of strong, healthy oxen. Angus patted one of his prized animals on the rump. "Aye!" he boomed in his heavy accent, "these lads'll drag you through mud right up to yer eyeballs! Just keep crackin' the whip on 'em, all the way to your new home."

"*Wa-do.* Thank you, Mr. Reid," Charlie shook his head no, "but we only need them until we get past Hopkinsville. We're not asking for charity."

Reid, himself a proud and independent man, recognized and respected the same quality in others. "Oh, 'tisn't charity, lad," he said with a chuckle. "Angus Reid doesn't give 'em away! Tell you true, I'm a tired old man. I'd just ruther not have to swap 'em out again." The old Scot lowered his tired bones onto a fallen log and pulled out a sheep-bladder flask. "My boys an' me put up plenty of hay and grain this summer. If you get back this way in the spring, maybe we'll trade back. Yer mules'll be nice and fat by then." He lifted the flask. "Fine Scotch whiskey. Made it myself." Reid took a long, satisfying drink and passed the container to Charlie, who indulged himself in an even longer draft. The old Scot smiled, pleased to have his whiskey received with such heartfelt appreciation. Charlie wiped his mouth with the back of his hand and coughed from the strong spirits, bringing another chuckle from the

Scot.

Both men reacted to a flurry of activity only a few wagons away. Following the initial rush for food and shoes offered by the people of Hopkinsville, a firm spot of ground had been chosen to stockpile the rest of the goods until an orderly and equitable distribution could be made. Many of the Cherokees had already formed a line, waiting patiently for a meager ration of supplies and clothing. But Sergeant Charles DeKalb, backed by his own men—Corporals Stevens, Thorpe, Evans and Whitaker—had pushed the Cherokees back. Access was still granted, however, to the whites carrying armloads of goods to add to the pile.

"Stay back! All of you!" DeKalb shouted at the Cherokees. "You're worse than a bunch of vultures!"

It took only a few seconds for Charlie Swimmer, followed by the hobbling Angus Reid, to reach the scene. Martha and Eva, with Sally tagging along, hurried up from the other direction. Close behind them came Sergeant Robert Barton. Old *Tsunaluska* stepped forward, remaining dignified in his anger.

"The contractors—who were paid in advance—don't show up. If they do come, the supplies are ruined. Rotten. Full of weevils and worms," the old chief challenged DeKalb.

"Take it up with the contractors," DeKalb snarled. "This food will be used to feed army troops."

Charlie stopped only inches from DeKalb. "The removal was put under the control of Chief Ross and the Cherokees. You're not in charge here," he said firmly.

DeKalb, incensed that a lowly Cherokee Indian would dare come so close, pushed Charlie back and drew his pistol. "Long as I'm army and you're civilian—long as I'm white and you're not—you can bet your worthless Injun ass I'm in charge!" DeKalb yelled.

He cocked his pistol and took up a wide stance in front of the stockpiled goods. The Cherokees who had gathered were inflamed but not surprised. They had seen it all—had lived it all—before. But Sergeant DeKalb and his men had miscalculated the reaction of the whites from Hopkinsville. Their outrage at the soldier's behavior was evident in their faces.

Martha Swimmer helped her father to his feet. Then, in open defiance of DeKalb, she walked around him and began handing out food to Cherokee women waiting in line. Sally slipped past her mother and joined Martha. The child labored beneath the weight of a large ham which she deposited at the feet of an old Cherokee woman. When Martha returned for more goods, DeKalb stepped in her path.

"Get out of my way," she said fearlessly and pushed him aside. DeKalb back-handed her, knocking her to her knees in the freezing mud. Charlie immediately moved toward his daughter, but DeKalb brandished his pistol as a warning to Charlie and the other Cherokees to stay back. The incident had suddenly escalated, prompting Evans and Thorpe to draw their pistols in anticipation of trouble. From the other side of the crowd, Sergeant Robert Barton drew his own pistol and started walking toward them.

"I'm tellin' you!" DeKalb shouted at the Cherokees, "Stay back! These goods is now property of the United States Army!"

Martha sprang back to her feet and dabbed at the blood flowing from the corner of her mouth. She saw Robert approaching. When he had reached them, Barton raised his pistol, aiming it directly at DeKalb, who didn't take him seriously. Not until Barton walked right up and placed the muzzle against the side of DeKalb's head. The other soldiers were stunned by Barton's actions.

"You'd better think real hard on what you're doing, boy," DeKalb's voice cracked a little through his attempted bravado. "I'll have you court-martialed just for holding a gun to my head."

Barton's voice was more of a growl, with a hotter ire than any of them had ever heard from him. "I warned you, DeKalb! You'd go too far one day..." They remained frozen until Robert finally lowered his pistol and went to see about Martha. Released from immediate danger, DeKalb recovered his arrogant smirk.

"It's all right, Robert," Martha clung to his arm. "It isn't worth it."

"No," Barton corrected her firmly. "It's *not* all right. Take the food. All of you!" He waved the crowd toward the pile of goods. "And the clothes. Take what you need."

If the Cherokees were allowed to take the goods, DeKalb realized, he would have lost the confrontation to Barton. Worse, he would have lost face in front of these Indians. An unbearable thought. With his lip curled in a familiar sneer, DeKalb pointed his pistol at Martha. She glared defiantly. DeKalb shifted the gun down, aiming at the face of a terrified Sally, then brought it back up to Martha.

"I could shoot her or the kid right now and nobody'd do nothing about it," he directed his words to Barton. "They're just Cherokees."

Without a single word of warning or a moment's hesitation, Robert Barton raised his pistol and fired, hitting DeKalb in the center of the chest. DeKalb staggered backward but didn't go down immediately. With his head cocked a little to one side, he looked at Barton in shocked disbelief, then down at his wound and finally back up to Barton. DeKalb opened his mouth to speak but no words came out. Only a gush of blood. His eyes went distant and glazed just before they rolled up in his head and he fell backwards.

The attenuation of the pistol's report had left a vacuous silence. All eyes were on Sergeant Robert Barton. He stepped across the fellow soldier he had just shot, calmly went to his friend, Corporal Miles Franklin, and gave up his pistol. Robert then unbuckled his saber and offered it as well.

"Corporal Franklin," he said with full military solemnity, "I'm surrendering my arms and submitting myself to be placed under arrest for the murder of Sergeant Charles DeKalb, United States Army."

The young corporal was completely bewildered. He looked for help to the other soldiers who were equally stunned. "Sergeant...you did what you had to do..."

"I killed the man, Corporal," Barton insisted. "You all saw it," he turned to the crowd of witnesses.

The stiff-jointed Angus Reid hobbled forward with the aid of his cane. "What I saw was that man..." he pointed to the fallen DeKalb, "...threatening to shoot that woman..." his shaking finger shifted to Martha, "...and this wee bairn..." he pointed last to Sally. "*That's* what *I* saw."

One of the Hopkinsville women who had earlier spoken with Chief Ross and Quatie stepped out of the crowd and gestured toward Robert. "And then we all saw this brave man come to their rescue."

"And we'd swear to it before God and any court in the land," her friend added.

There was another long silence. Finally Charlie Swimmer grabbed a shovel and started digging a grave in the roadside ditch right beside the body of Sergeant DeKalb. After Charlie had turned the first few muddy shovelfuls, Corporal Franklin and two Hopkinsville men scrambled for more shovels and began digging. The armed Kentuckians kept a watchful eye on Stevens, Thorpe, Evans and Whitaker while the women began distributing the food, blankets, shoes and clothing to the Cherokees.

After a few minutes Evans and Thorpe left the scene, followed shortly by Stevens and Whitaker. They walked back down the line of wagons toward the rear of the train. The Hopkinsville men permitted them to pass, content to defuse the situation by getting the soldiers away from the scene. Neither Sergeant Barton nor Corporal Franklin was certain what to do next. Barton's eyes found *Gu-wi-s-gu-wi*, who had hurried from midway down the line to investigate the pistol shot. He looked at Barton, his sympathy and respect for the young soldier clearly evident.

Chief *Tsunaluska* conferred aside with John Ross. He spoke in whispers with an occasional glance toward the crowd of whites who had manifested such kindness and compassion toward their people. Their eyes drifted down to where DeKalb was being buried. A *yo-neg* soldier's own vile hatred had cost him his life. And for what? Ross went to stand with Charlie and Martha Swimmer. *Tsunaluska* shook his head at the tragedy of it all and started slowly back down the line of wagons.

"Choona-looskie?" a scratchy, old voice came softly from the crowd. *Tsunaluska* stopped and looked back at the weathered old man, squinting inquisitively at him. With his quivering cane the slow moving Kentuckian limped a little apart from the others. A leathered old battle scar ran from the left side of his forehead across the bridge of his nose and down into the beard on his right cheek. *Tsunaluska* studied him, straining to remember.

"You know me?" the old Cherokee asked.

"You Choona-looskie, ain't you?"

"Who are you?"

"Name's Tillman," the old man smacked his toothless gums together. "Jonathan Tillman. We fought together under Andy Jackson at Horseshoe Bend on the Tallapoosie. I was there when you saved Old Hick'ry from gettin' his head split open by a Creek Red Stick warrior. Don't you remember?"

The clarity of recognition gradually swept *Tsunaluska*'s expression as the battle of many years hence flickered to life in his memory. He extended his hand and the two old warriors grasped each other's forearm in greeting.

"*Si-yo*, Tillman. I remember The Horseshoe. My life—the lives of many of our warriors—were at stake for you and your country. That day I thought Jackson was my best friend. But Jackson didn't do me right as a friend that saved his life. And your country does my people no justice now."

Tillman took a silver flask from his coat pocket and offered it to *Tsunaluska*. The old chief accepted, grateful for a taste of good whiskey.

"You're right," Tillman agreed with the Cherokee's bitter indictment. "We fought again' this. Hard as we could. Even went down to Tennessee. Tried to persuade Jackson to get Van Buren to back off. Didn't do no good," Tillman lamented. His eyes slipped out of focus as though replaying the scene at The Hermitage in his mind. He snapped back to the moment and made a sweeping gesture with an arthritic hand toward the mixed crowd of Cherokees and his own people of Hopkinsville. "But we come down here to do what we could."

"We will not forget your kindness," *Tsunaluska* said. He gave back the flask and placed a hand of gratitude on Tillman's shoulder. Tillman took a drink. A light snow began to fall. The two men watched their people intermingling like old friends.

* * * * * * *

On the move once more, the Cherokee wagons were strung out from horizon to horizon. The unravelled string of travellers snaked toward the northwest, the only thing moving in a pristine landscape that appeared locked in the grip of a cold, white stillness. The snowfall had lasted several hours, ending just before midnight. Those Cherokees who needed it most had been delivered into the comforting warmth of the Hopkinsville town hall. Medications were administered freely, and what wasn't used immediately had been packed to go with the Cherokees when they resumed their journey. It wasn't enough, the citizens of Hopkinsville knew, but it was the best they could do. Outside, those Cherokees who couldn't fit into the town hall huddled in the lee of their wagons and the hide-covered lean-to's that had been assembled.

The next morning ushered in a brilliant sunrise on a cold but beautiful, clear day. The removal travellers leaned into the blustery wind, their newly acquired shoes, blankets and coats a welcome defense against the bitter cold.

Despite the hospitable welcome, the much needed rest and the fresh supply of medicine, one night of proper care was not a cure-all. Many Cherokees were still very weak and seriously ill. They were forced to continue riding on the over-crowded wagons. Each day hunters went off, only to return hours later with empty hunting sacks, hurrying to catch up to the wagons. Most of the game had either been decimated by the harsh winter or depleted by earlier emigrants, including Creeks, Choctaws and Chickasaws who had been driven westward in the years preceding the Cherokee removal.

Robert Barton rode beside the Swimmer wagon, but he kept his eyes straight ahead, displaying the same somber expression he had worn since the shooting of Charles DeKalb. From the wagon Martha watched him with concern. Her heart longed for him, ached at his pain, twisted itself into knots because of the impenetrable wall he had erected around himself. Charlie Swimmer had grown increasingly fond of the handsome *yo-neg*, though he had never gone out of his way to make his feelings known. The courageous way in which Barton had come to the defense of Martha and Sally had removed all barriers. Here, indeed, was a white man with a true heart. A *Tsa-la-gi* heart. Charlie and Eva, like Martha, were worried about the young man, but they said nothing.

* * * * * * *

Some of the wagons carrying the sickest of the travellers had finally been forced to stop beside stubbled fields lying cold and cramped beneath a glazed hoarfrost. Dr. Rawles was aided by Dr. Hamilton and the two Hopkinsville physicians who had volunteered to travel on with the Cherokees. They were all near collapse but did their best to treat the ill with limited resources. With the ranks of the sick and the dying swelling each day, the medical supplies and added blankets brought from Hopkinsville soon ran out. The doctors had been assisted, as usual, by Quatie Ross and a host of other women—Cherokee, black and white—in caring for the afflicted. Cherokee medicine men worked shoulder to shoulder beside white doctors, chanting, administering root teas, herbal concoctions and plasters.

Another wagon pulled out of the train to join the Cherokees' roadside hospital. Quatie Ross deposited a sick four-year-old girl on the tailgate of the hospital wagon where Dr. Rawles, himself fighting a nagging cough, was working on a Cherokee woman and her six-year-old son. Rawles pulled the blanket tightly around the woman's shoulders and gave instructions to Martha Swimmer who had been assisting him all morning.

"Half a grain of opium and twenty grains of calomel. Fifteen grains for the boy," Rawles said. Martha tugged at his sleeve.

"Doctor, we're almost out."

"Of calomel?"

"Calomel. Opium. Laudanum. Everything," she confirmed. Rawles rummaged hurriedly through near-empty boxes inside the wagon. His disappointed expression confirmed Martha's inventory report. "What do we do when it's all gone?" she asked.

Rawles looked at the next wagon. A Cherokee medicine man,

in a long black coat and a black hat that made him look more like one of the *yo-neg* doctors, was treating a sick old man with an herbal plaster. At the opposite end of the same wagon, one of the Hopkinsville doctors wore a traditional turban given to him in gratitude for helping a Cherokee family. Rawles shook his head at the irony of the image. He smiled at Martha and motioned toward the medicine man. "Then, I guess I'll have to start learning what they know, won't I?"

Martha dug through the near-empty medical supply boxes for the medicine he had instructed her to administer to the Cherokee woman and her son. Rawles slid down to examine the little girl Quatie had brought. It didn't take long to make his diagnosis. The child was burning with fever and had all the symptoms.

"Pneumonia," he said, shaking his head. "Seventh case today. And we've got dysentery, measles, influenza. We're running out of medicine, but we sure don't seem to be running out of diseases!" Rawles vented his frustration. When he looked down, Quatie's diminutive frame was doubled over the tailgate, so gripped by the coughing seizure that she couldn't draw air. "*Ma-di!* Come here!" Rawles called.

Martha brought the box of medicine, but before she could even set it down on the tailgate, Quatie was waving them off. She had defeated the cough and forced herself to draw only short, tiny breaths to keep from launching into another round.

"You take it, Dr. Rawles," Quatie pointed at the medicine. "You're the one who has to save these people."

Rawles helped her straighten up and put his hands on her shoulders. "I'm just treating the bodies, Mrs. Ross. You're keeping their spirits alive." He dug hurriedly through Martha's medicine box. By the time he had found a vial of laudanum, Quatie was already walking away, battling another cough.

* * * * * * *

By late afternoon the first Cherokee wagons, flanked by the road-weary who had been forced to walk, began arriving at the next designated campsite. From its worn appearance, the location had already served too many travellers in days past. *Tsunaluska* kneeled beside the stagnant pool, broke through the thin membrane of ice, cupped his hand and tasted the water. Immediately he spit it out. Other thirsty Cherokees arrived at the pool and dropped to their knees. Most of them also spit out the bitter water, but so great was the thirst of some that they forced themselves to drink. *Tsunaluska* looked around and spotted the Hopkinsville doctor wearing the Cherokee turban.

"The water is bad. Look..." *Tsunaluska* pointed across the pool to the slit-trench toilet left improperly covered by the previous campers. It had been dug much too close to the spring-fed pool and had seeped through the ground, polluting the water. At the far end lay two decaying corpses—they looked like Cherokee—that had been buried too shallow and too near the pool. The recent storms had washed away the dirt, leaving the bodies partially exposed and lying in the water.

"Hey! Don't drink that water!" the Hopkinsville doctor called to the Cherokees on the other side. "It's contaminated!" He pointed to the decomposing bodies. "From the corpses. And the sewer trenches!"

"It's poison!" *Tsunaluska* simplified the warning. "It'll make you sick!"

"We're already sick," a Cherokee boy dismissed them with a wave and drank more water.

"It'll kill you!" the doctor said.

"We're already dying!" the boy's father answered. "At least, for now, it quenches the thirst." He dipped his hand once more into the pool. The doctor looked helplessly at *Tsunaluska*. The old chief shook the polluted waters from his own hand and walked away. Both men felt frustrated, but they were powerless to control the others. Perhaps when more of the Cherokees and their leaders arrived, saner heads would prevail.

* * * * * * *

Campfires were spread like scattered fireflies along the trail and into the woods fifty to one hundred yards on either side of the road. By mid-afternoon the morning's welcome sunshine had yielded to a gathering cloud bank which, by nightfall, had given birth to new snow flurries swirling in a piercing cold.

Tsu-tsu Swimmer finished relieving himself at the slit-trench latrine and pulled up his trousers. He had waited in the cold for almost half an hour until there was no one else around. Twice he had approached, but before he could select the most private spot, he heard others coming and decided to wait. The Cherokees—by nature a clean and private people—had discovered on their first night in the concentration camps one of the subtle and insidious weapons their captors used against them. The loss of privacy. To these prisoners who had committed no crime, had broken no law, it went far beyond embarrassment. It was complete humiliation, being forced to relieve themselves and void their bowels within view—and hearing—of others. For many it was the ultimate shame. A young girl might look up and see through the thinning mist the very same young man who, just the night before, had looked longingly at her through the flames of the campfire. Perhaps she had held his eyes an extra second or two before looking away, indicating that she, too, was interested. But now, squatted over the trench, his discomfort equalled her own and he was powerless to muffle his own flatulence. And each knew that any subsequent locking of eyes across the fire would produce only a nervous redirection. No gazing. No games. No flirtations. No prolonged looks. Only shame and embarrassment.

Blowing to warm his freezing hands, *Tsu-tsu* hurried back to camp where he crawled back into the Swimmer wagon beneath the tattered tarp covering. Charlie and Eva had used their largest piece of canvas, together with a few animal hides, to form a tent slanting off to one side of the wagon. Directly beneath the wagon Martha sat on some animal skins, a blanket wrapped around her shoulders. Another blanket hung straight down from the side of the wagon to form a thin, fabric wall between Martha's area and that occupied by her parents. Another animal hide on the opposite side made up the outer wall of her little *room*.

The animal skin had been flapped open and draped across the wagon wheel. Martha could see Robert Barton sitting on a box in the snow just outside. He was motionless, staring out into the darkness. With a shallow pan she scooped the last of the coals from the dying fire beside Robert and placed the pan beneath the wagon to provide a little warmth. After watching Robert for a while, she reached out and took his arm. He yielded quietly, allowing himself to be pulled under the wagon. She lowered the animal skin flap, then took his face in both her hands.

"Robert, stop it! Put it behind you!"

"I killed him, *Ma-di*," Robert said in a vacant monotone and turned away. He felt uncomfortable looking at her in his criminal shame.

"You're a soldier. A warrior. Sometimes a warrior has to kill."

"But he wasn't the enemy," Barton became more animated. "He was one of my own!"

His answer angered Martha. "He wasn't the enemy?!" she

pulled him sharply around to face her. "He put his gun to my little sister's head—then pointed it right in my face—and he's not the enemy?!"

Robert knew he had hurt her. It was the last thing in the world he wanted to do. He realized just how profoundly he loved this fiery *Tsa-la-gi* girl. No, this *Tsa-la-gi woman*. He slipped his arm around her.

"I'm sorry, *Ma-di*," he said simply, taking her face in his hands just as she had done to him earlier. He lifted her chin and looked into her eyes. "I love you more than anything in this world," he said tenderly. "You're right. Anyone who would try to hurt you is my enemy. My worst enemy."

Martha kissed him. Barton was shy at first, but soon yielded to his own swelling passion. She pushed him down on the skins and drew the other hides and blankets over them. He felt her squirming and knew she must have been disrobing beneath the covers. When she stopped moving, he felt her hands on his chest, unbuttoning his tunic and pulling it open. He assisted by slipping his arms out of the garment and pushing it aside. Then he felt her press against him; felt her bare breasts against his naked chest. It was the warmest, softest, most exhilarating and titillating sensation he had ever known. So intense was his joy he could have wept, but weeping was quickly forgotten when her hand slipped down across his stomach and began removing his trousers.

* * * * * * *

Charlie and Eva lay together beneath their blankets a scant two yards away from Martha and Robert. Each pretended they couldn't hear the movement or the breathing from beyond the thin blanket dividing them. Sally, lying at their feet, coughed fitfully. Beside her Buck stirred. Eva sat up and patted them both to sleep, then slipped back beneath the blanket and rolled close to Charlie to whisper her report.

"*Sa-li* still has a fever."

"Get some medicine from the *yo-neg* doctor tomorrow," Charlie said softly. Eva pressed against him, absorbing his warmth. They had succeeded for a while in ignoring the activity beneath the wagon, but as the young lovers approached the pinnacle of their passion—and there was no mistaking they were, indeed, reaching that peak—Eva and Charlie could no longer pretend it wasn't happening.

"I hope she knows what she's doing," Charlie whispered.

"Sounds to me like they've figured it out," Eva said with a soft chuckle.

"You know what I mean," Charlie said. He had come to be very fond of Robert Barton, but this was his oldest daughter. His firstborn.

Eva slipped her arms around him. "Shut up and go to sleep," she whispered in his ear.

* * * * * * *

Martha and Robert, exhausted, lay entwined in their contentment. For this one night they remained oblivious to the suffering, the pain and the misery that had become their world. Slowly Martha raised her hand toward the underside of the wagon, tracing her fingers along its bottom. Suddenly she poked her index finger through the knothole in the board.

"Ow! My eye!" *Tsu-tsu* cried from the wagon bed above.

"Next time, mind your own business!" she barked up at him in a loud whisper. Robert, shocked and embarrassed, looked from Martha up to the knothole and back to Martha. She pulled the blanket up to completely cover them and drew him to her again.

CHAPTER
49

The *George Guess* and the *Vesper* dragged their Cherokee barges north on the Tennessee River toward the junction with the Ohio. The steamers strained and coughed, hissing and spitting in obvious need of repair. Although the day was crisp and cold, a few minutes on deck in the sunshine actually warmed a body to the point of feeling comfortable. It was a deceptive warmth, however, for the cold hand of death continued to book passage on every keelboat gliding smoothly along the glassy river.

Susanna Drummond Tanner came out of the barge house onto the deck to throw some garbage overboard. When she started back inside she spotted a young Cherokee mother sitting at the rail a few yards away holding her baby. For some time Susanna watched what she had initially perceived as a peaceful, idyllic scene. Then she noticed the woman's pendulum rocking was because her entire body was racked with inaudible sobs, and the child she clung to was limp. Susanna went to her, but she knew no words would help. A gentle touch of the woman's head, a consoling hand on the shoulder was all Susanna had to offer. She was relieved when two older *Tsa-la-gi* women showed up to take care of the situation, allowing her to go back inside. When she reached the doorway, *Tsisdu* came out leading Meg and *Me-li*.

A look from Susanna and a subtle eye signal toward the woman with the dead child told *Tsisdu* to steer the girls in the other direction. William came out behind them. He looked at the women as they softly began their Cherokee death chant.

"That's the sixth child to die in two days," Susanna said, her voice filled with pity for the lost and concern for the living children, including her own.

"I know," William said, sad and helpless.

"You never know which one could be next," she said. He knew her meaning. They looked back along the rail to *Tsisdu* and the girls. "Meg still has the flux. It's been way too long."

William drew a deep breath and leaned out over the rail, looking up the river. What was he hoping to see there? he wondered. Some mystical revelation that would relieve their concern?

"We're coming up to the Ohio," he said. "Lt. Deas says we should make Paducah by nightfall. We'll take on supplies there. Food, medicine. Hopefully more blankets and clothes. Maybe rest a couple of days while they make some repairs. If they can't find the parts for the *Vesper's* engine, they might have to transfer us to another steamer."

Susanna's voice was gritty with frustration. "And how many more children will die before we get to this wonderful new home in the west? How many more of the old ones?"

William cast his troubled thoughts to the river. He had no answers.

* * * * * * *

Near Paducah, Kentucky

The distant lights of Paducah reflected off the river's tranquil surface as the *Vesper* and the *George Guess* steamed past the confluence of the Tennessee and Ohio Rivers. On the pilot deck of the *Vesper*, Lieutenant Edward Deas smoked his pipe and gazed out at the port city off to their left. At their last stop to take on firewood, Lieutenant Whiteley had left the *George Guess* in the able hands of Lieutenant Barrett and joined Deas aboard the *Vesper*.

"She's a beautiful town," Whiteley noted.

"They're all beautiful at night, R. H.," Deas agreed. "Especially from a distance."

"Are we going to stop?"

"We'll dock just south of the city," Deas answered. "The supply contractors are supposed to meet us there."

"We're six days behind schedule. You think they'll still be around?"

"They want their money," Deas said, his pipe clasped between his teeth. "The ones that don't show are the ones who got paid in advance." The two pilots leaned out to look back at the keelboats. The fires on the upper decks were being extinguished one by one. The Cherokees moved back inside, away from the night chill. Deas recognized William Drummond, his beautiful daughter, Susanna, the twitchy-faced one they called Rabbit Man and a host of other Cherokees he had come to know quite well.

* * * * * * *

Five crude wooden docks jutted out like wide-spread fingers sifting the Ohio at the ferry just before Paducah where the river flowed to the northwest. The *Vesper* and the *George Guess* tied up there, with the keelboats strung upstream behind them to the southeast. Torches, oil lanterns and candles dotted the night. Their phantasmic shadows gave the quiet but teeming bustle of activity a distinctively netherworld appearance.

Lieutenant Deas, William Drummond, his friend, the Rabbit Man, and a number of other Cherokee barge leaders surrounded the fire *Tsisdu* had built as soon as he hit shore, knowing they would need its warmth. The last of the Cherokees leaving the keelboats scattered along the bank. Here and there more fires sprang to life to ward off the clutching cold. Deas and the men with him watched a torch bobbing toward them in the darkness as a shadowy figure approached from the direction of the ferry shack. Finally they recognized the messenger as their own Lieutenant Whiteley.

"The ferry man says the suppliers were here," Whiteley reported. "They left a little more than an hour ago."

Deas kicked a rock into the fire. "The bastards! They knew we were coming!"

"I thought you said they'd be here because they want to get paid," Whiteley reminded Deas of their earlier conversation. Deas felt embarrassed by having missed the call. He put his back to the fire as though to warm himself. In reality, he preferred casting his anger to the darkness rather than getting into it with Whiteley. He was glad when William came to his defense.

"Ordinarily the lieutenant would be right. But sometimes these contractors have their own agenda."

"I don't get it," Whiteley argued in frustration. "Either they're here or they're not."

"It isn't quite that simple," William calmly pointed out.

"Maybe we could get a couple of horses," Whiteley suggested. "Send someone after them."

"Oh, they're not far away, believe me," Deas assured him. "I've run into this before. They'll stay hidden for a few hours. Let the cold set in. Then they'll show up when everyone's freezing and starving."

"And raise their prices," Whiteley said, beginning to understand.

"And we'll be glad to pay," William added. It was a scheme with which the Cherokees—land route and river travellers alike—had become all too familiar.

* * * * * * *

Camp fires dotted the landscape up and down the river bank

where the *Tsa-la-gi* hovered together against the bone chilling cold. They made the most of every available threadbare piece of blanket or clothing. Exhausted, hungry and sick, many of them lay shivering on the ground with only a single blanket or a worn animal hide and strained without success toward elusive sleep. William sat by his fire, knees drawn up in front of him, his large, angular hands wrapped around a tin cup of steaming coffee. *Tsisdu* appeared out of the darkness to join him.

"Someone's coming," the Rabbit Man said.

William got up, looking and listening in the direction from which *Tsisdu* had come. "Probably the supply wagons," he said in response to Susanna's questioning look. She threw off her own tattered blanket and started to get up. William held out a hand to stop her. "Stay here. We don't want them in the camp," he said, then left with *Tsisdu*.

They met up with other Cherokee men and went together to join Deas and Whiteley and a handful of soldiers at the northernmost edge of the encampment. All the men had blankets draped around their shoulders and two of the enlisted men carried torches. Once assembled, they climbed the steep slope up to the road that ran parallel to the river high above the camp.

Just as Deas had predicted, when they reached the top, they saw emerging from the woods across the high road a long train of supply wagons. Whites in warm long coats carried torches and lanterns to light the way. By the time they stopped there were fifteen supply schooners strung along the road.

The suppliers refused to drive their wagons the additional half mile to the switch-back leading down to the river bank where the steamers and the barges were tied up. They wouldn't say why. They simply refused. *Of course*, someone threw in from the darkness, *if the Cherokees were willing to pay an additional ten dollars per wagon...*

It took the better part of an hour for *Tsisdu* and some of the other Cherokees to go back down to the ferry station, wake someone and make arrangements to rent wagons and mule teams. They then had to go the long way around to reach the supply wagons on the high road. William waited with Deas and the soldiers and a few Cherokees. Thinking he recognized a couple of Georgians he had encountered before—Brantley and Solmes, he thought were their names—William casually lifted the tarp from one of the supply wagons. His finger traced lightly across the logo—*Tanner Overland Freight*—and he wondered about the name imprinted there.

584

"Thirty cents a pound," the one called Brantley said smugly before he would allow the transfer of goods to begin.

"Thirty cents!" *Tsisdu* protested. "You got corn meal in them sacks or gold?!"

"That's outrageous," Deas shook his head. "These people don't have that kind of money."

"I thought the price had already been agreed on," Whiteley said.

"Thirty cents. That's the price. Take it or leave it," Brantley spat out his obviously well-rehearsed demand.

"We'll pay," William said, stepping in to join Deas and *Tsisdu*. "We have no choice." He motioned to the other Cherokees to start transferring the bags from the supply wagons to their temporary transport vehicles. Lieutenant Whiteley watched the Cherokees begin and then confronted Brantley once more.

"My God, man! Have you no conscience? You're no better than a common thief!"

Brantley and his cohorts bristled at the accusation but kept their composure while William passed the payment to the man named Solmes.

"That ain't enough," Solmes said. William doubted seriously if the man could count at all and knew for certain he couldn't have tallied so quickly—or accurately—what he had just received in the dark.

"What are you talking about?" William countered his challenge.

"It's forty cents the pound," Solmes insisted.

"He said thirty!" William thumbed back toward Brantley.

"Price just went up."

"Forty is out of the question!"

"Mouth off again, and it'll be fifty," Solmes said. He was making them pay for Lieutenant Whiteley's *common thief* remark.

"We agreed on the price! That's all we'll pay!" William wouldn't budge.

"You'll pay forty or you can get it someplace else!" Brantley swaggered over to lend his authority to the negotiation. William glared at him without answering. Brantley ordered a couple of his fellow Georgians to begin carting the bags of flour and corn meal back to the Tanner Overland wagons.

"Don't touch those bags!" William shouted at the loaders, then firmly defied Brantley's demand. "We're not paying forty." Brantley was about to respond but bit off his reply. He was looking past William to something in the darkness beyond. A chill of revulsion went up William's back when he heard the familiar voice behind him.

"You're right, Mr. Drummond. You're not paying forty. The price is now sixty."

William's old nemesis, Titus Ogilvie, stepped his horse out of the darkness at the edge of the road into the undulating glow of the torches. It was his preferred and predictable way—staying back in the shadows, allowing the drama to unfold; coming forth at the climactic moment to seize the spotlight and, if things worked according to his plan, to deliver the death blow. Riding beside Titus on Stick, William's own black gelding, was Ogilvie's dimwitted son, Alton. William's eyes narrowed to angry slits. He strode deliberately toward Titus, keeping his eyes on Alton as the son dismounted.

"You'll pay our price or you and the rest of these Injuns'll starve," Alton said confidently, determined to make his father proud. "It's up to you. And every time you open your mouth, the price goes up."

Without answering, William kept walking straight toward him. Alton stepped back, his hand going cautiously to the butt of the pistol stuck in his belt. William snatched Stick's reins from Alton. He stroked the animal and spoke softly.

"Hey, boy! I've been worried about you." Stick flubbered with recognition and affectionately nibbled at William's arm.

"What the hell you think you're doing?" Alton snarled.

"This is my horse," William growled down at the shorter man, then started leading Stick back toward the Cherokee wagons. Alton drew his pistol, but Titus held up his hand to stop his son. It was apparent to all that the older Ogilvie was thoroughly enjoying the little scenario he had so carefully orchestrated. He leaned forward in the saddle and smiled down at William.

"Perhaps you've forgotten, Drummond. You're no longer a man of property."

William kept walking with the gelding, not even looking at Titus. "I don't know how you came by this horse, but we both know you stole it. I'm taking him back."

Alton aimed his gun at William's back. "Stop right there, you thievin' son of a bitch, or I'll drop you!"

Lieutenant Deas and two of the soldiers moved swiftly to block Alton's view of William. "You aren't going to shoot anyone. Put that gun away," Deas pointed at Alton.

"Ain't nobody here scared o' you soldier boys," Solmes

sneered. "Why don't y'all jes' git on back to your boat?"

Alton shifted, trying to get a clear look at William, but the soldiers wouldn't let it happen. "Paw! He's stealin' my horse!" Alton whined.

Resting his bulk on elbows propped on his saddle, Titus shook his head at the endless stupidity of his progeny. But Alton shocked them all by cocking his pistol and getting off a shot when a narrow view of William suddenly presented itself. The slug hit William in the right shoulder, throwing him forward on his knees. Stick bolted sharply to one side.

William fought to draw a breath, stunned by the raging fire that engulfed the entire right side of his body. He clutched at his shoulder. Deas aimed his pistol at Alton, who was caught off guard by the lieutenant's quick and decisive action. Brantley, Solmes and the rest of Ogilvie's men drew their pistols, not looking to start anything but remaining watchful, wary. The Cherokees—none of whom were armed—kept a cautious eye on everyone.

"I warned you," Alton yelled at William. "Everybody knows what happens to a horse thief!" Realizing he had ignited an already volatile situation, Alton panicked. He grabbed Solmes' pistol and dashed to William slumped and bleeding at the edge of the road. He aimed the pistol point blank at the man he had already shot once. "You stole my horse!"

Deas pointed his gun at Alton's head. Whiteley and the other soldiers turned their pistols on Brantley, Solmes and the rest of Ogilvie's men.

"Drop the gun! Now!" Deas shouted. Alton looked from William to Deas to his father, uncertain what to do.

"That's enough, boy," Titus said. He climbed laboriously down from his horse. "Don't mess around and get yourself killed."

Alton, ordinarily quick to comply with his father's orders, was wide-eyed and out of control. He circled around to the edge of the road to face the crowd, his pistol still aimed at William's head. But before anyone could fire, Alton's expression changed from crazed anger to pained confusion. Blood gurgled up in his throat and erupted from his mouth. His eyes went down to the large, crimson covered pitchfork tines jutting out through the front of his shirt and coat. The pistol in his hand sagged before it discharged into the ground right in front of William. Alton dropped to his knees and fell forward. The pitchfork that had run him through swayed back and forth, creating a grotesque pendulum shadow in the shimmering torch light.

William fought the invading unconsciousness that threatened to swallow him. With great effort he lifted his head to look up where Alton had been standing and found himself staring at his benefactor. William could only figure the pain of his wound had caused him to hallucinate, for he was looking into the face of none other than his old friend, Ezekiel Campbell.

With the guns of Lieutenants Deas and Whiteley and the other soldiers trained on them, the rest of Ogilvie's men deemed it wise to lower their weapons. Two of the soldiers, aided by a couple of the Cherokees, made the rounds to collect the guns from the supply men. Deas, Ogilvie and their respective followers looked on in amazement when Ezekiel and six other black men, armed with pitchforks and sticks—and one with an old blunderbuss—stepped from the darkness.

But Titus Ogilvie's main concern was not a handful of blacks who had mysteriously appeared out of the trees. He saw his son lying dead in the mud with Ezekiel standing over him. Like an enraged lioness protecting its cub, Titus drew his knife, raised it with both hands and charged at Ezekiel.

A single shot shattered the night. Ogilvie's momentum carried the limping, staggering behemoth several more yards before he dropped the knife and fell face down in the mud at Ezekiel's feet beside the body of his son. The soldiers assumed one of their own had shot Titus. But that was not the case. They looked from one to the other to identify the shooter and discovered Peter Tanner standing at the tree line where Titus had earlier emerged. The smoking pistol hung loose in one hand, his ever-present corn jug in the other. Peter's clothes were dirty and rumpled, his eyes clouded with the permanent glaze of a non-stop drinker. William, his own eyes fogged by pain, looked at his son-in-law.

"Peter...? Is that you?"

"Mistah Tanner?" At first Ezekiel hadn't recognized the man he had known since Peter was a bratty little boy back in Pine Hill, Georgia. Lieutenant Deas kept his pistol trained on Brantley, Solmes and the others while he side-stepped to check on William. Together he and Ezekiel helped William to his feet. William clung to Ezekiel's arm. They turned their eyes on Peter, who rocked unsteadily and tilted the jug for another drink. Fortified once more, he gawked incredulously at Titus lying in the mud, the father's outstretched hands only inches from his dead son's feet.

"I missed..." Peter slurred his words.

"No, you didn't," William said weakly with gratitude. "You

saved our lives."

Peter shook his head, pointing the jug at Ezekiel. "I was aimin' at the nigger. Titus got in the way." He staggered toward them, gawking down at the bullet wound in Titus Ogilvie's back. "We were partners, him and me," Peter said to no one in particular.

"Partners?" William asked. He winced painfully when Ezekiel began carefully removing his coat. Peter made an exaggerated nod and pointed to the side of the nearest supply wagon.

"See? He couldn't get contracts, so we was using my name..." He looked around at the wagons. The consequence of his actions were beginning to take shape in his mash-clouded mind. "I reckon now it's all mine. Maybe I'll finally get some respect..." Like a tired old man, Peter lowered himself to sit on the wagon tongue and took another drink, then waved magnanimously at the supply wagons. "Go ahead. Take it. Take it all. Five cents a pound," he said.

Brantley, Solmes and the rest of Ogilvie's men were stunned speechless at the insanity of their *other boss*. Deas, Whiteley and the Cherokees recognized that fortune had finally favored them for a change. Peter took another drink and gestured with the little jug toward the Cherokees.

"I hate to see kids go hungry. Seen enough of that in them damn camps..." A long silence followed Peter's declaration. No one moved. Again Peter waved flamboyantly. "Go ahead! Take it!"

"Five cents, Mister Tanner?" Brantley inched closer to Peter. "You know what you're sayin'?"

"Shut up!" Peter snapped. "I'm the boss now! I said five cents a pound! Take it!"

Gradually the Cherokees moved to the supply wagons, threw back the rest of the tarps and began toting bags to their rented transports. It would be morning before they got them all loaded onto the *Vesper*, the *George Guess* and the keelboats. But there was no rush, because the steam engine repairs were expected to take several days.

William pressed a torn piece of blanket against the exit wound in the front of his shoulder while Ezekiel ripped the rest of the fabric into strips to bandage the bullet hole in the back. Peter watched them with the fascination drunks often have with mysteries of the mundane.

"I'm sorry you got shot, Mr. Drummond," Peter's apology sounded sincere. "He was a strange one, that Alton. Something like this was bound to happen sooner or later."

"Are you going to be all right, son?" William asked.

Peter sighed heavily. "Oh...I'll be all right. I'm a prominent businessman now. Remember?" William blinked. What could he say? He allowed Ezekiel to lead him to the Cherokee wagons for a ride back to camp. "William..." Peter said softly. Ezekiel and William stopped, waiting for him to finish. "Don't tell Susanna," Peter's voice was heavy with a genuine sadness. "That you saw me. Here. Like this. Please. Leave a man a shred of dignity. You know?"

William looked down at what remained of the young man who had once carried the promise of a brilliant military career. "Take care of yourself, Peter," he said, convinced he would never see Meg's father again. Peter lifted his jug in acknowledgement of William's parting words.

William looked into the ebony face of his old friend and, misty eyed, managed a smile. Much to the shy Ezekiel's discomfort, the employer he had known for so many years as a subdued and unemotional man, put his good arm around him in an affectionate hug.

"It's good to see you, Zeke," William's voice faltered.

"You still bleedin', Mistah William," Ezekiel answered, embarrassed. "We best get you some doctor help."

* * * * * * *

Peter watched Ezekiel and three of his black friends gently load William onto the first Cherokee wagon ready to roll. Ezekiel made sure Stick was securely tied to the tailgate. They departed immediately, escorted by Lieutenant Deas and two enlisted men, leaving Whiteley and the other soldiers to oversee the transport of the remaining supplies.

When the last Cherokee wagon had disappeared into the night, Peter allowed his eyes to stumble back to the Ogilvies lying in the mud. He shook his head, thinking perhaps he had merely had too much to drink. But when he looked again, there was no doubt that the baleen blob face down in the mud before him had, indeed, moved. A large air bubble erupted just before Titus' head pushed up, completely covered in road muck. Despite the mask of sludge, Peter clearly recognized the painfully distorted grimace of his partner. After Peter, Brantley was the first to see Titus move. His eyes widened in disbelief. He rushed to their fallen leader, drawing the attention of the others. As though he had been waiting for confirmation that someone else had also seen it, Peter finally rose from the wagon tongue.

"Titus?...Partner?" he asked tentatively.

Brantley rolled the mud-covered Ogilvie onto his side, but Titus pushed him away and sat up, clutching painfully at his wound.

"Go fetch a doctor!" Peter waved excitedly to Solmes. "Over at the Indian camp! Hurry!"

Solmes raced off into the darkness, taking the shortcut down the embankment—the same route by which William, Deas and the others had arrived. Titus scraped the mud from his eyes.

"Who shot me?" he demanded. The rest of the supply men looked at Peter, who glared back at them.

"One of them niggers," Peter lied. "There was a whole gang of 'em."

Titus looked at his dead son, then scanned the rest of the area. "Then how come I don't see no dead niggers?"

Peter pondered the question, carefully formulating the most plausible answer. "They ran off." Yes. That sounded good. "They ran off with the Indians," he added, hoping to convince himself as well as Titus.

Ogilvie accepted the answer for the moment. He gazed down at Alton, whose boot was within arm's reach, and patted the back of his lifeless son's leg. "He's dead, Tanner. I've lost both my boys."

Peter didn't know what to say. Finally he asked, "Are you going to die?"

Ogilvie rolled his eyes with the realization that he had already inherited a replacement for his idiot son. He flinched with intense pain and looked up at Brantley. "Well, don't just stand there! Get me a blanket before I freeze to death!"

This simple request had all the supply men looking at each other. Brantley cleared his throat and weakly confessed, "We don't have...there ain't no blankets. We sold 'em all...to the Injuns..."

It took all the strength of Brantley and three other men to pull the grimacing, bleeding Ogilvie up out of the mud. Peter took off his jacket and put it around Titus' shoulders. Brantley and the others sat him on the tailgate of the nearest wagon and offered him whiskey. Racked with pain and gasping for breath, Titus looked around at the empty wagons. He took a good long drink, then asked, "So...how much did you get? Forty cents a pound? Fifty?"

No one spoke, but all eyes went to Peter, who scratched at the back of his head and squinted off into the darkness in the direction the Cherokees had taken, wishing he might somehow call them back and raise the price.

* * * * * * *

Solmes's pleas for medical assistance from the Indian camp had, for the most part, fallen on deaf ears. The Cherokee supply wagons had reached camp just minutes before him, but the story had spread rapidly. There were still too many sick Cherokees who required immediate care to spare a doctor for two or three hours to go up on the high road to treat one man, especially when that man was Titus Ogilvie. Solmes was given an astringent with which to cleanse Titus's wound. When he asked for a couple of blankets, he was allowed two for which he was required to pay two dollars each.

After William's wound was properly cleansed and dressed, he sat by the fire, surrounded by the Cherokees who had brought him back to camp and by the black men who had saved them. Eventually they were joined by the wives of the black men, including Reba. The inebriating smell of fresh cornbread cooking and slabs of bacon frying filled the night air even before the last of the transport wagons rolled through the camp, distributing supplies to the Cherokees scattered up and down the river bank. New blankets were passed out along with new shoes and a few coats—welcome contributions, though not nearly enough to meet the needs of all the travellers.

Once word of the confrontation with the suppliers and the ensuing shooting had raced through the camp, other Cherokees began drifting to William's fire. Reba sat on a log directly across from William. Ezekiel stood behind her.

"I'm telling you, Reba," William recounted the incident, "there I was, lying in the mud, my shoulder on fire but thanking God my life had been spared. Then I looked up and saw Ezekiel. My old heart almost failed me!"

"That's right, Mistah William," Reba said with her familiar cackle. "That ugly nigger'd scare jes' 'bout anybody to death! But you doin' fine now, so we can go find Miz 'Liz'beth." William's expression darkened, his eyes searching the ground at Reba's feet. "Oh, Lawdy! He'p me, Jesus!" she cried out. In her anguish, she looked away from William and out beyond the fire, straight at Susanna and *Tsisdu*, who were standing only a few feet away with rest of the curious Cherokees. Though Reba had looked right at her, the changes in Susanna's appearance had been so drastic that the black woman didn't even recognize the girl she had delivered into this world and had helped raise from a baby. Susanna was holding Meg, whose hair was braided and adorned with the ever-present eagle feather. She lay asleep on her mother's shoulder, her back to the fire. Reba clutched at her breast with one hand while the other extended trembling toward the heavens. The tears flowed down her face. "That woman was a saint! An' now she sho' 'nuff the pride of God's angels! He should'a took Reba and let Miz 'Liz'beth march on!"

Reba's loud wailing woke Meg. She rubbed her eyes, certain she had heard a familiar voice. She twisted in her mother's arms to look around. Susanna quietly deposited Meg in Reba's lap. At first Reba thought she had merely been handed a Cherokee child as a gesture of consolation for her grief. It took her a moment to recognize the baby, and still Reba didn't know Susanna.

"Oh, Lawd, my little Meggie! Would you look at this sweet chil'!" The tears continued, but they were tears of joy. "And the Lawd say: *Suffer the little chilluns to come unto me...*," she cried loudly, then added in an emotion-filled whisper, "Thank you, Jesus! Thank you, Jesus!"

She clung to Meg, rocking back and forth. The child squirmed free enough to push back and look up at Reba. She touched the tears streaming down the black woman's face, then gently patted each cheek to console the dear woman who had also helped deliver her into this world.

"And where's yo' Momma, little angel?" Reba quizzed.

"I'm right here, Reba," Susanna said from only inches away. Reba knew the voice to be Susanna's, but when she looked up, her jaw slacked with the shock of recognition. Susanna's skin had been darkened by the sun and her hair was done up in Cherokee fashion. She looked much like any of the other Cherokee women around her.

"Sweet Jesus, they sho' 'nuff gon' have to put me in the groun' now!" Reba exclaimed. Her hand covered her mouth and she shook her head in amazement. "Zeke! You might as well start diggin'!"

"I've missed you, Reba," Susanna's eyes were filling with tears. "It's so good to see you."

"That did it! I'm dyin'," Reba said, laughing and crying at the same time. "Take me home, Jesus!"

William and Ezekiel chuckled at the antics of this woman who had always been such a strong figure in all their lives. Ezekiel squinted past Reba, studying the young woman before him.

"Is that really you, Missy?"

"Yes, Ezekiel," Susanna said. Like Reba, her words came out a mixture of laughter and crying. "And I want to thank you for saving my father's life."

"Aw, it weren't nothin', Missy," Ezekiel's reaction, as always, was one of humility. He couldn't recall Susanna Drummond ever having thanked him for anything her entire life. He squinted at her again and repeated, "Is that really you?"

"Stop gawkin', fool! Course it's her," Reba said, swatting at him. For the first time Reba noticed the other little girl clinging to Susanna's dress and knew intuitively this was more than just another Cherokee child in the crowd. "And who's this little sweet potato?" she opened her arms, beckoning *Me-li* to join her and Meg.

"This is *Me-li*. Mary," Susanna made the official introduction. "She's with us now."

"My mommie's in the river," *Me-li* informed Reba.

A solemn look passed between Reba and Susanna—a look which, without the details, conveyed the gist of the tragedy. Without responding directly to *Me-li's* pronouncement, Reba did what she did best. She pulled the child to her, hugged her and smothered her with much needed love and affection. Even Meg patted her new *sister* on the head with her little fingers. Once *Me-li* was firmly ensconced beside Meg in the lap of this doting, grandmotherly *gŭ-ni-ge* woman, Reba brushed some stray wisps of hair back from Meg's face and looked up at Susanna.

"What day is today?" she asked simply.

"Goodness! I couldn't tell you," Susanna, for the first time, realized she had lost all track of days and weeks. "I believe it must be December."

William broke into a smile. He knew what Reba was getting at. "December fifth, to be exact," he said, and winced with pain when he attempted to shift to a more comfortable position.

"Umm-hmm," Reba agreed. "An' that means some little angel is one year old today!" She squeezed Meg and showered her with kisses.

"My God!" Susanna was stunned. "It's Meg's birthday!" She looked at William. "I—with everything that's happened—how could I forget?"

"Don't feel bad," William consoled his daughter. "I knew exactly what day it was and still forgot it was her birthday."

"I'm such a terrible mother!" Susanna laughed, embarrassed. She picked Meg up from Reba's lap as though the child herself had comprehended the unforgivable oversight.

"Naw," Reba said. "Don't mean you a bad Momma. Jes' means you still need Reba 'round to think of these things."

594

Susanna took the black woman's hand and squeezed it with great affection.

"That we do," William agreed. "That we do."

* * * * * * *

The rest of the supplies had been distributed. Campfires burned brighter. A distant fiddle played a lively tune—a rarity in these times. The crowd that had gathered around the Drummonds gradually dispersed to begin their own humble celebration. So many were still weak and ill that the festivities consisted of little more than a decent meal, some medication and a good night's sleep.

A black iron pot had been found and Reba cooked a batch of fry bread to go with the fresh coffee delivered with the new supplies. William, Susanna, *Tsisdu*, Meg and *Me-li* shared the evening with Reba and Ezekiel as though they had never been apart. *Me-li* had taken to Reba and was soon clinging to her leg while Meg squirmed in the black woman's lap. Susanna sat with her father, making sure he was comfortably propped against the pile of clothes and blankets with minimum pressure on the shoulder. His eyes remained half closed the rest of the evening, drifting in and out of whiskey-pampered sleep. Susanna kept her hand on his arm while she talked to Reba.

"So, tell us, how did you come to be here? How did you ever find us?"

"We got us a place 'bout twenty-five, thirty miles north. 'Tween here and Jonesboro," Ezekiel explained. He leaned forward to stoke up the coals and add a few sticks of wood.

Reba fed a piece of fry bread dipped in warm milk to each of the little girls, then began her tale. "We run into ol' Joshua and his wife, 'Tunia. They was travelin' with Mistah Charlie Pierce, 'cept Mistah Pierce set 'em free and they headed on up north."

"You remember Josh," Ezekiel broke in. "He helped us cut them stumps outa the meadow down by the creek—when was it?—back in the summer of twenty-nine, I believe..."

"Shut up, Zeke! Don't nobody care what you an' that nigger done ten years ago!" Reba barked good naturedly, then continued to relate her tale to Susanna and William, who was alert for the time being. "Anyhow, 'Tunia say she overheard Mistah Pierce talkin' 'bout his brother comin' up on the river. He talked 'bout some of the folks comin' with 'em, and he said Drummond, so we knowed it had to be y'all. We been 'spectin' these boats in here 'bout fo'-five days now. We was camped jes' outside of Paducah—up close to them others that come in by land."

"Chief Ross is there," Ezekiel said, glancing at Reba to see if it was all right for him to speak before adding, "And I seen Charlie Swimmer an' his bunch. I could take ol' Stick to him. He can bring him on."

"That'd be good," William said softly. He had thought that, if nothing else, he'd just give the horse to Ezekiel. But William knew he'd need Stick once they were in the west and Ezekiel's suggestion made sense.

"You saw the Swimmers? How are they?" Susanna leaned forward with great interest.

Reba shook her head in amazement once again. "Lawdy, Missy! You jes' keep on surprisin' ol' Reba! I thought you couldn't abide them folks."

"A lot has changed, Reba," Susanna reminded her.

"Well, Miss Eva and Martha and the younguns is all good. They oldest boy got his arm cut up pretty bad. We heard lots of folks been dyin'—on the river, too."

"We was worried sick," Ezekiel added.

"Hush up, Zeke! Who's tellin' this?" Reba scolded again, then repeated his exact words. "We was worried sick."

William's head was back and his eyes were closed. He had heard it all and couldn't resist a soft chuckle. "Just like being back home," he smiled and surrendered to the welcome blackness of sleep.

* * * * * * *

Bellows blew the coals to a brilliant red. Smithy tongs carried bolts and bands of metal to waiting anvils where they were pounded and shaped to make much needed repairs to the *Vesper* and the *George Guess*. The eastern horizon was dappled with a wintery orange hue pregnant with sunrise. Yet to the north lay a low, thick cloud formation that promised some tumultuous activity before day's end. Even so, the dock area along the Ohio just south of Paducah was a hive of Cherokees, swarming in and out among the work areas set up by the extra blacksmiths brought in by Lieutenant Deas.

The Drummonds—and all those camped in their vicinity—awoke to the intoxicating aroma of bacon, fry bread, eggs scrambled with fried wild onions and potatoes, corn pone and hoecakes. Reba and Ezekiel, along with their black friends who had accompanied them down from Illinois, prepared a marvelous

596

breakfast, the likes of which these road weary and river worn travellers hadn't enjoyed for a long, long time.

Charlie and Eva Swimmer, accompanied by Martha, *Tsu-tsu*, Buck and Sally, had ridden Angus Reid's oxen up from the land travellers camp in the wee hours upon hearing that the river folk had put in below Paducah. Robert Barton had become inseparable from his beloved Martha. He now sported a week's growth of beard and wore a traditional Cherokee hunting jacket instead of his army tunic. His entire military demeanor had disappeared since the shooting of Charles DeKalb. Robert refused to let anyone, even his closest friend, Miles Franklin, address him as *Sergeant*.

Susanna delivered a tin cup of steaming coffee to William, who welcomed it with a twinge of pain when he tried to sit up. Together, Reba and Susanna changed his bandage and put his right arm in a sling which they comfortably but securely bound to his body beneath his coat. *Tsisdu*, Meg and *Me-li* were close by. The possessions brought ashore had been repacked, tightly bound and sat ready to go back onto the keelboat.

William forced himself up from his comfortable seat to join Charlie and Ezekiel, who were standing off to one side. He knew from their hushed tones and furtive glances they were discussing something important. Charlie waited until Susanna handed them each a fresh cup of coffee and rejoined Reba, Eva and the other women before resuming his report.

"The Paducah sheriff and some of his men came to our camp in the middle of the night."

"That figures," William said.

"A *yo-neg* supply contractor was killed," Charlie explained. "Sheriff said it was a pitchfork. Another one was wounded pretty bad. Shot in the back. They claimed they were ambushed by a bunch of *Tsa-la-gi's* and *gŭ-ni-ge's*."

"I wouldn't know anything about it," William shrugged innocently. Charlie looked to Ezekiel with a subtle smile.

"Zeke don't know nothin'," the black man echoed with a rare, wry smile of his own. "Jes' come down to visit. Now I'm goin' home."

The loud bray of a steam whistle drew everyone to the river. Chugging into view through the morning mist that hung like milky cotton on the Ohio was the steamship *Victoria*, angling toward the same docks where the *Vesper* and the *George Guess* were tied up. William, Charlie and Ezekiel were joined by *Tsisdu* and a host of Cherokee men. They studied the steamer that was easily half again as large as the *Vesper* and by all appearances newer and in much better condition.

Two hours later, while repairs continued on the *Vesper* and the *George Guess*, more than twenty wagons began their descent down the sloping switchback from the high road. It was Chief John Ross with his extended family and their possessions. They stopped to visit and to warm themselves at William's fire while their belongings—including the boxes filled with important tribal documents—were loaded aboard the new steamer.

"I've hired the *Victoria*, *Wi-li*," Ross explained. "Going by land is taking too long. I thought it would be good for morale if I travelled with the overland group. But George Lowrey, Elijah and Charles Hicks—all those who left before the weather turned—they'll be out west in dire need of strong leadership. Going by river will get us there faster."

"I don't know, *Gu-wi-s-gu-wi*," William recalled once having proposed that very idea, but now he offered a different perspective. "We've had nothing but trouble on the river. We should've reached Ft. Smith a long time ago."

Ross listened patiently as William unfolded a moving account of all the problems they had encountered. Then Ross confided to the man he had come to trust, "I must confess—I have my selfish reasons. Quatie won't last much longer if we stay on the trail. That must sound terrible, knowing so many of our people are dying and there's little or nothing we can do to stop it."

"Don't feel guilty for trying to save your wife, *Gu-wi-s-gu-wi*," William reassured the chief. "I, of all people, understand. I'd give anything to still have Elizabeth."

"I want you to come with us. You and your family," Ross offered.

"Are you sure there's room?"

"We'll make room," Ross said. "I'll need you in the west, *Wi-li*. Your ships won't be ready for a few days. And we'll be travelling without keelboats. We need to get there. Fast."

William looked out at the *Victoria* and pondered the chief's offer. The clouds the Cherokees had been cautiously watching to the north swept down upon them sooner than they expected. A light snow was falling. The early sporadic flurries were hardly noticed but promised to make more of an impact as the day wore on. The cold dampness sent stabbing pains surging through William's wounded shoulder. He and Ross watched four Cherokee men carry a crudely fashioned litter bearing Quatie Ross down toward the *Victoria*. Dr.

Rawles stuck close to the stretcher, signalling the men to stop when they reached *Gu-wi-s-gu-wi*. When they saw Quatie being carried in this manner, Susanna, Reba, Eva and Martha—with Robert Barton at her side—hurried toward them.

"I don't like the water," Quatie weakly touched her husband's hand.

"If you don't get on this boat, you'll be dead inside of a week," Dr. Rawles chided her gently.

"I could die tomorrow on this boat," she scolded back. "A lot of our people are dying. I don't want special treatment."

Susanna gave her a consoling pat on the arm, tucked the blanket around her and wiped a couple of snowflakes from her forehead. "Believe me, Quatie, there's nothing special about being on these boats!"

* * * * * * *

The time had come for Reba, Ezekiel and their black friends to head back to Illinois. The snow was falling harder and promised to get worse before it got better. They needed to make as much distance as possible before nightfall. The good-byes were always more difficult for the women than for the men. At least on the surface. Eyes were moist, if not flowing. The children sensed their mothers' emotion but didn't know how to interpret the situation.

Eva embraced Reba, then clung to the black woman's hands and said, "Truth is, we might never see each other again."

"You hush, Miz Eva. Y'all gon' be jes' fine."

"I hope so, Reba. I do," Eva said. Reba reached for Susanna, tears welling up for both of them.

"If you was still sassy and mean, this'd be a whole lots easier, Missy," Reba forced a laugh only to keep from crying. Susanna shifted Meg to her other hip and hugged the black woman for a long time. Finally, Reba held her at arm's length and took Susanna's free hand in her own. She felt the heavy silver on Susanna's finger and lifted it for a look.

"That's a spooky lookin' ring, Missy. What is that, a wolf?"

"Yes, a wolf," Susanna looked at the ring.

"Now where would you be gettin' a ring like that?" Reba asked.

Susanna smiled. "You wouldn't believe me if I told you."

"Reba done seen the change in you, girl! Reba'd believe anything now!" the black woman cackled, then grew serious. "You got yo' Momma's goodness in you, Missy. I always knew it. You take care of Mistah William and these precious babies." Reba drowned Meg and *Me-li* in a final flurry of hugs and kisses.

"I wish you and Ezekiel were coming with us," Susanna clung to Reba's arm.

"We'll miss you something awful, chil'," Reba said. She wiped the tears from Susanna's cheek with her broad, flat thumb. "Things don't work out, y'all know you got a place to come to. You too, Miss Eva."

"*Wa-do*, Reba. Thank you," Eva said. The women exchanged their final hugs. *Me-li* went from one to the other, hugging each woman's leg, then stretched up to hug Meg, balanced on Susanna's hip. *Me-li* didn't know exactly what was going on, but it was evident everyone was sad and needed hugs. And she wanted to contribute.

* * * * * * *

It was a dolorous parting for all of them when the four groups prepared to go their separate ways—Reba, Ezekiel and their black friends headed back up into Illinois; Charlie Swimmer, his family and all the rest who would go on by land with Peter Hildebrand's party; those who had come on the *Vesper* and the *George Guess* and would wait another day or two for the completion of repairs; and, finally, Chief Ross, his extended family and those who would accompany them aboard the *Victoria*, including the Drummonds.

After dividing the contents of a tobacco pouch, Charlie Swimmer and Ezekiel Campbell loaded and lit their pipes. They would smoke together for the last time. Both men knew there was little likelihood they would ever see each other again, but neither mentioned it. They had known each other for years, had worked shoulder to shoulder for much of that time. Each had great respect for the other as a hard worker and a fair and honest man. In their minds no greater tribute could be bestowed.

From a few yards away they watched William Drummond, the man they had both worked for. The man they admired and respected. William said his good-byes to Reba and the rest of the Swimmer family. He hugged Eva, thanking her for her friendship and kindness toward Elizabeth when they were in the camps. When he embraced Reba, her tears flowed again. It was difficult for her to let go. She finally released him and wiped her eyes with her apron while William said a parting word to Martha and Robert, mussed

Buck's hair, then hoisted Sally with his good arm and chatted with her about her doll.

"Take care of yo'self, Charlie Swimmer," Ezekiel said.

"You, too, Zeke," Charlie replied.

"I'll be clearin' stumps come spring. If you up my way an' need work..."

"I hope to be clearin' stumps myself," Charlie answered. It was their way of saying *I intend to survive and be doing well come Spring. Hope you survive and are doing well, too.* No further comment or interpretation was required.

William handed Sally to her mother and joined the men. He shook the hand of his old friend, Ezekiel. The two men gripped firmly. Again, words were unnecessary. Ezekiel looked around cautiously. Satisfied they weren't being watched by any soldiers or government agents, he pulled a pistol from beneath his coat and slipped it to William.

"Thanks, Ezekiel, but I'd better not," William declined. "Cherokees aren't supposed to carry guns on this trip."

"And white folks like that Ogilvie boy ain't s'pose to be shootin' at you, neither," Ezekiel argued with irrefutable logic.

"You don't sic a toothless dog to fight a bobcat," Charlie was backing Ezekiel on this one.

"Take it, Father." Susanna had come up behind William and made it three against one. She gave Ezekiel a strong, affectionate hug, smiling at his embarrassment. "Thank you again, Ezekiel, for everything. You take good care of Reba."

"Oh, I s'pect Reba'll take care of Reba," he discharged his embarrassment in a soft chuckle. "Don't you worry none 'bout that!"

A shrill steam whistle sounded from the *Victoria*. Susanna took her father's arm. "We'd better go, *E-to-da*. I think they're ready."

"*E-to-da!* Listen to you," Charlie grinned. "You'll make a *Tsa-la-gi* yet!"

"Take care of Eva and the girls." Susanna squeezed Charlie's arm.

"Good-bye, Miss Susie," Charlie said with a slight bow.

* * * * * * *

From the hillside overlooking the Ohio just south of Paducah, Lieutenant Edward Deas watched the steamship *Victoria*, weighted almost to the water line, pull away from its moorings, chugging, steaming, hissing, vomiting its thick, black smoke against the dull gray clouds. Beside Deas stood the tall, thin, red haired Sergeant Haney. With sad expressions they witnessed the departure of so many Cherokees they had befriended in the course of their journey. They held their hands high—part wave and part salute. From the deck of the *Victoria*, a few of the *Tsa-la-gi*, including the strange little man they called *Tsisdu*—or Rabbit Man—waved back.

"Not a bad lot, when you think about it," Sergeant Haney said. "Pretty decent folks."

"A noble people," Deas agreed. "This whole removal is a dark stain on the fabric of our country's honor, Sergeant Haney."

"Maybe their journey will be a little smoother from here on. Even on the *Vesper* and the *George Guess*," the sergeant offered a positive thought.

"I fear the worst lies ahead for them," the lieutenant shook his head. "May God Almighty prove me wrong."

* * * * * * *

William Drummond stood with Chief John Ross on the lower foredeck of the heavily loaded *Victoria*. They peered ahead down the river of an uncertain future. The wind had picked up and more black-bellied clouds were congregating in the rapidly darkening sky. Meg clung tightly to her mother. *Me-li* ran to take *Tsisdu's* hand when she saw him coming from the rear deck. He joined them at the side rail just abaft of the huge paddle wheel. Susanna studied the eddies created by the Victoria's wake, then looked back upstream toward Paducah. *Tsisdu* scooped *Me-li* up in his arms and moved in beside Susanna. His nose made the familiar twitch just before he pointed downstream.

"The river flows this way. You have to forget what lies back there," he said.

Her eyes burned with an intensity he found unnerving. Her response was firm but without anger. "I know our future is in the west. But I buried my mother back there. Don't tell me I have to forget her!"

Tsisdu dropped his head, realizing she was right. When he lifted his eyes to make an apology, *Tsisdu* noticed Susanna's expression had changed to one of alarm. Looking past him toward the aft deck, she shoved Meg into his arms and hurried along the rail.

602

The rear of the *Victoria* was crowded with boxes, crates, trunks and bundles. The cargo had been stacked as high as possible on the windward side to provide relief from the stinging cold for those forced to huddle there because there wasn't enough room inside to house them all. Make-shift beds of bags and softer parcels had been fashioned for the seriously ill. And weaving in and out among them, dispensing medicine and loving care, was the reason for Susanna's shocked reaction—Quatie Ross.

Susanna reached Quatie at about the same time John Ross came down the ladder from the upper deck. Quatie couldn't decipher their words above the din of the steam engine and the paddle wheel. She pretended not to understand when they insisted on ushering her back inside the lower cabin.

* * * * * * *

By the time the *Victoria* had gotten under way, the land travellers had taken the ferry to the Illinois side of the Ohio, across from Paducah. The road ran along a ridge high above and parallel to the river for a while before it forked. One leg continued north toward Jonesboro. The other curved off to the west to follow the river. This was the path taken by Hildebrand's long train of wagons, carts and Cherokees on foot. From the high ground of the northern fork, Ezekiel and Reba waved to their Cherokee and black friends headed west. In the distance they could see the trail of black smoke from the *Victoria* and watched the steamer snake her way along the river and disappear around the bend.

CHAPTER
50

Two days out of Paducah the weather had become even darker and wetter, sharpening the teeth of the vicious cold that gnawed its way into the land travellers' joints. At a crossroads in southern Illinois five wagons pulled off and set up a temporary blacksmith station to repair broken wagon tongues, single- and double-traces and broken wheels or to re-shoe horses and mules. Those performing smithy duties considered the hard work fair exchange for an afternoon of hovering over a warm fire. A number of local whites had appeared, some as curious spectators, others to sell goods at outrageously inflated prices, and a few who actually offered to help.

Charlie Swimmer pulled his wagon to the side of the road. Word had travelled back down the line about the blacksmith setup, and Charlie had hoped to make it with a broken wheel to the crossroads, but the spokes were too rotten and the axle hub was badly cracked. Eva, Martha and Sally rode Stick on ahead, accompanying another family. They would wait at the crossroads. *Tsu-tsu* and Buck unloaded the wagon while Charlie cut a strong sapling which they would leverage against a large rock to raise the axle. No one mentioned *Tsu-tsu's* earlier injury, but everyone was careful to avoid any mishaps.

Just up the road from them a local white settler leaned against the tailgate of his wagon full of new wheels, wagon parts and harness accessories. His hands were tucked deep inside the pockets of his warm, fleece-lined coat and he wore a confident smirk.

"Can we fix it, *E-to-da?*" Buck asked his father.

"Not this time," Charlie said. "The wood's all rotten."

"I got wheels," the *yo-neg* called out in the overly friendly tone of a salesman stroking a potential customer. Charlie eyed him with suspicion.

"How much?"

"How much you got?"

"If you're like most everyone else along this road, probably not enough!" Charlie said with open bitterness.

"Oh, you got money," the white man laughed. "I *know* you got money. You just don't wanna let go of it. You Cherokees is tighter than any Scot I ever knew back in Edinburgh!"

Charlie paused from trimming the end of the sapling with his dull hatchet and stretched his sore back. "What little money I've got, we need to get started in the west."

"Ain't nothin' to start if you never even get there," the *yo-neg*, like any salesman, had an excuse for every answer, an answer for every excuse.

Charlie pondered his options. In truth, he realized he had no options. He had a broken wheel and they couldn't go on without a replacement.

"All right...how much?" he asked reluctantly.

"Well, now, let's see..." the cat saw an opportunity to toy a bit with the cornered mouse. "Trade in that old rim you got there, get yerself a whole new wheel, I figure oughta run you about twenty-five dollars..."

Charlie scowled and went back to his work. He had known better, but he felt he at least had to try. A scorpion is a scorpion is a scorpion. He would simply paint in his mind a picture of the road which didn't include this *yo-neg* and his wagon load of outrageously overpriced new wheels. Charlie maneuvered the sapling into position beneath the axle. He looked up to see a tall, lanky, young man about thirty years old, with rough chiseled features and an unruly shock of coal black hair. This newcomer was rolling a wheel straight toward the Swimmer wagon.

"I've got a wheel here. Won't cost you near twenty-five dollars," the lanky young man called out.

Charlie expected the price would still be far beyond his means. "How much?"

"Don't know, just yet," the stranger replied. "But I promise, you'll be able to afford it." He smiled at *Tsu-tsu*. "Hello there, young man."

Tsu-tsu stared back him but didn't speak. The first wheel-seller was miffed at this intruder's attempt to steal his customer. "Hey! Who asked you to come hornin' in on my deal?"

"I'm sorry," the lanky stranger apologized, feigning ignorance. "Had you struck an agreement with this gentleman?" he asked Charlie.

"For twenty-five dollars?!" Charlie snorted.

"Well, then..." the tall stranger said, "looks like this wheel will fit your wagon just fine." He leaned the wheel against the Swimmer wagon. Despite the cold, he pushed up his sleeves and went to work. Charlie and *Tsu-tsu* moved the old wheel out of the way. The first *yo-neg* wheel-seller, cursing under his breath, climbed into his wagon and drove on up the line. The tall, lanky man smiled again at Buck and *Tsu-tsu*, talking as he worked.

"I'm from up near Springfield, myself. Doing a little surveying down this way. Been following the situation of the Cherokees. A lot of people in this country are outraged at what's happened."

"Yes," Charlie agreed, adding with unmistakable cynicism, "we've met many people along the trail who were outraged. But no one was able to help. Not when it really counted." The stranger, on his knees in the mud, paused from his work, moved by the *Tsa-la-gi's* words. "If you really want to change things," Charlie went on, "you have to do something *before* it's too late. For us...it's too late."

The young man looked around at the Cherokees and blacks streaming along the road and at the others working on broken down wagons and carts. "Words I shall remember, Mister...?"

"Swimmer. Charlie Swimmer. My sons, Martin and Buck." When introducing *Tsu-tsu* to a white man, Charlie often used his English name.

The stranger nodded to each one. "Mr. Swimmer. Martin. Buck. Let's get this wheel set." He got into a crouch and was about to lift the new wheel onto the axle when Charlie put a hand out to stop him.

"How much does it cost?"

The young man rose and stepped back. He ran his long, bony fingers through his thick hair. "Tell you the truth, I don't want your money."

"Well, I don't want your charity," Charlie countered.

"I'm not offering charity. I was thinkin' I'd be taking this..." He lifted one of the boys' blow gun from the wagon, running his fingers along it with an appreciative look. Charlie was suspicious, but the young man's admiration seemed genuine.

"I saw some lads this morning hunting with one of these," the tall, lanky man said. He stroked the smooth finish of the five-foot-long reed. "It was amazing. They hit a rabbit at—must've been ten, twelve yards. On the run!"

Tsu-tsu handed him one of the darts and showed him how to fit it into one end, tapping it down the into the chute a couple of inches. The stranger looked around for a target. Buck pointed to his father's animal-hide water flask hanging from the side of the wagon. The tall, young man aimed and blew. He was as stunned as anyone and as delighted as a child when the dart actually hit the skin bag. Charlie watched the slender stream of water shooting out onto the ground. No one spoke until the bag had completely deflated. Charlie shot a perturbed look at *Tsu-tsu*, Buck and their

606

new playmate, who grinned sheepishly.

"Well...I'll just take my new blow gun and..." he said, gesturing toward the trail. His long strides carried him back to his cart where he took the mule by the harness and led him away.

"*Yo-neg!*" Charlie called out. The young man stopped and looked back. "You didn't tell us your name."

"Lincoln. The name's Abraham Lincoln."

"*Wa-do*, Abraham Lincoln. Thanks for the wheel," Charlie said.

"You're very welcome, Charlie Swimmer. Boys," Abe waved once more to *Tsu-tsu* and Buck. "And thanks for the blow gun."

Tsu-tsu smiled and waved back. He had decided he liked the gawky stranger, though he couldn't say exactly why. There was a certain quality there, *Tsu-tsu* thought. Secretly he prided himself on his ability—since he was quite young—to discern particular qualities in individuals. And during his brief years he had seldom been wrong. From the time he was Buck's age he would diligently study any man his father spoke with, whether on the streets of Pine Hill—or Titusville—or at a council meeting at Red Clay or New Echota or simply a chance encounter somewhere along the road. It was a talent he wasn't quite sure what to do with. He had shared it with no one. Perhaps when he was older, he thought, it would be useful to him.

There were a lot of things *Tsu-tsu* kept to himself. Though he loved his father dearly and respected no man more, something inside had always told *Tsu-tsu* he wouldn't be satisfied just being a farmer, a blacksmith and healer of horses like Charlie. There was certainly no shame in being those things, but for himself *Tsu-tsu* saw more. Much more. Exactly what, he wasn't sure. But that, he was confident, would come as he grew older.

Beginning with the roundup, and then the imprisonment and now the forced march in the dead of winter, *Tsu-tsu* had found himself becoming increasingly interested in the *Tsa-la-gi* tribal leaders, especially at this time when leadership was proving so vital at every turn. Perhaps that was it, he thought. He would become a leader among his people. A chief. He loved that he could read and write in both English and his native tongue—and had found he had a penchant for picking up Latin and Greek as well as French and Spanish. He had read old copies of the *Cherokee Phoenix* newspaper, comparing the Cherokee text with its juxtaposed English translation. He greatly admired men like John Ridge and Elias Boudinot. They had gone to the great universities in New England and had brought back a level of education and sophistication unsurpassed among native peoples. At the same time *Tsu-tsu* admired the traditionalist views of *Gu-wi-s-gu-wi* who, ironically, was himself only one-eighth Cherokee. *Tsu-tsu* had even decided perhaps it wasn't too bold to dream he might someday become principal chief of the *Tsa-la-gi*. He would bring peace to the hostile factions within the nation and would become a great spokesman for his people and the preservation of their traditional ways. In addition he would gain for the Cherokees world-wide recognition through the skills of statesmanship he would develop. He would, of course, through all this, be recognized as a courageous and indefatigable warrior. And exceedingly handsome. That would be important.

* * * * * * *

The day's travel had been greatly curtailed by the need all up and down the six-hundred-plus wagon train for extensive repairs. To compound the difficulties, the temperature had plummeted and the *Tsa-la-gi* found themselves shortly after noon buffeted by a driving snow storm. The wind flung snow and sleet furiously into their narrowed eyes, stinging, forcing them to view the dismal day through ice-crusted lashes.

The road lay blanketed beneath a blinding whiteness, the path identifiable only by its shallow, flattened trough and the absence of trees and brush. Occasionally the upper part of a rotting wheel left alongside the road by those who had gone before protruded through the frozen top crust, its rimless black spokes pointing accusingly to the heavens.

By dusk Hildebrand's scouts had discovered a deserted house located a quarter mile off the main road, set back near a creek that would provide ample fresh water for the entire group. The two-story structure's advanced state of dilapidation told of its long time abandonment. The front porch was partially collapsed, the window shutters dangled precariously and a large limb had fallen from an adjacent oak and punctured the roof. Trees and shrubs, once pruned and trimmed, had grown unchecked for years. Some of the men had to hack a path through the brush down to the creek.

With his one good arm, *Tsu-tsu* Swimmer carried a bucket of water back up to the old house. Wagons had been parked randomly among the trees throughout the grounds and overflowing into the woods beyond. Mules, horses and oxen were tethered on the south side of the estate, their backs turned to the blustery north wind that brought fresh sleet and snow. Numerous fires had been started—not without considerable difficulty—in search of some relief from the freezing rain that lashed at them in savage parabolas. Dark, blanket-wrapped human forms cowered silent and motionless in tight circles around the crackling blazes as the Cherokees hunkered down for another miserable night on the trail. *Tsu-tsu* waited outside the door while two Cherokee men carried a sick old woman into the house which served as a make-shift hospital. A refuge for the most severely stricken.

Those inside listened to the wind pushing against the creaky building with agonizing rage. It was as though the huddled fugitives were being held accountable for some unspecified transgression, and the relentless storm seemed determined to exact a vengeful toll.

Tsu-tsu watched his sister dip hot water from the large pan heating on a potbelly stove in the center of the spacious room. When she had finished, he curled one arm around the bucket of fresh water and emptied it into the great pan.

"Keep it coming, little brother," Martha said.

"Stop calling me *little*," he insisted. Martha saw the hurt in his face. She pulled his sleeve back down over his wounded arm.

"You're right, *Tsu-tsu*," she said with affection. "You're a man now. No more *u-s-di*. I'm sorry."

He stood taller with her praise. "I'd better get more water."

Another sick child was brought in just as Eva came from an adjoining room to fill another pan with hot water. She and her two oldest children surveyed the over-crowded hospital. Bodies lay practically on top of each other and every space in between was taken up by those attending them. "There just isn't any more room," Eva said. They watched to see where the new child would be laid.

"And half of these will be dead before morning," Martha added with a cynicism darker than her years warranted. Eva touched *Tsu-tsu's* forehead, then Martha's face, feeling for signs of fever.

"How are you two?"

"Fine," *Tsu-tsu* assured her.

"All right, *e-ge-i*," *Ma-di* echoed.

"Where are Sally and Buck?"

"Outside with Father," *Tsu-tsu* answered.

"Good," Eva said. "I know it's cold, but I don't want the little ones in here. Go on," she nudged *Tsu-tsu* back toward the door. Balancing himself with the bucket, he picked his way back through groaning and coughing bodies to go for more water. Like *Tsu-tsu*, Eva and Martha began negotiating the human maze to help the doctors and medicine men care for the sick.

* * * * * * *

On his way back down to the creek for more water, *Tsu-tsu* circled around to check on his father and Buck and Sally. More importantly, he would hover beside their little fire and steal a few seconds of glorious warmth. Near his family's campsite *Tsu-tsu* passed one ancient Cherokee man whom he had seen a few times on the journey but didn't know personally. Wrapped in a threadbare blanket, the old one moved slowly—almost in a trance—among his people, from wagon to wagon, campfire to campfire. Despite their recent acquisition of supplies at Paducah, Kentucky, the Cherokees hadn't received nearly enough clothing and blankets to sustain them against such a fierce storm. After the driest, hottest summer even the old ones could recall, the *Tsa-la-gi* found themselves besieged by the bitterest, harshest winter in memory.

Tsu-tsu warmed himself at his family's fire. He watched the old man stop a couple of fires down where a young Cherokee mother sat with her two shivering children. The old one bent down to the seated trio and exchanged a few words with the mother. Then he unwrapped his own blanket and put it around the little girl, who appeared to be about the age of *Tsu-tsu's* little sister, Sally. It was, *Tsu-tsu* thought, an amazing gesture of kindness, but what occurred next he found even more incredible. The ancient one removed his shirt and wrapped it around the little boy—perhaps a year older than the little girl—leaving the old man bare-chested against the brutal wind and freezing rain.

Tsu-tsu imagined what the young mother was saying as she waved her hands and shook her head in protest, reluctant to accept the gifts that would leave the old man mortally exposed. But the ancient one held up both hands to silence her. From this distance *Tsu-tsu* couldn't see the tears in the mother's eyes, but there was no mistaking the immeasurable gratitude in her expression for his tremendous sacrifice. When the old one had finished wrapping the shirt around the boy, the mother reached out and touched his leathery old hand. Then, like *Tsu-tsu*, her eyes followed the ancient, time-creased warrior as he walked off into the night, naked from the waist up.

610

* * * * * * *

The ubiquitous soft moans of the afflicted mingled with the low chants of medicine men and medicine women, drifting through the old abandoned house like troubled, disembodied spirits wandering lost between two worlds. By the flickering light of the stove, a few candles and oil lanterns, the handful of white doctors, assisted by Eva Swimmer and other Cherokee and black women, moved like phantoms among the ill. Fortunately, many of the sick had, from sheer exhaustion, drifted off to sleep. And no one doubted that morning light would reveal a number who had slipped into a deeper slumber from which there was no awakening.

Martha Swimmer and Robert Barton sat on the floor near one of the lanterns. Robert wrote in his journal by the faint light. *Ma-di*, a thin blanket wrapped around her, clung to his arm, both for affection and from a gripping sense of helpless desperation. They looked across the darkened room when an unusually loud moan filled the air, followed by the raspy flight of another Cherokee's last breath. The shadowy form of a doctor pulled the blanket off the deceased and tossed it onto a pile in the corner.

Martha squeezed Robert's arm a little tighter and drew closer, reading along as he wrote in his journal...

> *Those most gravely ill have been gathered into this abandoned house. A fresh blizzard rages outside. Cholera is rampant. Within a few feet of us tonight, already four have died and dozens more lie awaiting the call of the Reaper. Yet there are no loud lamentations. True to their Cherokee blood, they gaze upon the departed with manly sorrow. At morning's first light, they will, in their silent dignity, hack out of the frozen ground a narrow bed in which to lay their loved ones. Poor, destitute and unbefriended as they are, they would command the respect of the coldest stranger....*

* * * * * * *

The old *Tsa-la-gi* who had given up his blanket and shirt to a needy boy and girl stood facing east into the morning's first gray light. His eyes were rigid, open, his arms outstretched, holding on to the limbs of the small trees on either side of him. His face, shoulders and arms were decked with snow and ice and his long, white hair stuck out almost horizontally to his right—the south. During the night the relentless north wind and the driving sleet had combined to create a rigid sculpture.

Charlie Swimmer, *Tsu-tsu* and two other Cherokee men pried the old man's frozen fingers from the ice-covered limbs. Among those who had gathered to watch was the young mother. Her two children were still wrapped in the deceased warrior's blanket and shirt.

* * * * * * *

Exactly as Robert Barton had foretold in his journal the night before, the digging of graves in the frozen ground had begun. By the time the rest of the encampment was beginning to stir from beneath the layer of new snow that had blanketed them during the night, Charlie, *Tsu-tsu* and the others were lowering the old man into a shallow grave. In front of the house a *yo-neg* doctor took back an armload of blankets from an old Cherokee woman. She had collected the diseased covers of those who had perished during the night. Her bony, trembling hand reached out longingly when he tossed the blankets onto the fire burning just off the south end of the rotting porch.

"I'm sorry, *E-li-si*," the doctor said with genuine sorrow. "These blankets are infected. They must be destroyed."

Silent and forlorn, the old woman's eyes lingered on the flames. Again her hand stretched out as though to caress the blankets' warmth one last time, then, shivering from the cold, she hobbled off in search of the wagon she was to ride in.

Unable to man a shovel with only one good arm, *Tsu-tsu* left the old man's grave and took Buck with him to harness the oxen. With her tattered, wedding-gown doll tucked securely under one arm, Sally scraped away a patch of snow and pulled off a few blades of dead grass which she offered to *Tsu-s-qua-ne-gi-dŭ*, her pet goat. She kept the little bleater on a short rope and maintained a watchful eye, lest her only friend fall into the wrong hands and end up as someone's breakfast or lunch. *Tsu-tsu* and Buck had warned her, and she hadn't forgotten.

612

51

Arkansas Territory

Another abandoned dwelling—a one room cabin with a dirt floor—provided shelter from the storm for Johnny Fields, Michael Drummond and their fugitive band of *thievin', murderin' outlaw Injuns*, as they had been described throughout the territory. With no furniture in the little hovel, they were forced to sit on the packed dirt floor that smelled like moldy soil too long denied sunshine and fresh air. The smoke from the fire in the middle of the room escaped through a hole in the roof. The silence was marked by an occasional hiss when the snow on the roof melted, dripped down inside the cabin and splattered into the fire.

Ne-di and Betty Jo Proctor occupied one side of the room with their children, Jack and Janie, who entertained themselves with a quiet game of stick war. *Tsa-tsi* Starr sat with his back against the door, his hat pulled low over his eyes, but they all knew he wasn't asleep. He had a keenness of hearing that amazed those who knew him. He would hear anyone approaching—on horseback or on foot—long before any of the rest of them. Long enough, in fact, to save their lives.

Agnes sat close to Johnny. She made grooming gestures, touched him and leaned against him at every opportunity. It was her way of reinforcing an intimacy which Johnny didn't share. He sharpened his knife on a piece of stone, giving the task his undivided concentration. Michael and Annie sat across from them with little James. The tension between *Tsi-mi's* parents was palpable. The subject was difficult for them to discuss.

"You know if you go back, we can't go with you," Annie said. The hurt in her voice was evident, though she tried to mask it as subdued anger. "So, you'll just leave us here?"

"I don't want to leave you, Annie," Michael protested. How could he make her understand? "It's just that...I want to see my family."

Annie looked up from braiding *Tsi-mi's* hair with a confused expression that said *Don't you know your mother is dead?* Then she realized that, of course, he didn't. She softened and touched his hand. "I know you miss your family, *Mi-ki*. But you don't need to go back to Georgia. You'll see your sister soon."

"My sister?!" Michael looked at her strangely. "I'm talking

about my mother and father. My sister doesn't give a damn about me."

"If you believe that, you don't know your sister," Annie smiled.

Michael thought she was only trying to confuse the issue. He'd been contemplating a trip back to Georgia to see his parents, and she found the idea unsettling. He drew in a long, calculated breath, determined to remain calm. He didn't want it to degenerate into an emotional argument.

"Annie, I know sometimes you think you know things. You see things. But this makes no sense at all."

"Give it time, *Mi-ki*. Give it time," she said with that *I-know-something-you-don't* tone that he hated and loved at the same time.

"*Mi-ki*. Time, *Mi-ki*," James parroted her words. Michael and Annie each centered on their son for a while, a practice they both understood and often used to dissipate the tension between them. Finally, Michael looked up at her.

"What? You're saying my family is coming here? Why the hell would they do that?" he asked. Annie shrugged with an innocent *I-don't-have-all-the-answers* look that only irritated Michael further. "First break in the weather, I'm heading back," he announced emphatically, adding, "and I'm taking *Tsi-mi* with me. You can come or you can stay." He involved himself with cleaning his pistol. That was that. He'd made up his mind. He had spoken. Annie shook her head, irritated at his stubbornness, but she didn't respond. She pulled Jimmy to her, focusing once more on her son.

Johnny tested the sharpened blade of his knife against the ball of his thumb, then held it in the flame before stropping it on a piece of saddle leather. Michael sensed Johnny had something to say and looked at his friend, waiting.

"I'm not saying you *should* go..." Johnny finally spoke softly. He glanced at Annie, not wishing to incur her wrath. "But if you *do*, I'll go with you."

"I'm going, too," *E-gi-ni* put in. The rest—even *Tsa-tsi* and *Ne-di*—were puzzled by her firm pronouncement. "I just want to be where you are, Johnny."

"Why?" he asked innocently. She tugged at him affectionately, certain he was only teasing.

Annie leaned close to Michael. She had been carefully formulating exactly what she wanted to say. Her voice was low but iced with determination. "If you leave us—living like this—in empty cabins and in caves—don't bother to come back."

614

He finished carefully wiping the gun before he looked up at his wife. There was no doubt she meant every word she had spoken.

"What makes you say my family is coming here?" Michael referred to her earlier declaration.

"I'm not sure," she shook her head. "I just know you'll see your family." She pushed *Tsi-mi* toward his father and checked on the two squirrels and four birds cooking on green sticks. Michael pondered the dilemma, weighing his options.

"I'm gonna hang around here for a while," he announced.

Johnny nodded with a little smile of understanding. *E-gi-ni*, convinced the threat of Johnny's leaving had passed, leaned her head against his back and slipped her arms around his waist. He glanced down at her hands clasped in front of him but otherwise ignored her.

"I think I'm going to ride over toward Little Rock," he told Michael.

"No!" *E-gi-ni* blurted out. "Why would you go there?"

Again Johnny ignored Agnes, directing his words to Michael. "We never really got rid of Tom Carver and his gang. I got a feeling he's up to no good."

"It's the middle of winter," *E-gi-ni* cut in. "There won't be anyone on the roads for him to rob 'til spring."

Michael and Johnny exchanged a look. They were both becoming annoyed with her repeated interruptions. But it was Annie who spoke for them.

"Be quiet, Agnes." *E-gi-ni* threw Annie a harsh look and said no more. Sulking, she busied herself going through the motions of straightening Johnny's bedroll for the tenth time.

"Here. You might need this," Michael handed Johnny the pearl-handled Collier repeating pistol he had just cleaned. Johnny grunted his gratitude and took the weapon.

"You coming, *Tsa-tsi*? *Ne-di*?" Johnny asked the other two members of their vigilante squad.

"I'll go," *Tsa-tsi* said. Ned grunted affirmatively with a single nod. *E-gi-ni* refused to look at any of them. She didn't want them to see her biting her lip or to catch the glistening wetness in her eyes. She only turned around when she heard the scraping of the cabin door on the dirt floor.

"Hurry back to me, *Tsa-ni*," she said, forcing a coy smile.

Johnny, again embarrassed by this emotional link which existed only in *E-gi-ni's* mind—and, apparently, in her heart—acted like he hadn't heard her. He looked only at Michael.

"We'll be back in no time."

CHAPTER

52

Mississippi River
Cape Girardeau, Missouri

Cape Girardeau was a huddling of some two thousand marrow-frozen souls in a snow-covered, wind-beaten village with its muted streets and dung-steamed alleys clinging tenaciously to the river's edge. The town was spread up and down the western bank of the Mississippi, long from north to south but never venturing too far from the river bank. The lifeless day drew to a close with the gray sky becoming even darker. Here and there lamps were lit, casting their golden glow through snow-banked windows to the mostly empty streets outside.

A few of the hardier citizens—and the more curious—were drawn to the river which was filled with huge, jagged ice flows that had broken loose upstream. Jack Harshaw was an old farmer with twelve hundred eighty acres southwest of town where he grew corn and wheat and ran two hundred head of beef cattle. He and his dog had come into town in his one-horse buggy. They finished loading a few supplies shortly after midday and spent the rest of the afternoon lingering around the potbelly stove inside the general store, dreading the long ride back to the farm. But as the day waxed long, Jack knew they'd better get started. He stopped his buggy directly behind the eight or ten citizens gathered to stare across the river at the east bank. Hundreds of Cherokees had been arriving all day. When Jack came to a halt, his white, short-haired terrier mutt named Lady squirmed into his lap. Through the swirling snow they watched the Cherokee wagons rolling up to the banks only to discover their progress halted by dangerously large ice chunks, grinding, screeching and cracking violently in a thunderous cacophony. It would have been suicide to attempt crossing by ferry, and it didn't appear the river would freeze solid enough for them to cross the ice.

"It's them. The Cherokees," Jack heard from Mr. Haliburton, one of the town's prominent citizens.

"They should've been through here weeks ago," added a slender Scot named MacLeod who continually made little snorting sounds through his nose when he spoke.

"Ain't no way they're gettin' across this river now," offered Simon Dexter, a one-armed old veteran of 1814 who had fought

616

beside the Cherokees twenty-five years ago and had a great respect for them.

"And it'll freeze up even more tonight," MacLeod put in.

Mrs. Haliburton pulled her luxurious long pelisse tightly around her and held her hat on to keep the wind from stealing it. "It's shameful, what they're doing to those poor people," she reflected on the Cherokee's plight.

"What *they're doing*?" her husband asked with an amused expression. "Who's *they*?"

"*They* is us!" MacLeod set her straight.

"Not me!" exclaimed Dexter. "I ain't done nothin' to them folks."

"It's *our* congress, *our* president, *our* army," MacLeod explained. "Same as if we was right there doin' it ourselves."

"Well, I can't take 'em *all* in," Dexter, the old veteran, announced, "but as many as can fit is welcome out at my place."

"Mine, too," Jack Harshaw echoed from his buggy seat. "I got a new barn that'll hold a bunch of 'em."

"Yeah, that's a real generous offer, Harshaw," Haliburton scoffed, "and a safe one...seein' as how ain't no way they're gettin' across this frozen river."

"I think it's amazing they've made it this far. Driven from their homes in the dead of winter," Mrs. Haliburton sympathized with the beleaguered travellers.

The only other woman present, Matilda Smoot, was head of the local Presbyterian ladies association. "Well, I don't like 'em being here," she snorted with righteous contempt. "It ain't Christian. Them mixin' with decent white folks. We can't have it."

Matilda's remark drew dark looks from the others, but no one responded until Mr. Haliburton said, "Well, it don't matter much. Once they get across, like as not they'll just keep moving. They got a good three...four hundred miles yet to go."

* * * * * * *

By dusk countless twinkling camp fires were scattered up and down the eastern bank of the Mississippi. The Cherokees prepared to burrow in for another freezing night. At the Swimmer camp Charlie and Buck added to the fire the skimpy handful of damp twigs they had managed to find scattered in the snow. Charlie drew the tattered blanket a little tighter around Eva and Sally. They had both taken ill on the latest leg of their journey. Martha added some herbs to a small pot of water boiling over the fire.

"They're really sick, *E-to-da*," she said with quiet concern, glancing at her mother and little sister. "Especially *Sa-li*."

"She'll be all right. She's strong," Charlie said unconvincingly. Martha locked onto him until he met her eye. Realizing she knew he had no answer, he looked away, helpless, frustrated, and walked off through the snow.

* * * * * * *

Standing at the water's edge, *Tsu-tsu* gazed across the river at the scattered lights of the sprawling village on the opposite shore. His father appeared beside him.

"I'm going over there tomorrow," *Tsu-tsu* announced in a low, matter-of-fact tone. "To find some *yo-neg* medicine for *Sa-li* and *E-ge-i*."

"No. It's too dangerous," Charlie said. Father and son watched the huge ice flows crash into each other.

"I can cross on the ice."

"We'll have to wait 'til it warms up and the ferry boats can get us across," Charlie put a hand on his son's shoulder.

"It's been a bad winter, *E-to-da*. That could take weeks. Mother and Sally will die," *Tsu-tsu* argued.

"We'll just have to use *Tsa-la-gi* medicine," his father said. They headed back toward the campfire. Mixed with the grating and grinding of the ice in the river came a chorus of bereaved wailing and the chanting of Cherokee medicine men and medicine women that had become their quotidian evening song.

* * * * * * *

The frozen landscape lay broad and desolate in the frigid morning gray. The Reverend Evan Jones's long, unbraided hair flowed from beneath his wide-brimmed black hat and waved in the icy wind blowing in off the Mississippi. He stood at the head of the two graves hacked out of the cold and lifeless earth for the corpses of a Cherokee mother and her child. Very vocal and animated in his delivery, Reverend Jones loudly punctuated each phrase with a plea to *Tsi-sa*—Jesus—and a grunt, which was met each time by murmurs of agreement from the Cherokees gathered for the burial service.

"We give these beloved unto Heaven! *Tsi-sa*! Uh! The souls

of Sarah and little Jane *Ta-no-wi*, *Tsi-sa*! Uh!"

"Amen! *Tsi-sa*! Amen!" came from the huddled crowd, which included Peter Hildebrand, many of the Cherokee leaders and even one of the *yo-neg* doctors who had fought valiantly but in vain to save the mother and daughter.

"Take them to your bosom, *Tsi-sa*! Uh! Too many mothers have died! *Tsi-sa*! Uh! Too many daughters have died! *Tsi-sa*! Uh! Too many fathers and sons! *Tsi-sa*! Uh!"

"Amen! Yes, Lord Jesus! *Tsi-sa*!"

"Embrace the spirit of this mother! Uh! Hold fast this precious child! *Tsi-sa*! Uh!" Evans concluded. At a signal from the preacher, the blanket-wrapped bodies—without benefit of coffins—were lowered into the frozen ground.

The tears on Martha's cheeks had turned to ice in the blustery wind. She pulled Robert closer. His youthful beard, thin and stringy, had grown even longer and there remained little vestige of his U. S. military affiliation. Charlie, on Martha's other side, looked around as though searching for something...or someone. She sensed that his thoughts, like her own, had drifted back across the camp to the rest of their family.

Eva's cough was weak but incessant. Gaunt and hollow-eyed, she inspected the fire, wondering if it were possible to get closer without actually igniting herself. Sally lay with her head in her mother's lap. Glancing down at her daughter, Eva's heart skipped in panic. Then Sally stirred, coughing in a shallow, fitful sleep. Buck, long Sally's tormentor, now sat beside her, a hand resting on her shoulder, watching over his sister.

At the graveside, Martha noticed her father's expression had grown even more distressed. He continued to glance around nervously, first in one direction, then another. Before she could ask what was troubling him, they were drawn back to the funeral when Sam *Ta-no-wi*, the surviving husband and father, stepped away from the graves and raised his hand to the gathering. His face was twisted with a mixture of bone-gnawing grief and a soul-consuming anger. His voice wasn't loud, but it burned with conviction.

"I, Sam *Ta-no-wi*, will have revenge!" he announced, holding his hand above his head. "I will kill Major Ridge, John Ridge, Buck Watie and every other man who signed the treaty that brought us here! It is the law of our people! If there are true *Tsa-la-gi* men who can hear my words, you will join me! I have spoken! Uh!" He looked back down at the graves of his wife and daughter one last time before pushing his way through the murmuring crowd. After

619

Sam had gone, Charlie resumed looking around...searching....

* * * * * * *

Robert Barton, with the aid of his friend, Miles Franklin, and two Cherokee men pulled the drenched and rigid body of *Tsu-tsu* Swimmer from the icy Mississippi. The frothy water dripped in silver strings back into the river like drool from the frozen, hungry beast most reluctant to yield up its latest morsel. Intent, as he had promised, on obtaining medicine for his mother and sister, *Tsu-tsu* had gone about a mile upstream and jumped onto the largest piece of ice that came close enough to shore. He planned to work his way across the river, moving from one piece of ice to another, timing the current to leap to the opposite shore at Cape Girardeau. Somehow he lost his balance and fell into the river. The ice flows had pushed his body back toward the bank where it became entangled in the branches of a dead tree a half mile below the Cherokee encampment.

Charlie had been summoned as soon as *Tsu-tsu's* body was spotted. He rushed down the bank and grabbed his son, embracing the cold, lifeless corpse. Martha reached the top of the bank and looked down at her father and her dead brother. Her face twisted in horror and she had to be restrained by the other Cherokees. She watched as her father pushed the others away and lifted the rigid, frozen body in his powerful arms. Six times he tried to ascend the slippery bank and lost his footing. Each time he slid back down, the others offered to help, but he stubbornly refused. On the seventh try he made it to the top and accepted Martha's extended hand to help him up over the precipice.

Martha had seen people die almost every day during the months in the concentration camp and on the road. But her mind—her heart and her soul—could not accept this grotesquely stiff and cyanotic scarecrow image of her little brother as the latest sacrifice to the inevitability of death.

* * * * * * *

When Eva Swimmer was told that her son had perished, she was so weak her reaction appeared strangely subdued to those around her. Deep, exhausted sobs slipped into another coughing attack. Sally seemed to understand that her brother was dead. She cried weakly and clung to her wedding dress doll. Buck struggled to hold back his tears, refusing to let himself cry. He was now the

620

young man of the family. He had to be strong. *Tsu-tsu* would have insisted on it.

Charlie and Martha stood clinging to each other at the burial. Both preachers—Jesse Bushyhead and Evan Jones—were there. The wind had grown even stronger, scratching the throat and lungs with each breath. The snow swirled around them like the icy vapor of departed Cherokee spirits, twisting and spiraling as though confusion about their destiny in this life had followed them into the next. Robert Barton and Miles Franklin were there and a couple of Cherokee leaders, but the storm had become so intense that others who would normally have attended were forced to seek shelter.

A few took wagons to the eastern edge of the Cherokee camp where government contractors—including Titus Ogilvie and Peter Tanner of *Tanner Overland Freight*—had caught up with them and were selling second-rate, inferior supplies at outrageously inflated prices. And precisely as the contractors had greedily anticipated, the Cherokees were more than willing to pay.

* * * * * * *

At the exact hour that *Tsu-tsu* Swimmer's body was being lowered into a black hole chipped out of the frozen banks of an icy, angry Mississippi River, President Martin Van Buren was preparing to address a joint session of the United States Congress. He stroked his familiar mutton-chop side burns and waited for the buzz to subside before beginning his speech.

> *"It affords me sincere pleasure to be able to apprise you of the entire removal of the Cherokee Nation of Indians to their new homes west of the Mississippi. The measures authorized by Congress have had the happiest effects, and the Cherokees have emigrated without any apparent reluctance...."*

The rocky mixture of mud and ice was pushed in over *Tsu-tsu's* blanketed body. His wounded arm was still wrapped in rags. The mushy earth was tamped down by shovels and boots.

> *".......and in a letter which I have recently received from Secretary of State Poinsett, he writes: The generous and enlightened policy toward the Indians has been ably and judiciously carried into effect...with*

promptness and praiseworthy humanity. They have been treated with kind and grateful feelings...not only without violence, but with very proper regard for the interest of the people."

* * * * * * *

Twenty-seven days later the Cherokees were still dug in on the east bank of the Great Father of Waters. For almost four weeks they had been subjected to punishing blizzard conditions. On those few days when there had been a clear sky—no clouds, no snow or sleet—the temperature had been even colder. The Cherokees felt themselves trapped within the hostile circumference of a great, white well whose top opened to an icy, unreachable blue.

On the western bank of the Mississippi, the same group of Cape Girardeau's good citizens gathered once again to ponder the *Cherokee problem*. A microcosm of the entire community, they reflected the attitudes of sympathy, antipathy, indifference and irresolution.

"It's a month next Tuesday," Mr. Haliburton said, and no one was certain exactly what he meant. Was he merely marking the calendar? Was there a hidden shred of compassion for the starving, freezing Cherokees on the other side of the river?

"It must be just awful for them," Mrs. Haliburton said. "They've been burying ten—sometimes twenty people a day over there!"

"Well, it hasn't been easy for us, either," important church leader, Matilda Smoot, lamented. "Worrying they might sneak across the river some night and start murdering decent Christian folk in their sleep."

"Good Lord, Matilda! How you do go on!" Mrs. Haliburton clucked.

MacLeod was disgusted with Matilda's stupidity. "If they could sneak across the river, don't you think they'd have done it and been gone long ago?"

But Matilda had the perfectly rational explanation. "They are Indians, don't forget," she reminded them. "You can never tell with those people."

Simon Dexter had, on numerous occasions, come down to peer across the river, wondering if, by chance, he might spot one or two of the Cherokees he had fought with under Andy Jackson at Horseshoe Bend and New Orleans. It was too far to see, but he had come anyway. You never knew. He continued gazing across at the Cherokees and responded glibly to Mrs. Smoot.

"You might, indeed, be murdered in your sleep some night, Matilda, but I'm not so sure it'll be at the hand of a Cherokee."

The others suppressed smiles and chuckles. Matilda Smoot stuttered and hissed, unable to put together a scathing—albeit righteous—rejoinder.

"I hope the river clears soon," Mrs. Haliburton concluded. "For their sake. And God preserve them from Matilda and her *decent Christian folk.*"

In a repeat performance of their countless exchanges over the years, Matilda Smoot stomped off in a huff, tracking through the snow back toward the village. Gradually, the rest of them broke up and drifted off to their comfortably warm houses to sit by a crackling fire, perhaps to sip whiskey and warm milk and decry the unfortunate fate of the hapless Indians.

Arkansas River
South of Little Rock

The *Victoria* strained and chugged through the night, clawing her way through the blinding snow and sleet that had begun late in the afternoon as a series of scattered flurries and mushy, frozen rain. The steamer inched her way upstream, pushed at a sharp angle by the near gale-force northwesterly head winds dangerously close to the large tree limbs overhanging the east bank.

The captain of the *Victoria* was Colin MacKenzie, a portly, bearded man in his mid-thirties who spoke with a pronouncedly nasal Appalachian twang. On the *Victoria*'s bridge he, along with Chief Ross, William Drummond and two other Cherokees, clung to whatever was at hand to keep from being tossed about. It was especially tricky for William to hold on with his left hand and concentrate on not hitting his right arm and wounded shoulder. The helmsman, a tall, sinewy Virginian with a bushy moustache, struggled to steer the boat away from the tree-lined bank.

"We've made good time the last few days," *Gu-wi-s-gu-wi* shouted above the roar of the storm and the rhythmic pounding of the steamer's giant pistons. "Now this weather will steal it back from us."

"Lost time's the least of our worries right now, Chief Ross," Captain MacKenzie spoke, straining to see out into the night. "This here's a bad stretch of river. Even if we stay off the sand bars and steer clear of some pretty treacherous rocks, we can still get ripped apart by them trees." No sooner had he spoken than the *Victoria* lurched sharply to starboard. "Hard to port! Hard to port!" MacKenzie shouted to the helmsman whose sturdy forearms delineated every pumped and rigid muscle as he fought the huge wheel.

"What was that? It felt like rocks!" Ross called out.

"Sand bar," the captain corrected him. The *Victoria* scraped bottom before sliding gradually back into deeper water. "We were lucky this time."

"Lucky?" William asked.

"We're still movin', ain't we?" the captain grinned. But their good fortune was short lived. The words were scarcely out of his mouth before they were thrown forward with a mighty force. The

Victoria had struck another sand bar. This time, there was no scraping free, no movement. The vessel was stuck.

* * * * * * *

Susanna and a few Cherokee women—including Quatie Ross, against the protests of all the others—were busy tending the sick when the *Victoria* struck the last sand bar. They were tossed about like Meg's doll, slammed to the deck and driven against each other, the bulkheads or boxes and crates. Grabbing whatever they could to stabilize themselves, they tried to help the afflicted who had been tossed from their beds. When the groans of discomfort and the cries of shock subsided, there was a period of quiet, marked only by the howling of the storm. Most of those who had fallen were getting to their feet when the *Victoria* moaned as though echoing the spirits of her ailing passengers. She heaved and crunched and finally slipped away from the sand bar.

* * * * * * *

On the pilot's deck the rotund captain exhaled a great sigh of relief when the boat began to inch forward once more. He announced his decision to Ross, William and the others.

"I've steered through here a hunnert times by moonlight, but in a storm like this, you can't see nothin' and it's nigh impossible with this wind. We're stopping here. Best tell your people, Chief. They'll want to get off and make camp quick, before they all freeze to death."

Gu-wi-s-gu-wi, William and the other Cherokees moved among the passengers informing them of the situation. William found Susanna. Working with only one hand and arm, he helped her restore the sick and frightened children to their make-shift cots. He noticed his daughter was wearing no coat or blanket, only her thin dress. When he took off his coat and attempted to put it around her, she pushed it away, forcing him to shout above the wailing wind.

"Put it on!"

"I'm all right, Father! You keep it!"

William blocked her path and wouldn't let her pass. "I've already lost your mother...I don't think I could handle it if..." he trailed off, unable to utter the words. She relented, allowing him to wrap the coat around her and steer her toward the rear deck. "We're getting off here! It's too dangerous to go on!"

"Now?! Here?!"

The word spread rapidly. The sick ones were told to stay in their beds until someone came to help them ashore. William and Susanna went out on deck. Near the stern they ran into *Tsisdu*, maneuvering to the lee side, out of the driving sleet with *Me-li* tucked inside his coat.

"Where's Meg?" Susanna shouted with concern.

"I thought she was with you, but I was coming to make sure," *Tsisdu* bellowed.

"Oh, God!" Susanna's hand covered her mouth. She began frantically looking around. Then she heard a voice from the darkness behind them.

"Is someone looking for a little girl?" Quatie Ross, with Meg in tow, had come from the other side of the boat. The chief's wife took the blanket from her shoulders and wrapped it around Meg.

"Meg! What on earth, child!" Susanna rushed to her and scooped Meg up in her arms.

"Mommie..." the child was more frightened by the adults' reaction than by having been momentarily separated in the darkness. Susanna removed the blanket and tried to give it back to Quatie, but the chief's wife adamantly replaced it around Meg, pulling it up over the child's head.

"No. Keep this baby wrapped up!" Quatie insisted. "I found her near the back of the boat. No telling how long she'd been wandering around." She and Susanna both shot scolding looks at *Tsisdu*, who ducked his eyes, embarrassed and ashamed.

"I must have dozed off..." he confessed.

"It's all right," William said. "Meg's safe now. Come on, we have to get our things!" *Tsisdu* began removing his coat to give to Quatie—just as William had done for Susanna—but Quatie stopped him.

"No, I'll be all right."

John Ross came toward them, struggling to maintain his balance on the icy deck of the constantly shifting boat. He carried an old, wadded up blanket.

"*Gu-wi-s-gu-wi*! You'd better get her out of this before she catches her death!" William pointed at Quatie.

Ross was already flapping out the old blanket. He put it around Quatie's shoulders and drew it closed in front, then pulled her close and put his arms around her, perhaps to warm her from the cold...or simply as a gesture of affection for the woman he was afraid of losing.

626

"I'll outlive you all," Quatie protested. "You'll see..." She coughed and snuggled closer to her husband. Either she knew it was time to give in or she simply no longer had the strength to resist. She allowed *Gu-wi-s-gu-wi* to lead her back toward the *Victoria's* large, common room that was their hospital. They were almost thrown overboard when the *Victoria* slammed against the river bank. The top of one of the smoke stacks had been clipped by a large tree limb. The railing and support posts at the starboard corner of the upper deck were crushed by the giant, gnarled limbs of a huge oak that loomed like a shadowy ogre, ready to devour anyone or anything attempting to enter its domain.

* * * * * * *

Along the east bank of the Arkansas River the Cherokees crouched against the driving wind and intermittent sleet that stung the skin like a thousand ice wasps. Many careful and concentrated attempts were required to kindle a fire, the ephemeral sparks and first tiny flames protectively nurtured like a fragile newborn. Back and forth the Cherokees scurried, off the *Victoria* with belongings, then back on again in search of misplaced items or a lost child, or to help someone ashore, streaming in multiple directions like busy insects in the darkness. William, *Tsisdu* and John Ross stood near the gang plank with the *Victoria's* captain and members of his engine crew.

"How does it look, Captain MacKenzie?" the chief asked.

The captain pulled his mackinaw collar up to cover his frozen ears. "Even if this storm breaks by sunrise, the *Victoria* ain't goin' nowhere," he said. "Not for at least a week."

"A week?!" William was stunned.

"We cracked the main piston shaft when we hit the bank, and that tree ate us up top side," MacKenzie reported. The engine crewmen grunted their confirmation.

"We can't stay here a week!" *Gu-wi-s-gu-wi* insisted.

The captain rubbed his face and puffed his cheeks full of air, trying to think of an alternative. "You can take the road on up to Little Rock," he finally spoke. "My brother runs a boat—the *Tecumseh*—from there all the way to Ft. Gibson."

"How are we supposed to carry all our things?" *Tsisdu* asked.

The captain shrugged. "Might be a few farmers in the area that'll sell you a wagon or two."

"That won't help," William shook his head. "Not with this

many people."

"We'll just have to leave what we can't carry," Ross concluded. He knew Captain MacKenzie's solution was the only workable one.

"It's either that or wait 'til we get her patched up," the captain replied. He politely said good night to the Cherokee leaders and went with his men back aboard the steamer. *Gu-wi-s-gu-wi* and the Cherokees looked at the boat, then scanned the undulating swarm of *Tsa-la-gi* travellers busily preparing to battle the long, harsh night.

* * * * * * *

February 1, 1839
South of Little Rock

The Cherokees who had begun their journey on the trail—with the exception of William Drummond and his family, who had started out on the keelboats behind the *Vesper* and the *George Guess*—now found themselves once again on land. The snow and sleet had withdrawn in a temporary truce shortly after daybreak. Still, the *Tsa-la-gi* were forced to battle the slippery, frozen mud on their northward march headlong into the brutal assault of the fierce, icy winds.

William and *Tsisdu* were bent beneath the weight of large loads, forced to concentrate on every step. Though by far the larger of the two men, William—because of his wound—carried the smaller bundle, balanced on his left shoulder. For either of them, a misplaced foot here, an unseen patch of ice there, coupled with a timely gust of wind could send them toppling. It had already happened several times. Getting back up and regaining control of the oversized load was more physically exhausting than transporting the cargo itself. Meg rode strapped to Susanna's back in the traditional manner, held in place by a strip of blanket supported from Susanna's forehead. *Me-li* clung to her hand and fought to keep up the grueling pace.

Of the few wagons they had managed to acquire near the Arkansas River, one was filled with the Ross's belongings, including the invaluable tribal papers. The rest of the wagons provided transportation for the sick, the very young and the very old. Chief Ross walked beside the wagon that carried the Cherokee documents. Quatie, at his side, slipped on a patch of frozen mud and grabbed his

628

arm to keep from falling. She regained her footing, but they had gone only a few steps when she collapsed completely. The wagon stopped. Ross lifted his wife and deposited her gently in the rear with others too ill to walk.

Shortly after midday a few of the younger men went off into the woods to hunt. They moved in a northerly direction parallel to the main trail and would rejoin the group a few hours later. They had been gone little more than an hour when, to everyone's delight, one of the hunters burst from the woods to stop the party. The hunt had been more successful than anticipated, providing not one deer but two! Chief Ross decided it would be good for body and soul to stop right then and there. By the time the men appeared bearing the two large bucks—suspended upside down on poles between the hunters' shoulders—two large fires were already blazing. Before the animals were skinned and prepared for cooking, thanks was offered to *Ye-ho-wa* and to the spirits of the slain animals for the ultimate sacrifice they had made on behalf of their *Tsa-la-gi* brothers and sisters.

The next few hours were spent resting and feasting on roast venison. Stomachs were filled—for the time being, at least—and the spirits of the weak and afflicted immeasurably lifted. When the last bones had been picked clean and the fires extinguished, the Cherokees resumed their languid crawl toward Little Rock, hoping to eke out a few more miles before making camp for the night. At least, they thought, their stomachs were full and, if they could only stay warm, they might get a good night's sleep.

* * * * * * *

By the end of the day the wind had died down, leaving the Cherokees to face another bitterly cold night. A full moon hung against a star-speckled onyx sky. Larger than normal fires blazed in the clearing where the travellers had made camp. In contrast to the urgent scrambling of the night before, the *Tsa-la-gi* moved about with a universal gravity.

Chief Ross had stretched a tarp from the side of his wagon to form an open-sided tent. Quatie lay on a make-shift bed of blankets piled atop a row of boxes. *Gu-wi-s-gu-wi* sat beside her. Across from him a Cherokee medicine man worked patiently over Quatie, chanting and mumbling almost inaudibly, entreating the spirit world to strengthen her.

The cycle of rejuvenation among the Cherokees proved to be

629

short lived. Word spread rapidly throughout the camp that their Healing Angel, Quatie, was down, and it was serious. Before long, members of the chief's family had gathered quietly and were joined by William, his granddaughter, Meg and *Me-li*. All three open sides of the shelter were filled with the faces of concerned Cherokees, looking on from a respectful distance.

Susanna pressed through the crowd and handed a cup to the medicine man. He sniffed it, tasted it, then carefully passed it across the bed to chief Ross. Gently the *di-da-nŭ-wi-s-gi* lifted Quatie's head.

"*Gu-wi-s-gu-wi...*" she said in a weak, scratchy whisper.

"Drink, Quatie," he urged her softly, holding the cup to her lips. But she was too weak. The liquid ran out of her mouth and down her chin. With the little strength left her, she pushed the cup away and placed her hand on her husband's.

"*Gu-wi-s-gu-wi...*I'm so thirsty..." she said. "If I could just have some water..."

"Could someone get some water?" the chief called to the onlookers.

"...snow..." Quatie whispered.

"What?" he bent closer.

"Please, *Gu-wi-s-gu-wi*...get me some snow...it's so pure...so cool...please..."

He looked around and saw everyone staring at him. He understood their immobile silence, frozen in their grave concern for this woman they all adored. He would get the snow himself. Gently he lowered her head back onto the blankets and pressed through his people in search of a patch of unspoiled snow. As soon as he was gone, Quatie beckoned weakly to Susanna, who came closer and took Quatie's hand.

"It won't be long now, Susie..." Quatie managed a faint smile.

"Don't talk that way, Quatie," Susanna tried to sound encouraging.

"Look after *Gu-wi-s-gu-wi*. Promise me," the chief's wife pleaded. "See that he marries again. The burden of leading our nation is great. He's not a man meant to be alone."

"Shh. The two of you will grow old together," Susanna placed her other hand on Quatie's forehead. "You said it yourself—you'll outlive us all."

Quatie coughed. It was a quiet, weak and shallow cough. "Take care of the children..." she said, looking around at the little faces in the crowd. "...the children..." She stretched her hand out toward Meg, standing a few feet away. Slowly the hand lowered. Quatie exhaled one last, raspy breath and closed her eyes in peace. Susanna gasped and looked around for her father.

Standing beside William was John Ross who had returned with a double handful of fresh, pure snow. He looked down at his beloved Quatie. His cupped hands relaxed and the powdery flakes swirled around him like a dancing spirit as he moved slowly toward the bed.

* * * * * * *

Though no official announcement had gone out, the remainder of the Cherokees in camp were drawn toward the shelter where the beloved wife of their chief had just died. With the large campfires blazing and the light of the full moon glistening off the snow-covered ground, the camp was exceptionally bright. The emigrants had no idea they were being observed from a thick copse of trees that capped a rise in the terrain a few hundred yards away.

Tom Carver had rebuilt his gang to six men, five not counting himself. Whenever one or two drifted away or got killed in a robbery—as had happened too often to suit him in the past few months—he always managed to enlist replacements. The successors were usually men from Texas or from Indian Territory who had run afoul of the law in the past and were looking for an opportunity to line their pockets with enough money to keep them in whiskey and whores.

"Just a bunch of Cherokees. Don't look to me like they got much," said Harrison, a square-jawed, red-faced man. Both his nostrils had been slit in a knife fight and fluttered a little each time he exhaled through his nose. He had been too drunk at the time to feel the pain and too drunk too many times since to remember exactly when and where it had happened.

"Money. That's what they got," Tom Carver corrected the new man. "Ain't you learned nothin' yet, Harrison?"

Holt, almost a duplicate of Harrison, except with nostrils intact and a chin much more pointed, looked at the gang leader. "Money? Them Injuns's got money?"

"Allotment money, Holt. From the gov'ment," Carver kept his eyes on their moonlit prey in the distance.

"And we're gonna get it, right?" Harrison just wanted to be sure he was clear on the plan. Carver looked at him and shook his head. Where do I find them, he wondered. Can a man truly be this

631

stupid?

The third new gang member, Hansen, was a small, ferret-faced smallpox survivor with a pitted complexion. At first Carver though it was a good omen that three men—all of their names beginning with the same letter—had appeared to join his gang just when he was in need of reinforcements. Given their pronounced lack of substance between the ears, however, Carver had since decided it was nothing more than random happenstance. Hensen nudged Holt and gestured toward the Indian camp. Carver looked back to the Cherokees to see what Hansen had pointed out.

Susanna Drummond Tanner, emotionally devastated by the death of her friend, Quatie Ross, pushed through the crowd surrounding the tarp shelter and walked away to be alone. With her hair down, long and flowing, she looked stunning beneath the light of the full moon. She went past the other wagons, beyond the last blazing fire and glided silently into the trees.

"She's purty, ain't she," Harrison stated the obvious. Tom Carver's lip on the unscarred side of his face curled into a lecherous sneer.

"Watch yer mouth, Harrison. That's my woman you're talking about."

"Gosh, you know her, Tom?"

Carver slapped Harrison with his hat. "Damn, Harrison, you're dumber'n mud!"

"But you said..." Harrison was now confused.

"We gonna hit 'em tonight, Tom?" Holt asked.

Carver answered Holt but kept his eyes on Susanna. "No. Not with 'em all together like this. Too hard to handle. The road goes through a narrow valley a few miles this side of Little Rock."

"And we'll be waitin' for 'em, right?" Harrison asked and received another look of hopeless disdain from the gang leader. Carver—by nature mistrustful—had begun to suspect Harrison was up to something, just pretending to be such a clod. He had to be. No human could really be that stupid, he thought. Tom shook his head and rolled his eyes, then started back toward their horses tied up at the rear of the grove. Harrison looked to Holt for confirmation. "So, we are gonna rob 'em, right, Holt?"

"Yeah, Harrison," Holt answered in a patronizing tone. "Looks that way."

He had been with Harrison long enough to know the man was totally incapable of guile. He truly *was* that stupid. And if Harrison didn't end up getting them all killed, Holt knew that with time Tom

632

Carver would come to understand the oafish simpleton for what he was: perhaps the most inept criminal ever to strap on a gun. With a final glance at the distant Cherokees—just to make certain he had it clear in his mind—Harrison followed Holt to the horses.

* * * * * * *

The solemn sunrise burial was attended by all the Cherokees and the few blacks travelling with them. Quatie Ross's body was wrapped in the same blanket *Gu-wi-s-gu-wi* had placed around her aboard the *Victoria*. The Cherokee preacher read from a tattered old Bible, its thin pages rustled by the chilled breeze. John Ross hadn't slept. His shoulders drooped and his eyes were sunken in their sockets, sad, exhausted.

Susanna, red-eyed and pensive, stood silent with Meg and *Me-li* beside her. For the second time in a few short weeks she felt an emptiness, the depths of which she would never have thought possible. She watched them lower into the trailside grave the body of this little woman of indefatigable physical energy and spiritual strength. The woman who, more than anyone since the death of her own mother, had—without judgement or criticism—lovingly coached Susanna from a spoiled, self-indulgent, finishing-school princess, *yoneg* debutante into someone capable of seeing beyond herself. Quatie had taught her the importance of helping others, especially the children. *Take care of the children...the children*, Susanna recalled The Angel's final words.

Tsisdu and William, like the others, were subdued in their guarded concern for the chief. They all kept a distance, granting closer access to the members of *Gu-wi-s-gu-wi's* immediate family who had lost a mother, an aunt, a sister-in-law. Somewhere at the back of the crowd a couple of Cherokee women were joined by the emotion-filled voices of the black women in a softly harmonized spiritual hymn. An old Cherokee man played a mournful dirge on his fiddle and was accompanied by a mixed-blood of Scottish descent—a distant cousin of John Ross—who, like other displaced Cherokees, had somehow managed to transport an old bagpipe all this way. For this special occasion he had donned his tattered old kilt of the Ross Clan tartan—triple dark stripes, two narrow sets between wider ones, all on a background of red. No one laughed—or even smiled—at the odd mixture of Scottish traditional kilt combined with knee-high Cherokee boots, hunting jacket and turban. Such attire was worn as a gesture of supreme honor and respect, reserved only for the highest, most serious ceremonies.

* * * * * * *

Two hours later the fires had all been extinguished and the Ross party was once again on the move. Faces were grim and sorrowful, plodding onward, determined, bracing into the cold northwesterly wind. John Ross rode in the wagon that carried the tribe's national papers and documents. He sat with his hands folded in his lap, his eyes straight ahead in a mournful trance. Cherokees walked beside the wagon, their hands resting on a side board, the tailgate, or hooked onto a piece of the mules' harness. In this manner the entire band moved silently for miles. No one—not even the children—uttered a word.

CHAPTER
54

A farm in eastern Missouri

Eighteen miles south of Cape Girardeau, Jack Harshaw's large new barn sat on a flat piece of ground at the intersection of two expansive fields cleared for cultivation. One stretched west, the other extended southward. The Harshaw's house, a spacious, rectangular two-story wooden structure with a massive stone fireplace on either end, butted up against a row of trees on the north side that sheltered it from the icy winds blowing down off the plains. A wagon path led from the house out to the main road almost a quarter mile away.

The weather around and to the north of Cape Girardeau, while still punishingly cold, had finally cleared long enough to free the river of the treacherous ice that had held the Cherokees prisoner for so many weeks. The ferry took three days to transport all the emigrants across, causing concern among the *Tsa-la-gi* that another storm might come up, leaving them divided by the great river.

Many of the riverside village's good citizens had sacrificed hours of sleep and the warm comfort of their homes to stand guard at the edge of town to protect their women and children, *just in case the Injuns got antsy and decided to try anything funny.* Others, like 1814 veteran Simon Dexter, brought what blankets and food they could gather—which wasn't much, since Cape Girardeau had been socked in by the same storm that had hammered away at the Cherokees. But it was the warmth of the effort more than the thickness of the stew that brought a smile and heartfelt gratitude to a handful of Missourians and a few *Tsa-la-gi.*

Wagons pulled into the open area around Harshaw's barn, crowding into any available space. Some who had been forced to walk shuffled in and stopped, gazing around at the beautiful farm blanketed with snow. Others found a seat on a wagon tailgate or a pile of hay for a much needed rest. After weeks of freezing nights and bitterly cold days, this day had proven unseasonably warm, a welcome relief to all, particularly those who were sick.

Charlie Swimmer stood between Eva and Martha, the three of them shoulder to shoulder with a host of other Cherokees, including Peter Hildebrand and many of the leaders of his group. Eyes were wide. Jaws hung slack. A huge pit—six feet wide by forty feet long—had been dug behind the Harshaw barn. The trench was filled with glowing red coals, and suspended above it were fifteen sides of freshly slaughtered beef and pork.

Beaming at his guests from across the roasting meat was Jack Harshaw. Behind him were his wife, his four sons and their wives, three daughters and their husbands and at least fifteen grandchildren, all busy setting out large platters of food on make-shift plank tables. Robust fires had already been started, strategically placed around the entire area to provide both light and warmth for the night that would soon be upon them.

With quiet astonishment the gathering Cherokees surveyed the meat cooking over the pit, the food on the tables, the crackling fires. It was for them an unprecedented show of hospitality. Except for the generosity of the good folks of Hopkinsville, Kentucky and a handful from Cape Girardeau, they had never experienced such kindness from *yo-negs*. What they *had* endured in the past year was the clawing stench and choking dust of the camps. The pervasive suffering, the insidious assault of disease and the deaths that inevitably followed. The endless miles through mud, sleet, snow and ice on the trail. The maggot-infested meat eaten in huddled desperation in the dark. Vomiting rotten meal, or worse, heaving blood. All these things had taught those *Tsa-la-gi* who didn't already know it something of the darkness of the white man's heart.

To suddenly experience such a humane reception was a difficult adjustment. They were Cherokee. Harshaw was a *yo-neg*. Understandably, questions filled their minds. *What was he after? What did he want?* The *Tsa-la-gi* were speechless, most of them even suspicious. They glanced toward the house and barn, expecting to see a mob of hateful *yo-negs* descending upon them. But no such enemies appeared. Finally, Sally Swimmer, her doll clutched tightly under one arm, ventured out to one of Harshaw's granddaughters who was swabbing a side of beef with a sauce-soaked rag on the end of a stick. Tentatively Sally put forth her finger, touched the side of beef and tasted the sauce. Pronouncing it good with a broad smile, she extended her doll for the little Harshaw girl to play with.

* * * * * * *

It had been a day like many of the Cherokees had never known. For those who had, it was a day the likes of which they had never expected to see again. The supply of fresh food appeared endless. As soon as a side of beef was hauled to a big butcher's table to be carved, another took its place over the coals.

The barn was the largest any of these Cherokees had ever seen. Even larger, Charlie Swimmer thought, than William Drummond's barn back in Georgia. Throughout the afternoon the Cherokees milled around, eating, resting, eating, visiting, eating some more. A number of them moved inside the barn when the late afternoon chill began to set in. They rested on the ground, on piles of hay, on wooden boxes or on their own parcels. The women and children of the Harshaw family circulated among them, cheerfully filling cups and gourds from jugs of cider or steaming pots of coffee. Some of the Cherokee and black women eventually felt comfortable enough to help serve from platters of bread and meat or large bowls filled with boiled potatoes and plump, juicy cobs of tender corn. A fire was built in a black iron cauldron in the center of the barn, with the hay and straw pushed back to a safe distance.

From inside, the Cherokees looked out through the broad doors and saw their friends and loved ones still eating, warmed by the fires, for once undaunted by the approach of another cold, Missouri winter night. Somewhere a fiddle began to play, but this time it wasn't the dolorous tones of a requiem. The Scottish-Irish influence among the mixed-bloods was evinced by the numerous jigs and highland tunes.

Some of the sickest travellers were made comfortable in the barn. Others chose to remain near their wagons. But without a doubt, the doctors and those who had spent weeks helping them tend the sick and the dying for eighteen to twenty hours each day saw a definite impact. Not a single Cherokee died that day on the Harshaw farm. It was the first day without a fatality any of them could remember since leaving Rattlesnake Springs, Tennessee.

Sally, Buck and a flock of Cherokee youngsters followed two of the Harshaw grandchildren on an egg gathering expedition around the barn and through the large chicken coop halfway between the barn and the house. Hens squawked and fluttered out of the shed or rose up to join other chickens roosting in the barn's rafters. With all the cooking going on, Sally made frequent trips out to the Swimmer wagon to make sure *Tsu-s-qua-ne-gi-dŭ*, her pet goat, didn't mistakenly end up skewered on a roasting spit.

Three Cherokee fiddlers—an ancient man, a middle-aged woman and a teenage boy—were joined by one of Jack Harshaw's sons in sawing out a medley of familiar folk tunes. A couple more of the Harshaw brothers played their banjos and one of the sisters had excavated a long-forgotten concertina. With the yuletide season fast upon them, Christmas songs—in both English and Cherokee—were

637

enjoyed by all.

Martha Swimmer and Robert Barton spent most of the evening inside. When the fiddles and banjos broke into a jig, Robert jumped up and pulled Martha out to join him in the center of the barn. He began dancing an old Scottish step his grandmother had taught him. *Ma-di* was reluctant, embarrassed at first, but seeing Robert happy for the first time in so long made her smile. She would at least make an attempt to learn the dance. In short order they were joined by more young Cherokees and even a few older couples. The oldest of the Harshaw grandchildren, a handsome sixteen year old boy, drew an attractive young Cherokee girl to the cleared area that served as a *dance floor.* It wasn't the governor's ball, but it was the closest thing to fun these people had experienced since being driven from their cabins and herded into concentration camps more than six months earlier. Six months that for many had obscured the normal perceptions of time and felt more like six years.

The music and dancing continued into the night. At one end of the barn Jack Harshaw coaxed his white terrier-mutt, Lady, through a series of yelping *songs* and dances and tricks to the delight of the Cherokees surrounding him—old, young and in between.

Charlie Swimmer couldn't help chuckling at the old man and his dog. But when he glanced up at Eva, she was distant, staring past the jumping mutt, out through the barn door and into the night. Charlie knew that in this grieving mother's mind was the vision of their son, *Tsu-tsu.* And Charlie knew that deep inside, her spirit desperately longed to see their son bounding in with that familiar mischievous smile he always displayed when teasing Buck or Sally. So strongly did she feel it that Charlie found himself glancing occasionally toward the barn door. He adjusted the shawl on her shoulders and put a comforting arm around his wife, the woman who had born him four beautiful children. The woman who had, at one time or another, nursed them all back from death's door. The woman who had watched her firstborn son rolled up in a threadbare blanket and pushed into a narrow grave in the frozen ground. She would eat the food and appreciate the warm fire, but Eva Swimmer wouldn't laugh at jumping dogs or dance any Scottish jigs this night.

"*Tsu-tsu* would have loved this," Charlie said softly. Her eyes were brimming with tears. She slipped her arm through his. They left Jack to his dog tricks and watched the young couples dancing in the center of the barn. They followed their daughter, Martha, and the young *yo-neg* soldier she had grown to love.

638

Later in the evening the Scottish-Irish music gradually yielded to the soft, steady rhythm of two Cherokee drums that had survived the journey. They were soon accompanied by the shuffle of Cherokee boots and the *chatter-clack* of Cherokee shells. Lacking real turtle shells, some of the older Cherokee girls had gathered small stones and hard kernels of feed corn. They wrapped them in tiny pouches formed from a torn blanket, an old sash or even the bottom of a threadbare dress. These were tied to their legs just below the knees or at the ankles. Thus adorned, the girls began circling slowly to start a traditional *stomp dance*. Soon two young men joined them, and before long there were others. The *Tsa-la-gi* knew it was a little late in the season for their traditional *A-to-hu-na*, or *Reconciliation and Friendship* ceremony, but in their collective hearts they felt this was the closest to it they were likely to come this year.

Martha had made an honest—if somewhat awkward—attempt at the Scottish jig. Now it was Robert's turn to learn a new dance. She was pleased at how adeptly he picked it up and how much he enjoyed the traditional dance of her people. They moved in a large circle, stomping to the heartbeat *thump-THUMP-thump-THUMP* and the high-pitched wailing of the Cherokee singers seated around the drums. So engaged were Robert and Martha with each other that neither noticed the two army corporals, Thorpe and Evans, in the shadows near the side door. These men had no friends among the Cherokees. They didn't know anyone in Missouri. They had but one thing to occupy their thoughts. And that one thing was Robert Barton. Barton—the man who had killed their friend, Sergeant Charles DeKalb. Barton—the man who, in their estimation, was a murderer and a deserter.

* * * * * * *

How long had it been, many of the Cherokees tried to remember, since any of them had been so full and warm and smiling. And the *yo-negs* there—Jack Harshaw and his entire extended family—regarded it equally as a joyous celebration. They mixed freely and socialized with both the *Tsa-la-gi* and the blacks travelling with them. Throughout the day, Harshaw's daughters and daughters-in-law had been collecting their children's hand-me-down clothes. By late afternoon they were sharing a wonderful time with the Cherokee and black women, holding the clothes up to the children hovering close by and convincing them to try on the garments. Once their natural shyness had been overcome, the Cherokee and black children delighted in their new apparel, whether for its stylishness, bright color or the warmth it promised against the cold days and bitter nights ahead.

By nightfall, more of Jack's friends and distant relatives from the vicinity had joined the festivities, a welcome social break from the frozen isolation of a hard Missouri winter. Simon Dexter, the one-armed veteran of The Horseshoe and New Orleans had ridden out from Cape Girardeau. Even among this single group of Cherokees he found three old warriors—including *Tsunaluska*—he had fought beside against the British under Andy Jackson. The old men—white, black and *Tsa-la-gi*—exchanged tobacco, cider, memories and lies while children played all around them, their differences non-existent in a one-night, make-believe world of peace and brotherhood.

As the evening wore on, more wood was piled onto the fires which would burn all night. Eventually many of the Cherokees—especially the ill and the weak—began curling up in their blankets in the wagons where space permitted or on the ground beneath the wagons. They all tried to get as close as possible to the fires and didn't mind the noisy revelers or that the party might last the entire night. It would be better than the moaning of the ill, the final gasps of the dying, the wailing of the bereaved and the howling winds of the soul-devouring storms they had endured for weeks. The drums, fiddles, bagpipes, the stomping, the laughter and shrieking of the children were the stuff of pleasant dreams and of visions gifted from The Great Spirit.

Exhausted but relaxed and rejuvenated, Robert Barton took Martha's hand to lead her from the noisy festivities out into the chilly night. When they reached the barn's side door, they found their path blocked by Thorpe and Evans. No words were exchanged at first, but the corporals' glares issued a silent challenge.

"Step aside, Thorpe," Robert said in a low voice.

Evans looked down at Robert's feet and pointed to the knee-high, fringed leather Cherokee boots he had adopted. "You're out of uniform, *Sergeant* Barton," he sneered with caustic emphasis on the military rank.

"And you're in my way, *Corporal* Evans," Barton answered with equal acerbity.

"It's all right, Robert. Let it go." Martha pressed her hand against his back, urging him to go. When she attempted to move past the soldiers, Thorpe held out his arm to block her path. Martha looked down at his arm, which was pressed against her breasts. Barton saw the same thing. He calmly placed his hand on Thorpe's chest, then, in an instant, he twisted the army tunic so tightly up beneath Thorpe's chin that he gasped for air. Robert pulled him close, their noses almost touching, his voice soft but deadly.

"If you ever touch this woman again, I will tear this arm off and beat you to death with it."

With his free hand, Barton grabbed Thorpe's wrist and twisted the arm behind his back. He shoved Thorpe into Evans, knocking both men out of Martha's path. Pushing past them, Robert and Martha went out into the cold night air.

"This ain't over, Barton!" Thorpe called after them.

"Not by a long shot, it ain't!" Evans echoed.

Barton wanted to go back and finish it right then and there, but Martha seized his arm and forced him to keep walking. With a safe distance between them and the barn door, Martha let the knife slip from concealment against the inside of her forearm down into her hand. She restored it to the sheath hidden inside her waistband. Robert watched her with astonishment.

"*Ma-di!*"

"Don't worry, *'Tsu-ts'*," she smiled up at him. "I wasn't going to let them hurt you."

*   *   *   *   *   *   *

Robert and Martha strolled around in the night, past groups of Cherokees enjoying a late meal of roast pork and fry bread; past a circle of blacks eating and softly singing spirituals in their own unique style; past a forum of Cherokee leaders engaged in animated but friendly debate on national politics with some of Jack Harshaw's sons and sons-in-law. At one fire near the perimeter, Sam *Ta-no-wi*—sullen and morose—methodically sharpened his knife on a stone. He was surrounded by men and older boys of dark countenance. Their conversation in guardedly hushed tones wasn't lively like the others, and their minds were clearly not on food, music or dancing.

A frail Cherokee woman lay knotted in her blanket beneath a nearby wagon. The glow from the fire caressed her wrinkled face. Her glazed eyes stayed a while on Sam *Ta-no-wi* and the men with him. Then she pulled her blanket tightly around her and closed her eyes to sleep. She had seen men like these before down through her many years. Knew their looks. Had heard the dark whisperings of betrayal, blood and revenge. If she closed her eyes, she wouldn't see.

And soon the music would fade, the fires would dim, Cherokees would seek the warmth of their blankets for a good night's sleep on a full stomach, and the whispers of blood would be consumed by the hiss and howl of an arctic wind.

* * * * * * *

A few of the once legion fires still crackled. Most of them had been reduced to cooling ashes or piles of glowing embers. A pair of Cherokee boots moved cautiously among the sleeping, careful not to disturb anyone before arriving at the dormant form of Corporal Miles Franklin rolled up in his blanket against the leeward side of the barn. Robert Barton, carrying his carefully folded army tunic, his saber, his pistol and army boots, dropped quietly to his knees beside his friend. He gently placed a hand over Franklin's mouth and nudged him awake.

"*Ma-di* and I are leaving," Barton whispered.

"What?" Franklin slurred groggily. He pushed Robert's hand from his mouth and rubbed his face.

"We have to," Barton leaned close, keeping his voice low. "I've thought it over. It's the only way."

"What are you saying?"

"You know what I'm saying, Miles. And you know what you have to do." Barton set the pile of military paraphernalia on the ground beside Franklin.

"Is this because of DeKalb?" Franklin asked. He was finally awake enough to grasp the situation. "Robert, that's all behind you. He's dead."

"Yeah, but Thorpe and Evans aren't!"

Franklin placed a hand atop the military items, then looked back up at his friend. "Where will you go?"

"I don't know. Somewhere in Missouri. We'll get us a little farm."

Franklin shook his head, at a loss for words. "Robert..."

"I know..." Robert pulled something from inside his shirt and added it to the pile. "Here's a letter to my mother. I'd like you to post it when you get back east."

Franklin slipped the letter inside his jacket. Barton clasped his friend's hand firmly, then pulled Miles close and hugged him.

* * * * * * *

While Robert was with Miles Franklin, Martha had gone to say good-bye to her family. She spoke softly with Eva and rested her hand lovingly on her father's chest. When Eva reached to wake up Buck and Sally, Martha stopped her.

"No!" she whispered. "If they wake up, I won't be able to leave them." She gently touched the sleeping children and kissed each on the forehead. Buck stirred but didn't waken. Martha tucked the little wedding-dress doll—now dirty and ragged—firmly under Sally's arm.

Robert Barton slipped beneath the edge of the tarp hanging off the side of the wagon. Eva and Charlie looked at him and he at them, each trying to interpret the other's expression. Eva took Robert's face in her hands, pulled him close and kissed him on each cheek.

"She was my first," Eva's voice was soft with emotion. "You treat her like a princess."

"She *is* a princess, Mrs. Swimmer. She always will be," he reassured her. Martha joined them in a three-way hug. Robert shifted to face Charlie, who remained stone-faced as he firmly gripped Barton's forearm.

"Take care of her, *yo-neg*. Give her many sons..."

"And a few daughters..." Barton added with a smile at Martha.

"Will we ever...?" Eva wanted to know if she would ever see her daughter again but couldn't bring herself to finish the question.

"We will come and find you," Barton squeezed her hand.

"Someday," Martha said.

"It could be a while," Robert admitted, adding, "but we *will* see you again."

Charlie pulled the tarp back a few inches and looked out at the sky graying in the east. "You'd better go. It'll be getting light soon." He gently pushed them out, holding on to Martha's hand an extra moment before letting her slip away.

* * * * * * *

Sunrise over southeastern Missouri found two figures walking on either side of a horse piled high with their possessions—black specters against the desolate expanse of a pristine blanket left by the night's snow storm. Red-orange streaks of light glistening on the snow shot out like tiny fingers across the southbound path of Robert Barton and Martha Swimmer. They had left behind them their family and friends amid the early stirring Cherokees who would soon be leaving Jack Harshaw's farm.

Once they got back on the trail, the train of Cherokee wagons was strung out for more than two miles, inching northwest across the blinding white stillness. Gallons of hot coffee, hundreds of eggs, pounds of bacon and ham had been served as a send-off breakfast for the Cherokees, who didn't fail to show their heartfelt gratitude to Jack Harshaw, his friends and entire extended family. It had been an evening none of them would forget. The *Tsa-la-gi*, though they had little to offer, left behind gifts of appreciation. A silver belt buckle, a turban, a sash, an arrow or a blow gun and a couple of darts. A few Cherokee boots were exchanged for thicker, warmer *yo-neg* boots; doe-skin hunting jackets swapped for fur-lined mackinaws. When the wagons began rolling out, good-byes were said, hands were shaken, children were hugged, and hastily formed friendships that in all likelihood would never go any further took their first steps toward becoming but a pleasant memory.

Onward through the white nothingness of snowbound Missouri they would roll, through Jackson, Fredericktown, Farmington and Potosi. On west to Rolla, then bending south toward Lebanon, Springfield, Aurora and Monett, eventually cutting across the extreme northwest corner of Arkansas and finally into Indian Territory. And more *Tsa-la-gi* would die. This they knew. Some would freeze. Some would starve. Others would succumb to pneumonia, whooping cough, consumption, flux and all the other insidious enemies so adept at invading their tents, their bodies, their souls.

* * * * * * *

The same old Cherokee woman, who the night before had quietly observed Sam *Ta-no-wi* and his friends, pulled her blanket tightly around her and folded a corner of it across her face. Like others around her, she glanced off to the north, hoping to outrace the ominous blizzard-laden clouds bearing down upon them, their gray cotton underbellies deceptively streaked with a playful sunrise orange. The expressions of other travellers could not be called light-hearted, but there was, for a brief time, a renewed strength and determination.

Charlie Swimmer walked beside their wagon and Eva rode William Drummond's black gelding, Stick. Nothing had been said all morning while they were preparing to leave the Harshaw farm. No soldiers had come along to inquire after Robert or to take a head count. None of their Cherokee friends had noticed Martha's absence, or, if they had, were discreet enough not to mention it. Eva glanced lovingly at her little ones in the wagon. Her first born son was gone forever. Her oldest daughter had gone off to make a life of her own. Buck and Sally had become all the more precious in her eyes.

Sally, as always, clung to her ragged, wedding-dress doll. She crouched in the front corner of the wagon, looking around for the older sister she worshipped. She didn't see Martha, yet somehow she knew not to ask. Buck held fast to *Tsu-s-qua-ne-gi-dŭ*, the pet goat, which had been allowed to ride in the wagon with them. Buck studied his mother and father and knew something had happened and knew it involved his sister, *Ma-di*, but, like Sally, he knew better than to mention it.

They had been on the trail only a short time before Corporal Miles Franklin overtook them from the rear of the wagon train. He slowed his horse, keeping pace with the Swimmer wagon. Though he didn't speak, everything that needed to be said was communicated with knowing looks and furtive glances. Charlie acknowledged Franklin with a slight nod, which was returned by the corporal. From his horse, Miles reached into the wagon and pulled the tattered blanket a little closer around Sally before riding on up the line. Twice he glanced back, as though simply surveying the wagons, horses and walking refugees strung out on the road behind him as far as he could see.

55

Arkansas Territory

The hills rose and fell in all directions, coming down at steep angles from opposite sides of the road to form a narrow pass barely wide enough for two wagons to travel abreast. The first of the Ross wagons appeared sometime late in the afternoon. The Cherokees' every movement was being monitored through a spy glass by the outlaw, Tom Carver, from the cover of the scrub oak and cedars covering a distant hill northeast of the pass. The rest of Carver's gang sat quietly on their horses back in the trees, awaiting the signal that would send them to the location Carver had selected for the ambush. The gang had camped just north of the Cherokees the night before and rode hard all morning to arrive in time for Carver to plan every detail of the robbery. He also wanted time to check out the area to make sure their little business venture didn't get interrupted by those pesky *Injun vigilantes*.

Carver collapsed the eye piece and pointed with his left hand—missing two fingers—to the spot on the trail some distance ahead of the Cherokees. "That's where we'll wait for 'em."

Holt indicated a curve just before the selected robbery site and added, "And jump 'em when they come around that bend in the trail?"

Carver shook his head no. "It's gettin' late. Like as not they'll make camp in that little stretch there." He referred to an elongated area that widened a little on either side of the road in the narrow valley formed between the hills. "Strung out. Not all bunched together like before. We just let 'em get all settled in. Thinkin' they're safe. Roust 'em out in the middle of the night. Scares 'em half to death. Hell, they won't know if there's eight of us or fifty."

Harrison looked around at the others and made a quick count. "There's eight of us, Tom," he offered helpfully in his usual servile manner, then added, "But yeah—that's how I figure it. Rob 'em in the middle of the night."

"Good, Harrison," Carver growled. "That's real good. Why don't you just take over and run things from here on?"

"Wull, gee, Tom," Harrison whined, "I didn't mean it like that..."

Carver jerked his horse around and started down the hill

toward the pre-determined spot where they would wait while the Cherokees made camp. During his careful descent of the steep trail, Carver kept looking around. Though he had taken great pains throughout the day to make sure they weren't being followed, Carver couldn't shake the nagging feeling that all was not entirely well, which accounted for much of his irritability with his own men.

And well the outlaw leader should have been concerned, for while he had failed to catch even a glimpse of anything untoward, he and his gang had, indeed, been under the relentless scrutiny of Johnny Fields, *Tsa-tsi* Starr and *Ne-di* Proctor every step of the way. Johnny swept his spy glass away from the Carver Gang descending the back side of the hill and down to the trail and the Cherokees.

"I thought they wouldn't be coming in groups this big 'til spring," *Tsa-tsi* noted.

"They're sitting ducks for Carver," *Ne-di* said.

"There's eight of them. Three of us," Johnny announced.

The usually stone-faced *Tsa-tsi* cracked a rare smile. "Too bad for them, *'Tsu-ts'*," he said. Johnny slipped the spy glass back into his pocket and the trio of vigilantes crept back to their horses.

* * * * * * *

Tom Carver had been accurate in his prediction of where the Cherokees would make camp. Chief Ross gave the order to stop just before sundown, allowing the travellers time to cut firewood before dark, which would come a little earlier than normal because of the high hills to the west. A stream that paralleled the road at the base of the eastern hills would provide an adequate supply of fresh water.

Throughout the forest that blanketed the hills and bordered the road up and down the narrow canyon echoed the *thwack-thwack* of hatchets and axes splitting wood. Susanna Drummond Tanner halted after a few blows of the hand ax to check on Meg and *Me-li*. She had positioned them near the stream with strict orders to play there with Meg's doll. Each time she paused, the sound of other Cherokees making camp for the night filtered to her through the woods. After a half hour of chopping, Susanna buried the ax blade in the fallen log and gathered up the pieces she had cut. She gave *Me-li* some wood to carry and Meg, with her doll under one arm, picked up a single piece in the other hand.

"Take these back to Grandpa before it gets dark," Susanna told the girls, pointing them in the right direction. "You can help him build the fire."

Meg dropped her one stick of firewood and grabbed *Me-li's* skirt as they headed back toward camp. Susanna watched them for a while to be certain they were going the right way, then kneeled with her bucket to fill it from the stream. Just before the lip of the bucket touched the glassy smooth surface of the water, Susanna froze, captivated by the reflection before her. She lifted her eyes and looked across to the clearing on the other side of the creek.

In the shadow of the trees—his back turned three-quarters to her—stood the same half-eagle, half-man phantom Susanna had experienced that frightful night near Decatur, Alabama. She remained on her knees at the water's edge, watching the man-creature which, this time, appeared completely unaware of her presence. He raised his huge wings and made a singularly emphatic flapping motion as though trying to lift off the ground and take flight, but he achieved no elevation. After two or three more futile attempts, he rotated toward Susanna. Mesmerized, she watched his eagle head undergo a metamorphosis, transforming into the head of a man. She couldn't clearly see his face, but from the shadows his eyes burned like hot coals. He folded his large wings in front of him like closing the fabric of a stylish cloak then rapidly whipped them open again. Magically suspended waist-high about three feet in front of him was a brightly glowing ball of fire, like the flaming tip of a torch, but without the handle.

The eagle-man—now more man-eagle—stared at the flame which illuminated his face. For the first time Susanna saw his features—a strikingly handsome young man about her own age, give or take a year or two, obviously Indian, Cherokee she presumed but didn't know why she felt that way. She found herself drawn to his eyes. Eyes that were intensely passionate. She continued to watch, entranced. The flame hovered for a while, then lifted slowly into the night sky. The man-eagle never took his eyes off the burning orb, even when he began his own gradual ascent. His massive wings were widespread but not flapping. Susanna never once blinked until a gust of wind hit her in the face. She flinched for only an instant, but when she looked back, the vision had vanished. She lifted her eyes to the sky where she had last seen the ball of fire—the spot now occupied by the full moon.

* * * * * * *

Susanna brought an armload of firewood and a pail of water back to camp. The girls were adding tiny sticks and slivers of

648

kindling to the fire William had started. Across from them sat *Tsisdu*, smoking his pipe and gazing into the crystal shafts held in the open bandanna. Susanna, quiet and pensive, replenished the water in the pot hanging over the fire and stirred the soup. William picked up each little girl for an affectionate hug then rose stiffly and brushed his fingers along the side of his daughter's head.

"I'm going to check on *Gu-wi-s-gu-wi*," he said.

"All right, Father," she answered blankly, lost in her own thoughts. He didn't ask what was on her mind. He knew she would tell him when—and only when—she was ready. William walked off into the darkness, headed for Chief Ross's camp. Susanna watched the girls poking at the fire.

"I have just seen something," she said to the strange Rabbit Man without looking at him.

"I know," he answered, not taking his eyes off the crystals.

Startled by his response, she looked at him. He must have misunderstood her, she thought. "In the woods," she explained. "There was a man..."

"I know," *Tsisdu* repeated.

"Why do you say that, Rabbit Man?" she snapped at him irritably. "You have no idea what I'm talking about! You always do that. Acting like you know some great mystery!" She trained her eyes on the girls. She didn't want to look at this little man she sometimes found so annoying.

He looked up at her for the first time. "You saw the eagle-man." Why did she fight him so fiercely in these spiritual matters, he wondered.

With a shocked expression, she spun back to face him, her voice a breathless whisper. "Were you following me? You saw him, too?" *Tsisdu* merely lifted the bandanna with the crystals, indicating the source of his knowledge, but Susanna wasn't convinced. "Then what else did you see?"

"I saw the fire."

Their eyes locked. There was a simple, if mysterious honesty there that made her want to accept him at his word. To believe that he had, indeed, shared her vision, possibly through his crystals. But she didn't entirely rule out the possibility that he had simply spied on her.

"What does it mean?" she challenged.

He studied his crystals in silence, then answered without lifting his eyes. "The fire comes from the belly."

"From the belly?"

"From *your* belly."

"That doesn't make any sense," she shook her head. "Does that mean I'm going to be sick? With cholera? Dysentery? Am I going to die?"

The Rabbit Man looked up at her and smiled. "We're *all* going to die. But you have many years ahead of you. Many roads to travel."

"Then what does the ball of fire mean?" she insisted.

"It is a light," he replied. "For the *Tsa-la-gi*. To lead them." Each time he spoke, she thought, his words became more abstruse. *Tsisdu* touched his stomach in answer to her puzzled look. "From here. You will give them a leader. A light in the darkness."

"You mean Meg?!" she almost laughed.

He shook his head no. "There will be another...."

Susanna finally tore her eyes from him and dipped a modest portion of soup into her cup. "Well," she said flatly, "you can put your crystals away, Rabbit Man. You're not the Archangel Michael, and I don't intend to have any more children. You're way off the mark with this little Annunciation." She rose and walked to the edge of the campsite, facing the darkness. "Crazy old fool...." she mumbled to herself.

Sipping from the cup of warm soup, Susanna stared into the darkness of the trees for a while to clear her mind. Her focus gradually shifted to something in the undergrowth a few yards away. It appeared to be the shadowy figure of a man, barely visible, the moonlight reflecting off the pistol in his hand. After the phantasmagoric vision she had experienced earlier, she was reluctant to believe her eyes. But the figure remained. The pistol remained. And the terrifying reality of what was about to unfold gripped her by the throat. Susanna dropped the cup of soup and ran straight back toward the campfire where she grabbed Meg and *Me-li* just as they were crawling into their bedrolls.

"*Tsisdu!* Someone's out there!" she yelled to the Rabbit Man. Holding tightly to the startled girls, Susanna bolted for the woods, away from where she had seen the gunman. She would find Chief Ross's camp and her father.

In an instant she regretted having insisted on making their camp farther than usual from the others. Following the crushing loss of her dear friend, Quatie Ross, Susanna had felt the need for solitude. And now that distance threatened to be their undoing. Susanna ran. She scooped Meg up and carried her and was literally dragging *Me-li*. They heard the distant shouts—and the shots—of the robbers attacking the other Cherokee campsites. When Susanna thought they had gone far enough to escape immediate danger, she slowed to a fast walk, allowing herself and the girls to catch their breath.

They had only gone a few paces when Tom Carver's horse exploded from the thick brush right in front of them. Susanna knew she would never forget the evil in the eyes that leered down at her.

Things were working out exactly as Carver had planned. Susanna ran in another direction, toward some trees with low hanging branches which, she hoped, would impede a rider's progress. But again they were blocked when Holt appeared before them. Susanna spun around to go in the opposite direction, but *Me-li's* hand slipped free and she fell. Carver dismounted. Susanna pulled *Me-li* to her feet and pushed both girls behind her.

The scar-faced outlaw lowered his mask, grinned at her, then spit a string of tobacco juice into a patch of snow. He saw her involuntary look of revulsion and lashed out with his good hand, striking Susanna in the face. The forceful blow knocked her to the ground halfway across the tiny clearing. Her first thought was to get back to the girls, but her mind was clouded from the blow and when she tried to get up, her arm buckled beneath her. Out of the corner of her eye she saw Holt position himself to seal her off from the children. She saw the terror-filled faces of Meg and *Me-li*. This time she put both hands beneath her to push herself up off the ground. She heard the crunch of Carver's boots in the snow beside her and looked up just in time to see it coming. He kicked her shoulder, spinning her sideways, landing her on her back.

Carver dropped to one knee, the tip of his large knife pressed against her upper lip directly beneath her nose. Her eyes cut to the side past his leg. She caught a glimpse of the girls. Holt, on his knees between them, held them tightly with a fistful of each child's hair. Susanna knew what she had to do. There was no one else to help them. In all likelihood, no one had even heard her screams. She knew her father, *Tsisdu* and the others were busy fending for themselves. Carefully she pushed the knife blade away from her face with a finger.

"That...that really isn't necessary," she said, struggling to suppress the quiver in her voice and replace it with what she hoped would sound like a coy, seductive tone. If it was as transparent to him as it felt to her, she thought, she and the girls were as good as dead. She had no idea if her ploy had worked until Carver emitted a lustful little laugh. Never taking his eyes off her, he slipped the knife back into the scabbard on his belt. His thick, coarse hand caressed her face and brushed back a few strands before closing on a fist full of her long, brown locks. He rose and jerked her violently to her feet, then pushed her to a large oak tree, pressing against her, deliberately blocking her view of Meg and *Me-li*. The rough bark cut sharply into her back. Carver began groping her, his mouth open and drooling in his bobbing pursuit to kiss her. He laughed, enjoying the cat-and-mouse chase of trying to corner her elusive lips.

"That's good. Hard-to-get. I like that," he chuckled, then clutched her face in his vice-like grip and kissed her full on the mouth, so hard that when he finally broke the kiss, a trickle of blood ran down from where her lip had been cut by teeth—hers on the inside, his outside. The outlaw's fetid breath filled her nostrils when his serpentine tongue rolled out and licked the blood from her chin. His hand slid from her face down to her neck, not choking, but in a position to do so in an instant. With his disfigured left hand, Carver ripped open the front of Susanna's dress and began fondling her breasts. He shifted slightly to one side to view his handiwork, allowing her a fleeting glance toward the girls. They were still firmly in the grasp of Holt, who was voyeuristically enjoying the show.

"That's nice," Carver growled as he squeezed her breast. "You got big 'uns."

Her eyes rolled back in her head and she fought the urge to surrender to unconsciousness, but she couldn't afford the luxury of that escape. She had to save Meg and *Me-li*. She knew that if she didn't, Carver and Holt would rape the children after having her and conclude their little party by killing all three. She struggled for breath and arched her back, pushing her breasts up toward him.

"You like that...?" she again tried to sound seductive. She had worked a hand free and slid it down the front of his chest to his waist where she began unfastening the front of his trousers. Carver grunted his pleasure and continued to fondle her, his eyes closed in ecstasy, his right hand still resting on her throat. She felt his bristly beard and scratchy moustache when his rough, chapped lips closed around her nipple. *Control*, she told herself repeatedly. *Keep yourself under control.* The hand—with the two missing fingers—that had been holding her breasts slipped inside the torn dress, down across her stomach and into her private area. The scarred stubs of the third and fourth fingers dug against her pubic mound while the other two probed between her legs. Her eyes darted side to side, desperately trying to get another glimpse of the girls. Slicing into her consciousness for the first time were the distant shouts, the screams and the sounds of fighting taking place between other Cherokees and their attackers.

Susanna's fingers closed around Carver's hardness and she felt the vomit rise up in her throat. The bark cut deeper into her back with his intensified thrusting as she massaged him with her hand. He lifted his head from her breast and pressed in for another kiss. She forced her face up toward his to appear willing...even eager. But just before their lips met, Carver's head jerked backwards, his eyes widened, his face contorted with intense pain and confusion. He staggered back a step and gaped down at his own knife buried almost to the hilt in his left side. The handle was tilted down at an angle where she had driven it in just below his rib cage. Susanna, frozen with terror, remained pressed against the tree. Carver placed both hands around the knife handle, hesitated, then thrust down and out with a painful grunt. The blade made a sickening slurpy-suck sound when it exited his body, releasing behind it a gushing crimson river.

Hearing Carver, Holt strained to see what was going on. He had anticipated a moan of orgastic ecstasy, but this had sounded more like a gasping groan of intense pain. With Carver's back to him, Holt couldn't see that the entire front of the gang leader's stomach and left leg were already drenched with blood.

"You all right, Tom?" Holt asked tentatively.

He saw Carver stagger forward toward Susanna, stumbling, with his pants halfway down to his knees, his erection exposed. He extended the knife toward her, his twisted expression a mixture of anger and death-beckoning pain. His knees buckled and he fell forward against her.

"Damn, Tom!" Holt let loose a lusty, guttural laugh. "Save some for the rest of us!"

Susanna was pinned against the tree, the dying man's face pressed against hers. She knew she had little time to complete her task. There was no way of knowing what Holt might do once he realized she had killed his friend. He might run away like the coward he was, or he might, in a fit of vengeance, take out his own knife and slit the throats of Meg and *Me-li* before she could reach him. Wrenching the knife from Carver's hand, she gripped its wet, sticky handle and plunged it once more into his midsection, driving it up and in with all her strength. Blood shot from his mouth, covering her face and running down over her bare breasts. She looked directly into his blood-shot eyes—now frozen in death—with a burning hatred she wouldn't have thought herself capable of feeling.

Summoning her remaining strength, Susanna heaved him off of her. He fell to his knees, his weight balanced back against his heels, eliciting another crude laugh from Holt. "Take it easy! You gonna wear yourself out!" He strained to see through the darkness. Susanna pulled the front of her blood stained dress closed and stepped around the dead man. "Oh, yeah!" Holt squealed with anticipation. "Come on over here and I'll make a *real* woman outa you..." Holt rose from his kneeling position, releasing his grip on the girls' hair. He began opening the front of his trousers and had taken a couple of steps toward Susanna in the darkness when he froze with scrotum-shriveling understanding. A shaft of moonlight reflected off the blade hanging at Susanna's side. Holt held out his hand toward her. "Stop right there!" he tried to make his voice forceful. "Harrison! Hansen!" he screamed into the night. "You boys all right?" He nervously fumbled his pistol from his belt and cocked it, pointing it at Susanna. "I'll shoot, you murderin' Injun bitch!" Susanna kept coming toward him, her eyes burning into his, never leaving his face. He whipped the pistol around, pointing it at Meg and *Me-li*. "I'll kill them nits of yours, too!"

Everything was moving in expanded time for Susanna. Every twitch he made, every step she took, the blinking of his eyes—each fragment of a second lengthened into minutes. Holt looked at her and was almost overcome by the hypnotic power of her eyes. Had he survived to tell the tale, Holt would have been branded a liar, for no one would have believed what he would have sworn upon his own mother's soul he had seen. The eyes. The incredible—and inhuman!—eyes. Eyes like he had seen only once before. The eyes of a wolf that had attacked and nearly killed him when he had tried his hand at trapping up north before opting for the more leisurely life of a highwayman. He watched the eyes of this killer she-wolf who had come to protect her young and he knew he was about to die. He saw the bared fangs of the charging beast. His arm felt like lead, his finger on the trigger paralyzed in arthritic fear. Somehow he managed to raise the pistol point blank at the wolf lunging for his throat.

The shot split the night, bringing a shriek from Meg and *Me-li*. Until then they had remained silent in the face of the incomprehensible yet terrifying events. Susanna lurched to a stop with Carver's knife still raised for the attack. At her feet lay the outlaw Holt, the side of his head blown away. The girls began to cry.

Susanna was close enough for them to see she was half naked and covered in blood. She rushed to them, fell to her knees and embraced them both. Only then did Susanna look around her. She spotted the man a few feet away in the shadows, holding the smoking pistol.

Staring back at Susanna and the two little girls was Johnny Fields. Instinctively, Susanna brandished the knife and looked around, uncertain if he was her benefactor or another gang member who'd been aiming at her and merely missed. Satisfied there were no others emerging from the brush, Susanna came back to Johnny. She looked into his eyes.

"My God!" she gasped in a hoarse whisper. "It's you!"

Johnny looked behind him to make sure there was no one else. "You know me?" he asked, puzzled.

"Who are you?" she demanded.

He spoke to her in Cherokee, hoping to calm her, telling her everything was all right and he wasn't going to hurt them. She kept her eye on him, still cautious, but no longer frightened. She lowered the knife and pulled the girls close to her once more.

"*Da-qua-to-a Tsa-ni,*" Johnny told them his name.

Susanna shook her head, indicating she didn't understand. "I only know a few words."

"My name is Johnny," he repeated in English. He stuck his pistol back into his belt and squatted to present a less intimidating profile, smiling at the girls. "*Si-yo.* I'm Johnny."

"Susanna," she responded, then added, "Drummond. Tanner."

"That's a lot of names," he rose and held out his hand. "I think you'd better come with me."

Once again Susanna pulled the girls close, eyeing Johnny with renewed suspicion. Yet, she realized, there wasn't the feeling of fear and apprehension she had expected, and she found his smile strangely disarming.

"You really are the *u-ni-tsi wa-ya,* aren't you?" his smile broadened.

"What?"

"Mother wolf. You're like a mother wolf."

Susanna was gripped by the frantic, almost panic-stricken need to find William. "Where's my father? Can you take me to my father? I have to find my father," she rattled off rapidly.

"I don't know where your father is," Johnny shook his head, "but you'll be safe with me. I promise." He asked the girls, "*Ga-to-*

no de-tsa-to-a?"

Meg didn't understand, but *Me-li* told him her name, then added a phrase in Cherokee.

"What did she say?" Susanna asked.

"Her mother is in the river," Johnny translated, then said to Meg, "*Ni-hi tso-du-ha.*"

"She doesn't..." Susanna trailed off, apologetically.

"I said she's very pretty," Johnny explained. Again their eyes met and Susanna felt a sense of peace. "Like her mother."

"Were you...out there...tonight?" she didn't really know how to ask him. If this *wasn't* the man-eagle she had seen in the forest, then he would surely think her insane. And if it *was* him, then she would think herself insane for having imagined him as part eagle.

"I've been tracking these men for a couple of days now," he answered, misinterpreting her meaning. He motioned toward his horse tied to a tree at the edge of the clearing. "*Tsi-ne-na,*" he said, smiling again. "We'd better get moving, *U-ni-tsi wa-ya.*"

"That's right. Mother wolf. And don't you forget it."

She took his hand, allowing him to help her to her feet. Johnny lifted *Me-li* and Susanna picked up Meg. They started toward his horse.

"Susie..." he called from behind her. She spun around, shocked to hear the pet name only her closest family had ever used. He picked up Carver's knife, wiped the blade on his pants leg and held it out toward her.

"Why did you call me that?" her voice was once more low and challenging.

"Mother Wolf might need this," he ignored her question.

"You keep it," she said.

"Even Mother Wolf should never travel unarmed in this territory," he took the sheath off Carver's body, inserted the knife and held it out toward her. Susanna finished tying up the torn front of her dress and stuck the knife under the sash around her waist. Johnny took the reins of Carver's horse and led the animal to Susanna. She glanced at the slumped body of the outlaw gang leader. The emotions of the terrifyingly traumatic incident were beginning to seep through her defenses.

"I never thought in my entire life I would ever kill another human being."

"Human?! Him?!" Johnny scoffed.

"He's dead!"

"Guys like him aren't human," Johnny said. "You gotta look

at it like it's—like it's—hell, it's no different than killin' a hog. Stick him, then get outa the way 'til he's done bleedin'.'"

"I'm sorry. I don't share your calloused view," she said, looking at Holt.

"Just wait," he said with a cynical chuckle. "You run into enough of his kind—and out here, you will!—you'll change your tune."

"Shouldn't we bury them?"

He was incredulous. "Don't you know what he was about to do to you?"

"Yes," she said calmly, feeling a need to reach back and find some significant vestige of her civilized self, something to swallow up that fleeting instant of intense satisfaction she had felt when she drove the deadly blade into Carver's gut. "I am quite aware...of what he..."

"And when he got done, he'd have cut your throat. And then him and his friends would've taken their time with these little girls. And when they were finished, they'd've left all three of you for the buzzards." His words echoed the very thoughts—and fears—that had earlier flashed through her mind.

"So now it's repay the deed in kind?" she resisted his reasoning. "And what does that make me?"

"Don't *make* you nothing," Johnny shrugged and hoisted *Meli* up onto his saddle. "Just how it *is*."

He took Meg from Susanna and set her on the ground, then placed his hands firmly on Susanna's waist and boosted her up onto Carver's horse. Again their eyes met. At close range. There was something at work here that each felt, yet neither understood. He, of course, knew exactly who she was. She had told him her name. It was the sister of his friend, Michael Drummond. How she had come to be here remained—for now—a mystery. But that riddle would be answered soon enough, he figured.

And she knew him. The eagle-man who had changed into the man-eagle. The face, the eyes were the same. Of this she was certain. It was a vision forever etched in her memory, her very spirit. Yet, how could such a thing be? It was, indeed, a mystery. And she wondered if it would ever make sense to her. She kept her eyes on him and shifted back in the saddle. He lifted Meg to sit in front of her, then gave Susanna the reins. Their hands touched and she felt the electricity. It was all too confusing and she was determined to push it from her mind. This man had appeared out of the darkness and had saved their lives. For that she was grateful.

What relationship he might bear to some aquiline apparition she had seen—or imagined—on a dark night in the forest was most likely a connection that existed only in the stressful jungle of her own fears and insecurities. That's what she would do. She would put it out of her mind.

Johnny sprang into the saddle behind *Me-li* and brought his horse even with Carver's mount—now Susanna's. Their faces were inches apart.

"Let's go find your father," he said in a hypnotic voice that told her he would *not* be so easily banished from her consciousness.

Johnny bolted his horse in the direction of the rest of the Cherokee campsites. Holding Meg tightly in front of her, Susanna whipped her horse around to follow.

* * * * * * *

Johnny was the first to reach the abandoned Drummond campsite, followed shortly by Susanna. She reined up sharply.

"Here! This was our camp!" she cried. She slowed the spinning horse enough to grab one of their bags off a stump and tied it to the saddle in front of Meg.

More shots rang out in the distance, but before they could decide which direction to take, they heard someone thrashing through the underbrush, coming toward them.

"Susie! Susanna!" William called out.

"Father! Over here!"

William burst into the camp clearing. "Susie! Thank God!" he exclaimed and stuck the pistol Ezekiel had given him back into his belt. "Are you all right? Meg? Mary?" He saw *Me-li* on the horse with Johnny.

More shots rang out, closer than before. "Come on, William! Let's get out of here! *Tsi-ne-na!*" Johnny shouted. Susanna grabbed the reins of Johnny's horse and jerked the animal's head around.

"All right! Who are you! How did you know his name?!" she demanded. Before he could answer, William came close enough to see Susanna was covered with blood.

"My God! What happened to you?!"

"Mother Wolf can take care of herself," Johnny assured him.

"I'm all right, Father," Susanna confirmed. "What happened?"

"There were robbers! One of them was about to shoot *Gu-wi-s-gu-wi*. Then these other two came out of nowhere!" He looked at

Johnny. "Are they with you?"

"That was *Tsa-tsi* and *Ne-di*."

"Well, they made short work of those outlaws!"

Johnny eased his horse forward and transferred *Me-li* to the other horse behind Susanna. "Hold on tight, *Me-li*" he said, touching her face in a comforting gesture. Johnny then extended his hand down to William. "Come on! We've got to get out of here!" As if on cue, his warning was punctuated by more shots followed by a lot of shouting from the trees just west of them.

"Maybe we should wait for the army," William hesitated. "We sent a couple of riders on ahead to Ft. Smith."

"I don't think you want to do that," Johnny said. He pulled another pistol from his belt and extended it toward William.

"No!" Susanna screamed instinctively. She drew the big knife from her waistband, thinking Johnny was pointing the weapon at her father.

"Wait!" William jumped in her path, holding up his hand to stop her. The horse spooked, almost unseating Susanna and both little girls before William grabbed the reins and brought the animal under control. Puzzled and amazed, Susanna watched William take the pistol from Johnny and examine it closely. He looked up at Johnny and said softly, "This belongs to my son!" He showed Susanna the Collier. "This is Michael's pistol!"

Susanna had gradually shifted Carver's horse close enough for her to reach Johnny with the knife. He felt the steel press against the side of his neck.

"What have you done to my brother?"

Johnny couldn't resist a smile at her feisty nature. He grinned at William. "Is she always this nasty?"

"Do you know my son? Where is Michael?" William's voice was charged with excitement. And once again, before Johnny could answer, more shots were fired. Johnny reached for William.

"Let's go! Get on!"

William looked at the pistol one more time and made up his mind. He took the offered hand and climbed up behind Johnny.

The thin string of smoke twirled its way up from the chimney and hung lazily against the cold, crisp blue sky. Set deep in the woods of western Arkansas, the abandoned cabin that served as the raiders' hideout had been patched and made, if not comfortable, at least modestly inhabitable, though it had never been intended to house ten people. But it was warmer and drier than any of their previous hideouts and it lay far enough off the beaten path to offer the seclusion they required. The trail leading in from the road twisted for a good two miles through the trees, up, down and around the hills before climbing toward the clearing. The cabin sat near the top of a thickly wooded hill populated with live oaks, blackjack, hickory, a few sweetgums and birch. There were willows near the creek tucked along the western rim of the slope behind the cabin. Escape routes to the north, south and west had been mapped out and had even been shown to the older children, Jack and Janie Proctor, in the event they became separated from their parents in a hasty retreat. But so far it had been unnecessary to implement any such contingency. They had remained here unmolested longer than at any previous hideout—cave or cabin.

Michael Drummond came from the woods, his rifle in one hand, the two wild turkeys he had killed in the other. It was the first clear day this corner of the territory had seen for weeks, and the sun felt warm on his face. He smelled the fry-bread Annie and Betty Jo Proctor were cooking and knew his son, *Tsi-mi*, along with Jack and Janie, would be counting the drops of dough as they plopped into the hot grease where they would magically expand to four or five times their original size. The children would watch them bubble, waiting patiently for these wonderful treats which, piping hot, they would dip into the pot of honey, the last of three such pots they had discovered in the cabin.

Annie and Betty Jo went about their work, affectionately nudging the children out of their way from time to time. The two women exchanged a knowing look after glancing at *E-gi-ni*, who sat pouting in the corner. Silently she rubbed oil into the saddle that had belonged to her late brother, *Do-tsu-wa*. When Michael entered with the two birds, James ran excitedly to him.

"*E-to-da!*" *Tsi-mi* squealed. "*Gŭ-ni! Gŭ-ni!*" he poked each bird with an inquisitive, chubby finger.

Michael leaned the rifle against the wall and scooped his son up in one arm. Annie relieved Michael of the birds and gave him a peck on the cheek.

"Well! He finally hit something!" she teased.

"We'll eat good," Michael slapped her affectionately on the behind. "For a couple of days, anyway."

Annie had just flopped the turkey's up onto the table when everyone froze at the distant sound of a shrill whistle. They counted silently to three and the whistle was repeated. *E-gi-ni* sprang for the door.

"Johnny's back!"

Everyone headed outside to greet the returning warriors. It had been unanimously decided that the women and children would no longer accompany the men on their dangerous missions. And they had agreed that—on a rotating basis—one of the men would always remain with the women and children when the others went out. True, it had reduced their numbers in dealing with highwaymen and marauders, but the growing bounty on their heads—put there by the U. S. Army—necessitated a home guard. Even though the double whistles were the pre-arranged signal for friendly approach, Michael grabbed the rifle leaning beside the door just as a precaution, hanging it loosely in the crook of his arm.

E-gi-ni was the first out the door, followed by Jimmy, then Michael and Annie. Janie and Jack charged past them and Betty Jo stopped in the doorway, wiping her hands on her dress before shading her eyes against the sun. Coming toward them up the narrow, sloping trail were *Tsa-tsi* Starr and *Ne-di* Proctor, riding single file. Behind them walked Susanna, leading Tom Carver's horse with Meg and *Me-li* aboard. Johnny walked beside the other horse ridden by William.

"There's someone with them," Annie said nervously. Both Susanna and William had undergone such transformation that, through the trees and shadows at this distance, Michael didn't recognize his own family.

"Looks like a man, a woman and a couple of kids," he shaded his eyes, straining for a better look.

"Great," *E-gi-ni* grumbled. "More mouths to feed."

Michael shared her concern, but for different reasons. "We agreed—we never bring in strangers," he said.

Annie's concern had vanished, replaced by the beginnings of a smile. She still couldn't see—with her eyes—but she could *see*.

"They aren't strangers," she said in a matter-of-fact tone.

Michael looked at her, puzzled. She flashed him her familiar raised-eyebrow smile and casually walked back to sit in the doorway at Betty Jo's feet where she pulled *Tsi-mi* between her knees. Michael, still alert and curious, leaned back against the wall beside the door, the rifle propped against the cabin beside him. They would wait. Once *Tsa-tsi*, *Ne-di* and their visitors emerged from the trees into the sunlight, things would become clear. Either they were captives—which no one seriously considered—or they were friends who, for whatever reason, had run afoul of the authorities and were in need of a safe haven.

E-gi-ni couldn't wait. She trotted a few paces down the grade to be the first to greet her Johnny. Behind *Tsa-tsi* and *Ne-di* she saw Susanna leading the horse. And walking close beside Johnny. They weren't touching, but their close proximity didn't go unnoticed. *E-gi-ni's* only outward reaction was a subtle narrowing of the eyes to a squint, which most would have attributed to the sun in her face.

When the group finally reached the cabin, William stiffly dismounted. Janie and Jack raced out to *Ne-di*. Jimmy scampered out behind them and bumped right into William, who scooped him up with his left arm. Jimmy laughed, patted William's cheeks and then squirmed to get down. William lowered the child who immediately ran away, pausing to look back at the tall, older man who had just held him. William was transfixed. Jimmy began circling Jack and Janie, showing off as little boys will do. William continued up toward the cabin, but stopped abruptly. There, a few feet away, was his son, Michael. The two men recognized one another, but it took a while to absorb the marked changes each had undergone since they were last together. Michael's hair hung below his shoulders, and although it was mid-winter, his skin was still darkly tanned. William, older, thinner and much grayer than Michael remembered him, had also acquired a beard over the last several months. Stooped by the burden of the past year, he looked considerably shorter than his six-foot-four-inch height.

"Michael! Son!"

Michael rushed to embrace his father. Susanna had taken Meg off the horse and was holding the wide-eyed, curious little nymph on her hip. They were only a few feet away from Michael, but, as had happened with Reba and Ezekiel near Paducah, Kentucky, Susanna remained unrecognized. Michael looked right at her over William's shoulder and didn't know her. She kept her expression blank, betraying nothing. She had come to enjoy the *incognito* effect wrought by the many changes she had undergone. Michael stepped back from the embrace, holding his father at arm's length.

"I can't believe it! What are you doing here?"

"You don't know? We're *Tsa-la-gi*, son."

Michael was dumbstruck. "We're...?"

"Cherokee," William repeated.

"But I got your letter. There was nothing about..."

"It all happened after that letter," William explained. "It was my great grandmother. Titus Ogilvie dug it out of the records. They came and took our farm. Everything. We're here for the same reason all the other Cherokees are here."

Michael looked around—still not recognizing Susanna—his brow knit with concern. "Where's Mother?"

William looked at the ground and ran his fingers through his lengthening gray hair before facing his son. His eyes spoke the answer sooner than the words. "There were camps. Like prisons. Hundreds died. Your mother's health..." his voice trailed off into a sad, raspy sigh. Again Michael embraced his father, each man choking back the tears.

"What's this about?" Michael asked when they separated. He gestured at William's right arm which, partly from habit, partly from lingering discomfort, he often kept stiffly bent and pressed against his side as though it were still in a sling.

"This? Another gift from the Ogilvie's—the youngest boy. They followed us all the way to Kentucky. Believe it or not, he was riding Stick! He must have stolen him from Chief Ross or Charlie Swimmer. I'll tell you all about it..." William wasn't in the mood to detail their journey just yet.

When they started toward the cabin, Michael held onto the arm of the man he had missed so painfully. Only now did he acknowledged to himself how much of a struggle it had been to swallow the longing and the sadness.

"Annie was right," Michael forced a little laugh. "She said you'd be here."

"Annie? She said that?" William found it odd. After a couple of steps, he stopped and looked back at Susanna and Meg. Michael studied the woman who was standing close to Johnny. She spoke in low tones, her hand resting in a familiar way on Johnny's arm—a gesture that didn't register with William but did not go unnoted by Michael, Annie and *E-gi-ni*.

"Looks like *Tsa-ni* found something interesting," Michael commented. *E-gi-ni* overheard him. She stared down the path at Johnny and Susanna, her head cocked a little to one side, hand on hip, waiting impatiently for Johnny to hurry up the path to embrace *his woman.*

Johnny shifted his position, giving Michael a clear view of the woman who finally made eye contact with him and smiled. Michael's eyes widened with recognition and amazement. They moved toward each other, hesitant at first, then hurrying the last few steps into a loving embrace—something which in the animosity of years past neither would have dreamed possible. But Michael couldn't hug her for long. He held her back for another look, taking in her long, braided hair done up in a twist behind her head. Her skin, once a shielded alabaster, was tanned so darkly from the summer sun that it hadn't lost its deep, olive hue even in the intervening weeks of winter.

"I can't believe this is my sister! It's impossible. *Tsa-ni!* This is Susie! My sister!" he blurted out what everyone else apparently already knew.

"We've met," Susanna said, looking back at Johnny.

"He saved our lives! We were attacked," William, like Susanna and Michael, was still amazed by their fortuitous, circumstantial—some might even say divinely orchestrated—meeting.

"Carver's gang," Johnny answered Michael's questioning look. With a glance at Susanna he added, "He won't be bothering any more *Tsa-la-gi*. You should have seen her. A real she-wolf!"

"Susanna?" Michael's astonishment continued to grow.

"Gutted him like a hog," Johnny confirmed. "Except he wasn't hanging by his heels."

"Please. That's enough!" Susanna didn't want to relive the horror.

"I'm sorry," Johnny apologized, realizing it was still a sensitive issue for her. Their eyes dwelt in each other. Much too long to suit *E-gi-ni*, who wedged herself between them. She slipped her arms around Johnny's waist and gave him a hug.

"I'm so glad you're safe. I was so worried," she said as one might to a husband. Johnny, embarrassed, officially introduced *E-gi-ni*.

"Susanna. Mr. Drummond. This is Agnes."

"*E-gi-ni*," she corrected him, insisting on the *Tsa-la-gi* form of her name. She thought that, in some way, it linked her closer to Johnny than this almost-*yo-neg*, *Tsa-la-gi*-only-by-accident intruder ever hoped to be. "Johnny and I have been together since...since my brother got killed...saving *Tsa-ni's* life."

"I see," Susanna said in an off-handed way that made *E-gi-ni* wonder how much Johnny had told Susanna—or had *not* told her—on their ride back to the cabin.

"You must be exhausted, *Tsa-ni*. Come on." *E-gi-ni* pulled him away and up toward the cabin. Johnny looked back at Susanna, who smiled, enjoying his obvious discomfort. Michael came up beside her and spoke to Meg in a gentle tone.

"And this little lady is...?" Michael assumed she was Susanna's but wanted a formal introduction.

"This is Meg. Margaret Elizabeth," Susanna told him. Meg leaned against her mother's leg until Susanna picked her up.

"Good. That's a good name," Michael gave his sister an approving nod. "Hello, Meg. I'm your Uncle Michael."

Meg looked at her mother, not understanding, and shyly buried her face in Susanna's shoulder. Michael quietly asked his sister, "And where is Meg's father...?"

In Susanna's shrug of dismissal Michael saw the remnants of her pain. "In a drunken stupor somewhere, I suppose. Or dead, if there's any justice in the world." She forced a smile and beckoned to the other little girl who had almost been forgotten. "And this is Mary. *Me-li*. She's with us now."

"Hello, *Me-li*," Michael smiled at the shy waif who tried to remain hidden behind Susanna. Michael looked around and spotted James playing with Janie and Jack across the clearing. "*Tsi-mi! E-he-na! Tsi-mi!*" he called. James broke away from his familiar playmates and ran to his father.

Annie appeared with a platter of food from the cabin, stopping right in front of Susanna.

"*Si-yo, 'ge-yu-ts'*," Annie said softly, welcoming her sister-in-law in Cherokee. Susanna grasped the full meaning of acceptance carried in the greeting.

"*Si-yo, 'ge-yu-ts'*," she repeated the salutation.

Annie handed the tray of food to Michael and picked *Tsi-mi* up. "This is your grandfather," she told her son and held him close to William.

"Yes. We met. Earlier," William smiled at the beautiful child who before today had existed only in his imagination.

"And this is your cousin, Meg," Michael said, indicating the little girl balanced on Susanna's hip.

"Meg! Meg! Meg!" *Tsi-mi* repeated the name. They touched each other curiously as children do, each one eyeing the other up and down. William picked up *Me-li* and stepped in close to join them. He felt the family bond he had longed for so many times when they were on the river and on their overland journey. *Me-li's* arm was on William's shoulder, her little fingers twisting in the long hair on the back of his neck. She waited for *Tsi-mi* to look at her long enough for her to tell him.

"My mother is in the river," she said softly. *Tsi-mi* stared at her, not understanding. Annie lovingly touched the little girl's face.

* * * * * * *

No one complained about the cabin being crowded that night. The reunited family and the rest of the raiders sat around the blazing fire. Behind them the remains of a two-turkey feast and fry-bread still covered the table. *E-gi-ni* was careful to keep herself positioned between Johnny and Susanna, frequently touching him and making her customary possessive grooming gestures. The children played around and under the table with the stripped turkey bones and made frequent trips to the stove in search of a remnant of fry-bread left in the warming pan, deaf to the repeated motherly cautions not to burn themselves.

William had brought them up to date on their journey to this point. He had been reluctant to abandon Chief Ross, but Susanna's bloody condition following her ordeal with Carver, combined with Johnny's unexpected presentation of Michael's Collier repeating pistol had persuaded him. They had spoken little on the ride back to the secluded cabin, but *Tsa-tsi* and *Ne-di* had quietly reassured him that the Carver gang's robbery attempt had been successfully thwarted and *Gu-wi-s-gu-wi* and the rest of his party were safe.

Susanna dug through the lone pack she had managed to grab from the camp when Johnny rescued them from the Carver gang. She found the letter pouch Elizabeth had given her.

"It's from Mother," she said, caressing the old leather. "She made me promise to give it to you."

Michael took it from her. Sensing its importance, he handled it with great care. "What is it?"

"I don't know," Susanna said strangely. "A letter, I suppose. She wouldn't let us look. She said only you were to open it."

Michael broke the wax seal, unbuckled the tiny leather straps and opened the pouch. Gently he unfolded the single piece of paper that was now weathered and stained. He looked on one side then turned it over. To their astonishment, the paper was completely blank. Michael and Susanna looked at each other, then to their father, who could only shake his head. No one understood until

Annie explained. She spoke with the quiet confidence of one who had been there when Elizabeth had first sealed the pouch.

"The message is that the two of you are brother and sister and should be together," she said, then looked at each one before adding, "and love each other. Remember how you used to fight all the time?"

Brother and sister caught each other's eye. Smiles gave way to soft laughter.

"God, we hated each other!" Michael said with a grin.

"When you left, I said as far as I was concerned, it was good riddance," Susanna confessed, gazing past him as though replaying that distant moment outside the Atlanta mansion the night of the governor's ball. "I never thought I'd be so glad to see you. And you, too, Annie," she said in a penitent tone. "I was so cruel to you. Please forgive me. I hope we can be friends."

"Not just friends, Susanna," Annie smiled. "We're family."

Michael took his sister's hands and studied her. "I still can't believe it's you," he said, shaking his head incredulously.

Hours more were passed conversing, reminiscing and catching up. *Tsi-mi* lay asleep in the lap of his father who sat with his father, smoking a pipe which they shared with Johnny and *Ne-di* and *Tsa-tsi*. Betty Jo and *E-gi-ni* were at the other end of the single, long room, almost finished with the after-meal clean up. Betty Jo, as usual, worked quietly, without complaining. *E-gi-ni* continuously glanced at the others. Though Susanna was talking mostly to Michael, she had positioned herself so there was frequent eye contact with Johnny. *E-gi-ni* noticed. And so did Annie.

"Peter was in charge of the prison camp," Susanna continued her account of their days at Coosawattee.

"Why didn't he get you out of there?" Michael asked.

"We couldn't leave. We're Cherokee. It still sounds strange to say that. And Peter...well..."

"You don't want to talk about Peter, do you?" Michael sensed her reluctance.

"No. She doesn't," Johnny answered for her. Everyone looked at him, puzzled by his unexpected interjection.

"No. I don't want to talk about Peter," Susanna confirmed.

E-gi-ni looked from Johnny to Susanna. And back to Johnny. *What was going on here?* She bit her lip and said nothing, but she was definitely not pleased with the nearly palpable energy crackling between her man and this intruder.

Susanna changed the subject. "So, Michael. You and Johnny

have been protecting Cherokees from the likes of this Tom Carver. You're sort of a Cherokee Robin Hood?"

That was it for *E-gi-ni*. She startled everyone by noisily dropping a tin plate into the wash bucket. She had never heard of a robin hood, but she would not have her man likened to a timid little song bird! "My Johnny is no robin. No *Tsi-s-quo-quo*. He is *wo-ha-li*! An eagle!"

"An eagle," Susanna repeated softly, looking into Johnny's eyes. "Yes. I know."

* * * * * * *

Full of good food and warmed by the fire, the children were soon ready for sleep, as were a number of the adults. The cabin, now home to fourteen—nine adults and five children, offered no real privacy for anyone. Sleeping areas had been unofficially staked out but no clear lines were drawn. *Ne-di* and Betty Jo had retired to the far end of the rectangular cabin with Jack and Janie. *Tsa-tsi* assumed his customary position where he would sleep sitting on the floor, his back against the wall beside the door. *Tsi-mi* Drummond slept in his mother's arms. Annie leaned against Michael whose back was against the wall near the fireplace. The on-going conversation among her, Michael, William and Susanna was kept low so as not to disturb the others. Johnny sat on the opposite side of the fireplace across from Michael. He drifted in and out of sleep, his head tilted back against the wall. Each time he awoke, his drowsy eyes found Susanna, a fact of which she was keenly aware. *E-gi-ni* slept on the floor beside Johnny. Her hand rested on his leg just above the ankle as though holding on to her prized possession.

Michael tried to explain to his father that he and his family weren't living like outlaws on the run because of the incident back in Georgia involving Titus Ogilvie. *Ne-di* and *Tsa-tsi* had fled west following their escape from the cave in North Carolina the day Annie's father was killed and Michael and James were captured.

"No one out here knew anything about the governor's ball," Michael said, "and we haven't lived like this the whole time."

"No. Sometimes it's been in caves," Annie teased with a seed of truth.

"Caves?!" Susanna found the idea appalling.

"Stop it, Annie! She's teasing," Michael calmed his sister. "We had a nice farm over near Ft. Coffee. That's where Jimmy was born. But the *yo-neg* soldiers came and burned it down."

668

"We got out just minutes ahead of them," Annie added.

"Certainly you don't plan to live like fugitives for the rest of your lives!" William found it all too incredible.

"That's what I'm telling you," Michael's sounded exasperated. "None of this was planned. But it's out of our hands now."

"I won't have my grandchildren growing up like this," William said. He touched *Tsi-mi*, and looked down at Meg, asleep in Susanna's arms, and *Me-li* on the floor just beyond.

"Do we have a choice?" Annie asked softly.

William pursed his mouth and gnawed the inside of his nether lip. It had been a lifelong habit when probing the complexities of a multi-faceted problem. Finally he had formulated what he thought was a workable answer.

"I'll go over to Ft. Smith and talk to General Arbuckle."

"He's a hard man," Michael countered. "And he hates Indians. Especially Cherokees!"

"Nonsense," William said, recalling the genuinely sympathetic position taken by General Winfield Scott. They were all intelligent men. They merely needed to come together, discuss the problem openly and honestly and arrive at an equitable resolution.

"You're forgetting, Father. You're not a respected attorney out here," Susanna reminded him. "You're just another Cherokee Indian."

"Well, at least we're together as a family. It's going to be all right," William conceded her point. He would come up with another plan tomorrow. But he was convinced he could work things out. This is what he had done all his adult life. And he would do it again for his children and his grandchildren. It would be all right.

"No, it's not all right, Father," Michael knew too well his father's mannerism that began *Well, at least...* It only meant William was postponing the battle until he had devised a strategy to guarantee his victory. But this was much more serious, and Michael had to make him understand. "You and Susie—and Meg—you'll be in serious trouble if you're caught here with us. Johnny and me—and *Tsa-tsi* and *Ne-di*—we're fugitives. There's a price on our heads. If the army or the territory marshall find us, they'll kill us."

William pondered the gravity of his son's words. He looked around at the rest of the people in the cabin. "What about Betty Jo and their children? And Agnes?"

"They made their choice," Annie said. "We all did."

William put his hand on his son's shoulder and looked him in the eye. "Well, I've made my choice. Susie?" They awaited

Susanna's verdict. She looked down at Meg, then at *Tsi-mi* and Annie.

"I think Meg has taken quite a shine to her cousin Jimmy. How could I separate them now? We're family."

Michael was pleased with his sister's decision, but his concern for their safety remained. "I hope you know what you're doing."

PART III

More than 2,000 Cherokees died in the concentration camps before their westward journey had even begun. Another estimated 2,000 died on the Trail Of Tears during the harsh winter of 1838-39. In all, nearly one-fourth of the entire tribe perished.

The last group of Cherokees arrived in Indian Territory on March 24, 1839, after 185 brutal days on the road.

Many Cherokees who had recently arrived, along with others who had been in the west for some time, gathered to meet them.

57

Near Ft. Gibson, Indian Territory

The beautiful meadow, budding with the signs of spring, was already crowded with Cherokees by mid morning, and more continued to pour in from the surrounding farms and towns. Many were Old Settlers—Cherokees who had been in the west since shortly after the turn of the century. President Jefferson and the politicians of his day had begun making speeches and public statements that became, for the Cherokee and many other Indian tribes in the eastern part of the continent, the handwriting on the wall. Another group had even split off from the Old Settlers and had moved down into the rolling hills and thick pine forests of East Texas. The terrain, the climate and the red clay soil there reminded them of their beloved homeland in northern Georgia.

For the Old Settlers who had been in Indian Territory more than three decades, the forced removal of their fellow Cherokees from the southeast meant reunion with family and friends they hadn't seen in a long time. It also created some apprehension and anxiety on the part of many. They had established their own leadership out west. They had their own chiefs, their own way of doing things. Their government structure was less rigid than in the east. Without the influence of mixed-bloods with their eastern university educations, printing presses and fancy ways of talking and speech-making, the Old Settlers had reverted to a primarily agrarian society. Their government was as undemanding and unobtrusive as they could make it, and most of them preferred it that way. There was a growing fear among the Old Settlers that the advent of the national tribal council and all the eastern leaders would impose upon them strictures neither warranted nor welcome. But on this day, they had gathered to greet old friends and relatives and even strangers who shared their heritage, their ancestry, their *Tsa-la-gi* blood.

Joining the Old Settlers were the Cherokees who had arrived more recently. Many, like Major Ridge and his followers, who had come to be known as *The Treaty Party*, had begun migrating west soon after the Treaty Of New Echota was ratified by the U. S. Senate in May of 1836.

The rest of the Cherokees gathering near Ft. Gibson were those who had been rounded up beginning in the early summer of

1838. The ones who had been held in filthy, disease infested concentration camps for weeks—some for *months*—before being packed onto keelboats and dragged behind steamboats up and down the rivers or forced to endure untold hardships of disease, starvation and the savage elements on the overland trail. These Cherokees had come to be identified as members of *The Ross Party.*

On this day, leaders of all factions hoped to set aside their differences in a heartfelt celebration of triumph of the *Tsa-la-gi* Spirit as the last of the land travellers arrived. Those who had come to this place on the Trail Of Tears, as well as those who had already been in the west for a couple of years, sincerely hoped the new arrivals would find a good place to live. Things would settle down. Crops would be planted. Cabins and frame houses would be erected. Green Corn dances and Ripe Corn and Great New Moon ceremonies would be celebrated. There would be Bouncing Bush feasts and the *U-ku,* or Chief Dance, and stomp dances and hog fries and *A-ne-tsa,* the stick-ball games. And for some of the mixed-bloods who had grown accustomed to such things back east, even the occasional cotillion with orchestra.

But shoulder to shoulder with these benevolent thoughts and good wishes marched a bitter, more realistic expectation, cloaked darkly in a brooding vengeance and the bloody raiment of tribal law. Thoughts of conspiracy and plotting and meetings in the night, leading inevitably to a cycle of death. Suspicion. Accusation. Revenge. And more death and continued division among their people.

The mood—on the surface at least—was festive, but controlled. A speakers' platform had been erected on one side of the meadow adjacent to some trees. Presumably, the tribal leaders—of whichever faction—would make speeches. A company of soldiers from Ft. Gibson were stationed around the meadow to keep things orderly, but so far there had been no sign of any disturbance.

In charge of the military detail was Sergeant Wakefield, the one who had arrested Michael Drummond at his farm and carted him off to jail at Ft. Smith just across the line in Arkansas Territory. Following Johnny Fields' escape from the Ft. Smith stockade and the death of Sergeant Lawrence Bolton—both of which Wakefield had taken personally—the sergeant's request for reassignment to Ft. Gibson, Indian Territory, had been granted. This, he was convinced, would place him in closer proximity and afford him better opportunities to track down and bring to justice these murdering outlaw savages. Wakefield and a squad of his men mingled among the Cherokees. Their demeanor was low-keyed, but their watchful eyes constantly roamed the ever-thickening crowd. From atop his horse, Wakefield studied the Cherokees streaming past him or surveyed groups gathered in the shade of the sprawling oaks and elm trees.

The venerable, white-haired Major Ridge moved among the people, visiting old friends he hadn't seen since leaving in the early spring of '37. With him were his son, John Ridge, and nephews, Elias Boudinot and Elias's brother, Stand Watie, along with other members of The Treaty Party. They made a point throughout the morning of remaining on the opposite side of the meadow from the speaker's platform where John Ross, his brother, Lewis, Hair Conrad, George Lowrey and other eastern tribal leaders had been assembled. The Ross Party mingled with the Old Settlers, hoping to allay their political fears and to enlist their support in reestablishing the national government structure in the west. Most of the Old Settlers, however, remained noncommittal, preferring to adopt a wait-and-see attitude. And between the other two groups—the Treaty Party and the Ross Party—there were the inevitable looks, whispers and nudges, each group clearly aware of the other, yet neither eager to initiate contact.

Sergeant Wakefield rode his horse at a leisurely walk amid the throng, enjoying the smell of the beef, pork and turkey that filled the air from the roasting pits heating up in anticipation of the final arrivals. He saw many faces that were vaguely familiar from his duties at the supply depot and others who, he figured, had arrived more recently or who got their supplies and allotments elsewhere. But the constantly moving eyes in his otherwise expressionless countenance were searching for two faces in particular—Michael Drummond and Johnny Fields. Wakefield eased his horse past an older man surrounded by his family—sons, daughters, grandchildren—and headed for the water barrel adjacent to the speakers platform to refill his canteen.

When Wakefield moved on across the meadow, the old man and his family breathed easier and exchanged looks of relief. The sergeant would have had no reason to recognize William Drummond. The men he was looking for—Michael and Johnny—had been carrying *Tsi-mi* and Meg on their shoulders and had kept their hats pulled low on their faces. He might have recognized Annie, but, like Susanna, Betty Jo and *E-gi-ni*, her head was covered and she kept her eyes down. *Tsa-tsi* and *Ne-di* carried Jack and Janie Proctor, holding them so as to obscure Wakefield's view of their faces.

Johnny walked beside Susanna—close enough to bump shoulders on occasion on their slow progress across the meadow. Annie sped up a little to come even with Michael and Johnny.

"Don't get cocky, you two," she warned. "You know good and well who they're looking for."

"These soldiers are looking for you?" Susanna asked. The hard reality of their outlaw status and the tales told at the cabin suddenly became chillingly clear.

Johnny downplayed the significance of the army presence with a bit of bravado. "Let's just say, we know them and they know us."

"Maybe we should go," Susanna urged.

"We'll be all right," Michael's attempt to reassure his sister wasn't entirely convincing. Annie flashed Susanna a look that said *I've heard that one before!*

William's wounded right shoulder was healing nicely, but it tired quickly. He shifted *Me-li* to his left hip and continued searching faces in the crowd. Somehow the child anticipated his intention.

"Can we find *Tsisdu*?" she asked softly.

"Yes. I'm hoping he'll be here today," William said. He had grown most fond of the twitchy-faced, wiry little man and had missed him tremendously since the night he, Susanna and the girls had ridden away with Johnny, leaving *Tsisdu* behind with *Gu-wi-s-gu-wi's* band south of Little Rock. And William knew how much Meg and *Me-li* had come to love the eccentric little diviner, with his tall tales and his bandanna-wrapped crystals.

"*Rabbit Man*, I call him," Susanna told the others about their friend. "We met him on the river. He saved *Me-li* from drowning. He's an odd one, but you'll like him. He reads the crystals."

"You believe in the crystals?" Johnny looked at her.

"Well, I didn't at first..."

"But now?" he bumped her, teasing.

"Now I'm not so sure," Susanna admitted. "Some of the things he said are...well...interesting, to say the least."

"You're not at all like Michael described you."

Susanna smiled, pleased that Michael had told Johnny about her and, knowing those reports had probably been less than favorable, equally pleased she now presented an image more to his liking. "Perhaps, I'm no longer the sister he described," she replied.

E-gi-ni appeared from behind and wedged herself in between Johnny and Susanna. She brought Meg down from Johnny's shoulders.

"Here. Let me take her."

Meg wasn't especially fond of *E-gi-ni*. She squirmed and leaned, reaching for her mother, and *E-gi-ni* was glad to hand the child over. Meg would keep Susanna occupied and there would be less of what *E-gi-ni* suspected was not-so-accidental bumping and not-so-innocent touching. And she was determined this time to maintain her rightful position at Johnny's side.

The entire entourage came to a halt, almost running into the back of William, who had stopped a few feet away from a group of Cherokee men smoking their pipes, whittling and telling stories. There among them, wearing a bright red turban, was the wiry, animated Rabbit Man, *Tsisdu*, engaged in an exaggerated recounting of some adventure back in the old country.

"*Si-yo! Tsisdu! Tsisdu!*" *Me-li* was the first to call out to him.

Johnny leaned across in front of *E-gi-ni* and said softly to Susanna, "There's your Rabbit Man."

"Where...?"

She stepped out in front of *E-gi-ni* to look past her father.

"There. With those men. See? In the red turban," Johnny pointed him out. Susanna finally spotted *Tsisdu*.

"Wait a minute! How did you know?!" she asked in amazement.

Tsisdu looked around and located the little voice that had called his name. A grin spread across his face, and his nose crinkled with its characteristic twitch. He limped hurriedly toward them. *Me-li* leaned out of William's arms to be taken by *Tsisdu*.

"*Tsisdu! Tsisdu!*" she squealed.

"I've been looking for you all morning," William said.

"I was hoping you'd be here," *Tsisdu* held *Me-li* perched on one arm while he shook William's hand vigorously. "I see you found your son," he nodded to Michael.

"Just as you predicted," William grinned. "And how we found him is an amazing story. We—"

Tsisdu's eyes widened and he stepped past William. To the astonishment of the others, Johnny stepped out to greet him.

"*Sa-lo-li! U-we-tsi!*" *Tsisdu* called his son by his pet name, Squirrel.

"*E-to-da!*" Johnny acknowledged his father with a broad smile and a big embrace. *Me-li* hugged them both, finding it all just so much fun. Susanna, her hand covering her mouth in disbelief, joined

676

them. When Johnny and his father broke their embrace, *Tsisdu* saw her.

"Susie! We were so worried about you and the girls!"

"*Tsisdu! Tsisdu!*" Meg echoed *Me-li's* earlier squeals, equally delighted to see her friend and favorite story teller. She jumped from her mother's arms, and *Tsisdu* found himself in the familiar role of holding his two special girls. It was clear to everyone they truly adored this peculiar little one-eyed man.

Annie bumped hard into Michael and stepped in front of him. "*Ha-nu-wa!*" she warned.

Their joyous reunion had attracted the idle curiosity of a soldier leaning against the speaker's platform a few yards away. Annie had succeeded in blocking the corporal's view of Michael and Johnny. Michael kept his back to the soldier as he bent down and picked up *Tsi-mi*. The entire group drifted like a single, pulsating organism toward the shade opposite the platform. The soldier followed them for a while with his eyes, then soon lost interest. He pulled out his tobacco pouch and casually began stuffing his cheeks.

William and the others adeptly put a few trees between themselves and the soldier. But before the celebration with *Tsisdu* could resume, shouts came from the far end of the meadow out near the road.

"They're here!"

"Here they come!"

"It's them! I see them!"

The sea of waiting Cherokees ebbed across the meadow toward the road leading in from the northeast. The last group of the *Tsa-la-gi* to be forcefully removed from their beloved homeland had finally arrived. The long anticipated reunions between friends and family began as soon as the first wagons rolled in. Each road-weary traveller immediately searched the crowd for a familiar face. For many, that desperately sought countenance would not appear. The long carried dread of a loved one lost became heart-wrenching reality as that loved one's death was reported. A new arrival, unable to find the friend or relative whose image had sustained the exhausted traveller over so many hard miles, sought someone who knew for certain. Someone to verify the rumors.

Was my sister just unable to come to the celebration today?

Did my brother perish on the trail?

When did he die?

Where?

Did you see her buried? Where? Where exactly?

Were you there, or did you just hear it from someone who heard it from someone else?

But the predominant emotion was one of overwhelming relief. Despite what had happened to them, the losses—material, personal, spiritual—which they had suffered, the torture, the pain, the indignities they had endured, it was over. They had made it. They were here. Theirs was the fire that knew no extinction. The fire of the Eternal Flame. It was time to make a new start. They would weep for the loved ones who had perished. They would mourn the loss of a friend, a relative, a history, a homeland. But tomorrow they would pick up the pieces and start anew. Such had always been the spirit of the *Tsa-la-gi*, and this would be no different. Theirs was the fire that knew no extinction. Baked by scorching sun, choked by dust, deluged by floods, frozen by bitter cold, whipped and beaten by the scourge of *yo-neg* greed and hatred, they would rise again from the ashes, as suggested by the name of their former newspaper, *The Cherokee Phoenix*, for theirs was the fire that knew no extinction.

* * * * * * *

Members of the Ross Party greeted as many of the arrivals as possible, out of heartfelt gladness that they had survived the trip, but also not without an eye to shoring up their political position. At the same time, members of the Ridge faction, or the Treaty Party, were equally busy greeting the newcomers in an attempt to establish good will. Some Cherokees had come west under better circumstances than others—in less inclement weather and with better access to government provisions. But they were all here now, and they were all brothers and sisters with one common goal: to restore the once proud *Tsa-la-gi* nation.

The truth was that most of these hungry, sick and exhausted travellers had little or no interest in matters political. The cry of their stomachs drowned out the polemics of those who had come to greet them with an agenda. Their eyes were on the sides of beef and pork and the roasting spits crowded with turkey, chicken, quail, pheasant, rabbit and squirrel as they waited patiently in line for what, to them, was a king's feast.

William and Susanna finally located the Swimmers. When Sally saw Meg, she ran to hug the younger child as though she were being reunited with her lost little sister. Eva and Susanna shared a similar reunion, with as few words but with considerably more emotion. It was at once a reunion of joy and sadness. They were thrilled to find each other, but the news of *Tsu-Tsu's* drowning in the frozen waters of the Mississippi left the Drummonds devastated.

No one ever revealed why *Tsu-tsu* had come to be in the icy river in the first place. Charlie had vowed to take to his grave the conversation he'd shared with his son when *Tsu-tsu* announced his intention to cross to Cape Girardeau to get medicine for his mother and Sally. It was better, Charlie thought, that Eva never know, lest she spend the rest of her life blaming herself. Her baby had died going to get medicine for her. Charlie had known and hadn't stopped him. Each carried questions that would forever remain unuttered. And forever unanswered. Eva's unsolved mystery would always be *What was my son doing in that deadly river?* And Charlie would never stop asking himself *Why didn't I prevent my son from going near that deadly river?* Mother and father would openly and lovingly recall their son's life, but neither would ever discuss the details of *Tsu-tsu's* tragic and untimely passing.

The Drummond party and the Swimmer family waited together for their food. There was nothing either could say that the other hadn't already experienced. Perhaps in years to come, when the pain had numbed, they would sit around the fire and talk about their survival of this incredible ordeal. For now, silence better suited the soul's palate.

The adults watched Sally showing Janie Proctor the wedding-dress doll she had tenaciously clung to throughout the entire trip. Buck Swimmer had immediately befriended Jack Proctor. The two of them decided it would be the manly thing to take the younger, less experienced *Tsi-mi* Drummond under their wing. They would keep an eye on him while the grown ups visited, and there were many important things which they—being much older and wiser—could teach him.

Despite the sadness of their losses, the Drummonds and the Swimmers and all those who comprised their extended family had much to be thankful for on this day of celebration. They would eat good food. They would spend the day together. They would visit friends, lending words of consolation and encouragement. They would talk of planting and of hunting. They would plan for the future but they would never forget the past. Or their homes in Georgia, Tennessee, Alabama, North Carolina. Homes that had been theirs and their fathers' and their fathers' before them. Homes given to them by The Great Spirit. Homes taken away by a president, a government, an army of a nation that had come to their country, had seen their forested hills and majestic mountains, their

679

pristine rivers, lakes and streams, their fertile valleys and had decided all these things were good. And they wanted them. And the *Tsa-la-gi* must be driven out. In the name of God, progress and civilization. The *Tsa-la-gi* would never forget.

* * * * * * *

Throughout the afternoon the river of newly arriving Cherokees continued to flow into the meadow. The last group, knowing they were almost to their new home, had allowed themselves to become strung out much longer than usual along the road. Some, eager to arrive, had arisen early, broken camp and gotten on their way.

Others realized their long and arduous journey was nearing an end. The weather was good. They would make their destination easily before nightfall. These had lingered, resting a little longer before taking to the road. Death and tragedy had been the driving animus in their miserable lives for the past several months. But their relief at having survived and their eagerness to begin a new life that would be—most of them believed—free from the oppressive yoke of a *yo-neg* government, couldn't help but generate a festive spirit.

E-gi-ni managed for most of the day to keep herself between Johnny and Susanna. She pouted, she primped and preened, she touched and cooed. And finally she convinced Johnny to take a walk with her—far away from the others—to a grove of trees at the far side of the meadow where she made a last-ditch plea.

"Who are you trying to fool, Johnny? You're no father. No family man. You're an outlaw! You need a *Tsa-la-gi* woman!" she petitioned, hoping to persuade him that she had only his best interest at heart.

"She is—" Johnny was about to say Susanna was *Tsa-la-gi*, otherwise she wouldn't be here. *E-gi-ni* saw it coming and cut him off.

"A *real* *Tsa-la-gi* woman!" she growled with disdain at the idea of calling this newcomer, this intruder, a *Tsa-la-gi*. "Not some finishing-school princess! Married to a *yo-neg a-ya-wi-s-gi!* A soldier! A white soldier!"

Johnny looked back across the meadow to where Susanna was talking to Eva Swimmer. Probably reminiscing about some incident involving *Tsu-tsu*, the son Eva had lost, he thought. Something prompted Susanna to pause and glance in their direction.

"I hate her," *E-gi-ni* said softly, almost with a tone of defeat.

680

She slammed her hand against the tree's rough bark. Johnny put his hands on her shoulders and turned her to face him. He kept her at arms length when she tried to rush into his arms. This was good, she thought. This could work. She saw it in his eyes—he had been moved. She was getting close. She just had to learn how to play him. This was good.

"Listen to me, *E-gi-ni*," he said with firmness while trying to remain kind. "I am *not* your husband. I am *not* your lover. Your brother was my friend. He saved my life. I tried to be a friend to you when we lost *Do-tsu-wa*. A *friend*. If you took it any other way, I'm sorry."

This was *not* what she wanted to hear. Not what she thought he would say. "But...what about all those nights...?" she reminded him of the many times she had slipped beneath his blanket and they had been together as man and woman. As lovers. As husband and wife.

"*You* came to *my* bed. I never asked you."

E-gi-ni felt the fire rise in her throat. He was allowed to feel sorry for her in her grief. She could turn that to her advantage. He was allowed to hold her and comfort her. She could make that work, too. But it was a grave mistake to tell her he had *entered* her only out of pity. That he had been inside her merely because she had been there. A convenience. A mounting of circumstance. Her desperate plea for love transformed itself into the fury of rejection. "You never said *No*! You never asked me to leave you alone!"

"To tell you the truth, I just felt—"

She put her hand to his lips to silence him. "Stop! If you say you just felt sorry for me, I swear, I'll take that knife you're wearing and cut off your *wa-ta-li*!"

Johnny believed her. He tried to sound compassionate and, at the same time, he declared himself innocent of wrong doing. "I was going to say, I just felt we were marking time until—"

Again she cut him off. Johnny saw that her mind was made up. Whatever he said—short of *I'm sorry and I love you*—would be wrong. "Until something better came along?" she finished for him, then added, "Something a little *whiter?*"

"You'll make someone a wonderful wife someday, *E-gi-ni*. It just won't be with me."

"You're damned right it won't!" she snapped bitterly and stormed off before he could reply. He took a few steps after her.

"Agnes! *E-gi-ni*!"

"She sounded upset."

He knew the voice from off to his right. Susanna, after seeing them earlier, had come along the edge of the meadow, arriving only seconds before *E-gi-ni* stormed off.

"She was just saying good-bye," Johnny lied. But he knew it wasn't really lying, because she *knew* he was lying. "She said to give you her best," he added. Susanna smiled and stepped close to him. She took a strand of his hair delicately between her finger, twisting it coyly before giving it a playful but painful tug. "Ow!" Johnny pulled away and looked at her.

"You liar."

"Wait," he said, pretending to jog his memory. "Come to think of it, I believe what she said was: we should both rot in hell."

"Now, *that* I believe." Susanna patted his stomach affectionately. "Come on. You must be starved. Let's feed you." Together they walked back across the meadow toward the roasting pits where food was still being served.

* * * * * * *

After a delicious meal of roasted wild turkey, fry bread and boiled corn, William loaded his pipe and went for a stroll around the meadow. Major Ridge—in the company of his son, John, and his nephew, Elias Boudinot—hailed William who, deep in thought, was about to pass them by.

"*Si-yo, Wi-li* Drummond! I didn't expect to see you here!"

William joined them and greeted John, Elias and the others before replying. "As it turns out, Major Ridge, I, too, am Cherokee."

"You always were, *Wi-li*" The Ridge said with obvious affection. "You always were. It isn't easy being Cherokee in these times."

"But it must be quite easy being *chief* of the Cherokees. So many appear to be doing it so well," the voice, thick with challenging sarcasm, came from the group approaching them. The speaker was Lewis Ross, accompanied by his brother, Chief John Ross, the Hicks brothers, George Lowrey and a handful of other tribal leaders. The chilled tension was instantly palpable between the two factions.

"But no doubt, *Gu-wi-s-gu-wi*, you're hard at work sorting it all out for the rest of us," Ridge rebounded the insult in his booming, sonorous voice.

Elias Boudinot stepped up beside his uncle. "And I'm sure you're convinced there's no room in the equation for a wag like John Rogers, who's only been chief out here for twenty years."

"Of course not!" John Ridge chimed in with artful sarcasm. "That would only muddy the waters of *true* Cherokee leadership."

"Gentlemen! Gentlemen! Please!" William positioned himself at an equal distance between the two groups. He had hoped to avoid the confrontation everyone had been predicting—some perhaps even eagerly anticipating. "Over the years, I've come to know most of you. There are great leaders on both sides of this issue. Men of great abilities. All with the welfare of the Cherokee nation foremost in their hearts. Men I number as my friends, and now, as Cherokee brothers. If ever there was a need for cooperation and diplomacy, God knows, that time is now!"

A long silence followed as the men of each faction considered their friend's entreaty. It was young John Ridge who finally answered William. "Cooperation and diplomacy. Friendship and Cherokee brotherhood. Noble words indeed, *Wi-li* Drummond," he said with sincerity, then glared fiercely at the Ross group. "But words which, I fear, serve only to cloak the darker designs of those bent on a bloody revenge."

Boudinot added to his cousin's denouncement. "Revenge against a group of *Tsa-la-gi* whose only sin was trying to save our people from the torturous trip they have just been forced to endure...at the expense of how many lives? The number we're hearing is over four thousand!"

"Four thousand Cherokees, *Gu-wi-s-gu-wi*," John took up the torch. "Four thousand of our people! All because of your self-serving, bull-headed stubbornness and pride!"

Tempers were clearly rising, and those on the outer fringes of the Ross contention began to press forward, ready for a scrap. William felt helpless as he watched the posturing and pointing from both sides. Hair Conrad raised an accusing finger at the leaders of the Treaty Party. "The deaths in those camps and on this Trail Of Tears are on *your* heads, not ours!"

Finally, John Ross stepped into the middle ground beside William and held up a hand toward each side, lobbying, as he always had, for a peaceful solution. "Stop it! *Wi-li* is right. This kind of talk only fans the flames of discord. We need to hold a council. Where everyone can be heard. And there should be no more talk of revenge. Against anyone! And no more of this foolish arguing! We'll talk when heads are cooler."

Gu-wi-s-gu-wi said good-bye to William and walked away, motioning for his people to follow. George Lowrey, Charles and Elijah Hicks and Hair Conrad went right away, but several of the fringe Ross faction, including Sam *Ta-no-wi*, lingered. They talked among themselves, casting an occasional furtive glance at the Ridge enclave who had turned their backs in a familiar Cherokee gesture intended to snub the other party.

CHAPTER
58

Ft. Gibson, Indian Territory

Ft. Gibson served as the hub of activity for the military as well as the Indian agents and all other governmental and quasi-governmental dealings with the native Americans who had been forcefully removed to Indian Territory. At times there was hardly room to pass in the middle of the street—let alone on the plank sidewalks in front of the buildings. There were soldiers, Cherokees, Creeks, Chickasaws, Choctaws and members of other tribes. There were civilian suppliers hoping to land a fat government contract or, having one, making sure their own employees weren't stealing from them the money they had stolen from the government and from the Indians.

The headquarters building stood on slightly higher ground at the eastern end of the main thoroughfare that ran through the center of the Ft. Gibson compound. Other buildings—trading posts, saloons, general merchandise establishments—had sprung up outside the fort, suggesting the beginnings of what would undoubtedly become a thriving little town.

Sixty-three year old General Matthew Arbuckle was Commander of U. S. Armed Forces in the Arkansas and Indian Territories. Had his copious eyebrows been evenly distributed over his cheeks and chin, he would have had a thick, healthy beard. An irascible, doughty old man who hated his job, hated Indians and hated everything about Indian Territory, Arbuckle spent most of his time in his headquarters at Ft. Gibson, eating or drinking the whiskey provided him by the contractors. In exchange, Arbuckle made sure that he—and those under him—conveniently looked the other way while the whiskey peddlers plied their trade just outside the gates and wherever else in the Territory they wished. But Arbuckle was strict about having no whiskey inside Ft. Gibson itself. Except, of course, for his own private cabinet to accommodate himself and his officers.

Arbuckle sat behind his huge, mahogany desk picking incessantly at his teeth. He was intent on dislodging an irritating shred of meat, once part of the carcass littering the huge platter on the serving cart off to the side.

"These are mighty serious charges, Corporal," the general studied the two young soldiers facing him from across the desk.

Lounging in a comfortable chair placed conveniently near the food cart was Major Tyler who had come over from Ft. Smith. The general's aide refilled the major's whiskey glass, then executed a tight circle to resume his statue-like stance in the corner behind Arbuckle. Major Tyler swished the amber reinforcements lazily in his glass and studied Corporals Thorpe and Evans. The two of them had initially reported to him in Ft. Smith with the charges they had just repeated to General Arbuckle. A sentry was positioned near the door, and in front of him stood the accused, Corporal Miles Franklin.

"I know it's serious, General Arbuckle," Thorpe said, then indicated the pile of gear—boots, saber, tunic—lying on the corner of the desk. "But there's your proof, right there."

The general sucked at his teeth with determination and probed with the splinter of wood. With his other hand he pulled experimentally at the dewlaps of skin that flowed over his uniform collar. His lips puckered around the wooden pick with resolve before he finally answered.

"I see no *proof* of anything, Corporal, except that this Sergeant—" he exhaled heavily and leaned forward to pick up Major Tyler's report from the desk. "Robert Barton," he read, then dropped the paper on the desk and relaxed back into his chair. "This Sergeant Barton—he isn't here and these are his things—or so you claim."

"That's what I'm saying, sir," Thorpe insisted. "He deserted!"

Evans held his hat subserviently in front of him and dipped deferentially before speaking. "Begging the general's pardon, sir, but what about Sergeant DeKalb?"

With a look of irritation at the second accuser, Arbuckle forced himself forward once more to read from the report. He scanned it, dropped it and continued digging at his teeth. "Sergeant Charles DeKalb..."

"A fine soldier, General," Thorpe testified, adding the forgotten, "Sir."

Arbuckle pointed at the pile of gear with his toothpick. "And you're saying this Sergeant Barton murdered Sergeant...?"

"DeKalb, sir," the aide filled in from his position in the corner.

Arbuckle was quite satisfied to have his assistant spare him the effort. "Any witnesses?" he raised his eyebrows at Thorpe and Evans.

"None listed in the charges, sir," the aide answered.

"Oh, there was plenty of folks seen it, General. I can tell you that," Evans testified vigorously.

"But none of them would come forward?" Arbuckle was puzzled. "Wouldn't even give you a statement?"

Tyler leaned forward for the first time and asserted with importance, "So, basically, all we have is your word against his." Tyler gestured with his near-empty whiskey glass at Miles. Corporal Franklin concentrated on a point on the wall just above the general's head and repeated his well rehearsed story.

"Sergeant Robert Barton died of pneumonia on the morning of February 18, 1839, outside of Lebanon, Missouri and was buried alongside the road in a large grave with six Cherokee adults and two black children. Go dig 'em up, if you don't believe me." Franklin's testimony was so gripping even Thorpe and Evans were momentarily confused.

"I never saw him die, General. I swear it," Thorpe felt he needed to explain to Arbuckle why he had neglected to consider this important piece of information. Evans shook his head, dismissing Franklin's account.

"We would'a seen him buried. We would'a been there."

Tyler pointed at Thorpe and Evans. "Were either of you at Sergeant—"

"DeKalb," the aide repeated.

"Were you at DeKalb's funeral?" Tyler completed his question. Thorpe and Evans looked at each other, now more confused than ever. The major was suggesting that if they weren't at DeKalb's interment, yet accepted his death, why were they disputing the death of Sergeant Barton merely on the grounds they hadn't attended his burial. "Were you? Did you see DeKalb buried?" Tyler repeated.

"Well...no...I mean, we seen him killed, but we had to get goin'," Thorpe put forth the most obvious interpretation.

"But Barton! We seen him one day — and the next day he's gone!" Evans protested.

Miles raised a finger politely and took a step forward, confident he could put the entire issue to rest with a simple explanation. "General, we were strung up and down the road for miles. I sometimes went five, six days—even a week!—without seeing either Corporal Thorpe or Corporal Evans. God knows what they were off doing." The subtle implication that they might have been engaged in unofficial—perhaps even illegal—activities had not been missed by Thorpe and Evans, so Franklin was certain Major

Tyler and General Arbuckle had gotten the message as well.

"We wasn't doin' nothin'!" Thorpe blurted out.

"That's probably very true, General," Miles admitted. His double meaning elicited a hint of a smile from the general's lips wrapped around his toothpick. "Perhaps they even deserted for a few days. Then later rejoined the party—out of remorse, patriotism—or fear of being caught and court-martialed? My point is, a lot happened out there on the trail. And on the morning of February 18, I buried Cavalry Sergeant Robert Barton, United States Army."

General Arbuckle stared across the desk at the three corporals. He rolled the end of the toothpick between his thumb and forefinger as he pondered the dilemma with the gravity of Mighty Solomon. Then suddenly he smiled broadly and displayed the shred of meat impaled on the wooden splinter.

"Got it!" he exclaimed with delight.

"Very good, sir," the aide cheered from the corner. Thorpe and Evans exchanged another confused glance, and Miles Franklin realized he was off the hook. General Matthew Arbuckle simply didn't care. The incident in question hadn't occurred in Ft. Gibson. It hadn't occurred in Indian Territory. It hadn't even occurred anywhere in Arbuckle's jurisdiction. The important thing was the general had successfully extracted that annoying scrap of meat from between his teeth.

59

Near Ft. Gibson, Indian Territory

The last of the Cherokees to come west on the Trail Of Tears pulled into the meadow near Ft. Gibson around sundown. A few of the earlier arrivals had already gone on with family or friends, but most had stayed to welcome the last to reach their new home. The supply of good food was inexhaustible, a true miracle for those who had faced starvation most of the winter. The conversations were long and rich, some even peppered with laughter. The younger men and older boys organized an impromptu *a-ne-tsa*, or stick ball game, in the center of the meadow. It was a shorter than normal field of play with the goal posts set on opposite sides of the meadow. Players, for the most part, ran stiffly and slowly. But the sheer joy of the traditional game was evident. Sticks were pegged into the ground by the older men each time a goal was scored.

A few brief speeches had been made from the specially constructed platform. There were frequent prayers from the many Cherokee Christian ministers who had travelled west. Some delivered long, rambling treatises of gratitude to the Almighty for having allowed them to complete their journey. Others offered lengthy exhortations for protection in the coming days, the wisdom to make sound choices in selecting where they would finally settle and earnest entreaties for ample rain, healthy crops and bountiful harvests in the summer and fall to come.

When the red-orange fireball began to dip below the western horizon, fires twinkled to life around the meadow. The stick ball players rejoined friends and family for another serving of roasted meat and boiled potatoes. William stole a few minutes with Michael and *Tsi-mi* for a walk around the tree-lined meadow, ever mindful of the bored and resentful soldiers who had been ordered to remain until the last Cherokee had departed.

"I've been offered some good land on Honey Creek," William told his son.

"Up near Major Ridge's place?" Michael figured The Ridge, or his son and nephew, had extended the offer, hoping to gain an important ally in the inevitable struggle for tribal control that would soon unfold. "That's some beautiful country," Michael added noncommittally, not wanting to influence his father's decision one way or the other.

"And *Gu-wi-s-gu-wi* wants me to settle near Park Hill," William continued. "Says he'll do whatever it takes to make it happen."

Michael stopped and caught William's arm with a serious look. "What do *you* want, Father?"

"What do *I* want? I want for all this to stop. I want to get settled. Put down some roots before my time is up." He affectionately mussed the hair of his adoring grandson. "I want more of these beautiful grandchildren. I want them to be able to live in peace. And that's what your mother would have wanted, too."

"That sounds wonderful, Father. But I don't see it happening. Not for a while, anyway." He found it strange, playing the pragmatic advocate to the unrealistic dreams of his father. All his life these roles had been reversed. But William didn't consider his views unrealistic or unattainable.

"Don't say that," he countered. "The hard part is over. We survived! We're together again. That's the important thing. I'm sure this business with the army will blow over in time."

Michael was about to respond when both men stopped, their discussion interrupted by the sounds of men arguing somewhere in the darkness across the meadow. These weren't the opinionated, assertive voices of a friendly political debate, at which the Cherokees were unsurpassed among the native tribes. These voices were tense. Antagonistic. Belligerent.

"The Ross Party and the Treaty Party are at it again," William said.

They listened for a while before Michael spoke. "I'm afraid there are much bigger storms brewing than my *business* with the army, Father."

They had located the disturbance across the meadow and watched the shadowy forms shifting around one of the fires. From their position Michael and William couldn't determine which group was which. They were all *Tsa-la-gi* silhouettes, standing around the same fire, born of the same spirit. But because of their losses and their suffering, many were prepared to invite the mark of Cain upon themselves. William and Michael walked sadly back toward their family.

* * * * * * *

Johnny, Michael and the rest of the renegade clan made the long ride back to their hideout cabin late in the night. The celebration in the meadow near Ft. Gibson had been a long and relaxing day, and the only enemy they found themselves battling was the enticement of satiated slumber. The children were crumpled in sleep, held on the horses by their parents. *Me-li* rode in front of her beloved *Tsisdu* on Stick, William's black gelding. *E-gi-ni* hung back, bitter and sulking. *Tsisdu* pulled out and waited patiently for her to catch up. When she saw him, she stopped her horse, keeping a distance between them.

"Come on, *E-gi-ni*. Stay with the rest of us, *'Ge-yu-ts'*. We're a family here," *Tsisdu* implored.

She looked off into the night. *Tsisdu* allowed the rest of the group to go on ahead, but still *E-gi-ni* refused to budge. Realizing she wasn't going to join them, *Tsisdu* trotted Stick to catch up to the others. Once the others were well on their way, *E-gi-ni* finally followed, holding her horse to a slow walk.

* * * * * * *

The night was pleasantly cool but not so chilled as to make sleep uncomfortable. They didn't even bother to build a fire, immediately putting the children to bed on their pallets and blankets on the floor. In less than an hour the cabin breathed with the heavy snoring of its dormant inhabitants.

But not everyone was asleep. Susanna raised up on one elbow and looked at the darkened forms of Meg and *Me-li*. In the moonlight filtering in through the window she saw the bare spot on the floor where *E-gi-ni* usually slept. Susanna's eyes swung around to Johnny near the opposite wall. He, too, was aware that *E-gi-ni* was gone and looked back across the room at Susanna.

Out at the remuda where the horses were tethered on the south slope behind the cabin, *E-gi-ni* finished strapping her belongings onto the beautifully crafted saddle her brother, *Do-tsu-wa*, had bequeathed to her. Hanging from the saddle was Redbird's elaborately designed, silver inlaid gun belt and holster. *E-gi-ni* stroked Johnny's horse lovingly along the side of his muscled neck. The horse jerked his head back and turned away, a gesture she interpreted as a sign, a confirmation of Johnny's rejection of her.

"*Ha-wa, so-qui-li*," she said. "You are just like *Tsa-ni*. You run from my touch." She mounted her horse and rode quietly off through the trees in the bright moonlight. She would swing wide of the cabin and come out on the narrow trail heading east toward the main road.

From the pitch black shadows at the side of the cabin, Susanna, wrapped in her blanket, watched *E-gi-ni* and made no attempt to stop her. She listened until the sound of *Do-tsu-wa's* horse was gone, then looked out into the beautiful night for a long time. When she turned to go back inside, Susanna was startled to find Johnny standing directly behind her. She searched his face carefully, trying to gauge his reaction to *E-gi-ni's* departure. His arms came out from under his own blanket and he rested his hands on Susanna's shoulders. She took the front corners of his blanket and pulled, drawing his face down to hers. She kissed him—with a tenderness at first that gradually yielded to a heated passion.

Johnny's desire intensified. He felt his own weighted swelling which, he knew, she must also have felt pressing against her. Then Susanna broke the kiss. He looked puzzled, but allowed her to lead him to the other side of the firewood stacked a few feet from the cabin. There she let her own blanket fall to the ground and dropped to her knees. Again she pulled on his blanket, bringing him down in front of her. He leaned forward and kissed her again. Susanna felt the heat of his mouth, inhaled the sweetness of his breath. As the kiss intensified, Johnny opened his blanket wide with both arms to take her inside. Her eyes widened. For an instant she saw before her the man-eagle of her earlier visions spread his wings to their full span and close them to completely encircle her. The apparition man-eagle lowered himself over her and she closed her eyes, the images alternating in her mind with the real man in her arms. Johnny covered them with his blanket and Susanna plunged herself into the passionate love-making with a fire she had never known—would never have dreamed possible.

* * * * * * *

Tsisdu lay on his stomach, propped up on his elbows. The ragged bandanna lay open before him, illuminated by the moonbeams from the window. The Rabbit Man peered into the crystals, pleased with what he saw there. He wrapped the tattered fabric around the glass shafts and tucked them beneath his turban, folded neatly on the floor beside his sleeping mat. With a twitch of his nose and a smile seen only by the Little People, the *Yŭ-wi-tsu-na-s-ti-ga*, he closed his eye.

CHAPTER

60

June 21, 1839

William Drummond had chosen neither the acreage that Chief John Ross had picked out for him near Park Hill nor the section of rich bottom land in the Honey Creek area suggested by Major Ridge. His half-finished cabin sat in a clearing on a slightly elevated plot of ground overlooking a beautiful meadow, bordered on one side by woods and on another by a flowing stream. William thought it ironic that he had located approximately midway between the other two properties, reflecting his stance between the positions espoused by *Gu-wi-s-gu-wi's* Ross Party and The Ridge's Treaty Party.

Michael and Johnny hoisted a log high over their heads and *Tsisdu*, standing on a ladder, helped guide it into place. Meg, almost nineteen months old, *Me-li*, six-and-a-half, and *Tsi-mi*, two, fought over who would deliver the hammer to *Tsisdu* and the spikes he would drive into the log joints. In the shade of the tallest wall Susanna and Annie mixed mortar in a large wooden tub and scooped it into the cracks between the logs as the wall took shape. Michael and Johnny went to retrieve another log from the pile at the edge of the woods.

William swung his shiny, new ax with power and confidence. The bark and wood chips flew from the notch he was cutting in the end of the log. He paused, buried the blade in the top of a stump and wiped the sweat from his face, then rotated his right shoulder—the one that had taken a slug from Alton Ogilvie's pistol. The work, combined with the sun's warmth, had proven therapeutic, restoring it to full capacity. William walked over to where *Tsisdu* was spiking the latest log into place and scooped a gourd dipper of sweet, fresh spring water from the bucket sitting in the shade.

"It's going to be a nice home, *E-to-da*," Annie dug a handful of mortar from the tub.

"Oh, this is only temporary, Annie," he said.

"Temporary?" Susanna stopped smoothing the mortar between the logs.

"A year from now we'll have a big new house right over there," he pointed to a spot a hundred feet closer to the creek. "Just like back home. I've got it all right up here," he tapped the side of his head.

"Then *I* will live *here*. In this cabin," *Tsisdu* pointed to their current project. "I'll help your father work the farm." He pounded the last spike into the log and studied William's reaction to the announcement of his future plans.

"That's pretty much the way I see it," William agreed. *Tsisdu* grinned, twitched his nose and winked at *Me-li* and Meg. Johnny and Michael, after placing the next log to be notched and trimmed into the X-frames, joined William at the water bucket.

"She's looking good. Real good," Michael assessed their progress.

"And soon as we're finished, I'm going over to Ft. Gibson and talk to General Arbuckle." William broached the subject he knew irritated Michael.

"We've been through all that, Father."

William ignored Michael's objection. Like a true lawyer, he would pound and pound his point until the other side relented. "If we clear the air on this whole matter, then you and Annie and Jimmy can live here with peace of mind. We're going to be a family again. I don't want this to be just another hideout for a bunch of renegade outlaws and fugitives from justice."

"Listen to me, Father," Michael dropped the gourd back into the water bucket. "All we have to do is just let it go. Don't say anything to anyone. Time will go by and it'll all be forgotten. If you go there stirring things up with Arbuckle, it'll only remind them of something they can do on a slow afternoon. Next thing you know, there's a patrol riding this way."

William decided to work the parental guilt angle. "There was a time you wouldn't have dared dispute your father."

"Michael's not disputing you, Father. But he's dealt with these people before," Susanna injected.

He found it remarkable that Susanna had come to Michael's defense on several occasions since arriving in the west. William couldn't recall them ever having agreed on anything in their entire lives, much less one interceding on the other's behalf. Now, he noticed, they teamed up against him at every opportunity. He shot Susanna an annoyed look and held up a hand to cut her off, then walked back toward his log and ax. Michael shrugged to his sister.

"I can't believe I'm defending you!" Susanna laughed, then pointed toward the road. "Good," she commented on the approaching riders. "We can use the help."

Michael and Johnny walked across the clearing to greet *Tsa-tsi* and *Ne-di*, riding up from the main road at the bottom of the grade about two hundred yards from the cabin. Michael and Johnny noted their visitors' grave expressions. They obviously hadn't come to offer help with an old fashioned cabin raising. *Tsa-tsi* and *Ne-di* stopped at some distance from the construction site and waited for Michael and Johnny to join them so their conversation could remain private. While they watched the horses nibbling the tender spring grass, *Tsa-tsi* and *Ne-di* told Michael and Johnny about a meeting scheduled for that night. Their movements were nervous, their eyes avoided direct contact as they spoke.

"What kind of meeting?" Michael asked.

Ne-di and *Tsa-tsi* cut furtive glances up toward William and the women.

"Meeting about what?" Johnny repeated Michael's question.

Ned's voice was soft and evasive. "About laws."

"Laws? What laws?" Michael pressed for more.

"*Tsa-la-gi* laws," *Tsa-tsi* said, staring at the horses.

"Blood laws," *Ne-di* added. Michael and Johnny exchanged a look of immediate understanding. There had been hints and rumors for weeks that there might be some sort of revenge plotted against the men who had signed the Treaty of New Echota, the final stroke that had robbed the Cherokees of their homeland. Michael and Johnny had both decided they wanted nothing to do with such madness.

"I don't think so," Michael declined the implied invitation. *Tsa-tsi* and *Ne-di* waited for an explanation. A simple refusal wouldn't suffice. Michael stared at them and said no more. His answer was *No* and that was that. It would have to be enough.

"*Tsa-ni?*" Ned asked in a quiet tone.

Johnny looked them straight in the eye and said without hesitation, "I'm with *Mi-ki*."

William paused from planing the top of the next cabin log and looked down toward the four young men. *Tsisdu*, who was trimming the notch cut out near the log's end, stopped and looked at William, then down toward Michael, Johnny, *Tsa-tsi* and *Ne-di*.

"Those boys are acting awfully secretive," William mused. "What do you suppose that's all about?"

A troubled look clouded *Tsisdu's* face. "About dying..." he said in a distant voice.

"Who died?"

Tsisdu intently studied the four young men with the same expression William had observed before when the Rabbit Man *saw* things in his crystals. "No one. Yet. But there will be blood. A lot of blood."

Again William looked down toward the road. Ned and George continued their attempts to persuade Michael and Johnny.

"A lot of people will be wondering why you two aren't there," Ned said.

"Let them wonder," Johnny answered.

"*Tsa-ni*, we need all the friends we can get!" *Tsa-tsi* couldn't understand Johnny's flippant dismissal of such an important meeting.

"We already have too many enemies, *'Tsu-ts'*," Ned reminded him.

Michael squatted in the shade and tugged thoughtfully at the long stems of grass while he listened. When Ned and *Tsa-tsi* had finished, Michael rose abruptly and sternly scolded his friends.

"What's gotten into you two? Sure, we had to kill sometimes—to save ourselves. Our families. Or to protect innocent people. But we're not murderers who run around slaughtering our own *Tsa-la-gi* brothers! Some of these men I've known since I was a child!"

Ned and *Tsa-tsi* shuffled and ducked their eyes, shamed by Michael's words. "Here comes your father," *Tsa-tsi* cautioned.

"Why all the secrecy, lads?" William asked. *Ne-di* and *Tsa-tsi* averted their eyes while mumbling their perfunctory greetings. A long silence followed until William faced his son. "What's going on, Michael?"

"There's a meeting tonight. Over at the council grounds."

William flashed a cold, hard glare at each young man. All four refused to look at him. "The Takatoka Council House? At Double Springs?" he pressed them, directing his words mostly to Ned and George. "That meeting's been going on for two weeks! We went for a couple of days, but folks have lives to live. Things to do. Can't meet forever. What on earth could they still be meeting about?" Michael knew his father well enough to know he was fully aware of the purpose behind the proposed late-night meeting. William saw the swift glance pass between Ned and *Tsa-tsi*—silent agreement not to reveal more than they had to. "This is about blood laws, isn't it?" William wouldn't let up. *Tsa-tsi* and *Ne-di* directed their *We will say no more—it's your turn to answer* looks at Michael and Johnny. "I know what's going on," William continued. "These men who want revenge—they're good men—but they lost everything back home. They watched their families and friends die in the camps or on the Trail of Tears. And now someone has to pay."

Tsa-tsi had intended not to speak but found himself

responding in a rare display of emotion. "The men who signed that treaty gave away our homeland!" he blurted.

"Come on!" Johnny broke in. "The *yo-negs* would have taken it sooner or later! You know that!"

"The law is the law! *Tsa-la-gi* law!" *Ne-di* shot back with an outburst as uncharacteristic as *Tsa-tsi's*.

"Law?!" Michael scoffed at their reasoning. "You're one to talk about the law! After all we've been through!"

William had been thoughtfully observing this microcosm of the factionalism which, like insatiable moths, was eating away at the very fabric of the Cherokee nation. Emotional battles raging between friends and brothers. He shocked them all when he said, "Michael, I think you should go to this meeting." He fielded their incredulous looks and explained his thinking. "You can be the voice of reason. Make sure this foolishness doesn't go any further."

Tsa-tsi looked William directly in the eye for the first time. "I don't mean to be rude, *Wi-li*, but this doesn't concern you."

William's face grew flushed and he swelled with controlled rage to his full six-foot-four height, towering over the much shorter *Tsa-tsi*. "Doesn't concern me?!" his voice came as a beastly growl, restrained only by his years of practiced control. "According to the law—and based on what we've been through—I'm as Cherokee as you are! I lost everything I'd worked a lifetime to build! I buried my Elizabeth—Michael's mother!—in that damn camp! I watched my friends die out there on that trail and on the river like so many sick cattle! How dare you say it doesn't concern me!"

William stormed back up toward the cabin. His loud tirade had drawn the attention of Annie and Susanna who stopped their mortar work to look at the men. Johnny and Michael had nothing more to say to their friends. *Ne-di* and *Tsa-tsi* were clearly embarrassed at having insulted Michael's father.

* * * * * * *

The cabin work halted well before dark. Following the confrontation with *Tsa-tsi* and *Ne-di*, William had attacked his work with a wrathful vigor that kept the rest of them—even Michael and Johnny—scrambling to keep up. The two younger men relaxed in the cool shade. Michael sharpened William's ax. Johnny, drenched with sweat, leaned against the stack of logs already notched and ready to put into place the following day. His head was tilted back, his eyes closed. He listened to Meg and *Me-li* splashing in a shallow part of the creek closest to the cabin. He loved the girls, and the sound of their voices was sweet music to him. Susanna brought a bucket of water and playfully doused him with a dipper full, then slid down beside him and wiped his face with her skirt before giving him another dipper to drink. She adored watching his every move and gesture. Affectionately, she leaned against him and playfully bit his muscular shoulder.

"Do you think we can...maybe...take a walk tonight? A long walk?" she said, her eyes searching his, a finger hooked inside the top of his trousers at the side. It pleased him that she never hid how much she wanted him. Since beginning construction on the cabin, they had all been sleeping in close proximity at the end of their exhausting days. Johnny and Susanna—like Michael and Annie—had found little time or space for intimacy.

"A long walk?" he repeated with a sly grin.

"A *very* long walk."

"In the forest? With the wild animals?" he teased.

"There's only one wild animal you need to worry about," she purred and nibbled at his ear. "I love you, John Fields...*Tsa-ni*," she whispered.

"*U-ni-tsi Wa-ya*..." he said.

"That's right! Mother wolf! And don't you forget it!" Susanna emitted a low growl that softened to a purr, then pushed him over and crawled on top of him, biting his neck playfully.

"*Tsa-ni*. We need to get going," Michael said from the other side of the log pile. He dried his forearms after washing up. Susanna rolled off of Johnny and looked up at her brother.

"Going where?"

"Something we have to do, Susie," Michael was deliberately evasive.

"What?" She sat on her knees, looking at Johnny. "What about our walk?"

Johnny got up and brushed himself off, picked the gourd up off the grass and dropped it back into the water bucket. "Soon. We'll do it soon." Johnny bent down and kissed her on the top of her head. He gripped her hair tightly and waded into her eyes, then jumped over the pile of logs and walked away with Michael toward their horses.

"What's going on? Michael? Johnny?" she called, but they kept walking. She stared after them, puzzled and concerned. This wasn't like Johnny—not even like Michael since they had been reunited. There was something they weren't telling her.

* * * * * * *

Takatoka Council House
Double Springs, Indian Territory

More than a hundred Cherokee men were still at the council house, open on all seven sides in the traditional *Tsa-la-gi* design. The light from candles and oil lanterns, combined with the flame of the seven-wood council fire, cast eerie, dancing shadows that exaggerated the animated debate and exhortations of the men. Armed Cherokees were evenly spaced about the perimeter of the grounds, relaxed but alert, watching the horses and keeping a sharp eye on all paths leading to and from the council house.

Many of the men inside wore black bandannas over their faces. Others had the same bandannas hanging loosely around their necks, unconcerned about who might see them. The more secretive wore hoods with eye holes, with a hat or a Cherokee turban on top. Michael and Johnny sat quietly on the outer edge. For them, it was an interesting irony. Men—including their friends, *Tsa-tsi* Starr and *Ne-di* Proctor—who had spoken so righteously of blood law, of tribal code and tradition, nevertheless found it necessary to hide their faces. Deeds ordained by law, spirits crying out for vengeance from their graves back at the concentration camps or along the Trail of Tears wouldn't, it seemed to them, demand secret meetings and midnight plottings.

This council session wasn't at all what Michael and Johnny had anticipated. Perhaps they hadn't really known what to expect, but this they found most unsettling. Neither of them had spoken at the meeting as William had hoped. The decisions, they knew, had already been made. They were witness merely to the formalities.

When the debates and discussions subsided, the Cherokees seated themselves on the benches facing the center of the council house. A mixed-blood, serving as temporary court clerk, called out the names of the accused. Three full-bloods—representing the clans of the accused—pronounced the verdict and sentence.

"John Bell," the clerk read dryly.

"Guilty. Sentenced to die," the clan judges declared in unison.

"James Starr," the clerk said.

"Guilty. Death."

"George Adair."

"Guilty," said the judges. "He must die."

"And from the Deer Clan..." the clerk picked up another piece of paper. The first three judges stepped back and were replaced by three members of the *A-ni-ka-wi* who would pass judgement on the accused of their clan.

"We have decided," the first Deer Clan judge announced solemnly.

"The Ridge. Also called Major Ridge," the clerk read.

The second Deer Clan judge spoke. "For dealing away ancestral tribal land without the approval and permission of the national council and the *Tsa-la-gi* people: guilty."

A mild flurry of murmurs and whispers rippled through the gathering. The clerk waited for things to settle down before reciting the rest of the names. "John Ridge, son of Major Ridge. *Ga-la-gi-na*, also called Buck Watie, also called Elias Boudinot. And Stand Watie. All *A-ni-ka-wi*. The Deer Clan."

All three judges spoke at once. "Guilty. All guilty."

"All sentenced according to tribal law."

"Death."

This brought the loudest reaction of all from the Cherokees. Michael and Johnny saw men they recognized among the unmasked and hoodless—including *Tsa-tsi* and *Ne-di*. Michael knew many of these men had been on the trail with his father. Michael's and Johnny's eyes eventually came back to each other and they realized this entire thing was bigger than either of them could have known. And more ominously, they understood it had given birth to its own momentum that would not be denied. Could not be stopped.

Once all the accused had been named, the judgements pronounced and the sentences handed down, the clerk produced a ratty old hat filled with little pieces of paper. "Each man draws a slip of paper," he announced. "If the one you draw has an *X*, you have been selected to carry out the sentence." He paused, then put it in simpler terms. "You will be an executioner..."

The hat went around from man to man. Johnny kept a close eye on the hat and was able to spot the first piece drawn with an *X*. Michael didn't need to see the paper. He read the result in each man's face. The first to draw an assassin's mark was John Vann, his expression somber, his commitment determined. Around went the hat. Draw after draw. Then the face of a man called Daniel Colston registered the next *X*. The hat kept moving until it came to Johnny and Michael. They declined to take a slip, looking at each other, then up to the Cherokee holding the hat in front of them. Their hesitation drew strong looks from others in the council house, but

Michael and Johnny steadfastly refused to participate. The hat went on to Ned and George. Each drew a slip of paper. Michael had the distinct impression that he and Johnny were more relieved than *Ne-di* and *Tsa-tsi* that they had drawn blank papers and wouldn't be serving as sanctioned assassins.

The hat was passed to the man standing just beyond Ned. It was Allen Ross, the son of Chief John Ross. His hand went out, but the hat was pulled back and young Ross appeared confused. The leader of the meeting—a man neither Michael nor Johnny recognized behind his black mask—approached the chief's son.

"We have another job for you, Allen Ross," the masked leader said. "You will make sure your father stays at home. We must protect *Gu-wi-s-gu-wi*. He must know nothing of this until the blood of the traitors who betrayed our homeland soaks the new ground."

Young Ross nodded with understanding and the hat moved on. After all the slips had been drawn, the meeting's leader instructed those who had pulled an *X* to file silently out into the night. Michael and Johnny rose to leave, but when they reached the edge of the council house, their way was blocked by three Cherokee men, two wearing bandannas and the third with a hood. Michael and Johnny looked behind them, surprised to find *Ne-di* and *Tsa-tsi* cutting off any retreat in that direction.

"Sorry, *Tsa-ni*. *Mi-ki*," Ned said, his voice relaxed but determined. "We can't let you go yet."

"What the hell are you talking about?" Michael was incensed.

"You wouldn't draw from the hat," *Tsa-tsi* explained.

Ned tried to defuse the situation. He knew Michael's temper and hoped his friend wouldn't cause trouble. "That was your choice. It's all right. But..."

"But they're afraid you might try to warn them," *Tsa-tsi* finished.

"Get out of my way, *Tsa-tsi*," Michael said.

"Don't make this any tougher than it is, *Mi-ki*." Michael heard in Ned's voice a coldness he wouldn't have anticipated from this man who had stood shoulder to shoulder with him and looked into the gaping jaws of death.

"We're leaving, Ned," Johnny put it plainly and stepped toward the open night, but the three masked Cherokees stood their ground. Michael's hand closed around the handle of the knife attached to his belt. He looked intently at each of the men blocking his way.

"I'm going home now," Michael announced. "Any man who

tries to stop me will find himself tripping over his own intestines." Michael then took an angle past the masked Cherokees who had blocked their path. *Tsa-tsi* grabbed Michael's arm.

"Wait!" *Tsa-tsi* said. "We'll go with you."

"Good," *Ne-di* agreed. "We'll stay at your place tonight."

This was good, Michael and Johnny thought. At least *Ne-di* and *Tsa-tsi* wouldn't be riding through the night to slaughter anyone. The other Cherokees accepted this arrangement and stepped aside without incident or comment, allowing them to pass.

CHAPTER

61

Painted white and situated in the midst of an expansive, immaculate lawn, the home of John Ridge near Honey Creek was a beautiful, two-story structure that would have been the envy of his wife's *yo-neg* relatives back in Connecticut. An uninformed traveller going by on the road this cool, clear June night might have thought he was passing the elegant home of a territorial governor or a successful local business magnate. But John and his wife, the former Sarah Northrup, liked having a big house and made it a warm and loving home for their six children. Looking to the future, they saw perhaps even more children and, eventually, daughters-in-law and sons-in-law, followed by innumerable grandchildren.

Sarah kissed her son, twelve-year-old John Rollin Ridge, and sent him upstairs to bed. Tall for his age, yet slender and graceful, he balanced the silver candle holder to light his way, proud that, as the oldest, he had been allowed to stay up a half hour longer than the other children. He was prouder still that he was trusted to take the candle upstairs by himself and safely extinguish it before going to sleep. He thought perhaps he might read by its light for while, in case any of the other children were still awake. They would be doubly envious—not only of his stay-up-late privileges, but of his ability to read as well. And should the other children all be asleep, there was a good chance Miss Sophie, the nanny-teacher who had joined them in the west, might still be awake in her room across the hall. She would certainly be pleased to know he was reading before going to sleep.

Sarah watched him ascend the stairs, then returned to the kitchen and poured a cup of cider for herself and her husband. She had absolutely adored John since he first charmed, courted and wed her when he was a university student in New England. After she set the kettle back on the stove, John pulled her to his side and slipped his arm around her waist.

"John. My dear, sweet John," she ran her fingers up the back of his neck and through his thick, black hair. "For the first time I'm starting to feel like things are really going to work out. Miss Sophie's come to help teach the children. You and Samuel have been able to resume translating the Bible into Cherokee."

"I wish I shared your enthusiasm, Sarah," he said with more concern in his voice than she liked to hear. He stared pensively into the fire through the open door of the pot-bellied stove. She kissed him on the forehead and slid into the chair next to his. She knew his anxiety had nothing to do with their friend.

Samuel Austin Worcester, John's long time companion, had devoted much of his life to helping John and his cousin, Elias Boudinot, publish *The Cherokee Phoenix* in both their native language and in English. Worcester had also helped translate their tribal constitution and other important documents into English. But for his efforts, Worcester had brought years of hardship upon himself and his family. He had endured the ignominy of unjust imprisonment for his unwavering commitment to the *Tsa-la-gi* when Georgia passed racially biased laws designed solely to dispossess the Indians. His unflagging support of Cherokee rights—as well as the rights of Creeks and Choctaws—had earned him a four year sentence at hard labor for defying the state of Georgia when he refused to obey their racist, anti-Indian laws.

In 1832, the U. S. Supreme Court, in the landmark case of *Worcester v. State of Georgia*, had ruled as unconstitutional not only the law which had imprisoned Samuel and other missionaries for their work among the Cherokees, but the entire section of Georgia laws known as the *Indian codes*. But the Cherokees' jubilation had been short lived. On hearing of the court's ruling, President Andrew Jackson was reported to have said of the Chief Justice, "John Marshall has made his decision; let him enforce it now, if he can!"

For his lifetime of dedication to the *Tsa-la-gi*, Worcester had come to be highly revered throughout the tribe and had been given the honored yet affectionate name of *A-tse-nŭ-s-ti, The One Sent*, or *The Messenger*. He had been a key figure in implementing Sequoyah's system of Cherokee writing and bringing the tribe from a strictly oral language to near complete literacy within the span of a single generation. For some time John and Samuel had been working on a complete translation of the Holy Bible into Cherokee and hoped to secure another printing press which they would set up in the west.

"Are you still troubling yourself trying to fathom John Ross's next move?" Sarah asked.

She knew her husband well. Knew how his mind worked. He sipped his cider for a time, then finally voiced his thoughts. "I've heard that Ross stayed on at the Takatoka meeting after we left. Held his own council for a couple of days after Chief Brown had officially closed the meeting," he said. "At least that's the rumor going around."

She forced a soft laugh, hoping it might bring him some

comfort if he thought she considered his worries unimportant. "And if I know *Gu-wi-s-gu-wi*, that's exactly what happened."

"This thing isn't over yet. I can feel it," John's fears wouldn't be easily allayed.

She patted the top of his hand on the table. "What happens happens, *Tsa-ni*." His hand enveloped hers, almost clinging. "What John Ross—or anyone else—decides to do, you can't control." His eyes drifted to the rifle in the corner near the door. Only recently had he even considered keeping a loaded gun in his house. All the children had been strictly prohibited from going near it, each one charged with policing the others. Yet it was a constant source of concern for Sarah—every time she heard a loud noise or noticed one of the children absent from the room.

"Stand Watie says we have to be prepared," he said.

"And what, exactly, is your cousin preparing for?" she asked.

He looked at her for a long time before responding.

"I think we all know the answer to that. But I'll tell you this: I won't spend the rest of my days looking over my shoulder. I refuse to live that way."

His words had a sobering effect, vanquishing her earlier attempts at minimizing the gravity of the situation. "I'm sure everything will be all right," she said unconvincingly. Like her husband, Sarah gazed into the flames within the stove.

* * * * * * *

For Michael and Johnny there was a quiet yet palpable tension between them and their former raider comrades, *Ne-di* and *Tsa-tsi*. Recent events and present circumstances had put a strain on their once inviolable friendship. But Michael was pleased that they had elected, along with him and Johnny, to distance themselves from the sinister plot.

"This won't prove anything," Michael commented on the proposed assassinations. "You know that."

"It's something that has to be done," *Tsa-tsi* answered.

"It'll be the end of all this," Ned added. "The end of *Ge-tsi-ka-hŭ-da A-ne-gŭ-i*. The Trail Of Tears."

"No, my friend," Michael shook his head, realizing his words were wasted. "This is only the beginning. I'm just glad we have no part in it."

* * * * * * *

The gray stillness before dawn was shattered by the call of a crow from the treetops surrounding John Ridge's home. Another crow answered from across the clearing and the two large, black birds lifted themselves against the reddening sky, disappearing from the view of twenty-five mounted Cherokees who waited quietly in the shadows of the trees. They had been there for hours, and would wait even longer.

The first golden-red glow of sunrise shimmered on the leaves of the hickory and chestnut trees and bathed the Ridge house in a pinkish-orange tint. The black-masked Cherokees hadn't yet detected any movement from inside. The doorknob turned and the back door was pushed open by a Cherokee boot. Within seconds, three pairs of feet were moving quietly, swiftly up the stairs, stopping at a creaky stair, then moving on.

The three masked men reached the second floor landing without incident. The first carried a pistol, the other two had large, broad-blade knives. The leader stepped to the window and looked out. The other twenty-two members of the execution party had formed a semi-circle in front of the Ridge house. Satisfied that all escape routes were sealed off, the lead assassin eased opened a door and looked in on the six Ridge children asleep in the large dormitory style room lined with three beds on either side. He pulled the door closed and opened another down the hallway. Seeing the couple asleep in the bed, the first assassin started in, but one of the others caught his arm and shook his head *No*. This wasn't the Ridges, but Sarah's sister and brother-in-law who had recently arrived from the east to summer with the Ridges in their new home.

Neither John nor Sarah moved when the executioners entered their bedroom. They didn't waken when the pistol was placed against John's temple. When the hammer cocked, John stirred and coughed lightly in his sleep. The finger closed around the trigger and squeezed. There was a loud click. The powder sputtered and the pistol failed to fire. John's eyes popped open, his nostrils filled with the acrid burn of the fizzled gunpowder. He found himself staring up at the three masked strangers at the side of his bed. His eyes cut to the pistol and his comprehension was immediate.

John's attackers didn't anticipated his speedy reaction. He twisted the pistol out of the assassin's hand as the three men seized him. Sarah awoke, terrified to see the intruders dragging her husband from their bed. John struggled fiercely.

"What are you doing here?! Who are you?! What do you want?!" he demanded. But he knew too well the answers to his questions.

"No! Leave him alone! John!" Sarah screamed. She lunged and caught his ankle, but the men pulled harder and she lost her grip. Sarah leaped from the bed and fearlessly attacked the nearest assassin, trying to pull him away from her husband. The Cherokee intruder slung her hard against an oak armoire and she fell to the floor, momentarily dazed. Though John was thin and wiry, he fought ferociously. Still, he was no match for three larger men. They dragged him flailing and kicking from the bedroom and down the stairs. Knowing what lay in store, John screamed—not from fear but to warn his in-laws, Miss Sophie and the children to hide or, by whatever means at their disposal, prepare to defend themselves. As he was going down the stairs, John caught a glimpse of his brother-in-law and the three oldest children emerging, puzzled, groggy, from their rooms. Sarah stumbled past them to the edge of the landing.

The Cherokees waiting outside heard the struggle, and they heard the terrified screams and shouts of Sarah Ridge just before the door flew open. The three assassins, with John Ridge yelling and swearing, exploded into the bright sunlight. Immediately the twenty-two death riders closed to form a tight circle around the three executioners and their prisoner. In desperation, John wrestled the pistol away from his attacker a second time, pointed it directly at the assassin and pulled the trigger. Just as before, the pistol failed to fire. The other two men grabbed John's arms, overpowering the smaller man. They held his limbs outstretched while the first assassin drew his knife and plunged it into John's stomach.

They had come to complete a grim task which each man felt was fully ordained by tribal blood laws. But each of the assassins had gained an immense respect for the valiant spirit of this diminutive Cherokee. Even with the life flowing out of him, John fought and raged like a wounded panther. In accordance with the custom in such assassinations, once John had been stabbed, the three men took him by the arms and legs and threw his body as high in the air as they could. John landed on his back with a thud, the wind knocked out of him. The throwing was intended to expand the wound, burst any penetrated organs and hasten the bleeding—both internal and external. Bravely, John rolled over and struggled to his hands and knees, the blood pouring from his stomach wound and from his mouth.

From the doorway Sarah screamed, her face twisted in anguish. Six men promptly broke from the circle and forced Sarah, her sister and brother-in-law back inside at gunpoint. They could watch through the windows—their cries, screams and shouts muffled—while each man in the circle drew his knife and drove it into the body of John Ridge. In all, he received a total of twenty-five stab wounds.

John was stretched out face down, motionless in a pool of his own blood. In single file, each of the group ceremoniously passed over him and stomped the body. Many of those present were having second thoughts. Because of John's incredible endurance, some felt the Great Spirit was somehow protecting him and, in fact, they might not be able to kill him. The more superstitious among them became even more apprehensive when, despite the stabbing, the throwing and the stomping, John raised himself up on one elbow. They watched in awe as this courageous man, swaying weakly, turned himself to face the house, trying to peer through the feet and legs of his attackers for one final glimpse of his beloved Sarah and the children he so adored. He cringed at the thought of them seeing him like this, yet he wanted with all the life remaining in him for their faces to be the final image he took from this world.

Thinking John must surely be dead following the stabbing and stomping, some of the assassins had allowed the door to be opened. Sarah fought in vain to get through the throng of armed men. With only a glimpse now and then, she saw his lips form the words *gŭ-ge-yu-i*, I love you. But there was no sound. Only more blood.

The guards holding Sarah at bay finally allowed her brother-in-law to come out. He pushed his way through the men. Many of them still held their bloody knives loosely at their sides. Grasping John under the armpits, Sarah's brother-in-law tried to drag him back toward the house, but the body had gone limp and was slippery with blood.

"For the love of God! Can't some of you help me?!" he cried. The others remained still and looked blankly at him without answering.

"Let's go," the primary assassin finally said to the others. "Our work is done!" One of the men standing close to John pulled down his black bandanna mask. It was Sam *Ta-no-wi*. At the frozen graveside of his own wife and child he had bitterly vowed this season would come to pass. For him it was a personal vendetta. Sam *Ta-no-wi*, truth be told, couldn't have cared less about allegiance to ancient tribal laws.

"He isn't dead!" Sam's vengeful hatred would be assuaged only when the job was finished. The main executioner looked down at John Ridge. Their eyes met and John blinked once when he heard his assassin's pronouncement.

"Yes. He's dead."

John Ridge's eyes had already begun to lose focus by the time his brother-in-law, slipping and sliding in the blood, dragged him back toward the house.

* * * * * * *

Dr. Sam Worcester was a tall, thin man just over forty. He liked to rise early to split firewood in the cool of the morning on the shady side of his house situated near Park Hill. June 22, 1839 had begun for Samuel with his routine ritual—prayer of gratitude for granting him another day, beseeching the Almighty to guide him toward the ultimate fulfillment of God's plan for his life; a cup of coffee lovingly prepared by his devoted wife; a game of yarn ball with the family cat; a rapid review of the previous night's scripture translations, with corrections if necessary; then out the door to finish his chores.

Samuel paused from his wood splitting when his house guest, Elias Boudinot, shirtsleeves rolled up, came out of the house carrying a steaming cup of coffee. He waited for a second cup poured by Mrs. Worcester, a slender woman with her hair pulled straight back in a bun at the base of her neck. Her outward features were stern and unexpressive, but to all who knew her she was a kind and gentle soul. She retreated back into the house and was replaced in the doorway by Delight Boudinot, Elias's beautiful new bride. Like his cousin John's wife, Sarah Ridge, Delight was a long way from her New England origins. With one arm wrapped around a large bowl of batter. She vigorously stirred the contents with a long, wooden spoon.

"Now don't go wandering off before breakfast, Buck. It'll be ready soon."

He had been born Buck, or *Ga-la-gi-na*, Watie. During his tenure at the university in the east he had been befriended and so greatly influenced by a kind and supportive man named Elias Boudinot that, out of reverence and respect, he adopted the older man's name as his own.

"Yes, my Delight," he answered. "Maybe I'll just pop over for a minute to see how the roof's coming."

"Not until after you eat! I know you," she scolded lovingly. She was, indeed, his delight. A woman whose stunning physical beauty was matched by her gracious heart. And her strength of will rivaled his own. All these things about her he idolized.

"All too well," he said, stepping back up on the stoop to give her a kiss. "You do indeed!" Elias's first wife, Harriet Gold, who had been hanged in effigy in her hometown of Cornwall, Connecticut after committing the unpardonable sin of miscegenation in marrying an Indian, had died from complications of pregnancy in the summer of 1836. In a relatively short time Elias had taken as his wife the lovely Delight Sargent, a young woman who had worked as a Christian missionary among the Cherokees for some years. They were staying with their closest friends, the Worcesters, while their new home was being constructed a scant two hundred yards away across the meadow.

Elias took the second cup of coffee to Samuel. The two men looked out toward the construction site where already the sounds of sawing and hammering drifted across to them. Despite Delight's admonition, Elias wanted to have a look at the progress on the roof.

"Sam, I think I'll go over for just a minute or two and—"

"—and check on the carpenters?" Sam interrupted with a knowing smile. "Not again, Elias!"

"Well, it *is* my new house, Samuel," Elias laughed. "I want it to be perfect."

"That's what you said yesterday. And the day before. And you never get back until sundown."

Elias knew well the reason behind Samuel's protest. With the other business and political interests sapping so much of John Ridge's energy, their long-time work with Worcester had fallen mainly on Boudinot's shoulders.

"Don't worry, we'll get the Bible translated into Cherokee. I promise!"

"Once a man of great promise...now just a man of promises," Samuel teased. "Go. Go. Build your house!" He gathered up an armload of firewood and headed back inside.

* * * * * * *

For Elias it was a short and pleasant stroll. A team of Cherokee, Choctaw and Creek carpenters were already hard at work on his new house. He circled the project, examining the framing and the roof work. Elias waved casually to the four men who appeared unexpectedly, coming toward him from the trees at the edge of the meadow.

710

"*Si-yo, Ga-la-gi-na!*" one of them called in a friendly tone.

"Buck," the second man greeted him.

"*Si-yo!*" Elias responded. "What can I do for you this morning?"

"We need *nŭ-wo-ti,*" the second man requested medicine. "My children are sick."

"And my wife and son," the first man added. "Yesterday they were fine. But this morning..." he shrugged at the unexplained onset of their maladies.

"We figured it would be quickest to get something from Doctor Sam," the second man pressed right to the point.

"Makes sense," Elias agreed. "We'll see what he has."

"*Wa-do, Ga-la-gi-na,*" the first man thanked him.

Elias started back across the meadow toward Worcester's house. Samuel kept his medicine shelves well stocked and often treated Cherokees who came to his door, day or night. And when a patient was unable to travel, Worcester gladly went to towns and isolated cabins on the rivers or deep in the hills. On other occasions, a husband or wife, a father or mother might come to his door and describe in detail the symptoms of a loved one's ailment. Worcester would make his diagnosis and dispense medication for conditions that didn't sound life-threatening.

As they crossed the meadow, the first man dropped a little behind Elias. "Did you bring in the *di-da-nŭ-wi-s-gi?*" Elias asked. Many Cherokees didn't consult with Worcester or any other white doctor until after the Cherokee medicine man had been called in, and then only with the *di-da-nŭ-wi-s-gi's* consent—or at least in the absence of protest.

The second man, keeping pace with Elias, explained. "The *di-da-nŭ-wi-s-gi's* making medicine. But we want some from Doctor Sam, too. Take no chances."

When they reached the halfway point between the construction site and Worcester's house, the first man drew his knife, ran up behind Elias, and stabbed him in the back. Boudinot let out a piercing scream and fell to his knees in the tall, dew-soaked grass. The assassin pulled the knife out and pushed his victim to the ground. Rolling onto his side, Elias looked up just as the second man pulled a tomahawk from beneath his coat. Silhouetted against the rising sun, he raised the war hatchet high above his head.

Realizing that his remaining time on this earth numbered at best a few seconds, Boudinot screamed even louder in a blood-curdling death cry. He watched the tomahawk's descent through the

711

slow, thick syrup of protracted time. Before his last cry had echoed across the meadow, darkness swept over Elias Boudinot with the bone-crunching blow that split his skull.

The carpenters had heard Elias, but when they started toward the center of the meadow, the other two Cherokees who had stayed behind drew their pistols and prevented them from going to their employer's aid.

Mrs. Worcester and Delight Boudinot had also heard the chilling screams. They rushed from the house and were joined by Samuel coming from the woodpile. They started across the meadow but were unable to see Boudinot in the tall grass.

"Elias! Elias! Where are you?!" Delight's voice was charged with panic.

The two assassins ran back toward the construction site where they collected the other two Cherokees. All four disappeared into the woods.

"There! Those men!" Samuel was the first to see them. "Who are you?! Where's Elias?!" he shouted. He wanted to go after them, but he knew from the blood-curdling scream they had heard it was more important to find his friend. Along with his wife and Delight, Samuel stumbled frantically around in the grass until he spotted something off to his left. He couldn't see distinctly, but he knew it had to be Elias. "Over here!" he called to the women. They thrashed through the tall grass to join Samuel just as he reached the body. Delight dropped to her knees beside her beloved husband, cradling his bloody head in her lap.

"Elias! God, please! No!" her cry rose from the depths of her soul. He looked up at her one last time and his eyes went blank in death. Thirty mounted assassins—led by the four who had so cravenly deceived and then slaughtered the young Cherokee leader—exploded from the trees, thundering past only inches from the body of Elias Boudinot and his distraught wife and friends. They crossed the meadow and made for the woods which would eventually take them out to the main road.

* * * * * * *

Stand Watie, brother of Elias Boudinot, was unloading burlap bags of seed from a wagon and stacking them on the plank walkway in front of the Ridge's general store near Honey Creek. He had been unable to sleep and thought he might as well get an early start on the shipment that had arrived late the evening before. Already the day promised to be as warm and humid as the previous one. Watie, a short, muscular man, easily tossed the heavy bag into place atop the others and looked up, alerted by the sound of hoofbeats approaching at a dead run.

The Choctaw carpenter had been dispatched by Dr. Worcester on his best horse, Comet, to go and tell Stand Watie the terrible news about his brother and to warn him his own life was in danger. In truth, Worcester suspected it might be too late, but he had to try. The Choctaw messenger rode Comet to a sliding halt, almost slamming into Watie who grabbed the reins and brought the lathered mount under control.

"What's wrong? What are you doing with Sam Worcester's horse?" Watie demanded.

"Your brother is dead, Watie!" the Choctaw informed him. "Boudinot is dead. Doctor Sam sent me to warn you."

"*Ga-la-gi-na*?!" Watie said incredulously. "What happened?"

"There was at least two dozen. Maybe more," the Choctaw reported. "They might be coming for you, too!"

Stand Watie's first thought was for the safety of his cousin, John Ridge and his family. "Hurry!" he barked at the messenger. "You have to go tell John and Sarah!" The Choctaw wheeled Comet around and raced away. Neither man was aware that the ground at Honey Creek already flowed red with the blood of John Ridge.

* * * * * * *

Major Ridge got up long before sunrise to prepare for his trip. He had received word the day before that a dear friend, a black man he'd known since childhood, had taken seriously ill. Fourteen-year-old Theodore, the sick man's grandson, had been given the great responsibility of riding to Indian Territory to accompany Major Ridge back to Van Buren. The stately, silver-haired Major Ridge sat regally in the saddle as they crossed the border into Arkansas Territory near Little Rock Creek. Theodore, splendidly attired in his tight white trousers and green riding jacket, respectfully rode a few paces behind the awe-inspiring Cherokee legend.

"Your grandfather's been a good friend to me for many years, Theodore," the Major said, motioning for Theodore to bring his horse alongside. "I hope he can hang on until we get there."

Theodore trotted his horse forward. He enjoyed the company of the Cherokee leader. Despite his stern appearance, The Ridge had treated Theodore cordially, chatting freely with him over dinner and an early breakfast that morning. The Major had even winked and poured a half inch of good whiskey for the young man on the front porch where they sat in the cool air after the evening meal.

"When he took sick in the night, Grandmama say go fetch The Major," he repeated his well-rehearsed account, bringing a smile from The Ridge, who had already heard it at least five times. "Grandpa couldn't talk so good, but you could tell he say yo' name."

"I've known him since we were boys growing up in Tennessee. Back east," The Ridge recounted.

"I don't recall much about that place, Mistah Ridge," Theodore said.

"You must've been—what?—maybe six when you came out west?"

"Yes, suh," Theodore answered. "Five, I think."

"Well, it's a beautiful place, Theodore," Ridge recalled the land of his ancestors. "A beautiful place. We all hated to leave it. It was our home." He heaved a long and ponderous sigh, adrift in the recollection of some fond and distant memory.

"Yes, suh," Theodore agreed politely. A pebble that fell near him caused Theodore to glance up to a large rock formation hanging over the south side of the road. He and The Major were in the shadows, but Theodore caught the unmistakable glint of the morning sunlight off rifle barrels jutting out from between the rocks high above. Alertly he cut his eyes to the woods flanking them on the other side. There were no sun flashes, but he could clearly make out rifle barrels protruding from the trees bordering the road. "Mistah Ridge!" he yelled, thinking they were about to be robbed.

Before either of them could react, a score of rifle barrels spat their fire. The impact of any one of the bullets at such close range would have been enough to knock The Ridge from his horse. But he had been caught in a cross fire. The force of the shots from one side strangely balanced the impact from the other, keeping the Cherokee leader in the saddle. He had been hit at least five or six times in the head, back and chest.

Theodore's horse bolted sideways, almost unseating the young rider, who gaped in wide-eyed disbelief at the incredible sight before him. The Major's horse, startled by the gunshots, its reins dangling loose, spun wildly in the road. Finally the animal raised up on his hind legs, dumping the dead *Tsa-la-gi* leader in the dust before bolting into the woods.

The black-masked assassins rose from their hiding place in the rocks above and the others stepped out into the road from the cover of the trees. Theodore's slender legs flailed wildly as he kicked his horse and rode for his life. A couple of ineffectual shots were fired, but none came close. Theodore, low in the saddle against the horse's neck, disappeared around the turn in the road. No one pursued him. The masked executioners hadn't come to kill a young black boy. They encircled the lifeless corpse of Major Ridge lying crumpled in the middle of an Arkansas highway. One by one they passed over him and stomped the lifeless body.

Johnny and Michael slipped out from among the sleeping women and children. They built a fire near some trees down by the road where Ned and George had slept on the ground. The tension among them from the night before lingered, thickening in the silence of the morning air. *Tsisdu* had risen before any of the others. He sat on a stump smoking his pipe.

Michael dipped coffee for himself and Johnny from the black pot *Tsisdu* had brought down from the cabin. He filled a third cup and was about to hand it to Ned when he noticed *Tsisdu* staring up the road. Michael followed *Tsisdu's* line of sight to the trees about two hundred yards away. In the low-lying fog awaiting the burn off by the morning sun, Michael saw a Cherokee man squatting beside a tree. He appeared to be gnawing on a piece of dried meat. A few feet away from him, another Cherokee in a similar squat was smoking his pipe. A third leaned against a tree, his chin propped on the muzzle of his long rifle. Michael spun around to face Ned, whose hand was outstretched to receive the coffee. Instead, Michael poured the brew onto the ground and hung the tin cup back on the end of the iron rod supporting the pot.

"You're not here as our friends, are you?" Michael asked the question to which he already knew the answer. "They're only here to keep an eye on us, *'Tsu-ts'*," he said to Johnny. "To keep us from warning the others."

"I know. I saw them around midnight. We're their prisoners, *'Tsu-ts'*. Like it or not."

"Don't say that," *Tsa-tsi* implored them. "You are our brothers. *Tso-s-da-da-nŭ*, both of you."

"Not after this, *Tsa-tsi*," Michael said flatly, the pain of betrayal in his voice.

"It had to be this way, *Mi-ki*," Ned tried to persuade them.

"Did it?" Michael challenged. "I don't think so." He started to turn away but Ned caught his arm. Michael pulled free. As far as he was concerned, there was nothing more to say.

"If a warrior is wounded—and the flesh is rotten—you sometimes have to cut off an arm or a leg to save the warrior," Ned presented his hyperbolic argument.

"Not when you've survived the battle and there's a chance to heal!" Michael fired back.

"You boys came back awfully late last night," William's voice caught them off guard. The appearance of Michael's father brought their conversation to an abrupt halt. *Tsisdu* got up from his stump and ambled over to the fire. He poured from the pot and handed the cup to William. *"Wa-do, 'Tsu-ts',"* William thanked the Rabbit Man. "You been down here all night?"

"Mostly. Off and on," *Tsisdu* answered, stretching his sore back.

"How did the meeting go?" William asked his son and Johnny. There was a long silence. In the distance, one of the Cherokee horses whinnied. William squinted through the mist and saw the men waiting up the road. He looked back to Michael and Johnny for an explanation.

"They're planning to kill Major Ridge!" Michael blurted out. "And John and Elias and the others!"

William looked to Ned and *Tsa-tsi* for confirmation. Their silent lips and evasive eyes spoke volumes. *Tsisdu* gestured with his pipe toward the other Cherokees, motionless spirits in the drifting fog.

"They're here to *protect* us," the Rabbit Man said sarcastically.

"It's the law. It has to be this way," Ned repeated his rote argument.

Michael threw his coffee cup down and went to get his horse. "It does *not* have to be this way! I'm going to warn them! *Tsa-ni?*" he looked at the only friend he had left, asking for his help. Johnny dropped his cup beside the fire and hurried to join Michael.

"I'll ride to Honey Creek," he said. "You go to Park Hill."

They sprang onto their unsaddled horses and pulled up beside the fire. Michael drew his Collier repeating pistol from his belt. "I'll kill any man who tries to stop me!" he glared down at *Ne-di* and *Tsa-tsi*. There was no doubt in their minds he meant every word. Johnny and Michael took off. Ned and George trotted out to the middle of the road with William right behind them.

"*Mi-ki!* It's too late!" *Ne-di* shouted.

"It's over. It's done by now," *Tsa-tsi* called.

The riders stopped and turned their horses around. Behind them the other Cherokees emerged from the woods and rode away in the morning mist, their watchdog duty served. Michael looked into his father's eyes. Memories flooded back from three years earlier when he had been powerless to save his best friend, James Walker. Once again, Michael felt he had failed someone he should have been able to rescue. His jaw tightened with swallowed anger and frustration.

"I know, son. I know," were the only words William could find.

Michael stopped beside Ned and *Tsa-tsi*. "Get on your horses and get out of here," his voice was low and tinged with sadness. "Don't ever come back. You're not my brothers. No, *tso-s-da-da-nŭ*! I turn my back on you! From now on, you don't exist." Michael rode back up toward the cabin. Johnny followed, pulling alongside Michael.

Ned took a couple of steps after them. "*Mi-ki! Tsa-ni!*" he called, knowing there would be no reply.

William's indignant glare at *Ne-di* and *Tsa-tsi* echoed his son's banishment of their former friends. He followed Michael and Johnny up to the cabin. *Ne-di* and *Tsa-tsi* looked with pleading to *Tsisdu*, squatting by the fire. With a stick the Rabbit Man tilted the pot until the last of the coffee extinguished the fire with an ominous hiss amid billows of steam and smoke.

* * * * * * *

A circle of heavily armed Cherokees stood arm's length apart, surrounding the home of principal chief John Ross near Park Hill. Their backs were to the house, their eyes watchful to intercept any family member, friend or clansman of the slain Treaty Party who might appear, intent upon revenge against the chief. Horses were tied to trees in the yard or grazed inside the circle of men.

When William, Michael and Johnny rode up from the main road, the *Tsa-la-gi* guards closed ranks to block their path. William didn't recognize any of the men in this immediate part of the circle, and none of them knew William. A rifle was raised in challenge, then a pistol. A hand glided smoothly to a knife on the belt.

"I need to see *Gu-wi-s-gu-wi*," William said.

"Someone will have to vouch for you," the guard with the rifle answered. Michael recognized one of the men the raiders had once saved.

"You know us!" he said, pointing to the man.

"We saved you from those *yo-neg* outlaws on the Arkansas River!" Johnny added.

"We know you, but we don't know your intentions," the Cherokee from the river replied. He felt uncomfortable challenging the men who had rescued him and his family.

"It's all right!" came a voice from inside the circle. William

718

looked past the guards to see John Howard Payne, the journalist friend of John Ross. He had come west to continue chronicling the fate of the Cherokee nation. "Let them through! I'll vouch for them," he called to the guards. The Cherokees parted and allowed the riders through. Once inside the circle, the three men dismounted. William exchanged a subdued greeting with Payne. The amenities of their reunion were kept to a minimum and they soon started toward the house. Michael and Johnny stayed outside with the horses. The man from the river came over to chat with them.

John Ross was greatly distressed by the shocking news of the morning's tragic events. He was also concerned for his own safety. Highly agitated, he paced around the large main room of his expansive new house that—with the contributed labor of many skilled workers—had gone up in a very short time following his arrival in the west. Because he was the political opponent—some might even say the enemy—of Major Ridge and the Treaty Party, he would be the first to come under suspicion of having engineered the executions. Consequently, he would become the primary target for blood vengeance by the clan and family members of the slain men.

William and Payne entered and stood quietly near the door. George Lowrey, Charles Hicks and many other tribal leaders sat around the room, smoking their pipes and conversing in low tones commensurate with the funereal atmosphere. Ross spotted William and Payne.

"I knew something was wrong when all these men started showing up," he said. *Gu-wi-s-gu-wi* figured the assassination conspirators had arranged for the chief's *protection* to begin even before the first execution took place at Honey Creek.

"*Gu-wi-s-gu-wi*, everyone knows you had nothing to do with the murders," William reassured the chief.

"Do they?" Ross countered, not so easily pacified. "We have reports that Stand Watie is on his way here right now to exact his swift revenge!"

George Lowrey rose from the table and greeted William. They hadn't seen each other for some time. "One of the Spear brothers was ambushed by a cousin of The Ridge," he reported on the bloody cycle that always followed such killings. "Money Talker, Joseph Beanstalk, Bird Doublehead. All dead."

"Revenge is swift, indeed," Charles Hicks added.

"Were they involved in the executions?" William asked.

"How should I know?!" Ross fired back, already sensitive to

the flood of insinuations, allegations and accusations he knew would be forthcoming.

William took no offense to the chief's outburst. "What do we do?"

"We wait. That's what we do," Payne answered. "Passions are running high right now. We need time."

"We don't have time!" the chief clenched his fist, holding it up as though to ward off some unseen assailant. "Something like this is just what the *yo-negs* want. They'll use it as an excuse to tear our nation apart. They'll destroy everything we've worked for! This will pit brother against brother! Father against son..." his eyes burned into the conscience of his son, Allen, whose job it had been to make sure his father's alibi was irrefutable and his house was secured against retaliation from the moment the assassinations began.

* * * * * * *

General Matthew Arbuckle, commander of all military forces in the Arkansas and Indian Territories, was usually low keyed and easy going, but on this morning he was in a state of unmitigated fury. The alert and ubiquitous *aide* kept silently to one side while the general paced back and forth behind his expansive desk in the Ft. Gibson headquarters. Major Tyler had come over from Ft. Smith the day before on other business and sorely wished he could extricate himself from this sticky situation and return to his own post. His only consolation was that the general's wrath wasn't directed at him. The target of Arbuckle's blistering tirade was Rufus Stone, United States Marshal for the Arkansas and Indian Territories. News of John Ridge's and Elias Boudinot's slaying had reached Ft. Gibson shortly after the body of esteemed Cherokee tribal leader, Major Ridge, had been found lying murdered in the middle of the road to Van Buren.

Stone, in his late forties, was a weathered man with a bit of a paunch. His gray-flecked beard was neatly trimmed and his blue eyes, usually narrowed to a sun squint, burned this morning with resentment toward Arbuckle. Stone wasn't a man who took well to a verbal lashing, especially in the presence of others. Under ordinary circumstances, had a man addressed him in the manner and tone now being used by the general, Stone would have either decked him on the spot or, if in a more mellow frame of mind, would simply have walked away.

"You're the U. S. Marshal here, Stone! And you don't know what the hell's going on in your own territory?!"

"It's your territory as well, General!" Stone fired back defensively.

"For military matters, yes!" Arbuckle acknowledged, then countered with sarcasm. "Have we been invaded by a foreign army? Is there officially an Indian uprising?"

"Some say it could come to that," Stone reminded him.

"Hell. Why not just let 'em kill each other?" Major Tyler interjected, ostensibly in jest but with a seed of seriousness. "Makes all our jobs easier."

Stone had run into Tyler before and didn't like the man. "I'll tell you why, Major. Indians get tired of killing Indians real quick. Then they start killing white folks."

"You're right about that, Marshal Stone," the general was forced to agree. "And neither of us has the manpower to take on a full-scale uprising right now."

"What about the Cherokee police? The *Light Horse*," Tyler suggested, not wanting his contributions to be entirely dismissed.

"That's just it," Stone countered. "They're Cherokee. How eager you think they'll be to turn on their own?"

"Fact is, they're *Indians*," Arbuckle summed it all up. "Can't trust them."

"I'm going to need to deputize some men," Stone concluded.

"Take some of the wagoners and contractors who followed the Indians out," the general was ahead of him. "All they've been doing is hanging around, getting drunk and causing trouble anyway. It'll give 'em something to do."

"There is one other thing we can try, General..." The marshal's tone caught Arbuckle's attention. He peered at Stone over the top of his wire-rimmed glasses, waiting to hear the lawman's proposal.

* * * * * * *

Later that same evening Marshal Rufus Stone stood before a gathering of shabby and unruly whites. Most of them had served as wagoners and contractors who had sold to, cheated or stolen from the Cherokees throughout the removal. Scurrilous men for the most part, vile and offensive, they would be deputized to form Stone's posse in the pursuit and apprehension of the murderers of the Cherokee Treaty Party. Most of them were already drunk and disorderly—as they usually were by this time each evening—but Stone knew there was nothing he could do about it. He had called them together for one reason.

"The United States owes a debt of gratitude to the brave men who have assembled here to help preserve law and order in the Territory," he began, knowing such polemics were of no interest whatsoever to the men before him. They had one question in their minds, perhaps two. *What's in it for me?* and, for some, *Do I get to kill some Indians?* "I'm Territorial Marshal Rufus Stone," he introduced himself. "I'll be officially deputizing you men as Assistant U. S. Marshals. You'll be divided into three groups. Each group will be led by either myself or one of my regular Deputy Marshals...Bill Haines and Henry Willard..." Stone indicated his two deputies—both stern-faced men, trail worn and sun-dried. Haines was tall and lanky with a thick, blonde moustache, an odd mismatch for his coal black hair. Willard was short, thick and stumpy. He sported thick, bushy sideburns but no chin whiskers. Standing with Haines and Willard were some of the men who had been deputized earlier in the afternoon to form the first of Stone's groups. Among them were Titus Ogilvie and Peter Tanner. Peter, as usual, was drunk and glassy-eyed. His greatest challenge was trying to remember exactly why he was there. Titus, as usual, was already plotting a way to turn the situation to his advantage. He was confident that by the time they were to report the next morning he would have the details all worked out.

* * * * * * *

The crudely hand-lettered reward poster—written in both English and the Cherokee symbols—offered a reward *for information leading to the capture of anyone involved in the murders of Cherokees John Ridge, Major Ridge, Elias Boudinot or other assassinated members of the Treaty Party*. Marshal Rufus Stone nailed the paper to the tree adjacent to the Van Buren road. He lowered the hammer and stepped back to assess his work. With him were his newly appointed *deputies*, including Titus Ogilvie's devoted myrmidons, Brantley and Solmes. The hot morning sun, coupled with the steamy humidity, promised another sweltering day. Only about two-thirds of the men Marshal Stone had deputized the night before were at the gates of the Ft. Gibson compound early the next morning. In truth, Stone had anticipated fewer than half of them would show.

"I don't read. What's it say, Marshal?" Solmes asked and

wiped his runny nose on the back of his hand.

"There's a reward. For turning in anyone connected with the Cherokee murders," Stone answered loud enough for all to hear. He suspected most of them shared their spokesman's illiteracy.

"You mean we can get money if we bring in some Injuns? Jes' 'cuz they killed some other Injuns?" Solmes scratched his head, puzzled by the proposition but delighted at the idea of making such easy money. He failed to understand that the posted reward was for members of the Cherokee community, not white deputy marshals.

"Dead or alive?" Brantley asked. Stone shot them a harsh look and mounted his horse. He was having second thoughts about the idea he had proposed to Arbuckle—and which the general had enthusiastically endorsed—to simply offer money to any Cherokee willing to implicate any other Cherokee in the assassinations. Any allegation resulting in the arrest of a Cherokee they could haul back to the Ft. Gibson stockade meant cash for the accuser. And the charges, Marshal Stone and General Arbuckle had agreed, didn't require concrete substantiation. No proof beyond a reasonable doubt. *Just get me some bodies we can swing from a rope*, Arbuckle had whispered at the end of their meeting. Stone was counting on there being enough desperate Indians who had either gambled away and drunk their money up or had been robbed or scammed out of their allotments to come forward with information that would help resolve this annoying situation.

"You're not here to kill anybody," Stone reminded them. "And no, you don't get any money. This is your civic duty," he bellowed before riding out. Brantley and Solmes were the last to mount up and follow.

"*Civic duty?*" Brantley asked Solmes. "What the hell's that?"

Solmes, battling some pollen-induced allergy, pressed a thumb to one nostril and from the other blasted a clump of mucoid encrustations the size of a hickory nut. "If we ain't gettin' no money outa this deal, what are we doin' here?"

Brantley had no answer, but he offered a thought that might at least pass for consolation. "Maybe we'll get to kill us a Injun or two anyway." Solmes raised his eyebrows and smiled. It was something they could look forward to.

"Yeah. 'At's a good idea. You got good brains," he complimented Brantley's intellectual prowess.

* * * * * * *

Throughout the rest of the day Marshal Stone and his battalion of deputies scoured the northeast corner of Indian Territory. Posters were nailed up at every crossroads and watering hole, every village, bridge and ferry. By early afternoon, a group of deputized wagoners and contractors were dragging a Cherokee man from his cabin. The defiant *Tsa-la-gi* freely and proudly admitted having been at the Takatoka meeting when the assassinations were planned. He had ridden with his brothers to the home of John Ridge near Honey Creek. He insisted that he had done nothing wrong. He had only fulfilled Cherokee tribal law and he would not go with them.

After the conspirator was subjected to vigorous physical persuasion at the hands of the white deputies, the accompanying Cherokee Light Horse—the tribe's official police force—stepped in and took custody of the admitted assassin, hoisting him onto one of their own horses.

The marshal sat on his horse at an intersection on the Ft. Gibson road and counted out wrinkled notes and some coins to the reward-seeking mixed-blood who had led them to their first capture. As he thumbed through his money, the mixed-blood felt the burning eyes of the man he had betrayed. The response to the posters had exceeded Stone's expectations. News had travelled fast that the *yonegs* were paying good money for reporting anyone evenly remotely associated with the conspiracy. A couple of men in no way involved with plotting or carrying out the executions were fingered for personal reasons. One had impregnated another man's wife, and a second had stolen a pig. It was an opportunity—and a lucrative one—to settle old, unrelated personal scores, and the whites obviously didn't care whether or not those they rounded up were guilty of the Treaty Party killings.

* * * * * * *

One of the men who had stabbed John Ridge was dragged from his cabin, his wife and children screaming and crying behind him. Ironically, it was a scene not unlike the very one in which he himself had participated. This time, however, it wasn't a posse of rowdy, drunken *yo-neg* deputies but members of the *A-ni-ka-wi*, the Deer Clan, who, in accordance with Cherokee tradition, were honor bound to exact revenge for the murders of their clansmen. *A-ni-ka-wi* men held the conspirator's arms outstretched while the others stabbed him multiple times. They then tossed him high into the air, allowing his wounded body to land with a thud, his organs exploding inside him, blood gushing from his mouth. The anguish he saw in the faces of his wife and children mirrored the horror he had witnessed in the countenances of Sarah Ridge, young John Rollin Ridge and his brothers and sisters.

* * * * * * *

All the walls of William Drummond's new cabin were in place and the roof was more than half finished. Moonlight flooded in through the open space that, hopefully, would be completed before the next rainfall. Annie and Susanna worked their soothing magic to settle the three children to sleep opposite where William, Michael, Johnny and *Tsisdu* huddled around the blaze crackling in the new stone fireplace.

The night's tranquility was splintered by thundering hoofbeats. Immediately the lanterns and candles were extinguished. *Tsisdu* doused the fire with the contents of the coffee pot while the others reached for their guns. The women lay down on either side of the children and placed their hands over the mouths of Meg, *Tsi-mi* and *Me-li*. The men were on their knees, guns ready, peering out the window opening. In the moonlight they could barely distinguish a group of riders galloping past on the road almost two hundred yards from the cabin.

"Light Horse?" William asked in a whisper, "or *yo-negs*?"

"Couldn't tell," Michael answered softly.

"What difference does it make, as long as they leave us alone," they heard Susanna say from the darkness.

"I want to see!" *Tsi-mi* said loudly.

"Me, too! I want to see!" Meg and *Me-li* parroted him. They squirmed free of the women and raced to the window. Jimmy stretched up as high as he could and *Me-li* lifted Meg up to look out. With the hoofbeats receding in the distance, the adults breathed easier. A couple of candles were relit but the fireplace remained dark and the children were herded back to bed.

* * * * * * *

By the next day Rufus Stone had decided to call in more territorial deputies and divide the *ad hoc* posse into smaller squads to cover more territory. Interim Deputies Brantley and Solmes had, as usual, aligned themselves with Titus Ogilvie and Peter Tanner.

The four of them silently agreed to hang near the back of the group each time an accused Cherokee conspirator was apprehended. Ogilvie's plan didn't include becoming involved with the actual arrest. God forbid there should be a struggle. Someone could get hurt.

At a cabin in the hills southeast of Ft. Gibson, Titus and his men watched the Cherokee Light Horse take the prisoner away. They sat patiently while Marshal Stone's regular deputy, Bill Haines, counted out money to the man who had led them to the accused assassin. After making the payment, Haines motioned for Ogilvie and the others to follow, then galloped to join the Light Horse, their prisoner and the rest of the posse. Titus and his men, however, remained behind. They watched the Cherokee pocket his money, get on his mule and ride away. Titus signalled to Brantley and Solmes before he and Peter rode after Haines.

Brantley and Solmes kept their horses at a walk a few yards behind the Cherokee and his mule until Titus, Tanner, Haines and the others were well out of view. Then, with a precision not often found in men of such limited mental acuity, they executed their plan. After pulling alongside the mule on either side, Solmes grabbed the reins. Brantley drew his pistol and held it inches from the Cherokee's face. With one hand in the air to indicate surrender, the Cherokee slowly removed from his coat pocket the cash Haines had just paid him. Once Brantley had the money, Solmes released the reins and motioned the Cherokee on his way.

"Let's go get some whiskey!" Solmes grinned. Brantley scowled at him for the distraction and had to start counting the money again.

Brantley finally finished the tally, then summarily dismissed the whiskey idea. "Are you crazy?! Mr. O.'ll kick our ass!" With an air of obedient urgency, he rode off to catch up with the others.

"Damn!" Solmes grumbled, "cain't get no whiskey. Ain't killed no Injuns..." Disappointed, he trotted after Brantley. "Hey!" he yelled. "How come we let him go? We could'a kilt him!"

* * * * * * *

By nightfall the different posse groups, led by Haines, Willard or one of the additional deputies Marshal Stone had called in, were making their way back to Ft. Gibson. Stone's intention, with Arbuckle's blessing, was to defuse the volatile Cherokee assassination-revenge situation. At the same time the marshal was trying not to create a new crisis by having his men become embroiled in some skirmish or, worse, wiped out in an ambush in the middle of the night.

When the last group rode in, the Cherokee Light Horse police took their prisoners to the stockade where they would be held until enough of them had been captured to make a grand display of their hanging. General Arbuckle hoped such a widely publicized event would discourage any future assassination plots—tribal laws notwithstanding. The white posse members, in contrast, were interested at the end of each day only in finding food, whiskey, card games and prostitutes, courtesy of the many operations thriving in the woods just outside Ft. Gibson.

As they rode in, none of them—Cherokee Light Horse or white deputy—noticed the dark, blanket-wrapped form slinking along the boardwalk to the door of General Arbuckle's office. After a brief, muffled exchanged with the sentry, the shadowy figure was ushered inside.

*   *   *   *   *   *   *

General Arbuckle's *aide* paused to adjust the wick of the oil lantern to a brighter burn, then continued penning the testimony just given by their late-night visitor. He blotted the statement dry and blew on it three times before sliding it along the desk. General Arbuckle was seated in his large chair, his tunic unbuttoned, boots standing on the floor beside the desk, a cup of whiskey and warm milk next to the large Bible open in front of him. He tilted his head back and looked down at the statement, reading through the tiny, wire-rimmed spectacles perched on his bulbous nose. When finished, he looked over the glasses to the person standing across from him.

"You're telling me these men are the key conspirators in the Treaty Party assassinations?" A muffled grunt from the hooded shadow confirmed his statement. Arbuckle took a sip from the cup, wiped away the milk moustache and exhaled heavily—his eyes never leaving the informant. "You realize, of course, you won't receive any reward money until *after* these people are taken into custody."

"I don't want your money," the informant spoke softly, lowering the blanket from her head. "I just want to do what's right," *E-gi-ni* Redbird said.

The general tapped his fingers thoughtfully on the desk, studying the woman before him. "So do I...so do I," he said, then motioned to the sentry standing just inside the door.

* * * * * * *

The heavy wooden stockade door creaked opened and the two soldiers pushed *E-gi-ni* into the cell. When she regained her balance, she threw the blanket on the cot by the wall and protested vehemently. "Why are you doing this?! I didn't even ask for a reward! I gave you good information!"

"A little *too* good, according to the general," one of the sentries agreed.

The second guard held up a forearm to keep her from coming closer to the cell door. "General Arbuckle says anybody that knows so much details had to be in on the conspiracy."

As soon as the key had turned in the lock, *E-gi-ni* rushed to the tiny peep-hole. "This isn't right! You can't do this!" she shrieked, her voice acrid with outraged betrayal.

"Just following the general's orders," the first sentry shrugged.

With her face pressed against the tiny bars, *E-gi-ni's* eyes filled with tears. She bit her lip and listened to the hollow echo of the soldiers' retreating footsteps.

CHAPTER

63

The events of recent days had overwhelmed William and his family. Many of their friends had been slaughtered in the bloodbath of clan revenge following the Treaty Party assassinations. And the tragedy was compounded in knowing that many of the executioners, as William had often said, were basically good men who sadly had been misguided into believing that tribal blood laws must be obeyed. To these men, the actions of the Treaty Party had resulted in the deaths of parents, spouses, children or other family and friends, and the spirits of those loved ones untimely taken cried out for revenge.

The Drummonds hadn't built a fire for the past four nights. The days had been hot and the evenings unusually warm. After the children fell asleep, Susanna and her father went for a stroll along the creek behind the cabin.

"I remember the long walks we used to take back home," William recalled fondly.

"This is home now," Susanna smiled in the darkness. She had come to love the night when things were peaceful. "I never thought I'd say this, but it really is a beautiful place."

They walked on a little farther before William spoke. "So much has happened in such a short time. Yet, it feels like an eternity since your mother and I waited up all night when Meg was born." Susanna caught up with him and slipped her hand into his as she had done when she was just a little girl. He squeezed her hand gently. "I'm so proud of you, Susie. Proud of who you've become. And Michael, too. It's funny. We always had such grand expectations for our children—your mother and I. You would grow up to be the sophisticated wife of some fine young man, perhaps with a brilliant military career ahead of him. Michael would join me in the law practice, then go on to become senator, governor...who knows...even president. And now..."

"Yes," she laughed softly, "look at us now."

"Don't say it like that," William tugged at her hand affectionately. "I could die tonight—go to be with your mother—and know we've done well. And whatever happens, you...and Michael...and Meg..."

"And Johnny," she put in.

William smiled. "And Johnny...all of you...will be all right."

It was a while before Susanna responded, this time with a serious tone. "I wonder sometimes. Back home, they hunted us like animals. The whites did. Rounded us up and threw us into those camps. So many died. And then the terrible journey to get here. So many more were lost. Some—like Mother—not even Cherokee!"

"But we survived," William reminded her. "We made it."

"And now look what's happening," Susanna made her point. "The whites don't have to kill us. We've turned on each other. Cherokee killing Cherokee. When will it all end?"

They stopped and William gazed up through the trees at the star-flecked sky. "I wish I could tell you. I really wish I could," he sighed. They both looked up for a while, then continued their walk in pensive silence.

* * * * * * *

Marshal Rufus Stone had been wakened and summoned to General Arbuckle's office only minutes after the soldiers escorted *E-gi-ni* Redbird to her cell. He read the statement and listened to the general's impressions of the girl's story, then paid a visit to the stockade.

E-gi-ni gave him a near verbatim repeat performance that, to the marshal, appeared a bit too well rehearsed. Nevertheless, she had furnished them detailed descriptions of the alleged conspirators and specific directions on where to find them. Stone and his men had already rounded up more than twenty-five Cherokees. Many of them, the marshal suspected, were guilty of nothing, but he and Arbuckle were willing to sacrifice them on the altar of political expediency. He needed the ring leaders, the featured players, not just the spear carriers in this little Cherokee blood drama which had already thrown a mantle of embarrassment on the U. S. Marshal service in Washington, D.C.

What's wrong in the Arkansas and Indian Territories, the widely published inquiries came, *that the U. S. Marshal can't control a few hundred Indians who're already sick and down-trodden after a brutal winter's march just to get there?*

And if their informant's story proved false, so what? They would have wasted an evening and inconvenienced a handful of Cherokees.

Stone called his deputies, Haines and Willard, away from a card game and a round of drinks that was clearly not their first. Haines was sent off to fetch three of the Cherokee Light Horse for their late night ride. The marshal then hand-picked four other whites—the ones who appeared the least inebriated—and thought it curious when four more volunteered. These were men who, to Stone's recollection, hadn't acquitted themselves with any distinction in the last several days. In fact, he barely remembered them at all. But when Haines reappeared with the Light Horse, Titus Ogilvie, Peter Tanner and their dimwitted henchmen, Brantley and Solmes, were saddled and ready to ride.

* * * * * * *

The cool evening breeze brought welcome relief from the day's heat. While Susanna was out walking with William, Johnny remained in the cabin, sitting on the floor beside his father near the open window. *Tsisdu* smoked his pipe and alternated between gazing out the window and watching the children he adored. Meg sat on the floor between Johnny's legs, leaning back against him. Annie and Michael played quietly with *Tsi-mi*. *Me-li* painstakingly transferred three baby kittens from a wooden box in the corner to a basket. She proceeded around the room to ceremoniously deliver one to *Tsi-mi* and another to Meg.

The pregnant cat had mysteriously appeared at the cabin late one night, meowing as if asking permission to enter, though she could easily have sprung through the open unfinished window casings. Her ears had been ripped and gnawed almost to the skull, and half her tail was missing. The children instantly adopted her and *Tsisdu* prepared an herbal concoction, most of which ended up on *Tsi-mi*, Meg and *Me-li*. The children named the cat Molly and prepared a bed in an old wooden government allotment box in the corner. They went to sleep one night and awoke the next morning to the miracle of tiny, spastic angels. Each day they attended their new charges with adult solemnity, having been cautioned about the possible tragic results of handling the kittens too often before they gained their strength. *Tsi-mi* was the first to discover one morning that two of them had begun to open their eyes. A few days later all three kittens were wide-eyed and all sanctions had been lifted. They were now fair game for holding, cuddling and tucking inside a shirt or a dress.

"*We-si! We-si-u-s-di!*" Meg cooed softly to the little cat in her high-pitched, baby-talk voice.

"*Tso-i we-si,*" *Me-li* announced the three kittens and counted them out—one, two, three. "*Sa-wu. Ta-li. Tso-i.*" That had become their names. One, Two and Three in Cherokee. The adults, watching the children play with the kittens, exchanged concerned looks at the sudden rumbling vibrations of distant hoofbeats.

"They're coming here," *Tsisdu* said softly.

"They've never stopped here before," Annie said, but she shared his sense of foreboding.

"They're coming here," *Tsisdu* repeated with an ominous tone. They were all aware of the territorial marshal's round up of accused assassins, but, knowing their own innocence, their greater concern had always been that Sergeant Wakefield might ride up some day—or night—and there would be an ugly situation. Johnny got to his feet and deposited Meg at Annie's side, then herded *Me-li* along so all three children were together before he joined Michael at the doorway. *Tsisdu* had been right. The bobbing torches illuminated the riders and horses coming up the gentle grade from the main road.

"I'll talk to them," Johnny said.

Michael studied them. "They don't look like talkers to me." He motioned to his wife. "Annie—take the children out back. By the creek. Father and Susie are out there."

"Go with them, *E-to-da*," Johnny told *Tsisdu*.

Hurriedly, but without panic, Michael checked his Collier repeating pistol, shoved it into his belt and grabbed one of the rifles. Johnny took the other. Young as they were, Meg, *Tsi-mi* and *Me-li* had learned the necessity of silence and the value of speed in these urgent moments. Just before Annie, *Tsisdu* and the children left, Michael went to them. Annie looked up into his eyes. Her hand rested on his forearm. She felt the tension, despite his attempt to convey a business-as-usual air.

"Be careful, *Mi-ki*," she said softly.

"I'm sure it's nothing. Go on," he knew she could read his every thought, but it was a little lie they each used only to alleviate the other's anxiety at times like this. When she turned to go, Annie almost tripped over Meg, crouched in the darkness, straining her eyes in search of something. Annie took Meg's hand and herded *Tsi-mi* and *Me-li* out the back door. Michael watched them go, then rejoined Johnny at the front. He never noticed the tattered wedding-dress doll his boot pushed farther behind the door.

"Hurry," Johnny whispered loudly to his father. *Tsisdu* grabbed another rifle and fumbled around in the darkness, then rushed out into the night to join Annie and the children. Meg and *Tsi-mi* kept their eyes on the basket of kittens *Me-li* carried. Molly meowed with motherly concern and trotted behind them on the narrow footpath.

Johnny and Michael squatted at the front window opening and watched the riders approaching at a moderate, steady pace. Rufus Stone was in the lead, flanked on either side by his deputies, the lanky Haines and the shorter, thicker Willard. Immediately behind them were the three Cherokee Light Horse, followed by the posse of white volunteers. Titus Ogilvie, Peter Tanner, Brantley and Solmes brought up the rear. They were blocked from Michael's view by the other riders and too far away to be recognized in the darkness.

* * * * * * *

In the woods behind the cabin, Annie, *Tsisdu* and the children glided swiftly along the path that went straight to, then ran eastward along the creek. Annie stopped to look back in the direction of the cabin. She was hit with a barrage of hideous images—too rapid and too disturbing to interpret. But she recognized the visceral jolt in the pit of her stomach that always accompanied a prescience of death.

"*Tsi-ne-na!* Let's go!" *Tsisdu* called in an urgent whisper. "We need to find *Wi-li* and *Se-ho-ya!*"

"I want Mommy..." Meg whimpered.

Annie scooped Jimmy up and hurried to join *Tsisdu* and the girls.

* * * * * * *

Marshal Stone signalled to stop when they were still twenty yards from the cabin. Stone rode out from the rest and cautiously approached the darkened structure.

"Hello! Anybody home?" The marshal hadn't really expected a response. He directed Haines and two of the Light Horse to circle around back to prevent an escape. Stone, a methodical, by-the-book lawman, breathed heavily, waiting patiently for the three men to reach their deployment positions.

Michael and Johnny, from deep in the shadows, tried to get a look at the men outside. "See anyone you know?" Michael whispered. Johnny leaned out past him just enough to rapidly scan the few faces illuminated by the torches. No one looked familiar. He shook his head no.

At the rear of the posse Peter Tanner took a long drink before offering the whiskey to Titus Ogilvie. With a sidelong look of disgust, Titus thoroughly wiped the mouth of the flask before drinking. Brantley held out his hand, anticipating the whiskey would be passed his way.

"Ought to be some decent money this time," he said conspiratorially. "There's a whole bunch of 'em. I heard the marshal say."

Titus swallowed with a wheezing exhalation and passed the flask back to Peter. He gave it a shake to check its level, then drained the last few drops. Disappointed, Brantley let his hand drop. They looked back to the cabin.

"This is Rufus Stone," the lawman hailed in a loud, official voice. "U. S. Territorial Marshal. I can see somebody in there. Come on out."

Several minutes passed before Johnny and Michael finally stepped out the front door. They held their guns in plain sight, hanging loosely at their side in a non-threatening posture. Stone's trained eye sized the pair up quickly. He motioned for Deputy Willard to ride closer with his torch. The marshal unfolded a piece of paper, squinting to read in the flickering light.

"Are you...John Fields and Michael Drummond?"

Titus Ogilvie's head snapped. Had his ears deceived him? Could it be? They had come along because they'd been told there were a number of Cherokees to be captured. Unaware that the informant sat languishing in the Ft. Gibson stockade, they were counting on a big reward payoff. There would be ample opportunity under cover of darkness to relieve the accuser of his newly acquired wealth. Not once had the names of the accused been mentioned. The marshal had directions on how to get here, Peter Tanner had a flask to relieve the boredom and Titus Ogilvie had a plan to acquire the money. What more did they need to know?

"What did he say?" Titus looked at Peter, Brantley and Solmes.

Johnny and Michael exchanged a long look, trying to decide whether they should identify themselves.

"Are you John Fields and Michael Drummond?" Stone repeated. Still they didn't answer. The marshal queried the one remaining Light Horse, who sat just beyond Deputy Willard. "Do you recognize these men?"

"I know Fields," the Cherokee policeman pointed to Johnny. His finger drifted to Michael and he added, "Never seen this one."

With Johnny positively identified, Michael saw no reason to hold back. "I'm Michael Drummond," he thrust his chin out. "What do you want?"

Titus Ogilvie maneuvered his horse out of the cluster and up toward the cabin. With the typically delayed reaction of a drunk, Peter finally followed, but he was in such a fog he still hadn't made the connection or simply hadn't heard the name. Marshal Stone kept his voice friendly but official. He eyed with quiet caution the weapons Johnny and Michael hadn't bothered to conceal.

"You wanna put down your guns? I got a warrant here for your arrest."

"What are the charges?" Michael asked.

He was certain they were finally being apprehended for the incident at Ft. Smith months earlier in which Sergeant Bolton had been killed. Michael would draw this out to buy Annie, *Tsisdu* and the children additional time to get farther away from the cabin. He figured the marshal—probably at General Arbuckle's behest—had used the activity surrounding the assassinations to do a little house cleaning. *While you're out rounding up Indians*, Arbuckle probably said, *bring in these two if you run across them.* Michael was somewhat surprised at the absence of Sergeant Wakefield. It hadn't occurred to Michael or Johnny that this visit could be linked to the murders of the Treaty Party leaders.

"Who else is in the house?" Stone asked, ignoring Michael's inquiry about the charges.

"Nobody," Johnny answered.

Stone motioned for Willard, still holding the torch, to check inside. While the deputy examined the cabin, the marshal continued with Michael and Johnny. "I also have warrants for Susanna Drummond Tanner and William Drummond." He folded the paper and stuck it back in his pocket.

Peter finally grasped a shred of recognition through the whiskey haze. "Did I hear...? Did he say...?"

Titus guided his mount up near the Light Horse policeman and looked down at Michael with elated outrage. It was an opportunity for sweet revenge which Titus had long since—and with great reluctance—accepted as having eluded him forever. "I don't believe it! My God, I don't believe it!"

"You know this man?" the marshal twisted in his saddle to face Ogilvie.

"Know him!?" Titus snorted. "Oh, indeed! Too well, I know him!"

The faces weren't clearly distinguishable behind the glaring torches, but Michael recognized the voice oozing from the shadowy bulk.

"Ogilvie?!" Titus side-stepped his horse toward Stone until he came into the circle of the torches' glow. "It *is* you! Well, I'll be damned!" Michael exclaimed.

"You will, indeed, be damned, young Drummond. If I have anything to say about it." Titus could scarcely control his growing excitement.

"Well, you *don't* have nothin' to say about it, Ogilvie, so just back off," the marshal ordered. Titus held up his hands in a placating gesture and looked at Peter with a wry grin. After awkwardly turning his horse in a full circle, Peter finally positioned himself beside Titus. He gawked at Michael and continually rolled his eyes as though these physical efforts might somehow clear his blurred vision and steady the image before him.

"Michael?" he slurred the name, bending forward in the saddle. "Michael Drummond?"

"Peter?!" Michael was as astonished to see his brother-in-law as he had been to find himself once again facing Titus Ogilvie.

"That's right, Drummond," Titus chuckled, relishing the stare-down between the two lifelong enemies. "Your beloved brother-in-law. The *General* himself!"

"This was *U-ni-tsi Wa-ya's* husband?" Johnny asked, stunned. "This drunk?"

Because of his inebriated state and his life-long ignorance of the *Tsa-la-gi* language, Peter had missed Johnny's *Mother Wolf* reference to his wife—or *former* wife.

"Where's Susanna? And my daughter...?" Peter's tongue moved heavily in his mouth like a molasses covered finger through baled cotton. "They're dead, aren't they? I knew it. Susanna was always weak...frail...she should have stayed with me..." His rambling voice cracked as though he might cry at any moment.

"This ain't no damn family reunion," Stone growled. His eyes never left Michael's and Johnny's weapons. "We're here to take these people prisoner."

"Damn! I need a drink!" Peter removed his hat and used his sleeve to wipe the sweat and matted hair from his forehead. With his other hand he searched from pocket to pocket for a flask.

* * * * * * *

William and Susanna had reached the little falls where the creek flowed over a granite outcropping and angled down toward a little valley. After a period of tranquil contemplation they started back but had gone only a short distance when Susanna halted, holding her hand up to stop William.

"Someone's coming..."

No sooner had she spoken than Annie, *Tsisdu* and the children emerged from the black tunnel formed by the low branches overhanging the narrow path. *Tsisdu* carried the rifle and a fist full of other items he had grabbed from the cabin.

"*Tsisdu*! What's the matter?" William asked.

"What is it, Annie?" Susanna stooped to meet Meg who ran on ahead to her mother. Annie motioned them to be quiet, but no one was going to silence Meg.

"Mommy! I'm scared!" she said loudly, clinging to Susanna.

* * * * * * *

After searching the cabin, Deputy Willard came out and shook his head, indicating he had found nothing. Stone leaned down toward Michael. His voice was controlled, patient, almost paternal.

"Son, we ain't leavin' here without all the people named on these here warrants," he said, pausing to let the point sink in. Then he added, "Now don't make us go chasin' through the woods in the middle of the night. Somebody's gonna get hurt."

Michael appreciated the marshal's attitude. Stone was no fool and knew most likely there were children involved. Michael chose his words prudently so as not to sound argumentative. "Marshal, with all due respect, we have a right to know what we're being charged with."

"You're nothin' but a God damn murderin' Injun, boy! You got no rights!" Titus Ogilvie bellowed, his face puffed with rage.

"Shut up, Ogilvie!" the marshal barked. He didn't like being interrupted, he didn't like anyone interfering with his job, and he didn't like the fat man before him. "I don't want to hear another word outa you! You got that?!" Titus looked up, he looked down, he looked sideways, but he wouldn't look at Rufus Stone. Even in the dim torchlight, the others saw Ogilvie's face redden with anger and humiliation. Satisfied he had made his point, Stone turned back to Michael. "We have a witness says you all conspired to assassinate the Ridges and num'rous other Cherokee leaders."

"That's a damn lie!" Johnny blurted out. "We had nothing to do with it! We wanted to warn them!"

"So you *did* know they was gonna be killed," Deputy Willard smirked with pride, convinced he'd tricked the devious Injun into an admission of complicity.

"That don't mean we killed 'em!" Johnny fired back.

Stone's hand shifted casually to rest on the handle of his pistol, just in case. "Settle down, boys. You'll get your chance to be heard."

Johnny would not be silenced. "Yeah. We know what kind of chance a Cherokee gets!"

The situation was getting out of hand. It was time to disarm the prisoners. "I *asked* you once," Stone said in a calm but undeniably firm tone, "now I'm *telling* you—put them guns down."

The Light Horse rider nodded to Johnny and Michael, urging them to comply. Leather creaked and horses shifted as other members of the posse positioned themselves for easy access to their weapons. Titus Ogilvie pulled a pistol from his belt, holding it loosely at his side. He would love nothing more than the slightest provocation. One step in his direction by either Johnny or Michael. One wrong twitch or suspicious move. Sure, Stone would howl and, no doubt, dismiss him from the posse, but Titus didn't care. One chance. That's all he wanted.

Johnny looked to Michael, who only had to give a sign and Johnny would launch them into a blazing gunfight that would undoubtedly end their lives. Unnoticed by Marshal Stone, Michael glanced toward the woods, then laid down his rifle and his Collier repeating pistol. But Johnny had caught Michael's reminder of their greater obligation. Their families were out there. If this could be resolved without bloodshed, they might live to see their women and the children they loved. Johnny took a deep breath to calm his warrior spirit and laid his rifle down beside Michael's.

"You got some horses?" Stone asked once the weapons were out of hand.

"I heard some out back," Willard interjected, convinced these Indians would, by nature, have lied about it had he not exposed the truth.

Stone studied the two suspects, then played his next card. "We're taking all the horses when we go, boys. So, if you got women and kids back up in them woods, you gotta ask yourself—you really wanna leave 'em, with trash like this runnin' around loose—" he said and looked directly at Titus Ogilvie, "—knowin' they's out there? And you're sittin' in jail?"

A shot rang out and Marshal Rufus Stone fell from his horse. The dark stain spreading over the front of his shirt looked black beneath the torches and the moonlight. All eyes turned to Titus Ogilvie who still held the smoking pistol.

"You watch who you calling trash!" he said, sneering down at the man he had just gut shot.

* * * * * * *

William, *Tsisdu*, Annie, Susanna and the children all stopped abruptly as the shot echoed through the forest. The adults exchanged worried looks and the children's apprehension fed off the grownups. They didn't know exactly what was going on, but even the youngest knew the meaning of gunshots in the middle of the night and knew it couldn't be good.

* * * * * * *

Titus Ogilvie drew a second pistol from his belt—the same one his late son, Alton, had used to shoot William Drummond. He alertly scrutinized the stunned faces before him. He knew he must promptly gauge which son-of-a-bitch would make trouble. His first concern was Willard and Haines, Stone's official deputies. For all Titus knew, they might also have been long-time friends. But he saw no challenge in any of their eyes, only shock and fear. He looked back down at Stone who had propped himself up on one elbow. His other hand clutched his stomach as though he could stop the bleeding or at least hold his life inside for a few precious seconds longer.

"I'm relievin' you of your duties, Marshal Stone. I'll be in charge now," Ogilvie said, his official announcement laced with sarcasm. Titus moved his horse close to Willard, who couldn't take his eyes off the wounded marshal. Ogilvie snatched the torch from Willard and trotted toward the cabin.

In a delayed reaction, all the pieces finally clicked into place in Willard's mind. His boss—a United States Territorial Marshal—had just been murdered in cold blood by some rag-tag, temporary deputy. Willard drew his pistol and aimed it at Ogilvie. The deputy thought seriously about shooting Titus in the back, but he knew he wouldn't. He would take him in to face the justice system he'd been trained to respect, serve and obey. But before he could order Ogilvie to stop and surrender his weapons, another shot was fired. The side of Willard's head erupted in a shower of blood, hair, flesh and bone fragment. He fell from his horse, landing beside

Marshal Stone.

Titus snapped around in time to see Willard fall. He could tell the deputy's gun had been pointed at his back. He looked across at Peter Tanner, his pistol smoking, trying to steady his horse which had been startled by the blast.

"Mighty fine shot, General! Much obliged," Ogilvie praised his drunken friend, then casually tossed the torch into the cabin through the window opening. Michael and Johnny made a move toward the guns on the ground, but Titus spurred his horse to cut them off. At a signal from Ogilvie, Solmes sprang from his horse and retrieved the weapons. He tossed one rifle up to Brantley and took the other for himself. Solmes then picked up the Collier repeating pistol, examined it curiously, cocked it and grinned with the excitement of a child discovering a new toy.

* * * * * * *

When the second shot sounded, Annie and Susanna had stopped on the trail. The men they loved were at that cabin and there was shooting. They didn't know exactly what was going on or what they could do to help, but they knew they had to get there. Annie passed *Tsi-mi* to *Tsisdu* and Susanna handed Meg to William. The women ran toward the cabin, with *Tsisdu*, William and the children hurrying after them.

* * * * * * *

Despite his serious wound, Marshal Stone clung to life. Still holding his bloody stomach with one hand, he got to his knees, forming a three-point stance with the other hand. The Light Horse tribal policeman closest to Stone jumped down from his horse to help the marshal. Startled by the sudden dismount, Solmes spun and fired the Collier, instantly killing the Cherokee.

"Damn, Solmes! You got him!" Brantley exclaimed. "Well, there you go! You got to kill yerself a Injun!" Solmes looked at the dead Light Horse and at the smoking Collier, then grinned up at Brantley, who was pointing impatiently to the marshal. "Get the money! The reward money!" Brantley yelled.

With supreme effort, Stone straightened up from his tripod position and rocked back to sit on his heels. He shook his head weakly and held up a hand. Blood poured from his mouth, and his voice was barely audible.

"I don't have the money..."

Displeased by this response, Solmes kicked the marshal hard in the groin. Stone doubled over with a bottomless groan. Then, in a remarkable display of endurance, he straightened back up on his knees. This time Solmes fired the Collier point blank into the marshal's face, sprawling him backwards across the body of Deputy Willard. Solmes grinned up at Titus Ogilvie.

"This here's a great little gun, Mister O.! Don't even have to reload! Just keep on shootin'!"

The remaining Light Horse Cherokees returned from the rear of the cabin and Deputy Haines came around the other end. They had heard the shots and, from the other side, had seen Ogilvie throw the torch into the cabin. The additional shots brought them to investigate. It took only an instant for Haines and the two Light Horse Cherokees to figure out what had happened when they saw the bodies of Marshal Stone, Deputy Willard and the dead Light Horse policeman.

The other *yo-neg* posse men were forced to decide. Their fickle allegiance lay with whoever was in power, which, at the moment, appeared to be Titus Ogilvie. Two of the whites drew their guns and fired, killing one of the Light Horse and wounding the other. Johnny and Michael were the closest to Haines and the wounded Cherokee. They waved frantically for the two men to keep riding toward the road.

"Go!" they shouted. *"Do-yi! Do-yi!* Get out of here!"

To reach the road, Haines and the wounded Light Horse would have to go right past the men who were shooting at them. Bending low on their mounts, they sprinted past the *yo-negs*, hoping a few seconds would carry them far enough into the darkness to render them more shadow than substance as targets. As they raced by, the rest of the posse opened fire. The wounded Cherokee was struck twice, falling dead from the horse which raced on without him. But they missed Deputy Haines altogether. Peter Tanner had just finished reloading his pistol after shooting Deputy Willard. Despite his drunken state, he calmly aimed and fired. Haines raised up in the saddle, his hat and the top of his skull gone. The horse carried him a few yards more before he flipped backwards, his limp arms and legs flailing wildly before the body came to rest in a crumpled heap. The other posse men were visibly impressed with Peter's marksmanship.

Titus had seen it all before. While he appreciated the accomplishment, there was no time to sing Peter's praises. Ogilvie threw a rope around Michael and jerked it tight, binding Michael's arms to his side. Johnny grabbed the rope, creating enough slack for Michael to wriggle one arm free. Titus backed his horse up, pulling the rope taut again. He pulled Michael and Johnny close enough for Peter to crack Johnny on the head with the butt of his pistol. Johnny fell unconscious beside the bodies of Marshal Stone, Deputy Willard and the first Light Horse Cherokee killed by Solmes.

Titus yelled for Brantley to circle behind Michael and throw another rope. This one landed around Michael's neck. It was easier for all of them to see in the added light from the fire. The flames lapped up the side of the cabin door and above the windows to ignite the thatch roof, creating grotesquely twitching shadows all about the clearing. With the help of the other posse men, Michael was dragged, kicking and choking, to the largest pine William and *Tsisdu* had left standing to shade the cabin.

A disappointed Solmes finished rifling through the pockets of the blood-drenched marshal. "He was right," Solmes whined. "Ain't no damn money!" Frustrated, he pressed the Collier against the dead marshal's ribs and fired another slug into the corpse. In a pointless display of domination at once childlike and fiendish, he put the gun barrel to the head of Deputy Willard and fired. Next he placed the Collier to the back of Johnny's skull. He had pulled the trigger to within a hair of firing when Titus screamed.

"Solmes! Get your sorry ass over here!" Reluctantly Solmes released the trigger and started toward the tree where Michael swung wildly, suspended in mid air. He hung on desperately to the rope around his throat with his one free hand to keep from choking and to prevent his neck from being snapped. "Bring him down! Bring him down!" Titus yelled. "Can't you idiots do anything right?! When you hang a man, you got to tie his hands and feet!"

Brantley and another posse member thought they had done a pretty good job. With grumbling disappointment, they began lowering Michael, slacking the rope in repeated jerky motions to the delight of the onlookers. Titus side-stepped his horse over to Peter who had renewed his pocket-probing search for that elusive, tucked-away flask.

"If I recall, General, you prefer a firing squad to hanging," Titus joked. "Let me show you how it's done."

Peter's blank look flickered to life with the recollection of James Walker's execution.

"Yeah..." Peter answered and was about to say more, but Titus had already spurred his horse back toward the tree. He yanked the rope, slamming Michael hard against the trunk of the large pine, then tossed the other end to Brantley and Solmes.

"Tie him to the tree! What the hell you waitin' for?!" Ogilvie growled with exasperation. Eagerly the two henchmen pulled the rope tightly around Michael's neck and circled the tree, binding their prisoner firmly to the thick, rosin-speckled trunk. Ogilvie laboriously lowered his bulky mass from his horse.

* * * * * * *

Annie and Susanna, ahead of the men and children on the narrow trail in the woods, stopped when they reached a break in the trees. They could see the glow of the fire against the night sky and knew the cabin had been set ablaze. Their anxious concern for the men they loved drove them on as fast as they could go. They knew *Tsisdu*, William and the children were somewhere behind them, but foremost in the women's minds was getting to the cabin to see about Michael and Johnny.

* * * * * * *

Savoring this deliciously chilled serving of revenge, Titus Ogilvie pressed his oily face up close. Michael could smell the fat man's rancid breath even through the smoke from the burning cabin. Brantley, standing just behind Titus, kept the rope pulled tight. It wasn't the first time Michael Drummond had glared into Titus Ogilvie's blood-shot, beady eyes, but he realized it might well be the last. He knew that his wife and sister, his father and his son were out in those woods, and he hoped Annie and *Tsisdu* had kept them all going, as far away from the cabin as they could get. Whatever was about to happen to him, Michael thought, he was glad his loved ones weren't there to witness it. And he knew Johnny would have felt the same way.

"You disgusting pig!" Michael spat the words out with all the repugnance he could pack into his rope constricted voice. "I should have gutted you when I had the chance!"

Titus's lip rolled up in the start of a sneer, but so rapturous was this moment for him he couldn't prevent it from spreading into a full-faced, wicked grin.

"Aye! 'Tis true, Drummond. And now you're gonna find out just *how* true." He tugged sharply on the rope, snapping Michael's head hard against the tree and bringing his face even closer—so close, it appeared to the onlookers, that he might kiss Michael on the ear. "And it gives me more pleasure than you can imagine," he whispered. "I just wish my two boys were here to share in the fun!"

Bracing his hand against the tree, Titus wrapped his fat, grimy fingers around the rope and pulled, watching the twisted fibers cut into Michael's throat, depriving him of air. He studied with curious amusement the veins bulging in the neck and on the side of his torture victim's head. He watched the tiny saliva bubbles escape from between Michael's tightly clenched, cyanotic lips. Gradually Titus relaxed his grip, allowing Michael only a fleeting taste of the smokey, life-sustaining air before he repeated the grueling choke cycle.

Solmes danced with anticipation. He didn't know why, but he'd always loved watching a man die, especially when it was slow and painful. When he was drunk—if the subject happened to come up—he sometimes admitted it had even given him a hard one a couple of times. Solmes remembered telling on many a cold, rainy night by the campfire how *Mister O.* and *Mister T.* had thrown together a firing squad made up of young Cherokees. How Titus and Peter were going to force the Injun boys to execute James Walker. And how, at the last second, young Drummond had jumped in and shot his best friend smack between the eyes.

"You gonna make that other Injun kill him, Mister O.? That'd be funny!"

Ogilvie knew Solmes seldom had anything intelligible—much less intelligent—to say, but this idea struck his fancy. He squeezed the rope tighter around Michael's neck and pointed to Johnny.

"What say, Drummond? Shall we wake up your friend over there? Let him be our one-man, Cherokee firing squad? Does that ring a bell? Bring back old memories?"

Ogilvie didn't really expect Michael to reply, and he certainly hadn't anticipated the answer he got. The ropes held Michael's upper torso, binding his arms, chest and neck, but his captors had forgotten about his legs. The fringed boot flashed out and kicked Titus on the side of his crippled knee, dropping the fat man like a cannon ball rolling off the end of a caisson. Titus released the rope, and Michael greedily sucked in the precious air. But Brantley lunged in and drove his fist into Michael's stomach, taking his breath away.

Peter half-climbed, half-fell from his horse and staggered up to Michael. Ogilvie grabbed the back of Brantley's belt for balance and, bracing against the tree, painfully pulled himself to his feet. He snatched the large knife from Brantley's belt, then jerked the rope so hard Michael's head slammed against the tree, cutting off his air once again. With sweat rolling off the end of his nose, Titus was back in his captive's face, panting heavily.

A trickle of blood ran down from the tip of the knife pressed against Michael's cheek. Michael could see—and smell—Ogilvie's abscess infected gums when the fat man snarled, "I oughta just cut your murdering Cherokee heart out right now and feed it to the God damn dogs!"

Peter leaned in over Ogilvie's shoulder, his own putrid, alcoholic breath mixing with Titus's to overwhelm the olfactory senses of their prisoner. "I always knew you'd end up this way, Michael," Peter lectured. "From the time we were kids. You were always the trouble maker. I tried to tell you. Now look at you!"

"Look at yourself, Peter!" Michael's words came out in a choked, scratchy whisper. "You're nothing but a filthy drunk!"

"You watch your mouth, boy!" Peter wedged himself in front of Titus and punched Michael in the face.

Michael's head recoiled from the blow and snapped right back to his assailant. Mustering everything he could from his dry, sticky mouth, he spat in Peter's face. Peter absently smeared the pinkish glob across his scraggly beard with the back of his hand. A lifetime of hatred for his brother-in-law burned through the haze of his drunken stupor. By this disrespectful act, Michael had sealed his own fate. Peter stepped back and clamped a hand on Ogilvie's shoulder—more to steady himself than from any sense of camaraderie.

"How do you want to do this, Titus?" he asked.

The fat man's eyes narrowed to slits. Raising Brantley's knife, Titus lunged toward the young man he so utterly despised. Michael brought his foot up again, but this time Ogilvie was prepared. He dodged the defensive maneuver and drove the knife straight for Michael's face, then deliberately veered off at the last instant to miss by only inches, driving the broad blade into the bark beside Michael's head. Titus stepped back and replayed his evil grin as he pulled the tiny stopper from his powder horn and began reloading his pistol.

* * * * * * *

Annie and Susanna were the first to reach the edge of the woods near the cabin, but it didn't take long for William and *Tsisdu*, with Jimmy and the girls, to catch up. The women were frantic.

Through the heavy growth of bushes and smaller trees they could see the cabin engulfed in flames. They could see the posse members surrounding their two leaders who were facing someone tied to the big pine tree. Though their view was partially obscured, they assumed the captive was either Johnny or Michael. They figured the other to be the pair of legs with Cherokee boots extending past a pile of corpses a few yards from the tree. When *Tsisdu* arrived, he crouched and parted the bushes. Susanna squatted beside him. From this angle they had an unobstructed view of the body on the ground beside the bloody corpses. It was, indeed, Johnny. She gripped Rabbit Man's shoulder.

"It's all right," *Tsisdu* reassured her. "He's not dead. *Tsani*'s alive."

Annie joined them, dropping to her knees on the other side of *Tsisdu*. They could also see the tree where Michael was tied and Peter and Titus were loading their pistols. Annie looked back into the brush behind them. William deposited *Tsi-mi* and the girls beside a tree and instructed them to hold hands, admonishing all three not to move and to keep silent. William then came up behind *Tsisdu* and the women. He was carrying one of the rifles. Susanna picked up *Tsisdu's* rifle. She had never fired one, but she would do whatever she had to do.

"No!" Annie called in a loud whisper.

"We've got to do something!"

Tsisdu silenced them with a chopping gesture. His words came in a rapid-fire whisper. "You'll get off one shot! Even if you hit one of them, there's plenty left to kill Michael and Johnny and then come after us...and the little ones!"

Susie's face twisted with indecision. She wasn't convinced that sitting idly by and doing nothing was the right answer. Annie empathized with her dilemma, but Susanna was acting on impulse.

"The muzzle flash," Annie whispered and pointed to the end of the gun Susanna held. "They'd know exactly where we are!"

"What do we do?" William asked, deferring to the Rabbit Man's leadership in this situation.

Tsisdu picked up the other items he had brought from the cabin. In their hasty retreat through the darkness, the others hadn't noticed. There were two Cherokee blow guns. *Tsisdu* handed one to Annie, then opened a small draw-string pouch suspended on a leather strap around his neck. He produced a tiny vial into which he dipped four darts. Holding them by their feathered ends, he cautiously handed two of them to Annie.

746

"Can you do it?" the Rabbit Man asked. Annie answered with a brave but unconvincing nod.

"What is that?" Susanna whispered.

"Poison? Is it poison?" William put his hand gently on Annie's shoulder. "Be careful!"

Susanna was less than persuaded of their success. "What if you miss? Or hit Johnny or Michael!"

"We won't miss—," *Tsisdu* said and looked at Annie, "—will we?" Again Annie tried not to reveal that she didn't entirely share his confidence.

William looked back through the brush toward the cabin and grabbed *Tsisdu's* arm. Johnny's eyes were open—though glazed—as he began to stir back to consciousness. He pushed himself up on one elbow and felt the gash in his scalp. His back was to the tree where Michael was tied. Johnny blinked and rolled his eyes, attempting to clear his head. He found himself staring straight at *Tsisdu* and the others. Certain he had seen some movement, something in the brush, Johnny squinted, trying to focus. It took a few seconds for the image to coalesce—it was his father, motioning for him to stay down.

Though still dazed, Johnny instantly knew the significance of the message. He stole a glimpse at the burning cabin and the men surrounding Michael before lowering his head back to the ground. The unfired pistols of Marshal Stone and Deputy Willard were within his reach. Johnny heard the men behind him and felt greatly disadvantaged that they were out of his field of vision. He assumed none of them had seen him raise up, or they would have already reacted. Johnny wondered if Michael had noticed.

"I thought you was gonna make that other Injun shoot him," Brantley reminded Titus.

Ogilvie shook his head no. "This one's all mine."

"No, Titus," Peter cut in, his hate-filled glare still riveted on Michael. "I get a piece of this, too."

"All right," Ogilvie agreed. He had no problem with that. "We'll *both* be the firing squad."

"Whatcha want us to do with that other'n?" Solmes asked about Johnny. He got the answer he had hoped for.

Ogilvie's eyes remained on Michael. "Hang him. Shoot him. Gut him. I don't give a shit. This is the one I want."

He glanced at Peter who acknowledged he was ready. The two men backed off a few paces, readying their pistols. Michael glared defiantly back at them. His thoughts flashed back to that day when James Walker had been tied to the post, about to be executed by young Cherokee boys Peter Tanner had forced to become old men in the span of a few seconds one sunny, Georgia afternoon. And though on that day Michael had watched his friend from a distance, this time he was seeing it all from right inside James Walker's head, intertwined with his spirit, looking out upon his own final minutes in this world.

Michael wanted both Peter Tanner and Titus Ogilvie to see in his eyes the scornful disdain and complete lack of fear right up until the instant they pulled their triggers and ended his life. At the same time he wanted to close his eyes and savor the vision of his beautiful Annie and his precious little *Tsi-mi* as the final thought and image to usher him into the spirit world. To his astonishment, Michael found himself doing both. Thoughts of Annie filled him—dancing with her in the Walker cabin at Christmas; making love to her in their forest glade; the beautiful anguish of her giving birth to their son; those mystical twinklings when she was connected to a different dimension, receiving her own strange and often portentous visions. Thoughts of *Tsi-mi*—taking his first wobbly step, then learning to run; going through a phase where he had insisted on walking only backwards, giggling all the while; his first words coming sporadically, then a flood of chatter; making them roar with laughter when he tried in vain to capture an elusive beetle. Yet, Michael found, his eyes remained open, watching every move of the two men before him.

Titus flashed his characteristic, lip-twisting, evil grin and pulled the hammer back on his old flint-lock, single-shot pistol. Peter's hatred of Michael for being everything he could not be—and for a lifetime of reminding him of that irrefutable fact—continued to slice out through his whiskey-glazed eyes. He cocked his pistol.

Solmes stepped up beside Titus and offered him Michael's Collier repeater. "You wanna use this one, Mister O.?" he snickered. "If you miss, you just shoot again!"

Without taking his eyes off Michael, Ogilvie pushed Solmes aside. "I won't miss," he growled.

Solmes shrugged to Brantley as if to say, *What the hell, I tried.*

"I thought it'd be funny—shootin' him with his own gun," Brantley said with a sympathetic shrug.

"After he's dead, I'm keepin' this gun," Solmes announced emphatically.

"You two shut up!" Ogilvie barked, then asked Peter, "You

ready, General?"

"Ready."

Peter's anticipation of killing Michael far outweighed the familiar sting of Titus's sarcastic reference to his never-to-be-achieved military rank. The two men spread out double arm's length apart and slowly raised their guns.

The events of the next few seconds were a divinely orchestrated ballet of flawless timing. *Tsisdu's* blow gun slipped between the branches of a low, thick bush. From the brush where Annie had taken up position, her blow gun appeared as well. Michael took a deep breath—his last, he figured—and continued glaring at his executioners.

From his blind position on the ground, Johnny knew time had run out. He had seen his father out there and knew that some sort of plan had been devised. But what was the plan? What should he do to help? What if it didn't work? What if they missed? They wouldn't be able to prevent Michael's murder and would only ensure their own. Johnny knew that when he moved, it would have to be fast. He held his breath, extended one arm and snatched the two pistols from the bodies of the dead marshal and his deputy. He shifted his head to steal a partial view of what was going on behind him.

Peter Tanner's and Titus Ogilvie's pistols came up in unison. Each man took aim. Peter, in military fashion, tried to focus his blood-shot eyes on the prisoner's heart. Ogilvie, however, wanted to see Michael's head explode. He pointed his gun at Michael's face, just above those damnable, defiant eyes.

Annie struggled to still her trembling hands and aimed her blow gun. *Tsisdu* sighted down the length of the slender reed. Susanna and William raised their rifles. They would fire only when it became necessary. Susanna cut a fleeting glance back to the tree where Meg, *Tsi-mi* and *Me-li* were holding hands, encircling the tree where William had left them. Their little faces registered both fear and their lack of understanding, but they remained obediently silent.

Ogilvie's fat finger closed around the trigger. Peter's finger began to squeeze. Johnny knew it was time to act. His plan flashed through his mind—flip over and, hopefully, get both Peter and Ogilvie. At least he would distract them from shooting *Mi-ki*. He knew such action would draw fire from all the others. Whatever his father and William were going to do, they'd better be ready to do it now. It was Johnny's and Michael's only chance. Johnny was about to move but froze when he spotted *Tsisdu's* blow gun and one of the rifles. He heard the puff of air and the soft *pfffttt* of *Tsisdu's* airborne dart. Titus heard it, too—an eye-blink before the poisoned missile buried itself in the side of his neck. Peter had also heard the strange sound. When he looked toward Ogilvie, his head moved just enough so that Annie's dart—which otherwise would have sailed right past him, missing by inches—pierced his cheek.

Brantley whipped his rifle up to a shoot-from-the-hip position and spun around, but he saw nothing. Solmes cocked the Collier repeating pistol and lowered himself into a crouch. The other four *yo-neg* posse men were fearfully wide-eyed and anxious. Perhaps, it occurred to them, they had too hastily realigned their loyalties after all. Was there someone other than Titus Ogilvie in charge—or soon to be in charge?

Titus clutched at the dart stuck in the grimy, sweaty roll of his fat neck. He scanned the brush and trees at the edge of the clearing in search of the shooter. Again he heard the *pfffttt* and this time actually saw the spinning, feather-tailed projectile coming right at him. But it was too late. His delayed, evasive twist came only after the second dart had already buried itself in the front of his throat. Titus looked at Peter Tanner, whose mouth was frozen wide open. He could see the tip of the dart inside Peter's mouth where it had completely penetrated his cheek and embedded itself in the side of the tongue.

Peter, still uncertain what had happened, gaped back at Titus, his forehead knit in pained confusion. The other posse members, equally bewildered, had no idea what to do. With one swift pull, Peter removed the poisoned dart and dropped it at his feet. He seemed unaffected by the blood flowing both from his mouth and from the cheek wound. Ogilvie tugged frantically at the second dart in his throat until it finally came out. Believing he had withstood the attack, Titus threw both darts in the direction of the brush and fanned his cocked pistol back and forth in search of his phantom attackers.

"Come on out, ye God damn cowards!" Titus screamed. "You sneaking Injun bastards!" Thinking he had seen some movement, Titus fired. Peter pivoted and shot in the same general direction, as did Brantley and Solmes, though none of them had the faintest idea what they were shooting at.

Susanna had retreated to the children's tree and made them all lie flat on the ground. She knelt beside them, still holding onto the rifle. Her other hand rested on Meg's back. She peered through the trees to where she knew William had positioned himself. He

750

aimed and fired his rifle. Out in the clearing, a large dark spot began spreading downward from the middle of Solmes's chest. He staggered backwards until he hit a tree and slid down into a grotesque sitting position, his head slumped forward as though watching his own life flow out of the gaping wound.

Just as Annie had predicted, the rifle's muzzle flash had betrayed William's position. The other posse men fired in his direction. But William had remembered his daughter-in-law's warning and immediately after shooting had taken cover behind a tree, speedily reloading while the *yo-neg's* bullets whizzed all around him.

Seeing her father under heavy fire, Susanna left the children and scrambled to a thick live oak tree. She braced the butt of the rifle against the trunk, pointed it in what she hoped was the right direction and pulled the trigger. When she looked out through the brush, it was evident she had hit nothing, but, like William, she had given away her location. Brantley and the other four *yo-neg* posse men knew that whoever had shot at them from the woods would be reloading. They charged the positions held by William and Susanna.

Johnny had been lying in the open, fully exposed. Any movement up until then would have immediately brought the *yo-neg's* fire and certain death. The gunfire from the woods was the distraction he needed. He rolled over, raised up onto his elbows, braced himself against the bodies of Stone and Willard and fired the two pistols simultaneously, killing Brantley and one of the other posse men. Seeing two of his companions fall, another white deputy dropped to his knee and aimed his pistol at Johnny's exposed flank.

"*Tsa-ni! Ha-nu-wa!*" Michael shouted in a hoarse, rope-choked whisper. He could do nothing but watch the battle unfold before him. He saw Johnny grab Stone's second pistol, roll to one side and come up on one knee, firing the pistol an instant before the *yo-neg* could squeeze off a shot. Johnny's bullet hit the *yo-neg* in the groin and sent him rolling on the ground with a piercing scream that soon trailed off into a death groan.

The two remaining *yo-neg* posse men had seen enough. They had come along, like Brantley and Solmes, in hopes of winding up with a few extra coins in their pockets or, at worst, a chance to beat up—maybe even kill—an Indian or two. But this had gotten way out of hand. Now their sole interest lay in saving their own asses. They scurried to the nearest horses, leaped into the saddle and rode away into the night.

Titus Ogilvie and Peter Tanner hurried to finish reloading

their pistols so they could turn them on Johnny. With his last shot, Johnny had left himself vulnerable in the middle of the clearing. Brantley's pistol lay on the ground near its owner's body. Johnny dove for the gun, scooped it up and rolled to a prone position. He aimed at Ogilvie—the closest to him—and pulled the trigger only to hear the sickening *click* of the empty pistol.

Peter staggered toward Johnny. He motioned with his pistol to Titus and slurred a few words intended to communicate that he would take care of Johnny while Ogilvie finished with Michael. But Ogilvie's first concern was for his own safety. They were still under attack from those bastards in the woods who, with ample time to reload, would soon be ready to fire another volley. He stumbled to the cover of the tree where Michael was still bound. From there he watched Tanner force Johnny to his feet. Peter, with his gun at the back of Johnny's neck, placed one hand on his shoulder and kept him at arm's length, using him as a protective barrier between himself and their hidden attackers.

"Put the guns down," William called out gruffly from the darkness, "or we'll drop you where you stand."

"You heard him," *Tsisdu* said loudly from his position opposite William. "We have you surrounded!"

From her location, Susanna made sure her rifle barrel was visible but kept herself hidden from view and said nothing.

"Lay down the guns and we won't shoot you!" William yelled. "You have our word!"

"Your word?" Titus called mockingly from behind the tree. "What the hell is that? Who are you?" Ogilvie had no idea where William Drummond was in the west and hadn't recognized the voice.

At Annie's position off to his left, Ogilvie saw the brush move. He fired in a panic. The bullet struck a tree and sent a spray of bark flying into the darkness. Another rifle shot from William's position hit the ground with a cloud of dust right beside Peter's foot. Peter staggered back a step or two, maintaining a firm grip on Johnny's shoulder. He constantly shifted his human shield and discovered that he wasn't a particularly brave soldier when fixed in the sights of an unseen enemy.

"Put it down!" William called out again in a loud, authoritative voice. Peter blinked once with drunken deliberation, then lowered his gun to the ground. He looked at the tree where Titus, his hands quivering uncontrollably, was spilling gunpowder all over himself as he desperately tried to pour it down the muzzle of his pistol. Ogilvie glanced nervously toward the brush where he had just fired and his eyes widened in disbelief. Annie Walker Drummond stepped out into the open, her blow gun hanging loosely in her hand. From a few yards off to Annie's left, Susanna emerged. Her rifle was aimed at Peter. So drastic had been the changes in his appearance that she didn't know him. Nor did Peter recognize his own wife, the mother of his child. He squinted past Susanna at Annie.

"*You!*" he said. The right side of his face was swollen and his tongue thick in his mouth. "I know you!"

Here before him, unmistakable, even in his drunken state, stood that same brazen Cherokee wench who had been the cause of the near-deadly confrontation between Michael Drummond and Titus Ogilvie that night almost three years ago. Peter recalled, too, from the sour-mash bog in the recesses of his mind, that she and Michael had run away somewhere out west and, by God, there they were! Incredible!

"Yes. *Me,*" Annie answered calmly. Her first impulse was to run straight to Michael, but she was afraid to risk it just yet. Ogilvie still held what she had to assume was a loaded pistol.

Titus took a closer look at the Cherokee woman Peter seemed to know. "Well, I'll be God damned!" he exclaimed with his characteristic sneer. "It's the squaw-princess of the governor's ball."

"And me," Susanna said boldly.

Peter still didn't recognize Susanna in the shifting light of the burning cabin. She appeared to be *just another damned Cherokee woman.* Susanna kept her empty rifle trained on him while Johnny picked up the pistol Peter had dropped. He rushed to Susanna and she touched his face lovingly, then his bloody head.

"I was so worried..."

"I'm all right," Johnny said.

Peter looked from Susanna to Annie. And back to Susanna. The wounded side of his face was growing increasingly round and puffy. "You mean we were attacked by a couple of *women?*" Peter's words came out slow and viscous. He looked around. He knew it had been a man's voice—strong and commanding—that ordered them to put down their guns. And a second man's voice from the darkness across the clearing. Why, then, didn't they show themselves? Was it to further humiliate him?

Johnny suspected Susanna's rifle hadn't been reloaded, but he played the bluff out just as she had begun it. He took the rifle from Susanna and kept it trained on Peter while they circled around to the tree where Michael was tied. Johnny turned the rifle on Titus and ordered him to put down his pistol. Once Ogilvie had complied,

Annie ran to the tree.

"You're truly pathetic, Peter," Susanna said with sickened disgust. Recognition was instantaneous from the tone and inflection of the scathing way she had uttered his name. His mouth opened even wider, and he scarcely noticed when William and *Tsisdu* stepped out from the brush.

"Susanna?! I thought—but—Michael said you were dead!" Peter whimpered thickly.

Susanna began untying the rope around Michael's chest and arms. Annie pulled Brantley's knife from the bark beside Michael's head and cut the rope around his neck.

"No! *You* said it, Peter. Not me," Michael answered while hungrily inhaling deep breaths of the smoke-filled air.

"Well, obviously, I'm *not* dead, am I?" Susanna said.

"And Margaret Elizabeth?" Peter asked. "Is she...?" Susanna didn't mask her revulsion at Peter's appearance. He read her thoughts and felt compelled to regain the long-lost control over her that he never really had. "Answer me, damn it!" he tried to shout, but his words tripped out thick and garbled—almost unintelligible. "Where is my daughter?!"

Susanna refused to answer. Peter saw her disgust rapidly changing to a searing anger, despite the tears welling up in her eyes. He turned to look at the man walking up to him out of the smoke.

"Mister Drummond!" Peter was genuinely surprised.

"Peter?!" William was equally taken aback. "I didn't recognize you!"

Peter looked down at himself. "Yeah. I guess I've changed some." His eyes went back to Susanna. He sucked on his tongue thoughtfully, concentrating on making his words clear. "Where's Margaret Elizabeth?" he acrimoniously repeated his earlier demand.

William placed a hand on Peter's shoulder. He spoke softly, and not without compassion. "Peter...there isn't much time. Don't waste it on anger." Puzzled, Peter looked from William to *Tsisdu*, then back to Susanna.

"What are you going to do? Kill us?" Titus Ogilvie asked.

"We already did that," Annie answered in her usual succinct manner. Peter misunderstood their meaning, fully expecting that he and Titus were about to be shot.

"So. This is what it comes to?" he looked at Susanna. "You're simply going to murder your husband? Just like that?"

Johnny put his arm around Susanna and glared at Peter. "*This* is my husband," Susanna proudly proclaimed.

It was just one more in a sequence of shocks for Peter. "A Cherokee?" he shook his head in disbelief. "You're choosing *him* over *me*? A Cher...o...kee..." It took a lifetime—or the remainder of one—for the final word to escape his lips. The poison had seized him, constricting his throat almost closed. A trickle of fresh blood streamed out his nose. Peter doubled over, gasping for breath. His eyes came back to the dart lying beside his boot. For the first time he understood what they had been trying to tell him. He raised his head, his desperate eyes jumping wildly from Susanna to Johnny and then to William.

And for the first time, Titus Ogilvie manifested genuine fear. "Tanner! What's wrong?" he screamed then looked at the others. "What the hell's wrong with him?!"

Peter, wheezing and gasping, picked up the dart with a trembling hand. He held it up for Ogilvie to see before it slipped from his fingers and fluttered back to the ground. Instinctively, Ogilvie's hand went to the bloody dart wound in his throat, then spidered around to the side of his neck.

They watched Peter Tanner die, with only the hissing and crackling of the burning cabin for his midnight requiem. Peter dropped to all fours in the dirt like a sick dog. His back arched in weak, painful spasms as he fought for each precious mouthful of air. Filthy, bleeding, sad and pathetic, he raised his head for the last time and looked up at Susanna. With tear-filled eyes he mouthed the words, *I'm sorry, Susanna...* Peter Tanner collapsed on his side, drew into a fetal position and breathed his last.

"You've murdered us!" Titus tried to shout, but his own throat had begun to constrict, making his would-be exclamation little more than a raspy screech. "Poisoned by a bunch of God damn Indians!"

Annie stepped closer to him, no longer fearful of any harm from this contemptible, sweaty, fat, dying wretch. "The same *bunch of God damn Indians* you came here to kill?" she asked tersely.

Ogilvie, defiant and hate-filled to the last, turned his familiar sneer on Michael. "You need to teach your squaw some manners when she talks to a white man."

Michael started toward Ogilvie, but Annie held out her arm to stop him. "Never mind," she said. "It doesn't matter now."

Titus's sneer faded into a grimace of pain. His bulky system had finally succumbed to the venom's deadly potency. He bent double as Peter had done. His throat had swollen closed and he gasped desperately for air. Then he dropped to his knees and convulsed uncontrollably. Yet, even in the spastic throes of an agonizing death, Titus Ogilvie couldn't let go of his hatred. He groped clumsily to retrieve a tiny pistol from the inside pocket of his coat.

"Michael! Watch out!" Susanna was the first to see it. But Michael wasn't overly concerned. Titus fumbled to cock the tiny hammer, but he lost control and flipped the weapon in the dirt, out of reach. Blood began to flow from the fat man's nose and mouth. Crimson bubbles erupted in showers from his nostrils and lips with each wheezing gasp. Titus looked up at William. Unlike Peter, there was no apology on his lips.

"I win, Drummond..." he proclaimed.

"You *win*?" Susanna was puzzled by his words.

"Like I always said..." Titus began, then choked, coughed and somehow managed a weak laugh. "I'd rather be *dead* than be a *God damn Indian...*"

William squatted and studied the dying pig for whom there was, apparently, not the faintest hope of redemption.

"Then I guess you win, Ogilvie," William agreed.

With a final scratchy exhalation, Titus Ogilvie flopped face down in the dirt. There was silent realization among the rest of them that it was finally over. William looked sadly at the blazing cabin that represented so many hours of hard work for all of them.

"Get the children," *Tsisdu* said.

Annie shouted toward the woods. "*Di-ni-yo-tli! E-he-na! E-hi-na-go-i!*" she urged them to come on out.

Me-li emerged from the brush, leading Meg by the hand. Annie and Susanna started toward them, but Annie's eyes remained on the trail, waiting for *Tsi-mi* to appear.

"*Tsi-mi!*" she called again, louder. "*E-hi-na-go-i!* Come on out! It's all right." Annie breathed a sigh of relief when, from another part of the brush, Jimmy appeared and started toward her.

Johnny looked at the burning cabin and called to the others, "Get the buckets! Hurry!"

"No! It's too late, *Tsa-ni*," William said. His voice sounded very tired. "It's too late."

Johnny knew William was right. Helplessly, they watched the flames devour their handiwork. William smiled at the sight of *Me-li* and Meg running to Susanna and flying into her arms. That single image, William knew, would give him the strength to start again from nothing. To rebuild the cabin. To dig deeper and plant the roots here in this place he had chosen for his family.

Beyond Susanna and the girls, *Tsi-mi* scurried toward his mother. His path took him past the tree where Solmes sat motionless against the trunk. The arm flashed out and grabbed the child, pulling the startled, screaming toddler into his lap. Solmes raised Michael's Collier repeating pistol to his young hostage's head. His audience was paralyzed by the sudden turn of events, just when they thought their nightmare had ended. Solmes rolled his eyes, battling the darkness, struggling to stay conscious.

"All right...." the words came out weak but determined. "Y'all gonna get me to a doctor. Quick!"

William was still holding the rifle. He took a step in their direction, but Solmes saw him and pressed the pistol harder against Jimmy's head.

"Don't test me, old man!" Solmes growled, wide-eyed. "Put down that gun!"

William stopped but didn't drop the rifle. When Solmes cocked the hammer of the Collier, William held up a hand and lowered the rifle to the ground.

"Come here..." Solmes demanded. William didn't move. "Now, God damn it!" the wounded man's attempt to shout degenerated into a cough. William complied, stepping closer to Solmes and his grandson.

"All right," William spoke calmly, not wanting to agitate Solmes further. "We'll get a wagon. We'll get you to a doctor. Just let the boy go..."

Without warning, Solmes whipped the pistol away from Jimmy and fired point blank, hitting William dead center in the chest. As the shot reverberated in the night, Jimmy's high-pitched shriek was followed instantly by the screams of Susanna and the girls. Solmes looked at them, puzzled. The reason for his actions should have been self-explanatory, he thought.

"Well, ain't no damn Injun gonna tell me what to do," he explained.

William lay on his back, fighting to keep his eyes open. The pain in his chest was like nothing he had ever known; like nothing he would have thought humanly possible to endure; such gripping, all-consuming pain that he knew death would come soon and found himself begging it to hurry. Everything in his field of vision moved in extremely protracted time. Michael and Susanna were coming toward him. It was evident in their horrified expressions and the nature of their movements that they were running, but to William it looked and felt like it would take hours for them to reach him.

With supreme effort he turned his head to one side and saw, only a few feet away, Titus Ogilvie's grinning death mask as though the fat man's corpse would, indeed, have the last laugh.

"Father! *E-to-da!*"

William heard his children calling as they approached. But their voices, deep and unnatural, echoed like rumblings from a dark pit somewhere deep within the earth.

William's eyes were drawn beyond his son and daughter to the opening of the narrow trail leading into the woods. The same trail where only a short time earlier he and Susanna had gone walking. There, in the glow of the burning cabin and the sparse scattering of moonlight, he saw Elizabeth. His beloved Elizabeth. She looked so beautiful, so hale and healthy, as she had many years ago when first he loved her. It felt so natural that she should be standing there, giving him that bashful half-wave of hers he had always found so precious. A half step behind her was an older couple. William recognized his parents. He hadn't seen them in so many years. And there was his older brother, Matthew, whom as a young man William had idolized. He had died of blood poisoning from wounds received at New Orleans in 1814. And Katherine, William's beautiful sister, five years his senior, tall, with flowing reddish-blonde hair. She was holding the tiny baby girl whose troubled birth had taken them both in 1805. William found it pleasantly odd that they all appeared more real than wraithy.

What had they been doing all this time? the thought flashed through his mind. Had Matthew been hunting? He loved to hunt. Had Katherine named her baby? What did she call her?

Looking past them, he saw even more people—mostly old folks, but there was also a young couple and even a small child. William felt these were people he should know, but it would take him a while to sort it all out. He was confident it would all come to him shortly. Then his eyes wandered a little farther to a stooped old Cherokee woman standing a little apart from the rest. This, William knew instantly, was Rebeka Fields, his *Tsa-la-gi* great-grandmother, whose precious blood—no matter how fractional—flowed in his own veins and had ultimately brought him to this place. Just behind his great grandmother stood a young Cherokee woman whose dress was soaked and clung heavily to her lithe frame. Her wet hair was plastered to the sides of her face.

William briefly took his eyes off Elizabeth and the other apparitions in the woods and found his cherished grandson, James Walker Drummond. *Tsi-mi* was crying. He cringed with his hands cupped over his ears, frightened by the deafening shot just fired only inches from his head.

Elizabeth, too, looked at their grandson, so helpless in the grasp of this wicked, evil man with his dirty, bloody face and wild-eyed expression. She saw Solmes's mouth as William had seen it—spewing its evil in twisted, time-stretched contortions while he waved the Collier pistol and barked his commands. He looked to them both like a man drowning in thick honey. Strange, William thought, that he couldn't *hear* the words so much as *see* them erupting in bursts of black and putrid yellow-green and with a stench more foul than diseased feces and rotting flesh. And somehow William knew that Elizabeth and those with her perceived it just as he did.

"He's beautiful, William!" Elizabeth's soothing voice was the only thing that lessened the pain in his chest. "Our little Jimmy. Don't worry about him. He's going to be all right." As always, she knew her husband's mind. The only thing preventing him from getting to his feet and joining her for a nice walk along the creek trail was his concern for their grandson. Already he felt disappointed that he wouldn't get to see him become a man.

"You'll see. We'll watch him grow up," Elizabeth reassured him.

Like pounding thunder *Tsisdu's* footsteps echoed in William's brain as the Rabbit Man rushed to his fallen friend. William held up his hand to signal there was no need to hurry. *Tsisdu* stopped short and watched in amazement as William rose to his feet. There was only a faint discoloration on his shirt where he had been shot, as though the bright crimson stain had simply dried up and faded away. William approached *Tsisdu* and placed a consoling hand on his friend's shoulder before continuing past him. *Tsisdu* was the only one of the adults who saw William walk over to Solmes and little *Tsi-mi*. With great affection, William touched the head of his grandson. He lifted the boy's chin to look up into his grandfather's face.

"Don't be afraid, little man," William said softly.

Tsi-mi smiled and stopped crying. He, like Rabbit Man, watched his Grandpa *Wi-li* join those waiting for him at the edge of the clearing. Besides *Tsisdu* and *Tsi-mi*, *Me-li* was the only other one who found reason to look toward the woods. Her eyes lit up at the sight of the woman in the wet dress. *Me-li's* mother gave her a little wave and a warm, loving smile. *Me-li* wanted to go to her, but when Solmes shot William, Meg had clamped onto *Me-li's* arm and wouldn't let go.

When William reached Elizabeth, he tenderly touched her face. He bent slightly and she tiptoed up to kiss him on his cheek, then slipped her arm around him, as she had always done. With the others gathered behind them, they walked off into the dark tunnel of the forest path.

* * * * * * *

Michael and Susanna cradled their father's lifeless body. Johnny, Annie and *Tsisdu* stood close by. When they realized that William was dead, Michael picked up the rifle lying at his father's feet. He stood up and faced Solmes, only to discover his own Collier pistol aimed right at him.

"You wanna be next?" Solmes snarled. Michael stopped.

"*Tsa-ni*...get your gun ready," he said calmly, making sure Solmes heard every word. "When he shoots me, kill him."

"*Mi-ki*! Don't!" Annie showed more emotion than she had displayed all evening.

"You son of a bitch!" Solmes growled. He shoved the gun toward Michael and pulled the trigger.

Click.

He rotated the barrel.

Click.

The repeating pistol's final shot had killed William Drummond. Michael started again toward Solmes, but the wounded man whipped out his Bowie knife—identical to the one Brantley had carried—and held it to Jimmy's throat. Michael pulled up short.

"Oh, you're a *bad Injun*, are you?" Solmes was confident he had regained the upper hand. "Come on! Let's see just how bad you are!"

Michael's goal was to keep the *yo-neg's* attention on himself and away from his son. If he mishandled it, Solmes could—and would—in one sweeping motion, decapitate *Tsi-mi*.

"You're a dead man, mister," Michael pointed at Solmes.

"I'm the *law*!" Solmes corrected him. "I'm takin' you in and gettin' a big reward! Now you get a wagon hitched up! We're goin' back to Ft. Gibson."

Tsi-mi craned around on Solmes's lap to look toward the forest trail. He caught a final glimpse of his Grandpa *Wi-li* and the others as they disappeared into the darkness. Once they were gone, *Tsi-mi* looked back to his father. Annie stepped to Michael's side, clinging to his arm. Johnny and *Tsisdu* kept their eyes on the blade pressed against Jimmy's neck.

Susanna gently pushed Meg and *Me-li* toward *Tsisdu* and whispered, "Stay with Rabbit Man." In slow, deliberate movements, she rose and started walking toward the man threatening to kill her nephew. Solmes watched her with squint-eyed suspicion. He pressed the knife harder against the boy's throat.

"Stop right there!" he barked. Solmes looked past her to Johnny and *Tsisdu*. "I don't see no wagon! I don't see no horses! Move, God damn it!" he strained to yell, his bellow trailing off into another blood-spitting cough that sprayed the side of *Tsi-mi's* face with red and black flecks.

"Please. Let the little boy go," Susanna said as compassionately as she could.

"Shut up! Git back over there with the others!" Solmes ordered, pointing with the big knife toward *Tsisdu* and the girls.

"Please don't hurt my son," Annie pleaded.

Solmes studied both women. He was white and a man, so he knew he was double smarter than a couple of *Injun squaws*. He had their little game all figured out.

"If you're thinkin' you'll just let me sit here 'til I bleed to death, I'll be takin' this little nit bastard with me! Believe it!" he snarled. Susanna gave him a firm *You're the boss* nod.

"*Tsa-ni. Tsisdu.* Get the wagon ready."

Johnny looked at Susanna. Had she gone completely crazy? With a quick head shake, *Tsisdu* signalled his son not to interfere.

"Do it!" Susanna barked sharply.

"You heard her!" Solmes snapped.

Tsisdu deposited Meg and *Me-li* beside Annie and Michael, then started for the wagon. Johnny picked up the rope near the tree where Michael had been tied and coiled it as he walked toward the harness hanging from two posts off to one side of the cabin. As the men went into action, Susanna turned back to Solmes.

"Please, let the boy go," she said calmly, hoping to persuade him it was the best plan. "Take me instead." She inched closer. Solmes raised up slightly, pressing back against the tree. He kept his grip on *Tsi-mi*.

Annie and Michael, helplessly frozen, looked from Susanna to Solmes. Michael had never seen his sister like this. He'd heard bits and pieces of her encounter with Tom Carver—a man who had almost killed them both—but only now could Michael fully appreciate the horrors she had suffered. There was no denying she had about her a captivating aura. It was at once serene and forceful—at least by outward appearances. Michael slipped his arm around Annie, hoping to give Solmes the impression that they were both terrified and posed no threat. Solmes got the message. He looked past them and was satisfied that Johnny and his father were preparing the wagon.

Good, he thought, *these damned Injuns're finally showin' some proper respect for a white man.*

What Solmes had *not* seen was Michael's fingers closing around the handle of Brantley's knife—identical to the one he was holding to *Tsi-mi's* throat. Annie had earlier placed the weapon in the back of her waistband after cutting the rope from around Michael's throat.

Susanna took a small step toward Solmes, shifting her angle to obstruct his vision of Michael and Annie. She couldn't see them behind her and she was unaware of the knife, but she knew they would be desperately thinking of something, and perhaps this little maneuver would help in some way.

"Let him go. Please, sir" Susanna repeated in a soft, subservient tone. "I can take care of that wound. I was trained as a nurse back in Georgia." When she had almost reached him, she squatted cautiously and dropped to her knees in the dirt. Susanna extended her hand toward him as one might to a cornered, wounded animal. He allowed her close enough to touch his shirt. She gently pulled it open to reveal the gaping, discolored gunshot wound.

"Stay back!" he snapped. Instantly she withdrew her hand.

Summoning all the powers within her—those she knew of and those she didn't—Susanna forced herself to ignore the knife and talk to this man as though he were a close friend who had suffered an accident requiring immediate attention.

"You'll never make it to Ft. Gibson if we don't do something about this," she said in a kind voice.

Out by the wagon, Johnny had stopped to watch Susanna, hypnotized by her controlled, calculated performance. Then his eyes went to something that sent a chill up his back. Cupped in Susanna's right hand—hidden from Solmes—was the tiny pistol Titus Ogilvie had dropped in the dirt only seconds before his death.

"Be careful, *U-ni-tsi Wa-ya,*" he cautioned his Mother Wolf in a voice so low only he could hear.

In response to Susanna's prognosis, Solmes looked down at his wound. It was, indeed, a sickening sight. He looked back up at her with pleading in his eyes. "You really a nurse?" he asked in a tone softer than he had used all night.

"Of course," she assured him. "I was once married to Major Tanner," she glanced toward Peter's body, then at Meg. "That's our little girl." With her left hand she wadded up the tail of his shirt and pressed it gently against the wound. He flinched but allowed her to continue.

"I know," he said. "The General—that's what we call him—he told us. He said you was part Cherokee, but not really. I never quite figured that one out." Solmes watched her use part of his shirt to dab carefully at the clotted blood crusted around the bullet hole.

"Yes. It's quite a mystery," she agreed absently, concentrating on the wound. Susanna hoped she appeared outwardly calm, because she felt her pounding heart was about to explode. It required every fiber of her being to sustain this ruse, with her murdered father lying only a few feet away and the lives of the rest of them—especially *Tsi-mi*—in imminent danger. She drew a deep breath and looked down at the dirt, then leaned toward him slightly. Balancing on her right hand—the one holding the pistol—she continued blotting gently at his wound. When the edge of his dirty shirt became blood-soaked, Susanna sat back on her knees and began ripping material from the lower part of her dress, being mindful to conceal the weapon. She folded the torn fabric to form a large pad. With both hands Susanna resumed gently wiping the sweat, the dirt and the combination of fresh and dried blood from around the wound.

Like all the others, Jimmy's eyes were on his Aunt Susie. Once in a while he glanced at his mother and father, or at Meg and *Me-li*, who still didn't comprehend what it was all about. Even *Tsisdu* and Johnny—who were supposed to be hitching the horse to the wagon, had stopped to watch Susanna and Solmes. She looked kindly into the outlaw's face and brought the folded cloth up to wipe a spot above his brow. She hesitated when he tensed up, then delicately blotting his forehead. Instinctively, *Tsi-mi* reached for his aunt, but Solmes jerked him back. Susanna concentrated on Solmes and ignored her nephew.

Even in his critical condition, the degenerate Solmes ogled Susanna's ample breasts right in front of him. He moved the knife from Jimmy's throat and cut the string holding together the top of her dress. With the tip he pushed aside the garment, exposing her. Grotesque memories of her ordeal with Tom Carver flooded Susanna. When she began this venture—to gain the wounded man's confidence and somehow rescue *Tsi-mi*, even if it meant killing this man—it hadn't occurred to her that the mission might become sexual. It unnerved her. Perhaps, she thought, the one positive flicker to emerge from the Carver nightmare was to prepare her for this moment.

Control, she screamed inside her head, just as she had with Carver. *Control. Control. Keep control.*

It had worked before and she desperately needed that same centeredness now. Her hands began to tremble and she bit her tongue. Hard. If she thought about the pain in her mouth, maybe her hand would stop shaking. She knew Solmes was out of bullets, but he could end her and *Tsi-mi's* lives with two flicks of his knife.

A shiver went through Annie as well. She felt the pain of what Susanna was subjecting herself to for the sake of Annie's and Michael's son. She had heard—in much more graphic detail than any of the men—Susanna's chilling account of the Tom Carver incident. Images of Annie's own horrifying rape and the murder of her mother at the hands of Cephus Ogilvie and Randolph Bogen flashed through her mind.

Suddenly it struck Susanna—if the blade was touching her breast, that meant it was away from *Tsi-mi's* throat. This was the moment.

Do it! Do it now! Don't think about it! Just do it!

Her hand dropped from Solmes's face and grabbed the knife with the wad of rags. At the same time, she shoved the pistol's stubby barrel into Solmes's eye socket. But just as she pulled the trigger, Solmes wrenched sharply to the side. The gun fired, hitting the tree trunk beside his head, showering them with bark, splinters and the burning sting of gunpowder. Solmes jerked on the knife, slicing through the rags and cutting Susanna's hand. Only the thickness of the cloth had prevented her from losing all four fingers.

Once the knife was free, Solmes made a wide, slashing swipe at Susanna. She lunged to one side, eluding the blow. With his free hand Solmes grabbed Jimmy's hair and pulled the screeching boy's head back, exposing his throat. When Solmes raised the knife to drive it home, Susanna grabbed his wrist. For a man so seriously wounded and having lost so much blood, he proved remarkably strong. Her hand, slippery with her own blood, began losing its grip. The knife trembled between them, mere inches from each one's face. The quivering steel moved downward. Susanna saw her own blood on the blade and fought with all her strength, but Solmes was gradually overcoming her resistance. The knife descended steadily toward *Tsi-mi*, who was squirming, screaming and crying.

Solmes's arm suddenly went limp. Susanna jumped at the loud *tthhwwaaacck* of the knife thrown with such force it buried itself almost to the hilt in Solmes's neck, pinning him to the trunk of the tree. His eyes, bloodshot and dilated, remained open, frozen in shock. Susanna didn't have to look behind her. She knew Michael would be there. The thought flashed through her mind of all those times when they were young that she had ridiculed him and James Walker for playing with knives and had chided her father for praising their ability to throw them with such accuracy.

The floodgates finally burst. Susanna pried the knife from Solmes's hand and pulled *Tsi-mi* off his lap. Sobbing uncontrollably, she closed the front of her dress—almost demurely—as though a quiet modesty dictated that the spiritless, hollow eyes of the dead man should not ogle her. Then she began plunging the knife into Solmes's lifeless body with frenzied repetition. Annie grabbed *Tsi-mi* and pulled him to her. Michael knelt beside his sister and held her tightly until she stopped stabbing the corpse. Johnny reached them and lifted Susanna up, taking her into his arms, oblivious to the blood she smeared all over him from her badly cut hand.

The children looked to the edge of the clearing when Molly appeared at the opening of the forest trail. She meowed pitifully at the burning cabin, then licked the kittens huddled against her.

* * * * * * *

The night was eerily still, as though the planet had slowed or altogether stopped in its rotation. The hiss and crackle of the fire was amplified by the absence of shouting and shooting, gasping, choking and dying. The flames from the burning cabin created strangely animated silhouettes of the corpses strewn about the grounds. *Tsisdu's* own shadow stretched far out in front of him and reached the others long before he arrived to join them. The children whimpered, the women sobbed, the men heaved great sighs of relief and shock and sadness. Smoke and glowing sparks caught in the updraft swirled into the night sky like souls of the dead—some destined to grow cold in the night air, others to burn for eternity.

From their perch on the gnarled, uppermost limb of a lifeless tree, a pair of large, shiny black ravens beckoned to restless souls across the lush, green tops of the summer forest. From their lofty vantage point they saw the smokey tendrils from the charred Drummond cabin lifting against the cobalt sky. And they cocked their heads and listened with corvoid curiosity to the *Tsa-la-gi* male voices blending in a traditional mourning song. Two skin-covered drums rendered a steady rhythm. The male voices faded, replaced by a single female with the languishing strains of *Amazing Grace...*

> *U-di-la-nŭ-hi u-we-tsi*
> *I-ga-gu-yŭ-he-i...*

After the first couple of lines, the males joined in. They were accompanied by a fiddle, played by an old Cherokee man William had befriended in the concentration camp.

> *Hna-quo tso-e wi-u-lo-se*
> *I-ga-gu-yŭ-ho-nŭ...*

No one moved. No one spoke. The simple grave—with its hand-painted marker written in both English and Cherokee—lay near the edge of the cabin clearing, not more than five paces from the spot where William was slain. The acrid smell of ash and burnt logs filled the nostrils of the mourners, but no one complained. Michael stood quietly beside Annie, with *Tsi-mi* clinging to her leg. Next to them were Susanna and Johnny, holding Meg, and the Rabbit Man with *Me-li*.

Tsisdu had ridden in the night to inform Annie's uncle, Andrew Sixkiller, and William's long time friend, Charlie Swimmer. In the few short hours since then, word had spread to many cabins and farms. Friends and family began arriving before dawn. They waited quietly out near the road until Michael came down to talk with them and show them where to dig the grave.

Andrew and Rebecca brought Annie's other aunt, the widow of John Sixkiller, whose husband was killed on the day Annie's father was shot and Michael and James were captured at the caves in the Snowbirds. Andrew's sons, Mark and Timothy, now sixteen and fourteen, helped prepare the grave. Tiana, twelve, and Nancy, eight, quietly tended to the smaller children. Betty Jo Proctor and her children, Janie and Jack, had ridden all the way on a mule. *Ne-di* was conspicuous in his absence.

A young family of blacks—a mother, father and their three

children—stood quietly to one side. Somehow—and no one bothered to ask—they had learned of William's death and appeared coming up the road just before the burial service began. Reba had befriended them in the early days at Coosawattee. After Reba and Ezekiel had left for Illinois, Elizabeth and the young couple had shared their longing for their dear friends. Elizabeth, normally quiet and reserved, had kept them in stitches relating the exploits of her beloved Reba and the ever reliable Ezekiel. Tales of runaway mules, of legendary cooking, of running battles between Reba and Susanna as a child, of Ezekiel rescuing William after an angry bull had chased him up a tree.

Charlie and Eva Swimmer, with Buck and Sally between them, stood opposite Michael and Annie. They had brought with them the Cherokee preacher, *O-ga-na-ya*, who concluded the ceremony by reading the familiar Hundred Twenty-First Psalm so popular among those Cherokees who counted themselves Christian.

Ga-du-si wi-di-ga-ga-ni na-hna tsŭ-di-da-le-hŭ-s-ga a-qua-li-ni-go hi-s-di-s-gi u-di-la-nŭ-hi. A-gi-s-de-li-s-gi na-s-gi u-wo-e-nŭ-hi ga-nu-la-di a-le e-lo-hi.

When *O-ga-na-ya* finished, there was a long silence, punctuated only by the amen of the ravens' cry as they lifted themselves against the brightening summer sky and disappeared beyond the trees. Behind the mourners, the Drummonds' horses—saddled and loaded with bedrolls and tightly baled possessions—stomped and snorted, impatient to get on the trail.

* * * * * * *

Friends and loved ones had come to pay their last respects to a man who had always been honest, fair, sincere and compassionate with each of them. They lingered awhile after the ground had closed over the body. There was no traditional meal, no sitting around talking about family, no watching the children, no recounting stories of days gone by, particularly stories involving the deceased. They all knew what lay ahead for the surviving members of *Wi-li* Drummond's family. There would be legal repercussions for the incident of the night before. And everyone understood why those involved weren't staying around to explain their version to the authorities. It was only a matter of time before an army patrol or a civilian posse came searching for the marshal and deputies who had been dispatched to this location.

The remains of Titus Ogilvie, Peter Tanner, Marshal Rufus Stone, his deputies Haines and Willard, along with Ogilvie's brutal henchmen, Solmes and Brantley, would never be found. Charlie Swimmer and Andrew Sixkiller had seen to that. The bodies of the murdered Cherokee Light Horse had been delivered to their families in the early hours before dawn. Their next of kin, in their grief, had heard the truth and in no way held Michael, Johnny or any of their family responsible.

* * * * * * * *

Susanna tied the last parcel on the back of Stick, her father's leggy black gelding. Then she inserted one final item into the folds of the outer blanket. It was the leather pouch her mother had given her to deliver to Michael.

"You're taking that old thing?" she heard from behind her. Susanna turned with a smile for her brother. *Tsi-mi* sat on Michael's shoulders.

"I know we have to travel light," she said. "You think I should leave it?"

"No. You should keep it. Always. It brought us together. It's part of us now." Michael put his arm around his sister and gave her an affectionate hug, something he couldn't remember ever having done in all their years in Georgia.

"I guess Mother knew what she was doing," Susanna pulled the edge of the blanket down over the letter pouch. Johnny Fields joined them, leading his horse with Meg in the saddle. Behind him came *Tsisdu*, leading Michael's horse. The young black father brought Annie's mount. There was little conversation. Mostly just knowing looks, laden with understanding of what lay ahead.

Me-li stood at the edge of the clearing where, the night before, she, *Tsisdu* and *Tsi-mi* had seen a host of special visitors.

"My mother is in the forest," she explained to the three black children and left it at that. The black children stared blankly at her, then looked into the woods where *Me-li* was pointing.

All the preparations had been made. The men huddled near the animals and milled around, speaking in low tones. Someone slipped an extra pistol to Johnny. Without his knowledge, a new rifle was tied to Michael's saddle. And to the new rifle, *Tsisdu* attached a blow gun, then dropped a handful of new, handmade darts into the saddle bag. Traditionally, the blow gun had never

768

really been considered a weapon among the *Tsa-la-gi*. It had always been used primarily for hunting small game—squirrels, rabbits, a turkey now and then. But the events of the night before had—for this family, at least—proven the reed's value, elevating it to a higher status. A large knife passed from hand to hand, eventually finding its way into Johnny's saddle bag. A couple of extra powder horns were bound to a saddle, along with a bag of lead pistol balls and hand-made cartridges for the Collier repeating pistol.

Charlie Swimmer shook hands with Johnny, Uncle Andrew and the young black father. They knew him only as Samuel, but he had been accepted as a friend of the family. Charlie then embraced Michael.

"Would you stop back by Park Hill on your way home?" Michael requested. "Say good-bye to Chief Ross for us. Father would like that."

"*Gu-wi-s-gu-wi* wanted to come, but the army is still watching him close."

"He was afraid he might bring you more trouble," Andrew confirmed Charlie's explanation.

"Tell him we understand," Michael said. "*Wa-do, O-ga-na-ya*," he thanked the *Tsa-la-gi* clergyman who had just left the group of women and children.

"*Wi-li* was a good man." *O-ga-na-ya* placed his hand on Michael's shoulder. "A friend to all *Tsa-la-gi*. *Tsi-sa* will like him. *A-da-nŭ-do*, The Great Spirit, will smile."

One of the men lit a pipe and started it around. Each man would smoke, and the cycle would repeat itself as often as time allowed before the journey began. The women put together last minute items of clothing, food, herbs and medicinal preparations. And even among the women weapons were not forgotten. Rebecca gave Annie a knife. Widow Sixkiller pressed a small, ancient pistol into Susanna's hand. At first Susanna politely declined, but the older woman was persistent. She lifted her dress to show Susanna where to hide the gun. The other women tried to keep from laughing.

Me-li, *Tsi-mi* and Meg ceremoniously transferred loving ownership of two of Molly's kittens to their friends. *Sa-wu*, One, went to Janie and Jack Proctor. *Ta-li*, Two, was adopted by the three black children. Each kitten was received with a flood of affectionate cuddling and cooing. Looks to parents for permission were met with warm, approving smiles. Low-keyed but vigorous discussions of new names for the kittens began immediately among their new owners. The third kitten—which the children had originally called *Tso-i*, or Three—was officially renamed *Tsi-s-du-s-di*, or Little Rabbit, not for any leporine characteristics, but because its defective left eye wasn't fully developed and remained closed almost to a slit. *Little Rabbit* would stay to keep Molly and its namesake, *Tsisdu*, company.

* * * * * * *

A half hour later everyone was ready to leave. There were two groups, each headed in a different direction. The Swimmers, the Sixkillers, Samuel and his family and *O-ga-na-ya* would disperse north and east back to their homes. Michael, Annie, *Tsi-mi*, Susanna, Johnny, Meg and *Me-li* would be on the trail. Sally Swimmer ran to Meg and gave her the wedding-dress doll Susanna had made for her long ago in the concentration camp. The doll was tattered and dirty, but easily recognized by Meg as a replacement for her own beloved child that had perished in the cabin fire.

"Give it back, Meggie," Susanna said softly. "That's *Sa-li's* special doll."

"Please," Eva pleaded softly. "Let Meg take it."

"But Sally's had it for so long," Susanna said, recalling how nasty she had once been to the sweet child. And how much joy she had seen in Sally's eyes when she first received her baby. "She and this doll have been through so much together."

"That's why she wants Meg to have it," Eva explained. "To *Sa-li* it's a friend to protect you on a long and dangerous journey. She believes it got her here safely. Now, she wants Meg to be safe. We all do."

Susanna lovingly cupped Sally's cheeks before she and Eva embraced. It was an emotional moment for both women—made lighter when Sally and Meg mimicked their mothers' hug exactly. It wasn't an easy parting for these friends who had endured so much together.

"Do you really have to go?" Eva Swimmer asked one last time. Charlie looked to Michael for an answer to the same question.

"Too many people in Ft. Gibson know where the marshal and his men were headed last night. How long you reckon before they start showing up here?" Michael said softly. They all knew he was right.

"Where will you go?" Charlie asked.

Uncle Andrew drew them all together for one last word prior

to their departure. With one arm around Michael's shoulder and the other around Johnny, he looked at each of them before he spoke.

"When you get to Texas, find *Di-wa-li*. The Bowl."

"*Di-wa-li?*" Johnny was unfamiliar with the name.

"Chief John Bowl," Andrew explained. "My father knew him. Ran with the Chickamaugans. He took a bunch of *Tsa-la-gi* down into East Texas twenty-odd years ago. I've been to see him. It's beautiful country there. The hills are gentle, the earth is red and the pines are tall. You'll think you're back home in Georgia."

"How do we find him?" Michael asked.

"Cross the Red River," Andrew said, pointing in the direction they would go. "Ride south. If you reach Nacogdoches, you went too far."

"Nacogdoches," Michael repeated the strange sounding Caddo name. "We'll find him."

"If you need help in Texas," Andrew added, "you can ask *Go-la-nŭ.*"

"*Go-la-nŭ?* The Raven? You mean Sam Houston?" Johnny had heard of the Tennesseean who had been adopted by the *Tsa-la-gi*. They all knew of Houston's exploits in the past few years in the newly formed Republic of Texas.

"The Bowl knows him. He can protect you. He's a big shot down there. You might find him at Washington-On-The-Brazos. I've known him since we were boys back in Tennessee," Andrew said. "He's a good man."

Annie clung to her uncle in a parting hug. "*Wa-do, E-du-tsi*. Thank you for everything. Both of you." She pulled Aunt Rebecca into the embrace.

Tsisdu waited for the opportunity to catch Susanna's eye. He touched his stomach and said, "The fire. Remember the fire."

Susanna leaned and whispered, "I think it's already getting warm!"

Tsisdu grinned broadly. Johnny joined them.

"What are you two so happy about?" he asked. "This is supposed to be a sad time."

"Happy is the underbelly of sad," *Tsisdu* said. Susanna hugged the grandfather of her unborn child and kissed him on the cheek.

"Good-bye, Rabbit Man. *Wa-do*," she said. "For everything."

Johnny and his father looked into each other's eyes. There were no words. For years they had been apart, then together for too short a time. Now Johnny was forced to go away. Perhaps they wouldn't see one another again in this life.

"*Do-na-da-go-hŭ-i, Sa-lo-li*," *Tsisdu* said good-bye to his son, calling him by his pet name, Squirrel.

"Good-bye, *E-to-da*," Johnny said softly.

* * * * * * *

Michael rode alone out in front. Behind him came Annie, with Jimmy in front of her and their effects stacked high in the back. Behind Annie was Susanna on Stick. She rode alone, but carried more baggage than any of the other horses. Then came Meg and *Me-li*, their horse also piled high with belongings. *Me-li* sat in front and pretended to be in control of their mount, which was, in fact, tied to Stick. Bringing up the rear was Johnny. A rifle lay casually across the front of his saddle. His and Michael's horses were the least burdened to allow defensive maneuverability in the event of an emergency.

They twisted their way along the winding trail that would lead them south toward Texas. Meg clung tightly to the ragged wedding-dress doll given to her by Sally Swimmer. With the other hand she adjusted the feather she had worn tied to a tiny braid since the morning Susanna placed it there following the eagle-man's visitation in the night forest.

None of them were sure of the path, never having been this way before. They would ride with the sunrise on their left, the sunset on their right and keep going. Just keep going. Eventually they would reach the Red River and cross into a new world. A new life for all of them.

EPILOGUE

The table in Grandma Mary Pierce's living-dining room was strewn with empty pizza boxes and soda cans on one end; on the other end were the items she had laid out so precisely in the beginning. A feather once worn in a little girl's hair. An old, empty letter pouch, cracked and dried. A silver ring with a beautifully engraved wolf's head. None of these things had held any meaning for me when her story began.

I leaned lazily against the front porch post that held up the sagging roof and thought about those objects on the table and about many details of the incredible story I had just heard. As I peered into the darkness, I felt and heard Grandma Mary swaying gently back and forth in the rocker I had carried out onto the porch so she could enjoy the cool night air.

I glanced back at her smoking her tiny, hand-carved pipe. Then I lifted the old clay jug to my lips and drained the last of her homemade blackberry wine. There were things stirring inside me I had never felt before. I fought hard to convince myself it was merely a tummy full of pizza and some astonishingly tasty wine, but deep inside I knew it was much more.

We listened to the crickets and the night birds. Boomer, the old hound dog, grunted from beneath the porch, grateful for the company. Behind me I heard Grandma strike another match to rekindle her pipe. A loose porch board creaked methodically beneath the rocking chair.

"So...now you know where you came from," she said with a sense that she had finally fulfilled a long awaited mission.

"Incredible...." was all I could say.

"What do you think about being *Tsa-la-gi*?" she asked.

"Tell you the truth," I admitted, "I've never given it a lot of thought, one way or the other."

"*Tsa-la-gi* is in your blood, Liz," she said. "But you don't know what it means for you. You will have to learn. In that way, you are like her."

"Like who?" I asked, facing her.

"Like Susanna Fields."

"*Fields!*" I said excitedly. "Then she *did* marry Johnny."

"In the *Tsa-la-gi* way."

"Then Meg must have been your—what?—your great

grandmother?" I asked, proud I had unravelled the connection. But she shook her head no.

"It was *Me-li*," she looked up at me with that twinkle in her eye. She had set me up. She knew I would make the wrong assumption and was tickled when I fell for it.

"*Me-li*! Mary! The little girl from the river!"

"Susanna and Johnny raised her as their own," Grandma explained. It hadn't even occurred to me that Grandma Mary had descended from *Me-li*, but then I thought of Grandma's name—Mary—and felt like an idiot.

"And that's where you got your name! Mary Susanna," I was determined to win at least one point. Grandma conceded it with an approving nod. "How can you remember all this after so many years?" I asked.

She rocked back and forth a few times before she answered, studying her pipe as she spoke. "It is important to remember, '*ge-yu-ts*'. To know where you *came from* is to know who you *are*." Then she raised her eyes to mine and said in a voice I knew I would never forget, "And, above all, remember this: *Tsa-la-gi* is a lot more than just the blood. It's Power of the Spirit. Strength of the Will. Courage of the Heart."

She nursed the little pipe and rocked gently, as though comforted by the steady creaking of the loose porch plank. I looked down at this withered little woman. I had seen her only a few times my entire life, but now I felt incredibly close to her. I leaned down and kissed this dear old spirit on the forehead. It caught her by surprise, but I knew she was pleased.

"I'm glad you told me these things, Grandma Mary," I said. She held onto my arm and pulled herself up out of the rocking chair. From her pocket she retrieved my watch which she had earlier confiscated and placed it in my palm.

"It's late. You sleep on the couch. We'll talk more tomorrow," she said. Grandma opened the screen door, then stopped and looked past me out into the night. A little smile toyed at the corners of her mouth.

"What?" I asked.

"They are close by," she said softly.

"Who?"

"*Yŭ-wi-tsu-na-s-ti-ga*."

"Wait! Don't tell me," I said, racking my brain, determined to remember. "That's the *Little People*." She patted my hand with approval. I looked out into the darkness but saw only trees, shadows and the porch light reflecting off a myriad of flying insects. "How do you know?" I asked. "Can you see them?"

"Sometimes. Sometimes you just know they're out there."

We went inside. I paused to sneak another look out into the night, but still I saw nothing. Then as the screen door slammed shut I glanced back and, for a fleeting instant, I could've sworn I had seen glowing eyes and the shadowy form of a wolf near the tree line at the edge of the clearing. It was just sitting there, staring at the house. At me.

* * * * * * *

Grandma Mary was up early the next morning, stirring around in the kitchen. She made a fresh pot of coffee and rattled the pots and pans just enough to make sure I woke up. Once I sat up on the couch and rubbed my way through the lingering blueberry haze, she peeked in and apologized, pretending she had intended to let me sleep. But I didn't mind. I wasn't certain at just what point during the night my thoughts had given way to imagination, or when imagination had yielded to the Dream Time. But despite the effects of Grandma's homemade wine, I felt more rested, more energized than I'd ever been. And a fresh batch of her delicious fry bread, dripping with butter and honey, accompanied by two cups of steaming hot coffee was the best breakfast I'd ever eaten.

The things from Grandma's special box, dragged out the day before as visual aids for the amazing story she had told, were still spread on the table. We didn't talk during the meal. I spent most of the time looking at one item after another, replaying in my mind the part of the story each represented.

When the last piece of uneaten fry bread had been tossed out just beyond the porch for Boomer, Grandma began meticulously repacking the old wooden box that was home to all these artifacts. With loving care she restored each piece to its designated spot in its predetermined order. The amulet Annie had worn around her neck, which Michael Drummond had placed there following the death of her father, Thomas Walker. The leather pouch Elizabeth Drummond had cleverly used to reunite her son and daughter. The feather worn by Meg Tanner after her mother had found it on the forest floor following her mystical encounter with the eagle-man. Some crystals rolled in the frayed remnants of an old bandanna. The threadbare remains of a faded rag doll, created from what had once been a beautiful wedding dress. A rusty old pearl-handled pistol, some blow darts and a few other odds and ends. Each in its own place.

I watched her shriveled finger slip through the last item on the table—the wolf's head ring worn by Susanna Drummond Tanner Fields. To my astonishment, she didn't put the ring back into the box. Instead, she closed the box lid and held out her hand toward me.

"No, Grandma Mary!" I shook my head and gently pushed her hand away. "I couldn't."

Firmly, she thrust it back at me. "Take it," she insisted. "I'm ninety years old. I won't be here forever. You will take it and you will tell your children. And their children."

I looked into my grandmother's wrinkled face and those twinkling eyes with a depth of love and appreciation I wouldn't anticipated. Whatever force, whatever spirit had brought us together at this time in our lives, I knew this was a sacred, ceremonial transferring of the flame. How many years, I wondered, had this dear, patient, delightful little old woman been sitting here in this little cabin in this little clearing in this little corner of Cherokee country in eastern Oklahoma just waiting for one of her grandchildren to come here and listen to her story. A chill went up my back at the thought of how much I had *not* wanted to come here in the first place, and how eager I'd been to merely dump off the fruitcake and hand lotion and be on my way.

She placed the exquisitely carved silver ring in my hand. I felt a peculiar heat emanating from the ring—a warmth far greater than could have been generated by her hand. But I didn't question. I didn't recoil. With this consecrated ritual, she had passed to me the obligation to keep the story alive.

"Yes, I will...*E-li-si*" I made a solemn promise, calling her *grandmother* in Cherokee for the first time in my life. She picked up the old wooden box and held it close with her eyes shut. It was like she was saying good-bye to an infant grandchild. Then she placed it in my arms, compounding tenfold my shock at receiving the wolf ring. I reached out and gently touched this dear old woman's face. She lovingly patted my hand on her cheek.

"You go now," she said with that gleam in her eye. "Come back in another eight years. If I'm still here, maybe I'll tell you the story of *this*." With her crooked, arthritic finger she tapped the wooden box she had just given me.

"Everything has its own story, doesn't it?"

"Everything."

I tried to hand the box back to her but, like with the ring, she insisted I keep it. Somehow she knew I would go through it again and again, each time recounting in my mind that part of the story represented by each icon. I wondered if I would ever know it as well as she did, but she assured me it had all taken place long before her time, too, and she had learned it just as I would learn it.

Together we went through the squeaky old screen door and out onto the front porch. Vaporous shreds of fog drifted aimlessly like an undulating white miasma over the countryside. It would hover there in the draws and valleys until the sun came to burn it away. A couple of chickens fluttered off the hood of my car. I cradled the old box as though it were my first born. And, in a trans-zoetic sense, I suppose it was! I looked down at my grandmother.

"I'll be back at semester break, *E-li-si Me-li*," I said. I could tell she was pleased I had begun using Cherokee. "And I'm bringing Michael with me. We're spending Christmas with you this year!"

"Oh, no, no," she teased with a smile. "You'll have all those parties with your friends. And Michael is a busy young man. He has no time for the foolish tales of an old woman."

Now wise to her manipulations, I grinned, then hugged her and kissed her on the cheek and trotted out to the Corolla. I opened the door, but before I could get in, she called to me from the porch.

"If you do come, don't bring any more fruitcake," she said. "I only ate it to be nice."

"Deal!" I laughed. "But only if you save us a jug of that blackberry wine."

When I drove away I saw her in my rear-view mirror, still waving from beside the screen door. Boomer raised up on his front legs and I knew he'd be back down on the cool sand before my car was even out of sight.

* * * * * * *

I drove slowly along the rough, tree-lined dirt lane that would lead me to the gravel county road which, in turn, would take me back to Highway 51. After going through a bumpy stretch of chuckholes, I glanced down at the box on the seat beside me to make sure it was all right. Just looking at it brought another smile to my face. But when I looked back up, I slammed on the brakes and my hand shot out to protect the box.

I had caught a glimpse of something in my peripheral vision off to the right side of the road. It was like that subtle change of color and light when someone in another room moves past a door that is barely cracked open, and you know that when you look, nothing will be there. A fog as palpable as cotton hung suspended above a narrow corn field backed up against the same woods that surrounded Grandma's place. There, at the edge near the road I saw what appeared to be a creature that was half eagle and half man, like the one so vividly described as appearing to Susanna Drummond. I felt a rush in the pit of my stomach when he looked directly at me, his wings open and outstretched.

"Oh, my God!" I gasped in a soft whisper. What else could I say? I was amazed I could even draw breath for this short utterance. I buried my face in my hands for an instant and shook my head. Maybe the blackberry wine hadn't been such a good idea after all, I thought. I had taken my eyes off the creature for no more than two or three seconds. As if drawn by an irresistible magnet, I raised my eyes to look. The fog in thin, wispy fingers, drifted apart just long enough to show me the large, dark scarecrow amid the dried, broken shocks, skeletal remains of the recent harvest. Its arms were outstretched with tattered sleeves rippling in the feathery breeze.

I don't know how long I sat there gaping at the steering wheel or looking down at the box on the seat beside me. Finally, I heaved a profound sigh of relief and drove on. The sun was coming up and the fog grew thinner with each passing second. I came to the end of the narrow lane and stopped. I wanted to be sure I turned in the right direction. I eased out across the ditch and went left. The gravel rocks peppered the underside of my car when the tires caught and pulled me up onto the county road.

Then I stopped the car again. I knew I'd made the correct choice—to go left. I looked all around—to both sides and behind me—and saw no one, yet I had the distinct feeling I was being watched. Once again I checked on the box. Thoughts of the previous day and of the evening spent with Grandma Mary flashed through my mind. Thoughts of the things she had said, the story she had told, and I knew. I knew. I didn't have to look. They were in the top of the tall pine off to my left and slightly behind me, watching. I was convinced that if I looked, I would see them. Three of the Little People—*Yŭ-wi-tsu-na-s-ti-ga*, Grandma had called them —resting comfortably on the uppermost branches, smoking a tiny pipe passed back and forth among them. I felt they were watching me and something else at the same time. And I knew if I looked far to my left through the trees flanking the gravel road, I would see what they saw.

My first impulse was to keep my eyes straight ahead and

drive on. But I found myself turning to look. In the shadows where the sun hadn't yet reached, the fog still clung to the ground. The trees stood like darkly uniformed sentinels keeping watch over their guarded secrets. Mists and vapors drifted weightlessly on the delicate morning breeze and slipped along the forest floor like a kitten beneath a bed sheet.

The fog shifted and I saw in the distance five horses moving at an angle away from me, headed in a southerly direction. The rider in front moved his head from side to side as though cautiously watching, searching. The horse behind him—a leggy, black gelding— carried a woman and a little boy. Third came another woman who frequently looked back at the two little girls on the horse behind hers. Had she looked up, her eyes would have been staring directly into mine. Once she raised up and peered past the little girls, across the baggage piled high on the horses, to the young man who brought up the rear. I thought I saw her smile. But they were a long way off and the fog was shifting back and forth with a tide-like ebb and flow.

I eased my foot back onto the accelerator and moved along the gravel road. I would soon be roaring down the highway toward Texas, knowing that the people I had just seen through the fog-shrouded trees would be there before me. More than a hundred and fifty years before me. I smiled and wished them a safe journey, then placed my hand gently on the old wooden box and felt very close to the riders I had seen moving quietly through the forest.

Glossary
of
Cherokee (*Tsa-la-gi*)
Words and Phrases

English — Cherokee

The pronunciation guides presented here are approximations and are not intended to capture all the linguistic subtleties or to account for all the variations in the Cherokee language. There are several excellent tapes and books available for those interested in learning to speak Cherokee.

In Cherokee, the "d" often shades to "t" (except for "da", "di" and "dla"), and the "g" often shades to "k" (except for "ga"). There is no soft "g" in English, as in the name "George". Where "oo" is used in this pronunciation guide, it is to be sounded as "oo" in *food* or *boot*.

A

a place to live — ti-s-qua-ni [tees kwah nee]
afraid — a-s-ga-s-di (or: a-s-ga-i-hŭ*) [ahs gahs dee / ahs gah ee hŭh]
all right — ha-wa [hah wah]
ancient — hi-lŭ-hi-yu-i [hee lŭh hi yoo ee]
and — a-le [ah lay]
are here — a-ha-ni [ah hah nee]
Are you Cherokee? — hi-tsa-la-gi-s-go [hee cha la kees koh]
army (military) — a-ni-ya-wi-s-gi (*lit.*: soldiers) [ah nee yah wees kee]
arrow — ga-tli-da [gah tlee dah]
asleep — ga-li-ha [gah lee hah]
assassinate — a-da-hi-s-di [ah dah hees dee]
attorney — di-ti-yo-hi-hi [dee tee yo hee hee]
away — u-tsa-ti-na [oo cha tee nah]

B

babies — tsu-na-s-di-i [choo nahs dee ee]
baby — u-s-di-i [oos dee ee]
be quiet — e-tla-we-i [ay tlah way ee]
Becky (Rebecca) — We-gi [way kee]
bear — yo-nŭ [yo nŭh]
beautiful — u-wo-du-(hi) [oo whoa doo (hee)]

---

*   The highly nasalized "u", which is usually represented when writing the Cherokee sounds in English as the letter "v", will, for purposes of this book and its glossary, be shown as ŭ. Try to remember that it is sounded similar to the "u" in the English words "hung" or "sung" without pronouncing the "g" at the end.

beer — a-wo-gi-lŭ-s-gi [ah whoa kee lŭhs kee]
Bird Clan — (See CLAN)
black eyed susan (deer eye) — a-wi-a-gi-ta [ah wee ah kee tah]
black fox — gŭ-ni-ge tsu-li [gŭh nee gay choo lee]
boat — tsi-yu [chee yoo]
Blue Clan — (see CLAN)
bread — ga-du [gah doo]
brother-in-law — a-na-lo-si [ah nah los ee]
Buck (name) — Ga-la-gi-na [gah lah gee nah]

C

can't — tla-ye-li [tlah yay lee]
candy — ka-l'(i)-se-tsi [kal (ee) say chee]
carry him — e-ni-na-wi-dŭ [ay nee nah wee dŭh]
cat — we-si (or we-sa) [way see (or way sah)]
cattle — wa-ga [wah gah]
children — di-ni-yo-tli [dee nee yo tlee]
CLANS: (seven) ** — tsu-ni-yŭ-wi [choo nee yŭh wee]
    Bird — a-ni-tsi-s-qua [ah nee chees kwah]
    Blue — A-ni-sa-ha-ni (or A-ni-sa-**ho**-ni) [ah nee sah hah nee]
        (sometimes known as the Panther or Wild Cat Clan)
    Deer — A-ni-ka-wi [ah nee kah wee]
    Kitowah — A-ni-gi-du-wa-gi [ah nee kee too wah kee]
    Longhair — A-ni-gi-la-hi (or A-ni-gi-**lo**-hi) [ah nee kee lah hee]
        (also called The Twister, or Hair Hanging Down or Wind Clan)
    Paint — A-ni-wa-di (or A-ni-**wo**-di) [ah nee wah dee]
    Wolf (largest clan) — A-ni-wa-ya [ah nee wah yah]
    Wild Potato — A-ni-ga-ta-we-gi [a nee gah tah way kee]
        (also known as The Bear or The Racoon or The Blind Savannah
        Clan)
come in! — gi-yŭ-ha! [gee yŭh hah!]
come out — e-hi-na go-i [ay hee nah koh ee]
come here — e-he-na [ay hay nah]
Cooweescoowee — Gu-wi-s-gu-wi [koo wee skoo wee]
coward — u-s-ga-e-na [oos gah ay nah]

D

daughter-in-law — a-gi-lo-hi [ah gee lo hee]

** There were never more than seven clans at any one time. However, down through the years, a few of the clans have been known by other names. In other instances, a clan name might have been dropped and another added.

days — du-do-da-qui-sŭ [doo doe dah kwee sŭh]
    Monday — do-da-quo-nŭ-hi [doe dah kwo nŭh hee]
    Tuesday — ta-li-ne-i-ga [tah lee nay ee gah]
    Wednesday — tso-i-ne-i-ga [cho ee nay ee gah]
    Thursday — u-gi-ne-i-ga [oo kee nay ee gah]
    Friday — tsu-na-gi-lo-s-ti [choo nah kee lo stee]
    Saturday — do-da-qui-de-na [doe dah kwee day nah]
    Sunday — do-da-qua-s-gŭ-i [doe dah kwahs gŭh ee]
dead — u-yo-hu-sŭ [oo yo hoo sŭh]
death — a-yo-hu-hi-s-di [ah yo hoo hees dee]
deer — a-wi [ah wee]
Deer Clan — (see CLAN)
do you understand? — ho-li-gi-tsŭ [hoe lee gee chŭh]
do you have... — tsa-ha [cha hah]
do you know? — hi-ga-ta-ka-tsu [hee gah tah kah choo]
do you want {xxxx}? — tsa-du-li-ha-tsu {xxxx} [cha doo lee hah choo]
do you want bread? — tsa-du-li-ha-tsu ga-du [cha doo lee hah choo gah doo]
don't fight — Tle-s-di a-la-s-di [tlays dee ah lahs dee]
dog — gi-li [gee lee]
downstream — ge-i we-we-yŭ-i[gay ee way way yŭh ee]
drunk — u-di-ta-hŭ [oo dee tah hŭh]
duck — ka-wo-nu [kah whoa noo]

E

eagle — wo-ha-li (or u-wo-ha-li) [whoa hah lee / oo whoa hah lee]
eat — hi-ga [hee gah]
Ellen — E-li-ni [ay lee nee]
Eva — E-wi [ay wee]
executed — a-s-da-wa-dŭ i-ya-dŭ-ne-di [ahs dah wah dŭh ee yah dŭh nay
    dee]

F

fall (autumn) — u-la-go-we-s-di [oo lah koh ways dee]
far — i-nŭ [ee nŭh]
fat — ga-li-tso-hi-da [gah lee cho hee dah]
father — e-to-da (or: a-da-to-da) [ay toe dah / ah dah toe dah]
festivals (or ceremonies):
    New Green Corn — Se-lu Tsu-ni-gi-s-ti-s-ti [say loo choo nee kees tees
        tee]
    Ripe Corn — Do-na-go-hu-ni [doe nah koh hoo nee]
    Great New Moon (Cherokee New Year) — Nu-wa-ti-e-qua [noo wah tee
        ay kwah]
    Reconciliation / New Friends — A-to-hu-na [ah toe hoo nah]

Bouncing Bush Feast — E-la-wa-ta-le-gi [ay lah wah tah lay kee]
Peace Chief's Dance — U-ku [oo koo]
filthy — ga-da-ha [gah dah hah]
fire — a-tsi-lŭ [ah chee lŭh]
Fort Smith — u-ya-ti di-so-ya-i [oo yah tee dee so yah ee]
fox — tsu-li (or tsu-la) [choo lee / choo lah]

G

George — Tsa-tsi [cha chee]
girl — a-ge-yu-tsa ('ge-yu-ts') [ah gay yoo cha / gay yooch]
give it to him — e-ti-ŭ-s-di [ay tee ŭhs dee]
goat — tsu-s-qua-ne-gi-dŭ [choos kwah nay gee dŭh]
go to sleep — hi-lŭ-na [hee lŭh nah]
go out! — do-yi! [doe yee]
good-bye — (one to one) do-na-da-go-hŭ-i [doe nah dah koh hŭh ee]
    (one to several others) — do-da-da-go-hŭ-i [doe dah dah koh hŭh ee]
gone — u-ni-gi-sŭ [oo nee gee sŭh]
grandfather — e-du-du [ay doo doo]
grandmother — e-li-si [ay lee see]
grandson — u-li-si a-tsu-tsa [oo lee see ah choo cha]
Great Spirit, the — A-da-nŭ-do [ah dah nŭh doe]

H

he came to help — i-gi-s-de-nu-hi-ga [ee gees day noo hee gah]
hello — si-yo (*formal*: o-si-yo) [see yo / oh see yo]
horse — so-qui-li [so kwee lee]
how are you? — to-hi-tsu [toe hee choo]
how many — hi-la i-ga-i [hee lah ee gah ee]
hummingbird — wa-le-la (or wa-le-li) [wah lay lah / wah lay lee]
hurt — a-tsi-so-nŭ-nŭ [ah chee so nŭh nŭh]

I

I don't know — tla-ya-qua-n'-ta [tlah yah kwahn tah]
    (*tla* as separate word means "no" or "not". As a prefix with -yi- or -ya-
    negates a verb.)
I love you — gŭ-ge-yu-i [gŭh gay yoo ee]
I know — a-qua-n'-ta — [ah kwahn tah]
I have spoken — a-ya a-gi-ha [ah yah ah gee hah]
I go / I am going — ge-ga [gay gah]
I say (I am saying) — ga-di-a [gah dee ah]

784

I speak the truth — a-ya du-yu-go-dŭ-ne-ga [ah yah doo yoo koh dŭh nay gah]
I believe you — a-yŭ u-wo-hi-yu [ah yŭh oo whoa hee yoo]
I am happy — ga-li-e-li-ga [gah lee ay lee gah]
I want {xxxx} — {xxxx} a-qua-du-li-ha [ah kwah doo lee hah]
I want water — a-ma a-qua-du-li-ha [ah mah ah kwah doo lee hah]
I want bread — ga-du a-qua-du-li-ha [gah doo ah kwah doo lee hah]
if I can — e-li-ga-ya-i [ay lee gah yah ee]
Is he/she here? — e-to-i [ay toe ee]
it is cold — u-yŭ-tla [oo yŭh tlah]
it is not true — ŭ-yo ho-wa-yi-gi [ŭh yo ho wah yee kee]
it is going to rain — dŭ-ga-na-ni [dŭh gah nah nee]
it is raining — a-ga-s-ga [a gahs gah]
it is ready — u-s-qua-lŭ-hŭ [oos kwah lŭh hŭh]
it is snowing — gu-ti-ha [goo tee hah]
it is so — u-to-hi-yu-du-yu-dŭ-i [oo toe hee yoo doo yoo dŭh ee]

J

Jackson — Tse-gi-si-ni [cheh kee see nee]
James — Tsi-mi [chee mee]
Jesus — Tsi-sa [chee sah]

K

Kitowah Clan — (see CLAN)

L

let's go (present) — tsi-ne-na [chee nay nah]
let's go (future) — i-ne-sŭ-i [ee nay sŭh ee]
let's get away — i-da-da-nŭ-na [ee dah dah nŭh nah]
let's eat — i-ti-ga [ee tee gah]
liar — ga-ye-go-gi [gah yeh koh gee]
little — u-s-di (also: diminutive suffix) [oos dee]
Little People — yŭ-wi-tsu-na-s-ti-ga [yŭh wee choo nahs tee gah]
Long Hair Clan — (see CLAN)

M

Martha — Ma-di [mah dee]
Martin — Tsu-tsu [choo choo]
Mary — Me-li [may lee]
measles — u-ne-yo-ti-s-gi [oo nay yo tees kee]

medicine — nŭ-wo-ti [nŭh whoa tee]

medicine man — di-da-nŭ-wi-s-gi [dee dah nŭh wees kee]

Merry Christmas — Da-ni'-s-ta-yo'-hi-hŭ! [dah nees tah yo hee hŭh]

Meteor/comet (fire panther) — tlŭ-da-tsi gi-ga-ge-i [tlŭh dah chee gee gah gay ee]

mother — e-tsi-i (or: u-ni-tsi) [e chee ee / oo nee chee]

murder — a-da-hi-s-di [ah dah hees dee]

my friend — gi-na-li-i [gee nah lee ee]

my mother — e-ge-i [ay gay ee]

my son — u-we-tsi [oo way chee]

my, our — a-qua-tse-li [ah kwah chay lee]

my sister — tso-s-da-se-i [chos dah say ee]

my father — e-to-da [ay toe dah]

my name — da-qua-to-a [dah kwah toe ah]

my daughter — u-we-tsi a-ge-yŭ [oo way chee ah gay yŭh]

my brother — tso-s-da-da-nŭ [chos dah dah nŭh]

O

old woman — a-ya-yŭ li-ge-i [ah yah yŭh lee gay ee]

or — di-tli-hi [dee tlee hee]

P

Paint Clan — (see CLAN)

penis — wa-ta-li (slang) [wah tah lee]

people — yŭ-wi (when used by itself) [yŭh wee]

When indicating a tribe or a clan, a-ni [ah nee] is used.

pig — si-qua [see kwah]

pneumonia — go-la-e-hi u-di-le-hŭ-s-gi [koh lah ay hee oo dee lay hŭhs kee]

pregnant — a-ta-gu te-nŭ-hi [ah tah koo tay nŭh hee]

Q

quiet — e-lu-we-i [ay loo way ee]

R

rabbit — tsi-s-du [chees doo]

railroad — ta-lu-gi-s-gi nŭ-no-hi [tah loo kees kee nŭh no hee]

raven — go-la-nŭ [koh lah nŭh]

rat, mouse — tsi-s-de-tsi [chees day chee]

rattlesnake — u-tso'-n(a)-ti' [oo cho nah tee / oo chone tee]

Rebecca (Becky) — We-gi [way kee]

S

Sally — Sa-li (same as Sarah) [sah lee]
send him away — e-da-ni-gi-s-da [ay dah nee gees dah]
(she is) a mother — u-ta-ga-tŭ li-ge-i [oo tah gah tŭh lee gay ee]
slave — a-tsi-na-tla-i [ah chee nah tlah ee]
   (var. a-tsi-na-sa-i) [a chee nah sah ee]
slaves (black) — di-ge-tsi-na-tla-i [dee gay chee nah tlah ee]
snake — i-na-dŭ [ee nah dŭh]
so they say — na-s-gi na-ni-wi-a [nahs kee nah nee wee ah]
soldier(s) — *(sing.)* a-ya-wi-s-gi [ah yah wees kee];
   (pl.) a-ni-ya-wi-s-gi [ah nee yah wees kee]
spring (season) — gi-la-go-di [gee lah koh dee]
Stand Watie — De-ga-ta-ga [day gah tah gah]
summer — go-ge-yi (or go-gi) [koh gay yee / koh gee]]
sweet bread (cake) — ga-du u-ga-na-s-di [gah doo oo gah nahs dee]

T

that's right — u-to-hi-ya [oo toe hee yah]
The Little Men — a-ni-s-ga-ya tsu-s-di [ah nees gah yah choos dee]
Trail of Tears — Nu-na-da-u-l'-tsu-ni [noo nah dah oo'l choo nee] (*lit.* "The Trail Where They Cried")
Trail of Tears — Ge-tsi-ka-hŭ-da A-ne-gŭ-i [gay chee kah hŭh dah - Ah nay gŭh ee]
two hundred — ta-l'-s-go-hi-s-qua [tahls koh hees kwah]

U

uncle — e-du-tsi [ay doo chee]

V

very dangerous — u-na-ye-hi-s-ti [oo nah yay hees tee]
very good — o-s-ta [ohs tah]

W

warrior — da-nu-wa a-na-li-hi [dah noo wah ah nah lee hee]
Washington — Wa-sŭ-da-na [wah sŭh dah nah]
watch it! — ha-nu-wa [hah noo wah]
water moccasin — u'-ga-n'-te-na [oo gahn tay nah]
we are friends — i-ga-li-i [ee gah lee ee]

we are alike — i-gi-tlo-yi [ee gee tloh yee]
welcome — u-li-he-li-s-di [oo lee hay lees dee]
what is it? — ga-to-u-s-di [gah toe oos dee]
what is your name — ga-to-no de-tsa-to-a [gah toe no day cha toe ah]
where — ha-tlŭ [hah tlŭh]
whiskey — wi-s-gi [wees kee]
white(s) — u-ne-gŭ [oo nay gŭh]; or a-yo-ne-ga [ah yo nay gah];
    (*slang*: yo-neg [yo nek]
winter — go-la [koh lah]
wolf — wa-ya [wah yah]
wolf mother — u-ni-tsi wa-ya [oo nee chee wah yah]
Wolf Clan — (see CLAN)

Y

yes — ŭ-ŭ [ŭh ŭh]
yesterday — u-sŭ-hi [oo sŭh hee]
you can (may) talk — hi-wo-ni-ha [hee whoa nee hah]
you are pretty — ni-hi tso-du-ha [nee hee cho doo hah]

Cherokee — English

A

a-da-hi-s-di — [ah dah hees dee] — murder, assassinate
a-da-nŭ-do — [ah dah nŭh doe] — Great Spirit, the
a-ga-s-ga — [a gahs gah] — it is raining
a-ge-yu-tsa ('ge-yu-ts') — [ah gay yoo cha / gay yooch] — girl
a-gi-lo-hi — [ah kee lo hee] — daughter-in-law
a-ha-ni — [ah hah nee] — are here
a-le — [ah lay] — and
a-ma a-qua-du-li-ha — [ah mah ah kwah doo lee hah] — I want water
a-na-lo-si — [ah nah lo see] — brother-in-law
a-ni-gi-du-wa-gi — [ah nee kee too wah kee] — Kitowah Clan
a-ni-gi-la-hi — [ah nee kee lah hee] — Longhair Clan
a-ni-ka-wi — [ah nee kah wee] — Deer
a-ni-s-ga-ya tsu-s-di — [ah nees gah yah choos dee] — The Little Men
a-ni-sa-ha-ni — [ah nee sah hah nee] — Blue Clan
a-ni-tsi-s-qua — [ah nee chees kwah] — Bird Clan
a-ni-wa-di — [ah nee wah dee] — Paint Clan
a-ni-wa-ya — [ah nee wah yah] — Wolf Clan (largest clan)
a-ni-ya-wi-s-gi — [ah nee yah wees kee] — army (military)
{xxxx} a-qua-du-li-ha — [ah kwah doo lee hah] — I want {xxxx}
a-qua-n'-ta — [ah kwahn tah] — I know
a-qua-tse-li — [ah kwah chay lee] — my, our
a-s-da-wa-dŭ i-ya-dŭ-ne-di — [ahs dah wah dŭh ee yah dŭh nay dee] — executed
a-s-ga-s-di (or: a-s-ga-i-hŭ) — [ahs gahs dee / ahs gah ee hŭh] — afraid
a-ta-gu te-nŭ-hi — [ah tah koo tay nŭh hee] — pregnant
A-to-hu-na — [ah toe hoo nah] — Reconciliation / New Friends Festival
a-tse-nŭ-s-ti — [ah chay nŭhs tee] "One Sent", or Messenger (cf. Rev. Samuel Worcester)
a-tsi-lŭ — [ah chee lŭh] — fire
a-tsi-na-tla-i — [a chee nah tlah ee] — slave
    (*var.* a-tsi-na-sa-i [a chee nah sah ee]
a-tsi-so-nŭ-nŭ — [ah chee so nŭh nŭh] — hurt
a-wi — [ah wee] — deer
a-wi-a-gi-ta — [ah wee ah kee tah] — black eyed susan (deer eye)
a-wo-gi-lŭ-s-gi — [ah whoa kee lŭhs kee] — beer
a-ya du-yu-go-dŭ-ne-ga — [ah yah doo yoo koh dŭh nay gah] — I speak the truth
a-ya a-gi-ha — [ah yah ah gee hah] — I have spoken
a-ya-wi-s-gi — [ah yah wees kee] — soldier (*sing.*)
    a-ni-ya-wi-s-gi — [ah nee yah wees kee] — soldiers (*pl.*)

a-ya-yŭ li-ge-i — [ah yah yŭh lee gay ee] — old woman
a-yo-hu-hi-s-di — [ah yo hoo hees dee] — death
a-yŭ u-wo-hi-yu — [ah yŭh oo whoa hee yoo] — I believe you

D

da-ni'-s-ta-yo'-hi-hŭ! — [dah nees tah yo hee hŭh] — Merry Christmas
da-nu-wa a-na-li-hi — [dah noo wah ah nah lee hee] — warrior
da-qua-to-a — [dah kwah toe ah] — my name
De-ga-ta-ga — [day gah tah gah] — Stand Watie
di-da-nŭ-wi-s-gi — [dee dah nŭh wees kee] — medicine man
di-da-yo-li-hŭ dŭ-ga-le-ni-s-gŭ — [dee dah yo lee hŭh - dŭh gah lay nees gŭh] — good-bye
di-ge-tsi-na-tla-i — [dee gay chee nah tlah ee] — slaves (black)
di-ni-yo-tli — [dee nee yo tlee] — children
di-ti-yo-hi-hi — [dee tee yo hee hee] — attorney
di-tli-hi — [dee tlee hee] — or
do-da-da-go-hŭ-i — [doe dah dah koh hŭh ee] — good-bye (one to many)
do-na-da-go-hŭ-i — [doe nah dah koh hŭh ee] — good-bye (one to one)
do-da-qua-s-gŭ-i — [doe dah kwahs kŭh ee] — Sunday
do-da-qui-de-na — [doe dah kwee day nah] — Saturday
do-da-quo-nŭ-hi — [doe dah kwo nŭh hee] — Monday
Do-na-go-hu-ni — [doe nah koh hoo nee] — Ripe Corn Festival
do-yi! — [doe yee] — go out!
du-do-da-qui-sŭ — [doo doe dah kwee sŭh] — days
dŭ-ga-na-ni — [dŭh gah nah nee] — it is going to rain

E

e-da-ni-gi-s-da — [ay dah nee gees dah] — send him away
e-du-du — [ay doo doo] — grandfather
e-du-tsi — [ay doo chee] — uncle
e-ge-i — [ay gay ee] — my mother
e-he-na — [ay hay nah] — come here
e-hi na-go-i — [ay hee nah koh ee] — come out
E-la-wa-ta-le-gi — [ay lah wah tah lay kee] — Bouncing Bush Feast
e-li-ga-ya-i — [ay lee gah yah ee] — if I can
E-li-ni — [ay lee nee] — Ellen
e-li-si — [ay lee see] — grandmother
e-lu-we-i — [ay loo way ee] — quiet
e-ni-na-wi-dŭ — [ay nee nah wee dŭh] — carry him
e-ti-ŭ-s-di — [ay tee ŭhs dee] — give it to him
e-tla-we-i — [ay tlah way ee] — be quiet
e-to-da (or: a-da-to-da) — [ay toe dah / ah dah toe dah] — (my) father
e-tsi-i (or: u-ni-tsi) — [ay chee / oo nee chi] — mother

E-wi — [ay wee] — Eva

G

ga-da-ha — [gah dah hah] — filthy
ga-di-a — [gah dee ah] — I say; I am saying
ga-du a-qua-du-li-ha — [gah doo ah kwah doo lee hah] — I want bread
ga-du u-ga-na-s-di — [gah doo oo gah nahs dee] — sweet bread (cake)
ga-du — [gah doo] — bread
Ga-la-gi-na — [gah lah gee nah] — Buck (name)
ga-li-e-li-ga — [gah lee ay lee gah] — I am happy
ga-li-ha — [gah lee hah] — asleep
ga-li-tso-hi-da — [gah lee cho hee dah] — fat
ga-tli-da — [gah tlee dah] — arrow
ga-to-no de-tsa-to-a — [gah toe no day cha toe ah] — what is your name
ga-to-u-s-di — [gah toe oos dee] — what is it?
ga-ye-go-gi — [gah yeh koh gee] — liar
ge-ga — [gay gah] — I go / I am going
ge-i we-we-yŭ-i — [gay ee way way yŭh ee] — downstream
Ge-tsi-ka-hŭ-da A-ne-gŭ-i — [gay chee kah hŭh dah - Ah nay gŭh ee] —
    Trail of Tears
gi-la-go-di — [gee lah koh dee] — spring (season)
gi-li — [gee lee] — dog
gi-na-li-i — [gee nah lee ee] — my friend
gi-yŭ-ha! — [gee yŭh hah!] — come in!
go-ge-yi (or: go-gi) — [koh gay yee / koh gee] — summer
go-la — [koh lah] — winter
go-la-e-hi u-di-le-hŭ-s-gi — [koh lah ay hee oo dee lay hŭhs kee]
    — pneumonia
go-la-nŭ — [koh lah nŭh] — raven
gu-ti-ha — [goo tee hah] — it is snowing
Gu-wi-s-gu-wi — [koo wee skoo wee] — John Ross
gŭ-ge-yu-i — [gŭh gay yoo ee] — I love you
gŭ-ni-ge tsu-li — [gŭh nee gay choo lee] — black fox

H

ha-nu-wa — [hah noo wah] — watch it!
ha-tlŭ — [hah tlŭh] — where
ha-wa — [hah wah] — all right
hi-ga — [hee gah] — eat
hi-ga-ta-ka-tsu — [hee gah tah kah choo] — do you know?
hi-la i-ga-i — [hee lah ee gah ee] — how many
hi-lŭ-hi-yu-i — [hee lŭh hi yoo ee] — ancient
hi-lŭ-na — [hee lŭh nah] — go to sleep

hi-tsa-la-gi-s-go — [hee cha la kees koh] — Are you Cherokee?
hi-wo-ni-ha — [hee whoa nee hah] — you can (may) talk
ho-li-gi-tsŭ — [hoe lee gee chŭh] — do you understand?

I

i-da-da-nŭ-na — [ee dah dah nŭh nah] — let's get away
i-ga-li-i — [ee gah lee ee] — we are friends
i-gi-s-de-nu-hi-ga — [ee gees day noo hee gah] — he came to help
i-gi-tlo-yi — [ee gee tloh yee] — we are alike
i-na-dŭ — [ee nah dŭh] — snake
i-ne-sŭ-i — [ee nay sŭh ee] — let's go (future)
i-nŭ — [ee nŭh] — far
i-ti-ga — [ee tee gah] — let's eat

K

ka-l'(i)-se-tsi — [kal (ee) say chee] — candy
ka-wo-nu — [kah whoa noo] — duck

M

Ma-di — [mah dee] — Martha
Me-li — [may lee] — Mary

N

na-s-gi na-ni-wi-a — [nahs kee nah nee wee ah] — so they say
ni-hi tso-du-ha — [nee hee cho doo hah] — you are pretty
Nu-na-da-u-l'-tsu-ni — [noo nah dah oo'l choo nee] The Trail Of Tears
    (*lit.* "The Trail Where They Cried")
Nu-wa-ti-e-qua — [noo wah tee ay kwah] — Great New Moon Festival
    (Also the Cherokee New Year)
nŭ-wo-ti — [nŭh whoa tee] — medicine

O

o-s-ta — [ohs tah] — very good; very well

S

Sa-li — [sah lee] — Sarah (same as Sally)

Se-lu Tsu-ni-gi-s-ti-s-ti — [say loo choo nee kees tees tee] - New Green Corn
  Festival

si-yo (*formal*: o-si-yo) — [see yo / oh see yo] — hello

si-qua — [see kwah] — pig

so-qui-li — [so kwee lee] — horse

T

ta-li-ne-i-ga — [tah lee nay ee gah] — Tuesday

ta-l'-s-go-hi-s-qua — [tahls koh hees kwah] — two hundred

ta-lu-gi-s-gi nŭ-no-hi — [tah loo kees kee nŭh no hee] — railroad

ti-s-qua-ni — [tees kwah nee] — a place to live

tla-ya-qua-n'-ta — [tlah yah kwahn tah] — I don't know (*tla* as separate
  word mean "no"or "not". As a prefix with -yi- or -ya- negates a verb.)

tla-ye-li — [tlah yay lee] — can't

Tle-s-di a-la-s-di — [tlays dee ah lahs dee] — don't fight

tlŭ-da-tsi gi-ga-ge-i — [tlŭh dah chee gee gah gay ee] — Meteor/comet (fire
  panther)

tsa-du-li-ha-tsu {xxxx} — [cha doo lee hah choo] — do you want {xxxx}

tsa-du-li-ha-tsu ga-du — [cha doo lee hah choo gah doo] — do you want
  bread

tsa-ha — [cha hah] — do you have...

Tse-gi-si-ni — [cheh kee see nee] — Jackson

Tsi-mi — [chee mee] — James

tsi-ne-na — [chee nay nah] — let's go (present)

tsi-s-de-tsi — [chees day chee] — rat, mouse

tsi-s-du — [chees doo] — rabbit

Tsi-sa — [chee sah] — Jesus

tsi-yu — [chee yoo] — boat

tso-i-ne-i-ga — [cho ee nay ee gah] — Wednesday

tso-s-da-da-nŭ — [chos dah dah nŭh] — my brother

tso-s-da-se-i — [chos dah say ee] — my sister

tsu-li (or tsu-la) — [choo lee / choo lah] — fox

tsu-na-gi-lo-s-ti — [choo nah kee los tee] — Friday

tsu-na-s-di-i — [choo nahs dee ee] — babies

tsu-ni-yŭ-wi — [choo nee yŭh wee] — Clans

tsu-s-qua-ne-gi-dŭ — [choos kwah nay kee dŭh] — goat

Tsu-tsu — [choo choo] — Martin

U

u'-ga-n'-te-na — [oo gahn tay nah] — water moccasin
u-di-ta-hŭ — [oo dee tah hŭh] — drunk
u-gi-ne-i-ga — [oo kee nay ee gah] — Thursday
U-ku — [oo koo] — Peace Chief's Dance
u-la-go-we-s-di — [oo lah koh ways dee] — fall (autumn)
u-li-he-li-s-di — [oo lee hay lees dee] — welcome
u-li-si a-tsu-tsa — [oo lee see ah choo cha] — grandson
u-na-ye-hi-s-ti — [oo nah yay hees tee] — very dangerous
u-ne-gŭ (or: a-yo-ne-ga) — [oo nay gŭh] (*slang*: yo-neg [yo nek] — white(s)
u-ne-yo-ti-s-gi — [oo nay yo tees kee] — measles
u-ni-gi-sŭ — [oo nee gee sŭh] — gone
u-ni-tsi wa-ya — [oo nee chee wah yah] — wolf mother
u-s-di (also: diminutive suff.) — [oos dee] — little
u-s-di-i — [oos dee ee] — baby
u-s-ga-e-na — [oos gah ay nah] — coward
u-s-qua-lŭ-hŭ — [oos kwah lŭh hŭh] — it is ready
u-sŭ-hi — [oo sŭh hee] — yesterday
u-ta-ga-tŭ li-ge-i — [oo tah gah tŭh lee gay ee] — (she is) a mother
u-to-hi-ya — [oo toe hee yah] — that's right
u-to-hi-yu-du-yu-dŭ-i — [oo toe hee yoo doo yoo dŭh ee] — it is so
u-tsa-ti-na — [oo chah tee nah] — away
u-tso'-n(a)-ti' — [oo cho nah tee / oo chone tee] — rattlesnake
U-we-na-ni — [oo way nah nee] — Richard
u-we-tsi a-ge-yŭ — [oo way chee ah gay yŭh] — my daughter
u-we-tsi — [oo way chee] — my son
u-wo-du-(hi) — [oo whoa doo (hee)] — beautiful
u-ya-ti di-so-ya-i — [oo yah tee dee so yah ee] — Fort Smith
u-yo-hu-sŭ — [oo yo hoo sŭh] — dead
u-yŭ-tla — [oo yŭh tlah] — it is cold

Ŭ (the very nasalized "U")

ŭ-ŭ — [ŭh ŭh] — yes
ŭ-yo ho-wa-yi-gi — [ŭh yo ho wah yee kee] — it is not true

W

wa-ga — [wah gah] — cattle
wa-le-la (or wa-le-li) — [wah lay lah / wah lay lee] — hummingbird
wa-ta-li — [wah tah lee] — penis (slang)
wa-sŭ-da-na — [wah sŭh dah nah] — Washington
wa-ya — [wah yah] — wolf

794

We-gi — [way kee] — Rebecca (Becky)
wi-s-gi — [wees kee] — whiskey
wo-ha-li (or u-wo-ha-li) — [whoa hah lee / oo whoa ha lee] — eagle

Y

yo-nŭ — [yo nŭh] — bear
yŭ-wi — [yŭh wee] — people (when used by itself). When indicating a tribe
    or clan, a-ni is used.
yŭ-wi-tsu-na-s-ti-ga — [yŭh wee choo nahs tee gah] — Little People

Suggested Reading

Carter, Samuel. *Cherokee Sunset, A Nation Betrayed.* New York: Doubleday, 1976.

Collier, Peter. *When Shall They Rest? The Cherokee's Long Struggle With America.* New York: Dell, 1973.

Debo, Angie. *And Still The Waters Run, The Betrayal Of The Five Civilized Tribes.* Princeton: Princeton University Press, 1940.

Ehle, John. *Trail Of Tears, The Rise And Fall Of The Cherokee Nation.* New York: Doubleday, 1988.

Erdoes, Richard and Alfonso Ortiz. *American Indian Myths And Legends.* New York: Pantheon Books, 1984.

Foreman, Grant. *Indian Removal.* Norman: University of Oklahoma Press, 1932.

Foreman, Grant. *Sequoyah.* Norman: University of Oklahoma Press, 1938.

Hausman, Gerald. *Turtle Island Alphabet, A Lexicon Of Native American Symbols And Culture.* New York: St. Martin's Press, 1992.

Hifler, Joyce Sequiche. *A Cherokee Feast Of Days.* Tulsa: Council Oak Books, 1992.

Holmes, Ruth Bradley and Betty Sharp Smith. *Beginning Cherokee.* Norman: University of Oklahoma Press, 1976.

Jahoda, Gloria. *The Trail Of Tears, The Story Of The American Indian Removals 1813-1855.* New York: Wings Books, 1975.

Kilpatrick, Anna G. and Jack F. *Friends Of Thunder: Folktales Of The Oklahoma Cherokee.* Dallas: Southern Methodist University Press, 1964.

Klausner, Janet. *Sequoyah's Gift, A Portrait Of The Cherokee Leader.* New York: Harper Collins, 1993.

Mooney, James. *Historical Sketch Of The Cherokees.* Chicago: Aldine Publishing Company, 1975.

Mooney, James. *Myths Of The Cherokee And Sacred Myths Of The Cherokees.* Nashville: (reproduced), 1972.

Royce, Charles C. *The Cherokee Nation Of Indians.* Chicago: Aldine Publishing Company, 1975.

Starkey, Marion L. *The Cherokee Nation*. North Dighton: JG Press, 1995.

Steele, William O. *The Cherokee Crown Of Tannassy*. Winston-Salem: John F. Blair Publisher, 1977.

Strickland, Rennard. *Fire And The Spirits*. Norman: University of Oklahoma Press, 1975.

Woodward, Grace Steele. *The Cherokees*. Norman: University of Oklahoma Press, 1963.